THE
HELLBORN KING

THE HELLBORN KING SAGA, BOOK ONE

A fantasy novel by

CHRISTOPHER G. BRENNING

The Forlorn Sea
Rej Rhivoth
Teb River
Rit
The Hinterwood
Skaginlef
Siln River
Blackwolf Pass
Borjifa
Mot
The Bymist
Pelg
Khorrtal
Brimnora
Morden
Hok
Kepdon
The Great Sea
The Plainhold
Dellhaven
Mor Seveht
Greenwood Forest
Aret
Cardale
Naxonnos
Bentmont
Larssa
Vhos River
Willowsgrove
Glimmergulf
Corinope
Sothfort
Sommerwood River
The Everblue
CALDAKAS

ACKNOWLEDGMENTS

Before you begin this story, I would like to take a moment to say thank you, to you. From the youngest age, it was always my dream to be an entertainer. Through theater, music, and now writing, I've put my heart and soul into making that passion a reality through one medium after another. I've had success in the past, but telling stories is the one thing I've truly wanted to do. If not for you holding this book and taking the time to read it, my dream would be simply that; a dream, and nothing more. I would also like to thank all of my early readers. So many of you gave me invaluable feedback, and without your input, this book would not be what it is today. There's so many, I regret I cannot mention you all, but I would like to give special thanks to a few people in particular: Christopher Jackson, Nicholas Trent and the rest of the #g crew, as well as Rebecca Ramirez and Cheryl Timm. I would also like to thank my good friend Thomas Hunter, another one of my early readers and one of my greatest champions. Your help and your encouragement has meant the world to me. Thank you for helping me bring this project to life. Lastly, and most importantly, I would like to dedicate this to my mother, Karen. I know you would prefer reading your Agatha Christie novels over, say, epic fantasy, but I hope that I've made you proud *regardless*.

CONTENTS

PROLOGUE

THE STENCH OF DEATH HUNG HEAVY OVER THE KILLING GROUNDS, thick and stagnant in the summer heat. It wasn't the first time Alfrid Valens had seen a dead body. It was a soldier's duty to make as many of them as possible, after all. But what he saw brought him near to retching. The men were dead for a week, maybe more, just as the riders had said.

"Looks like they were right." Eryk coughed. He shielded his nose with the back of his hand.

It was a stupid and obvious thing to say, but Alfrid was at a loss for words. He stared at the ruin that used to be the King's soldiers, their features having withered away into nothingness. What was unmistakable, however, was the eagle sigil of Betanthia on their breastplates.

"What sort of brigands would do something like this and not take a single thing off the bodies?" Alfrid pondered out loud.

It seemed strange for anyone to attack a Betanthian patrol and not take their pick of the spoils. There was plenty of fine steel and provisions, all of which could fetch a decent coin. Or be put to good use if one were so inclined.

He swatted at a fly that danced around his face, then donned a crested steel helm over his mop of shaggy blonde hair. Alfrid Valens was the last son of a dying line and had produced no heirs for himself. His father reminded him of it often. He was every bit the image of Lord Cedric and just as stony and calculating, though a man of far fewer words, if such a thing was possible.

"You know these Northmen, they like to kill for sport," Eryk replied.

There was truth to what he said. The barbarian tribes were more akin to animals as opposed to men. But it was Dhuuld Lurrson's job to keep the peace in Khorrtal and the surrounding lands, a peace that was often precarious. That was the agreement, the price for their relative autonomy. What good was a chieftain who couldn't uphold his end of the bargain?

"It's possible." Alfrid turned away from the hideous mess before him. "Someone knows what happened here, and whoever is responsible needs to pay."

His father demanded nothing less. Cedric Valens would be waiting at Castle Morden for the offenders to return in irons so they could be promptly executed for their crimes. A good hanging could help to restore order, since Dhuuld seemed incapable of maintaining it by virtue alone. How could he allow such a thing to happen?

Alfrid had half a mind to ride to Khorrtal and wring the old man's neck until the answers came tumbling out of his mouth. The more he thought of it, the more appealing the idea sounded. Savage folk often needed reminders of their true place in the world, and perhaps a hangman's noose would be a reminder enough.

"I think we had best pay our barbarian friend a little visit," Alfrid declared. "These are his lands, and what happens here is his responsibility. Perhaps he's become a bit too comfortable in his station."

"Very good, Captain. Should we bury the dead first?"

The army had lingered long enough as it was. Staying here for a burial detail might only expose them to danger, the same danger that had sealed the fate of his countrymen.

"No," Alfrid said. "We'll leave that task to the Khorrtalli. This happened on their watch. So let them take care of it."

The road would be the most direct way to the village, but also the most dangerous. Its banks and surrounding fields were thick and overgrown and could be harboring any number of unseen threats. Even with three thousand soldiers at his back, Alfrid felt uneasy. He watched the tall grass rustling in the breeze, its blades whispering soft warnings. Something about the road seemed treacherous and uninviting, something he couldn't quite explain.

"Shall I get the men moving then?" Eryk asked.

Alfrid nodded. "We go around. And spread them out. Tell everyone to stay alert."

He climbed back into the saddle as his orders echoed down the line, his gaze still fixated on the road. The column began to shift and spread out until the men were nearly a quarter mile abreast. Khorrtal was a mere speck on the horizon, but within an hour, maybe two, they would arrive.

"Keep a sharp eye open, lads!" a Sergeant with a long poleaxe shouted to the infantrymen. Thousands of colorful kite shields bobbed up and down as the men trudged through the field, their long spears swaying like barren trees in the wind. The clattering of steel plate and the clinking of mail played like a symphony, though the song was of little reassurance.

Onward they rode. Eryk was babbling something, but his words seemed as distant as the village. Alfrid was too focused on their surroundings to take notice. He spied a flock of carrion crows circling in the dreary sky, cawing and complaining. It was difficult to comprehend that pieces of good Betanthian men were now in the bellies of those foul, winged creatures. The thought sickened him.

"Wouldn't you agree, Captain?" Eryk said, breaking Alfrid out of his distraction.

"What was that?" he asked, brow furrowed.

"The ground. It's like a bloody marsh, look at it!"

It was true. The field was becoming a soupy, saturated mess the further they rode. This year, the early summer rainy season was relentless, turning even the driest plains into lakes. Alfrid was beginning to regret not taking the road. He would have preferred solid ground over this, even if the risk were greater. His horse struggled to keep a solid footing, and the men seemed to be faring no better. Their pace had slowed to a crawl, but thankfully the field was not impassible. At least, not yet.

"We'll be through it soon enough," Alfrid said, though unsure if he believed it himself.

Why hasn't that old fool come out to meet us? he wondered.

He glanced over his shoulder at a rider carrying the King's standard. The blue cloth snapped and twisted in the wind, its eagle sigil appearing to flap its wings and take flight. Beside him, another horseman carried the blue and burgundy war flag of Castle Morden. The banners were large enough and bright enough to be seen a mile away, or more, yet still Dhuuld had not produced himself. Had the old man turned false, or was he simply too oblivious to take notice of an army marching through his lands? Either outcome would be unacceptable.

"You're doing it again," Eryk observed.

"Doing what?" Alfrid scoffed in annoyance.

"You're thinking too much. Try not to look so grim, it doesn't suit you."

Eryk was a good man and a good friend from their days before the army, though a bit loose in the tongue. He was all of twenty, nearly four years the junior of Alfrid. Much of their youth was spent chasing maidens in Willowsgrove and getting into scuffles with the other lads. There was something in his dopey face that could make Alfrid smile in even the direst situations, but today he wasn't smiling. Neither of them were.

"I can't help it. I'll feel a lot better once we get out of this stinking bog, or, whatever this is."

It was impossible not to notice the smell. It was a ripe, pungent scent of wet, rotten vegetation and stagnant water. Alfrid wasn't sure what smelled worse, the swampy field or the pile of dead men they had encountered. A sudden, hot gust swept through the plain, the tall grass shaking and hissing like snakes coiled to strike.

"I don't know about you, but I could use a good romp once we get to the village," Eryk said, smiling. "What do you say we have ourselves a go?"

"I'll pass. They smell like… like wet dog." Alfrid wrinkled his nose at the thought. He never cared for the women in the village, they were far too plain and dreary for his liking. But then again, he never cared for much of anyone in Khorrtal in the first place.

"What's the matter, you haven't lost your appetite, have you?"

It was utterly perplexing, yet somehow oddly impressive how Eryk could remain so aloof, even at the most inopportune moments. There were times when all Alfrid could do was marvel at his friend's utter lack of self-awareness, and this was one of them. He shook his head incredulously.

You truly are a piece of work, Eryk.

A rider appeared in the distance, a large, hulking thing of a man on the back of an equally massive warhorse. He was as black as a shadow, tall as a castle's keep, with a long crimson cape flapping behind him. Alfrid sighed in relief.

"About time he showed up. I ought to put the lash to him in front of the entire village for all of his—"

But something seemed odd and out of place. He remembered Dhuuld being smaller and thinner, not gaunt, but certainly not an imposing figure by any means. Alfrid leaned forward and squinted, his eyes straining to catch a better glimpse of the man, but he was too far away to see clearly. The rider sat motionless, save for the soft fluttering of his cape in the wind.

"What's the matter?" Eryk asked. "Why—"

"Shhhh! Be quiet!" Alfrid replied softly. He raised a hand in a friendly gesture toward the rider, but it hung in the air unanswered. Something was wrong. He could feel it. He raised his hand higher in case the man could not see, but still, there was no reply. The rider continued to sit idle and silent, like a lion sizing up its prey.

What in the world is going on here?

Alfrid heard something whoosh past him, like the air was torn asunder, though it was faint and hard to make out over the sucking sound of his horse's hooves in the mud. At first, he thought little of it until something pinged off his breastplate and fluttered into the weeds. Alarmed, he gave the reigns a frantic crack, but an arrow struck his horse in the neck, followed by another and yet another in a near instant. The beast wailed and fell screaming to the ground.

He landed with an awkward thud, his head rattling inside his steel helm like a pebble. Stunned and nearly unconscious, Alfrid stumbled to his feet, clasping his temples as a dull ringing filled his ears. As he turned, a savage beast of a man charged in, an axe in one hand and a short sword in the other. Roaring and swinging wildly, the bald barbarian attacked and nearly struck a killing blow.

Instinctively, Alfrid drew his arming sword and parried one strike, then another. He was seeing double and did not know which of the savages to attack. He answered with an arcing slash, but the beard of the warrior's axe hooked his blade and ripped it free from his grasp.

The Northman stepped in with a thrust, the sword point biting through the rings of mail just below Alfrid's breastplate. He heard the wet thump of steel sinking into his flesh, yet felt no pain. As it was wrenched free, a torrent of blood erupted from the wound, spilling onto the ground with a spurt. The barbarian gave him a shove and set off toward another target.

He couldn't remember falling or hitting the ground. The last thing Alfrid saw before his vision turned to black was the blurry, frantic chaos of battle, a horrific maelstrom of steel and flesh colliding violently with each other. Slowly he drifted off to sleep, a deep and welcoming sleep he might never wake from.

But his slumber would not last long. Alfrid awoke, gasping and choking in a sudden panic. He could still hear the clanging of steel and screams of dying men, though it was much quieter now. Coughing and spitting out a mouthful of dirty water, he tried to stand and retrieve his sword, but the sting of severed nerves wracked his body, sending him crashing back to the ground.

Alfrid groaned woefully and nearly vomited from the pain, his hands clutching at his lacerated bowels. When he pulled them away, he saw blood running between his fingers, warm and thick and nearly black from bile.

No... this... this cannot be...

Terror-stricken, Alfrid clutched his abdomen with one hand and grimaced, then began to drag himself forward with the other. He had to get away, as far away from here as he possibly could, and fast. It was the only thing he could do.

A pair of barbarians came sloshing through the red mud, laughing and jeering in a language he did not understand. Alfrid laid still, hoping they would mistake him for a corpse. However, he would not have to try hard, as he already appeared moments away from the grave.

Their hair and beards were long and untamed, their skin painted with a tapestry of blue runic tattoos. They wore leather, mail, animal furs, and bits of steel armor. One carried a two-handed great axe, which Alfrid had only ever used to split wood. He could only imagine the pain of having it split bone. The other carried a large wooden shield and an arming sword which appeared to be Betanthian forged, with its ornate handle and inch-wide fuller running down the blade's length.

The barbarians rifled through the belongings of one corpse after another, pilfering anything of value. They turned one body over and found a man still alive, moaning in agony and clutching a bloody chest wound. Alfrid watched through a half-opened eye as the Northmen pointed and laughed mockingly.

"No, please, no! I beg of you! Please!" the soldier cried out.

One of the savages plunged a blade deep into the man's guts, twisting and jerking the steel back and forth until he expired.

Alfrid shivered with fear, his bowels pulsing with a vicious, fiery ache. He waited patiently until the barbarians moved far enough away before he began crawling once again. He navigated a labyrinth of bodies, each more ravaged and ruined than the last, their faces forever frozen in terror.

He saw the cold, dead eyes of Eryk staring back at him. A thick river of blood snaked onto the ground, filling the space where his head and body once met.

I'm so sorry, my friend. I've failed you. I've failed everyone.

Alfrid wept softly, overcome with despair. He thought of surrendering to his wounds and joining his friend in the afterlife, if there even was one. There seemed little point in continuing on, not after such a devastating defeat. But no, Eryk would not want that. Instead, he would want Alfrid to escape, to live, and to grow old. And to avenge him, along with every other man that had met their demise on this day.

After whispering a soft goodbye, Alfrid continued on, hoping to reach the tall grass and find cover. As he lurched across the soupy earth, he heard a metallic crunching of armor from behind, the ground squishing with each step. A massive, black shadow crept across the field like an eclipse, bringing with it a sudden chill.

The huge barbarian halted, his bloodied sabatons resting mere feet from Alfrid's face. A small gathering of warriors congregated behind him, though all were mindful to keep their distance. His nearly seven-foot frame was imposing enough to make cowards of even the bravest men. He wore a suit of steel plate, so black it seemed to swallow the light around it.

After coughing out blood that was steadily filling his mouth, Alfrid turned, his eyes slowly moving upward. There would be no escape, not now.

"Well, I suppose this is it then…" he said helplessly through labored, panting breaths.

"For you, it most certainly is. But, for Betanthia, this is merely the beginning," the colossus responded. "Remember the Bloodbath at Borjifa? Of course you do, all of you Bethard underlings know the tale. The gods demand justice, and I am their champion."

The man's voice echoed from a blackened steel helm that encased his entire head. Shaped in the form of a skull, the helm had two long horns protruding from its brow and two smaller horns near the mandible.

"Get on with it, you fucking savage!" Alfrid shot back, spitting out a mouthful of blood in frail defiance.

"I would have your name first."

"Alfrid Valens. Remember it well, you swine. You will rue this day." His jaw quivered.

The barbarian removed his helm slowly and deliberately. Beads of sweat dripped down his bald head and ran across a stern and sour face. His eyes were nearly as black as the steel covering his massive, muscular frame. Several weeks of beard growth had formed across a chiseled jawline, his lips tight and forming into a half scowl, half smirk of amusement.

"Valens, you say? Then the fates are kind, it seems. I know your father well. We have a sort of history, you might say. But, worry not, son of Cedric. He will be joining you in the next life soon enough. I, Damien Dreadfire, will see to it that his line and the lines of every man responsible for Borjifa are extinguished forever. Never will the name of Valens be uttered again by anyone."

Alfrid's eyes drifted to the gray, overcast sky. He wished he could see the sun one final time and feel its warmth before departing this world, but it was not meant to be. He cursed himself for ever coming to this place, but it was too late now for such regrets.

"Father… I'm sorry…" Alfrid whispered. His cold and clammy body was warmed momentarily by a stream of fresh urine pooling around him.

Damien chuckled in amusement, then reached for the hilt of his bastard sword. In the hands of smaller men, it might very well be a greatsword. It was nearly five feet of expertly forged death. The length of the dark gray blade was washed with a thick layer of blood, and Alfrid supposed that soon enough, the sword would drink of his own blood as well.

The end was near, that much he knew. But every instinct, every fiber of his being, drove him toward survival, but little more could be done. Damien Dreadfire would never allow him to leave this place, and even if he did, there would be no recovering from such a grievous wound.

I'm tired. So… so very tired…

Alfrid broke into a fit of tears, the last of his strength flickering away like a candle about to expire.

"No, please, please, good sir, don't kill me. I had no involvement with Borjifa, I had only just joined the army when it happened. I wasn't there! Please! Your quarrel is not with me!" He tried to drag himself backward and away from the barbarian in one last effort to escape.

"Die now with dignity, son of Cedric. Azldyr has no sympathy for cowards. If your soul is untainted, you may very well enter Sjenohor this day."

"Please, I beg of you, I'll do anything!" Alfrid cried. "I'll give you anything, please just let me live!"

Damien Dreadfire took a step forward, his fearsome black armor clanking. His face was a roadmap of rage, vengeance, and a beastly hunger for death that could not be sated.

"I will be sure to let your father know that his son died begging in a puddle of his own blood and piss when I visit him shortly."

Defeated and exhausted, Alfrid lay flat on the ground, relieving the pressure on his wound. His skin had turned cold and icy blue as the last traces of life seeped from his abdomen. There would be little point resisting the inevitable now.

He grimaced in expectation of a sword strike, but instead, his face was greeted with a crushing stomp from Damien's armored foot. His skull gave way with a sickening crunch and sprayed blood and brain matter everywhere, some of which splashed against Dreadfire's hardened face. The now headless body of Alfrid Valens twitched once, then twice before becoming still.

With this terrible and decisive stroke, he had become one of the first casualties in a new conflict, the likes of which had not been seen for nearly four hundred years. War was not coming to the Kingdom of Betanthia, it was already here, and Damien Dreadfire was its architect.

EINARR

THE SWORD SANG A WET, THROATY SONG AS IT PASSED THROUGH THE foeman's neck. Its ovation was warm and red, and lingered in the air for half a heartbeat before drifting away on the wind. The man stepped back a pace, the light quickly diminishing in his eyes. Einarr Rolffson watched as his head gave a reverent bow, then tumbled to the ground, a fountain of blood erupting from his lifeless body.

Einarr wheeled around just as a Betanthian soldier swung a halberd with blinding speed, the blade coming mere inches from his face. He lunged backward, nearly losing his footing in the mud. Einarr's bastard sword rose to meet the halberd as it came screaming down again, both weapons clattering and rattling as they collided. He blocked the attack and attempted a quick thrust, but the polearm was too swift and countered it effortlessly.

The soldier was strong and knew his weapon well. Einarr feared he would not be able to defeat such an opponent, not like this. They danced side to side, carefully measuring each other's movements. The halberdier lunged, his spearpoint coming dangerously close, but Einarr was able to step away. A fierce wind blew his long brown hair around like a scarf, obscuring his vision. He wound up a two-handed slash in reply but tripped over a corpse and fell, splashing into a puddle of brownish-red water.

The enemy sneered and prepared to bring the axehead down in an overhead chop. Einarr half-sworded his blade and prepared to block the strike but knew it would do little against such a powerful attack. He winced in anticipation, but there was a sudden deep thumping sound, and a torrent of blood erupted from the Betanthian's mouth and nose. Again, the halberd came down, though this time limp and lame, and the soldier fell face first onto the ground, a one-handed axe protruding from the back of his skull.

"What's the matter, Rolffson?" Zander, the Zylmacian warchief, smirked. "Don't you fisher folk know how to fight?"

He reached down and wrenched his axe free, smiling. Bald and bare-chested, the wildman was showered in muck and blood and looked like something fresh out of a nightmare. Zander trudged onward, howling like a madman and eager to serve more death.

Einarr fought back to his feet, slapping a thick layer of mud off his hardened leather armor. He witnessed the last of the Betanthian army break ranks and attempt to flee, but the field was perilous and difficult to navigate. Men slipped and fell, clawing and scrambling over each other in a panicked rout.

They didn't make it far. Einarr watched as the warband descended upon the Betanthians like a pack of wolves. Their screams alone were enough to make him turn away. He had spilled a man's blood once before and only out of necessity, but this was another matter entirely. This was his first true battle.

So this is war. May the gods forgive us for what we have done.

Einarr took several deep breaths and coughed. The air was thick with humidity and even thicker with the smell of death. He could nearly taste it. He gripped his bastard sword tight and slogged away from the chaos, stepping over one body after another, eager to retire from the field.

Carrion crows overhead wasted little time and began swooping down to treat themselves to a fresh meal. It was too much to stomach.

He stepped over a pair of bodies and heard a pitiful groan from one of them. It was a Betanthian, grievously wounded and near death, and half-submerged in the mud. He clutched a ruined stump of an arm just below his shoulder, blood gushing uncontrollably onto the earth.

"P… please…" The soldier coughed and moaned.

There was little Einarr could do for the man. He felt pity in his heart, and even shame. From the youngest age, he was taught that all life was sacred and every living thing was connected.

"I'm sorry, Kholdyr. Forgive me for what I must do," Einarr said softly, his eyes drawn to the heavens.

A heavy steel breastplate encased the soldier's chest, protecting his heart and vital organs. Einarr raised his weapon but was unsure how to end the man's suffering. With a sigh, he turned the sword pommel up, drove the blade into the Betanthian's head, and pulled it free. It was an ugly thing to do, but necessary.

He ran a hand through his beard, flicking away specks of debris. The wet dirt tasted like blood. He spat a thick gobbet onto the ground, eager to cleanse the foulness from his lips. Cleansing his soul would be another matter entirely.

The battle had ended nearly as quickly as it began. Their attack was meticulously planned and perfectly executed, just as Damien said it would be. It was the culmination of two years of hard work and determination, bringing the last of the free northern tribes together, along with the western wildmen. Einarr didn't think it would be possible. Hardly anyone did. But here they stood, with their first battle won.

"Einarr!" Arik Akselson approached, a half a score of their Nothanek brethren beside him. Arik wore a breastplate of hardened leather and boar tusks with matching greaves and bracers. The others were in similarly basic attire. "Gods, can you believe it? We won! We actually won!"

It hardly seemed a fair fight, twelve thousand against a third of that, maybe less. But his kinsmen fought well, and bravely. This, too, was their first time on a proper battlefield, and it would seem out of place to deny them their due praise.

"Thank the gods, you all made it." Einarr embraced each of them, though Arik was the only man he somewhat knew.

"My father used to tell me stories of battle, but experiencing it is something else entirely!" Arik smiled incredulously.

It was an experience Einarr could have done without. It was not the Nothanek who spoiled for a fight, nor the Borjifans. None of them asked for this. No, King Marcellus Bethard and his armies had come in search of conquest and left death and ruin in their wake.

"Indeed," Einarr sighed. "I'm proud of you men, and certainly Damien will be grateful for your efforts. Do forgive me, but I must speak with him. I'll see you back at camp."

Arik slapped him on the back and took leave with the other Nothanek. Einarr scanned the terrible landscape in search of Dreadfire, trying not to focus too intensely on the horrific aftermath. He passed by Sylvia Stormguard, who knelt before an ever-growing pile of severed heads. She chanted softly and rhythmically as if in a trance. Her fair skin was covered head to toe in blue warpaint, her flowing mid-back length brown hair a mess of tangles and wet with blood. Einarr looked on uneasily as she took a knife to the face of a dead Betanthian, his skin already a shade of pale blue.

"Is this necessary, Stormguard? You cannot make them any deader than they already are." Einarr swallowed hard.

Sylvia glared at him with unusual intensity but could not maintain her expression for long. She smiled and bellowed heartily with laughter.

"It's an offering to the war god. We'll need his help if we're going to win this war." One of the carved symbols matched a runic tattoo underneath Sylvia's right eye; the sign of Azldyr. Others had been sliced into the dead flesh as well. "These easterners have no idea what they're in for."

Do I have any idea of what I'm in for?

"I never would have thought the Rhivothi were so… morbid in their offerings." The sight of mutilated heads sent bile into the back of Einarr's throat. He had no choice but to avert his eyes.

Sylvia Stormguard was drunk on the ecstasy of battle and hallucinating from mushrooms coursing through her. She shrugged off his comment and scoffed.

"I must ask, do all Nothanek have such fair stomachs, or are you the exception?"

"I'll forgive your insult, just this once," he said. "These men deserved death, but such desecration is unnecessary."

"Do you object to the gods' tribute?" the shieldmaiden shot back.

She was a crazed fanatic, to be sure, and though Einarr was confident enough in his strength and abilities, he kept a tight grip on a dagger sheathed behind his back.

"You assume too much. All life is sacred, Stormguard, even those of our enemies. Send them to the gods for judgment, yes, but this butchery is a step beyond."

"You have your ways, we have ours. To be granted favor with Azldyr, the proper rituals must be performed. He is the war god, after all. Like it or not, we'll need his help if we're ever going to see home again."

An awkward silence came between both warchiefs. Though Einarr disapproved of Sylvia's methods, they were nevertheless her own. The Nothanek and Rhivothi were not enemies as other tribes in the warband were, but their cultures differed in many ways. Nevertheless, in the spirit of their common purpose and goal, Einarr conceded Sylvia's point.

"Very well then." He cleared his throat. "Have you seen Damien? I must speak with him."

"Yes, he's the one who asked me to perform the sevelsej. Where he is now, I don't know." Sylvia laughed in anticipation as a wagon towed by two horses creaked and lurched across the spongy, blood-drenched soil.

The horses whinnied and hesitated from the smell of death but were whipped and compelled onward by their driver.

One by one, she loaded the pile of heads into the wagon. Each was placed in a specific order in accordance with whatever strange ritual she was whispering. Einarr watched as the shieldmaiden's eyes rolled into the back of her head as a song of ancient Khorrish words flowed across her tongue like a turbulent river.

When she came to the final head, Sylvia held it high and laughed. It was an ominous and possessed laugh, more like a crone's as opposed to a woman who looked to be in her twenties. An eyeless and mutilated face stared back at her accusingly.

"I call upon our honored ancestors to give us aid and comfort and let our enemies find none for themselves. Send forth your shades to torment those who have wronged us. Let their cities burn, and their houses crumble. Bring us fortune and victory." Sylvia completed her incantation, then kissed the head before placing it on the pile among the others.

Einarr tightened his face at the sight. This was the first time he had ever witnessed a Rhivothi death ritual. It brought back memories of stories his elders would share around a warm fire when he was a child. They sometimes spoke of the sorcerers of Rej Rhivoth, a strange northern coastal city that claimed the war god Azldyr as their patron. The elders spoke of black magic, dread curses, shapeshifting, and human sacrifice, but such tales always seemed more fantastical than real.

At least some of the stories are true, it seems.

"I've got one for you, Sylvia," a Rhivothi warrior said, flanked by a half-dozen of his kinsmen. Most of them were lightly armored, if at all. They were tall, fearsome, beastly-looking men, much larger and more robust than even the heartiest Nothanek. Between them was a young Betanthian soldier, battered, bloodied, and shaking as if taken by an affliction.

Gods, tell me they're not going to butcher this man!

Einarr took a step forward but thought better of interfering. Provoking the Rhivothi might prove treacherous. He could not risk the warband tearing itself apart, not after two years of forging it alongside Damien. And not after winning their first battle together.

"You there, on the wagon, and be quick about it!" Stormguard pointed her bloodied knife at the driver's seat.

The Betanthian soldier looked around uneasily, as if he could not understand what was happening. He was a young man, clean-shaven and with close-cropped black hair, and looked entirely out of place on a battlefield. One of the Rhivothi gave him a shove from behind with a single arm; the rest chuckled.

The soldier clawed up and onto the wagon like a frightened cat. Einarr let out a sigh of relief, grateful for Sylvia's mercy. He had witnessed enough death to last a lifetime, maybe longer. However, there was still some uncertainty about what the shieldmaiden intended to do next. A crowd was beginning to gather, their cheers and guttural bellows growing and intensifying like a gathering storm.

"Here he comes." She grinned.

Einarr turned and saw Damien Dreadfire, his blackened armor splashed with flecks of brown and red. He paused and basked in the ravenous reception of the warband, a content yet focused look across his stony face.

"Sons and daughters of the north! Of the west! This victory is yours!" Damien shouted, his voice carrying far and wide across the killing fields.

Twelve thousand warriors gave a thunderous reply and hoisted their weapons above their heads in jubilation.

"We have struck the first blow against Betanthia. The Bethards will watch as we lay waste to their foul kingdom! The gods demand blood! They cry out for justice! You are the instruments of their vengeance!"

The warriors roared their approval, beating their armored chests and clanging sword and axe against shield. Einarr joined in the revelry as the bloodied Northmen around him whipped one another into a near frenzy. Though he took displeasure in the excesses of Stormguard, Einarr was nevertheless proud to have taken the first step toward avenging the Bloodbath at Borjifa.

Damien's attention turned to the soldier on the wagon as the deafening war cries dissipated. Bloodied and light-headed from terror, the whelp trembled in fear as the Supreme Warlord approached. Einarr knew there would be no stopping whatever Damien intended to do, and was at peace with what might happen next. He knew that in the sight of the gods, he had at least tried his best to spare the prisoner.

"Go now, little dog, and tell your masters that soon they will meet their fate, for I am the fist of the war god! I am the bringer of blood and sorrow! I am the shadow of death! Tell them that Damien Dreadfire is coming for them. Do this, and you may keep your pathetic life. Do it not, and I will peel the flesh from your bones while you live."

Einarr was taken aback by Damien's decision. He sighed as a wave of relief washed over him. Perhaps Zifnir, goddess of peace and life, had seen enough and showed mercy to their captive. Regardless, it was a welcome turn of events.

"Ride now, and return to your commander. Go, and deliver my message while I still permit you to live."

Frantically, the soldier snapped the leather reins several times, the wagon's wheels creaking and groaning as they turned. Their wooden spokes dripped with muddied earth and the blood of slain men as the horses lurched forward and through the killing fields. The prisoner was met with insults and mocking cries as he passed by the victorious warriors, but soon enough, horse and rider diminished and disappeared over the horizon.

Let Damien celebrate with the men. We can speak later. I had best pray.

Einarr ventured away from the warband as they continued to loot the dead and celebrate their crushing victory with song and strong drink. A small grove of trees to the north of the battlefield provided some privacy where he could pray to the gods and thank them for their protection.

Standing beneath a cluster of sycamore trees, Einarr drew his bastard sword and dropped to one knee, clutching the hilt of his blade with both hands and bowing down in worship.

"Kholdyr, god of gods, hear my prayer. Forgive me for the blood I have spilled here today. Guide and protect me and all of the Nothanek, your faithful servants. Let your will reign supreme."

He sighed and drew a deep breath as a gentle breeze cleaned away the lingering scent of death in the air. "Zifnir, gentle mother. Thank you for your mercy. Carry the souls of our blessed dead to the fields of Sjenohor so they may find peace among their ancestors and feast from Kholdyr's bounty for all eternity."

Einarr raised his head toward the sky, ready to offer another prayer to the long list of gods the Nothanek revered. But he sensed prying eyes upon him and saw a shadow bleeding across the ground.

"Einarr," Damien Dreadfire said, his voice low and gravelly. "Waste not your time on prayers, my friend. The gods are already with us. Honor them instead with your sword arm."

"Yes, Damien, Azldyr's thirst must truly be quenched after today." The words were sour and left a foul taste in his mouth.

"Does something trouble you, my friend?" Dreadfire cocked his head. "Speak. You know there are no secrets between us."

"No, there is no trouble. You won a great victory here today, and tonight your men will drink and feast in your honor." Einarr tried to mask the disgust in his heart.

"Come now, Einarr, speak true," Damien demanded. "Something troubles you, and I would know the truth of it."

"I would never seek to deny you your vengeance, Damien. Gods know these men and their masters earned their deaths, and I will stand at your side until justice has been served. But I bore witness to

Stormguard desecrating the bodies of our enemies. As hated as they may be, no creature deserves to be defiled in such a manner. All life is sacred, even the most villainous among us."

Einarr's face tightened. Though he was the closest to Damien out of the other warchiefs and had known him the longest, something about the man was still indescribably frightening. Two years was enough to forge a solid friendship, but not nearly long enough to learn all of Damien's complexities and secrets he kept locked away in dark places.

"I understand your misgivings," Dreadfire said with an unusual calmness. "And on any other occasion, I might have agreed with you. Stormguard and her Rhivothi are fanatics for certain, and while they believe such butchery is an appeasement to Azldyr, I have my reasons for permitting the sevelsej."

"I still mourn for what happened at Borjifa, Damien. I am one of the few to have seen the aftermath with my own eyes. But…" Lost for words, Einarr threw his hands in the air.

"Do you not see?" Dreadfire's voice rose in intensity and urgency. "What we have started here cannot be undone! We are but twelve thousand! This was a small taste of what the Bethards can muster. There will be more, many more, that will come for us. If we are to win this war, then we must utilize every tool at our disposal." Damien's eyes reflected a deep, calculating, and burning hatred.

"But at what cost? And where does it all end?" Einarr asked hopelessly.

"When the gods have drunk their fill of Bethard blood, it will end. If you have not the stomach for it, you may take your leave back to Skaginlef, and I will think no less of you."

Einarr's mouth hung open as he watched Damien turn and start back toward the warband. He felt slighted. Embarrassed, even. Here he stood with Betanthian blood still wet on his armor, yet somehow his dedication to their cause was in question.

Is this how Damien sees me, as a man more concerned with my principles than fighting to protect our people?

The thought turned his stomach. Quickly, he sheathed his bastard sword and followed after Damien. The warlord did not break stride; his attention focused on disorderly celebrations taking place nearby.

"I swore a vow to you, Damien, and I intend to keep it. Think what you will of my beliefs, but I am no coward. I'll kill as many men as I must."

"I know, son of Rolff. I did not know your father in life, but from what I have heard, his reputation always preceded him. You are a credit to his lineage and to your people. Never forget that, or feel shame for your integrity. But remember, you must always fulfill your duty to the gods, no matter what they ask of us."

Such a compliment was something Einarr would never have expected from a man the likes of Damien Dreadfire, his surprise so great he could offer no reply. The remainder of their walk was silent as Einarr contemplated the full weight of his friend's words. A small part of him felt conflicted and uncertain. Einarr knew deep inside his heart that the principles Damien was lauding today might very well cause turmoil between them in the future. It was an unwelcome and unpleasant thought.

When they returned to the warband, Einarr noticed many warriors congregating around a small clearing. He craned his neck and saw nothing.

"What's going on here? Shouldn't we be making our way back to camp?"

Damien stared intently at the gathering, saying nothing. Einarr grew suspicious. He glanced around in uncertainty, but an eruption of cheers drew his attention. A half-dozen pikes were raised into the air, each bearing a skewered body. The men must have been Betanthian officers, as their breastplates bore a special insignia near their pauldrons.

Einarr felt a sudden, sick feeling in his stomach. He tried to look away, yet somehow he couldn't. It was a grisly monument to the day's work.

"Fear is our most lethal weapon, and I intend to wield it unflinchingly." Damien sneered, his black eyes glaring at the macabre display with bittersweet satisfaction.

Is this what lies in store for me, Kholdyr? Is this what I must be subjected to, for all my good intentions? Is this truly your will?

Damien placed a gauntleted hand on Einarr's shoulder. "Stay your misgivings, my friend. Such cruelty is necessary. The man who led this army was Alfrid Valens."

The name sounded familiar, yet Einarr could not place it. He cocked his head curiously.

"He is the son of Cedric Valens. You have seen his handiwork first-hand at Borjifa." Damien's mouth tightened into a frown. "Lord Valens is the man who led the attack against my people. And right now, he is garrisoned at Castle Morden. That is where these men are from. And after the wagon returns to the castle, he will be coming to seek revenge. That is when the next phase of my plan begins."

Such explanation did little to assuage the uncertainty in Einarr's heart.

"Is this a fight we can even win, Damien?"

"We must. We have no choice. We have to fight while the north still has some measure of strength left. But worry not, my friend. I have seen the path we must tread. I will not lead us astray. But for now, we must leave this place. Get the men moving, we march to the Hinterwood."

Einarr nodded, then made his way to a large gathering of warriors, mostly Zylmacians. Something about the western wildmen made him feel uneasy, even more so than the Rhivothi. From rumors he heard drifting throughout camp at night, the Zylmacians were as likely to skewer a Northman as they were a Betanthian.

He paused, cleared his throat, cupped both hands around his mouth, and shouted. "Listen here, men! Damien has ordered us to disperse at once. We must march with all haste!"

A few of the Nothanek obeyed, and even a score of Rhivothi, much to his surprise. But the wildmen remained, unphased and oblivious.

"Come now, we must leave at once!" he shouted, his throat burning.

A sudden horn blast rippled through the battlefield, drawing the attention of everyone around. Marvath Bonesplitter and a score of his kin muscled through a cluster of warriors and made their way to Einarr.

The last of the four warchiefs, he was a behemoth of a man who nearly rivaled Damien Dreadfire in height and muscle mass. His long, sandy-blonde hair and beard were stained red, as was his bare chest. He clutched a two-handed great axe in his hands, still dripping with fresh gore. Silence fell over the field, with all eyes turning toward him.

"Is there a problem here, Rolffson?" Marvath grunted. His eyes were wide and wild, much like Sylvia Stormguard's.

"It seems our men are too content in their looting and butchery to retire. We've lingered here too long. Damien has instructed us to leave this place at once."

"By his will, so be it," Marvath replied.

"Listen here, you swine!" Bonesplitter turned to the warriors and bellowed. "Your warlord has given you the order to disperse, and here you sit like a bunch of drunkards? Get your asses moving, or I'll take my axe to each and every one of you!" Marvath hoisted his weapon high.

The warriors grumbled, then gathered themselves and began their march. Zander and a handful of his wildmen continued to linger as if they had not heard the order, nor cared to heed the warning. Bonesplitter stormed over to them, fists clenched so tightly around the axe handle it nearly shattered from the pressure.

"That means you, westerner. Get moving." Marvath pointed the axe at Zander's face.

"I remember being told that my men and I have the right to plunder so long as we march under Damien's banner. Would you deny me what's rightfully mine?"

Such an intense staredown would have led to blows if Einarr had not intervened. Both men were fanatics in their own ways and were even more volatile and unpredictable when crossed with one another. He stepped forward and attempted to defuse the situation, asserting himself as Damien's right hand.

"You may stay and loot if you please, but you'll be left to face the Betanthian army alone when it comes to seek revenge. Are a few trinkets worth your life and the lives of your men?"

Running his tongue across half-rotten teeth, Zander sneered and chuckled, then gave Bonesplitter a nod of agreement. Without another word, the wildman turned away with his kinsmen in tow. Marvath stormed over to Damien, his bloodied face turning an even deeper shade of red in anger.

"Are you certain allowing these Zylmacians to march alongside us was wise? They are undisciplined, unruly, and led by a half-wit," Bonesplitter snarled.

"We need every man we can get, and even still, I fear it may not be enough," Damien lamented. "This force we defeated today was just a small taste of what the Bethards can send our way. Zander serves his purpose, and with time he will come to see how we do things in the north."

"If you say so." Marvath spat. "I still don't trust the man."

"Which is why I have you here to watch my back," Dreadfire replied, nodding to the Rhivothi fanatic.

Don't forget about me, Damien. Was I not the first one to swear to you?

Quickly, Einarr dismissed the slight, if it even was one. He knew of Bonesplitter's savagery and why Damien kept him close. It would certainly stand to reason that Einarr would want the largest and most violent man watching his back if needed.

Damien, Einarr, and Marvath walked through the wasteland of dead men to retrieve their horses. They paused and watched as the warband stirred and assembled, then began to move out. Long columns of warriors snaked out of the killing fields and toward the Hinterwood as the sun began its long descent.

"Never would I have imagined we would come this far," Damien reflected as he put a heel into the side of his large, black stallion.

"My lord?" Marvath asked curiously.

"Years of traveling around the Hinterwood and beyond, speaking with tribal leaders and forging this alliance. Years of careful planning and execution… and now here we are, with our first battle won."

"And you have done well. Word of this victory will spread, and others will flock to our cause. Have no fear; this is just the beginning," Marvath boasted. He brushed a windblown lock of blonde hair from his face.

Just the beginning… Do we even know what we have started?

Einarr's thoughts drifted back to Skaginlef and the quaint life he left behind. Though the harvest was many months away, he wondered if the war would permit him to return in time. If the gods were kind, they would see justice served swiftly and allow the Nothanek to see their homes and families again. Two years away felt like a dozen lifetimes. But it would be Einarr Rolffson's job to see his people through the next battle, and however many battles it would take until the war was over. It was a weighty responsibility, but one he agreed to freely.

"Fear, you say? A healthy dose of fear is necessary for our enemies, but also for ourselves," Damien said coldly. "It keeps you from becoming complacent. It keeps you from becoming too confident and underestimating your enemy."

With a grim understanding, Damien Dreadfire's eyes turned to the south. "And there is plenty over the horizon we must fear if we are to make it out of this war alive."

CEDRIC

WHERE IS MY SON? WHAT COULD POSSIBLY BE TAKING HIM SO LONG?
Lord Cedric Valens sighed deeply, his eyes fixed on the far-distant hills surrounding Castle Morden. As a lifelong military man and Commandant of Betanthia's western garrison, there were certain protocols he expected to be followed. The most important was communication, something his son Alfrid seemed to have forgotten as of late.

I knew it was too soon to be sending him out. I should have known better. Damn it, damn it all to hell!

Cedric turned away from the window in his bed-chamber, scowling. It was early, too early for his men to begin their daily training regimen, but time enough for his morning walk across the battlements. He descended from his chamber at the top of the inner keep. A dull, pulsating ache in his hip made each step more grueling than the last. It was one of many times Cedric wished he kept his private quarters on the lower level near his office, but it was seen as a lord's honor to reside above those he commands.

By the time he reached the bottom, he was already yearning for a nap. Cedric's body felt as if it were that of an eighty-four-year-old man instead of a forty-eight-year-old. After a good round of stretching, he stepped out into the bailey and was greeted by a gust of crisp morning air. The early summer rainy season had just run its course, and soon the nights and mornings would become just as unbearable as the afternoons.

Damned humidity. It just sucks the life right out of you. Give me a Cardale summer any day.

The capital was where he truly wished to be, not stuck at the edge of Betanthia's western border. As he walked through the empty bailey, Cedric Valens wondered if his promotion to Commandant was worth its cost. There was glory and respect to be found in the title, for certain, but the office came with its own share of hardships. Being shuttered away in the far reaches of the Kingdom was certainly not what he had envisioned.

He ascended a staircase in one of the four corner towers, his sore hip complaining with every step. A nearby sentry paused and saluted as he passed, then returned to patrol. There was safety to be found inside Castle Morden's walls, which were built using the largest and heaviest stone blocks ever fashioned, but it made climbing to the battlements all the more insufferable. And the scenery that lay beyond was nearly as dismal as the stronghold's stony gray facade.

Hills and more hills. What I wouldn't give to have warm sand between my toes again.

His first two laps around the battlements were especially painful, but the third was more tolerable. As the morning sky grew brighter, dirt and grime that tarnished the castle exterior became clearer. Castle Morden was completed only twenty years prior, but from the outside, it looked older and far more weathered. Cedric chuckled, thinking of how much his body had in common with the place he called home.

On any other day, he would oversee training for the recruits who arrived a fortnight prior. But as men began to saunter out into the courtyard, Cedric made a hasty retreat. The latest batch of peasants was proving to be extremely disappointing, to say the least. Watching them clumsily stumble through their morning drills was more than he could stomach, especially having grown used to commanding elite troops in the field. It was the last thing he needed to subject himself to, especially with Alfrid's whereabouts remaining uncertain.

Before he could find refuge back inside the keep, he was greeted by Lieutenant Ellis Byrne, an overly enthusiastic officer in his early twenties. His presence was insufferable more often than not, but at least he meant well.

"Good day to you, my lord," Ellis said cheerfully.

"If this counts as a good day to you, I'd hate to see what a bad day is." Cedric scowled and looked up at the gloomy sky with disdain. "Have we received any word from Alfrid's patrol?"

"As of this morning, no, my lord. Perhaps I could dispatch a rider to Khorrtal? It could be that Captain Valens has been too occupied to send word."

He sighed in frustration. Suppressing the disturbance in Khorrtal should have fallen to Commander Jaxson Holland and not Alfrid, but his field army of thirty thousand men had become bogged down for months on the Zylmacian borderlands, thanks to the non-stop rain. It was a source of endless frustration, to say the least.

"If we don't hear anything by midday, then yes, send a rider at once," Cedric ordered. "And have your man inform the good Captain that part of his responsibility is to send regular situation reports, as tedious and time-consuming as they may be."

His doubts about bringing Alfrid under his wing were growing. There was a good chance his son had become too comfortable in his station and thought that rules simply didn't apply to him. A strong reprimand would await Alfrid upon his return, one that would be done in front of the garrison to avoid any accusations of favoritism.

"Yes, my lord, I'll see to it." Ellis stiffened his back and saluted.

"I really do hate this forsaken place," Cedric whispered as he hobbled into the keep. The stress of thinking about Alfrid seemed to make his hip even worse, but there would be little use in dwelling on it now. There were enough duties requiring his attention, duties just as important as suppressing uprisings in the barbarian village of Khorrtal. He entered his office, shut the door, and sat behind his large, overcrowded desk.

Grain shipments from Mor Seveht. Iron ore from Hok. Now if only I could get some recruits that were worth a damn.

One by one, Cedric confronted each piece of parchment on his desk with the same indignation. He had been a soldier all his life, a man of action, but now reduced to busywork better suited for lesser men. It wasn't easy to oversee such a large stretch of frontier. There was always some report to be filed with Cardale or their liaison with the Blackthorn Knights. Whenever one paper was completed, it was time to draft another.

When he was about halfway finished, Cedric stood with a groan and stretched his aching legs, hips cracking and popping like the old chair he sat on. He looked down at the piles of paper and could not help but remember the most important dispatch was still missing.

Damn it Alfrid, how difficult is it to send a rider? Why must you put me through this? I suppose it's my fault. I should have taught you better.

He ran a hand through thin wisps of gray hair on the top of his head and looked around helplessly. It was the most unsettling feeling to know he could do nothing except wait. Across the room stood a tall bookshelf, its contents covered with a healthy layer of dust. Inside a pair of cabinet doors was a small cask of wine left inside for ages, so long that Cedric had almost forgotten about it.

He gently opened the doors, retrieved the cask, and sat it on his desk. Its contents sloshed around and suggested it was still quite full. Cedric returned to his seat with a grunt of discomfort, then dumped the remaining water inside a wooden cup onto the floor. As he poured the wine, he shook his head, knowing it was weak to succumb to such a vice.

After a few sips, he began to feel better and was able to finish trudging through the remainder of his paperwork. By the time Cedric finished, it was nearly supper time, but he didn't feel like eating. Instead, he shambled up the winding staircase, cask tucked gently under one arm, while the sounds of laughing and feasting echoed into the cavernous keep.

Upward he climbed, pausing every so often to nurse his aching hip and stare out of a westward-facing window. With longing eyes, he scanned the horizon, hoping against hope that from such a vantage point, he might spy a friendly rider approaching. But each time he stopped to look, it only brought more disappointment. Climbing to the top seemed to take an hour or more, and each time the wind blew, it felt as if the entire tower was swaying and shifting.

When Cedric finally arrived at his chamber, he set the cask down, slipped into his night clothes, and immediately went to bed. There were no dreams, only a pitch-black nothingness that lifted when he opened his eyes. A small sliver of sunlight poured through the window and kissed his face, beckoning him to rise and face a new day.

Begrudgingly, Cedric dragged himself from bed and downed a few mouthfuls of water to ease the slamming sensation in his head. Not even a cool morning breeze through the window could renew his body or spirit, but the daily routine was calling nevertheless.

After making his daily walk around the battlements, Cedric observed his men funneling into the bailey for their morning training. This was perhaps the most frustrating part of being in charge, watching young peasant boys make fools of themselves for hours on end. These were not real soldiers, and with each passing day, he wondered if they ever would be.

"Good da—, I mean, I trust you slept well, my lord?" Ellis Byrne babbled stupidly, hoping to avoid the same accosting from the day before.

"That was undoubtedly the worst sleep I've ever had," Cedric grumbled, though he took a bit of satisfaction from seeing the young Lieutenant squirm. "What do you have to report?"

"Nothing new, my lord. As always, I will inform you the second I hear anything."

Lord Valens shook his head, then resumed watching the recruits as they trained. It was a pitiful sight to behold. They swung wildly at each other with little regard for stance or technique, a sloppy and disappointing spectacle if there ever was one.

"These recruits get worse every year, I swear," he complained.

"Indeed, my lord. But have faith, we'll get them whipped into shape one way or another."

"Sometimes, I wonder if Cardale knows what goes on outside the city limits. It's as if they've forgotten we have a border to protect and need capable men to do it."

Ellis pursed his lips, unsure of how to respond.

"They scrape the bottom of the barrel and expect me to defend our lands with whatever they dredge up." Cedric spat. "These damn peasant boys they send me have grown fat and soft."

He peered down into the courtyard and squinted. "Except that one over there." He pointed at a short and gaunt recruit, struggling to keep a practice sword and shield upright.

"Look at him, Ellis. He looks like something the dogs dug up. Damn sod looks like he's about to piss himself!"

Cedric stormed across the battlements and shouted at the lad, who looked to be barely fifteen. He disappeared into the corner tower, then reappeared at ground level. Cedric's anger and frustration had boiled over to the point where he could no longer feel the pain in his hip.

"You there! Yes, you! Just what do you think you're doing?" His words thundered and drew the attention of everyone in the bailey. It grew quiet, save for a few muffled chuckles.

"I'm… I'm training, my lord," the young man stammered, his arms straining from the weight of weapons too large to handle. Sweat was seeping through his thin and slightly ragged brown tunic.

"Is this some kind of joke? Do you make a mockery of my garrison, boy? What's your name?"

"Spencer M…M… Morris, my lord."

"Well, Spencer Morris, Norris, whatever… What's a walking corpse like you doing in my castle? Shouldn't you be in a field somewhere pushing up wildflowers and feeding the crows? Hm?"

"I was conscripted, my lord. I was told I would learn to fight." Spencer's fearful eyes glanced up but immediately fell back to the ground.

"I'm surprised you could fight your way out of your mother's cunt!" Cedric shot back, drawing more chuckles. "Ellis! Front and center."

"Yes, my lord?" Lieutenant Byrne muscled through the gathering of men and presented himself.

"Take this one here to the stables. Perhaps shoveling horse shit all day will put some muscle on his bones. Get him out of my sight." He turned away from the young wretch in displeasure and made his way back up to the battlements.

Decades of faithful service to the crown, and for what? This? Cedric thought as he slogged up the stone steps. *I have done everything Marcellus has asked of me, I have stained my hands red for the man, and this is how he rewards me?*

Captain Declan Wilmot and Lieutenant Zakery Chambers stood near the entrance to the corner tower, snickering to themselves. They were dressed in casual attire instead of their officer's armor, with plain tunics and trousers on both of them. Although it was an annoyance to see their disregard for proper dress, Cedric had little energy to accost either of them.

"I'll never tire of watching you break in the recruits." Declan smiled, fighting back the urge to laugh.

"Someone has to put fear into these little boys," Cedric grunted, still fuming from the encounter. "I hate having to get my blood up, but it's become a necessity as of late. If they think I'm harsh, they should see what lies beyond these walls. Those savages out there aren't going to spare their lives, let alone their feelings."

Both officers saw that Cedric's words pained him. It had been far too long since the Mord had received word from Alfrid's patrol. A deep concern had grown throughout the ranks, though few dared to speak of it openly. Even though Cedric didn't know it, the entire stronghold shared his frustration and anxiety.

"That's why we're here, my lord. We'll make proper soldiers out of them in no time, have no fear. We haven't let you down yet," Zakery said reassuringly. He gave Declan a nod and a slight motion of his hand, compelling him to speak privately with their Commandant. Lieutenant Chambers dismissed himself, strode across the battlements, then disappeared into the tower.

The bailey was filled with clashing and clanging of sword on shield, thumping of arrows against targets, and grunts and shouts of men as they trained. Declan beckoned Cedric to follow him to the other end of the castle walls, where it was quieter.

"May we speak freely, my lord?"

"Very well. What troubles you?"

"It's not what troubles me; it's what troubles you. There isn't a man here that doesn't share your worry. I just want you to know we are all concerned for Alfrid, and we'll do whatever it takes to bring him home safely. We dispatched a rider yesterday afternoon, but it will take a few days before we hear anything."

"I've been commanding men since you first learned to hold a sword," Cedric said curtly. "I know how long these missions are supposed to take. And Alfrid knows the protocols. He knows to send riders and keep lines of communication open, or at least he bloody well should. No, something has gone terribly wrong. I can feel it in my bones."

"Commander Holland should be returning from deployment shortly, perhaps we could send him to investigate?"

Cedric scoffed at the mention of his name and stared out beyond the castle walls. "There's no telling when he'll be back. I wouldn't put much faith in the man."

Miles of green, rolling fields were a sight to behold, but their beauty was a mere facade. Beyond them was the domain of barbarians, men who refused to be conquered. Despite House Bethard's effort to bring civilization to all of Caldakas, there were still countless tribes who refused and clung to their old ways. Cedric had a special disdain for such men, having faced them more times than he could remember.

He thought back to his past encounters with the northern tribes. The Battle of Mosswood had been especially bloody and still left a foul taste in his mouth. He was young and naive and made many mistakes, costing untold Betanthian lives. The Battle of Borjifa was an experience he would just assume forget. No one dared speak of it aloud due to the rumors of what had transpired that day. The two sieges of Khorrtal were the most recent and proved to be his most successful. The barbarian city had begun to accept the Kingdom and its rule, though its surrounding lands were still hostile.

"With your permission, I'll take a detachment of riders and see to the matter personally," Declan Wilmot said, breaking Cedric out of his head.

As he made to speak, a sudden commotion by the gatehouse drew his attention. Men were hurriedly gathering in greater and greater numbers, their voices muffled and indiscernible.

"My lord! Come quickly!" someone cried out.

Cedric descended from the battlements to ground level and hurried to the source of the disturbance, impatiently ordering those in front of him to disperse. His heart fluttered and slammed, making it difficult to draw breath. This was the moment Castle Morden had been waiting for.

Finally, and it's about damn time too.

He was uncertain if he would hug Alfrid or slap him, but either way, Cedric was immensely grateful. A horse-drawn covered wagon sat in the entranceway to the bailey. Anxious soldiers had clustered around and prevented it from fully entering. Cedric found it curious, since Alfrid's patrol took no wagons with them and would never send a messenger in such a way. It made no sense, not when speed was the objective.

"Make way! Make way, I say!" Cedric barked.

As the wagon came fully into sight, he saw a shocked and heavily bloodied man slumped over on top. A hideous stench befouled the air, and the sound of thousands of flies was near deafening.

The young man was one of Morden's own and among the three thousand Alfrid took with him. Lord Valens shouted for fresh water and for the soldier to be brought down. He was unsure of what to make of the situation.

"Tell me, what did you see out there?" Cedric asked impatiently. "What of our detachment? What news do you bring? Speak!"

Still dazed, the soldier stared blankly into space and offered no reply. Cedric grabbed him by the shoulders and gave him a shake. "What of Captain Valens? What happened to my son?"

"They were everywhere," the man said in a faint and monotone voice. "We were just outside of Khorrtal when they set upon us. It all happened so fast. One minute, we were marching, and the next…" His lips tightened and quivered. "The last thing I remember was the screams. I went down, I'm not sure from what. When I came to, it was quiet. It was… I've never seen such a thing… I thought I was going to die right then and there, but he sent me back here… he… he told me…"

Cedric was unsatisfied with the cryptic answers. " I will ask you one final time, what happened to my son? And who was this man you speak of? Tell me now, or I'll have your head!"

The soldier turned to his Commandant, tears dripping from sunken and reddened eyes. "I'm not sure what happened to Captain Alfrid.

All I saw was death… death all around me. His name is… is Damien Dreadfire, that's what he said. He's coming. He's… he's coming…"

Silence fell over the Mord. Cedric stood quietly, his stomach clenched tightly as a fist. He turned to the rear of the wagon and approached, the overwhelming odor growing more intense and insufferable. His hand gripped the canvas bonnet hesitantly, then threw it back. A large swarm of flies erupted, the men nearby recoiling in disgust at the horrific sight before them.

The wagon was filled with severed heads, many of whom had eyes missing and mouths left agape. Strange runes were crudely carved into their faces, with different symbols under each eye. The growing summer heat caused them to decompose on the ride back. After a glance, Cedric closed the bonnet. Men retched and groaned, some leaving the courtyard altogether, their senses overcome by the bloody warning they had received.

"My lord, what do we do now?" Ellis coughed and covered his face.

"I want riders dispatched immediately."

His decades of experience with the barbarian tribes told him exactly what happened and what this macabre warning meant. It was, without a doubt, his worst nightmare come true.

"Send word to the High Marshal at Bentmont. Tell him to ready the Blackthorn and dispatch whatever men he can as quickly as possible. And notify the King. He's going to want to hear about this." Cedric moved briskly to the stables and continued issuing orders.

"Someone find Commander Holland and tell him to send his army to Khorrtal immediately. Have him meet me there. He is not, and I repeat, not to return to the castle," he demanded, mounting his horse.

"My lord, are you sure it's wise to leave? What if those fiends are headed this way?" Ellis asked with growing concern.

"They won't be. They know better than to attack fortifications. And I would rather our army meet them in the field instead of being trapped here. I've never lost a battle against these savages, and I don't intend to lose now," Cedric replied.

"Yes, my lord. Shall I accompany you?"

"No, you'll have command while I'm gone. I'm going out there to look for my son. Seal the gates behind me and double the wall guard. And when you write to the High Marshal, make a note of everything. Leave out no detail, do you understand me?"

"Absolutely, my lord. Shall I send word to Lord Vakaro as well?"

Cedric's face tightened. Lord Ridley Vakaro, the southern Commandant, was perhaps the only man in Betanthia that unsettled him. Endlessly resourceful and with a mean streak rivaling any barbarian, he was a force to be reckoned with. But he was far away, much farther away than the Blackthorn Knights in Bentmont.

"No, he'll never be able to arrive soon enough, even if he were to march today," Cedric lamented. "This is our fight. But we must have Commander Holland. Reaching him is imperative!"

"Yes, my lord, it will be done." Ellis gave a crisp salute and ran to the keep to fetch pen and parchment.

"Wilmot! Chambers! On me!" he cried out, then gave his steed a stern nudge with a bootheel and rode through the gate.

With little more than two hundred knights following him, Cedric Valens left the safety of Castle Morden and raced at speed to the northwest. Nearly two days of hard riding lay ahead. A messenger was sent to the east, and would ride hard for nearly half a day before passing it on to another who waited at various checkpoints across Betanthia.

The pace was brutal, and the day seemed to melt away as man and beast raced toward Khorrtal. With frantic determination, Cedric drove his white destrier as hard as possible, his knights struggling to keep pace. It wasn't until the horses tired and protested any further advance that he decided to make camp and rest. The next day would come soon enough, and he would need all the strength his mind and body could muster.

His meal that evening was meager, and his company even more so. It was nearly impossible to find rest, and Cedric had to rely on all of his discipline to keep his eyes shut. Alfrid was still out there, somewhere, or at least he hoped, and every minute that passed was another minute his son was left vulnerable. But even the strongest and heartiest of warriors needed rest, he thought, and soon the haze of the dream realm took hold.

Sleeping would prove to be treacherous. His dreams were filled with horrific images of fire and death, things he had seen many times before. But this time, it was different. At the center of the carnage was Alfrid, alone and surrounded by a ring of fire. Cedric tried to reach out and take hold of his son, but the heat was too intense. Again, he tried to rescue Alfrid, but each effort became increasingly difficult. Cedric stumbled back to withdraw from the heat, his skin nearly boiling.

The look of unbridled fear on Alfrid's face was unlike anything he had ever witnessed. His son writhed and screamed as the flames closed in, but neither made any audible noise. It seemed as if Cedric had gone deaf, yet he could hear his breathing and heart thumping. Suddenly, the indomitable inferno climbed higher and grew as bright as the sun. Cedric rose to try one final time, but his footing soon faltered. The once firm ground liquefied into a reddish-brown cocktail of blood and soil, trickling up from below at first but then gushing forth as if a valve had opened.

The thick cascade of gore and filth quickly turned into an ocean, and Cedric was forced to begin treading the foul water. He looked around frantically to where Alfrid was wreathed in fire, but he was nowhere to be found, and neither were the flames. Cedric saw nothing except a blackened sky above and an endless sea of blood below. Then, a figure appeared in the distance, walking above the reddish-black tides as if they were stone.

Whoever, or whatever it was, moved closer. It looked to be a man, unnaturally tall and built like a mountain. He wore a suit of black steel armor and was shrouded by a helm that looked like the head of a demon. From its dark eye slits came two soft embers, each twinkling softly before crackling and rising into an explosion of flames.

Cedric tried to swim away but felt bony fingers grasping his feet and legs. He screamed and flailed his arms in terror to try and stay afloat. The figure in black armor drew closer, then reached to take hold of him. Jagged claws on the man's gauntlets came inches away from Cedric's face when he finally awoke, the nightmare having thankfully ended.

A thick film of moisture coated his face, though he was unsure if it was sweat or morning dew. The sun was rising quickly, and with it, fear from the terrible nightmare subsided. All he felt was determination. Determination to see his son again and hold him close.

It was a dream, just a dream. Alfrid is still out there, and he needs you now.

There would be little time to eat a proper breakfast, not when Khorrtal was nearly within sight. Cedric took a few bites of bread and a few drinks from a waterskin, then mounted his destrier in a hurry. The commotion caused the knights to rouse from their slumber and take notice of their Commandant, prompting a hasty preparation for the ride ahead.

It was half-past noon when Lord Valens caught sight of a large swarm of birds circling in the distance. He immediately felt his hope fade into nothingness. Cedric paused at the base of a small hill, the final obstacle between him and whatever lay on the other side.

The smell of death was so nauseating it caused his horse to recoil. A certain part of him wanted to turn back, but he could not. In the deepest depths of his heart, Cedric knew the horrors waiting in the valley below, and that his son was likely down there, somewhere.

I can't leave him... not down there, and not like this. My boy deserves more than the hospitality of crows.

With as much courage as he could gather, Cedric jammed his heel into his steed and galloped over the hilltop. Once there, he gave pause. All he could do was stare in shock at the butchered remains of his men as a single tear slipped down his cheek.

MADELYN

A SHARP BANGING AGAINST THE DOOR ROUSED MADELYN EVERLY from her sleep. In her weary and half-conscious state, she couldn't make out what was said by whoever was on the other side. Perhaps it was a pressing matter needing a swift response, or it could simply be the usual monotony of her daily duties calling. She was almost too tired to care.

Madelyn stretched as she pulled the sheets back from her naked body, because what she really wanted was another twenty minutes of rest. But it was half past six, and time enough for her to get up and start the day. She rubbed the sleep from her steely-blue eyes and rose from bed slowly, her toes curling against a bearskin rug. Another day at Castle Thorn was calling.

A dingy mirror sat near a large bay window. She looked herself up and down briefly. Bruises from a sparring match two days ago still peppered her toned body, as well as scratches and bites from last night's tryst. Red nail marks on her arm would be easy to explain away, but a faint outline of teeth near a birthmark on her neck would speak volumes.

Her long, straight, hip-length hair was a knotted mess from the lust-fueled rendezvous of a few hours prior. While combing out the tangles, she could not help but replay the events in her head. He was a decent lover and knew a woman's body well, and had come to know her body many times over the past eight months. In fact, she was tempted to invite him back to her bedchamber come sundown, but she had a feeling today would be long and tiresome, as days in the Order often were. No matter.

Madelyn put her hair into a braid, then began deciding what to wear. Maybe today, she would dress in something more discreet so that none would raise suspicion over the markings on her body. After a few minutes of deliberation, she threw caution to the wind and settled on her usual attire. A simple yet figure-flattering white blouse and a black leather corset were her staples, with leggings and knee-high black leather boots, and a worn leather belt with several small pouches and a sheath for a dagger. She dressed in the same outfit, or one similar to it, almost every day, and she wasn't about to let other people's opinions dictate her sense of style.

Let them stare and ask questions if they want. I don't give a damn.

Her walk through the long, cavernous corridors always seemed to take ages. Castle Thorn felt empty no matter how many knights were inside, given it was one of the largest strongholds ever built. Madelyn ran her hand across the bare walls as she walked, feeling their rough yet surprisingly smooth surface. The stones were as black as obsidian and felt slightly damp from humidity. Sometimes, the blocks became so wet they appeared to be weeping.

An eastern breeze through a nearby window caught her attention. She paused and glanced out at the magnificence of Bentmont. From here, the view extended far into the surrounding countryside, even though her quarters were nowhere near the top of the keep. The stronghold cast a long shadow across Bentmont, so long that no matter where one might find themselves, they would always be in the presence of Castle Thorn.

She leaned slightly out the window and looked upward, the keep tower so tall it nearly disappeared into the heavens. There were times when Madelyn wondered how long it took to build such a castle, how many men labored to complete it, and what madman thought of its construction.

I can't decide which is taller, Castle Thorn or the Westwind Citadel. If I ever get back to Cardale, I'll have to find out!

It would certainly be a close contest. Sometimes when the weather was right, Castle Thorn's tower appeared to vanish into the clouds, giving the illusion it continued upward with no end. If it wasn't for the splendor of Bentmont surrounding such a monstrosity, one might never venture within a hundred leagues of it.

While descending the near thousands of stairs to ground level, she recalled a time when she constructed a wooden sled and slid all the way to the bottom. She couldn't have been more than seven, maybe eight at the time. The High Marshal was quite upset when he heard the racket, the great hall below filled with the most awful noise.

I caught a thrashing for that one, but it was worth it!

It was a fond memory. Though Castle Thorn was no ordinary home for a child, it was still home. And so was Bentmont, for that matter. There was a certain allure to it that she couldn't put her finger on. It was an old city, far older than Cardale, and in certain places, it showed. It was quieter by far, less populated than the capital, and lacked many of its problems. Crime was virtually non-existent due to the constant comings and goings of thousands of Blackthorn Knights, which made for many pleasant and worry-free adventures through the market stalls, even at late hours of the night.

After her long, winding trek to the bottom, she made her way to the grand chamber. Unlike the crisp air in the tower that was so clean she could practically taste it, here it stunk like horse dung. It was perhaps the worst part about summer, the heat making the stench nearly unbearable. It wafted throughout the lower level like a dense, putrid fog. Despite growing up here, the smell still made her wrinkle her nose and cough.

Whoever built this place obviously thought little about where to put the stables. Did they have to go so close to the keep doors? Ugh.

The High Marshal's voice echoed faintly into the hallway through a semi-closed door. Madelyn paused just before entering so as not to disturb whatever gathering was happening inside. It was not until she heard the meeting adjourning that she entered, an entourage of officers who passed by casting judgmental gazes.

Life as the only female Commander in the Blackthorn Knights was far from easy, but she had learned to take the good with the bad in stride. Nearly a decade of service to the Order would have been enough to earn any man unquestionable respect from his peers, but for her, reality was much different.

Despite being only twenty-five, Madelyn Everly had risen to the highest rank aside from the office of the High Marshal. After being found abandoned at the gates of Castle Thorn as a child, she was taken in by Jenson Powell and eventually raised to be a knight. She sometimes wondered if she had been shown favoritism over the years despite her accomplishments, and if her brethren in the Order bore resentment for it. Sometimes, it felt like it was the case.

Madelyn paid no attention to their whispers and made her way across the chamber, stopping at the end of a large oak table sitting at its center. The room was modestly adorned with black and gold banners of the Blackthorn Knights, and oil paintings of previous High Marshals who served throughout the centuries.

"Good morning, High Marshal." She bowed respectfully.

At the opposite end of the table sat Jenson Powell. Nearly two dozen chairs ran down the length of the table between them. He motioned for her to come closer.

"Good morning to you, Madelyn. I trust you are well?" Jenson asked without looking up from the parchments and books cluttered around him.

"Very well, sir. How can I be of service?"

High Marshal Powell paused for a second until he found the document he was looking for, then pushed the other papers aside and laid it down before her.

"A rider arrived in the night with a message from Castle Morden."

"Castle Morden?" She found it curious that anyone from the Mord was sending a communique to the Order. The northwestern frontier had been quiet for years and was defended by an entire field army.

Surely this must be a simple logistical matter? But if so, why is he bothering to tell me? I'm a Commander, not a clerk.

"Judging from the contents, it… doesn't look good," Jenson said through pursed lips.

"I beg your pardon, High Marshal, but I don't understand."

"Can I trust this matter will stay strictly confidential?" There was a certain seriousness behind Jenson Powell's hazel eyes, quite uncharacteristic for a man she had known for most of her life.

Madelyn nodded. Jenson handed over the communique, then ran a hand down his face. She quickly scanned the message but had to stop and reread it slowly, this time aloud.

"Morden garrison… attacked… patrol lost…" Her voice trailed off. "Is this authentic?"

"Yes. The dispatch bore the Commandant's seal."

The more gruesome details turned Madelyn's face green. It was the most unspeakable form of savagery one could imagine. She was unsure how to feel after reading about the fate of Alfrid Valens and his three thousand men, her emotions shifting from uneasiness to anger, and back to uneasiness again.

The message contained several drawings of strange runic symbols she had never seen. They certainly didn't represent any form of language spoken in the Kingdom, or even the few Droethien dialects one might encounter. No, this appeared to be something far, far older. Curiously she studied them.

"What are these drawings of? What are they supposed to mean?"

"I'm not sure, Madelyn, I've been sifting through my books on the histories, and I haven't been able to turn up anything. And there's nothing in the archives with any information, at least nothing I've found," Jenson replied with a sigh, then leaned back in his chair. The tarnished old wood groaned and popped from his weight.

"Regardless of what they mean, something has to be done about this attack. Is the King aware of what's happened?"

"Likely no, at least, not yet. The dispatch reached us first; another will reach Cardale within the week. I do believe that, Commander…" Jenson paused, straining to remember the correct name. "Commander Holland is still in the theater and will likely respond soon enough."

"So we should do nothing?" she asked petulantly.

"Not entirely," the High Marshal said, sensing her impatience. "The immediate threat can be dealt with well enough, but I'm far more interested in the long-term ramifications of this… this declaration of theirs, and what it ultimately might mean. We're here to safeguard Betanthia, Madelyn. It's our duty to be vigilant and proactive, and to see every potential outcome those fat, contented lords in Cardale cannot."

Madelyn smiled. There were often tensions between the King's advisors and the High Marshal over the security of Betanthia's borders. On more than one occasion, Lord Aldred Eldon chastised High Marshal Powell over his supposedly overzealous and, as Aldred put it, paranoid nature.

"There must be some meaning behind all of this, Madelyn," Jenson continued. "I want you to head to the Ivornorium and see what you can find. I know you're not fond of scholarly labor, but I want to keep this matter between us until we know more. Of my Commanders, I have the most faith in you."

His sentiment was touching. Madelyn never knew who her parents were; the only father figure she had was the High Marshal. Having devoted his life to the Order, Jenson Powell never wed nor bore children. It stood to reason he saw Madelyn as a daughter, though they never spoke of such things.

"I'll do my best, High Marshal. You can trust I'll keep this matter confidential."

Madelyn stood and saluted, then promptly left the grand chamber, the dispatch folded neatly inside a leather belt pouch. Upon reaching the bailey, she heard swords clacking against shields and grunts and shouts of recruits as they trained. Madelyn stepped out into the dirt courtyard and briefly surveyed the morning drills, which she seldom did. A blinding sun overpowered a patch of wispy clouds, shining so bright its rays pained her steely-blue eyes.

"Faster yah damn cravens, faster! You there, keep your guard up!" Hunter Northcott was an unattractive man with an even more unattractive voice. His thick harborman accent was unmistakable. Madelyn heard him walking among the recruits and accosting them at every opportunity. He was one of the more reliable Elites in the Order and mentored her many times. It was difficult to see his head of shaggy silver hair amidst a sea of steel helmets, but knowing he was there brought a smile to her face.

A half-dozen other officers were watching, but Madelyn was unsure who some of them were. The Order often rotated forces from frontline duty back to Castle Thorn, and many of the officers she had never seen before. One face she could never forget was that of the head cavalryman, First Lance Corbyn Scott. After all, they had burned the midnight oil in each other's arms just last night.

"Are you sure you've held a sword before? That performance was utterly disgraceful!" Corbyn spat, tossing his helmet and sparring sword to the ground. Locks of sweaty black hair fell over his caramel-colored eyes. He brushed them out of the way with his fingers.

"Yes, I've held a sword before. What sort of question is that?" the recruit shot back in defiance, callously dropping his helmet. The man lacked any form of discipline or respect despite appearing to be well into his thirties.

"Someone with that kind of ego sure as hell better deliver when the time comes. I can't tell you how many cocky recruits we get in here year after year. And every one of you thinks the same thing; that you can pick up a sword and master it in an afternoon. Well, let me tell you, you're nothing. A Droethien would cleave right through you without feeling a jolt in his sword arm."

The nameless recruit rolled his eyes and made to leave.

"And you know what happens the first time someone like you sees battle?" Corbyn continued his verbal assault. "The same thing every time. They get cut to ribbons and scream for their mothers while holding their guts. Learn some humility. It will serve you well one day."

The man muttered something, threw down his gauntlets, and loosened his steel breastplate that was digging into his sides. Madelyn exited the keep and traversed the bailey toward the gatehouse, trying not to pay attention to the sparring match, but the recruit quickly became focused on her.

"Now there's a sight! The High Marshal must have expensive taste when it comes to the local whores. Perhaps I'll fancy a go later tonight!"

The First Lance was having none of it. He stepped in close to the recruit and violently grabbed a handful of his manhood. Corbyn squeezed his testicles hard and twisted, causing the upstart recruit to yelp and turn red in a near instant.

"That's Madelyn Everly. Are you familiar with the name?" Corbyn growled.

"N… No… sir," the recruit croaked and grabbed him by the forearms, but the First Lance's grip was locked tight.

"How many Commanders are there in the Blackthorn Knights?" Corbyn squeezed harder, but the only reply was an incoherent groan.

"There are three. And you're looking at one of them."

He released his grip, the recruit stumbling backward and falling in a heap on the ground. Madelyn had to fight with all her discipline to avoid laughing at the exchange.

"You are never to disrespect her like that again, to her face or behind her back. Do you understand me? She's one of the finest leaders the Order has ever produced, and as Commander, she's never lost a single battle. Ever." Corbyn looked down at the recruit with disgust. "Now pick your gear up and find someone else to train you. I'm finished."

Madelyn smiled as she passed through the outer gatehouse. The First Lance was a good and kind man, though sometimes overzealous in his affections. She often found it amusing, but certainly flattering all the same. Were it any other day, she might have stayed longer and relished in the exchange, but the High Marshal was not a man to be kept waiting.

Madelyn always enjoyed walking the streets of Bentmont. It was an old city with a more modern and alluring charm than the capital. Centuries-old buildings made of brick and sandstone had weathered to a rusty brown color over the years, while fired clay roof tiles still retained their distinctive red hue. Miles of maze-like stone streets were narrow, save for the main avenues, making it a traveler's worst nightmare.

When not tending to her duties at Castle Thorn, Madelyn loved to wander throughout the city and explore new shops and taverns from the richest neighborhoods to the poorest. But today, she had little time for such leisure. She had to resist the urge to browse wares from Bentmont's leather workers and blacksmiths as she hurried to the Ivornorium. But ultimately, this was one battle she would lose. While shuffling, and at times, shoving her way through a massive crowd, she happened upon a merchant stable she had not seen before.

Don't do it. Don't you do it. You have business to attend to.

An olive-skinned merchant's wares were quite diverse. He had leather bracelets, belts, and bags of exquisite quality, but Madelyn had all those in plenty. Not even his unique and distinctive metalworks seemed to appeal to her. More than steel and leather, she fancied trinkets and keepsakes. She often considered it a stupid hobby, near to an obsession.

A wide array of small figurines immediately caught her attention. Some appeared carved out of animal bone or ivory, and some were crafted from bronze or copper. Madelyn picked up a figurine of a priestess and grinned. It was remarkably well-detailed, from its carving to its paint. Although she did not practice the old faith, the piece was still intriguing. Another statuette of a wild horse in mid-gallop made her heart swoon.

"How much for both of these?" she asked the merchantman excitedly.

"Ah, the lady has fine taste," the man said in a thick and somewhat familiar accent. Judging by his appearance, he could very well have been Droethien. "For you, hmmm… I say, five gold pieces."

The price was steeper than she hoped, and if the man was Droethien, there would be little success in haggling. But life as a knight was always uncertain, and she thought it would be better to enjoy the little things whenever possible. Madelyn reached into a belt pouch, produced a handful of coins, and then handed five to the merchant.

"Most thanks to you, my lady." The merchant suddenly had an idea flash in his eyes. He held up a finger to keep her attention, then ducked beneath his stall to fetch something. When he emerged, he held a small glass vial filled with opaque liquid.

"For your generosity, will you sample some of my finest perfume? It came to me just this week. Perhaps if the lady approves, she will buy next time, yes?"

Cautiously, Madelyn agreed. She wasn't the type of woman who enjoyed wearing fine dresses and perfumes, but free was a good enough price for anyone. She rolled back a sleeve on her white blouse and held out her wrist. The merchantman removed the small cork and dabbled a few drops on her fair skin.

The perfume was surprisingly sweet and pleasant, much to her delight. She thanked the merchant with a smile, then continued on, keepsakes in hand. As the market crowd grew in size, so too did the heat. Summer was in its infancy, and the heat would grow even more insufferable within the next few weeks. Madelyn much preferred the cool crispness of autumn and its magnificent colors and smells.

The Ivornorium appeared just ahead, its ancient yet remarkably intact white walls shining with sunlight. Gentle mists from the court-yard fountain greeted her, kissing her face lightly. Madelyn sought shelter beneath a tree within the well-landscaped grounds and stole a moment to cool off.

Rarely had she come to the Ivornorium, for scholarly works were of little interest to a warrior. The feel of forged steel in her hands was more desirable than the dusty pages of an old book. But the magnificence of such a place never ceased to inspire awe, and she often wondered how it managed to survive intact for centuries or more. Though Castle Thorn was one of the most impressive places in Bentmont, to Madelyn, it paled in comparison to the Ivornorium.

Constructed of pure marble, the ancient library was of classic Khorrish design and towered above everything around it. It was per-haps the first building in Betanthia to be constructed with a dome, which shone so brightly in the sun that it was painful to look at. At its entrance stood two rows of delicately carved marble columns, so tall it was a wonder how they were erected. Beyond it, an arched entryway was held secure by two imposing, reinforced doors of solid oak.

After a much-needed respite, she continued onward. Madelyn felt small and insignificant as she stood before the doors, which looked as if they required an entire forest to construct. She took hold of a smooth black ring handle and rapped it forcefully several times.

While waiting for an answer, she studied the columns and statues of kings and noblemen from centuries past, which decorated the edifice. It seemed like an eternity before the doors stirred, their large iron hinges moaning woefully as they were pulled open. Standing inside was Chronican Willard Mirren, an elderly man who greeted her with surprise and a smile.

"Ah, Commander Everly, it is an honor! What brings you to the Ivornorium on such a fine day? Come in, come in!" Willard waved excitedly and beckoned her forth, his hands bristling by his long, wispy silver beard.

"Willard! It's been far too long." She smiled as she entered. The smell of old books, burning candles, and a musty tinge drew her attention. It was a welcome relief from the lingering stench of horses in her nostrils.

"Indeed it has been, my dear! How have you been as of late?"

"I'm doing well, thank you for asking. I would be even better if it weren't for this heat." Madelyn ran a hand along the back of her sweaty neck. A few loose hairs from her braid clung to her sticky skin, and she brushed them free with her fingers. Much to her delight, the fragrance on her wrists seemed to become more prevalent as she perspired.

The cavernous hall contained nearly a dozen floors of bookshelves and a large parlor at its center. How many books the Ivornorium held was a mystery, but she could only suppose the number was into the thousands, maybe even tens of thousands.

"Allow me to offer you some refreshment then. Right this way," the Chronican said as he gathered up his flowing robes, which looked to be several sizes too large.

Madelyn smiled as Willard toddled to a table and fetched a pitcher of water, his steps labored from a noticeable hunch of his back. He was a sweet old man who felt almost like a grandfather. Madelyn grew sad with regret, for it had been too long since she had seen him last. It was also a reminder that she had never known her real family.

Since the day she was found outside Castle Thorn at age four, all Madelyn had known was the Order. But sometimes, family was more than just blood. Sometimes one's own blood could be more harsh and unforgiving than those who had chosen to be like family.

The old Chronican poured a generous amount of fresh water into a crude wooden cup, then handed it to her with unsteady hands.

"Thank you, Willard. You're too kind."

Madelyn sighed as the cool liquid touched her lips, and in a near instant, the cup was empty. Willard chuckled and offered more, but she declined and returned the cup.

"So, my dear," he said, "are you here on business, or have you come to keep an old man company?"

Madelyn wiped a few drops of water from her mouth with the back of her hand. "I just so happen to be here on business, yes. The High Marshal sent me. It's a sensitive matter, but I need your help, if you would be willing."

"Absolutely, Maddie! I'll do my best to be of assistance to you. I may be old, but I know every book and scroll in the Ivornorium, from floor to ceiling! And you can trust I will be very discreet, as always."

She felt a certain comfort when Willard called her Maddie, though she would likely skewer anyone else who dared to call her that.

"I'm glad to hear it." She removed the dispatch from her belt pouch, unfolded it, and handed it to the Chronican. "There was an attack in the west, Willard. It was… terrible, judging from the details. Whoever is responsible sent a wagon full of heads back to Castle Morden, with strange symbols carved into them. I was hoping you could tell me what these symbols mean."

Willard paused, his old eyes straining to read the small print. "Oh, dear. Quite… quite dreadful indeed." He studied the crude drawings of runic symbols and stroked his beard gently.

"Unfortunately, I don't know what they mean off the top of my head, but perhaps I can find some answers for you." He immediately led Madelyn across the great hall and up a large marble staircase, which split to the right and left. They climbed to the third floor, Willard pausing briefly to catch his breath. Once at the top, they continued down a row of bookshelves, nearly fifteen feet tall.

"Little is written about the tribes in the west, and the north for that matter." He coughed. "Sadly, many who venture to those lands seldom return, but a few old accounts are written here somewhere." Willard removed a book from the shelf, opened it, and flipped through a few pages before replacing it and withdrawing another. He mumbled while looking its contents over, then set it back where it belonged.

"I'm sorry, my dear, but it appears I've grown old. I cannot remember where to find the book you seek. I'm afraid this will take some work," he said, disappointed.

"It's alright, Willard. Just tell me where to look."

"It should be down this aisle or perhaps the next one over. I believe it's a black book, and you'll want to look for one that's quite worn, especially on the binding. If it's the one I'm thinking of, it will be very old, several hundred years old if I'm not mistaken."

Madelyn scoured the nearly endless wall of books before her while Willard took the next row over. Before she knew it, half a dozen books were in her hands. She took them over to a nearby desk, dropped them in a heap, then cracked open the first one. After skimming through it briefly, she discarded it and continued sifting through another.

The second book produced better results, as it chronicled the life of a northern chieftain named Kuggvord the Grim, who lived some four hundred years ago. The tale drew her fascination, and she soon found herself poring over its contents and making notes on fresh parchment.

She learned the northern people were deeply religious and believed their deities lived in the waters, trees, and living things of the forest. There were accounts of Kuggvord's conquest of the old kingdom after repeated incursions into their territory. With the blessing of the war god, and his two-handed greatsword named Ruin, the ancient warlord swept over the Plainhold like a scourge, sacking every city and stronghold in his path, putting all who opposed him to the sword.

While interesting, the book provided few answers as to the languages and religious symbols of the Northmen, and neither did the other books on the desk. Hours passed by. Madelyn grew frustrated, and Willard seemed to be faring no better. She stood and stretched, her muscles aching and joints popping in displeasure, then made her way to the old chronican.

"Any luck Willard? I've turned up nothing." She sighed in exhaustion and boredom. Her eyes were irritated from smoke piping out of numerous sconces on the walls.

"Unfortunately, no. I do apologize, my dear. I know it has to be here somewhere. In all my time as a Chronican, I have never forgotten where a text is. I've spent nearly fifty years among these books. I know them like they're my children! Or at least, I did."

Madelyn moved a few books to the side and sat on the table's edge. Something immediately caught her eye near the top of a shelf a few rows from where they were searching. Its binding was worn and nearly a charcoal gray, but it stood out from the other books around it.

"What about that one over there?"

Willard turned in his seat and squinted. "Hmm, perhaps, but that row is for books on medicine and the healing arts. But I suppose it couldn't hurt to check."

The Chronican rose slowly, and together they made their way to the bookshelf. Madelyn took hold of a nearby ladder, climbed it carefully, and reached up to grab the faded old book. A thick layer of dust coated its cracked and worn leather cover, which radiated with the stench of mildew. She flipped through and discovered many pages bore words and symbols in a language she did not recognize.

"I think this might be it!" Madelyn rushed back to the desk and laid the book open, though she was careful not to damage it. She stopped on a chapter containing many drawings of runes used by the Northmen and Zylmacian wildmen, then set the dispatch beside it for comparison.

"Willard, come see. This is what we were looking for!"

The Chronican toddled back to the desk and resumed his seat.

"Alright, Maddie, let me see." His frail fingers delicately turned page after page. "Hmm, here it talks about the various uses of runes. Offerings, protections, healing, and so on." He flipped to the next page, then the one after. "Ah, and here it speaks of the ancient gods and the symbols representing them."

Willard's glassy eyes lit up with excitement. "Let me see… This first sign represents Khol… Kholdyr, god of the sun and chieftain among the gods. No, no, that's not it."

He squinted hard at the book, then glanced at the dispatch. "The drawing in your message is a rune for Azldyr."

"Who is that?" Madelyn asked curiously, though she suspected such a barbaric-sounding name meant anything but good.

"He is the war god of the Northmen, also worshipped by the western wildmen and some in the south long ago. These other runes… I'm not quite… oh my…"

Madelyn felt her heart skip a beat. She was so anxious, her palms were becoming damp with sweat. She wiped them on her leggings.

So the High Marshal's suspicions were correct. This is the start of something much bigger, after all.

Such thoughts were disconcerting. She made certain to write down every detail.

"Summon. Offering. Mankind. These other runes, my dear… these are an invocation of the war god." Willard thumbed through the book a bit more, then pointed a gnarled finger at a paragraph. "This particular invocation is only used in the most serious of matters. There is only one record of their use, which coincides with a great atrocity hundreds of years ago by a warlord named…" His eyes squinted so hard they appeared closed.

"Kuggvord. I read about him in another book. It said he killed hundreds of thousands of men, women, and children in a blood feud," Madelyn said quietly. "Tell me true, do you think this could be happening all over again, or am I overthinking it?"

"From my knowledge of the northern people, they are not to be trifled with, and they hold their gods in the highest regard." Willard paused for a second to collect his thoughts. "It appears this matter is quite serious, my dear, or at least should be treated as such. Is anyone else aware of the message?"

Madelyn shook her head. "No, the High Marshal is the only one who knows, besides me. And now you."

"Good. Best to let him know what we've found here, and soon. I will let you know if I uncover anything else." Willard placed a gentle hand on her back. "Go now, Maddie, I'll take it from here."

"Thank you, Willard. It's been great to see you again. I'll come to visit soon, I promise." She smiled gently at the Chronican, then folded the dispatch and her notes together.

Hurriedly, she strode out of the Ivornorium and back into the sweltering heat. She made sure to pass by the fountains to catch another misty spray, which had attracted a flock of pigeons. It was reassuring to know she was not the only one struggling with such warmth.

While the trip to the Ivornorium seemed to last half the morning, the return to Castle Thorn felt like it was over in no time. The stronghold had grown quiet in her absence, and Madelyn saw an empty courtyard through an open portcullis, save for Jenson Powell and a handful of knights near the stables.

"High Marshal!" she called out, hands toying with each other. A pair of guards at the gatehouse snapped to attention and saluted as she passed.

"That will be all for now," Jenson Powell dismissed the knights before turning and meeting Madelyn near a gatehouse tower. Some of the men looked suspiciously at her but were quick to take their leave.

"Welcome back, Madelyn. Were you able to discover anything at the Ivornorium?"

"Yes. It's not as much information as I hoped, but the Chronican assures me he'll continue searching." She withdrew her notes and handed them to Jenson. "It's as you feared, High Marshal. If this is genuine, we're facing a full-scale invasion that hasn't been seen in centuries."

Jenson's mouth drew back into a frown. He shook his head in dismay. "Then we must act. It's our sworn duty to be proactive. I need you to ride to Cardale and present these findings to the King and his council."

He wants me to speak directly to the King?

She had been to the Westwind Citadel more times than she could remember but was never given the opportunity to speak with King Marcellus Bethard. Although, from the rumors she had heard in recent years, a meeting was probably the last thing she wanted to do.

"But, High Marshal, should I not head to Castle Morden? If the threat is real, we must reinforce our border as quickly as possible."

"You will, soon enough. The Blackthorn won't be able to take this task on alone. We need Cardale to prepare. Go now, make haste." Jenson turned to leave but stopped himself.

"Oh, and I almost forgot." He hefted a small sack from the inside pocket of his cloak and tossed it to her. "Find yourself a decent place to stay when you get there. I won't have you sleeping in the barracks like some enlisted soldier. You're on official business, so the least the Order can do is give you a decent roof over your head."

It was a kind gesture, and Madelyn smiled and thanked him. Regardless of what the High Marshal said at times or how he acted, she knew he cared about her wellbeing. In a way, he was as much a father figure as a superior, so Madelyn had twice the incentive not to fail.

The journey would take a week or so, depending on the swiftness of her horse. While she was disappointed in traveling east when the west needed aid, she would at least get to see the capital again, and Gareth Bethard as well. He was the eldest son of King Marcellus and heir to the throne. They remained close friends for many years, but Madelyn often suspected Gareth harbored greater feelings for her. But he was a good man, and kind, and well worth visiting once again.

After gathering the equipment and items she would need for the journey, she made her way to the stables and prepared to leave. There were dozens of stalls on either side of an open aisle, seemingly hundreds, where the Order housed and tended to its most prized possessions; their horses.

After passing by several stalls, some empty and some occupied, Madelyn found her horse, Nora. She was a Plainhold Strider, one of the tallest and most muscular of horse breeds, and quite aggressive. There seemed to be a mutual understanding between horse and rider, which made Madelyn fall in love with Nora during their first ride. She even turned down a prized stallion from the High Marshal upon being promoted to Commander because Nora was all she needed.

"Hey girl, how are you doing?"

Madelyn smiled and stroked Nora's long, soft snout. The stablekeepers kept her mount properly fed, groomed, and ready to be saddled. The horse nickered and exhaled in her face.

"It's good to see you too!" she laughed. "Are you ready to go for a ride?" Before Madelyn could saddle Nora, she heard the clacking of footsteps approaching.

"Hey! Are you planning on going somewhere?" Corbyn asked curiously.

Although she was happy to see him, she wasn't at the same time. "Yes, as a matter of fact," Madelyn replied, placing a leather saddle on her horse. "I have business in Cardale. The High Marshal's orders."

"Oh, I see…"

Corbyn leaned against the side of Nora's stall. Even though he had been training all morning under the hot sun, he smelled quite good. Madelyn knew what he was about to ask, and she would have to check her impulses. This mission was far too important for such distractions.

"I don't suppose you could use some company on your journey? The road to Cardale can be quite boring when you're alone."

"I'll be fine, thank you. I have urgent business, Corbyn. I'll be speaking to the King." Madelyn tightened down the saddle and tugged at it. "This is important. I need to keep my head clear."

"I promise you, I'll be as professional as possible. Come on, we both know the capital is a dangerous place, even for a knight."

Something in Corbyn Scott's caramel-colored eyes broke down all of her defenses. He was undoubtedly handsome and knew her more intimately than anyone. After chewing her lip and thinking carefully, she ultimately relented.

"Fine, but this is strictly business, ok? I can't stress the importance of this meeting enough. A lot is resting on my shoulders, and I can't be distracted by you." She placed a bridle around Nora's head, then loaded her equipment into saddlebags.

"Alright, alright. You don't have to tell me twice. What is it that's got you so, so… bothered?"

"I can't tell you, Corbyn. The High Marshal made it clear that no one except the King and his advisors are to know. So please, don't ask again."

Madelyn mounted her horse and took up the reins. With a gentle nudge of a boot heel, Nora walked out into the aisle.

"If you're coming, then I suggest you get ready fast. We don't want to keep Marcellus Bethard waiting."

LUCETTA

AN AFTERNOON SUN SHONE BRIGHTLY UPON THE SANDY-COLORED facade of Trace Bethard and his sister Lucetta Eldon's estate. Its modern architecture starkly contrasted the old, grey stone of the Westwind Citadel, which sat two miles away. Exotic fruit trees and tall arborvitae decorated a small, walled-in courtyard alongside sculpted fountains and marble benches. Servants moved about to and fro, preparing for the evening's feast, a scent of roasted meat and fresh incense thick in the air.

"Aldred! Come to dinner, darling. The table has been set. Your business can wait until afterward," shouted Lucetta as she entered the dining room. From there, she saw her husband's study at the end of a long hall.

"A king's advisor never rests, my dear," Lord Aldred Eldon said, sifting through a pile of messages he received throughout the day. His hands paused on a small scroll that arrived at dawn and was characteristic of those sent by the military. He toyed with it curiously.

"I'm sure Betanthia can get along just fine until after supper," Lucetta said, arms crossed, an annoyed expression souring her powdered face. As the daughter of King Marcellus Bethard, she was unaccustomed to waiting for anything or anyone, her husband included.

"Coming, my love." Aldred tossed the scroll down on his cluttered desk and made his way to the dining room.

The scent of roasted boar and sweet jasmine drifted like a cloud as the main course was prepared. Lord Aldred entered and was greeted by the curtsy of housemaids, the opulence of a bountiful feast, and the impatient stare of his wife.

"I suppose the King's affairs can wait awhile longer." Aldred seated himself at one end of the table, his mind still occupied. He was nearly twenty years Lucetta's senior and dedicated every waking moment to serving the King. She often wondered which Aldred loved more, his duties or her.

Lucetta smiled as her brother, Trace Bethard, entered and seated himself. He was a tall, stout man, half bald, clad in the finest silks, and nearly as powdered as she was. Trace was alone tonight, once again. His wife Esma had been absent for several weeks and was hardly seen by anyone. Lucetta cared little for her sister-in-law anyways, as she valued frivolities and social gatherings more than family business.

"Where is Esma? I assumed that she would be joining us this evening?" Lucetta lied, having come to expect the absence.

"She's with the noblewomen in Whitemont district doing who knows what. She won't be joining us this evening," Trace replied, lacking concern.

"It's a shame, really," she said lazily. She twisted a lock of long, curled auburn hair that hung just past her waistline, as she often did when irritated or deep in thought.

My brother marries a lesser lord's daughter and elevates her to our status. She holds our wealth and name and uses both to her advantage, but doesn't have the courtesy to eat at our table. How Trace can stomach such an insult is beyond me.

"Perhaps tomorrow, then?" Lucetta's smile was cynical.

Trace gave an indifferent shrug, then slid his chair closer to the table. The first course of the feast was finally being served. Freshly baked bread, honey-mustard eggs, sweet buttered corn, candied fruits, and a well-seasoned roasted boar. Generous portions were placed onto each of their plates. Complementing such fine foods were flagons of dark red wine of various vintages, each chosen with expert care.

After filling each cup to the brim, the servants bowed and retreated to the corners. Meagerness was not something the Bethards were known for. It was either all or nothing in every facet of life. The thought made Lucetta wonder if her eldest brother, Gareth, was even a Bethard at all. He was the crown prince, but behaved more like a peasant than anything.

He seemed to love common folk more than his siblings, a perceived slight Lucetta could never forgive. She could scarcely remember the last time they spoke to each other, though in reality, it was of no real consequence.

This is how royalty should live, she thought, chewing on a heel of fresh bread. *Not in taverns and low places with low people. If only I had been born a man and Gareth a woman, what a difference I would make for Betanthia.*

Conversation was absent at the table, a far cry from the previous night when they laughed, boasted, and shared their grand visions for the future. Lucetta could tell her husband's mind was somewhere else this evening, likely still focused on his damned papers.

Indeed, Aldred's expression and fidgeting fingers spoke volumes. Something was amiss; even Lucetta could sense it. He excused himself from the table and returned to his study without speaking a word. She sighed and scowled, then continued to eat.

"Trace, you must see the plans I drafted for a new estate. It's truly remarkable!" Lucetta was uncomfortable with the silence and annoyed at her distracted husband. She needed conversation to brighten a quickly souring mood.

Trace had a hint of annoyance about him as well. He swallowed a mouthful of wine after swishing it a few times to savor the taste. "We just remodeled the one in Dellhaven and, now, what? You want to build another?"

"Everyone has their talents, brother. You have your business ventures and trade agreements, and Aldred has the wherewithal to keep the Kingdom functioning on a daily basis."

"And where do your talents lie, sister?" Trace asked sarcastically.

"I have a creative mind. I have the ability to take nothing and make it into something," she answered proudly.

"Indeed. Every room in the estate is filled to the brim with your *somethings*."

"And what, pray tell, are you implying, Trace?" Lucetta frowned.

"Look around you. Every sculpture, every tapestry, everything, has been procured by you. Not a day goes by when I fail to notice something new. Is that not enough to satisfy your… creative urges?"

"Is that what you think of me, that I should be some lowly housewife, contenting myself with trappings and trinkets? No, I have much grander visions, and only those will satisfy my… creative urges."

"Your grander visions may drive this family into the poorhouse if you aren't more mindful of your spending. I can hardly keep track of your expenses as it is." It was Trace's turn to do some frowning of his own.

"Perhaps you should worry less about my expenses and more about taking charge of your marriage and doing some creating of your own. Heavens know this family needs heirs."

The insult left Trace seething, but there was little he could say without escalating the spat into a full-blown argument. He knew Lucetta was barren, and in times of anger, she would often project her frustration onto him. Having children of her own was the one thing she had always wanted since girlhood, but the fates decided otherwise. Instead, she found solace in an array of grand projects. From commissioning elaborate works of art to designing great buildings, there was no limit to her ambition.

"You needn't be so cruel, sister." Trace's eyes lowered to his plate. He picked at the remainder of his meal with a knife.

"Forgive me," Lucetta apologized, though, in reality, she was anything but sorry.

The dining room grew awkwardly silent, save for a soft chirping of crickets beyond an open window.

"So then," he said unexpectedly, "tell me about your newest project. Will you be adding another estate in Dellhaven?"

Lucetta appreciated the sentiment. It was kind of Trace to make peace and inquire about her endeavors. "No. I've grown quite displeased with Dellhaven these days."

"And why is that? I thought you adored the place."

"Dellhaven is lovely, to be certain," she sighed. "But it's become so crowded as of late. Nowadays, any low-born merchant or galley captain with enough coin seems to be buying their way in. It's far too loud and busy for my liking."

"As if a little added wealth is a bad thing?" Trace glanced briefly at the jeweled rings on his fingers as he sipped wine. "Dellhaven's success bodes well for us."

"It's not about the money, Trace. Money is simply a means to an end."

"And what end might that be, sister?" he asked inquisitively.

"The one thing you cannot put a price on." Lucetta paused for dramatic effect. "Peace of mind. You've been around this city far more than I have. Tell me with a straight face this is the same Cardale you remember as a child. Now… now you can hardly walk to the Citadel without a battalion of soldiers around you, it seems."

"Growing pains, sister. The price of our success. Cardale has twice the population from twenty years ago, and with each new conquest comes a fresh crop of slaves and wares from those regions. Everyone wants a piece of the action, it seems."

"Ever the scholar you are, brother," she said with a huff. "What *is* is quite different from what *should be*. I would gladly trade half the prosperity of Betanthia for twice the safety and peace of mind. Not all money is good money."

"So that's why you spend so much of it, to rid its corrupting influence from your sight!"

Trace was met with a glare so sharp it nearly severed him in two. He chuckled softly and grinned, amused at his quip.

"I'm just having a bit of fun, sister. I jest." He took another sip of wine. "You'll hear no disagreement from me, Cardale *has* fallen into disrepair since father turned ill. Have you tried speaking to Aldred about it?"

"I shouldn't have to, Trace. Aldred is father's advisor, not his custodian. The only one with any real responsibility is Gareth, but we all know how he chooses to spend his time."

Merely thinking about her eldest brother put off what remained of her appetite. It was supremely frustrating to sit back and watch Cardale stagnate under her father's absence and her brother's indifference, especially when she had limitless ideas to bring the city back to glory.

"I certainly won't be making any excuses for his behavior, but when did you speak to him last? I can't imagine life being all that pleasant when you're in such proximity to father. Gareth sees far more ugliness than we do."

"If he has such a fragile constitution, then he should renounce his claim to the throne," Lucetta proclaimed. "The last thing Betanthia needs is a weak, ineffectual man running it, especially with all the problems we face."

"That's a pretty simplistic point of view, Lucetta." He screwed up his face. "Try speaking to him sometime."

"I just… don't have any sympathy for him. And I won't apologize, either. If life is so difficult, then change it, don't wallow in your problems." Lucetta found herself consuming wine at a much faster pace than she was used to. Her head felt light and fuzzy.

"Being isolated from one's family can drive a person to all manners of indiscretion." Trace motioned to one of the servants for more refreshment. "Just try to be a bit more understanding, like I know you can be."

"Not only are you a scholar, but you're also a diplomat too, it seems," she said with a clever grin.

Trace chortled, then raised his glass to his sister and toasted. Throughout their conversation, both siblings seemed to have forgotten about Aldred, who remained conspicuously absent from the table. His food was no longer piping with steam and had grown cold. Lucetta took notice and wondered if her husband was even still at the estate.

"We don't have to discuss our brother now. Perhaps later, and with another glass of wine. Tell me more about your latest endeavor." Trace squirmed as if he could feel his purse strings tightening themselves at the thought of the expense, which would likely come from his pocket.

At first, Lucetta was excited to share her newest and most ambitious plans with her brother but was quickly overcome by anxiety. She wasn't sure if the wine was making her feel less certain or what else it might have been. Without answering, her attention turned to what remained of her meal.

"Come now!" he said reassuringly. "Tell me all about it. I truly wish to hear."

Aldred returned to the dining room, his face more sullen and serious. He reclaimed his seat and took several large gulps of wine, which was quite uncharacteristic of such a conservative man.

"What's the matter, my love?" Lucetta asked with worried eyes. She touched him gently on the arm.

"Terrible business, it seems. I'll spare you the details. It would not make for pleasant table conversation," Aldred said reluctantly, then pushed away his plate of cold food.

"Nonsense, something seems amiss with you. Please, do be open with us."

"Very well. Commandant Valens' son is dead, and so are three thousand of the King's soldiers." Aldred frowned. The reply was grim and frustrated.

"Dead?" Lucetta could barely believe what she was hearing. "How? How could this be possible? Where did it happen?"

"The attack was unprovoked, according to the dispatch. It seems Lord Valens sent a detachment of men to Khorrtal in response to unrest. Why he sent three thousand men is a bit of a mystery, but he must have wanted to make a show of force."

"It appears it wasn't enough," Trace chimed in. The look of concern on his face mirrored that of his sister.

"Indeed." Aldred nodded. "But that isn't the worst of it. I'm afraid if I say anymore, it may turn your stomachs."

Lucetta's hands grew sweaty. This was the first time she could recall the Kingdom coming under direct attack. Over the years, there had been border skirmishes with the Droethiens, and more recently, an incursion by the Zylmacian wildmen. But nothing on the scale of what Aldred was describing. She felt compelled to hear more, although there was an accompanying sense of dread over what he might say next.

"Please, Aldred, you must tell us. This is as much our kingdom as it is father's." A sharp pain in the center of Lucetta's head made it difficult to keep her eyes open. She closed and rubbed them for a few seconds but felt little relief.

"Very well." Aldred cleared his throat and glared at the servants so sharply they scattered like frightened cats. "There was a survivor from the attack. He was sent back to Castle Morden with… with a wagon… filled with the heads of the King's soldiers."

Lucetta's chair felt as if it had fallen out from underneath her. She instinctively gasped and covered her mouth, then looked in astonishment at Trace. Her brother swallowed hard, then glanced around the room uncomfortably.

"I do apologize for such unsavory talk, my dear." Aldred's eyes shifted back down to his plate. He stared at the now cold slices of meat with an ever-worsening frown, as if he was somehow seeing mangled bodies instead of a succulent meal.

"What does this mean, Aldred? Is… is war upon us?" It was a stupid question Lucetta immediately regretted asking. But inside her was a fleeting hope that this was an isolated incident.

"That remains to be seen, but perhaps not. Lord Valens has thirty thousand men under his command. The dispatch stated he was traveling at speed to Khorrtal with Commander Holland in pursuit. The rider also informed me that the Blackthorn have been notified, so I'm cautiously optimistic this situation will be resolved in short order."

Lucetta covered her mouth and fought the urge to weep. The thought of unwashed savages roaming the countryside, butchering, raping, and pillaging, was so frightening she began to tremble. Looking around the room, she noticed a dark, blurry spot in her vision. Curiously, the spot seemed to remain still, despite moving her eyes.

"I can assure you, my dear, everything will be alright. I must prepare a briefing for the King at once and meet with the rest of the council. Do excuse my absence for the rest of the evening." Aldred kissed Lucetta on the forehead and gently stroked her long auburn hair twice before disappearing to his study.

The smell of food on the table was enough to turn her stomach. After ensuring her husband was gone, she rose from her seat and retreated to her private chamber. A group of servants in the hall scattered in all directions, looking nearly as confused and distraught as their mistress.

Thankfully, Lucetta's chamber had been prepared hours earlier. The second-floor suite hosted an expansive study with adjacent lounging rooms and two large balconies, one facing the estate's courtyard, the other facing outwards toward Cardale. From the latter, she saw the looming majesty of the Westwind Citadel and nearly all the royal grounds.

On the near side of her study sat an oaken desk, cluttered with papers and drawings she had made over the last several weeks. A pair of bookshelves flanked the desk, though Lucetta had little time to enjoy any of their contents these days. As she entered, her attention turned to a small table on the other side of the room, with two high back chairs next to it. A fresh flagon of wine and a set of crystal glasses sat on the table. As she poured herself a generous serving, the shutting of the chamber door gave her a startle. Unbeknownst to her, Trace had followed closely behind.

"My apologies, sister. I didn't mean to frighten you." Her brother's face was grim and fraught with concern.

"I'm fine. You didn't need to follow me."

"Nonsense. The news Aldred spoke of. The attack. Is it really bothering you so much?"

"It's more than that, Trace," she said, then stepped onto the courtyard balcony.

The evening air was cool and quite pleasant. Warm sconce light radiated from the courtyard below as servants prepared for nightfall. Even the sight of the estate's gardens was not as comforting as it used to be. Lucetta sometimes wondered if she had grown too used to this place, but the outside world was dreadful and too dangerous to risk her safety.

"For once, let's not play this game where you pretend everything is alright when it clearly isn't. Come now. Whatever you say stays with me, as always."

"It isn't always pleasant to have oneself proven right," she mumbled into her wine glass.

"No need to be coy, sister. Proven right how?"

"Do you remember our conversation from the dinner table?" Lucetta asked in annoyance. "It all makes sense now, after everything Aldred told us of this attack."

Trace gave her a stupid and confused stare.

"Our capital has descended into chaos, and now our lands are being attacked from the outside. Can you not see, brother? This is how a nation falls; first from within, then from without."

Trace chuckled, though he tried to keep himself restrained. Wine was beginning to make his eyes slide down his chubby face.

"This isn't funny," she snarled. "Has the thought not occurred to you that maybe our enemies sense weakness and have grown bold because of it? Answer me with a straight face; when was the last time you heard of Betanthia coming under attack like this?"

"You worry too much, sister! Our lands are well-protected. Between our four Commandants and dozens of lords across the country, there are hundreds of thousands of men at arms to keep us safe. Whoever is responsible for this atrocity will be in chains or dead within a fortnight. It's really nothing to get upset about."

His words made sense, but were of little comfort. Lucetta shrugged them off and leaned against the balustrade.

"And as far as Cardale goes," Trace continued, "when is the last time you actually saw the city?"

"I see the city every day," she answered sarcastically, gesturing at the balcony on the opposite side of her chamber.

"No, I mean, when was the last time you actually walked the streets and saw with your own eyes what's going on out there? Cardale has undesirable areas, as with any major city, but there is so much wealth and potential out there. You really shouldn't be so quick to dismiss it."

"The last time I traveled to the Citadel, my caravan was greeted with rocks and the foulest language I've ever heard." Recalling the experience was stressful enough that she emptied her wine glass without knowing it.

"You have to take the good with the bad, sister. We're Bethards. Those living on the streets have nothing to lose, and sometimes, well, sometimes, they lash out. But Cardale isn't like that across the board, and I can't say I've had anything bad happen to me."

Of course not, Trace. You're a man. You can simply wear your cloak and disappear into a crowd. For me, it isn't so simple.

"I would urge you to see for yourself," Trace said, lifting his chin. "There's a lot of possibilities out there. In fact, I'm in the process of adding another branch to the family bank, and I've begun drawing up plans for a new arena—something to keep the common folk entertained. And, of course, we'll tax the betting money. The amount of gold we'll make will be staggering."

It was difficult to see her brother's excitement and not feel like she was wasting her life and talents by staying locked in the estate every day. Lucetta had always considered herself to be smarter than Trace. Far more, in fact. Sometimes, she wasn't sure who was more of a bumbling oaf, him or Gareth.

"I'm happy for you." Lucetta was anything but happy. "Maybe you're right, brother. Perhaps I should see the city for myself. Why should you be the only one who gets to live out their dreams?"

"Precisely," he said, smiling.

Together they sat in silence for the next half hour and continued to consume glass after glass of wine. Although she tried her best to remain stoic and act as if nothing was troubling her, Lucetta remained a mess of unraveling nerves. She caught herself glancing over at the other balcony and toward the Westwind Citadel. Her head was starting to ache from overthinking. Every time she heard the clopping of horse hooves on Auburn Row, a spike of anxiety rattled her body.

She was unsure when Aldred planned to leave for the Citadel. The thought of him overseeing Betanthia's first war in a generation was nearly too much to bear. He was a decent advisor, though in reality, he was more of an errand boy, and certainly not a warrior. Not like how her father, Marcellus Bethard, used to be.

"Sister, what troubles you now?" Trace was becoming annoyed with his sister's raw nerves.

"Nothing, I'm weary and need rest. We can speak more tomorrow." Lucetta gripped the side of her head and winced. A sharp, throbbing pain felt as if a band of horses was stampeding over her. The dark spot returned as well and was more pronounced this time.

"Is everything alright? Shall I fetch a physician?" Trace asked nervously. He moved to her side and placed a hand on her shoulder.

"No, I'll be alright. I've been having the worst headaches the last few days. Probably just from stress." The dark spot began to fade almost as quickly as it arrived, and so too did the pain. She let out a sigh of relief.

"Please, sister, get some rest. I'll come to check on you in the morning."

After planting a delicate kiss on her forehead, Trace left quietly. It was no lie; Lucetta had been under a great deal of stress lately, and an excess of wine was doing her no favors. Rest would be the best medicine. Cautiously, she made her way down the hall and toward the master bedchamber. It would be some time before Aldred would be joining her, if at all, given the news they had received. She changed out of her evening gown and into sleeping clothes.

As she lay on the soft, red satin bed sheets, she could not help but think about the attack in the west and what it meant, and what it would mean. Betanthia was the strongest force on the entire continent, that could not be disputed. But decades of relative peace may have bore unintended consequences. After generations of pushing the frontier and bringing new lands into the fold, perhaps the barbarian tribes had begun to sense weakness. Perhaps they would be coming to claim what was no longer theirs by right.

War was a terrifying prospect, but Lucetta reminded herself she was in Cardale, about as far as one could get from the western borderlands. Between the capital and the unknown stood dozens of lords and millions of soldiers and civilians who would fight to the death to protect their king and country.

But would they?

Given what little she had seen inside Cardale, she was suddenly unsure. But these were worries for men of war, not someone like her. No, she was better suited for what was right in front of her. Cardale needed to be safe, strong, and a bastion of stability for the entire Kingdom.

Moments before falling asleep, another thought entered her weary mind. What if the capital wasn't as troubled as she thought? What if this was more overthinking, brought on by boredom and dissatisfaction with life? It was difficult to be certain. But Trace was right, though Lucetta was loath to admit it. Perhaps the time had come to leave the protective walls of her estate and see the outside world with her own eyes, to put her mind and heart at ease.

Maybe I should see the city for myself. It's been too long. Why should I be stuck inside wallowing in fear while Trace is out making a name for himself? No, it isn't right. I owe it to myself to be more than this.

The thought made her smile, which was something she was doing far too less of these days. What she truly needed was faith. Faith in the Royal Guardsmen and the city watch, men charged with protecting her family. Faith in the Commandants and their legions of soldiers to defend Betanthia's borders. And faith in Aldred, the man tasked with holding it all together.

Maybe Trace was right, Lucetta thought while drifting off to sleep. *Cardale is a place of opportunity. And like all opportunities, they must be seized upon and taken, or they will be lost. Maybe it really is that simple. Maybe that's all I need to do, just reach out and take what is rightfully mine.*

CEDRIC II

THE SIGHT WAS ANY MAN'S WORST NIGHTMARE. PILES OF DEAD MEN littered the red-stained field, their broken bodies a monument of cruelty to those who had perpetrated such an atrocity. Hundreds of others lay headless and scattered about, their bloating corpses stripped of armor, clothing, and anything of value. Lord Cedric Valens and his knights had to cover their faces and shield themselves from thick clouds of flies and an even thicker smell of rot.

Cedric was lost for words. He was a man with many battles under his belt and had witnessed such savagery more than once, but this time was different. Because now, somewhere among the sea of corpses was his son's body, or so he feared.

I did this. I sent him here. Were it not for me, these men would still be alive. And my son... my poor son. Please forgive me. Please, be alive.

After dismounting, Cedric made his way down to the killing fields. Even though the men were dead, the presence of their lord was a courtesy owed to them, he thought. The ground was wet and smelled strongly of blood. Each step felt heavier and more difficult than the last, but he continued onward until he could walk no further.

This was not how the mission was supposed to end. Khorrtal was still a wild place, certainly. Despite its occupation, disturbances sometimes erupted, but never a full-blown rebellion. Were the Khorrtalli responsible for this butchery? Did they aid and abet it in some way? No, Cedric thought, they were too few to best three thousand of his seasoned soldiers. The lone survivor was undoubtedly correct; this was the work of an outside force, it must have been.

Cedric was no stranger to war. But in war, there were unspoken rules one would abide by. In many ways, the carnage of centuries past had become more refined, almost gentlemanly in a way. But what he witnessed looked to be the work of wild animals, much less men. How anyone could relish such unfathomable cruelty was beyond his understanding.

Slowly, his attention turned to the opposite end of the field. A half-dozen pikes stood, staked deep into the earth, with corpses skewered atop them. Many of the impaled were savaged beyond recognition. Because Cedric could not make out their features, there was a small, fleeting hope that Alfrid was not among them.

His hope, however, was soon shattered. One pike, in particular, towered higher than the rest. Unlike the men around it, the body at its end was not stripped of its armor and effects. Even without a head, its identity was unmistakable. The corpse wore a steel breastplate emblazoned with the King's colors and an insignia of an officer. Cedric saw it was a Captain's rank, despite the armor's soiled and damaged condition.

Little remained of Alfrid's head save for the base of a skull and chunks of matter still clinging to it. His lower half was stained black by blood that poured from a fatal wound before his body ran dry. Birds had already eaten their fill of the corpse and moved on to more suitable carrion.

Oh my boy, what have they done? What have they done to you?

It took every ounce of waning strength not to fall into a sobbing heap on the ground. Cedric heard muffled voices of his knights as they searched in vain for survivors. Even though he was screaming on the inside, he knew his knights would be looking for strength and courage from their leader.

"My lord, I… I have no words." Captain Declan Wilmot said as he moved to Cedric's side. He stared in horror at the sight of Alfrid's body, but looked away.

There was little Lord Valens could say. Even if he tried, the words might be enough to fracture the delicate hold he had over his emotions. Feeling ill and near to vomiting, Cedric turned and stumbled away, but everywhere he went, he was surrounded by death.

"You men, over there!" Declan shouted. A group of twenty knights came traversing over the dead. "Bring them down, right this instant. And find a cloak or something to… to cover him."

He avoided saying anything that might upset Cedric, but it was unnecessary. Lord Valens had ventured far enough from the massacre that he could hear nothing. After reaching the edge of the killing fields, he found solitude. Were it not for the cawing of hundreds, perhaps thousands of crows circling above, he might have found quiet as well. Their incessant noise was overpowering and stoked his temper into a raging inferno.

Silence… silence, you foul creatures, SILENCE!

In frustration, Cedric picked up a rock and heaved it into the sky, but it fell pitifully short and did nothing to coerce their silence. He slumped onto the ground, his heart empty yet full of unspeakable pain. Cedric glanced over one shoulder to see if his men were around. When he saw they weren't, he wept quietly.

His tears would not last long. In the distance came a deep rumble. At first, he thought it might be a sign of a coming storm, but the sky bore no clouds in any direction. As seconds passed, the sound became unmistakable. It was the beating of horse hooves, hundreds of them.

With burning hatred in his eyes, Cedric stood, drew his sword, and prepared to face whoever was approaching. Could it be the barbarians returning to finish their work? He could not be certain. It would be a clever plan, he thought. Killing Alfrid and forcing himself out into the open with only a few hundred knights would be a coup. Not only would the savages have wiped out most of Morden's defenders, but they would also have a lord's head to claim.

Come and get me, you bastards! House Valens won't be snuffed out so easily. I'll kill every last one of you myself!

Death was no longer a frightening prospect. With an unbreakable grip on his sword, Cedric scanned the distance, waiting to see who would come cresting over the hill. To his relief, and to his disappointment, he saw the King's colors peeking up like an eastern sunrise. As badly as he wanted to kill the men responsible, this was perhaps the better outcome.

Riding at the head of a column of several hundred knights was Commander Jaxson Holland, with thirty thousand men at arms at his back. They finally arrived after their months-long deployment to the Zylmacian borderlands. He was one of the most reliable leaders Cedric had ever known, but heavy storms of the waning rainy season slowed his return for weeks.

The inbound knights came to a sudden halt with the mere raise of their Commander's hand. Their horses were certainly thankful, as the oppressive stench made them neigh and stir. Jaxson dismounted and continued on foot. He was roughly ten years younger than Cedric but was not lacking in experience. If one were ignorant, they might have thought Jaxson was Lord Valens' son, not Alfrid. He wore the steel breastplate and mail of a senior officer. A half helm covered his bald and battle-scarred head.

"My lord." Jaxson saluted and bowed. "My sincerest condolences. I marched the men day and night; we came as quickly as we could. I regret it was not quick enough. I beg your forgiveness."

Being cross with Jaxson would be of no use. It certainly would not bring Alfrid back. And if it was anyone's fault, it was his own. There were always reservations in the back of his mind about bringing his son to the western frontier. Both he and Alfrid knew the dangers, and neither one had given the proper respect to a wild place such as Khorrtal.

"The rest of the army will be here by sundown," Jaxson continued. "I swear to you, my lord, we will find the fiends responsible for this, and we will make them pay."

Wearily, Cedric raised a hand in acknowledgment. He felt so exhausted, he thought about falling asleep right there among the dead. If he did, maybe the fates would be kind and take his breath away as he slept. It seemed like a good enough idea, and would mean he would be reunited with Alfrid in the next life.

"You're in command here, Jaxson. Do what you must. I am indisposed."

"Yes, my lord. I will see that these men get a proper burial." Commander Holland saluted, then returned to his knights.

With the utmost care and respect, Alfrid's remains were the first to be taken down and laid on the ground. Having noticed Cedric's grieved state, one of the knights removed his cloak and placed it delicately over the corpse. It was a small kindness, but one every man was grateful for.

The next several hours were spent gathering materials for as many pyres as could be constructed. There would be no time to dig graves for the fallen, as was customary in the Kingdom. Pyres had fallen out of favor among the populace generations ago, but it was often a necessity for military men. There would be no dignity in digging a pit and throwing the dead into a heap on top of one another. No, not for Alfrid. That simply wouldn't do.

By the time evening arrived, enough wood had been collected from the nearby outskirts of the Hinterwood. The knights were reluctant to venture any closer due to superstitions about the unfathomably large forest. But time was growing scarce, and Commander Holland did not want the perpetrators to slip too far from his grasp. Some of the fallen

82

would have to share a pyre, but at the very least, Alfrid was afforded his own.

Before the impromptu ceremony began, the footsteps of tens of thousands of men grew as loud as thunderclaps. The full body of Commander Holland's field army had arrived. Lord Valens paid them little attention, instead stealing every moment he could alongside his son.

"I never should have sent you here," Cedric said quietly, his lips quivering. "Not that I didn't trust you to lead these men. No, of that, I'm sure you did your very best and fought bravely. But it should have been me. I should have been the one to die here, and you should be the one to have lived."

A tear fell from his cold eyes. "You were the future of our house. You were supposed to marry, grow old, and be surrounded by your own children. I was supposed to be laid to rest long before you. And now it all ends. Thousands of years of Valens lineage all come to an end. But I could not be prouder to have you be the last of my line. Be at peace, my son."

Captain Wilmot and Lieutenant Chambers approached Alfrid's pyre with lit torches in hand. The knights of Castle Morden lit torches and waited for their Commandant before laying their men to rest. Reluctantly, Cedric took a torch from Declan's hand and stared into the orange flames that would soon claim his son's body. He turned to the gathered knights to speak but choked on his words.

"Let us never forget these men and their sacrifice for their country. They fought bravely, and now it falls to us to be brave and avenge their loss. May they find peace in the next life."

Goodbye, son, I love you.

After looking upon Alfrid's body one final time, Cedric placed the torch on the pyre. In unison, the knights put their torches to the rest of the fallen. The flames were small and subtle but quickly erupted and roared into a massive inferno. Cedric watched as the fire lapped at his son's body, slowly eating away at the cloak covering the space where his head once sat. But he could not bear to see such devastation again and turned away.

"My deepest condolences, my lord," Declan said, touching Cedric's shoulder. "Apologies if I'm speaking out of place, but if you wish to return to the Mord, we could—"

"And why would I do that?" Cedric shot back with searing anger.

"So you may grieve in peace. Commander Holland is more than capable of—"

"No, I'm not going anywhere. I will not rest until I choke the life from this, Damien Dreadfire, myself. He may have bested us once, but now he'll have to face our full might."

The grief in Cedric's heart soon gave way to the purest form of hatred one could imagine. He stormed off through the field of roaring pyres, unphased by their blistering heat. He would not find the man responsible tonight, but Cedric would be damned if he would rest while his son's murderer supped and slept as a free man.

"Chambers! My horse. Now!"

Before the Lieutenant could move, a squire rushed over with his horse in tow. Cedric mounted his destrier and gave the beast a sharp, violent kick. Even though sunlight was fading faster by the minute, clods of disturbed earth from an army on the march were still visible. Judging from the tracks, it appeared to be a large host, but nothing his force could not handle.

"Prepare to march! Prepare to march!" Declan shouted over the roar of burning pyres.

The order was repeated far and wide, and all thirty thousand men quickly fell into formation, following their Commandant into an uncertain night. Though they had been at a forced march for days, the army's resolve was firm.

"My lord," Commander Holland called out as he galloped toward Cedric. "Should we not rest the army? At least for the night? It'll be dark soon, and the men are tired."

"The only ones resting tonight are three thousand of our men and the beasts who murdered them. Will you rest now and allow this injustice to stand? That my son's killers are out there roaming free?"

"No, my lord. But nightfall is nearly here, and… these tracks appear to be headed into the Hinterwood."

"Is there an issue, Commander?" Cedric said with an ever-growing hostility.

"It's just… my lord, that forest is cursed. It's dangerous enough to pass through there in the daytime, let alone at night. The men are loath to go there in the dark."

Am I hearing what I think it is I'm hearing? Has Holland turned craven?

"The men will do exactly as they're told, and so will you, Commander. Now go and summon your best trackers. Find me a path forward."

Those savages will not find a moment's peace, not here or anywhere. I will hunt them to the very ends of the earth if I must, and I will take from them everything they have taken from me and more.

A half-dozen riders raced by Cedric and headed off toward the Hinterwood, where the path was leading them. He was never a man to buy into superstition. Stories about the forest were simply stories, he thought, grand tales the barbarians used to their advantage to keep Betanthia at bay.

If those animals think a few ghost stories will keep me from my vengeance, then they have made the gravest of errors.

CHARLOTTE

"GET OUT, YOU STUPID HAG! GET OUT!"

King Marcellus Bethard shouted, throwing an empty flagon of wine in anger. The fine silver nearly hit Queen Charlotte in the head as it clanged off the wall and bounced several times on the floor. The King was in an unusually foul mood this morning, but there was little guess as to why. Some days were certainly better than others, and to Charlotte Bethard's misfortune, this was not one of them.

Two girls who had shared Marcellus' bed that night scurried out from the still-darkened room, and in such a rush, they forgot to clothe themselves. It was a sight the Queen was used to seeing all too often, though each time brought a renewed anguish. Witnessing Marcellus' adultery had become so commonplace, she cursed herself for even bothering to see him.

"I would have thought you would be in a better mood this morning. Were your little whores not enough to satisfy you?"

Charlotte could hardly believe the words that had come out of her mouth. She gasped ever so slightly in anticipation of the King's wrath, though surprisingly, he seemed not to notice. Instead, Marcellus called out for another flagon of wine. Within moments, a servant hurried into the room with refreshment in hand.

"You're going to drink the Kingdom out of wine at this rate," Charlotte said, shaking her head.

"If all you've come here to do is berate me, then you can turn around and leave," King Marcellus slurred. He sniffed at the wine, then drank with the grace of a toddler.

"Have some dignity. You're the King, or have you forgotten? Your drinking and whoring has become so intolerable, I'm told even the commoners speak of it now."

"Piss on the commoners," Marcellus belched. "If I hear them say such things, I'll have all of their heads!"

Between her husband's insolence and the stench of wine and sex lingering in the air, the Queen's patience was at an end. She stormed across the chamber and threw open the curtains one by one.

Marcellus Bethard was a pitiful sight to behold. His strong, muscular frame had diminished so dramatically that he appeared as thin and frail as an elderly man. His hair had turned almost completely gray, while his once smooth and clean-shaven face became drooped, wrinkled, and covered in a scraggly silver beard.

"Damn you, woman!" Marcellus winced as bright rays of morning sunlight poured into the room.

Only then could Queen Charlotte see the full extent of filth and carnage. The sight sickened her.

"I've grown tired of this, Marcellus. I'm tired of seeing you waste away in this accursed chamber while your people and your family wonder what has become of you. You need to do something with yourself. Tend to your kingdom. See how your children are doing. Something!"

She moved to the door, but the King stumbled to his feet and stood in her path.

"And I've grown tired of you thinking I owe anyone an explanation for anything! I'm the king, do you understand? I will not be dishonored in my own hall by you or anyone else!"

"You dishonor yourself. You certainly don't need any help with that," Charlotte retorted.

The back of Marcellus' hand hit Charlotte so hard and fast she did not remember falling to the floor. For a moment, she forgot where she was and could hear nothing, save for a dull ringing in her ears. When the disorientation subsided, she saw the King looming over her.

"You watch your fucking mouth, woman! I fought for this kingdom with my own two hands. I've shed my own blood for this kingdom! I don't deserve to be spoken to in such a manner, and if you disrespect me again, I'm going to peel the skin from your body and nail it to the fucking wall!"

Charlotte's courage had all but left, leaving behind a frightened woman who knew the King's anger all too well. Clutching her injured head, she rose on unsteady legs and turned to leave. But before she could move, Marcellus grabbed her forcefully by the arm.

"Now, you remember what I said because next time, you won't be so lucky. In fact, don't show your face around here again, you crone." Charlotte gasped in pain, his grip tight as a vice.

Marcellus gave her a shove through the door and slammed it shut, a deafening crash echoing far throughout the cavernous hallway. The King had not always been so cold. Quite the contrary, once. Many years ago, when they were young, Marcellus Bethard was a man of strength, vigor, and honor. He was a loving husband who cared deeply for his family. Those were perhaps the most painful memories of all.

The King insisted on traveling with his armies to the northwestern frontier on several long campaigns. His conquest of the upper Plainhold had proven difficult for the northern Commandant to tackle on his own, so Marcellus marched with sixty thousand men to conquer and lay claim to the land. The war raged for nearly two bloody years, culminating with a battle at a village called Borjifa.

Fighting against the northern tribes was fierce, and during a pitched night battle, the King suffered a terrible injury. A blow to the head from a maul unhorsed him, and after winning their victory, the soldiers of Betanthia feared they would lose their king before sunrise. But Marcellus survived, though forever changed by a wound that nearly claimed his life.

Charlotte tried to keep this sad tale in mind, but it was of little comfort after years of seeing her husband change before her eyes. Sometimes, she wished he had simply died on the battlefield so he might be remembered as a man of honor and glory. Whatever Marcellus was now, it was far from the man she married.

Is this what my life has become? What did I ever do to deserve such cruelty? All I've ever done was try to be a good wife and mother…

Charlotte clasped shaking hands over her eyes and sobbed. She stood alone in an empty hall, with nothing but the walls of the Westwind Citadel to hear her cries. As she retreated to her chamber, a passing servant gave pause and bowed. The sorrow on Charlotte's face was plain, and the servant disappeared around the corner in short order.

The Queen's chamber had become like a prison in recent months, as it was the only place she could find refuge from the King. She was forbidden to leave the grounds, even with an appropriate escort. Recently, the edict became more restrictive, and she was now barred from leaving the palace altogether.

The Westwind Citadel itself seemed to be the very definition of chaos. It was so impossibly large that Charlotte was unsure if she had seen every room, despite living there for decades. From the outside, it was an imposing testament to the power of House Bethard. Tall, thick outer walls protected an expansive courtyard, gardens, and barracks from the outside world. But the Citadel was so incredibly massive that the walls did nothing to spoil its splendor for the commoners.

Nearly a dozen towers jutted from the earth like the fingers of giants, each clawing and grasping toward the heavens above. Every one of them held a commanding view over Cardale, which had swelled so monstrously in size there was hardly room left for further expansion.

Inside the palace was quite the opposite. It was far too large even for a dozen families. It contained many banquet halls, ballrooms, and bedrooms; each numbered into the twenties or more. The largest room of all, the throne room, sat empty for ages. The King had abdicated most of his daily responsibilities to his son-in-law and closest advisor, Lord Aldred.

Still, the throne room was always Charlotte's favorite place. It was cavernous, airy, and decorated with precious artwork from end to end. Marble statues lining the walls were old beyond time, with a few pieces dating back to the city's founding by the ancient Khorrish people. A solid block of marble was chiseled into a throne and sat at the top of a long flight of stairs, each appearing more like platforms. It was upholstered in red velvet and inlaid with golden trim and precious gemstones. It was the most awe-inspiring thing Charlotte could remember from her first visit to the Citadel when she was young.

But the palace had lost its magical allure. Instead, it was now her tormentor. All around her, memories of a happier life lingered like ghosts of long-lost relatives. Her memories were once comforting but were now sorrowful reminders of everything she used to love about being the queen. It was painful to go anywhere in the palace, but even more painful being shut in her quarters every day.

At least she had Gareth, her eldest son and heir to the throne. He was a good son and tried his best, but Charlotte began to sense something different about him lately. She had seen Gareth stumbling to his chambers, drunk and beside himself, on more than one occasion. Truly, the stresses of dealing with not only her problems, but also his father's behavior were taking a toll on him.

Her other two children, Trace and Lucetta, had started lives of their own. Though they lived only a short distance away at their estate, Charlotte hardly saw either one. They might as well have moved to the other side of the Kingdom, for as absent as they were. It was discouraging to be left alone, though she could hardly fault any of her children for avoiding such violence and toxicity.

Perhaps it's better this way. Perhaps I deserve this, after all.

Charlotte arrived at her chamber, shut the door behind her, and sighed. She sat at a small cherrywood desk facing an eastern sky. From there, an ocean breeze wafted in through the window. She always loved the scent of the sea, and every time the winds blew favorably, she thought of her visits to the royal estate in Dellhaven.

Such thoughts were always bittersweet. While gazing at the bustling city below, she slid open a desk drawer and retrieved a small dirk inside. Her fingers danced about its razor-sharp tip, struggling with the thought of whether to use it or not. The soft flesh on her wrist would cut easily, and within moments, her suffering would be over forever, she thought.

That's all it will take, and the pain will be gone. If I did it, would anyone care? Would anyone notice?

A gentle rapping at the door caught Charlotte's attention. She returned the dirk, closing the drawer as the door opened.

"Your Majesty, am I disturbing you?" Emilee Harper, her personal maidservant, asked as she entered. She wore a plain black gown with a white apron, typical for servant girls at the Citadel. Her curly brown hair was fastened into an elegant updo, accented with a modest silver circlet. It was perhaps the only thing to define her as the Queen's maidservant.

Charlotte gave no reply but turned halfway so Emilee could not see the swollen welt on her head. As the servant girl set to freshening up, she noticed the Queen's unusual silence. Her morning routine was often met with a heartfelt greeting or at least a tacit acknowledgment.

"Is everything alright, my queen?" Emilee cocked her head curiously.

The Queen was always kind to her, much more so than the King, but today Charlotte was loath to keep any company.

"I would like my privacy, Emilee. You're dismissed," Charlotte replied softly but with an unusual gruffness.

The maidservant was flabbergasted and quickly retreated into the hall. The Queen immediately regretted being so short with Emilee. After all, she was only doing her job. Fresh tears streamed down her face as she grappled with the thought that, perhaps, she was becoming more like the King every day.

This is not the life I pictured for myself. If my parents were here to see this, they would be outraged. Father would strangle Marcellus with his bare hands if he knew how I was being treated.

Charlotte wished she was back in her hometown of Glimmergulf, and young again. Life was simple, especially for a lord's daughter. House Taybor was certainly not one of the more noble houses of the Kingdom. There was seldom much to do at their plantation in Glimmergulf save for watching the field masters as they brought wagons of grains, fruits, and vegetables to the castle. From there, their wares would be cataloged and sent to Cardale or Bentmont for sale in the markets.

Charlotte often spent time outside with her embroidery. But when her father, Lord Fulton Taybor, wasn't looking, she would sneak into the stables and ride on one of his prized striders. She remembered playing with her favorite horse one sunny afternoon, whom she named Apple for his reddish hue. When she thought her father wasn't looking, she saddled Apple and rode him out into the fields, but Lord Taybor was just around the corner and became frightfully angry.

She tried to stop Apple and turn him around, but her father's commotion spooked the horse, and onward they rode until the plantation was nearly out of sight. That was the first time Charlotte could recall being struck. When she returned, Lord Fulton took a switch to the back of her thighs until they bled.

His apology came later that evening when they sat down for supper. It was then that he vowed never to strike her again, and never did for the rest of his life. But it would not be the last time she would feel a man's wrath.

The stinging of the welt on her head brought back memories of her father that night. "I should never have hit you, Charlotte. You're precious to me, and I swear that I will never raise my hand to you again no matter how cross I become. I love you."

If only Marcellus could be so noble and humble…

Her reflection in the mirror was pitiful to witness. Charlotte never remembered looking so aged and worn. Her long, brown hair began to show strands of silver-gray much sooner than her mother did at her age. When once the sight of her fading youth was distressing, Charlotte had more or less succumbed to such inevitability. The hazel eyes staring back in the mirror had not changed, but a slow creep of crow's feet at their corners was plain enough to see.

Is this to be my fate? That of a broken old woman?

Charlotte turned from the mirror in frustration, wishing Gareth was here to comfort her. Though, it wouldn't feel right to trouble him anymore. She stared out the window for a minute before rising and moving closer to it. She peered down at the gardens below, which seemed so small from such a dizzying height. They were still beautiful to behold, even from above. She remembered better times, caring for the flowers and getting lost in acres of maze-like hedges.

She wondered what it would feel like to fly through the air with nothing to impede her descent. All she would need to do is step onto the windowsill, close her eyes, and let go. It could possibly be one last moment of bliss before the ground would rush up to meet her. Charlotte hoped there wouldn't be pain.

With trembling hands, she grasped the edges of the windowsill and tried to step onto it, but her legs refused to budge. Though her mind was willing, her body was not yet ready. As the Queen struggled to regain control over her movements, thoughts of Gareth crept back into her mind. The gardens were his favorite place as well, and she could not bear the idea of him discovering her lifeless body lying among the flowers and hedges, shattered and broken from the fall.

I can't… I can't do it…

Sobbing, Charlotte slumped back from the windowsill and fell to the floor. She had been strong for so many years, especially after Marcellus' mind began to fade, but even the strongest steel bends and eventually breaks. Life was not supposed to be this difficult. Not for someone of her status. Charlotte would gladly trade every bit of wealth and privilege away if it would mean she could find peace.

The mournful weeping did not go unnoticed, however. At first, the door cracked open slowly but was thrown open in a hurry. Emilee must have been standing vigil outside the entire time. The maidservant rushed to Charlotte's side and embraced her.

"My queen!" Emilee said, astonished. "Whatever is the matter?"

After wiping water from her eyes, Charlotte moved a thick lock of hair behind her ear, revealing a welt the King had given her. Emilee gasped and sat stunned before embracing the Queen once again.

"Oh heavens! I… I…" the servant girl stammered, lost for words.

"It's so bad, Emilee. It just gets worse by the day."

"I don't even know what to say, my queen. This is shocking… this is appalling. I'll speak to Sir Edmund about it immediately."

The Captain of the Royal Guardsmen was a good man, but Charlotte was still terrified at the possibility of Marcellus finding out she told anyone of his abuse. She trembled furiously as if taken by a sudden chill.

"No, no, you mustn't!" Charlotte pleaded. "I cannot risk him finding out. Please, Emilee, don't do it."

The maidservant looked as if she was about to cry as well. "As you wish, my queen, but… there has to be something I can do for you. Please, allow me to help."

The only thing Charlotte wanted was her son. It didn't matter if her suffering was an inconvenience to him. Being alone and without family to comfort her was too great to bear.

"Please… Gareth… I want Gareth…"

"I'll fetch him right away, my queen. Please, take a deep breath and try to be calm. I'll be right back, ok?"

Emilee embraced her tightly, then left in search of the crown prince. As guilty as she felt for disturbing Gareth again, she needed to have him close by. Such isolation and abuse were more than anyone could endure alone, and Queen Charlotte feared that if something did not change soon, she might very well be dead.

MADELYN II

AFTER NEARLY A WEEK OF HARD RIDING, THE TALL PEAKS OF THE Westwind Citadel came into view. It was a lovely journey, and Corbyn kept his promise to be professional. There was a particularly chilly night they spent curled up beside a fire, but even still, he maintained decorum. Even though Madelyn was a skilled warrior and needed no one to look after her, having his strong, protective arms wrapped around her was pleasant nonetheless.

The full breadth of the city revealed itself as they crested a final hill. Madelyn paused for a moment and surveyed the landscape before her. Cardale was a gargantuan city, a literal forest of brick and stone buildings. Some towered so far into the sky that it was difficult to believe men could even build such things. The entire perimeter was surrounded by a fifty-foot wall that stretched and snaked for miles. A tall, reinforced gate stood at every mile marker, of which there were over two dozen.

While Bentmont was a city colored with a rusty-red hue, Cardale was almost entirely tan. It looked as pristine as a painting from a distance, but such appearances were deceptive. The capital was not all it seemed to be from the outside, and Madelyn knew this well enough from experience. It was some time since she last visited, and as they approached one of the massive and imposing gates, she was thankful to have Corbyn beside her.

This place never ceases to amaze me. But I could never picture myself living here. It's far too… too…

It was difficult for Madelyn to put her finger on why the capital wasn't to her liking. It was far larger and busier than Bentmont, but large and busy cities never bothered her. There was something unpleasant about it, though perhaps unpleasant was too strong of a word.

Although the gates were typically open during this time of day, they were always well-guarded. Half a dozen men stood vigil next to a pair of tall, thick wooden doors, checking the comings and goings of peasant and lord alike. Madelyn spied a score of archers pacing about the battlements above. One by one, they would disappear behind one of the many thousands of crenellations, only to appear a moment later, then disappear once again.

The men at the gate finished clearing a peasant man and his cart to enter when Madelyn and Corbyn trotted over. She chose to wear her armor for this very reason. Her polished steel breastplate shone like pure silver in the sun. Emblazoned on her left pauldron were the colors of the Blackthorn Knights; a horse in mid-gallop, ringed in a circle of thorns, against a black and gold backdrop. Her long, hip-length blonde hair was loose and flowing behind her like a golden cape.

Madelyn brought Nora to a halt as two guards approached. The remaining four looked on curiously.

"State your business," one of the men grunted. He seemed to recognize the heraldry but was hesitant to allow them free passage.

"I'm Commander Everly of the Blackthorn, here on urgent business on behalf of High Marshal Powell. I must speak with the King at once." She glanced down at the colors of the Order on her pauldron, then back at the guard.

"I'm afraid you'll need written approval from the high council in order to—"

Before the guard could finish speaking, another, more senior-looking man stepped forward and interrupted. It was apparent he had dealings with the Order in the past, either directly or by their frequent visits to the capital.

"That won't be necessary. Welcome to Cardale, Commander. Enjoy your visit."

Hastily, Madelyn and Corbyn were waved through, leaving the other guards staring at each other in bemusement. As she passed through the enormous gate, she could not help but notice significantly less farmland on the other side of the wall. A sizable portion of land had been developed, with hundreds of new dwellings springing up in the past year since she visited. It was fascinating to see how much Cardale had grown, but also a bit disheartening.

As the knights made their way down the western highway, curious onlookers stood in wonderment. Many looked as if they had never seen a knight before, or at least not very often. A group of young children stood clustered close together, whispering and pointing at Madelyn with little care for discretion. She met their inquisitiveness with a smile and a wave. It was heartwarming to see the eyes of a small blonde girl light up as if she was witnessing the arrival of the Queen herself.

After riding further, the full splendor of Cardale came into view. Tall masts from merchant ships at port jutted over the rooftops of far-distant buildings. An indiscernible murmur of hundreds of thousands of Cardaleians filled the air like an overture to a great symphony. And, of course, one could not fail to notice the smell. It was a curious amalgamation of salty sea water, fresh fish from the market, spices and incense, and the fetid stench of an overly taxed sewer system.

It was shocking to see how filthy the city had become. Madelyn was unaccustomed to seeing so many poor and destitute people wandering and lying about the streets, some begging for a spare coin and others seemingly lost in their misfortune. She spied a pack of mangy dogs as they tore into what she hoped was an animal carcass and not that of a human. She watched a middle-aged woman heave a bucket of putrid, dark liquid from a second-storey window onto the cobbles below. This was not the Cardale she remembered.

The western highway snaked through neighborhoods, past an abandoned temple that had become a refuge for the homeless and a small, newly-constructed marketplace. Fortunately, the city was not entirely consumed by poverty and squalor. Along the way to the city square, she passed by communities containing impressive-looking estates, some of which stood behind tall gates and walls. There was a greatly increased presence of city watchmen here, which gave some measure of safety.

"I find it interesting," Corbyn said. "The guards seem so defensive over who comes into the city, but not so much when it comes to the people living here."

"Well, you're certainly not wrong," Madelyn sighed in dismay. She resolved that if Gareth was at the Westwind Citadel, she would voice concern over the current state of Cardale. It would certainly be better to say it to the crown prince as opposed to the King, who undoubtedly would take offense. With Gareth, at least she had a sympathetic ear.

Madelyn began daydreaming about her meeting with the King. Doubt was slowly creeping into the back of her mind; doubt as to whether she could handle such a task in the first place. From what Gareth told her the last time they spoke, the King was unpredictable and often incapable of behaving like a civilized man.

It was not fear of physical harm that concerned Madelyn. It was what King Marcellus might do or accuse her of if she were to say something not to his liking. He was the sole source of power within Betanthia and could command the Royal Guardsmen to clap her in irons for whatever offense, regardless of her station in the Order. Hopefully, Sir Edmund would be able to accompany her as well. He was the Captain of the King's elite bodyguards and knew her cordially enough from her visits over the years. Surely, Sir Edmund would be able to keep Marcellus Bethard's madness under control, for her sake.

"I don't know about you, but I'm dying to get out of this saddle," Corbyn complained. "We should find somewhere to rest for a moment."

Not an unreasonable request, Madelyn supposed. She was feeling quite sore from a hard day of riding, and even Nora was beginning to protest. "Just a little bit further. I know a place where we can stay."

"Aren't we staying at the barracks?"

"No, not this time. The High Marshal decided to treat us, so we'll be staying at the Seascape Inn. It's close to the palace. I think you'll like it; I've stayed there before."

The remainder of their journey was brief, and soon enough, she heard rustling waters of the Camsby River, telling her the Seascape was nearby. Madelyn always enjoyed staying at the inn, which had a breathtaking view of the river and its mouth at the Great Sea. It was an elegant establishment, yet simple enough for her taste.

Upon seeing a weathered wooden sign hanging from the wall of the Seascape, Madelyn was able to breathe a sigh of relief. Before arriving at the door, she slid clumsily off Nora's saddle to stretch her aching legs. Madelyn's steel sabatons crunched and creaked against the cobblestones as she dismounted, echoing her own groans of discomfort.

A pair of ornate doors were propped open to allow for ventilation. From inside, a strong yet pleasant scent of incense drifted out. It was one of Madelyn's favorite things about Cardale; the variety of exotic foods, spices, and scents that were difficult to find anywhere else. There were few foreign traders in Bentmont, so selections at the marketplaces were mainly limited to what could be produced and sold locally.

After tying Nora to a hitching post, Madelyn limped inside the inn with Corbyn close behind. The last thing she wanted to do was sit any longer, but the idea of lying on a soft bed seemed refreshing enough. But after a week of uneventful travel, she had an itch to do a bit of exploring first.

Fortunately, there were still rooms available. Unfortunately, they were on the second and third floors. Not wanting to endure walking up more stairs than necessary, Madelyn settled on a second-floor suite. She removed a few coins from her purse and exchanged them for a skeleton key.

A pair of boys scurried out from a room behind the counter and ran outside to fetch their belongings. It was one of the courtesies Madelyn came to expect from the Seascape, and one of many things that brought her back with each visit to Cardale. She only wished there had been a room on the first floor instead of the second, so her legs might be spared. But a room is a room, and at least there was one.

Madelyn and Corbyn slogged up the stairs while the boys ran past them, gear in hand, and to their suite before they could reach the top. Though only in her twenties, Madelyn's body felt worn and ancient. Despite the ache of stiff muscles, it felt good to be moving under her own power again.

Their room was at the far end of a well-lit hallway. The boys waited anxiously for Madelyn and Corbyn to open the door, so they could get back to their activities. With a turn of the skeleton key, Madelyn entered, the boys rushing past her and placing their belongings against the wall.

For their efforts, she gave each of them a coin from her purse. They bashfully gave thanks, their eyes as wide and bright as the silver in their hands. In a flash, they disappeared into the hall, slamming the door behind them. Their reactions made Madelyn smile. Even if it was money given to her for personal expenses, it made her feel good to give to others. The Order could certainly afford a little charity.

"I think I'm going to lie down for a bit. Are you going anywhere?" Corbyn asked, struggling to remove his armor.

Plate steel was often a challenge to remove alone, so Madelyn offered a hand. In return, he assisted with removing her breastplate and pauldrons.

"For a bit. I'd like to stretch my legs some more, but I'll be back soon."

It was relieving to be free of the burden of steel armor. Her body felt much lighter, which made descending the stairs feel as if she was floating on air. The doors to the inn were still open, and the scents and sounds of Auburn Row called out to her. As she left the Seascape, she spied one of the helper boys feeding and brushing Nora, which made her smile.

The trip to Auburn Row and its market was brief. Madelyn paused for a moment while crossing a stone bridge over the Camsby River. Across from the market, the magnificence of the Westwind Citadel was plain to see. It was seat of Betanthia's might, the ultimate purpose behind her years of service. First and foremost, she served the Order, but the Order existed to safeguard the Bethard dynasty, and the Westwind Citadel was the manifestation of the power they commanded.

It was sometimes difficult to understand why a marketplace existed on Auburn Row, but she supposed it was somewhat obvious. How could one travel to Cardale and *not* pay a visit to the palace? It was likely the largest structure on Caldakas, far larger and more imposing than Castle Thorn, which was inconceivable. Madelyn could only guess how many generations of men had to labor in order to construct it.

Now that I can see it, the palace does look taller than Castle Thorn. It's larger than I remember.

After taking a moment to admire the palace, Madelyn started down Auburn Row. There were considerably more stalls now than she remembered, but little room was left for further expansion. Hawking of wares was never permitted so close to the Citadel, but in recent years, those seeking to engage in commerce on the Row were allowed to, provided they paid a tax.

About halfway through the marketplace, Madelyn happened upon a stall run by three exotic-looking women with dark, tan skin and hair as black as the night. She knew it was not uncommon to find Droethien merchants throughout the capital. Much more likely, in fact, than in Bentmont. Here, they sold a wide variety of handmade jewelry, from earrings to bracelets, to rings, and pieces so strange she had no idea what they were. A large rack hung an assortment of silk, linen, and woolen garments. Each was finely crafted, judging by what she saw.

Madelyn was never one to wear or even own jewelry, but the selections piqued her curiosity. She studied them carefully, feeling her coins burning a hole through her purse.

"A good day to you, my dear! Welcome, welcome! We have the finest silver and gemstones you will find east of the Plainhold, yes? Please, see for yourself!"

The woman's boast appeared to be no lie. Madelyn was captivated by intricate etchings on a large silver ring, which she slid onto her index finger, then held out her arm to examine. The piece had noticeable weight but felt comfortable otherwise. She knew she had to have it.

"I absolutely love this ring! I'd like to buy it. What's your price?" Without hesitation, she plunged a hand into her coin purse.

"Such a plain piece for such a pretty young lady, yes?" The woman smiled, the other two behind the stall snickering at one another.

It was a compliment Madelyn had received before, especially by Corbyn, but it always made her feel uncomfortable. She had never seen herself as a great beauty, and with her duties in the Order, her looks were often the furthest thing from her mind.

"I'm a simple girl," Madelyn said politely. "I've never cared for overly exquisite things. They're just... not to my liking."

"Ah, but have you ever seen how they look on you?" The merchant woman smiled. "Come, I will show you how we dress in the west, and if you like, then I offer you a discount, agreed?"

It's only a bit of fun, Madelyn. No one will ever know.

Anxiously, she agreed. If any of her brothers in the Order were to catch sight of her, she would never hear the end of it. Her whole life, she had grown up around fighting men and seldom had time to behave as anything other than a soldier, except in private.

"My name is Nya. Come, come. My girls and I will take great care."

The merchant woman looked her up and down. Nya quickly scurried about and gathered a few small, modest pieces of jewelry set with amber, a dress made of blue silk with gold trim, and sandals with straps around the ankle.

"Modest, yes. But beautiful and elegant at the same time. Please, put this on." Nya handed Madelyn the dress, her smile growing wider.

"I thought we were looking at jewelry…" Madelyn said apprehensively. She had never worn a silk gown, or any gown in her life, for that matter. The whole idea seemed strange to her.

"Ah, but what is the western style without the proper garment? Come, you will look as beautiful as the dawn. Nya promises this."

Madelyn was led to a stall where she could change. At first, she was uncertain, but after such a long journey from Bentmont, she deserved to be pampered. She took the gown behind the curtain and slipped into it. It was long and flowing, yet light and comfortable, and fastened around one shoulder. The silk felt cool against her skin; from what she saw, it complimented her figure nicely. When she stepped out, Nya and her two girls clapped and giggled.

"As always, Nya knows!" the merchant woman exclaimed. "Now come, we must finish."

She sat in a simple wicker chair and was immediately swarmed by the Droethiens. One of the girls ran her fingers through Madelyn's hair, then used a brush of boar bristles to untangle the knots. Another retrieved a metal file and glass bottles of paint, then began fixing her nails. Nya opened a kit of powdery makeup and dusted it carefully on her face and around her eyes.

The ordeal felt humiliating at first, but as Madelyn relaxed, her eyes closed, she began to enjoy it. Moments before falling asleep from the serenity of the experience, it was finished.

"Come, my dear, come see. You look like a proper western woman. Come, come!"

Nya led her to a tall mirror, its surface clean yet scarred with small pits. Nervously, Madelyn stepped in front of it and was immediately stunned by what she saw. The plain face she was used to seeing was now transformed. She looked more beautiful than she could have imagined.

Her long, blonde hair was put up, with a braided headband arcing across the front of her scalp, the length drawn back into a pinned-up mass of curls. Across her braid was a circlet of amber, delicately strung together. Madelyn's piercing steely-blue eyes were outlined in black makeup, the skin around them dusted into smokey rings. Her nails were painted like pure gold.

"Do you like?" Nya asked proudly.

Madelyn was lost for words. It felt as if the air was knocked from her lungs. She almost wanted to cry, but not tears of sadness or pain.

"Yes, I love it," she answered softly, studying herself.

"Good, good. For all of this, I charge, hmm, thirty silver. But for you, I say twenty, yes?"

There wasn't a moment of hesitation. Madelyn reached for her belt on top of her folded riding clothes. She thrust a hand inside her coin purse, removed four gold pieces, and handed them to Nya. The merchant woman bit into one of them to make certain, but was satisfied. One of the girls placed Madelyn's belongings into a small sack and handed it to her.

"You be sure to come back now, yes?" Nya asked inquisitively.

Madelyn smiled and nodded sheepishly. "I will. Thank you so much."

It was a strange feeling for a warrior to be more nervous about walking down the street as opposed to leading a charge into battle. This was not the first time she had been gussied up, but it was always in private and for herself to enjoy. And, of course, never in a style like this. But here she was, for all the world to see, and without her armor, in more ways than one.

As she walked down Auburn Row and back to the inn, Madelyn felt eyes upon her, hundreds of them. Most were curious because this *was* Cardale, after all, and she was styled as a Droethien. Not that it bothered her in the least, because she felt beautiful.

After arriving back at the Seascape, her pulse began to quicken. She feared Corbyn's reaction to seeing her in such a way. Although they were lovers and knew every inch of each other's bodies, she had never gone to such an effort to look beautiful for him, only for herself. And never quite like this. It was a flattering thought, at least, to know she was wanted for who she was without any unnecessary trappings.

Just breathe, Madelyn. It's fine. There's nothing to worry about.

Each step upstairs made her sore legs feel like they were turning to water. She was perhaps more unsettled with the idea of word spreading throughout the Order, which might take away from her fierce and dominating presence. Corbyn, however, was another matter entirely. He was no stranger to the Droethien borderlands and hated them as much as any Betanthian.

With a million thoughts racing through her head, Madelyn paused outside the door to their suite. After a few deep breaths and a quick adjustment to her dress, she entered slowly. She spied a platter of fresh meat and bread on the table, but Corbyn was nowhere to be found.

"Corbyn… are you here?" Madelyn asked, toying with the trim on her gown.

"Yes, I'm in the other room," he replied. "I had some food brought up, I'm guessing you're probably as hungry as—"

Corbyn froze in place as he rounded the corner. His mouth hung open like an unlatched door, his words turning to dust and falling away. His stunned reaction made Madelyn turn red with embarrassment.

"What's the matter?" she asked, scratching at the back of her neck.

"Nothing. You… you look… stunning beyond belief. I…"

Madelyn smiled, her face and chest becoming flush and warm. "Thank you, I was hoping you might like it. Please, just promise me you won't say anything to—"

"No," Corbyn interrupted, struggling to control his breathing. "No, I won't say anything at all."

Not that anyone was likely to believe him in the first place, or at least she hoped. Slowly, Madelyn walked toward Corbyn, discarding her sack of clothing on the floor. Their eyes met, and the world outside faded into the distant background.

"Shouldn't we… I mean, you… be preparing to see the King? This is a… very… important meeting after all…"

Corbyn's nervousness made her feel increasingly more confident. Madelyn was young, strong, and beautiful. And she knew it. Both lovers leaned in closer, each swimming in the endless oceans of their eyes until their lips touched. The kiss felt different from their hundreds of kisses before. This time, it wasn't a mere formality standing in the way of their bodies becoming entangled. No, this kiss was something more.

"The council meeting isn't until tomorrow." Madelyn leaned close to Corbyn's ear, then ran a hand through the smooth black hair above his neckline and whispered. "And besides, the King can wait."

CEDRIC III

T HE MARCH THROUGH THE HINTERWOOD WAS LONG AND PERILOUS. That night, it was bitterly cold and exceptionally dark. A waxing moon was shrouded by thick clouds, making it impossible to see even a foot ahead. The army's pace had slowed several times to a near crawl, prompting Lord Valens' fury. Rotating patrols of scouts performed admirably enough and kept the thirty thousand-man force on track, but as dawn drew closer, an undeniable truth began to rear its head; the men were exhausted and needed rest.

Begrudgingly, Cedric agreed to a quick respite. It would have been a lie to say he wasn't tired. The ordeal of saying goodbye to Alfrid left him as drained as an empty well. It made him feel old, far older than forty-eight years. There was apprehension about sleeping, however. The nightmares sure to haunt his dreams would be as unpleasant as the one he had before discovering Alfrid's body.

But Cedric did sleep, and thankfully there were no dreams. Or at least, none he could remember. Even his own mind seemed to have reached its limit. A morning sun filtered through a cathedral of pines when he woke. It had only been an hour, maybe two of rest, but it would suffice. Cedric Valens was a lifelong military man and had experienced far worse than a little fatigue.

"Get on your feet, men. There's no sleep while the enemy lives. Get moving!"

His order was met with exhausted groans and murmurs of agitation. Even Commander Holland seemed irritated at only having a moment to recover after such a grueling forced march. But he was loyal and dutiful, and after a few sips of what appeared to be wine, he was on his feet and assembling the men.

The Hinterwood was a strange and mystical place. For as long as Cedric could remember, it was a source of fantastical stories and rumors. The woods were purported to be haunted. It was said that upon death, barbarian spirits would return to wander there for all eternity. Even the trees seemed to have eyes. Their ancient, gnarled branches and trunks gave the feeling that Cedric's movements were being carefully studied.

Dense clouds of pollen, gnats, and humidity made marching insufferable. How anyone could stomach living in such a place was a mystery. But then again, the men responsible for killing Alfrid were more like beasts than humans. If that was the case, then it made perfect sense for Damien Dreadfire and his band of murderers to reside here.

The farthest Cedric could recall venturing into the wilderness was at the source of the Teb River, near Borjifa. But that campaign was years ago, and the terrain here was far different than what he was accustomed to. In the end, it would make no difference. Neither old wives' tales about the Hinterwood nor his men's reservations would deter him.

"My lord, the scouts have reported back," Commander Holland said. Cedric saw exhaustion on his face but had little sympathy. "We're hot on their trail. The tracks appear fresh, perhaps only a few days old."

"An army can cover quite a bit of ground in a few days," Cedric grumbled.

Even though Jaxson was someone he might consider a friend, it did little to stifle his resentment. Granted, *his* order sent Jaxson south to suppress a Zylmacian incursion. The western wildmen were as much of a threat as the Droethiens, though thankfully, they were easier to dispense.

Still, Cedric could not help but feel that with thirty thousand men plus Blackthorn auxiliaries, the borderland should have been secured in far less time. Within a month, he could have carved a swathe halfway through the Bymist, perhaps more.

If you were more diligent in your duties, my son might still be alive, Cedric thought, casting a glare toward Commander Holland. Part of him wished Jaxson was the one to have been killed instead. If it meant that Alfrid would still be alive, he would have sacrificed all thirty thousand men.

Soldiers are replaceable, Cedric reminded himself. *My son is not.*

The army continued its slog at a respectable pace. The further into the dense forest they marched, the more traveled it appeared, far from a deserted realm of ghosts many believed it to be. Many crude pathways were cleared to make the forest more accessible for those who dwelled there, and perhaps an army as well.

The southern edge of the Hinterwood contained mostly oak and maple trees, though an occasional evergreen was present. If it wasn't for tribes of bloodthirsty savages skulking about, the woods might otherwise be serene. An unusual amount of moss covered nearly every tree, including those that were fallen. Some were even completely enveloped in shaggy green blankets. It was a sight Cedric had not seen in all of his forty-eight years. He might have enjoyed the journey a bit more if not for a burning hatred in his heart. Indeed, the Hinterwood was a sight to behold.

You should have been here to experience this with me, son. We should have shared many more memories together.

As the morning sun drew higher, the summer heat rose to match it. To distract himself, Cedric recalled the time when Alfred was born. It was a cold winter but not particularly snowy. The midwives were uncertain if their baby would survive. It was weeks before Alfrid was expected to be born, and Olivia Valens' health was fast deteriorating.

He remembered the joy of Olivia giving birth to their first and only child, and the agony of losing her minutes after. It was a trade she gladly accepted and would have accepted, even if she knew it would require paying the ultimate price.

"Keep him safe, Cedric. Keep… him…"

Keep him safe. Those were Olivia's last words before she bled to death on the birthing table. And for two decades, Cedric did just that. But having seen the cruelty of the world, he knew Alfrid would have to learn to fight. He had seen too often what happened to those who could not. And the boy was small, far too small.

But Alfrid grew and learned well, and quickly. Cedric knew how badly his son wanted to follow in his footsteps. After all, he would inherit the title of Lord one day, and as a lord, he would be tasked with leading men into battle at the King's behest. There would only be one way to keep Alfrid safe: to bring his son under his command and supervision.

But all of Cedric's good intentions were for naught. He could not honor Olivia's promise, and now they were together in the next life. He never believed in the gods or a world beyond, but he hoped it was true for his family's sake. He could not bear the thought of never seeing his dearest son and wife again. The idea seemed too cruel to even contemplate.

"My lord," a voice interrupted. It was Jaxson, his face tightening. "Is everything alright?"

Pressure inside Cedric's head was agonizing, his brain throbbing with every heartbeat. His memories were becoming toxic, almost like poison, though more akin to drinking seawater.

"Fine, I'm… fine," he said, though clearly not.

"If I may speak plainly, my lord. There isn't a man who doesn't feel your loss. You don't have to be here. I… I know you want justice done, but—"

"But what?" Cedric interrupted. Lack of sleep and the weight of his despair made his fraying nerves show.

"You entrusted me to be your Commander for years now. And I haven't failed you yet. I beg your forgiveness, my lord, but I'm concerned. I'm concerned your rage will compromise the integrity of the army."

All Cedric could do was laugh, his thirty-four years of military service and experience suddenly called into question.

"My rage? My good man, you have yet to see my rage. And I find your lack of trust quite insulting. You *have* heard the story about how I was made a Commandant, have you not? Not even those deeds would qualify as rage. I'm far more calculating than you give me credit for, even under the most trying circumstances."

It was perhaps the only time Cedric had ever hinted at what took place at Borjifa, even without going into specifics. Those who whispered about that infamous day knew what he was capable of, even without rage. It was the King's orders, after all. At any cost, Marcellus Bethard told him, and Cedric did what was necessary. He had always done what was necessary.

"A thousand apologies, my lord. I meant no offense."

Despite being exhausted, grief-stricken, and overwhelmed with fury, Lords Valens was able to recognize the hostility in his tone. Though strict, he was always careful not to become a tyrant. Men would never freely follow such a leader into the fires of battle, and now was not the time for mistrust or disunity.

"None taken. I appreciate your efforts, Jaxson, and your sympathy. And you would be remiss in your duties if you were not looking out for the men's best interests."

Commander Holland seemed taken aback by Cedric's words, but the sentiment was nevertheless appreciated.

"And furthermore," Cedric continued, "after this campaign, I will petition the King to promote you to Commandant. I've grown too old for frontier life. And my fighting days are over, after I avenge my son's death."

"My lord… that… that is most generous of you. But why? Where will you go? What will you do?"

What would he do? It was a good and fair question. All Cedric had ever known was the army and the feel of a sword in his hand.

"I would like to spend the rest of my days in Cardale, perhaps even take up a seat on the King's council for a short while. This has been my whole life, Jaxson. The men. The fight. And it was good, but now I've grown tired."

"Nobody has earned the right more than you, my lord," Jaxson reflected. "There isn't a man here that wouldn't speak fondly of your character and abilities. I'm certain the King would be happy to grant you such a reward for your service."

Cardale was where Cedric felt he always belonged, living a life of peace and comfort. Crushing Damien Dreadfire's army and capturing new territory in the north would surely earn King Marcellus's favor. The only shame was that his son could not share in the glory and inherit his titles.

"Being a Commandant is a mighty responsibility. I will miss it, but at the same time, I won't." Cedric smiled, though it was empty. "Come, let's let the men rest for a moment. I need to get out of this saddle, my hips have had enough."

As the army was brought to a halt, Cedric rolled uncomfortably out of his saddle, a stinging soreness causing him to limp. He found shelter from the blazing sun underneath a giant beech tree. Even though sitting was the last thing he wanted to do, lying down provided a bit of relief.

Aside from the shuffling of thousands of feet and horse hooves and the clanking and crunching of armor, it was quite peaceful. Cedric took notice of the wind blowing through the trees and, of course, the birds. He heard soft songs of hundreds of birds and found them comforting; soothing, even. After the men had settled, it grew even quieter.

Squirrels scurried up the tall, ancient tree trunks for safety, while an occasional rabbit popped out of hiding to forage for food. Cedric even thought he saw a deer in the distance, standing as firmly as a statue at first but then quickly making its retreat. A subtle smell of old, fallen logs and fresh leaves mixed with the thick aroma of pine. The Hinterwood seemed less of a nightmare and more of a paradise.

Leaving the modern world behind and living in the woods did have an indescribable allure to it. Being surrounded by trees and wildlife most certainly would provide a more engaging experience than living among stone and squalor. If he were a younger man, Cedric might very well forsake his titles and leave Cardale to its devices. But he wasn't. And he had spent a lifetime in service to the crown and deserved the rewards owed to him.

He understood why many would choose this life instead of being amidst the clutter and busyness of a big city. Here, you could be free to do as you please, without noise or crime, or distractions.

I can see why the Northmen would defend such a place as fiercely as they do. If these were the King's woods, he would likely forbid any man to set foot in them but himself. I certainly would.

Slowly, he was beginning to empathize with his enemy. But such thoughts were fleeting and quickly melted away, twisting and morphing back into anger. Cedric had to remind himself why he was here. Alfrid was dead. The future of his house lay in ruins. And the man responsible was still out there, roaming free.

Declan soon appeared with food in hand. After catching sight of salted meat and bread, Cedric's stomach ached and groaned like a wounded beast. He had not eaten since the day he found Alfrid; it had only been a few bites of bread that morning.

"I figured you might be hungry," Captain Wilmot said with a half grin.

"Thank you, Declan. It's kind of you to look after me."

"It's what any good officer would do. Besides, you need to keep your strength up. Last I heard, our scouts say we're only a few days away from making contact. The Northmen aren't nearly as far away as they might think."

Nodding, Cedric bit into a slice of salted meat. His mouth watered instantly at the taste. "Good. As soon as we're finished, tell Commander Holland to get the men back on their feet. If we're this close, then I don't want to linger any longer than necessary."

"By your will, my lord."

Together they ate in silence. Cedric devoured his rations like a starving dog, having been encouraged by the news. In no time, he was climbing back into the saddle of his destrier, wincing as the sores on his body began screaming in protest. But neither pain nor hunger could keep Lord Valens from his revenge, not when the barbarians were so close.

GARETH

"**Y**OUR HIGHNESS, THE QUEEN REQUESTS YOUR PRESENCE."

The Royal Guardsman snapped his heels together and bowed before exiting Gareth Bethard's private quarters. The eldest son and heir of King Marcellus gave a deep sigh, rubbing his temples in annoyance that was quickly boiling into anger. This was the third time in the last two days.

Gareth stood and brushed his shoulder-length brown hair behind his ears, then gazed through the open balcony doors. A cool western breeze kissed his face and gently rustled a pair of red silk curtains. He contemplated ignoring the Queen's request, but failing to respond would most surely result in an even greater calamity, requiring far more effort to fix. It seemed, at least today, honoring his mother's request was the only option.

He walked lazily through the outer corridor and toward Queen Charlotte's chambers, imagining what new crisis he would encounter. He knew all too well the turmoil she was experiencing. Gareth could hardly recall the last time he spoke to Marcellus, for the two mixed as well as oil and water. Their last conversation ended so poorly he had sworn never to see his father again.

Why should I subject myself to such torture? What good will it do me?

Life as the crown prince was far from easy, and often, he wished such responsibility had fallen to another. The Westwind Citadel was not as glamorous or magical on the inside as an outsider might think. All the trappings of wealth and privilege were merely a facade. He often wondered how Betanthia managed to function with such turbulent disorder on a daily basis.

Just outside the Queen's door, Gareth heard faint sobbing. He paused in hesitation before entering, a lingering dread causing his pulse to quicken. It was not easy to bear the weight of Charlotte's emotional fragility, especially when he was struggling with demons of his own. As a consequence, Gareth had grown fond of strong drink as a means to cope with his troubles. The latest round of coping from the night before left his head swimming, even now.

"Yes, mother, what is it?" Gareth shuffled into the room.

Charlotte seemed not to notice. With her back turned to the door, she sat at her desk and looked at the city below. A muffled sniffle was evidence enough that she did not want Gareth to see her crying. He felt a sharp pang of guilt and moved to his mother's side. He then noticed a swollen red mark on the side of her head.

"Mother, what's the meaning of this?" Gareth gestured at the welt. Charlotte recoiled and attempted to hide it with her hair.

"Your father is at it again. This time he threatened to nail my skin to the wall. All because I told him to do something for once instead of sitting around drinking all day. He got so angry with me and wouldn't let me leave. That's when he struck me."

A deep, fiery rage began to burn inside Gareth's body. He felt a sudden lightheadedness from a rush of anger. "I've had enough of this. It's gone on far too long. I'll kill him. I'll kill him, and we'll be done with this madness forever."

Charlotte shot from her seat and gripped him by the arm, her hands trembling. "No! No, you mustn't. I'm sorry, I should never have troubled you. I just, I have no one else…"

"No, mother, stop it. I don't want to hear you make excuses for him. He should never, ever lay a hand on you. King or not, it isn't right. And he *has* no right either."

Gareth's head throbbed and felt near to bursting. The last thing he wanted was to get into another squabble between his parents, but this was an affront that could not be ignored.

"I know, and I'm sorry to bring you into this." Charlotte sniffled. "Could you just… talk to him? You're his eldest son; he'll listen to you."

"I've tried, mother, I've tried more times than I can even remember. When I speak to him, it's as if there's no awareness or understanding in his eyes. He just… stares at me, as if I were speaking Droethien or something…"

"It's so sad, Gareth. He isn't at all like the man he used to be. With each passing day, I recognize him a bit less."

Between excess drinking and the storm of stress raging in his head, Gareth felt as if he might black out. If Marcellus were not the king, the man would likely have been cast out as a common lunatic. But his privilege afforded endless pleasures and vices, which only seemed to hasten his degeneration. Gareth had seen it all too often in recent months.

"I will talk to him, but I can't keep doing this, mother. Just stay away from him. No law says you have to be in the same room together, or even in the same part of the palace, for that matter. There's only so much we can do; his mind is too far-gone. And yours will be too, if you keep subjecting yourself to this stress. Just stay away, like I've learned to."

The Queen gave a forced and weary smile, then nodded in agreement. She drew her graying, brown hair back and rubbed her reddened eyes. "I know, but it's just so hard when someone you used to love treats you like this. And I get little help from your siblings. They seem too busy these days to visit, even though I can see their estate from this very window."

"I understand, but let's remain calm now. There's no point in getting more worked up. I will handle it."

Queen Charlotte hugged Gareth tightly and gave her thanks. His mother's embrace was always somewhat bittersweet, though these days, he was becoming more and more disillusioned by it. He felt a hollow, cavernous space growing inside him that even Charlotte's love could not fill. Life inside the Westwind Citadel felt like it was slowly suffocating him to death.

Pulling away from his mother's embrace was not easy, but was necessary. Gareth often struggled to accept what his life had become. This was not the same home he was raised in. This was not the same family he once loved. Growing up, he would never have imagined the mighty Bethard family could become so fractured from within, and that he would be left to hold the pieces together.

It isn't fair. I never asked for any of this. I never wanted my life to turn out this way.

He had grown resentful of his two siblings, Trace and Lucetta. It was painful to remember how close they used to be as children, but after Marcellus' near-fatal injury, they made an escape to a new estate to avoid his toxicity. Even though Gareth saw their residence from his window, it felt like Trace and Lucetta were a million leagues away. He could not recall the last time either was available to help with their crippled father and distraught mother.

Is it really so much to ask? Are they that incapable of looking after their own family?

But he continued to try his hardest, despite it all. The tear-filled smile of his mother was motivation enough to keep moving forward, although, to Gareth, it felt more like an aimless stumble. There was so little time to focus on his life and the hopes and dreams he wanted to fulfill before having to bear the weight of the Kingdom on his shoulders one day.

Though he promised to speak to his father, Gareth instead felt the urge to flee the palace altogether. Certainly, there would be time enough to deal with Marcellus' abhorrent behavior. With great haste, he briskly traversed the winding corridors of the Westwind Citadel with only one thought in his mind. Though last night's drinking was excessive, even by his standards, his thirst was too great to ignore. Gareth could not be subjected to further conflict for the day, and the family would just have to get on well enough without him.

A unit of Royal Guardsmen at the Citadel's doors snapped to attention as Gareth made his way to the gardens, where he would often spend days getting lost. On more than one occasion, the Guardsmen had to locate him inside acres of winding mazes and carry him back to his chamber, drunk and despondent. Thankfully, his good friend, Sir Edmund Thomas, was the Captain of the Royal Guardsmen and always maintained a certain level of discretion, for his sake.

After a brief walk, he arrived at the outer gatehouse. Sir Edmund was always present at this time of day to oversee the shift change, and this day was no different Gareth saw his silver hair standing out among the younger men around him. Seeing Edmund going about his duties was a comfort and brought an increasingly infrequent smile to Gareth's face.

"Excellent to see you, sire. I trust you're having an enchanting day. Hm?" Edmund smirked.

"Please, don't start. I'm not in the mood."

"Again?" Edmund sighed. "You can't keep going on like this."

It was an exchange that had played out many times before, far more than anyone would perceive as normal. Gareth could tell it was beginning to wear on his friend as well.

"I would really prefer not to talk about it, Edmund. Not here, and not like this. It's an absolute nightmare in there, and I'm not going to deal with it anymore right now. I need a drink."

The pounding in his head began to worsen. It made him thirst for another drink, and fast. Despite the carnage it unleashed on his mind and body, his craving seemed to only grow by the day.

"You look like you need one! Come, let's get out of this dreary dump and soothe our spirits. Boys, don't burn the place down while I'm gone."

Edmund raised a hand and gave a quick wave to the dozen guards behind him before throwing his arm around Gareth and leaving the Citadel. Though he had fifty-five years of life to Gareth's twenty-eight, they were kindred spirits and spent a great deal of time in each other's company.

Together, they made their way onto Auburn Row. Instead of turning right and toward the heart of Cardale, they turned left. There they would find the merchant district near the docks, for that was where the best wines, rums, and whiskeys could be found. There was little danger in such an area. It was well-guarded, and Gareth was always one to dress modestly and never carry too much coin.

But despite its relative safety and frequent patrols, it was still Cardale. The city had grown famous for its lax enforcement of the law, with drunkenness, prostitution, and all manners of indecency on display. Such was life in a city numbering nearly half a million, from all reaches of Betanthia and beyond. Though it was loud and dirty, and at times dangerous, there was a certain charm to Cardale that Gareth could not put his finger on.

An unmistakable aroma from the fish market grew more potent with each step, and it set his already sour stomach to churning. The indiscernible babble of commoners shopping the day's catch was accompanied by gulls cawing as they swarmed around a handful of docked fishing vessels.

"Fresh fish! Lobsters and scallops! This batch here, fresh and ready for your kitchens!" a young, olive-skinned merchant bellowed from his stand.

Gareth wondered if he was a Droethien or a native of the southern peninsula. It was difficult to tell these days, especially with an influx of traders over the last decade.

I never used to see them in the capital, but now, it's like they're every-where I turn.

The merchantman's wares were indeed fresh, a stark contrast to the half-rotten stink from yesterday. Summer heat oftentimes made traversing the market only possible in the early morning hours. Gareth stopped to browse a variety of seafood as his stomach began aching for his first meal of the day.

Shortly ahead, the main artery running through the merchant district split and ran off in different directions, with each district containing its own selections of goods. Crown Ferry Road was where they were headed, which hosted some of the city's more notorious taverns. As Edmund and Gareth continued on toward their favorite watering hole, they passed by a man openly fornicating with a young woman, with seemingly no concern for the spectacle they were creating.

While some found it amusing, Edmund did not. He shot a passing patrol of city watchmen a hostile glare, then motioned to the blatant debauchery before their eyes. The watchmen took notice of Edmund's purple cloak and ornate silver breastplate and immediately sprung into action.

"Get moving, you lout!" one of the watchmen shouted, drawing a truncheon. He gave the man a swift clubbing, then sent both offenders scrambling to their feet to flee. "Save it for the Streets, filth! And don't let me catch you again!"

The Scarlet Streets seemed more of a manner of speaking than a physical place, or at least Gareth thought so. He heard rumors long ago that due to an excess of prostitution throughout the city and the inability of the watchmen to control it, a small enclave was established near the river. It was one place he never intended to visit, if it even existed, for his heart and mind already belonged to someone special.

Just ahead was the Hollow Stone, an establishment he found himself frequenting more as of late. Edmund shuffled ahead and opened the door, then beckoned Gareth to enter. It was one of the less scummy establishments on Crown Ferry Road, its patrons consisting of wealthier merchants and those with gold to spend in the greater markets.

The tavern smelled of spilled beer that had soaked into the floorboards over a generation or more. An occasional cloud of tobacco or herb smoke helped to mask the fetid odor, but Gareth visited so often that he hardly noticed any of the tavern's smells anymore.

Its patronage consisted of the typical sort for this time of day. A galley captain and his hands were in a far corner enjoying tankard after tankard of a frothy house ale. A merchant stood at the bar savoring a glass of red wine. His blue and gray silks suggested he was out of place at this particular establishment, but likely stopped for a quick drink or a particular vintage he could find nowhere else. The other patrons were little more than commoners; nameless and faceless people who went about their daily routines, their conversation little more than background noise.

"What will it be today?" Edmund asked redundantly, for he already knew the answer.

They were both connoisseurs of well-aged bourbon, a coincidence that laid the groundwork for a blossoming friendship over the years. Gareth reached into his pocket and threw a few coins onto the aged and worn table, its surface rough and discolored from years of drunken elbows sliding across it.

"To anyone else, I would say, surprise me, but I know better," Gareth said.

Sir Edmund gave an insidious grin. "I'll go easy on you today. The usual, then."

The elder Guardsman approached the bar, and with a simple wave, a middle-aged barkeep sprang into action. A cloud of spices and refuse from the outside market crept in through an open window, mixing with the aromas of various liquors and wines in the air. It was an interesting combination of scents, to be certain. Gareth loved it here, the sights and smells and scenery of the common man going about his day provided a sharp contrast to the life of luxury he always enjoyed. He often wondered if people in the tavern knew who he really was or if he was merely a friend of Edmund's.

"Two bourbons, comin' right up!"

The barkeep was quick to serve them, for it was just past three in the afternoon, and not particularly busy. Edmund returned with two wooden cups of bourbon. He sat one down in front of Gareth then planted himself in a creaky wooden chair beside him. Together they raised their drinks in a customary kickoff to their all too frequent drinking regimen.

"To peace of mind," Edmund toasted, tapping his cup gently against Gareth's.

Peace of mind… The one thing not even a Bethard can buy, it seems.

His first sip tasted simply divine. Gareth closed his eyes and swished the drink in his mouth, savoring every drop. Within moments, his nagging headache was fading until it was nearly gone, and a familiar warm tingle coursed through his body. It was almost enough to make him forget the events of that morning.

"I know you love your family, Gareth," Edmund said, breaking the comfortable silence. "And you have this strong sense of loyalty and duty towards them. I respect that. I really do. But it's not your job to fix any one of them, nor can you anyways. You'll only drive yourself mad if you keep this up. I've seen it wearing you down, and it's not good."

Gareth took another sip. "I know. Nobody knows better than me. I don't like living this way, but things are different when you're part of the ruling family, things are different."

Edmund pointed a finger in objection. "You are entitled to your own life, royalty or not. When was the last time you did something that made you happy?"

Sarcastically, Gareth hoisted his cup and gave it a shake.

"I'm not talking about that," Edmund grunted. "Come now, there must be something that gets you out of bed in the morning. What is it?"

It was a question he had given little thought to. In fact, the more Gareth thought about it, the more uncomfortable he felt. A glance at the other patrons inside the tavern brought with it a sobering self-reflection. All around him were men of varying ages from varying classes, each with a purpose and their own motivations. They seemed happy and carefree with goals, hopes, dreams, and business to attend to.

But Gareth had none of that. His days were spent trying to keep his family from tearing itself apart, and when he wasn't doing that, he would simply wander about the palace grounds or the city and drink. He was beginning to realize how badly his drinking had spiraled out of control.

"I don't remember the last time I was happy." Gareth's eyes fell to the table.

"Well, we need to work on that, then. As much as I enjoy our outings, this cannot be the only thing you do with your time. And I'm happy to help however I can, but first, we need to figure out what interests you."

It seemed like the more Edmund tried to help, the worse he began to feel. Gareth had no idea what it was he even enjoyed doing. He was never allowed to be his own person until King Marcellus began taking a turn for the worse. Twenty-eight years of life had passed, and he barely knew who he truly was.

"I wouldn't even know where to start, Edmund. I've lived a sheltered life. In fact, I never even ventured into the city on my own until, oh, what was it, a year ago, maybe two?"

"Well, I know just the thing, if you're willing to keep an open mind." Edmund motioned to the barkeep for another round. Gareth nodded, half in reluctance and half out of curiosity.

"I know it may sound crazy to you, but would you be willing to let me teach you to fight? I could show you everything I know: how to handle a spear and a sword, how to fight in formation and even on horseback if you're feeling adventurous enough."

Gareth laughed nervously. It was a fascinating proposition, but his first thought was what his mother would do if she found out. Queen Charlotte had always been protective over her children, and even now, at twenty-eight, Gareth found himself being treated as if he were eight.

"I… really? Why?"

"I've found that military training helps to center the mind and body," Edmund said reassuringly. "I've seen the most unruly recruits become confident and focused soldiers. I think it would do you a lot of good."

The barkeep brought over two fresh cups and retrieved the empty ones. Hastily he ran a discolored cloth over the tabletop and cleaned up splashes of spilled alcohol. Gareth's head was swimming again, and the bourbon gave him a much-needed boost of confidence.

"Yeah, that… that does sound interesting."

"Not only will it do wonders for you physically and mentally, but it'll also give you a great deal of credibility with the people. Everyone loves a warrior king." Edmund took a sip, then winked. "Especially the ladies. You'll be a hit."

A sudden rush nearly made Gareth faint. For almost a decade, he had been infatuated with Madelyn Everly, a Commander in the Blackthorn Knights. There were times when Gareth sensed Madelyn had given him a favorable eye, but certainly, a woman such as her could only respect a true man, a man of steel, not silks.

"So you'd like that?" Edmund asked.

Gareth was unaware he had been grinning ear to ear, lost in a daydream. He could picture it so clearly. In the vision, he was mounted on a fearsome warhorse, clad in shining steel armor, with Madelyn riding beside him. He was a conqueror, a leader of men, and a warrior king, as Edmund put it, and Madelyn his queen. Together, they could surely conquer Caldakas and usher in a new age of peace and enlightenment. He could go down in history as the greatest king of the entire Bethard dynasty.

"Yes, absolutely!" Gareth felt a warm sensation building in his cheeks. Edmund took notice and chuckled.

"So that's what young Gareth Bethard truly desires. I mention the ladies, and you turn as red as a tomato. So tell me, who is she?"

At first, he was hesitant to say. Madelyn was a commoner by birth, and it was forbidden for a member of the royal family to marry outside of their class. Even though he trusted Edmund with his life, there was lingering fear of his parents finding out. But still, Gareth could never forget the first time he laid eyes on her. They were both young, still in their teenage years. He knew, at first sight, she was the woman of his dreams.

"There's… no one in particular," Gareth stammered. He took a large gulp of bourbon and choked.

"Nonsense! You don't make it to fifty-five without learning a few things. You have the look of a man in love. Now, are you going to tell me about her, or am I going to have to force it out of you?" Edmund chuckled, his blue eyes lighting up like a summer sun reflecting against the sea.

"Alright, alright." Gareth went for another drink for some added courage but found his cup nearly empty. "Her name is Madelyn…"

"Wait… you wouldn't happen to be talking about Madelyn Everly? From the Blackthorn?"

Gareth wanted to run and hide like an embarrassed child. It could have been fear of his parent's disapproval if they were to find out or simply too much drink making him feel vulnerable. He felt ashamed, as if his affections were somehow dirty. Timidly he nodded.

"Well now!" Edmund bellowed. "That's a whole different breed of woman right there. But I suppose if you're going to aim somewhere, you should aim high."

Bashfully, Gareth shared a light-hearted laugh with his friend. The tavern began filling with more patrons, though both men seemed not to notice. Were it not for their intoxication, they might have been more discreet and considerate. But it was the first time in days that Gareth felt comfortable enough to open himself up.

"To be honest, you're the first person I've told. It's… it's forbidden, you know…"

"Bullshit," Edmund said, appearing to be cross. "I understand you're royalty, and there are certain rules you must abide by for now, but you know what? Once you're king, who will tell you what to do? Hm?"

"Yeah… yeah, you're right."

"No, I'm serious, Gareth. If that's the woman you want, then go and get her. But allow me to give you another piece of advice. First and foremost, you need to be the best man that you can be, *for yourself.* That's where it all starts. If you don't have any love and respect for yourself, how will someone like Madelyn ever love and respect you?"

It was the sort of fatherly advice Gareth was sorely lacking. Royal protocol dictated that the King be the one to find a suitable bride and arrange the marriage to a proper house, often to solidify alliances or consolidate political power. But maybe his father's injury had a silver lining to it. Marcellus Bethard's apathy could be the very thing to allow Gareth to follow his heart.

"And that's why I cherish your friendship, Edmund. You tell me things other people won't." He raised his cup to give a toast but forgot it was empty. No matter, it was the thought that counted.

"And you're receptive enough to listen to what I say. It gives me hope that your reign will be far different from your father's. But, I fear we must be heading back to the Citadel. Duty calls. Unless you wish to stay out?"

The day was so refreshing that Gareth had lost track of time. His outings with Edmund often turned into whole-day affairs, and today was no different. With the dinner crowd beginning to fill the Hollow Stone, he thought it best to return home. Though he enjoyed being among the people, he was aware of the dangers he faced as a member of the ruling family.

Together, Gareth and Sir Edmund shambled out of the tavern and back onto Crown Ferry Road. It was more crowded now than when they arrived. Being as intoxicated as he was, Gareth made sure to follow the elder Guardsman's purple cloak so as not to get swallowed up by an endless sea of commoners.

"What do you say we take a carriage back?" Edmund shouted over his shoulder. It was less of a question and more of a declaration.

After arriving at the closest intersection, Edmund flagged down the first driver he could find. It was a simple carriage driven by a simple-looking man and towed by a simple-looking brown horse. It was far from the most luxurious of transportation, but a black linen canopy would at least provide some relief from the sun.

Their ride to the Citadel was a blurry streak of colors and sounds that grew more indiscernible with each minute. Gareth immediately regretted drinking so much. It was excessive even by his standards, though somehow Edmund seemed to function just fine. He drifted off to sleep, but it seemed to last only seconds before he was shaken back to consciousness.

"Wake up, son, you're home." Edmund turned to one of his men. "Make sure he's fed and given plenty of water. And make sure he isn't disturbed. I don't want the Queen seeing him like this."

As Gareth poured himself out of the carriage and onto unsteady legs, another Guardsman approached. He gave Edmund a crisp salute and did his utmost to avoid looking at the Prince.

"I bring word, Captain." The Guardsman was young and nervous, probably fresh out of training. His overzealousness made the other sea-soned men smirk in amusement.

"I'm sure you do. Well, out with it, I'm about spent for one day." Edmund spat, then motioned for a waterskin. His thirst was so great the skin was empty in seconds.

"We've received word there will be a high council meeting tomorrow morning. The city watch said the Order has sent an emissary as well."

"It must be important, then," Edmund said, running an old hand across his stubbly face. "Pull an extra detail for security, just to be on the safe side. That many fine carriages rolling through the gates always generates curiosity."

"No carriages, sir. The watch says there's only two of them." The Guardsman shrugged.

"And who might this emissary be?" Edmund smiled mischievously and glanced over at Gareth. They both hoped for the same answer.

"Commander Everly, sir. Should I make space available for her and her entourage in the barracks?" the young Guardsman asked.

Could this be real? Or am I dreaming? He couldn't have said her name…

"Hmm… it must be urgent if they've sent someone like her. Yes, see to it right away."

Sir Edmund dismissed the Guardsman with a flick of his wrist. He turned to Gareth with a proud and satisfied look, more of a look a parent might give their child as opposed to one friend to another.

"Well then, the fates must be kind! It seems like you've had quite a stroke of luck! You need to get yourself sobered up and ready for tomorrow. If you're well enough, we can start your training at dawn. Nothing like a bit of swordplay in the morning to get a man's blood pumping."

It was nearly too much to take in. Madelyn had been away from Cardale for so long, and now, at one of the lowest points in his life, he would get another opportunity to see her. Gareth was beginning to have a moment of clarity, a rare occasion when the demons lingering in his mind were silent and not tormenting and jeering as they always did.

Edmund was right. Madelyn is a different breed of woman, and I have to be better. I must be better. It has to start with me...

It was difficult to stave off every feeling of doubt and insecurity threatening to override his newfound determination. But he knew that if he let another opportunity slip by, there would only be one person to blame.

Gareth straightened his back and smiled a drunken yet hopeful smile. "Bright and early, Edmund. I'll be ready."

EINARR II

Damien Dreadfire's warband continued their march through the southern edge of the Hinterwood, a dense canopy of trees screening their movement. The Supreme Warlord rode silently at the front of the formation, his warchiefs close behind. Their destination was another day to the northeast. Black and crimson banners bearing the runic symbol of Dreadfire himself danced gently across a warm breeze, a subtle ripple of their fabric resonating alongside the footfalls of two thousand heavy horses.

Einarr could scarcely believe the warband had swelled to such a formidable size within the past two years. He recalled the first time he met Damien following the terrible events at Borjifa. It was there Einarr swore his sword and the allegiance of his warriors to Dreadfire, a man he knew only by reputation. But now here they were, with one victory secured and the next battle drawing closer by the day.

Zander the Zylmacian broke ranks and rode alongside Sylvia Stormguard. He licked his lips and smiled while looking her up and down, though she pretended not to notice. She looked strikingly different off the battlefield, quite beautiful even, Einarr thought. The fierce Rhivothi shieldmaiden was clad in a wolf pelt cloak, leather cuirass, boots, and steel bracers. Her mid-back-length brown hair was brushed smooth and straight, accented with small braids. The dark eyeliner she wore complimented her nearly black eyes and the blue runic tattoos beneath them.

"Perhaps when we make camp, you and I can celebrate our victory the way we do in Zylmacia. The proper way." The wildman's smile grew wider and all the more unsavory.

"If it involves anything more than a horn of mead, you can forget about it. In fact, I'll pass on the mead. I'm not interested," Sylvia snorted without so much as a glance.

"They say Rhivothi women don't lay with men, but perhaps you can prove the rumors wrong. I'll be most accommodating."

Zander grabbed Sylvia's hand and pulled it toward his manhood. The shieldmaiden snatched it away and delivered a swift slap across his face.

"Oh, come now, love!" the wildman said, laughing. "One day, you might regret passing up your chance with me. When this war is over, I intend to be the most famous warrior since Kuggvord the Grim, with a soul name all my own!"

"You have to do something worthy to earn a soul name, you idiot," Marvath grunted, his annoyance boiling over. "Killing a few poorly trained boys is hardly impressive. And only a named warrior can name you."

"Why are you even interested in having a soul name?" Einarr complained, having grown tired of the conversation. "I didn't think you Zylmacians practiced northern customs."

"We don't, but I find the whole thing quite fascinating. To have a name and be feared and respected by everyone. One day they'll call me Zander the Unstoppable!"

"Touch me again, and they'll be calling you Zander the Cockless," Stormguard snarled.

The other warchiefs laughed. Even Damien appeared amused for a moment.

"Come now, everyone knows I'm the fiercest warrior west of the Bymist! How did you earn yours again? With that wicked tongue of yours?" Zander ran a hand across weeks' worth of beard growth, probably to nurse the stinging of her slap.

"She held off a band of brigands at Oldbridge single-handedly after her camp was attacked. And during a fierce thunderstorm, no less," Bonesplitter said as he rode closer. "They say she piled so many bodies on the bridge it slowed the enemy down until her men could regroup and drive them back. They say Azldyr himself charged her weapons with thunderbolts, and thus she was given her soul name that night. Would you like to hear how I earned mine?" he asked, eyes widening.

Zander raised his hands and smiled, content to concede, then fell back into formation. Marvath gave Sylvia a respectful nod, then rode ahead to Damien's side. Einarr could only wonder what sort of connection they shared, but perhaps with time, the answer would become clear.

After hours of riding, Damien raised his hand and brought his horse to a halt, having found a suitable spot to rest the warband until the following day.

"We make camp here for the night. Einarr, send out foraging parties and set a perimeter watch. We leave at first light. Our destination is not far now."

His command was faithfully executed. The day had grown late, and the warband began to secure themselves and prepare for a well-earned feast. Though all were still weary from battle and the grueling march north, their mood was jovial.

Zander approached Marvath and Einarr after camp was made, and nightfall loomed in the distant sky. They assisted in erecting the command tent, though the task was near completion. It seemed Zander intended to try and smooth things over between himself and Marvath, Einarr supposed, for the nomad was not one to be trifled with.

"I meant no disrespect to the lady, Bonesplitter, it was just a bit of fun. You northerners are so dreary all the time. Perhaps life among the trees has deprived you of proper sunlight."

"If you weren't such a damned fool, you might earn a bit of respect," Bonesplitter said.

The wildman chortled but offered no response. Einarr understood why Damien had allowed Zander and his warriors into their ranks. The Zylmacian wildmen made up a large portion of the warband, but that alone was not enough to earn respect from the other warchiefs. Marvath was the most hostile, but for what reason, Einarr could only speculate.

"A soul name is the highest of honors, for they recognize divine achievement" Marvath said. "A named warrior is to be respected at all times, regardless of what your cock tells you. Would you speak to Dreadfire in such a manner?" He pointed to Damien in the distance. "How do you think he got *his* name?"

Damien Dreadfire's silhouette stood large near the tree line, his massive frame casting an ominous shadow in the dying light. The three warchiefs stood silently and stared at their warlord as he overlooked their encampment. There was a certain aura to the man that could not be explained, for it radiated both darkness and light. Fire burned in his eyes, and ice water flowed through his veins, a tortured soul whose existence was forged out of steel and stone.

"I… uh…" Lost for words, Zander averted his eyes to the ground.

"Precisely. You don't know what some of us have endured to be named. A soul name is often a small consolation at best. Many of us would trade such an honor for what we had to sacrifice, without hesitation. So never disrespect Stormguard again, do you understand me?"

"Very well." Zander slinked away and off to his kin.

After finishing construction of the command tent, Einarr and Marvath took their leave and prepared for supper. Tonight they would drink and feast generously on rations they looted, though Einarr thought it was premature to celebrate much of anything. They won the opening skirmish of what was sure to be a long and bloody war, but it was important for the warriors to keep their health and spirits up.

Light from hundreds of campfires flickered across a darkening forest. There was celebration and feasting as song and story echoed throughout the encampment, with an occasional roar of laughter and cursing and cheering of a fistfight. The festivities were surprisingly modest, for the real battle was yet to come, a sobering fact on the minds of many.

Einarr and Marvath had taken to the outskirts of camp, where it was quieter. There they would be able to enjoy a well-earned meal in relative peace before returning to their duties the following day. They were joined by one of Bonesplitter's close friends from his tribe, Valerick the Red. He was an unpleasant man whom Einarr cared little for, due to the fact he bathed in animal blood before every battle. As a result, the man constantly smelled of death, his blonde hair and beard stained with a permanent brassy hue.

"Good evening to you, Marvath," Valerick said as he approached and sat beside the fire, a large black kettle resting above the flames. "So… what's the plan from here on out? How is Damien going to fight the Bethards in the middle of nowhere?"

The stench following Valerick was off-putting. Einarr inched closer to the kettle where he was preparing a stew. Thankfully, an aroma of fresh herbs helped to mask the disgusting smell. After a few stirs with a wooden spoon, his nostrils felt less offended.

"Damien will only fight on his terms, on the ground of his choosing," Bonesplitter stated. "He's leading us to Blackwolf Pass, I'm certain of it. I know these woods well. There's a valley about a quarter of a mile wide with tall hills on either side. That's where he plans to funnel our enemies."

"I can't say I've ever heard of it." Einarr shrugged.

"You should," said Bonesplitter, "it's the closest you'll be to Skaginlef since you left. You meek Teb dwellers must not venture very far."

Einarr's heart jumped with excitement at the mention of his village. "No, we don't. The river provides us with everything we need: fish, fresh water, and fertile land to farm. There's no need for us to go on adventures."

"It seems you're on quite the adventure already. Your singers will be sure to tell tales of Einarr the Explorer for hundreds of years."

Together, he and Bonesplitter shared a chuckle. It was a comforting thought to be remembered and spoken of in the histories, but it made his homesickness even stronger.

Valerick the Red seemed uncertain. "How can you be sure we're even being pursued?"

"Large armies leave large tracks, and after the little gift we sent back to the castle, they're sure to follow. At least if their trackers are worth a damn," Marvath replied. He picked up a bowl and poured a spoonful of piping hot stew into it. "I suspect they will be a few days behind us, a week maybe if they're slow. So eat heartily and get your rest. Tomorrow we make preparations."

Fresh venison, onions, and carrots permeated from the kettle like a fine perfume. Bonesplitter devoured his bowl with a savage appetite, then returned for more. Einarr and Valerick feasted, shared stories, and discussed their plans for the coming days. Damien spoke of the Bethard army before, and how each stretch of Betanthia's borders was protected by its own garrison. Dreadfire was unsure how many men they might be facing but had predicted it could be in the tens of thousands. It was enough to instill fear into any man's heart, however brave.

Such talk demanded a strong drink to accompany it. Casks of mead sat open throughout the encampment for all to enjoy. Einarr enjoyed the taste, for it reminded him of home. In less than an hour, he emptied nearly an entire cask with Valerick and Marvath. A strong and sudden rush of alcohol relaxed him and diminished his fear of the trials they were soon to face. Before drunkenness could overtake him, he decided to walk the encampment and visit with the warriors.

Einarr stumbled about with a fresh horn of mead in his hand and several more churning inside his stomach. He paused here and there and conversed with his Nothanek brethren and warriors from other tribes. His presence was met with appreciation and congratulations on their decisive victory.

As he continued from firepit to firepit, Einarr noticed the man responsible for their victory was absent. He saw Sylvia Stormguard drunk and vivacious alongside her shieldmaidens, more than two dozen strong and each as intoxicated as she was. As they danced and drank around a fire, they jeered and catcalled the men across them, some bearing their breasts while others shrieked with laughter. Einarr paused in amusement and watched, taking an overflowing gulp from his drinking horn and smiling as the scene unfolded.

A brave yet drunken Nothanek licked his lips and attempted to enter the raucous circle of women, only to be promptly laid out on his ass by a tall and muscular brunette. The others pointed and sneered, their shrill crowing echoing far and wide, much to his embarrassment. The man scurried back to his feet quickly, hoping few had witnessed his humiliation. Upon returning to his circle of companions, he was greeted with bellowing laughter and a round of jabs and jeers.

Moments like these were what Einarr lived for; strong drink, a bountiful feast, and the company of his northern kin among the trees and the gods. It was then he remembered why he wandered in the first place, and continued searching until he reached the camp's outer perimeter. In a pillar of rich white moonlight, Einarr spied Damien Dreadfire.

Damien was seated on a moss-covered log, alone and in silence, save for the rhythmic singing of a whetstone against the edge of his bastard sword. Einarr watched as the warlord ran the stone down the blade's length over and over again.

He approached on weary legs that grew more unstable with each swallow of mead. Damien shot to his feet upon hearing the footsteps, deciding whether to use the freshly sharpened sword or not. His arm was raised and ready to strike, but upon seeing Einarr, the blade was lowered, then rested at his side.

"Damien, why do you sit alone while your men drink and feast in honor of your victory?" Einarr asked as he clumsily sat on the log, mead splashing out of his drinking horn and onto his hand.

Dreadfire said nothing as he put the whetstone into a small leather pouch and tossed it next to his formidable suit of black armor. Damien looked over the length of his sword, eyes studying it carefully as moonlight danced off the dangerously sharp metal.

"It is not my victory. It belongs to everyone," Dreadfire uttered after a moment of silence, his mind most certainly preoccupied.

"You're wrong," Einarr stated boldly. "None of this would be possible were it not for you. The largest battle we're ever going to see draws near, against a foe who thought us too weak and divided to challenge their ambitions. But you… you brought these men together. You did what no one thought was possible."

Damien scoffed as his gaze shifted to the dark outlines of trees surrounding the encampment, and further still into the black abyss that had befallen the Hinterwood. Einarr was unable to read Damien's emotions in his drunken state, though something was amiss.

"What would you have me do on this night?" Dreadfire asked, turning toward Einarr, shadows and light dancing across his face.

"Go down there and be with your men."

"I will not celebrate before our victory is won. I need my wits to be as sharp as my steel." The Supreme Warlord rose and held his large bastard sword straight, examining it before returning the blade to its scabbard.

It was silent now, with nothing but the sounds of the forest to keep them company. At night was when the Hinterwood truly came alive.

The distant babbling of a river resonated throughout the trees while thousands of cicadas sang along in a loud, monotonous chorus. A peel of thunder occasionally rippled across the heavens, though judging from the sky, there looked to be no rain tonight, at least not here.

"Damien, I've known you longer than anyone. I was the first to swear myself and my men to you after Borjifa. So I will be honest." The mead coursing through Einarr's body made him bold, bolder than he would have otherwise been with a man as fearsome as Damien Dreadfire.

"I understand your purpose here is to kill and lead these men so they can kill as many of our enemies as need be. But armies are made up of men, and those men down there believe in you and your cause. They would follow you anywhere."

Einarr stood and turned toward the encampment, his tone growing softer yet grimmer. "And many of these men will likely not leave Blackwolf Pass alive. This place you have chosen will become a graveyard for our enemies and many of our own. You would honor them with your presence and give them courage."

He placed a hand on Damien's massive shoulders. "And courage they'll need. We will be heavily outnumbered if Cedric Valens sends his entire army against us. At least two to one, if the gods are merciful. Careful planning can only take us so far, it all comes down to the men wielding those spears and swords."

Damien nodded somberly in agreement. "Being drunk does not make you any less right."

"Sort of makes you long to live in the era of our grandfathers, does it not?" Einarr lamented. "At the very least, they had King Torbin's peace."

The mention of the Bethards agitated Dreadfire. He hawked and spat as if to cleanse his mouth of a foul taste.

"Torbin Bethard's peace was a lie, a lie our grandfathers foolishly believed. He made peace with our people so he could consolidate his forces to defend against the Droethiens. If our grandfathers were better warriors than diplomats, they would have seized the opportunity to strike. Their misguided desire for peace would prove to be our undoing."

There was little more Einarr could say. It was impossible to know how differently the present might have looked if the free northern tribes had chosen to fight instead of lay down their swords. Part of him wished his ancestors had greater foresight so he might be spared from having to make war in the face of greater odds. But there was little use in dwelling on thoughts of what might have been.

Damien appeared regretful for venting his frustrations. "I know you have made many sacrifices to stand alongside me, and for that, I am eternally grateful. It cannot be easy to be away from your lands and loved ones for so long."

"Well… many of my people march with me, so I'm never too far from home. All I want is to see them return to Skaginlef." A faux smile disguised Einarr's homesickness.

It was true, he did miss life on the Teb River, but the company of his tribesmen was enough to make his experience tolerable, even though some bore him resentment for fighting another man's war.

"There are many things you have yet to tell me about yourself, Einarr, and since we have shed blood together in the sight of the gods, that makes us brothers. Now tell me, is there someone at Skaginlef who awaits your return?" Dreadfire grabbed a skin of mead near his suit of armor and drank.

Memories flooded Einarr's mind, though most were sad to recall. Two years since the massacre at Borjifa had passed by in a flash. So much time was devoted to helping Damien build the warband's strength that Einarr seldom returned his thoughts to life before the war.

"There was once, yes."

Time had not healed Einarr's wounds. As hard as he tried to mask his sorrow, his voice wavered and betrayed him for just a moment.

Mead had withered his resolve, and though it seemed foolish to con-sume more, he continued to drink.

"It would be my honor for you to share your story with me, my friend. What happened?"

"There was this woman…" Einarr said solemnly. "Alina, she was called. Damien, if you had seen her, you would have thought it was Zifnir in the flesh. She had brown hair and green eyes. Gods she was beautiful. The very sight of her was enough to… enough to unleash the animal inside me, yet… yet tame the beast at the same time. Does this make sense to you?"

"Aye, it does. Tell me more."

"One day, I found the strength to approach her father. I asked for permission to court her, and to my surprise, I received his blessing. I felt as if I had died and been called home to Sjenohor, you know? We were soon to be married, but… she was taken by a fever unexpectedly."

A faint hint of mist filled Einarr's eyes and shimmered in the moon-light. He scratched the skin beneath one of his lids as if to soothe an itch and subtly wiped the water away, hoping Damien would not take notice.

"I could not bear to send her to the pyre, so I buried her beneath a cherry blossom tree on the banks of the Teb. It's beautiful. And I know that each spring when the tree blossoms, a part of her is reborn."

A melancholy smile was all Einarr could muster, but it was enough not to make him feel weak in Dreadfire's presence. He raised an empty drinking horn to the sky and toasted the gods and his lost love.

"I am sorry, Einarr. The gods were kind to bestow such a woman onto you, and cruel for taking her away. I will give my prayers to Zifnir in her honor."

"You have my thanks, Damien," Einarr whispered, bowing his head. "She died six months before Borjifa, so I know what it feels like to be dealt a terrible loss. That's why I pledged my support and the support of my people to you. I did not know you then, only by reputation, but what I saw in your eyes that day mirrored my anguish. I knew I could not leave others to suffer as I have suffered."

"You are a true friend and noble at heart." Damien Dreadfire's mighty hand landed on his back with a thud. It was one of the few showings of respect he had experienced, which Einarr was keenly aware of despite his inebriated state.

"I must confess I have few friends in my clan," Einarr said bitterly. "Most of them are here out of respect for our traditions. They were reluctant to leave their families and homes and wage another man's war."

"Is that why you sit and drink with me and not the Nothanek?" Damien asked. "Pay it no mind. Truly there must be more in this world for Einarr, son of Rolff. When you are not leading your people into battle and putting Bethard minions to the sword, what drives you? What makes you rise in the morning?"

Einarr chuckled, his sorrow lifting like fog in the morning sun. Though he was a humble man and carried himself accordingly, he was always proud to talk about his love of craftsmanship. Anxiously he rubbed the leathered, worn fingers on his right hand together, unaware he was doing it. Though it had been ages since he last constructed anything, his hands still remembered the feel of a hammer, axe, and fresh timber.

"I like to build. I like to cut trees and turn them into great works. I can't explain it, Damien. When I'm hewing the logs and transforming them into what I envision, I feel this… this connection to the earth and to the gods. It's a spiritual experience for me."

He was met with a surprised yet approving grin from Damien, another rarity in his experience. This certainly would be a night to remember, Einarr thought to himself.

"I can make most anything, you know," he boasted. "Weapons, ships, homesteads… I even built a new mead hall in Alina's honor. I was given a gift by the gods, for certain. Every chance I get, I craft something. Even if it's the smallest trinket."

He reached into a belt pouch and removed a carved icon. The wooden figure was barely larger than Einarr's thumb but contained the likeness of the war god, Azldyr, and the runes associated with his protection. He handed it to Damien with a slight reluctance.

"I've been carving this since we first broke camp and left for Khorrtal. It's an effigy of Azldyr. Though he is not the patron god of my people, I know we will need his help if we're to win this war. I would like for you to have it, and know he will keep your steel sharp and your sword arm strong, always."

Damien studied the carving in the moonlight, his eyes squinting to view its every detail. He clutched it in a closed fist and kissed the backside of his index finger.

"You honor me, Einarr. It will have a sacred place among my most prized treasures." Once more, Dreadfire examined the small piece, then placed it delicately inside a leather pouch for safekeeping.

"So Damien, you must do me the honor and tell me what your passion in life is, since you know my story now."

After emptying his meadskin, Damien stood and looked amusedly at Einarr. He discarded the empty skin near his greatsword, then started off to the warband, who were now properly celebrating.

"That is for another time. Come, we must see to our warriors."

As the night grew darker, fires burned brighter, and the men became more jubilant. Together, Einarr and Damien descended into the heart of camp, its energy primal and rejuvenating, and even seemed to lessen Einarr's drunkenness. The first warriors to spy their approach cheered and toasted and offered them fresh horns of mead.

"Men! Gather 'round!" Damien's call carried far and wide. Thousands of warriors paused and turned their attention. "It is my honor to stand beside you tonight in the presence of the gods."

The warband stirred and shambled closer.

"This host we have gathered represents the last of the old tribes and the bloodlines that gave birth to the mighty Khorrish nation."

Murmurs and a few lone cheers echoed throughout the trees.

"For hundreds of years, we have been hunted. We have suffered unspeakable atrocities. The Eveldanyr, our rightful kings, were put to the sword. Honoring our Khorrish heritage has been made punishable by death. We have been driven from our ancestral lands and pushed to the ends of the world. But no longer. Today, we push back!"

Twelve thousand voices erupted into a roaring fury. Damien raised his hand, the commotion coming to a swift end.

"The Bethards have cast aside their ancestral ways. They have abandoned the gods and forsaken any remaining bonds of brotherhood we once shared. They are the enemy, and together we will bring Azldyr's wrath upon them!"

Einarr's ears nearly bled from an eruption of deafening shouts and shrill cries around him.

"Now, let us drink and feast to our victory and all the victories to come!"

A large drum began thumping as the warband broke into jubilation. It was slow in tempo at first but began beating faster and faster, and soon more drums joined in. Music, dancing, laughter, and fighting filled the encampment. It was the greatest thing Einarr had ever witnessed, though now he was too drunk to enjoy it properly.

"Come, dance with me, Einarr!"

Sylvia crashed into Einarr and embraced him. Her pupils were wide as wagon wheels, though a faint and sweet scent on her breath was evidence enough of mushrooms. Sylvia was not possessed by battle rage, however, but seemed to radiate loving and playful energy. It must have been a different species of Rhivothi forest mushroom, he supposed.

"I really shouldn't. I need to rest," he complained.

"Oh, come on, dance with me! It'll be fun!"

Sylvia knocked Einarr's mead from his hand and spun him around by the arms. The motion nearly made him sick, and within a few twirls, he fell to the ground in a heap. Sylvia landed on top of him, their bodies tangled together.

They shared a lighthearted laugh. Before Einarr could speak, Sylvia pressed her face to his and kissed him. His surprise was enough to rouse him from his drunken weariness. Sylvia moaned, her body grinding slowly and rhythmically. But suddenly, the shieldmaiden realized what she was doing and rolled off him.

"I'm so sorry!" she laughed, her face turning rosy with embarrassment.

"It's quite alright, just a bit of fun." He smiled. "Enjoy the celebration."

Blushing and beside herself with amusement, Stormguard rose to her feet and stumbled off toward her Rhivothi shieldmaidens, who were overcome with amusement. Fortunately, Einarr was close to his tent and was able to haul himself inside. Despite pounding drums, songs, and laughter, he found sleep quickly. But the following morning, the weight of his indulgence reared its ugly head.

The ride to Blackwolf Pass was unbearable. Einarr found it difficult to remain mounted, and after drinking an entire waterskin, he only found the slightest relief. Rising humidity made an already stifling morning even more unbearable.

"What's the matter, Rolffson, you look ill," Bonesplitter quipped, to the amusement of the other warchiefs.

"Never mind me, I'll be fine." Einarr's face turned as green as the pines.

"This is it. This is where we will fight them," Damien said from the back of his massive war horse, his gaze fixed on a set of steep hilltops before them.

"If we can get them to commit. What's your plan?" Bonesplitter asked, surveying the area.

Dreadfire said nothing, but gave his horse a nudge and took off into the pass, the other warchiefs in close pursuit. The terrain was dramatically different from their last battlefield, which was flat and open. How the warband managed to pull off an ambush in such a location was a miracle unto itself. But here, Einarr knew they would hold an advantage.

"We will march through the pass first, so their trackers will think we have moved on. Once the bulk of their force is between the hills, we strike hard and fast. We will target their officers first, then break them thereafter. They will have nowhere to go." Damien pointed at the narrow portion of the pass.

"That's if they take the bait. What's the plan if they don't?" Zander asked, prompting ire from his cohorts.

"They'll take the bait, alright," Sylvia interjected. "I imagine old man Valens is heated after seeing his men become bird food. He'll make the mistake and go through the pass; he wants nothing more than to get a crack at us, I know it."

Zander gave an unsavory grin, and, no doubt, was thinking about how badly he'd like to get a crack at Sylvia. "No need for the hostility, love. Just making sure every option is being considered."

"I am of the same mind as Stormguard," Damien said, nodding. "I know the wrath of Cedric Valens. He will come for us as quickly as possible. But should he choose not to pursue through the pass, our attack will proceed as planned. Instead, our riders will circle behind his army and cut off their escape. These are our woods. Here, he will be outclassed."

GARETH II

Nervous anticipation kept Gareth awake all night. Only when hints of sun began to color the darkened sky was he able to steal a moment of rest. As he drifted off to sleep, a sudden yet soft rapping at his door jarred him awake. At first, Gareth shrugged it off and remained in bed, but slowly his door began to creak open.

"Bright and early, as promised." Sir Edmund said, poking his head inside. "Are you ready?"

I suppose we'll find out soon enough.

Wearily, Gareth rose and dressed in a plain white shirt, an old black doublet, a faded pair of tan trousers, and a brown cloak. Bread and water helped to soothe his lingering drunkenness but did little to calm his excitement. In a few hours, Madelyn would be here at the Westwind Citadel.

Together they strode down empty corridors, through the great hall, and across the courtyard to the barracks. A pair of patrolling Guardsmen paused and saluted as their captain and prince passed by. Gareth struggled to remember the last time he had been to the barracks, but the more he thought about it, the more it seemed like he had never been there. Although, there was always the possibility of stumbling in on a night of drunken wandering.

Once inside, they walked past dozens of bunks where scores of Guardsmen slept. It was surprising to see what amounted to a small army, with every man present sworn to defend the Bethard dynasty to whatever end. A stone staircase led to an underground chamber at the far side of the hall. The air was much cooler down there, perhaps even a bit chilly for his liking.

Once at the bottom, Gareth saw a vast array of weapon racks and training dummies. This was where the Royal Guardsmen honed their fighting skills. Edmund strutted into the center of the room, proudly holding his arms out.

"Here is where it all happens. We take men of any stripe or station and turn them into the best fighters Betanthia has to offer."

A young page passed by with an oil lantern, having finished lighting an array of candles and wall sconces. He bowed respectfully, then disappeared upstairs.

"Now," Edmund said, approaching a rack of weapons. "Now begins your introductory lesson."

Edmund hoisted a spear from the rack and tossed it to Gareth. He caught the weapon and looked at it curiously. "I was under the impression you were going to teach me swordplay. This is definitely not a sword."

"All in good time, Gareth, all in good time. The sword is something you will work up to. But this!" Edmund took up a spear of his own. "This is the most common weapon a soldier will face on the battlefield and is always the first weapon I train recruits to master. Why? Because it's the best weapon you can use."

"Better than a sword?" Gareth asked, confused.

The elder Guardsman assumed a fighting stance, gripping the spear with both hands. "Yes. With even rudimentary training, a spearman can go toe to toe with a moderately skilled swordsman and come out victorious nearly every time."

"And why is that?" Gareth stared at his weapon as if it were suddenly enchanted.

"Because…" Edmund stepped toward a dummy near the wall and thrust his spear into it, letting the shaft slide through his hands. The dummy rattled as it was struck. "You will have a significant reach advantage."

An impressive maneuver, but Gareth was not quite sold. The spear was such a simple weapon, intended for simple people, he thought. Growing up, he often heard tales of knights and warrior kings on the battlefield, wielding their shining blades and cutting through anyone who dared to stand in their path.

"But what happens if an opponent is able to get in close? You know, block the spear and charge in?"

Edmund smiled, then moved closer to the dummy. "Just remember, the spear is a tool, like anything else you see on these racks. *You* are the weapon. You have your hands, elbows, shoulders, knees, feet, and teeth. Even if you're disarmed, you can still fight and win if you know how."

"That doesn't sound very honorable to me, clawing at another man like some kind of beast…"

Suddenly, becoming a warrior seemed less appealing than a few minutes ago.

"Is there anything honorable about dying in a pool of your own blood and piss? I think not. But don't worry, I'll teach you everything I know, and there won't be a man around who will be able to best you."

Edmund moved to Gareth's side. "The first thing you need to do is work on your stance. It's the most important thing. Turn to your side, like this. No, a bit more. Now, grip the spear like so, your left hand facing up and your right hand facing down. Very good. Now, step forward and thrust with both arms."

It was a pitiful blow, the spear tip glancing off the dummy. Gareth sighed, his face turning red with embarrassment.

"It's alright," Edmund said. "Don't let yourself get discouraged. You're not going to become an expert in a day. I've seen far worse. Believe me."

Gareth took a deep breath, then resumed his stance. He gave the dummy a long look, then lunged toward it with a reckless thrust. Edmund smirked.

"Don't get too careless now; you're liable to get skewered if you disregard your technique. You have to be precise in your movements and deliberate in every strike. One mistake could end up costing you your life. Be patient. Your muscles will learn the movements soon enough."

They spent the next hour on his footwork and striking the dummy so many times his arms burned. It was exhausting and more physically demanding than Gareth anticipated, but Edmund would not let him quit. By the end of the session, he realized that years of drinking and lethargy had made him soft and weak. But a burning pain in his muscles felt good, almost euphoric.

Walking back upstairs was nearly impossible. But Gareth felt a strong desire to train again, and soon, much to his surprise. This could very well be a new addiction, he thought.

When they arrived at ground level, the barracks were empty. Its bunks looked inviting, but now was no time for a nap. As Gareth hobbled down the main hall, he noticed an open door that was previously closed. Curiously he looked inside, only to see hundreds, possibly thousands of weapons, shields, and pieces of armor.

This must be the armory.

Gareth entered and eyed all manner of weaponry, from swords and axes to polearms. They were stowed on racks running floor to ceiling, their numbers too great to count. He ran a hand across the smooth surface of an oval-shaped shield emblazoned with the golden eagle sigil of Betanthia. He could not help but smile as he picked up and studied a fearsome-looking spiked mace, then a bearded axe.

But one weapon, in particular, caught his eye. An arming sword in a silver sheath sat tucked away among a row of greatswords. Something about the blade seemed unusual, despite its simple appearance. Gareth picked it up and examined the grip, which was wrapped in blue leather. It was intriguing to see such a plain weapon housed in a Guardsman armory.

The sword's crossguard was just as undecorated, but was beset at the center with a single sapphire on each side. Slowly he unsheathed the sword and held it under the light of a nearby window slit. The steel sang quietly yet distinctly as it was freed from its scabbard. The blade appeared to be a shade of gray with a noticeable bluish tint and looked to be sharp beyond belief.

"It's beautiful," Gareth said as Edmund moved beside him.

"That? Oh… I don't believe I've seen that here before, or maybe just not for a long time." Edmund leaned in close and squinted. "It's certainly well-forged, but what it's doing in here, I have no idea."

"I think I'll keep it if that's alright," he said with a grin.

"Well, if you'd like a sword, I can have our smiths craft something more befitting. Something exquisitely etched, with gold inlays, I'm thinking." Edmund pondered.

"You know me, though. I prefer simple over extravagant."

"Then consider it yours. I won't try to tell my future king what he can and cannot have!"

It was true. Gareth didn't *need* permission to take the sword, but he was too respectful to just take something without asking, especially from a friend. Edmund helped fasten the weapon to his belt and made sure it was secure before they exited the armory. As he walked, Gareth gripped the hilt of his sword with one hand, beaming with pride.

"Now you know, you're going to have to come up with a name for the thing." Edmund chuckled.

"Why's that?"

"Well, it's considered bad luck not to name a horse, a ship, or a sword, so take it as a friendly word of advice."

He thought for a moment, but his mind was blank from exhaustion. "I don't know… I can't think of anything."

"Don't worry. The name will come to you soon enough. Or even better, maybe the sword will tell you its name."

"What do you mean? How exactly would a sword tell me its name?" He glanced down at the blade curiously.

Edmund smiled, his fifty-five years of experience shining through his blue eyes. "Every warrior's weapon is an extension of themselves. It's not just a sword. It's a part of you. Once you discover that connection, the blade will tell you its secrets. How it sits in your hand, how it wants to move and be handled in combat, and what its name is. You'll feel it in your heart when the time is right."

For the first time in ages, Gareth felt happy. Truly happy. He had just completed his first training session, and even though he learned nothing about swordplay, he found a weapon to call his own. Finally, there was purpose in life, something he could look forward to.

"But enough of old soldier's tales for now. How about you and I share a quick drink to celebrate?" Edmund gave him a gentle slap on the back as they left the barracks and ventured into the courtyard.

"I… don't know about that, Edmund."

The last thing he wanted was to be a sloppy, drunken mess in front of Madelyn. She was likely on her way to the Citadel already, and it was bad enough to be drenched in sticky sweat. All Gareth could think of was her. He considered maybe browsing the stalls on Auburn Row for a gift, since he knew of Madelyn's passion for collecting trinkets and other keepsakes.

"Nah, it'll be alright," Edmund said reassuringly. "Just a quick one, and only one. I promise."

"Very well," Gareth relented. "Let's head over to the Row, I'd like to look around while we're there."

"Now that's the spirit!" Sir Edmund squeezed him on the shoulder. Together, they passed through the outer gates and onto the avenue.

Auburn Row was deserted this time of the morning. In fact, only a handful of market stalls were even open. But thankfully, a block ahead was a small eatery, preparing a breakfast of eggs, bread, bacon, beef, and fish, whatever one might desire to start their day. Nearly a dozen crude tables and chairs were set under a sprawling canvas awning. Upon seeing Edmund and Gareth approaching, an old woman and her husband rushed to welcome and accommodate them.

"My prince!" The old man bowed so deeply, his knees nearly gave out.

Edmund was quick to check the man with a wave of his hand so as not to draw unwanted attention. The old man smiled meekly, hurried to a nearby table, and pulled a chair out for Gareth.

"Please, be seated!" The old man beamed. "What can I get for you, my pri—, I mean, Your... Highness..." He whispered, looking over his shoulder.

"Two cups of your finest bourbon. But make them small cups, if you wouldn't mind."

"And I'll take some bread, and that leg of lamb right there. I'm sorry, Edmund, I'm absolutely famished."

The old man gestured frantically to his wife. Within moments a fresh plate of food and a pair of drinks were served. With beastly hunger, Gareth devoured every last morsel before him. It felt like his first meal in years. As he chewed on the last bits of bread, he thought about falling asleep right then and there.

"And now, a toast to you." Edmund raised his cup. "To your first training session, and to many more."

Gareth raised his drink and thumped it against Edmund's. A few drops of bourbon splashed onto the tabletop, a crime if there ever was one. The spirit was not aged well by his standards but tasted refreshing nevertheless.

"Now, you have a young lady to see. Go on, go get her!"

Gareth downed the rest of his drink and embraced Edmund, then tossed a few coins on the table. His excitement of being in Madelyn's company nearly outweighed his curiosity as to why she had been sent to a council meeting in the first place.

Auburn Row was beginning to awaken for the day, but Gareth cared not. Any time spent away from the dreary Citadel was worth savoring, even though the palace loomed ominously behind him like a shadow. It was a constant reminder that he could not escape his reality, no matter where he was in Cardale.

As more stalls opened, Gareth searched for the perfect something to give Madelyn, though he unsure what to buy. While searching with no success, he happened upon a florist with a wide array of exotic flowers. Gareth never thought of Madelyn as the type of girl who liked flowers, but it would be a heartfelt gift nevertheless. He spotted the perfect one, a large rose with the most vibrant red petals he had ever seen.

"Ah, a lovely flower for a lucky lady!" a peasant woman behind the stand said.

He smiled and nodded, removing a coin from his purse. "Well, she's not one for flowers. Never has been. But it seems like a proper gift."

"Oh, I'm sure she'll adore it. It's always the thought that counts. Any gift, however large or small, can always make a lady feel special," she replied, her charm assuring Gareth his effort would not be wasted.

He held the rose carefully so as not to prick himself with its thorns, then started back to the palace briskly, turning briefly to give the woman a wave goodbye. With great haste, he arrived back at the gates to the Westwind Citadel with his gift in hand, as well as a healthy buzz.

You can do this, Gareth. You can do this. Remember, you're a prince.

He glanced around but saw neither Edmund nor Madelyn. He suspected the meeting was already underway, his heart clenching tight as a fist. Each step made his legs feel like he had just climbed a mountain, and his palms sweating so badly they were nearly dripping.

Gareth barely made it through the doors to the great hall when he detected a sweet scent in the air. Not the smell of his mother's perfume, or even his sister Lucetta's, he decided. In fact, it wasn't really a perfume in the first place. He looked around suspiciously and noticed Madelyn approaching from the corner of his eye. He scrambled to hide the rose inside an inner pocket of his cloak.

"Good day, my prince," Madelyn said politely, bowing.

"Please, call me Gareth. You know me well enough."

Madelyn appeared much the same as he remembered, though a bit older and more refined. Looking at her made it difficult to breathe.

"It's good to see you again, my lady," he continued. "You're looking quite lovely today."

"Oh, you're too kind. I just arrived from Bentmont yesterday. I could have slept for an entire week if I wasn't needed here today." Madelyn brushed stray hairs behind her ear as they locked eyes, but it was a fleeting moment. "Say, that's a nice sword you have there. May I see it?"

Gareth had forgotten the blade was still affixed to his belt. He felt embarrassed at first, since he had no experience with swordplay and dreaded being exposed, but Madelyn's excitement was too uplifting to deny her. Carefully, he removed the sword and handed it over.

The blade was plainer than the one she wore on her hip, but she seemed not to care. She inspected the weapon from end to end, then took several practice swings. Madelyn's motions were slow and calculated at first, but gradually her speed and flamboyance increased until she became a literal blur, the sword cleaving the air with a torrent of loud swishes and swooshes.

"Very impressive, I must say!" She smiled, handing the sword back to him. "It feels light and balanced, but not too stiff or so flimsy that it might break. May it serve you well!"

"Thank you!" he replied, struggling to sheathe the sword. "I was surprised when I heard you were coming. I trust the matter is of some importance?"

Together they walked up the grand staircase and to the council chamber on the next floor. It was difficult to stop his eyes from wandering as she walked ahead.

Of course, it's important, you fool. Why else would she be here?

"Unfortunately, yes. The High Marshal believes Betanthia is under dire threat. I was sent to speak to the King and his council personally."

"My father doesn't attend council meetings anymore," Gareth said sourly. "So I'm afraid everything must pass through Aldred first. Nobody deals with my father, not if they can avoid it."

"Do you speak to him at all?" Madelyn asked, dumbfounded.

The question was like peeling a scab off a fresh wound. Gareth could not recall the last time he had a real conversation with his father. It was insufferable to deal with King Marcellus in his diminished state, and the only logical alternative was to leave him alone entirely. Though, it seemed like Madelyn was expecting him to have more influence over the King, which, sadly, he did not.

"No, not really. I'm sure you've heard the stories, and maybe even seen with your own eyes over the years. My father is not the man he used to be. He doesn't listen to anyone in the family. He leaves everything up to Aldred, because Aldred is a good servant and never questions him."

Madelyn's face said it all. She seemed disappointed, perhaps even affronted by what she was hearing. Despite her younger age, she carried herself in a more seasoned and mature manner. Gareth began to tremble and sweat, fearing Madelyn was turned off by his indifference to the political side of his family. It was *his* birthright, after all.

"But, I, for one, am glad the High Marshal sent you. It's great to see you again." He smiled clumsily, desperate to change the subject as they arrived at the chamber. Madelyn smiled in kind, though it appeared to be forced. Courteously, Gareth opened the doors and beckoned her to enter first.

The council chamber was one of the larger rooms in the Westwind Citadel. At its center sat a long, rectangular table, a dozen chairs on either side and two at each end. The council was its smallest in a generation, consisting of only four members. But for their arrogance, Gareth felt the council was four members too large.

Lord Aldred and Sir Bryce stood leaning over a map sprawled open on the table. They appeared to have started the meeting early, judging by disheveled stacks of papers scattered about. The remaining council members had not yet arrived, however. As Gareth entered, he hung his cloak on a rack delicately, careful not to damage the flower inside.

"Good morning, councilmen." Madelyn saluted. "The High Marshal sends his regards on behalf of the Order."

At first, neither Aldred nor Sir Bryce looked up from the map. They continued their soft chatter as if no one were present. Madelyn stood, arms crossed, while Gareth took up a seat at the opposite end of the table.

"Good morning to you too, Commander," Sir Bryce finally responded.

He was the oldest of the King's council and by far the most distasteful. Gareth felt his blood boil as he watched the elder councilman eyeing Madelyn up and down. He wanted to leap across the table and wrap his hands around Bryce's wrinkled neck but thought better of it.

"I was hoping to have a word with the council, and the King if he's available," she said. "There has been an attack along the northwestern frontier. Three thousand men were killed, according to the report. It's feared that Commandant Valens' son was among them."

Disturbing news indeed. Gareth recoiled at the mention of the massacre, though the lack of interest by Aldred and Sir Bryce was even more troubling. Throughout his life, he had only known of victory through his father's conquests. And now, inexplicably, Betanthia had suffered a terrible defeat.

"We're well aware, Commander. We received word the other day," Sir Bryce said disinterestedly. "The matter has already been discussed at length."

"Lady Everly, we have taken steps to ensure the integrity of our borders, not that it's even necessary," Aldred said with a hint of condescension. "Commandant Valens is seeing to it personally. Have no fear."

Madelyn screwed up her face. "I beg your pardon, Lord Aldred, but the High Marshal believes this is a significant threat."

She removed the dispatch from a belt pouch, brought it to the councilmen, and laid it on the table. "Whoever is responsible for this attack sent a wagon full of heads back to Castle Morden. They were mutilated beyond recognition, and carved with a variety of symbols."

"Yes, Commander. We received the same dispatch as you did," Bryce said. He seemed less interested in the subject and more focused on what lay beneath Madelyn's garments.

"With all due respect, Sir, I was able to translate the symbols with the help of our Chronican." She removed another note and laid it alongside the first.

Gareth stood and moved closer, eager to see what she had discovered.

"This is serious," she said. "These symbols are an invocation of their war god. The north means to march against us in force. And after what happened outside Khorrtal, you can confidently say they already have."

"My lady, do not be troubled," Lord Aldred said, waving his hand lazily. "I was as concerned as you when I received word of the attack. But Sir Bryce knows the western frontier better than any man, and he assures me there is no greater threat to the Kingdom. The northern tribes are scattered and divided and pose no real danger to us. Our chain of command has contingencies for matters such as this."

Sir Bryce sneered, the wrinkles on his sixty-year-old face multiplying. "This attack, however uncivilized, is nothing more than the mewling of a few primitive sheepherders and tree worshippers. They will be found and crushed in short order. The High Marshal worries himself needlessly. Perhaps he is concerned that his charter will not be renewed if he doesn't find new ways to keep you all occupied?"

"As such, our attention is focused on more pressing matters of state," Aldred concluded.

The door to the council chambers opened, and in stepped the remaining councilmen. Lord Morgan Lawson was a wealthy nobleman who was the physical embodiment of decadence. He was old, though only slightly older than Aldred, a decade or so younger than Sir Bryce, and extremely plump.

Sir Tristan Conway could not be more the opposite. He was the youngest on the council and the son of an influential noble whose name Gareth couldn't be bothered to learn. The young councilman appeared small, almost childlike, next to a rotund Lord Lawson.

Gareth sensed growing awkwardness in the council chamber. He never cared much for Aldred and never thought of him as a brother-in-law. Why his sister chose to marry such a man was a mystery, though he suspected Aldred's position as his father's closest advisor had something to do with it.

"It seems we've missed out!" Sir Tristan quipped.

Lord Lawson snorted in reply, then waddled to his seat. "Indeed, indeed!"

Madelyn shot them a distasteful glare, then turned back to Lord Aldred. "Perhaps I might speak to the King, personally. I'm sure he will take less kindly to his men being butchered. I've always understood that any attack on the King's men is an attack on the King and his house. Unless the laws have changed?"

In frustration, she looked to Gareth for some measure of support. As badly as he wanted to speak on her behalf, he knew it would be futile. He knew Aldred looked down on him with seemingly nothing but contempt, and he could not bear the thought of being embarrassed in front of the woman he loved.

"The King cannot be troubled with such trivial affairs." Aldred waved his hand dismissively. "We have his full faith and blessing to handle situations such as these while he tends to more important affairs. Do remember that I sit at his right hand in all matters related to the security and prosperity of Betanthia."

A fire was burning inside Gareth's chest. If he could not defend himself, his house, and his birthright in front of Madelyn, he might destroy any opportunity to win her affection. But it was another argument on top of the endless sea of arguments he already had to endure. The stress was nearly too great to bear.

Come on, Gareth, say something. Don't just sit here and do nothing. For heaven's sake, say something! She needs you!

As Madelyn shook her head in disbelief, he gathered enough courage to stand and face his fears. He was determined not to let Aldred push him around, not this time.

"And I would remind you that I am your future king, and I believe this threat should be taken seriously," Gareth blurted, moving to Madelyn's side. "It's not every day a wagon full of heads shows up at the gates of one of our castles with runes of some war god carved into them. I've never heard of such a thing in all my life! How can you stand here with a straight face and say this is little more than business as usual?"

"Future king, my prince. Future," Sir Bryce reminded him. "We serve your father at his discretion. You do remember there is a *line* of succession, yes? And as of now, there is only one man at the head of that line."

Their contempt was seeping into the open. Madelyn stood with arms crossed, leaning her hip against the table, preparing to make an exit at any moment.

Aldred agreed with Sir Bryce and moved toward Gareth, then placed a hand on his shoulder. "Rest assured, my prince, everything is under control. The west has been quiet for years, save for the occasional raid on outlying villages or bandits strong-arming on the roads. I have never lost sleep over it, and I suggest you don't either. Now, can we be of any further assistance?"

Before Gareth could respond, Aldred turned his back and continued to pore over his map and the various plans and documents beside it.

Madelyn had already started for the door, unable to mask her annoyance any longer. Gareth took notice and followed, taking up his cloak while the councilmen muttered something behind his back. A pang of regret made his stomach groan and twist. The ordeal had been a complete mistake and had done nothing but serve him another humiliation. His worst fear had come true, and now whatever standing he held with Madelyn appeared in jeopardy.

A sharp clacking of footsteps echoed throughout the vaulted ceilings of the Citadel as she hurried down the grand staircase. Gareth decided to chase after her, though he was fraught with uncertainty. He could not let Madelyn return to Bentmont without attempting to save face, not after a year had passed without seeing her.

"Pompous fools. They've grown so fat and content they cannot see a threat when it's directly in front of them. It's maddening," she said, storming across the great hall.

"It's like this all the time, Madelyn. Were it not for my friendship with the Guardsmen, I fear they might assassinate the King and me and claim Betanthia for themselves. They're always more focused on what serves their interests, it seems."

"Have you tried talking to your father about any of this? I know you two aren't close, but he can't ignore everything you have to say. You're his son. You have every right to march right into his chamber and speak to him." Madelyn's steely-blue eyes had a great urgency behind them, her gaze piercing.

"I've wasted more effort on him than I should have. But for you, I'll speak to him again. I agree with you and the High Marshal; an attack is one thing, but what happened out west… that… that is a message. It's right to assume this is a warning of things to come and should be taken seriously. The Order has my support, and if you feel additional steps should be taken to safeguard the Kingdom, then so be it."

"Are you sure? Aldred and his lackeys seem to have a tight grip on what happens around—"

Gareth raised his hand and interrupted. "Yes, and if Aldred doesn't like it, then he can speak to me personally. He may be married to a Bethard, but that doesn't make him one."

Madelyn's stony demeanor began to soften. "Thank you, Gareth. I knew I could count on your support. When I get back to Bentmont, I'll let the High Marshal know."

"When do you plan on leaving?"

"In the morning," she sighed. "I don't think I'm up for such a long ride right now, not after this travesty of a meeting."

Nervously, Gareth reached into his cloak to retrieve the flower but thought better of it. Madelyn was still fuming. He was beginning to have doubts over whether to tell her anything in the first place. Talking to women was difficult enough, not nearly as easy as Sir Edmund made it sound, at least, not for him. And Madelyn was no ordinary woman.

"It was a pleasure to see you again, my pr— I mean, Gareth." She smiled, catching herself slipping back into old formality.

It was discouraging to hear, but Gareth returned the smile and watched as she strode across the courtyard toward the front gate.

"Madelyn!" he shouted. He wiped a river of sweat from his palms on his cloak.

She paused and turned abruptly. This was his moment. There would be no telling how long it might be until he would get another chance. And after giving Madelyn and the Order his blessing to act as they saw fit, it could be another year, or years until he might see her again. If at all.

"Perhaps we could walk through the gardens, or if you're hungry, we can go to the marketplace?" Gareth's heart thumped so hard his chest hurt.

"Maybe another time. It's been a long week, and I'm still very tired. But thank you," Madelyn replied, disinterested.

"You aren't staying at the barracks, are you?" he stammered, moving to her side.

The Royal Guardsmen were the fiercest killers in Betanthia. Not the safest company for a young woman, even one as capable as her.

"No, I'm staying at the Seascape Inn. Not that I would mind sleeping at the barracks, but apparently, the High Marshal isn't too fond of his only female Commander being among that many Cardaleian men. And in such proximity. So the Seascape it is, compliments of the Order."

"Now, what's wrong with a Cardale man?" Gareth smirked, feigning insult. He gave her a gentle nudge.

"Short on balls, even shorter on brains. Or is it the other way around?" She grinned with playful smugness.

"Very funny. But no, the Seascape is quite nice. The High Marshal has excellent taste to find such lodging for you."

"I chose it, thank you very much. The Order simply picked up the cost." Madelyn furrowed her brow as if to scold Gareth, but her rebuke was lighthearted.

Flummoxed yet on the verge of laughing, he threw his hands up and laughed. "Then the lady has impeccable taste."

Madelyn nodded toward the gatehouse, and together they exited from the palace grounds without an escort. Almost immediately after setting out onto Auburn Row, Gareth felt his mood lighten. Here he was, on a perfect summer day, with the woman of his dreams at his side.

The masses who frequented the Row were dispersing for lunch. Many shops and stalls along the boulevard temporarily closed as their owners took their afternoon break. There was silence for a moment as Gareth and Madelyn walked together in tandem, their attention drawn to the various food vendors, clothiers, and trinket peddlers they passed.

This was the happiest he had been in ages. He only wished Madelyn had been able to visit Cardale more often, but it mattered little. She was here now, and that was all he cared about.

All I want is for you to love me the way I love you. Is that so much to ask? I would treat you like a goddess and give you anything and everything in the world, and more.

As they crossed the bridge over the Camsby River, Madelyn stopped halfway and stared into the distance, leaning forward against the parapet. The waters danced vibrantly as a crisp yet gentle wind tugged at its surface. Daylight would become scarce in the coming hours, and there was nothing like a Cardale sunset. Every evening, a stunning tapestry of colors painted the heavens, its oranges and reds bleeding into a dying blue sky. Gareth thought about how lovely it would be to experience it with her.

"I've never enjoyed the capital's congestion, but it's beautiful. In its own way." Madelyn said, her words as smooth as the breeze.

She squinted and surveyed the buildings along the Camsby and how their colors seemed to shift and change depending on how the light hit them. Gareth stared at her breathlessly, his eyes studying every line of her face, and sighed in contentment.

He wanted nothing more than to take her in his arms and kiss her the way he always dreamt. He could nearly taste her sweetness on his lips. But it was only a thought, a passing vision of what might happen, if only the fates would allow it.

"Aye. This place does have a personality of its own." Gareth paused, a million thoughts racing through his mind, each one of them focused solely on her. "I'm glad you're here; it's been too long. I'm sorry today has been so disappointing. I hope, at least, it ends better than it began."

"Thank you," Madelyn said indifferently. "I'll be returning to Bentmont in the morning, so I think I'm going to turn in early. A week in the saddle is not pleasant, let me tell you. But again, I'm grateful for your support. I'll be sure to let the High Marshal know what you did today."

Together they continued on to the Seascape, only a short distance away. Gareth wished time would slow and allow him to live the moment for eternity, or at least a while longer. Time was dwindling away, and he knew if he didn't speak up, the opportunity would be lost, possibly forever. An ever-tightening knot in his chest made it difficult to breathe, let alone speak. But somehow, as they arrived outside of the inn, he managed to find the words.

"Well, I hope you have a good day, my pr—"

Before Madelyn could finish, Gareth stepped forward and took her by the hands. "There are many things I've wanted to say to you. I respect and admire you, Madelyn. I remember the first time I saw you, all those years ago. The Blackthorn arrived in Cardale for my father's birthday celebration. I remember seeing you on top of that white horse at the front of the column, alongside the High Marshal. Ever since that day, I've been utterly captivated by you."

"Yes, I remember it too. You were standing on the steps of the palace," Madelyn said sheepishly, trying to mask her discomfort.

"And from that moment, I … I just knew. As the years passed and I got to know you, the more I came to realize you are more than just a pretty face. The beauty within you radiates like starlight, and it makes you that much more irresistable to me." Gareth stopped suddenly, his mouth tightening into a frown.

Madelyn's eyes were slowly averting. She pulled away from his grasp and hastily fixed her hair, though it was already perfect.

"I have great affection for you, Madelyn. You're a kind yet fierce soul, and I would love nothing more than to have you be…" Gareth paused again, the words nearly choking him.

"I know what you're going to ask me, my prince." Her return to formality was grim. "I don't want to upset you, but I… I just…"

The world felt as if it had fallen away, leaving him alone and vulnerable. He wanted to scream and cry, but something inside refused to quit. Before he could say anything further, Madelyn interrupted him.

"You're a good man, and you'll be a fine king one day. But you and I are different people who want very different things in life. I hope you understand."

"But, I don't," Gareth mumbled pitifully, tears forming in his eyes.

"I'm flattered you think of me that way, but being a queen… it's just… not for me. I want to fight. I want to lead men into battle, and I've spent my whole life in pursuit of that goal. I've worked too hard to give it all up. I've never wanted to marry or have children. It's just not my destiny." Madelyn looked into his eyes, her resolve unshakable.

"But if you're queen, you can do whatever you like! You don't have to answer to anyone." Gareth's mind was racing so frantically, he nearly blacked out.

"I would be a bird in a cage. I can't do that, I need to fly free." Though Madelyn was determined and assertive, she was thankfully not cruel. She touched him gently on the arm as his head sunk lower. "I'm sorry."

Gareth's eyes turned so red there was no use holding back his tears. All he could do was clench his jaw and nod, his clothing a swampy mess of sweat and shame.

"Thank you for the walk," Madelyn said, making her way through the ornate doors of the Seascape. She stopped and turned suddenly. "There is one thing you could do for me, though, if it's not asking too much."

Still overcome with despair, Gareth's heart fluttered with hope, however fleeting.

"What would you ask of me?" he croaked.

"This city has changed a lot since I've been here last, and unfortunately, not for the better. It's filthy, Gareth. Wild animals run free, and the streets are overrun with poor, homeless people. Please, you must do something. And I don't mean simply passing the word on to Aldred or whoever else. Nothing will ever get done that way. This happened on their watch, and it's shameful. This is *your* city."

Her suggestion, however polite, seemed more like an insult than anything. Gareth had only traveled down Auburn Row and to the docks, so he was unaware of the things Madelyn was saying. But he had stomached enough defeat for one day, and simply nodded in reply.

He watched helplessly as Madelyn disappeared through the doors of the inn. All of his hopes and dreams were shattered. As he sniffled and went to wipe his tears, he felt a sudden, sharp prick. He remembered the flower was still inside his cloak. Carefully, he removed it and noticed the petals were damaged.

But it didn't matter anymore. Gareth sulked back to the bridge, feet dragging like a drunkard. The Camsby was still flowing serenely, much the opposite of the chaotic storm inside his head. He looked at the rose mournfully, then felt a tear fall and spatter on the backside of his hand.

I've made a fool of myself, and now Madelyn will never return my affection. I should never have listened to you, Edmund. I knew this was going to happen...

After wiping his eyes dry, Gareth let the rose slip from his fingers and fall into the water. The flower danced along the glassy surface and was carried further and further from sight until it disappeared, taking any chance of a future with Madelyn along with it.

His walk to the Westwind Citadel was as somber as a funeral procession. This was Gareth's first rejection, and it was difficult to swallow. He did not understand how any woman could turn down the chance to become a queen, so his mind arrived at the only possible conclusion; there was something wrong with *him*. There must have been something so off-putting about him as a person that not even the throne of

Betanthia was enough to win Madelyn's affection. And worse, she gave the matter no more than a second of thought.

I wish I were dead. I'm an utter failure, and nobody will ever want me.

Heartbroken and feeling as if his breath might give out, Gareth passed through the outer gates of the Citadel without acknowledgment from the guards. He didn't want to go home, but it was the only place he could go.

"Gareth!" A familiar voice called out. Sir Edmund appeared from inside the gatehouse but was paid no mind. Edmund could tell something was wrong. His mail and steel breastplate chimed softly as he hurried over.

"Is everything alright? "Edmund raised an eyebrow.

They walked in silence before Gareth sat on a weathered stone bench beneath a willow tree. A pair of Guardsmen on patrol drew close, but Edmund waved them off discreetly.

"I spoke with Madelyn," he sighed.

"Judging from the look on your face, it must not have gone well, I take it?"

"No," he sniffled. "Before the words left my mouth, she turned me down. I don't understand, I've always tried to be kind and good, but it isn't enough. Is there something wrong with me?"

Edmund patted him on the back. "No, lad, there's nothing wrong with you. It was a bold move, to be certain. But a man has to be bold. You will not gain a woman's respect by being anything but. And while she may have turned you down, you showed courage by asking her. She'll remember that."

"No, she won't." Tears were welling up in his eyes again. "She doesn't wish to marry or bear children. All I did was make a fool of myself."

"I make a fool of myself on a daily basis, but my men still respect me." Edmund smiled. "My point is, she may have turned you down, but that doesn't mean you'll never get a second chance. I know it's easy to let your mind run away when you're emotional, but remember, this isn't the end of the world. Who knows, if you stick to your training and try to be the best man you can be, she may very well come around."

Gareth sighed and nodded. "You're right. You're always right, Edmund."

The elder Guardsman bellowed with laughter. "Then I must have you fooled. I certainly don't have all the answers. I've just been around longer than you, that's all. And I've been through this before."

"Yes, but you have a way of bringing everything into perspective."

"Well, that perspective came at a cost. It always does. I've been through more wives than I can remember. And this last one, I had to ask her more than a dozen times to marry me before she finally relented. Sometimes I think she agreed just to shut me up!" Edmund laughed again.

"Listen here, lad." He leaned in closer. "If she's the one you want, don't give up. Be persistent, but be wise about it. Show her you're a man worth marrying. Be the best you can be, for yourself first and foremost. She's obviously not enticed by riches or power, so you have to impress her in other ways."

Gareth thought hard on Edmund's advice before sitting straight and facing his friend directly. "What more can a prince do?"

"Be honorable. Be brave. Take charge of your life and your duties. Be a real leader, not just one in name, like your father. Be passionate, yet be careful of wearing your heart on your sleeve. You'll impress her, in due time."

"Madelyn's a fighter," he complained. "She has been since she was a little girl. And that's all she wants to be."

"Aye, but we don't stay young and fierce forever. Give it time." Edmund rose from the bench with an aching groan.

"There was one thing she asked of me before we parted." Gareth stood on weary legs. "She told me Cardale is, well, filthy... and filled with squalor and poor people roaming about, and she told me I should do something about it.

"Well, there you have it!" Edmund said encouragingly. "Cardale could certainly use… a little attention. That's true enough. But this is good news! She's given you a task, and if you succeed, she'll see you're a man that can get things done. And, if you don't mind me saying this, I think a little responsibility would do you well. It'll keep your mind focused. Plus, with your training, you won't have time to think about what's going on between your mother and father."

Edmund smacked him on the arm, then walked back to the gatehouse. "You have a chance, Gareth! You just have to reach out and take it."

It seemed like a good idea at first, but not everything was as straightforward as Edmund liked to think. Aldred would certainly be an obstacle no matter what he tried to do. It was infuriating to think that, even though he was a prince, he was always treated like a bastard child when the Kingdom was his to inherit.

Why am I so concerned with what Aldred might say or do? I'm the crown prince, not him. What could he possibly do?

The more Gareth thought, the more it dawned on him that Aldred and the other councilmen were exploiting his lack of ambition. All he really had to do was begin asserting himself. The Queen most certainly would stand behind his endeavors, and it would prove most amusing for Aldred to try and tell his mother what to do.

His mood was improving so much that Madelyn's rejection started to hurt a little less. Instead, Gareth felt rejuvenated with determination. He entered the Citadel and ascended the steps of the great hall to his chamber above. While near the top, a Royal Guardsman descended the stairs and paused.

"So sorry to disturb you, Your Highness, but the Queen needs you. She says it's urgent."

Gareth shook his head and kept walking. "Whatever it is, I'll deal with it tomorrow. I've had enough for one day, and you can tell her I said that."

The prince then retired to his room, shut the door tightly, and locked it. With the assistance of a small cask of twelve-year bourbon, he would try and find sleep before the next morning's training session. Though it was painful to deny his mother's request, there was simply no coping with yet another catastrophe. Not today.

There would always be tomorrow to deal with his father, as he promised, and maybe chance enough to see Madelyn and smooth things over. Gareth's mind raced and wandered in anticipation of how the coming day would play out, but one drink after another helped him find peace. He needed rest and a renewed resolve if he was going to speak to the King, a dreadful thought ever-present in his mind.

LUCETTA II

THE DAY FELT AS IF IT WAS THE BLEAKEST IN HER LIFE. IT WAS DIFFICULT to remember the last time she set foot outside her estate. Had it been months or even years? Lucetta was beginning to feel more trapped and hopeless with each passing day. Not even hours spent in the splendor of her gardens could shake such melancholy feelings from her mind. A dozen-odd servants bustling about the estate took notice and were exceedingly cautious in their interactions.

Her husband was spending more time than usual at the Citadel. She felt he was using the western incursion as an excuse to be away from her. Trace had been absent as well, likely seeing to his banks or his docks, or his, well, whatever else he did. She felt truly alone.

Visiting the palace was simply out of the question. Dealing with her father was about as enjoyable as chewing gravel. The same could be said about her mother, although their interactions were more depressing than anything. It was hardly the sort of company she needed.

After wandering about the estate for an hour, Lucetta decided to return to her quarters. Her chamber had the luxury of two balconies, though she preferred overlooking her gardens. But today, the outside world was calling, a world she so wholeheartedly came to resent.

The winds were favorable today, and the stench of the docks was nearly unnoticeable. A gentle clopping of horse hooves and the droll murmur of common folk provided its usual mundane ambiance. From the balcony, she saw the palace looming large like a mountain. Lucetta stared at it long and hard, her thoughts surprisingly indifferent.

Maybe the failings of my family are, in fact, an opportunity for me. Maybe I've been too hard on the city and the people. Perhaps... I'm the one it's been waiting for... the one meant to save it.

It was an encouraging thought, but she remained skeptical until she could see with her own eyes what Cardale had become, as Trace suggested. Many years had passed since Lucetta traversed through the heart of the city. She came to realize the only times she left her estate were a rare trip to the Citadel or the odd holiday in Dellhaven.

When a servant knocked on the door, Lucetta bid her to enter. The young girl had come to refresh the room but instead was commanded to summon a carriage driver and an armed escort. While traveling incognito would provide greater security, Lucetta wasn't about to take chances. Not if her suspicions about Cardale were proven right.

Within twenty minutes, the servant girl returned and informed her a carriage was ready and waiting. A detachment of ten Royal Guardsmen would accompany her, with another dozen or so following close behind. With her heart pounding and nerves fraying in anticipation, Lucetta took a few swallows of wine and made certain a bottle would be traveling alongside her.

The carriage was well-armored and well-adorned. Its interior was befitting of a princess and was upholstered with cushions and pillows made from red velvet, as well as a rack for refreshments. On top of the carriage sat a driver and crossbowman.

Anxiety began rearing its head as the carriage door was shut and the wheels began turning. Even though she was surrounded by the fiercest men in Cardale, she felt naked and vulnerable. It wasn't until her entourage started down Aubrun Row that Lucetta accepted she was now fully in the hands of these men.

Throngs of people lining the boulevard parted and made way for their princess, though in actuality, they knew not who was inside. But the people had learned that not making way for the Guardsmen was to risk your own safety. Or perhaps your life.

She examined the market stalls as her carriage clattered down Auburn Row. This was but one of the many places where goods from across Betanthia would come to find buyers. There were all manners of textiles, spices, foods, jewelry, and so forth, each coming from the far corners of her family's lands, and even beyond. This was how the Bethards amassed so much wealth over the centuries, through conquest and trade. She found the whole experience terribly fascinating.

They passed by slave blocks on the next avenue. The racket was quite off-putting, as slave auctioneers competed to see who could speak the loudest and fastest and lure in the most buyers. There were many strange and exotic people on the blocks she had never seen before. Though Lucetta had spent her entire life in the company of servants and slaves, she only now realized how they were procured.

On one block stood a score of tall and burly men. Some had long hair that was so blonde it looked to be made of spun gold. Another auctioneer was peddling a family of what looked to be Droethiens, at least, judging from the stories she heard. They had dark hair and olive skin which only grew darker in the summer sun.

As slaves that were purchased were taken down from the block, a deep conflict took hold within her. If this was how such practice was truly done, then it was quite distasteful. Seeing mothers and fathers ripped away from their children was a sight she could not stomach. A drink of wine was necessary after witnessing such incivility.

She continued on toward the Camsby River running through the heart of Cardale. There were many stone bridges crossing the waterway, but Lucetta insisted on proceeding into the city center. She was unsettled by the slave markets, but if there was any chance of saving Cardale from itself, it was necessary to witness such things firsthand.

While traversing the bridge, she spied a dead body lying in the open. Animals and insects had robbed the corpse of its features, making it unclear if it was a man or a woman. The sight and smell were so horrifying she averted her eyes in a panic. How such an atrocity could be allowed on the streets was beyond belief.

Further down the road, she spied a pack of stray dogs. They were filthy, mangy beasts that growled and snapped at one another over whatever scraps they could scavenge. The guard's horses whinnied and stirred in distress, but a well-placed bolt from the crossbowman sent the mutts scurrying in all directions. The carrion they fought over stunk worse than the corpse on the bridge.

"Driver?" she asked, poking her head through an open window.

"Yes, my princess?" The driver leaned back, his eyes still fixed on the road ahead.

"Where exactly are we?"

"About a mile from the square, princess," the driver answered.

"I would like to be heading back to the estate shortly." A tremble in Lucetta's voice must have revealed her apprehension.

"Worry not, my princess. You're safe with us. We won't let any harm come to you."

As the column snaked its way through winding streets, they happened upon a more affluent area of Cardale. Here, the air wasn't stale and stinking of human waste. A thump and clack of armored footsteps brought Lucetta a sigh of relief. This was the first patrol of city watch she saw since departing. And it was plain to see why. Many of the homes were lavish, even by her own standards.

Cardale's accumulated wealth was laid bare before her eyes. One estate, in particular, looked to be recently constructed and nearly rivaled her own in splendor. Its landscape boasted an array of finely maintained trees and a decorative fountain at its center.

The resident nobleman was heading to a waiting carriage with a pair of bodyguards in tow. He was a loathsome-looking man, grown fat and soft, and swathed in rich black silks. The bodyguards stiffened their backs as a group of beggar children approached. They appeared to have wandered into the area in search of meat and bread, or perhaps the charity of a few coins.

In a fit of annoyance, the noble cursed and spat. One of the bodyguards drew a truncheon and began swinging wildly, striking at the youngsters, scattering them like frightened birds. A little girl, no older than six or seven, ran crying past Lucetta's carriage, clutching a wounded arm.

Her blood turned to molten iron in a near instant. Furiously, Lucetta stood, her body hanging halfway outside her carriage.

"Guards, stop that man!" she shouted.

Four Royal Guardsmen took off at a gallop, their purple cloaks flapping behind them, and immediately surrounded the fat noble, who seemed more annoyed at the inconvenience than concerned.

"What's the meaning of this? How dare you accost me in such a manner!" he protested.

The Guardsmen dismounted and remained in position until Lucetta's carriage stopped alongside them. She stormed out, cursing, her dress stuck to her sweaty skin.

"Just who do you think you are to detain me in such a manner?" the fat man complained.

He looked to his helpless bodyguards for support, but neither seemed keen on challenging the Guardsmen.

"And who do you think you are to speak to your princess in such a manner, toad?"

To the nobleman, Lucetta might very well have been speaking Droethien. He stared curiously, confused at what he was hearing.

Is this fool even aware he has a princess?

One of the Guardsmen took the end of his lance and slapped the noble on the back of the knees, sending him tumbling onto all fours.

"I beg your forgiveness, Princess," he said, stammering.

"Those children your men assaulted. What did they do to deserve such cruelty?" Lucetta felt her sun-kissed face burning with anger.

"You must understand, em… my princess, these children are everywhere. They move in hordes, thieving and begging, and even robbing those of us that aren't careful. I had to hire these men just to keep myself safe!"

Passersby and those who dwelled on the avenue were beginning to congregate. Lucetta heard hushed voices and saw them pointing out of the corner of her eye. She realized that most, if not all, had no idea who she was, though the banner flying from her carriage was unmistakable.

"Should it not be prudent, then, to gather your neighbors and find a solution to this crisis?" she growled, gesturing to the crowd. "Should it be such a burden to put a meal in a hungry child's stomach?"

The noble's face was so drenched with sweat, he looked as if he had fallen into the Camsby. With clasped and trembling hands, he looked back at his two bodyguards, who were equally as helpless as he was.

"What am I supposed to do, princess? Feed every child in the city? Every man and woman of wealth could bankrupt themselves with generosity, and it still would not be enough. Perhaps if… if House Bethard were… em… a bit more… "

"More what? What is your meaning?" Lucetta snapped. The nobleman appeared too frightened to offer a reply for fear of the consequences. "Speak plainly, and true. I would hear what you have to say."

"Your Highness, with the utmost respect… em… this is your city. King Marcellus and your family are the only ones who could make a real difference. Should not the burden of hungry children lie with… with…"

Although the nobleman was falling over himself to show respect, Lucetta was incensed. She couldn't well flog the man for telling the truth, and the truth was plain enough. He was right. This was her family's city, and its descent into decadence and squalor was the responsibility of House Bethard to remedy.

"Speak no more. Your concerns have been noted, and I will bring them to the King. In the meantime, try to be kinder to those who cannot help themselves."

"Yes, Your Highness, I will do just that. Thank you."

The fat man bowed so deeply his knees strained and quivered under his weight, then made a hasty retreat. She returned to her carriage and ordered the driver to depart immediately. By now, so many eyes were upon her it was becoming a security risk. But thankfully, before more of a scene could be made, she was on her way.

For the next half hour, Lucetta stewed in a storm of anger. She hated knowing that children were homeless and hungry on her streets. She hated the nobleman for treating them like stray animals. And lastly, she hated her father for letting it happen in the first place. Cardale had become a comedy of errors, and Lucetta was far from laughing.

"Your Highness, we're approaching the square now," the driver shouted, the carriage clunking over uneven cobblestones.

"Be quick about it. I'm not sure how much more of this heat I can manage," she complained.

Cardale's central square was a thing of beauty once. At least, she remembered it as such. She must have been a girl the last time she had seen it because the reality before her was dramatically different. A colossal marble statue at its center was dingy and covered with a layer of greenish grime. Vagrants were squatting near its base, drinking openly and some peddling all manner of wares, illicit or otherwise. A sprawling market of makeshift tents had been erected as well. What exactly they were selling or doing inside the tents, Lucetta could not be certain.

"Goodness… what in the world is going on here?" she asked the driver, stunned and lost for words.

"A little bit of everything, Your Highness. Many of the people here are homeless. Others are selling whatever they can get their hands on, legally or illegally. It's hard to say for certain; we try to stay away from this area."

"Where is the city watch? Why have they allowed this to happen in my family's square?"

"It's become a dangerous place, Your Highness." The driver shrugged helplessly. "The city watch only has so many men to go around. Most are needed in the wealthier neighborhoods and the markets to keep all the thieving down."

"This is entirely unacceptable!" she declared, fighting back an urge to cry.

A few vagrants took notice of the standard on her carriage and began to taunt and catcall. At first, they seemed lighthearted but quickly became agitated. Someone threw a rotten vegetable at the carriage. It splattered on the side and sent pieces of itself flying everywhere. The stench was terrible.

Others soon joined in, as shouts of "Bethard! There's a Bethard!" spread like wildfire. The Guardsmen were nervous, and without waiting for instructions, they turned the carriage around and made a swift retreat. Lucetta closed the window as a thunderous thump-thump-thumping of debris and rubbish peppered the wooden walls, a deafening roar leaving her stunned and afraid.

"Why are they doing this? Do they not realize I only wish to help them?" she stammered.

She poked her head outside a window in dismay but was immediately struck by a stone squarely on her temple. Millions of tiny, bright stars filled her vision. A shrill ringing in her ears was so piercing, she clasped her hands against her head to silence it, but the effort was futile. Only when the Guardsmen had retreated far enough away did the assault stop. She dragged the window shut, hoping to avoid being struck again.

After rubbing a swollen knot on her head, Lucetta noticed a few drops of blood on the palm of her hand. She nearly broke into a fit of sobbing but fought valiantly so the guards would not hear her cry.

"I think that's enough adventure for one day, Your Highness. What do you say?" the driver asked, his voice muffled.

She reached over to the wine rack, poured herself a generous serving, and drank it with a desperate thirst. After a second helping, her nerves began to settle, her head fuzzy and light instead of throbbing and heavy with pain. Bravely she opened the window to let fresh air in.

It was a relief to arrive at the Camsby bridge and be so close to home. Salty ocean water and fresh fish never smelled so good. The largest spire of the Westwind Citadel was visible just ahead, jutting dominantly into the heavens.

Her comfort was interrupted as they passed by the dead man from earlier. The corpse was no less terrifying than the first time she encountered it. How and why people continued to pass by such a horror without noticing was just as unsettling. But then, Lucetta was reminded of the inhumanity she witnessed in the square. Cardale was dead inside, dead as the corpse she stared at, or so it appeared.

The remainder of her trek went by in a flash, and before long, they were passing through the gates of her estate. After coming to a halt, the driver dismounted and opened the door. When she stepped out, the full extent of the attack was revealed. Her face tightened and twisted from the smell of rotting vegetables and who knows what else.

"Don't worry, Your Highness. We'll get it all cleaned up for you."

Save the effort. I don't believe I will be venturing out there again any-time soon.

Lucetta spent the rest of the day in her chamber with a steady supply of wine. Her time in the city had still left her shaken and horrified, even hours after it was over. Her trembling hands were soothed only after her third bottle had been depleted.

Supper time came and went without her. None dared to disturb her for fear of whatever alcohol-fueled rage might come out of her. But as evening turned to night, there was a quiet knock at her chamber door. After a minute passed, the door creaked open. She discreetly adjusted her hair so the lump on her head would not be visible.

"Lucetta? Darling, are you there?" Aldred asked quietly.

When there was no response, he showed himself in and shut the door softly. Aldred immediately sensed something was amiss. Empty bottles lay discarded on the floor, along with the day gown she wore. Instead, she sat in her night clothes on a couch, staring off at the wall, her mind elsewhere.

"Is everything alright? You didn't come down for supper."

Aldred sat at the end of the couch and placed his hand lovingly on her leg. Lucetta snapped back to reality and jumped as if being man-handled by the mob that sent her fleeing.

"It's alright, my love. You're safe." He reached out to touch her once more, but instead, she shifted herself away. "I didn't want to bring it up, but one of the Guardsmen informed me you took a tour around the city this afternoon. I… I heard about your… misfortune. I'm very sorry to hear what happened to you."

"Oh, Aldred! Aldred, it was terrible!" Lucetta cried, unable to mask her fear any longer. She fell into his arms, sobbing. "I only wanted to see what it's like out there and… there were so many. They were so angry, and… and they attacked me. They threw all sorts of vile things at me and were screaming. They hated me, and all I wanted to do was help…"

"There there, my love." Aldred stroked her long, auburn hair. "You're very brave. I wish you wouldn't have gone, but you're brave."

Suddenly, she was reminded of her husband's station as chief advisor to the King. The responsibility had fallen to him to manage the daily affairs of the Kingdom in her father's absent state. And with Gareth in dereliction of his duties as heir to the throne, there was no one left to blame but Aldred. This was *his* responsibility. No, it was his *fault.*

"Why is Cardale so… so… destitute?" She glared at her husband accusingly. "This is not how I remember it. No, when I was a child, it was nothing like this. Aldred, what happened?"

"This is a very large city, my love. It's grown and stretched beyond its means, but as it stands right now, things are relatively stable… despite today's unfortunate events, of course. I'm truly sorry for what happened to you. If I had known beforehand, I never would have let you go out there."

"Then why haven't you done something about it? How could you let Cardale descend into such… squalor? Aldred! There are dead people just… just lying about on the streets. In what world is this deemed acceptable?"

"It isn't," he sighed. "But times have been difficult, and resources are stretched thin. In the past, such tasks would be left up to the impoverished in return for coin. Or slaves, preferably. But the slave trade has dried up as of late. With your father in the state he's in, there haven't been new conquests for years. And as for the poor, there's so many now they can't be made to do much of anything."

"Then has it not crossed your mind that perhaps the city watch should be strengthened? Even a few hundred swords could make a world of difference. Conscript them if you have to!"

Lucetta was becoming so upset she felt lightheaded again. A dark blurry spot had returned to the corner of her eye as well.

"My dear." Aldred shifted closer. "It isn't that simple. The city watch is a volunteer force, and there aren't enough men willing to join up, aside from those who are starving and have no other option. And even then, those sorts make for poor recruits. More often than not, they use their newfound authority to their personal advantage. I've seen it time and time again."

Lucetta felt like Aldred was talking down to her as if she could not comprehend such matters. Her jaw tightened over the perceived slight. She was a Bethard, after all. Who was he to speak to a blood member of the ruling family in such a manner?

"Then perhaps you might send the military to crack down on the chaos unfolding only miles from our home! If these people get it in their heads that they've had enough of us, what's to stop the whole city from crashing our gates and leaving *our* bodies to rot in the streets?"

"There are… contingencies in place should the people turn hostile. But I fear using the military prematurely will only lead to unrest. I'm sorry, my love, but my hands are truly tied. As distasteful as you may find Cardale, it's the best we can hope for at this time."

Hope was something that felt more fleeting by the moment. In a struggle between rage and despair, the latter began winning out. Lucetta felt tears building in her eyes.

"I just can't accept this, Aldred. I can't. I don't know how I'm supposed to sleep at night knowing there are starving children on the streets, without a place to call home."

"I wish there were more I could do, my love, truly I do. As ugly as it may be, we at least have order. And without order, everyone would suffer, from the smallest babe to… to you and I." He kissed Lucetta on her forehead, then stood and made for the door. "Please try to get some rest. I'll see you in the morning."

She wasn't sure if it was the wine or the sheer audacity of her husband's indifference, but it took several minutes to realize what had just happened.

He honestly doesn't see anything wrong, does he? If he truly wanted to clean up this city, it would be done within a fortnight!

The Bethards were a family of power and resources, which could be used by the right man or woman with a strong will; a will to bring order to a city rotting from within. Her drunken mind drifted back to what she had witnessed earlier in the day. The dead body to the hungry children being beaten for being hungry, and of course, the rabid mob. Then, the most disturbing thought of all entered Lucetta's mind.

What if… what if there is no saving this city? What if it's just… too far gone to salvage?

No, that couldn't be the case, she thought. It was simply stress and an excess of wine that led her to such a conclusion. There was no way Cardale, the shining jewel of her family's kingdom, could have fallen so far from grace right under her nose.

She stumbled to her feet and shuffled over to the balcony facing the city. With dusk falling quickly, the oppressive afternoon heat relented. She could still hear the sounds of Auburn Row, though it had grown quiet. Cardale seemed so pleasant from where she stood, despite the terror she had faced.

Maybe… maybe it's not as horrible as it seems. Perhaps this was just a bad day, and tomorrow, things will be better.

Each attempt to rationalize what she had seen led her to the same depressing conclusion. Her eyes did not lie, nor did they betray. The city truly *had* become a filthy, poverty-ridden nightmare. And to make matters worse, her husband, who could turn things around if he desired, was indifferent. It felt like a betrayal, the same as if she had found another woman in Aldred's arms.

Lucetta stared at the Westwind Citadel, though drunkenness and the failing light made it difficult to see straight. The mere sight of the palace brought back more unpleasant memories than good. But despite her bitter feelings toward her parents, she knew if there were any hope for the people of Cardale, it would be found at the Citadel.

Reluctantly, she retired to the master bedchamber and fell onto her soft, oversized bed. There was no other choice. She would have to speak to her father and convince him to make the necessary changes to save Cardale, or grant her the authority to make those decisions instead. If no one had the courage to speak for the children the nobleman had beaten, it would have to be her.

Overwhelmed and racked with despair, and a head throbbing so badly it felt near to bursting, Lucetta laid on a soft satin pillow and cried herself to sleep.

CEDRIC IV

"We can't be much further now, my lord," Commander Holland said from horseback, surveying the terrain ahead. "The tracks appear to be recent. I do believe we've closed distance. Shall I send scouts ahead?"

"Very well, but only a few. I don't want to attract any unwanted attention, lest our position is revealed," Cedric grumbled, his bloodshot eyes struggling to remain open.

"You men, ride ahead and see what you can find. Report back immediately if you catch sight of them." Jaxson ordered a group of four light cavalrymen to advance ahead. He watched as they galloped off into the distance.

The army snaked and slithered six abreast through the foreboding trees, which only grew taller and denser the further they marched. Their pace had been relentless for days, and signs of fatigue were showing. Officers routinely had to confront stragglers, sometimes resorting to floggings in order to keep their formation together.

"Damn cursed forest, it never seems to end," Cedric complained, his face twisting into a vicious scowl. His enjoyment of the Hinterwood's splendor had long since faded. "I don't care how long it takes or how far we have to march. There's nowhere they can hide."

Jaxson looked at his lord, then his soldiers, and ran a hand down his sweat-coated face. "I'm concerned for the men, my lord. We're pushing too quickly. They won't be in any condition to fight if we keep this up. They aren't getting enough rest, especially in this heat."

"I'm the oldest here, Jaxson. If I can make it, so can they," Cedric shot back, his temper growing nearly as fiery as the summer sun.

"My lord, you are mounted, and they are on foot. I beseech you, look at them. Half are about ready to collapse." Jaxson turned and pointed.

Some of the soldiers were retching and groaning from lack of water. With a deep sigh, Cedric ran a hand across his thinning scalp, flicking away drops of perspiration.

"Very well. We rest for fifteen minutes," he conceded, then promptly dismounted.

Walking proved especially painful, as his saddle sores and aching hip had become inflamed. Thankfully, shade was plentiful. Cedric removed a waterskin from his saddlebag and drank it dry. The water inside had grown warm and foul but would be enough to stave off dehydration.

Orders were shouted down the length of the column, and within seconds the army came to a halt. Few were able to do more than collapse in the shade and stomach as much water as they could. Cedric heard coughing and complaining in abundance, clearing the anger that had clouded his mind. Jaxson was undoubtedly right. The men *were* being driven too hard.

"A wise decision, my lord," Declan gasped, staggering from his saddle. His fingers fumbled with the leather straps of his cuirass as he tried to remove it. The gambeson underneath was utterly drenched in sweat.

Cedric grumbled and looked away. "I will not risk those fiends escaping, not now. Not when we're so close. But I know our integrity must not suffer in the process."

"We cannot venture too far from water, my lord. And I haven't the faintest idea where to find any. I've seen no rivers or streams. Nothing," Declan croaked.

"Yes, but those savages know. If we maintain our pursuit, we will find water. Or them. And hopefully both. I know it's unpleasant business, but we have to keep moving. Send out more scouts and see if they can find water. Now, where's Lieutenant Chambers?" Cedric asked, rising from the ground on shaky legs.

"He's at the rear, my lord, when last I saw him," Declan replied, venting heat from the collar of his gambeson.

"Find him and tell him to get the men on their feet. We leave in five minutes."

Five minutes soon turned into twenty as the army struggled to get itself back in formation. The respite was desperately needed, and the men took their time with it. Lord Valens scowled but could do little else.

Despite exhaustion and thirst, he never once lost focus on the task at hand. It was impossible to forget the sight of Alfrid, dead and skewered at the end of a pike. No amount of discomfort could match the agony he endured mere days ago, agony that followed him closer than the thirty thousand men at his back.

Cedric's destrier protested as he climbed back into the saddle. Even his beast was acting like a petulant child. He gave the reins a sharp jerk in frustration. Jaxson moved to the front of the column where the cavalry was situated, while Declan stumbled off to the rear to get the men moving, leaving Cedric in solitude. His mind seemed to wander more when he was alone.

Alfrid, how I wish you were still with me. I failed you in life. But I will not fail you in death. I will avenge you. I swear it. If the gods are real, let them hear me and bear witness to this vow.

Cedric prodded his horse forward to retake his position at the head of the army. Being among the men always helped to stiffen his resolve.

He supposed another ten minutes had passed, but this time, he made certain everyone could hear him.

"Men! Forward… MARCH!" The forest thundered with the gravelly boom of his voice.

Moments later, the army stirred and regrouped, then began their march. For hours they continued, through hot sun and humid forest. The landscape began to shift and change the further they ventured. As the trees grew taller, so did the earth itself.

We must be nearing mountains.

He studied rising hills and rocky formations on the path ahead. The northern forests were ill-explored, and few maps or descriptions of the terrain existed. Maple, oak, birch, and aspen trees soon diminished and gave way to spruce, fir, and hemlock.

"Cedric," Jaxson uttered. "If I may be so bold. This quest looks to be folly."

Lord Valens raised a curious eyebrow. "And what makes you say that?"

"We have no idea where we are. We've moved too far from water, and the land here is inhospitable. Were it not for my respect for your title, and your loss, I would not have taken my men this far. Forgive me, my lord, but I must protest our advance."

Cedric studied the landscape around them, which now looked dramatically different from when they had first entered. A heavy odor of pine permeated the stagnant air, so thick he could taste it. Moss-covered rocks of ever-increasing size pimpled the rolling forested hills, rendering the army's formation lame.

Despite how far they had come, Jaxson was right. He was a Commander, after all, and was given such a title due to his excellent judgment. It would be reckless to disregard such a man outright. And his personal experience told him such conditions could not to be tolerated for long.

"I'm inclined to agree with you," Cedric conceded. "Have we news from our scouts?"

"I dispatched a rider half an hour ago to see what they have found, but so far, there's been no word." Jaxson shook his head. "With the utmost respect, my lord, I would advise we make camp as soon as possible. We'll be burying our men if we don't."

As much as it may pain me, he's right. An army in no condition to fight is no army at all.

"Very well, we will make camp as soon as we clear this pass. Send another patrol and find us a suitable location, and some water, immediately. Send out foraging parties as well. I'm sure the men could use a fresh meal."

Cedric felt defeated, but could not risk the army's integrity any longer.

"A wise decision, my lord. You heard the man, move ahead!" With a wave of his hand, Jaxson signaled a band of riders to advance forward through the pass. At first, the horses whined and refused, seemingly frightened by the foreboding landscape.

"Well, get on with it!" Jaxson barked, the riders struggling to regain control of their mounts.

"They won't budge, Commander. Something is spooking them," an armored cavalryman said, his horse neighing and beating its hoofs against the earth.

"I don't care if you have to flog the damn things! Your lord has issued you an order!" Jaxson shouted, his horse rearing and crying out.

"What in the hell is the problem here, Commander?" Cedric barked.

"Nothing, my lord. These are plains horses, they must not be used to the trees and hills."

A dreadful thought lingered and grew in the back of Cedric's mind, to the point where it could no longer be dismissed. He found himself glancing down at the tracks of Damien Dreadfire's army, perhaps as a way of assuring himself they were still on course. Nothing about the Hinterwood felt right. The trees themselves seemed to be watching, judging, and conspiring against him and his men. Foreigners to this land they were, and the land reminded them of it constantly.

After regaining control of their horses, the scouts rode ahead with all haste. The army was now well between steep, craggy hills of the pass, marching ten abreast, a growing uneasiness overriding their fatigue.

"I sure will be glad once we're out of this place," Jaxson said quietly.

"Agreed. But I think it's safe to say the stories of the Hinterwood are just stories. As imposing as these woods are, they're just trees and rocks. The Northmen use superstition as their armor, but if you can cut through it, they die just as easily as any other man," Lord Valens boasted.

"I admire your bravery. Of all the Commandants in the history of Betanthia, you're the only one who has managed to take an army this far. Even if we don't find this, Damien Dreadfire, the knowledge we gain from this expedition will be invaluable," Jaxson said encouragingly.

"Knowledge be damned. I would be content never to set foot in these accursed woods again. There's only one thing I want: that man's head mounted on my wall. But sadly, it looks to be little more than a dream at this point." The anger that burned through Cedric was beginning to return.

"Indeed, my lord, indeed. I share your disappointment," Commander Holland sighed.

"I feel like I've failed Alfrid. I sent him off to die, and now I cannot even bring his killers to justice. Do you understand how that feels, Jaxson, to know you're so close yet so far away?"

"I can only imagine, my lord, I can only imagine."

Both men shared the same frustrations and disappointment. But this strange land held too many secrets, the greatest of which, the location of Damien Dreadfire.

"He was my only child," Cedric lamented. " He was the best of me. He was… all I had left of my Olivia. And I failed her too. I don't know if the gods are real. I've never worshipped them a day in my life. But I would like to believe they're real, and that there's something more once this life is over. If it means I'll see them again, I'll pray every day for the rest of my life."

"Well, I've never spoken of my faith, because it's a deeply personal thing, but I do believe. And I've been praying for you and your family every day. I believe the gods are kind, and they—"

Jaxson fell silent. Cedric thought nothing of it but turned to see what the distraction was. A look of terror painted Commander Holland's face. A broadhead arrow stuck straight through the center of his neck, blood erupting from his mouth like a fountain. He fell, gurgling and writhing, clawing helplessly at the wooden shaft.

A shrill whistle filled the air, then another, then dozens more, followed by screams. The last of Jaxson's life spilled onto the dirt, and after a jerking spasm, his body went still. Lord Valens broke free from his disbelief and whirled around as a deluge of arrows began raining down.

"Ambush! Ambush! Form ranks, men, form ranks!" Zakery Chambers cried out from the middle of the column, raising his shield defensively.

There was no telling where the arrows were coming from. They seemed to fly forth from all directions, a great panic descending upon the army. Cavalry at the head of the column were heavily targeted, the wails of wounded and dying horses nearly drowning out the men.

"Get out of here! Ride! Ride!" Cedric yelled frantically to his cavalrymen as a projectile pierced his right thigh.

He snarled in pain and cracked the reins, but seconds later, his steed was peppered by a flurry of arrows and fell to the ground. As he lay next to his dying horse, he saw faint outlines of figures on top of the ridge, raining death down onto his soldiers.

"My lord!" an infantryman cried out, rushing to aid his Commandant.

With a shield raised high, he aided Cedric back onto his feet and was soon joined by several others.

"Get into formation, now!" Cedric barked, grimacing as pain pulsated through his leg.

Arrows continued to fall like a torrent of heavy rain. Lord Valens watched helplessly as more men fell around him.

"They're hitting us from both sides!" screamed a frantic soldier as he hid behind his kite shield.

"Form a second line to the north! Lock shields!" Cedric growled, limping to the center of a hastily formed shield wall.

He watched in dismay as his cavalry was wiped out, those who survived having run off through the pass.

Suddenly, a deafening roar came from the southern treeline at the column's rear. In an instant, thousands of warriors poured out from the trees and collided savagely with his disarrayed and exhausted soldiers. The barbarians were bare-chested or lightly armored in mail and leather and attacked fiercely with sword, spear, and axe.

Lord Valens was unsure of what was happening, but could faintly see Declan on horseback, frantically shifting his men around. For a moment, he believed the attack could be defeated, until Declan and his horse took a flurry of arrows, then fell away from sight.

"Lieutenant Chambers! Get these men out of the pass and repel this attack, or we're dead!" Cedric called out through the deafening noise of battle.

"Infantry! Push!" Zakery shouted at the center of a shield wall formation.

Another fierce roar erupted, this time from the north. Thousands of warriors crashed into the rear of the men defending against the first assault. They were heavily armored and equipped with spears, halberds, and other polearms. With the charge came a beating of war drums from the forest, deep and bellowing, and high in tempo.

Cedric watched as nearly a third of his army became enveloped and destroyed in seconds. His soldiers were being pushed into the pass by the attacking barbarians. Fear was spreading through the ranks, and cohesion beginning to break down.

But through the storm of combat, Lieutenant Chambers stood his ground and rallied their wavering army. Shield walls were formed on three sides to protect from arrows, and from Damien Dreadfire's attacking hoard behind them.

"My lord, the Lieutenant reports we're holding steady. What are your orders?" shouted an older soldier, shoving his way past the men circled around Cedric.

"We have to push through them. If we stay here, we're dead," Lord Valens croaked as he sat and clutched his bleeding leg.

"We're doing the best we can, my lord. The men are tired, but we'll give them hell. I'll send word to the Lieutenant." He disappeared back into the sea of soldiers.

Cedric fought through the pain and returned to his feet to survey the situation. To his dissatisfaction, the army had begun to cluster. Though they outnumbered the enemy, they lacked the stamina to push out of the pass. Incoming arrows had slowed to a trickle, a welcome reprieve if there ever was one.

Then the rocks came. Massive boulders were dislodged from the tops of both ridges and came tumbling down with terrifying speed. The men in their path were instantly crushed as the mighty stones plowed into the center of Cedric's army. Nearly all hope left Lord Valens as he watched Lieutenant Chambers scream and fall beneath a boulder, along with dozens of his men. Panic rushed through the ranks, and the lines quickly faltered.

With few options remaining, Cedric began to sound for a retreat, but before he could, another arrow struck, driving deep into his collarbone. The impact dropped him to the ground with a thud. Dazed and overwhelmed by pain, he attempted to rise but lacked strength.

There was no choice but to continue through the pass as first intended, then turn and establish a new line at its end. Cedric knew if he could do this, the tall, craggy hills would surround the enemy, and the tide of battle might be turned. But the ranks had clustered tighter, and tighter still until they squeezed and held Cedric so firm he could barely breathe.

Seconds later, a crushing tide of frantic men rushed toward him like a stampede of bulls. Some tried to lift him up but were caught in a tidal wave of routing men. As the army broke and fled through the pass, they unknowingly trampled over their lord in a frenzied panic.

The pain was severe, and he felt every foot crashing onto his body. Bones crunched and shattered, and organs ruptured from the relentless, crushing pressure. As the light in his eyes faded to black, Lord Valens' final thoughts were that of Alfrid and his Olivia. They would be seeing each other much sooner than he intended.

I'm sorry, my loves. Forgive me.

GARETH III

GARETH WOKE WITH A CRUSHING HEADACHE, LAST NIGHT'S drinking still visible in his bloodshot eyes. The future king of Betanthia poured himself out of bed and staggered to the far side of his chamber to fetch a flagon of water. He licked his dry, cracked lips and put the vessel to his mouth, emptying it in several large, desperate gulps. He discarded it onto the floor, panting and moaning like a wounded animal. It took every ounce of concentration to fight the urge to throw up.

I have got to stop. I can't keep doing this to myself. I'll die if I don't.

Today was a day Gareth dreaded facing, especially in such a condition. Even thinking of attending his daily training session was enough to rile his unsettled stomach. He decided it would be best to take the morning off, hoping Sir Edmund would raise little fuss. It would be stressful enough to face his father, and the last thing he needed was another argument on top of the one he was already anticipating.

And then, of course, there was Madelyn. An excess of alcohol from the night before had not soothed the sting of her rejection. If anything, his crushing hangover was a reminder of past failures as a person and prince. If he was to be the best man he could be, as Edmund had told him, his thirst would have to be conquered somehow.

Most days, Gareth gave little to no thought about his attire, especially during summer. But knowing he was soon to face his father and Madelyn shortly after, he decided on something more befitting of his status. A deep-red silk tunic and thin black trousers with black boots would suffice. Across his waist, he fastened a black leather belt and affixed a sheathed dirk to it. Simple, yet commanding. His hair was disheveled, but looked presentable enough after running his hands through it a few times.

A soft knocking at the door drew his attention. Before he could answer, the door cracked open, and Sir Edmund entered.

"I wasn't sure if you were awake! Or alive, for that matter." Edmund looked at him curiously. "You don't exactly look ready for sparring. Planning on going somewhere?"

"I promised my mother I would speak to my father, which I'm dreading," he said, sighing. "And I thought I would try to speak with Madelyn before she leaves for Bentmont. Who knows when I'll be able to see her again, with the coming war and all."

"War? What war might that be?"

Gareth could have punched himself squarely in the nose for such a blunder. He suddenly remembered that no one outside the council knew what was happening in the west. Thankfully, Edmund was a man he could trust.

"Well, the potential for a war." Gareth scratched the back of his neck. "It's a long story; I can fill you in later."

"Very well." Edmund shrugged. "So, does this mean you won't be training this morning?"

"Yes. No. I mean, correct. Besides, my body is so sore I can hardly feel a thing. I'll resume tomorrow. You can hold me to it."

"And I plan on it. Remember, consistency is key. Don't think you're getting out of it tomorrow!" Edmund turned and made his way into the hall. "And best of luck with your father. Try not to get too worked up when dealing with him. It's not worth it."

Sir Edmund left the door open, his boots clacking behind him. Gareth wished his friend would accompany him, though it would be of little use. He knew a fight with the King would be inevitable. It happened every time they spoke, and there was no reason to believe this time would be any different. But he made a promise to the Queen, and she was counting on him.

Gareth walked toward the King's chamber, dread creeping over him. There was always a fleeting chance that today would be one of Marcellus' better days. Maybe he would not be the drunken, raging tyrant he had turned into as of late, but in Gareth's experience, such luck was too good to be true.

Better get this over with. The longer you wait, the more likely you are to miss Madelyn before she leaves.

The King's chambers were protected by two Guardsmen clad in purple cloaks, mail, and ornate breastplates of polished steel, decorated in blue and gold. They stood silent and vigilant like statues, their gauntleted hands resting on the hilts of their greatswords. Ever-watchful eyes scanned the length of the hall through their nasal helmets and mail coifs.

As he approached, the senior Guardsman stepped forth and bowed. "Good morning, my prince. I must caution you, the King is not well today."

"The King is never well," Gareth said, wondering just how far-gone his father could be at such an early hour.

With a flick of his wrist, the guards parted and made way. His hand recoiled from the door for a second, but there was no turning back. As Gareth entered, a stench of alcohol and body odor affronted his nostrils, his face tightening in disgust.

The room was in shambles as if a whirlwind had swept through. Papers, clothing, spent casks, and flagons of wine littered the floor. Many of the drapes drawn shut, save for one on the far side of the room, behind Marcellus. He was sitting motionless on a wooden chair, surrounded by his filth and indifference. Gareth approached reluctantly, stepping gingerly over one mess after another.

"Father, I need to speak with you about something."

Each step brought more of Marcellus' disheveled appearance into view. The King's silvery thin hair was long and unkempt, as was his scraggly gray beard. His brown eyes were glazed over from lack of sleep and too much drink. A pitiful sight to behold. It was difficult, nearly impossible to believe this was the man responsible for bringing Betanthia some of its most glorious victories on the battlefield. But here Marcellus Bethard sat, a broken and empty husk of the man he used to be.

"Father?" Gareth uttered again.

The King turned slightly but was otherwise disinterested. He mumbled quietly and quickly, his words running clumsily into one another. Marcellus took a gulp of wine from a half-empty silver chalice, much of it running down his chin, and onto his stained gray tunic.

Gareth looked upon his father with both disdain and pity. As painful as it was, he remembered the man Marcellus used to be. As a boy, he recalled when the patriarch of House Bethard was strong and proud, a man of honor and duty. He had vivid memories of seeing his father leading the army off to distant lands and how inspiring and intimidating of a sight he was.

"I'm speaking to you," he said again. "Do you even hear me?"

"Damn stupid boy, leave me be! I suppose you've come to beg for more of my gold, is that it? That's all you and your cursed siblings seem to care about." Marcellus spat a purple gobbet onto the floor.

"I'm not here for your gold, father. Why do you assume we're here for something malicious whenever we come to see you? It isn't right, and it isn't fair to us." Gareth sighed in frustration. "I suppose you're unaware of what's been happening in your kingdom?"

Marcellus replied with silence.

"I'll tell you," he continued. "There's been an attack in the west. Thousands of men have been butchered. *Your* men."

The King laughed and swayed in his chair, sipping and slurping wine until it was nearly gone. "There are no armies in the west, I slayed them all! Me! I'm the one who conquered the world while you were hiding behind your mother's skirts!" Marcellus belched, then groaned.

His glassy eyes were distant and vacuous, his lips tinged purple.

"Except you didn't conquer the world," Gareth shot back. "You didn't conquer even half of Caldakas, and you certainly didn't wipe out the barbarians. They're back, and they murdered three thousand of your soldiers. Are you going to let such a crime go unanswered?"

The King said nothing.

"Clearly, you don't want me here," he said, his patience wearing thinner by the second. "And I don't want to be here either, but if you're going to be content with shutting yourself inside this pigsty for the remainder of your days, then do the honorable thing and abdicate. And not just abdicate your responsibilities to Aldred, as you've already done. But you should abdicate the throne and allow me to succeed you."

"And there it is!" Marcellus exclaimed feebly. He thrust a bony finger at Gareth accusingly. "You just want to be rid of me so you can seize power for yourself, power I fought my entire life to attain! Your damned mother probably put you up to this, didn't she?" Marcellus stood, stumbled, and nearly fell.

"I don't want to sit on your throne. Believe me, I don't. But someone needs to lead in your absence. Your paranoia is getting out of hand, father, and everyone suffers because of it. Your family isn't your enemy, whether you realize it or not. What have we ever done to offend you so?"

The King scoffed. "My family. Hah! My family cares so much about me. Tell me another one of your lies, boy."

"You are an insufferable old man. And I'm sick to death of you tormenting *my* mother. She's done nothing to deserve such treatment from you or anyone."

Gareth could hardly believe the words coming out of his mouth. A single bead of sweat ran down the middle of his forehead.

"You don't know the first thing about it, boy. Your mother is the one who—"

"I won't hear another word of it!" he exploded.

Every ounce of pent-up anger came spewing forth. The room was spinning and felt hot as a smelter, his vision turning a shade of red.

"She isn't your plaything," Gareth screamed. "She isn't some fool to be dragged out for your amusement! This had better be the final time you ever treat her in such a manner."

He started for the door but stopped halfway, unsatisfied with his rebuke.

"And another thing. You act like everything you own and control, all of your possessions, all of your money, even the entire fucking Kingdom, wouldn't eventually become mine after you die. I'm your heir, or have you forgotten that?"

Tension had reached a critical level and was near to exploding. Marcellus was shaking with rage, but Gareth did not relent. He could not.

"If we wanted you dead so badly, I would have paid an assassin to put you out of your misery long ago. Or perhaps I would come into your bedchamber in the dead of night and smother you with your own pillow. Furthermore, if I find out you've been threatening my mother again, you might wake one night to see me standing over you. You are a dishonorable man and a pathetic excuse for a king."

"Damn you, boy, you're no son of mine! You bastard! Get out! Get out and never come back! You hear me! I'll feast on your guts, you little shit!"

Marcellus erupted in rage and began throwing anything close at hand, spitting and cursing like a madman. While the King was melting down in anger, the door opened, and his sister Lucetta stepped inside.

As if the morning couldn't get worse than it already was, Gareth was now alone with the two people who despised him most. She was aghast at such a chaotic scene and shot him an ill-favored glare.

"What are you doing here?" she asked curtly.

"None of your business," he replied. "Not that it would matter much to you anyway. I assume you're here because you want something, am I right? Go on, sister, tell me what it is this time."

Without waiting for an answer, Gareth stormed into the hall and slammed the door, the guards nowhere to be found. Lucetta's unexpected presence was particularly enraging, given the circumstances. Although, there was a slight satisfaction in knowing his father's wrath would now be directed toward her.

Maybe now she'll see what I have to deal with on a daily basis. It might bring her some self-reflection, though I highly doubt it.

On the way back to his chamber, he passed Charlotte's room. The door was open, which was unusual as of late. Gareth peeked inside to make sure everything was alright. To his surprise, Trace was standing inside with the Queen.

"You're here too?" he asked in feigned surprise.

"It's good to see you, brother," Trace replied in his typical professional tone, even though such manners were appropriate for business affairs and not family discussions.

"I suppose wherever one of you goes, the other isn't far behind. But what I can't figure out is why you're both here. What new favor has she come to ask from our father?"

Queen Charlotte was shaken, having heard the fiery argument with Marcellus echoing down the hall. She sat at the edge of her bed, eyes and face swollen from crying.

"He's been up all night drinking and making an awful racket," she mumbled. "I've barely slept more than a few minutes. What in the world happened in there?"

"The same thing happens whenever I try to talk to him." Gareth frowned. "It never ends well. I did my best, mother. Truly I did. But every time we speak, I recognize him a little less. He's become insufferable."

"I know. This is what my life has become now," the Queen lamented. "I do appreciate you trying, Gareth."

"I'm just worried he will take it out on you now."

"If not this, it will be something else." Her lip quivered. "I don't want you to worry. This is my burden to bear, not yours. I should never have asked any of you to become entangled in this mess on my accord." She stood and moved to the window.

Seeing his mother so defeated and resigned to a life of misery was heart-wrenching. It was a helpless feeling to know she had to suffer so needlessly. If only the fates were kinder. If only Marcellus' breath would give out in the dead of night and relieve everyone of his cruelty.

"You mustn't let yourself be troubled, mother. This will pass." Trace tried to sound reassuring, but Gareth wondered if he was trying to reassure himself.

"Ignoring what goes on here won't make it go away, Trace," he said, scowling. "You're delusional if you think otherwise."

"I understand things around here are not ideal, but—"

"Ideal?" Gareth felt anger bursting from within him again. "It's about as far from ideal as you could get. But what would you know, Trace? We only see you when you're following behind Lucetta's skirts like an obedient dog. Because, of course, she only shows her face whenever she wants something. Tell me it isn't true. Tell me in that condescending tone you love to speak to me with."

"Gareth, please." His brother sighed. "This is your home. You live here, and you're the crown prince. I'm not sure what you expect from us. Lucetta will not inherit the throne, and neither will I, so we've made lives for ourselves outside of the palace. You cannot rightfully fault us for that. We do what we can when possible, and that's the best we can offer."

204

"Me being the heir to the throne doesn't absolve you of your responsibilities to our family."

"I never said it did," Trace protested.

"So do the honorable thing. You're still a Bethard, are you not? Or have you taken Esma's maiden name and disowned the rest of us?"

He always did think he was better than me. Ever since we were children, he would always treat me as if I was the younger sibling and he the elder.

A sharp click-clacking of hurried footsteps came rattling down the hall. Gareth grumbled and thought about escaping, knowing what was coming their way. Before he could move for the door, Lucetta came bursting in. Her eyes radiated a burning anger he had often seen in their father's eyes.

Those two are more similar than either one would care to admit.

"Just who do you think you are?" she shouted so loud it shook the windows, her face tight with animosity. "Do you know what I had to endure in there after you upset father the way you did?"

"If anyone has an idea, it would be mother and me, and certainly not you. We live with this chaos daily."

It was strangely satisfying to witness Lucetta get a small taste of what it was like around the Citadel as of late. Gareth felt not even the slightest bit of remorse for it either. If anything, it made him wish their father had scolded her even worse.

"Tell me, sister, how long has it been since you've come to visit just for the sake of visiting? The only time you see fit to grace us with your presence is when there's some task that needs father's assistance, or his blessing."

"Don't you dare insult me! You have no idea why I'm even here."

Gareth saw discoloration on the side of her cheek where a bruise seeped down from her temple. He decided the wound was too old to have been by Marcellus' hand. Could Aldred have pummeled her for some unknown reason?

"Not that it should even matter to you in the first place." Lucetta's face was becoming as red as her gown. "We're quite aware of how you spend your time and who you spend it with. So please, spare me your self-righteous indignation."

"How curious." Gareth glanced at Trace, who was tugging at the collar of his silk tunic. "I thought we were entitled to our own lives. Oh, but wait, that seems to apply only to you two. I beg your forgiveness; I'll be sure to live up to *your* standards in the future."

"Please, no more," Queen Charlotte implored her children breathlessly. "I cannot bear any more today. Please."

Fearing she might faint at any moment, Gareth rushed to his mother's side. Her skin felt cold and clammy, and she was shaking as if taken by a chill.

"I'm sorry, mother. You've been troubled enough." Gareth glared at his siblings. "Out! Both of you. She's been through far too much, and I won't have her disturbed any further. Go on, out! Out!"

Begrudgingly, Trace and Lucetta retreated from the chamber. It was quiet now, save for the Queen's whimpering. Gareth wrapped his arms around her gently.

"It's alright. Everything is going to be just fine, I promise."

A lone Guardsman opened the door halfway to see if everything was in order. Gareth gestured to his despondent mother with a nod. The guard disappeared to fetch Emilee, the Queen's favorite maidservant.

She arrived with all haste and rushed to Charlotte's side. Gareth's head was pounding so viciously that he could no longer bear it. The stress of not one but two hostile encounters conjured up an unquenchable thirst.

I need wine, ale, whiskey, anything. And I need it now.

Knowing the Queen was in good hands, Gareth saw himself out. He had endured enough abuse for one day and could stomach it no further. While traversing the long and winding corridors, he was chased down and accosted by a still-fuming Lucetta. She was even more hostile now that they were alone.

"I know you despise me, Gareth," his sister said bitterly. "And I must confess the feeling is quite mutual. If you were a better prince, I would have had no reason to come here today, and we could both spare ourselves the discomfort of being in each other's presence. Do you even know why I'm here?"

"No, and quite frankly, I don't care. You being here is more of a detriment than anything. I wish you would have stayed at your estate. Whatever business you have isn't here, that's for certain."

Lucetta appeared unphased by the slight. "I came to see father because this city has descended into squalor and desperately needs order and restoration. With all your gallivanting at taverns and who knows where else, I thought you would have noticed by now."

"Spare me," Gareth scoffed. "When did you suddenly develop such noble inclinations? We both know you're the sort that never does anything unless there's something in it for you. So tell me, sister, does the sight and smell of the common man offend you? Would you have them all expelled beyond the city walls to make your view a bit more pleasant?"

They passed through the throne room on the way to the great hall. It was still as vacant as it had been over recent years. The vaulted ceilings echoed with the click-clacking of Lucetta's footsteps as she continued her pursuit.

"You make me out to be some sort of selfish monster, yet I'm the only one in this family who wants to do something about it. If you can tell me straight-faced that you are alright with seeing dead people lying unattended in the streets, then perhaps you're the wrong person to be sitting there."

She gestured to the throne. It was often difficult to look at, knowing one day he would have to inherit the burden of his father's indifference. He sometimes wondered if there had been a mistake upon his birth, and he might not be a Bethard at all. There could not have been more distance between himself and Lucetta, siblings who once loved each other dearly as children.

"I'm sorry, sister. I'm sorry the world doesn't exist as you think it should. Such a tragedy that a half million odd souls outside this palace can't all be as well off as you, I know."

"Oh, please," Lucetta taunted. "You have such a childish outlook on everything."

"I've spent far more time than you out there among the common man, so don't you dare lecture me about anything. I would like nothing more than to have my own life and be free to take on more responsibilities in the Kingdom. I would, were it not for the daily crises I have to contend with. If you cared to be more involved with *our* parents, I would be able to do more for us and everyone. And, of course, if your husband would stop undermining me at every opportunity…"

Gareth turned away from the throne and continued to the great hall. He had seen enough of the accursed stone slab whose legacy always hung around his neck. His spiteful comment about Aldred incensed Lucetta.

"You leave him out of this," she barked. "Aldred is supposed to be an advisor, Gareth, not the surrogate king. He isn't supposed to have as much responsibility as he does, but because you aren't man enough to accept your duties—"

"Hold your tongue." He spun around and pointed a menacing finger mere inches from her face.

The exchange seemed only to amuse her, a subtle grin reflecting the smugness he had come to expect. Gareth quickened his pace and stormed through the great hall and out the front doors of the Citadel. Servants scattered in all directions to avoid the wrath of not one but two angry Bethards.

"You know what I say is true, brother. Being a king means you have to manage a range of responsibilities. Since you've proven unwilling and unable, perhaps you should consider abdicating your claim to the throne and allow Trace to sit in your stead."

You would certainly like that, wouldn't you?

It was becoming increasingly difficult to control his temper. Lucetta had expertly mastered the art of getting under his skin, and even though ages had passed since they were in each other's company, her skills were no less effective.

"I'm certain you would like nothing more than for Trace to sit on the throne," he snarled. "Our good, gentle brother Trace. I'm sure you would find it quite easy to pull his strings if he were king. With a simple snap of your fingers, he would do whatever you tell him to, like the good little whipped dog he is."

"How dare you! What has he ever done to deserve such an insult?" Lucetta may have appeared offended, but deep down inside, she knew it was true. He was sure of it.

"Nothing you haven't already told him to do. We all know how ambitious you are, Lucetta. And we all know it's because you cannot have children."

The slap came so fast Gareth couldn't see it coming. The gold rings on several of her fingers bit down hard against his cheekbones, sending a jolt of pain rattling through his head. Despite his anger, he immediately regretted such an underhanded comment. It was in poor taste and a painful reminder of his own failings in life. He was the eldest Bethard son and had no children of his own. But Lucetta was not able to make such a choice for herself. The fates had decided against it and left her barren.

Seeing his sister's rage and heartbreak was more than he could stomach. The day had barely begun, and he was already praying for it to end. And there was still the matter of speaking to Madelyn, the thought of which crept back into his mind.

"It's best if we don't speak for a while," he said without any apology. "I know you hate me, sister. I often wonder if I'll wake to find you standing over my bed one night, ready to plunge a dagger into my chest. Sometimes I wish you would."

And with that, he walked away.

That was wrong of me. I shouldn't have said such a thing to her. I have no doubt she would be a kinder person if the one thing she wanted were not taken away.

Now, more than ever, Gareth wanted a drink, and a strong one at that. His craving was so intense he felt tremors building in both hands. But now was no time to succumb to his awful addiction. There was another matter to attend to still.

On any other day, he could walk the streets of Cardale without an escort. His preference for modest attire helped him to blend in with the common folk, but with his fine silks on, it was another matter entirely. A trio of Guardsmen followed behind as he left the Westwind Citadel and started down Auburn Row. There was no time to change into something less conspicuous. And besides, Madelyn would need impressing.

I should have brought my sword. She seemed quite fascinated by it. Oh well, no matter.

A million thoughts raced through his mind, each leading in a different direction. Should he try to find a gift of some sort? Perhaps, but then it would be a matter of what to get. And what if it wasn't to her liking? Maybe he could go back and find something in the armory? No, there was no time. Gareth would have to do this unaided.

Before he knew it, the Seascape Inn was in sight. Desperately he hoped Madelyn had not left, although his opportunity was likely lost after the debacle at the palace. Before opening the ornate doors of the inn, Gareth wiped his hands on his tunic and exhaled a whirlwind of stress.

The lobby was empty, much to his surprise. The room felt larger inside than it looked outside, and was well-furnished and decorated, for an inn. This was the first time Gareth had ever been inside such an establishment. He always pictured such places to be little more than a collection of broom closets, with nothing but a straw bed and a candle inside. But this place was in a class all its own.

"Excuse me, is anyone there?"

A long counter on the other side of the lobby was vacant. He saw an impossibly thick ledger sitting open on top of its polished cherrywood surface, but there was no attendant. Gareth made his way over and searched around briefly. There was a room behind the counter. Its door was open, but there appeared to be no one in sight.

Am I too late? Has everyone left?

"Hello?" he called out again.

A faint creaking of floorboards emanated from the back room. Moments later, an elderly gentleman shuffled out, rubbed his eyes, and yawned.

"Yes? Is someone there?"

It took the old man a second to realize who he was speaking to. The innkeeper's fatigue fell away and was replaced by an ecstatic wonderment.

"Prince Gareth! I... I... Welcome! Welcome! This is most unexpected. How can I be of service to you?"

It was always an uncomfortable feeling whenever someone groveled. Gareth preferred to go unnoticed outside the palace to avoid such interactions. There was something satisfying about being treated like an everyday person instead of royalty.

"I was wondering if you could help me find someone. She's been a guest here for a few days."

"We've had quite a number of guests, my prince. What's her name?" The old innkeep flipped back a few pages in the ledger and squinted.

"Her name is Madelyn Everly. She's tall, about my height, and blonde."

"Hmm... Madelyn... Mad... elyn..."

An unsteady finger ran down one page and then another.

"I'm sorry, but I have no guest under that name."

"That's impossible!" Gareth exclaimed. "I saw her off to this very inn myself. Are you sure you're not mistaken? She's a member of the Blackthorn Knights."

"Ah yes, of course! Forgive my confusion, my prince." He closed the ledger. "We have frequent dealings with the Order whenever their officers travel to Cardale. For their safety, we do not include their names in our records. I believe she is still here. Her room is on the second floor at the end of the hall."

It was a relief to hear Madelyn was still at the inn, though a small part of him wished she had left. But this would be the only opportunity to speak before she was to travel off to the west, Gareth reminded himself. It was now or never.

His climb to the second floor was more grueling than it should have been. Each step made his legs feel as if he had scaled a mountain. Not even halfway up, he felt lightheaded and near to fainting. It took every ounce of willpower to drag himself onward.

Come on, Gareth, you can do this. If you don't, what will you think of yourself tomorrow?

Finally, he reached the second floor. It smelled of lemon and lavender, though not overpowering. Dozens of doors on either side of the hall were shut. Which rooms were occupied and which were vacant was impossible to tell. His footsteps were slow and light, and he heard muffled voices coming down the hall.

Could it be? Is she still here? But if that's her, who is she speaking to?

Gareth wiped a thin layer of sweat off his brow with the back of his sleeve. After inching closer to the door, the voices became more apparent. Yes, it was indeed Madelyn. His body suddenly felt weightless, as if falling endlessly from the sky. But there was another inside the room, someone he didn't recognize.

"I can't, Corbyn. We really must be getting back to Bentmont." Madelyn sounded annoyed and desperate.

A trunk lid slammed shut, and a few objects clattered as they fell, obscuring her words. Gareth used the sudden racket and crept closer to the door. Curiously he leaned down to the keyhole and listened.

"We don't need to make an event of it. We can be quick," the unknown man said. "I just can't stop thinking about how you looked the other day. I've never seen such beauty in all my life!"

Gareth heard a soft, wet kissing noise followed by a light exhale. He felt fear, panic, and anger washing over him. Frantically, he knelt beside the doorknob, peering through the keyhole to get a better view. He saw Madelyn standing near a vanity, with the unknown man embracing her from behind. Her face was a mixture of pleasure and displeasure.

"I said no, we don't have time for this. We need to…"

Madelyn fell silent as the man nibbled on her earlobe.

"Come now, love. We won't get another chance until we get back," he said with a grin.

No no no… this cannot be! Please, someone, tell me this is just a terrible dream!

Gareth's mind was a panicked maelstrom of despair, disbelief, anger, and hopelessness. Maybe his eyes were deceptive, he thought. Perhaps the encounter wasn't as it seemed, and Madelyn was being taken advantage of. He stepped back, a fiery hatred rising deep inside. His fists clenched so tightly his forearms were shaking.

I should march in there and put a stop to this. Who does this man think he is to touch her in such a manner?

Gareth reached for the dirk on his belt. He envisioned bursting through the door, confronting the man with steel in hand, and dispatching the would-be assailant in the nick of time. Madelyn's honor had to be defended from such treachery, and thankfully he was in the right place at the right time to do it.

I must do what needs to be done, for her sake.

Gareth moved back to the door with hardened resolve, ready to cut down the honorless dog inside. This would be his chance to prove to Madelyn that he was a man of action and capable of protecting her. He again leaned down to the keyhole to see if it was time to strike.

The bed creaked gently but grew louder and faster by the second. Gareth struggled to find a proper angle to see what was happening. His field of vision was narrow, but he saw Madelyn's naked body on the bed. Her long blonde hair danced like tall grass in the wind, her hips gyrating on top of the unknown man. Her ecstasy was unapologetic and laid bare for her lover to see.

Time itself came to an utter halt. Gareth might have thought he had died if not for the twisting and stabbing in his chest. The pain was so severe he clutched a hand to his breast and groaned. Near fainting, he stumbled back down the hall like a drunkard and paused at the top of the stairs. If only the flight were larger, he thought, then it would be easy enough to fling himself down it and be rid of his agony. Instead, he shambled down the steps one at a time until reaching the lobby.

The old man behind the counter appeared to be saying something. His lips were moving, but only a distant and muffled noise seemed to escape them. His sight was blurry, and the room began tilting and spinning erratically. Gareth had to fight the urge to throw up as he burst through the front door and spilled onto the cobbles outside. The Guardsmen sprang into action and rushed to aid their prince.

"Fetch the Captain and a carriage and as many men as possible. Go now, quickly!" an older Guardsman barked to a subordinate. He assisted Gareth over to a stone bench. Another drew his weapon and ordered everyone within earshot to stand back.

Every tear that fell from his eyes felt like razors. As Gareth sobbed, veins across his forehead bulged and looked as if they might burst from the pressure. It was the greatest and most devastating shock he had ever experienced. Madelyn was the love of his life, the one he wanted to spend eternity with. It was difficult enough to accept that she cared little for wealth and power or even kind words or deeds. But now, after witnessing her in bed with another man, it was clear his affection could never be reciprocated. Her heart belonged to another.

His vision suddenly turned black. He must have fainted. When he awoke, Sir Edmund was beside him inside a carriage.

"There you are," Edmund said, patting him on the shoulder. "You gave us all quite a scare, you know. What the hell happened back there?"

He was too exhausted to speak. Gareth propped himself up, but each bump in the road worsened the pressure and pain inside his throbbing head. Outside the carriage window stood hundreds of onlookers. Word must have spread about the incident and spread quickly. If his fractured heart wasn't enough to contend with, he now had to shoulder the embarrassment of commoners whispering and pointing.

"I don't want to talk about it."

"Very well, you don't have to if you don't want to." Edmund gave him another soft pat. "We'll be back to the Citadel shortly. You need to get some rest."

"No, I can't go back there." Gareth's heart quickened. "I can't be around anyone right now, I just can't…"

"It's alright; heavens know I can't *make* you do anything." Edmund scratched his chin. "If you'd like, you can stay in my room at the barracks for tonight. You'll find plenty of privacy there. The men know better than to go sniffing around my quarters. I promise your family won't find out about any of this."

A meek nod of agreement was all Edmund needed. It wasn't long before they arrived at the outer gates of the palace. It was a relief to be away from the public's prying eyes, but a dreadful feeling to be in such proximity to his family again. As soon as the carriage stopped, Gareth nearly tumbled out, then shambled off toward the barracks.

"I can have some food brought to the room if you'd like," Edmund offered. "Feel free to help yourself to my personal stash if you need to, but I would caution you against it. Sleep is what you need."

The elder Guardsman escorted Gareth inside and led him to the officer's quarters. Fortunately, at this time of day, most of the men were tending to their duties. Aside from the gardens, this was the one place within the palace grounds where he felt comfortable.

"There you go, lad, it's all yours." Edmund gestured to his chamber.

"Are you certain?"

"Absolutely! I'll spend the night with the boys. It'll be a good reminder to them that I'm always around. Some like to forget from time to time."

It was a modest accommodation for someone of Edmund's standing. It had the same plain and uncomfortable-looking rack as the other Guardsmen. Across the room was a simple desk cluttered with parchments. Behind it, a trio of shelves, just as overflowing. The only thing to distinguish Edmund's chamber from the rest of the barracks was a collection of souvenirs acquired from decades of adventure.

On the wall hung a round Droethien shield and dory. Beside it, a two-handed great axe, possibly belonging to a long-deceased barbarian. Other exotic weapons and a few pieces of armor sat on wooden busts. This was the first time Gareth had been inside his friend's chamber. And from what he saw, Edmund Thomas was every bit a warrior, as the stories said.

He turned to give his thanks but found the hall empty. He sighed and shut the door. It seemed too early for sleep, but the day was long and emotionally exhausting. Edmund's bed was indeed as uncomfortable as it looked, but within a few minutes, he passed out cold.

When Gareth awoke, it was dark outside. The barracks had fallen silent, the Guardsmen sleeping peacefully in their bunks. He sat up and groaned, and felt desperately thirsty. Edmund's alcohol stash sat on a shelf near a large wooden chest. Even though he didn't feel like getting drunk, it was the closest thing at hand.

There were a few bottles of bourbon and a small amount of wine. He opened a fresh wineskin and drank it nearly dry with several massive swallows. It was surprisingly sweet and went down as easily as water. It would soon prove to be a mistake, however. Instead of relaxation, he felt claustrophobic.

I have to get out of here right now. And I never want to come back.

He scrounged through some of Edmund's civilian clothes and found a plain brown tunic and hooded cloak to serve as a disguise. Hastily, Gareth threw the clothes over his own, grabbed what remained of the wineskin, and left the barracks. Alone, the prince of Betanthia ventured out into the night, vowing never to return.

EINARR III

"**M**y lord! My lord! The enemy are routing! They have lost heart and now flee!"

The scout shouted frantically, racing down a craggy hillside toward Damien Dreadfire, who sat armored and mounted on the back of a black war horse. Fighting continued to rage, so terrible and deafening it echoed through the pass and off the surrounding trees. Dreadfire's two-thousand-strong cavalry sat patiently as the chaos escalated, thus far content to kill only a few scouts who dared to venture ahead.

"Are you certain? Are their ranks broken?" Damien asked impatiently, his horse kicking at the dusty earth.

"Yes, my lord, they have scattered and now flee through the pass! They're headed this way!" the scout doubled over, gasping for air.

"The time has come, my friend. Are you ready?" Damien turned to Einarr, his face as grim and stony as the hills surrounding the killing grounds.

All Einarr could do was nod. Fear and hesitation turned his bowels into a writhing ball of snakes. This was the largest battle he had ever participated in, far more significant than the massacre outside of Khorrtal. Despite an encouraging report, he felt his hands shaking. It felt bizarre to wear ringmail and a breastplate that once belonged to a

Betanthian soldier. He would need extra protection on horseback, he thought, but death still clung to the metal.

As if somehow able to sense his fear, Damien placed an armored hand on his shoulder. The gesture was of little comfort but forced Einarr to sit straight and mask his fear.

"Take heart. It will all be over soon. Remember Borjifa."

"I'm ready, Damien, to whatever end. By your command, we ride."

A satisfied, bloodthirsty grin manifested across Dreadfire's face before disappearing underneath his blackened steel helm. Einarr sat and stared into the endless dark void of the helmet's eye slits. He sometimes wondered if the demonic visage was, in fact, Damien's true face, a reflection of inner darkness and wrath that began to define him.

"The hour is upon us! Our enemy has lost heart and now flee like the cowards they are!" the warlord bellowed.

A camp follower rushed forward and handed Damien a heavy, pointed lance, which he hoisted above his head with a single hand.

"Let us finish what our brave warriors have started! Honor the gods, and avenge Borjifa!"

Two thousand riders cried out, lifted their lances and sabers into the air, then shifted and organized into a large column. Einarr took position at Damien's right hand and prepared to enter the raging battle. Hastily, he donned an antlered half-helm and drew his bastard sword. It was hardly appropriate for a cavalry charge, but a flood of adrenaline coursing through his veins made the sword feel almost weightless.

"Gods be with us!" Einarr called out, more for his courage than the men's.

"Gods be with us!" the riders echoed in reply.

An unexpected gust of wind rattled the trees and made it seem as if Azldyr himself had responded in favor. Damien drove an armored heel into the side of his horse and began the charge into Blackwolf Pass. Without hesitation, Einarr followed in close pursuit. A thundering of horse hooves sounded like a violent storm had swept over the forest, so deafening the chaos of battle fell silent.

They rounded the craggy inlet of Blackwolf Pass and transitioned from a column to a wedge formation. From the back of his horse, Einarr saw the Betanthians were pushed deep into the pass, within striking distance. Secretly, he wished the battle was miles away and decided by the time he arrived, but the fates were not so lenient.

Hundreds, perhaps thousands of panicked Betanthians broke ranks and routed, which proved encouraging. Less than half continued to stand their ground and fight against an endless onslaught of the warband, who by some divine grace had done what Einarr thought was near impossible.

Gods! Even now, they outnumber us! And yet the battle turns in our favor?

Einarr watched as Damien delivered the pointed end of his lance into the first soldier he encountered. A shower of splinters erupted as the wooden shaft split and shattered into fragments. As he collided with his foes, Einarr lost all sense of himself. He swung his bastard sword single-handedly into one fleeing man, then another, and yet another.

The body of their cavalry slammed into Cedric Valens' army, causing the fleeing enemy to halt and turn back toward their brethren. Frantically, they searched for another escape route, but to their dismay, they were entirely surrounded. This was the moment Einarr had anticipated. Together, he and Damien charged into the enemy mass as far as they could, hacking and slashing at whatever stood before them.

A charging soldier thrust a spear into the neck of Einarr's horse. The beast thrashed about, wailing and moaning, then fell with a thud. Luckily, he was thrown before the horse could land on top of him. Einarr regained his footing as a soldier bore down on him with a short sword. He parried a wild slash, then another, and prepared to answer in kind. But the frenzied foe was suddenly skewered from behind by a Nothanek lancer.

The enemy had grown exhausted. They were without leadership and more afraid than he was. One by one, Einarr continued to cut down any man who stood in his path. He paused to observe another mass of cavalry slam headlong into a formation of clustered soldiers. A resounding crash was so deafening that nearly every man on both sides turned in awe to witness the calamity. Only then Einarr noticed that Damien Dreadfire had dismounted and ventured deep into the enemy ranks, cutting through dozens of Betanthians like a man possessed.

Dear gods, he's going to get himself killed!

A different kind of fear swept over Einarr. He knew if Damien were to fall, the warband might lose heart, and the war would be lost before it had truly begun. Frantically, he pushed and shoved his way forward, desperate to reach Dreadfire.

I'm never going to make it! Gods, please, give me strength!

He called out Damien's name several times but to no avail. The battle had become a blur, a disjointed melee without organized lines to separate friend from foe. A giant soldier clad in steel plate charged toward Einarr from his left and swung an arming sword so quickly, it nearly struck. Einarr lept back and parried with his bastard sword, then continued to exchange blows, their steel clattering and crashing together.

Another violent swing of the soldier's sword nearly caught Einarr in his side, but he was able to deflect the blade and drive it into the ground along with his own. Instinctively, Einarr drew a slender yet lengthy dagger and plunged it into the soft flesh of the man's neck, dropping him as a fountain of blood erupted from the wound, then his mouth.

Valuable time was lost in the exchange. Damien was nearly out of sight, and there was little more Einarr could do. There were too many enemies around him now, so many that pursuing any further might mean his own life. But hope was not lost. He saw the Rhivothi closing in quickly, much to his relief.

"Damien!" Sylvia Stormguard cried out. The shieldmaiden charged, and slammed a round shield into a soldier sprinting toward Dreadfire, knocking the man to the ground. She hacked and chopped him to pieces with a one-handed axe as if he were mutton. Together, they stood their ground and fought with legendary fury. An ever-growing mound of corpses soon piled up around them.

Bonesplitter's roar carried over the clashing of steel and the wails of dying men. Seeing the fanatic and his kin dispatching their enemy with frightening speed was a welcome sight. The typically reserved warchief had entered into a full-blown battle rage, the swings of his great-axe enough to overpower an angry bear.

The killing had become terribly lopsided. Hundreds of Betanthians threw down their weapons and pleaded for mercy. Within an instant, the fighting had come to an end. It took a concerted effort by Einarr to restrain those around him until further orders could be given. A great cloud of dust had been kicked up from the fierce fighting. It began to drift and settle, a stagnant warm breeze blowing through the pass.

"Where is he?" Dreadfire shouted.

Those who surrendered were set on their knees at swordpoint. Some quivered and panicked, though most were exhausted and had given up the last of their hope. Damien approached a man within the group of prisoners and hoisted him off the ground by the neck with a single arm.

"Where is Cedric Valens? Where is he?" The warlord's eyes burned with an unadulterated hatred.

"I… I don't… know."

Choking and gasping, the soldier clawed at Damien's massive hand. He jerked and thrashed about wildly but was released and dropped like a grain sack.

Einarr approached to offer his congratulations on a stunning victory, but Damien was consumed by rage. He glared at Einarr with fire burning deep in his eyes.

"Find that man, and bring him to me," Dreadfire demanded.

It was the only time Einarr had been dictated to in such a manner by Damien, but he paid it no mind. Most of the warriors around him were blood drunk, and he himself had not come down from the rush of battle. Einarr hoisted two prisoners onto their feet with relative ease.

"You, and you, listen carefully. If you value your lives, you will find your commander and bring him forth immediately. Do you understand?"

They nodded frantically and were shoved forward, a handful of warriors accompanying them. Einarr followed closely behind, scanning the massive piles of dead for signs of anything that might identify a lord of Betanthia. Many of the slain were so mangled and crushed it was difficult to tell if they were once human beings.

It didn't take long for the prisoners to locate Lord Valens. Einarr supposed one or both of them must have been near their commander during the battle. To his disappointment, they motioned toward a pile of corpses. Any hopes of capturing Cedric the Butcher alive were gone.

After securing the prisoners, Einarr approached the mound of bodies and sifted through them individually. Many were cleaved and butchered beyond recognition, while those at the bottom appeared to have no such injuries. No, these men were trampled to death, he concluded.

Near to abandoning his search, something unusual caught Einarr's eye. It was the golden trim of what looked to be a cloak. Upon further inspection, it remained attached to a body. His armor bore the King's eagle insignia on his breastplate, and the fineries about his neck, wrists, and fingers gave little doubt this was indeed Cedric Valens.

"Damien!" Einarr shouted, still gazing upon the dead man.

It was a terrible sight, but he could not look away. Cedric's face was smashed into a pulpy ruin. Pieces of broken skull jutted from his flesh like the rocks surrounding Blackwolf Pass. Blood and brain matter pooled in deep pits from the footfalls of men who unknowingly killed their lord.

Einarr heard heavy crunching of plate armor as Dreadfire drew closer. Like heat from a massive bonfire, he could almost feel the warlord's anger.

"Here, Damien. This is him."

He would have liked for Lord Valens to answer for his atrocities against the northern tribes, but such justice would now belong to the gods. Damien's face was a mess of despair, disappointment, and rage.

"For everything you did in life, you deserved to die kicking and screaming by my hands." Damien hawked his throat and spat on Cedric's corpse.

Victory brought little satisfaction to the Supreme Warlord, as Einarr suspected it would not. Damien lusted for revenge, a chance to confront a ghost from his past, and exact righteous vengeance. But the twisted and broken body of Lord Valens would deny him such catharsis.

"I'm truly sorry, my friend," Einarr said softly enough for only Damien to hear. "Trust that even now, Kholdyr sets his wrath upon this monster. He will not get off so easily."

The sentiment did nothing to lessen Dreadfire's anger. This was the moment he dreamt of and labored toward for years. But now that it was over, he seemed to be anything but satisfied.

"It is as the crone says, then. It seems that the fates are set in stone."

Einarr cocked his head. This was the first time he heard Damien speak of such a person. Granted, many camp followers of all ages and persuasions had accompanied the warband on their journey. He sometimes heard of the older women being referred to as crones by his kinsmen, but never in a condescending way. No, instead, they were always spoken of in whispers and wonderment. Some claimed the crones were mystics, who were either blessed with the gift of foresight or had acquired it unscrupulously.

"Who do you speak of, Damien?" asked Einarr, unsure if he truly wished to know. The Nothanek were deeply religious, after all, and shunned the use of black magic.

"Her name is Lazilyth."

It was a name unfamiliar. Perhaps it was a Rhivothi woman or maybe even a survivor from Borjifa.

"And what did she tell you?"

Briefly, Damien Dreadfire's gaze drifted and became lost amidst the endless breadth of the forest. It was the only time Einarr had seen what resembled fear in Damien's black eyes.

"She told me I would taste revenge, but it would turn to dust in my mouth. And the more revenge I seek, the more bitter the taste will become. And I will find the one to either unite or destroy all the free northern peoples, and the task would fall to me to lead this person true."

Such a revelation was shocking to hear. All this time, Einarr thought Damien was the man to unite the remaining tribes. He had spent two years bringing together the Nothanek, the Rhivothi, and the western Zylmacians. And this was still the beginning. Word of their victory at Blackwolf Pass would surely inspire more to rally to their cause.

"Are you certain, Damien?" Einarr asked cautiously. "After all, you've done what no man has done in four hundred years. Are you sure the one to unite the tribes isn't *you*?"

"No. I am simply the instrument of the gods' vengeance. The crone told me I will find her, the last of the Eveldanyr, the one with the power to usher our people into a new era or bring about our destruction."

Her? Einarr thought.

Who might this woman be? Was it Stormguard and her Rhivothi warriors, or was there another who had yet to reveal herself? Such questions made Einarr's weary mind even more exhausted. However, it was intriguing and exhilarating to hear that the Eveldanyr might still exist somewhere in the world.

In ancient times, the Eveldanyr were chieftains of lesser tribes. They were fair and just and thought to be the gods' emissaries. Many old traditions spoke of how the Eveldanyr were mystics and purveyors of arcane arts, all of which were lost to time and Betanthian conquest. If the crone was right and one of them still existed, it might very well mean a shift in the balance of power.

This could be the key to everything. Why did Damien not tell me this until now?

The warlord looked down one final time at Cedric Valens' remains. "It seems today, at least, she is proven correct. Strip his armor and weapons and put them in the wagons. Leave his body for the birds."

"It will be done," Einarr said. "And what of the prisoners?"

Cold and emotionless, Dreadfire glanced at hundreds of soldiers kneeling in the blood and gore of their brethren, then back at him.

"Kill them. Blackwolf Pass will be their burial ground."

The command sent a cold chill running through his body, as if his blood had turned to ice water. Damien had asked many things of Einarr over the years but never once ordered he commit an atrocity. Every fiber of morality within him screamed to stop, to not bring the sword down on defeated and humiliated men.

This is not the Nothanek way, Damien. You know this, yet you demand this task of me? How could I slay these men under the sight of the gods? This is not battle; that time has passed. This is murder.

The warband was watching. Einarr knew if he failed to follow Damien's order, he would lose his station as first among equals. Thousands of men were looking at him, each waiting with bated breath for the order.

Turning away from Damien, Einarr raised his hand into the air. Warriors drew steel and readied their weapons to strike. Others began to chant and stir, baying for more blood.

"No, please! Mercy! We beg of you! Mercy!"

Cries from the prisoner ranks filled him with disgust, not for their weakness but for the slaughter he was about to commit.

Gods forgive me for what I am about to do. But I have pledged myself to Damien, and to avenge your faithful worshippers who these men and their ilk murdered. Let Kholdyr decide if their spirits are clean.

Einarr looked one final time at the men he was about to dispatch and forced himself to feel nothing. He gave the order with a swing of his arm. Warriors began hacking, slashing, and cleaving with merciless fury. Some attempted to flee, but their efforts were in vain.

The killing fields grew silent moments before a roar of victory filled Blackwolf Pass. Rabid screams and cheers soon turned to chants of "Dreadfire! Dreadfire! Dreadfire!" as the warband paid homage to he who had brought yet another victory.

"My lord!" Marvath Bonesplitter cried out, muscling through the gathering. "Twice now, you have brought us victory! Twice you have upheld your vow. Let us remember this day for all time!"

Still hallucinating on mushrooms and seething with fury, Marvath hoisted a bloodied great axe with one hand and beat his bare chest with the other.

"You have honored us with victory, Damien, and we honor you!" Zander stepped forth, his bald head splashed with dirt and gore.

Bonesplitter shot him a distasteful glare. "All hail Lord Dreadfire!" The Rhivothi nomad cried out. The warband echoed his sentiment.

Marvath made to speak again, but Damien silenced everyone with a slicing gesture of his hand. It seemed to catch Bonesplitter off guard, but he checked and contented himself with another leer at Zander as the warriors grew silent.

"You have fought well this day, every one of you." Damien's voice carried an aura of disappointment but remained as stoic as ever.

"Once, we were but separate tribes who stood apart from one another. Though we share the same Khorrish blood, we became lost and divided. We broke faith with one another, and the gods saw fit to punish us for it. But here we stand, united once more. Together we have done what no man thought possible. We have spilled oceans of Betanthian blood, and we have achieved victory."

Hairs on the back of Einarr's neck stood on end. The Bloodbath at Borjifa had finally been avenged, he thought, and the Nothanek would soon return home. Skaginlef would only be days away, a week at most. He smiled first, then laughed, then nearly wept in joy at the thought of it.

Home. I could be back before the harvest! How good it will be to see everyone again. And to visit Alina, beneath her tree…

"Now, we march to Castle Morden!" Dreadfire roared.

His decree was met with resounding approval, but Einarr stood in disbelief. This was the moment he dreamt of for two years, the day Betanthia would be made to answer for their crimes. But Damien's bloodlust had apparently not been sated.

What? Damien, why? What madness has come over you? Victory is yours, there is no need to fight on!

"Gather your spoils and make for camp," the warlord commanded. "We march, come the morning."

Einarr stood silent as warriors stripped the dead of their weapons, armor, jewelry, and clothing. Even the Nothanek were taking part in the looting, but he had not the heart to stop them. Any hope of returning home was gone, and though Skaginlef was so close, it now seemed like it was a million miles away.

His fear during battle was nothing compared to the thought of attacking Castle Morden. Many years ago, he witnessed firsthand the terrible cost fortifications could inflict upon an attacking force. But those he encountered were crude wooden walls and palisades. This castle was made of stone and mortar, designed for only one purpose; to keep men out and break their will to attack.

The aftermath of a battle was hardly a time to protest, but Einarr prayed he might find Damien in a more agreeable state, given their victory. He spied the warlord making his way on foot through the pass. His suit of blackened plate armor must have been unbearable in the heat, as he had begun to strip pieces of it off.

"Damien, forgive me." Einarr's throat was as dry as the earth. "Are you sure it's wise to march on Morden? Some of these men have never seen a castle, let alone attack one."

"We must, my friend. If we do not, they will continue to threaten our lands. If we do not take that castle, we will never be free from danger."

"But the day is yours! The war is over! We set out to bring vengeance to Lord Valens and avenge Borjifa, and we've done just that." Einarr's brown eyes could not hide his desperation.

"This war is far from over, Einarr. You know it deep down inside you. Do you think Betanthia will do nothing after what we have done today? No, they will keep coming, and in far greater numbers. If we do not take Castle Morden, they will have a haven to stage their next assault on our lands."

The price of Einarr's vow was laid out before him. While they had won the day, it was folly to think King Marcellus would let their actions go unanswered. Thoughts of Skaginlef suffering the wrath of Betanthia because of loyalty were too great to bear. His village lay only a short distance from Borjifa, and it could very well be the Nothanek that suffered the next atrocity.

"Take heart, Einarr," Damien continued. "We have destroyed their western army, and the castle should be lightly defended. If we are swift, we can take it with minimal loss."

Should be. There are a lot of things that should be, yet aren't...

"You haven't led us astray, Damien. If this is the best course, then I'm with you."

Einarr was beginning to resent himself. There was always a sinking feeling within him that oaths and honor might come back with unintended consequences. His walk back to camp was in silence from the stifling heat, which had only begun to plateau. Einarr and Damien parted ways; each focused on removing their armor and finding the closest waterskin.

He spent the afternoon beneath the shade of a pine tree. The sun had fallen lower in the sky, providing a small measure of relief. For hours Einarr sat, replaying the battle in his mind. He could not shake the feeling of terror after charging into a frenzied mass of humanity tearing each other to pieces.

He could not believe surviving such a battle was possible, let alone coming out victorious. The face of every man Einarr cut down was seared into his memory. Though he had not the stomach for mead, it became necessary. He still heard the panicked screams of the men Damien ordered executed, which would forever ring in his ears.

The Nothanek were filtering back to camp, and each man who passed by paid their respects. Arik Akselson stopped to give his compliments, but Einarr failed to notice, his eyes staring off into the forest. Had loyalty and devotion to Damien's cause led him to abandon the defining principles of his people? He reflected long and hard on such thoughts.

Is this what I've become now? An executioner? A butcher? Is this how one builds a better world, on the backs of slain men?

"There you are! I thought we might have lost you."

Not even Sylvia Stormguard's bare midriff was enough to garner his attention. The shieldmaiden was carrying her armor, wearing only short, thin linens beneath it. She sat beside him to share a waterskin.

"What's the matter, Einarr? We made history today. You should be celebrating."

Her reply was silence. Sylvia's battle rage had succumbed to exhaustion and blistering heat, and with a clearer head, she could sense something was amiss. "Tell me, what troubles you?"

"I'm just thinking, that's all," he replied.

"Thinking?" Sylvia chuckled. "There will be plenty of time for that later. Come, have a drink with me. Don't be such a stick in the mud. You're still alive, aren't you?"

Leaving her weapons and armor where they lay, Sylvia rose, then pulled Einarr to his feet with surprising ease. The shieldmaiden was quite strong for her size. He gave a half-hearted smile, then followed her reluctantly to a broad canopy tent where camp followers prepared casks of refreshment. A middle-aged woman quickly supplied them with a horn of mead and a skin of water.

"Now, do you care to tell me why your spirits are so low? Judging by your face, you look as if we lost today," Stormguard observed.

"I'm just thinking… about everything that's happened and where it will lead. What happened here today… isn't the end. No, this is just the beginning."

"You're not the only one who has fears, Einarr. If you look hard enough, you can see it in every man and woman's eyes. But we do what we must because this is the path the gods have laid before us."

"I don't disagree," Einarr conceded. "But there will be hell to pay for what we've done here, make no mistake about it, Sylvia. And when Betanthia's vengeance arrives, Skaginlef may be the first to suffer. We're the closest settlement to the border since Borjifa was wiped out. I don't want my village and people to suffer the same fate."

"And why would it? We defeated an army much larger than our own. Our borders will be well-protected."

"The men we killed today are a fraction of what Marcellus Bethard can muster. And Skaginlef lies only a few days from here. I don't think there are enough warriors in all the north to stop a full-scale invasion."

Dreadful thoughts of the Teb running red with Nothanek blood crept into Einarr's mind. He could picture it so plainly, as if he were there in that very moment. He saw butchered bodies strewn about the village, the homes they once occupied wreathed in flames. The mead hall built in honor of Alina's life had become a raging inferno, its thick beams crackling and snapping in the heat, before finally collapsing into a pile of cinders. A disturbing vision, and one he could not let come to pass.

"Then it stands to reason; we must take Castle Morden." Sylvia grasped him by the arm. "We cannot allow them to keep their foothold so close to our lands."

Yes, you're right. Einarr wanted to say but held his tongue.

There would be little use in dwelling on such dark thoughts now. If this was the path the gods started him down, as Sylvia said, then they would see that no calamities would befall the Nothanek.

"You care about your people, and that's nothing to be ashamed of," she said. "Just remember, Einarr, to make each day count because none of us know when the gods will decide our time."

She speaks like a priest. I would never have imagined such a fearsome warrior could be so pious.

Einarr felt the warmth of Sylvia's lips pressing softly against his cheek. It was the second time she touched him in such a way. Before he could react, she ventured away to be with her kin. He brushed a long, knotted lock of brown hair behind his ear and watched as she disappeared.

He spent the waning afternoon hours recovering from battle and the sticky, sweltering heat. Einarr nearly found sleep by sunset, but as the temperature finally relented, the warband came alive. Though Dreadfire had given orders to disperse the following morning, no order would stop the warriors from celebrating their most historic victory.

Burning wood and roasting meat were enough to turn Einarr's stomach into a snarling beast. He remembered he had not eaten since morning. With reluctance, he emerged and sought his supper. Few noticed as he moved throughout camp and over to a roaring fire, where venison was roasting on a spit.

The meat was succulent, but he suspected it might be tainted. A pungent scent was offending his nostrils. Einarr sniffed his meal but noticed nothing. A soft breeze began to blow, and he quickly discovered the stench was not coming from his supper, but Blackwolf Pass.

It was enough to send a cold chill throughout his body and soul. Apprehensively, Einarr looked westward into the darkness. He wondered if the next massacre would be at Castle Morden, and if it might be their men littering the battlefield this time around.

Gods, protect us.

LUCETTA III

"**A**BSOLUTELY NOT," ALDRED GROWLED, GLANCING UP FROM A MESS of papers.

Lucetta was stunned. She stood motionless, processing the shock, unable to utter a single word. After returning home alongside Trace, she stormed into her husband's study to have a word. The conversation already proved to be a mistake.

"I'm sorry, my dear, but I cannot allow you to do that."

After her disastrous trip to the Citadel, she only wanted Aldred to provide the means to clean up the city. She wasn't asking for the impossible, merely men and resources to police the streets better and keep them clean.

"And why not, Aldred? Have you forgotten that I am the King's daughter?" She fiddled with the skirts on her flowing, cream-colored gown.

"I'm reminded of it constantly," he complained. "You must understand, my love, the only ones with authority to order such an endeavor are the King and his council. The laws were written that way for a reason."

"It seems extraordinarily unjust that a Bethard should have to be told anything by anyone." She crossed her arms.

"Please, try not to take offense when I say this. But you and Trace are lesser-born children. And even though Gareth is the heir, he still has no authority to make policy until he assumes the throne. If the law allowed any member of the royal family to do whatever they pleased, then Betanthia would be a disorderly mess. Anyone with a drop of Bethard blood would behave as if they were king."

How dare you call me lesser born. You may as well have slandered me as a commoner! You were nothing but a simple lord before I married you, and lords are plentiful enough.

Anger festering inside her was boiling to the surface. Lucetta had half a mind to leave and spend the following year in Dellhaven if this was the sort of treatment she could expect. It wasn't as if she was asking for something selfish, no—quite the opposite. Improving Cardale's safety and sanitation was an endeavor anyone of sound mind would support, or so she thought.

"So, if you're not going to allow me to straighten this city up, then I can expect you to handle the task?"

After a deep sigh, Aldred rubbed his temples. "I'm very busy right now, my dear. And as I've told you, resources are stretched thin. I'll do my best if I get an opportunity."

Useless. My husband is useless when it matters most. All of his meetings and paper shuffling, and for what?

"Very well then." She stormed out of Aldred's office, shoving past a servant crossing her path.

Trace sat in the dining room, waiting patiently. He stood and made to speak, but Lucetta was quite finished with conversation.

"Sister, may I have a word?"

"I'm going to kill him, Trace. I'm absolutely going to kill him! This is all Gareth's fault."

She was a raging inferno of hatred. Lucetta hurried down the hall and upstairs for privacy so no one could see her anger and distress. Trace followed, huffing, struggling to keep pace, and muttering something indiscernible. Not that it mattered. Nothing he could say would make her feel any better.

"Lucetta. Lucetta!" Trace panted and wheezed and turned a shade of red. His weight and the toll it was taking on his body were concerning.

The door was left open by a maidservant going about her daily cleaning. Luckily for the girl, she replenished a flagon of wine on the table, thus avoiding her mistress's wrath. The maid needed no cue to dismiss herself and made a hasty exit.

"What do you want, Trace?" Lucetta made her way to the wine.

"Can we just talk for a minute?" he gasped.

"What's there to talk about? You saw what Gareth did and how he behaved towards me. It's despicable! And now, because of him, there's no telling when father will be right-minded enough to speak to again!"

Lucetta was seething, the stress nearly too great to handle. Her head ached and throbbed so badly she was nearly in tears. The dark spot in her vision had returned, though this time, it seemed to move about freely from side to side, and was greater in size. She was beginning to think her recent anguish was driving her to madness.

"I know, the whole situation was far from ideal. And the timing couldn't have been worse." Trace sat down to catch his breath.

"Timing? This has nothing to do with timing. No, this has everything to do with our useless brother. In fact, he's worse than useless. He's a detriment."

"Do you even know why he was there?" Trace asked, coughing. "I spoke with mother. Things are getting out of hand over there. Gareth was only trying to protect her. Look, my brother and I have our problems. I cannot remember the last time we had a civil conversation. But you must give him more credit than that."

"How noble of him. Gareth now decides he's going to look out for our family. No, I don't believe it for one second. I find it far more believable that he angered father to get back at me. He's always trying to make a fool of us, don't you see?"

Trace wrinkled his chubby face. He looked terribly confused, as if he had suddenly become too stupid to comprehend anything.

"Sister, I think you're being a bit paranoid. How would Gareth know you were planning on speaking with father?"

It's good to see whose side you're truly on, Trace. After everything we've endured, you're now going to take Gareth's side over mine? How dare you.

"The Guardsmen could have told him we were coming," she hissed. "He's friends with Sir Edmund, that degenerate drunkard. The two of them are probably laughing at us right now."

Merely thinking about being ridiculed made Lucetta's blood boil. Her brother, however, seemed unconvinced.

"Sister, you're taking this too far. You haven't been the same since you went out into the city. I fear that blow to your head may have—"

"May have what, Trace? May have what?" she shrieked angrily, then picked up an empty glass from the table and threw it at her brother's head. It missed and shattered into a hundred pieces against the wall. "Are you trying to say I've gone as mad as father after a little pebble hit me on the head? Is that what you're trying to say?"

Stunned and in disbelief, her brother rose from his chair on trembling legs and stammered in his defense. But it would be to no avail.

"Just get out!" Lucetta screamed and thrust a finger toward the door.

Trace threw his hands up and left without further incident. The door sounded as if it had cracked from the force he used to slam it, but soon enough, it grew silent. After pausing to catch her breath, she stormed over to the vanity to fix her face before dinner. The summer heat and burning intensity of her anger caused her liberal application of makeup to run and smear. She touched up the damage but wondered why making herself presentable for ingrates such as her brother and husband was even necessary.

After combing out her hair and adjusting it to her liking, Lucetta took deep breaths to quell her anger and regain her composure. Dinner would be awkward enough after such a heated argument, but knowing

Trace, he would forget soon enough. While turning to the door, she was suddenly frightened and nearly jumped out of her skin.

Sitting on a chair across the room was a woman she had never seen before. Lucetta nearly screamed in panic but was overcome with shock. How the woman had managed to get inside her chamber was dumbfounding. She appeared tall and slender, with hair to her collarbone, as pitch black as her low-cut, form-fitting silk dress. Her skin was nearly milk white, but perhaps the most frightening thing was the eyes. Bright, orange-red eyes that radiated pure dread.

"Who… who are you? And what are you doing here?" Lucetta stammered. She thought of calling out to the guards, but the words stuck in her throat and refused to budge.

The shadowy woman said nothing but stared back so menacingly it nearly brought her to tears.

"Please…" she squeaked. "Take what you want and leave."

The intruder rose and drifted forward on a cushion of air. As she drew closer, Lucetta noticed her face appeared oddly familiar. It was almost as if she was looking at a reflection of herself, but at the same time, distinctly different. She was beautiful and shapely, but also the most terrifying thing one could imagine.

"I don't want any trouble, please! Please just go…"

"Oh, but you do want trouble," the strange woman said. Her voice was as smooth as satin, yet it sounded like several others were speaking as well. "You want it oh so badly."

"I don't understand," Lucetta stammered. "How… how did…"

Before she could utter another word, the mysterious woman lurched forward, coming mere inches from her face. "Enough with your sniveling. You are a pathetic little child, and you always have been."

A sudden knocking at the door was the most welcome thing Lucetta had heard in ages. Before she could call out to whoever was on the other side, the door cracked open slightly.

"Your Highness," a young servant girl said, stepping inside the chamber. "Sorry to disturb you, but… I thought I would notify you… that dinner will be served shortly."

Frantically, Lucetta glanced at the servant girl and then at the mysterious woman. She thought to cry out for help but noticed the girl paid no attention to the intruder. Even as the stranger passed in front of her and laughed, the servant did not react in the slightest.

"Sorry to disturb you, Your Highness." The servant girl appeared uncomfortable by the awkward silence and quickly dismissed herself.

Am I dreaming? This is the most bizarre thing I have ever experienced. What is going on?!?

"Now, since we were so rudely interrupted," the uninvited guest said, pacing about.

"Who are you?" Lucetta asked timidly. "And what business do you have here?"

The woman cackled in amusement. "You know who I am, child. You have seen me every day."

She passed in front of the vanity but gave no reflection. Lucetta stepped to the side and peered at the mirror from one angle, then another. But the truth was undeniable. The woman in black gave no evidence of her existence beyond what the naked eye could see.

"This… this can't be… You're not real! You're just some, some figment of my imagination. I must be losing my mind."

The shadowy woman sneered, then, with blinding speed, reached forward, grabbed a handful of her auburn hair, and yanked it backward. A jolt of pain nearly made her scream. Lucetta gasped in surprise, but the woman clasped an icy-cold hand over her mouth. A wave of terror washed over her as she realized this was no hallucination.

"Grow up." The intruder smirked. "You have always been a scared little girl. Even with all your wealth and status and delusions of power, you are nothing. Nothing."

It was true. Her whole life, she was always afraid of one thing or another. Whether it was fear of the dark, or wandering into the chambers beneath the Citadel, there was always terror lurking in the back of her mind. As she grew into adulthood, old fears were replaced by new ones. Later in life, she began fearing the confines of marriage and her father's wrath, and witnessing her family's thousand-year legacy come to ruin.

"How do you know?" Lucetta whimpered.

"I know you better than you know yourself," the woman in black said ominously. "If you were not so weak and naive, then you would see the truth, and I would have no reason to be here."

"What truth is it you speak of?"

The entity started toward a lounging room adjacent to the study. She turned and glared, her orange-red eyes glowing and pulsating as if fueled by fire.

"Maybe, just maybe, the fate of your family's kingdom lies not with its princes, but with its princesses." The woman smiled. "Speak a word of this to anyone, and you will die. I will see you soon."

Having spoken her piece, the shadowy woman turned and disappeared into the lounge. After a few seconds had passed, Lucetta worked up the courage to follow. Apprehensively, she paused at the doorway, then peered around the corner. To her horror, she saw only an empty room.

She was terrified. Too terrified to breathe. But as one minute passed, then another, she realized the ghastly encounter had ended and let out a blood-curdling scream.

Six guards charged upstairs and found her in the master bedchamber. She sat curled in a ball in the far corner, shaking and unresponsive. Two attempted to see if she was alright, while the other four searched every room from top to bottom.

After the second floor was scoured and secured, Aldred and Trace were allowed upstairs. They hurried down the hall and into the bedchamber.

"Lucetta! Darling, what's the matter?" Aldred reached out to help her, but she shrieked and pulled away, nearly climbing the wall in terror. The guards took hold of her.

"No! Let me go! Let me go!"

She screamed and thrashed like a wild animal. Her husband and brother looked at each other in confusion, then carried her onto the bed.

"What happened, sister? Are you alright?" Trace asked, then turned to one of the guards. "Have you checked the estate? Did anyone make it inside?"

"We've searched top to bottom, Your Highness, and we haven't turned up anything. We'll keep checking until we're certain it's safe. But for now, we'll stay here."

Both men clutched their swords and scanned the room, ready to act in case the intruder reemerged.

"My dear, what is it? Tell me, what happened?" Aldred never looked more worried or disturbed.

No, I cannot tell them. They would never believe me even if I did. And besides, she might be watching… even now.

And so Lucetta said nothing, much to her husband's dismay.

"She needs rest, Aldred," Trace said, sweat dripping down his forehead. "The stress she's been under lately has been quite taxing. And I'm afraid the trauma of her trip through the city has not yet passed."

"Yes, true enough. I have noticed the change in her these past few days." Aldred turned to one of the guards. "I would like both of you to stand vigil over the room for now, so she feels safe. She needs to rest." He leaned down and kissed her softly on the head. "Now, please, my dear, get some sleep. You're quite safe here. There's nothing to be afraid of, I promise."

Maybe it was just the result of stress, Lucetta thought to herself. She certainly had enough of it over the past several days, more than over the past several years combined. And it was comforting to know her husband and brother were genuinely concerned for her wellbeing. She gave Aldred a meek nod, then shifted and settled herself into bed. Perhaps sleep would do some good.

No more than a second of comfort passed before Lucetta sensed an indescribable dread taking hold once more. Something felt wrong, terribly wrong. Though the heat was sweltering and made the upper floors unbearable at times, her skin turned cold as if a bitter wind swept through the window.

The room began to swirl and become blurry. She was fainting, she knew it. In an instant, her vision turned as black as night. At first, there was nothing, but then a small dot of light appeared. It was faint, then quickly brightened and came into view as if she had opened her eyes for the first time.

Cardale's central square was filled with people. How she managed to get here was a mystery. There seemed to be ten thousand or more gathered, many agitated and jeering, though some laughed and celebrated. Lucetta looked around but could not see over the heads of those around her. The crowd appeared focused on what was happening in middle of the square. She pushed and forced her way through to gain a better view.

A man's voice rang out to silence the massive crowd. After a few attempts, it grew quiet, but still, she could see nothing. Onward she trudged, until spying a barricade with a company of city watchmen around it. She sighed in relief and approached.

"You there! I'm Princess Lucetta Eldon, and I demand you take me to the palace immediately!"

The order went unacknowledged. She moved closer and went to repeat herself but quickly realized he could not see her. Even those she muscled past failed to notice. Curiously, she thrust a finger into the watchman's shoulder.

What in the heavens is going on here?

Lucetta waved her hand in front of the man's face, but still nothing. She decided to cross the barricade and see if it would provoke a response, but still, there was nothing.

Can no one see me? Is this some kind of nightmare?

The experience felt real enough. Searing rays from an afternoon sun. A stale stench of unwashed commoners and their weight as she shoved past them. It could have been a dream, but if it was, then it was the most vivid she had ever experienced.

"Good people of Cardale!" a hulking man in a shimmering steel breastplate cried out. From the insignia near his pauldron, he looked to be an officer of some sort, perhaps even a lord. "You have gathered here today to witness the King's justice. Before you stands the accused."

He gestured to a woman standing on top of a wooden barrel on a gallows. A long hempen rope coiled tightly around her neck, both hands bound behind her back with irons. She was unwashed and wore a simple roughspun gown nearly as soiled as she was. Lucetta moved in closer past the defensive line of watchmen, straining to see the face of the one sentenced to death.

"She is guilty of bribery, murder, and treason of the highest order. Having stood trial before the King's court, she has been found guilty on all counts and sentenced to hang by the neck until dead."

The crowd whispered and stirred. Some booed and taunted. Some flung whatever manner of refuse they could get their hands on. There was little doubt they held no sympathy for the woman, whoever she might be. Lucetta climbed the gallows steps and stood feet away from the prisoner. A hangman clad in a black hood passed by and stood silent.

"Do you have any final words?" the officer asked contemptuously.

The prisoner said nothing but looked up with teary eyes. Lucetta gasped in shock as she saw the woman in black, the one who appeared inside her home. Although she was dirty and her hair was a long mess of tangles, her face was unmistakable. She looked up to the heavens pitifully and whispered.

"I'm sorry, mother."

The officer gave a nod, and a hooded executioner stepped forward, then kicked the barrel out from under the woman's feet. The rope snapped tautly, the crowd roaring as she choked and thrashed helplessly like a worm on a hook. It was over quickly. The woman's body twitched one final time, then went still.

"Good riddance, you bloody traitor," someone said.

What had she done to deserve such a fate? Only the most dastardly criminals were executed publically, so her crime must have been especially heinous. As Lucetta looked into the woman's poor, dead eyes, she could not help but feel pity. It wasn't proper for someone to die like this.

The sun suddenly grew brighter and brighter, a strange sensation washing over her body. Lucetta raised a hand to shield the blinding light, but she awoke in her bedchamber within a second.

It was all a dream, thankfully. The guards Aldred posted outside the chamber still stood vigilantly in the hall. Every window was closed and locked, which made her chamber feel like an iron smelter. And to make matters worse, she was still in her day gown, the thick, layered linen thoroughly drenched in sweat.

Something stirred at the end of the hall, frightening her beyond belief. She peered through the door and watched as the woman in black stepped out of her private chamber. Wide-eyed and terror-stricken, Lucetta watched as the entity turned and sneered, then pressed a single finger to her pale, dead lips and whispered.

"Shhhhhh…"

GARETH IV

Each day had become a long, unrecognizable blur. Gareth had never been more distraught and alone in his entire life. The shock of witnessing his first love in bed with another man had proven too torturous to bear. His only comfort was in taverns and back alleys during the day and alone on the docks at night. Gareth made certain to avoid the usual establishments because Sir Edmund and his men were likely scouring Crown Ferry Road and beyond.

The last thing he wanted was to be found by Edmund or by anyone, for that matter. Returning to the Westwind Citadel would result in a fierce scolding from his mother or his Guardsman friend, which would only worsen matters. Though Gareth was twenty-eight, he had the emotional maturity of a man half his age. That painful realization came one night as he walked along the water's edge by the docks.

I've been denied so much in my life. So many experiences. So many lessons. This isn't how I want to live. Maybe I should abdicate my claim to Trace, go off into the wilderness somewhere, and learn how to become a man.

As appealing as it sounded, there also came an understanding that even if he wanted to run, he wouldn't know how to live off the land. Since the day Gareth was born, countless servants tended to his every need, day and night. Such pampering left little room to grow and develop the skills necessary to survive in a harsh world. In many ways, the common folk he loved to walk among were wealthier than he was.

A full moon cast its warm glow on gently rippling waves. Gareth sat at the edge of the docks with either his fourth or fifth skin of wine; it was difficult to tell how many he had consumed. It was peaceful outside, and the temperature quite pleasant. A massive freighter bobbed gently two piers down. A gull squawked overhead as it foraged for fish at the market. Calm waters lapped lazily at the wooden dock pilings. It was the first time in days he felt somewhat at peace.

I wonder where that ship has been and where it's going. I wonder if they would take me with them, for the right coin, of course.

The thought brought a hint of a smile. There wasn't much for him in Cardale besides his mother and Sir Edmund. But the world outside Betanthia was large, and somewhere was a new place to call home. There had to be more to this life than being locked away in a palace of suffering.

After a few more swallows, the wine was gone. Gareth basked in a cool, salty breeze but grew restless. He felt like walking, and the city's heart was calling like a long-lost friend. The pier wobbled and swayed beneath his feet as he departed, though it could have been the wine taking effect. Thankfully, Crown Ferry Road was vacant, without so much as a patrol from the city watch.

The streets of Cardale were just as empty and quiet. While it was pleasant to traverse the city without throngs of people about, it was also more dangerous. There was no telling when a thief or cutthroat might spring from the shadows with steel in hand and bad intentions in his heart. Gareth kept his dirk at the ready, though in such an inebriated state, he was unlikely to fight off much of anyone.

No matter. If someone knifes me to death, my suffering will be over. Maybe it would be for the better.

He staggered through avenues and alleys with no clear destination in mind. Many places were unfamiliar and not particularly appealing. One thing became abundantly clear; Lucetta was indeed correct. The city *had* descended into abject squalor.

A putrid stench was the first thing Gareth took notice of. The stink of sewage was most offensive and managed to sober him up a bit, albeit briefly. A rat, nearly the size of a small dog, scurried out from a barrel, giving him a sudden scare. Somewhere in a dark corner, a homeless old man groaned pitifully, either from drunkenness or death's cold embrace.

Perhaps I was too harsh on Lucetta. She certainly appears to be right about the condition of the city. And so is Madelyn, for that matter. They've seen what I could not.

Though he tried to forget, the image of his love in ecstasy with another man still lingered. Such thoughts continued to haunt him, turning his sadness into anger, then sadness again. If only he was more aware and gave every princely responsibility the attention required, then perhaps she would not have been so quick to lay on her rejection.

Face it; you're a failure—Lucetta's right about you. If you had self-awareness, Madelyn would have been throwing herself at you.

He knew his shortcomings, every one of them. Gareth recalled a conversation with his father, though it was more of an argument than anything. The details of why they fought were lost to time but likely centered around Marcellus' increasingly tyrannical behavior toward the Queen.

"You're soft and weak, just like your mother," the King said, scowling. "You've got too much of that Taybor blood in you. Sometimes I wonder if you're even my son."

It wasn't an easy thing to confront one's failings. For his entire life, all Gareth ever tried to do was be reliable to the people who mattered most; his family. But sadly, he had given too much to others and taken too little for himself. Now nearly thirty years old, he had no idea who he was.

Edmund was right; I have no focus. No center. They're all right about me.

There was no other time in his life that he wanted to die as badly as right then. He was a failure not only to himself but to everyone else. As Gareth stumbled through dark and empty streets, drinking himself to death or paying a vagrant to cut his throat seemed more appealing.

Nobody will miss me except maybe mother. I seem to be doing far more harm by being alive than if I were dead.

Aimless and stumbling, he wandered about for another hour. A warm glow of red street lanterns illuminated the road ahead. Perhaps this was the fabled Scarlet Streets he had always heard about. Against better judgment, he started down it. Though Cardale was dark and quiet as its people slept, the Scarlet Streets were bustling with activity. Here was where men with proper coin could seek comfort from women of the night.

The Scarlet Streets had grown from a single stretch of road into an entire neighborhood in recent years, and one of ill repute. Gareth had never visited this place nor attempted to find it, and for good reason. On nights when he craved the warmth of a woman, there was always a tavern wench on Crown Ferry Road who was willing to accommodate. And better yet, they were always discreet. At least, most of the time.

The scandal that would erupt if he were found walking the Streets would surely be the talk of Cardale. It would validate every criticism of Lucetta's, and prove he was unfit to be the patriarch of House Bethard. Were it not for his utter despair and blinding drunkenness, Gareth might have turned around and started back home.

It doesn't matter anymore. If I live to see tomorrow, it will be by some miracle. I might as well have one last bit of joy before the end.

Gareth drew up the hood of Edmund's brown cloak and tried to appear as inconspicuous as possible. The first establishment he passed seemed to be little more than a tavern, though the muffled moans from a second-storey balcony suggested otherwise. Each building after was virtually identical, each smelling of sex and cheap wine, and filled with seedy clientele who cast suspicious eyes as he passed. Even though the Streets were cleaner than the slums he had traversed, it was mere window dressing for the debauchery and filth taking place for what seemed like miles.

The first two blocks appeared to host affordable establishments for the common man. Many appeared to be little more than tumbledown shacks and shanties, their edifices weathered and crumbling from decades of neglect. Here, Cardale revealed its sleazy, dark underbelly. It was good that Gareth took Edmund's tunic and cloak for a disguise, or else anyone might knife him without hesitation and strip his corpse bare.

In the hall of a brothel, a singer plucked lute strings and sang a sloppy rendition of a song. A dozen harlots and their patrons laughed, jested, and sang along. They were drunk and unruly, and Gareth could hardly tell what song it was. He paused for a second to witness the spectacle, then moved on.

A stray cat darted out from a shadow, turned and hissed, then slinked away. At a brothel across the street, a pair of burly doormen ejected a hostile patron while a frightened woman cowered behind them. She stood naked with only a sheet for cover and pointed to the offender accusingly, shouting obscenities.

This was certainly no place for a prince, or any man with a shred of dignity, for that matter. Curiosity drove him further down the Streets until he caught the familiar scent of the Camsby River. For a moment, Gareth thought he was back at Crown Ferry Road, where the river's mouth met the Great Sea, but a glow of red street lanterns reminded him that this was anywhere but familiar territory.

The buildings along this stretch of the Camsby were not of weathered and rotten wood, like the ones he passed by. These were much taller and made of stone, with fired clay roof tiles. The expansive glass windows of a brothel revealed a massive chandelier inside. Dozens of candles and crystals reflected light and bright colors throughout the lobby. It almost appeared as one of Cardale's finer inns, though the truth was much more indecent.

This almost looks like the Seascape… Madelyn's favorite inn…

Suddenly, it all made sense. The more upscale establishments were lined up and down the river; he could see it. The waterway would allow wealthy patrons to arrive via a small boat and secretly slip away unnoticed. Gareth pondered curiously, then stumbled to the brothel, careful to mask his face from a few odd passers-by. Thankfully, they paid him no attention otherwise.

The White Rose. Sounds… intriguing.

His forehead was slick with sweat as he stared at an ornate sign hanging outside a pair of cherry-colored doors. With hesitation and a rapidly pounding heart, Gareth entered and glanced around the lobby suspiciously. Certainly, this was a brothel, despite appearing to be anything but. A conspicuous silence juxtaposed raucous debauchery emanating from the lesser-refined establishments.

A red curtain behind the counter rustled, drawing his attention. A tall and shapely woman stepped from behind it in a tasteful yet revealing green gown. Half of her curled, red hair was pulled together into an elaborate updo, while the remaining length swayed gently across her tailbone as she approached.

"Welcome to the White Rose. I am Mistress Abigail. How may I be of service?"

Her high coastal accent was soft yet noticeable. Gold bracelets around her wrists jingled softly as her hands clasped together.

I shouldn't be here. What on earth are you doing, Gareth? Leave now! Leave now before you do something you'll regret!

It was difficult to look away from such a fine specimen of a woman. She was elegant and refined, perhaps of noble birth. There was no indication she was a courtesan or a purveyor of them, but looks were often deceiving in Cardale. Her eyes were like polished emeralds, accented by a dusting of makeup that allowed her freckles to show through. Each glance at Mistress Abigail's beauty made Gareth's heart flutter and breath quicken.

"I… um…" He fought back a belch and fought harder not to pass out on the floor.

It was all becoming too much. The despair. Feelings of failure and worthlessness. Being in such a strange and forbidden place. And his liver reaching its limit. The room was spinning, his stomach becoming more agitated by the second. Mistress Abigail paused and cocked her head. Her bright green eyes widened when she recognized the identity of her newest patron.

"By the gods! It can't be! My prince!" Abigail said louder than she should have, but checked herself accordingly. "My apologies, Your Highness. Please, come in! I would never have expected to see…"

Before she could finish speaking, Gareth stumbled and fell backward onto a table, spilling its adornments on the floor. An unlit candelabra fell with a crash and a clang, and a small porcelain vase shattered into dozens of small, jagged pieces.

"Are you unwell, my prince?"

A more rhetorical question than anything. Abigail saw he was drunk and distraught. She helped Gareth onto a sofa upholstered in red velvet, then rushed to fetch a water pitcher. When she returned, he snatched it away and downed the vessel like a man dying of thirst. For all he knew, he likely was.

"What brings you to the Streets, Your Highness? We get our share of merchants and the odd noble here and there, but never someone of your stature."

Abigail sat next to him and crossed her legs. Even in such an obliterated state, it was impossible not to stare at such a beautiful woman.

Slowly his eyes crept up and down her soft, smooth thighs. He could also sense eyes upon him, unfamiliar eyes studying him intently.

"I'm… I'm not well… I…" The words slowly oozed from his mouth like molasses.

Heavens, what are you doing? You have to get out of here. She recognizes you! If word were to spread that you were inside a brothel, you'll lose every-thing—every shred of respect and dignity, gone. And think of what mother would say!

Though his body was clumsy and uncontrollable, his mind was sur-prisingly sharp. Coming to the Scarlet Streets was a mistake; if he didn't leave fast, it might be the ultimate mistake. He tried to stand, but to no avail.

"I… I have to… to… leave… I… I…"

"No, please, you can't be seen on the Streets like this. You'll be robbed and left for dead! Please, my prince, allow me to help you." Mistress Abigail could sense his distress. "I swear to you I will main-tain the utmost discretion. It's the cornerstone of my business, you know. I wouldn't be here if I spoke of every man who walked through the door."

After fighting back fresh tears, Gareth nodded meekly. There was little he could do in such a condition. Abigail stood and helped him up, and together they retreated to a more secluded location, away from prying eyes. It appeared to be a private lounging room, or it could have been an office. After stumbling to another comfortable-looking sofa, Gareth fell in a heap.

Several of the White Rose's working girls peered curiously through a curtain on the other side of the room. They pointed and whispered with little care for discretion. Soon, more gathered as word spread through-out the brothel. Mistress Abigail was displeased by their eavesdropping.

"Girls, you had best not neglect your customers, or else you'll have to find another establishment to work at."

"We're not neglecting anyone, miss," a thin redhead in a peach-colored dress said, pushing past the curtain. "It's a slow night, and… and we heard that… that…"

"We come to see if it's true!" another girl said as she entered. She had long, dark, curly hair, and eyes the color of midnight. Her skin was light and fair in contrast. "Is it true, miss? Is he… is that the Prince?"

More girls continued to pile up outside the lounge. Gareth saw them staring back at him, though with his vision blurred, he could not tell just how many there were. It looked as if the Streets had poured into the White Stone to witness his presence. They were smiling and pointing; some even giggled.

"Yes, it is," Abigail replied, crossing her arms. "And if you breathe a word of this to anyone, you'll be found floating in the Camsby. Do you understand me?"

A somber seriousness came over the curious girls.

"He wandered in here unintentionally, but the fates are kind," Abigail said, then offered him more water. "If this were any other establishment, I shudder to think of what might happen to him. But this is the White Rose, and we will treat our prince as we would any other patron. With discretion. Now, someone see him off to the upper suite. Poor thing needs to rest."

Nearly twenty girls came spilling over one another like a wave against the seashore, each volunteering and vying for the opportunity. Whether for bragging rights or genuine attraction, it mattered little. Their commotion was nearly too much for Gareth to handle. He clasped both hands against his aching head and groaned.

"I want to, I want to!" a tall, lean brunette bellowed over the others.

"No, me! Please, me!" the thin redhead said. She shoved her way to the front of the group.

"Silence, all of you!" Mistress Abigail fumed. She could not have looked more disappointed and angry if she had tried. "Since you have utterly lost your wits, we'll leave it up to the prince to decide."

She placed a soft hand on his shoulder. "My prince, which of these lovely ladies would you like to look after you for the night?"

The notion of sleeping with anyone made Gareth even more uncomfortable. He stumbled in out of curiosity, not to seek a romp in the bedroom. Thankfully, Abigail was quick to sense his discomfort. She was quite experienced with men and knew how to read them well enough.

"I can assure you, Your Highness; there's no pressure. I would feel much more at ease if someone watched over you for the night. What you do, or don't do, is entirely up to you. The White Rose's hospitality is yours."

The working girls lined up so he could make a selection, but it was all too overwhelming. His eyes could not help but focus on a skinny blonde near the center of the lineup. She was cute but hardly resembled the woman he truly yearned for.

"Her." Gareth pointed.

The blonde girl smiled and curtseyed, then took him by the hand. She led the way through another door on the opposite end of the room. They traversed a long hallway decorated with paintings and tapestries, with doors to the right and left every so often. The brothel must have been well-constructed, as no sound from inside made its way out.

Gareth used every ounce of strength to stay afoot as the girl led him through a set of wide double doors. The suite was unlike anything outside the Westwind Citadel, its splendor rivaling his bedchamber.

Many finer details were little more than a blur, but the wooden floors were polished to such a shine they almost hurt to look at. The walls and furniture were colored in deep reds and soft beige hues, but he was only interested in the bed. It looked even more luxurious and comfortable than his own.

"My name is Clara," said the skinny blonde girl. "How may I be of service to you, Your Highness?"

"Water," he groaned.

Clumsily, he unfastened his cloak and tried to remove his boots but lost balance and toppled onto the floor. Clara quickly fetched a crystal goblet of water as he picked himself up. No matter how much he drank, the relentless grip of wine was too great to overcome.

"Allow me to help you, my prince." She loosened the straps on his boots and slid them off.

Before he could gulp down the remaining water, Gareth's vision went black. He collapsed unconscious onto the bed and fell into a deep sleep.

He dreamt of Madelyn standing beside his bedchamber window. She wore a blue and white gown draped to the floor. Her hair was loose and brushed until it shone like gold. On her head sat a silver crown lined with sapphires. Her belly was large with child; his child. She turned to him and smiled so warmly, it felt like pure sunlight.

Gareth joined by her side. They held each other and kissed with fiery passion. Madelyn took his hand and placed it on her belly, and together they felt a soft kick from the baby inside. It was all he had ever wanted, and he was finally at peace at that perfect moment.

"It's a boy," she whispered lovingly in his ear. "I just know it."

"I love you." It was all Gareth could muster. He was going to be a father, and together with the woman of his dreams, they would raise a future king and further the Bethard dynasty.

"I love you too," she said sweetly, then kissed him again.

It all felt so real. Madelyn's touch. The warmth of sunlight on his face and the feeling of inner peace. But deep down, Gareth knew it was just a dream. He prayed silently to whoever or whatever might hear him that he could stay here forever. But sadly, it was not meant to be. The dream world was beginning to dissolve and fade away.

Suddenly, he awoke. The heavenly encounter with his love was over. Little remained except sadness and emptiness. It was just a dream, and now he was back in a place he did not want to be, with a woman he did not want to be with.

"Did you sleep well, my prince?" Clara asked with a grin, her fingers toying with the edges of his tunic.

"I… yes, I think so."

Oh heavens, I didn't… I couldn't have done… could I?

"Pardon me for asking, but, did… did… we?"

If word got out that he had been to the Scarlet Streets and slept with a whore, it would be the end of him.

"No, Your Highness. You slept like a baby, and I was here to ensure you were alright. Men are known to drown in their vomit when they're that drunk, but you made it through just fine. Not that I wouldn't fancy a go, if you desire."

He sighed in relief. "No, it's… quite alright. You have my thanks for looking after me. And for your discretion, I hope."

Clara smiled and rolled from her side onto her belly.

"Of course, my prince, you have nothing to worry about. Not like anyone would believe me anyways. The Prince of Betanthia, here at the White Rose. And in my bed! Nobody would ever believe it!"

Thank goodness for small mercies. I pray you're right.

"You've done me a kind service. You have my gratitude."

He reached into a belt pouch, removed a few pieces of gold, and placed them in Clara's hand. To his surprise, the girl seemed less impressed by the coins and more by his presence.

"You're too kind, my prince. Our hospitality is yours, for as long as you require it."

Though he had just awakened, he was still exhausted. The ravages of wine had depleted Gareth's body of strength, and seconds later, his head fell back onto the pillow. This time there were no dreams, at least none he could remember. When his eyes opened, it was late evening.

The doors were left shut, and Clara had taken her leave. On a nearby table sat two silver flagons, one filled with water and the other with wine. It was a kind gesture. Gareth sat up, head swimming and throbbing with pain. After putting on his boots and cloak, he went to the table for refreshment. It was then that some of Edmund Thomas' old wisdom, if one could call it such, came back to him.

"Drink to sober up, I always say," the elder Guardsman once said, laughing.

Although Gareth had no stomach for wine, the thundering in his head was too intense to tolerate. He emptied most of the wine in a few large, desperate swallows. Before long, the pressure and pain gave way to a warm, light sensation that trickled down his body.

I've lingered here too long. If I don't return to the Citadel soon, they'll send the whole eastern garrison out looking for me.

The hall outside was empty and still. He walked carefully back to the lounge, focused solely on leaving without being noticed. Gareth peered past the curtain and found Mistress Abigail sitting at a desk, poring over the day's business. A quill in her right hand scratched ink into the pages of a thick ledger.

"My prince!" Her emerald eyes shimmered. "I trust you're well-rested and taken care of?"

"Yes. Your girl... Clara is it, was most accommodating. I cannot thank you enough for your hospitality. I don't know what would have happened if I hadn't found this place."

"You're very kind, and I'm honored we could host you. I can assure you; the girls will never speak of this to anyone, aside from themselves."

"Yes, of course. You have my thanks." Gareth bowed his head.

When Abigail stood from behind the desk, it was hard not to stare. She wore a form-fitting dress as red as her hair, a silver necklace hanging down across her breasts. Such beauty was intimidating to behold.

"I'm sure you'll be wanting to return to the palace. I've arranged safe transport for you, if you so desire. Now is a perfect time; night has fallen, and the city should be empty."

It was embarrassing to think of being shuffled off into the darkness like some lecherous lordling, but there was little choice otherwise. One way or another, he had to leave and return home.

"Very well."

He was taken to the cellar of the White Rose, and through a door leading outside. A small dock sat tucked away inside a cove within the stone walls lining the canal. It would be difficult to see such a place from above, much to his relief. In the water was a small boat with a covered roof. It would be enough to ensure a safe return and shield him from prying eyes.

"Thank you for your visit, my prince. Do remember us."

Mistress Abigail gave a flowing curtsy, then retreated back inside. The boatman wore a hooded cloak, shrouding his appearance. He waited patiently for Gareth to board, and cast off into the dying night.

With a straight oar, the skipper propelled them down the river and toward its mouth at the Great Sea. The waters were still and smooth, a welcome mercy with how unpleasant Gareth's stomach felt. But a rush of wine took hold once again. As often as Edmund's advice proved right, his adage began proving itself unwise.

As the boat made its way out into the mouth of the Camsby, the Westwind Citadel came into view. Gareth felt dizzy for half a second, afraid of what he was returning to. Hopefully, the Queen would not have noticed his absence. The King most certainly could care less about his safety, even if he had turned up dead on the Streets. Though, in all likelihood, the only person who would truly care would be Edmund.

I swear, sometimes the man acts like he's my true father. And the way he guards me, you wouldn't think otherwise.

The boatman rowed into a slip at the end of the docks. Here, the piers were old and unused. Many were aged and crumbling from the unyielding erosion of seawater and time. It was a perfect spot to disembark. Gareth tossed a gold coin to the boatman for his service, stepped onto the creaky pier, and started toward home.

Auburn Row was nearly as empty as Crown Ferry Road, save for rats scurrying near a food vendor's stall and the occasional complaining of a gull. He saw the soft glow of torches at the Citadel's gatehouse, light dancing playfully off the polished steel breastplates of Guardsmen standing vigil.

Best get this done and over with…

Gareth's head ached like an axeman was splitting his skull like a fallen log. A desperate thirst was also returning and getting worse as he anticipated the inevitable dressing-down from Sir Edmund. Passing through the gatehouse proved easy enough. The Guardsmen stood at attention and gave only the most necessary of looks, though he could feel their judgment. He managed only a few steps before a familiar voice called out from across the night-drenched courtyard.

"Gareth!" Sir Edmund shouted. "Where in the hell have you been? I've had patrols all over the damn city looking for you!"

An exhausted sigh and roll of his eyes were Gareth's only answer. He was focused solely on finding another skin of wine and drinking himself to sleep. Possibly even to death if the fates were kind.

"I'm talking to you. What in the hell were you thinking, disappearing like that?" Edmund moved around in front of Gareth, impeding his path.

"I don't want to talk about it."

"Well, we're a little past that now, aren't we?" Sir Edmund growled. "Do you realize the position you put me in? You've been gone for days! Do you realize what would have happened if you decided not to return?"

I wonder if anyone aside from you even noticed I wasn't here.

"I'm in no mood for lectures tonight, Edmund. Leave it alone."

"No. No, I will not," the elder Guardsman said curtly. "For all the years I have watched over you, and for everything I've done to try to help you, I'm owed an explanation."

"I need a drink," he muttered.

Gareth's head was throbbing even worse. He moved to the bubbling fountain at the courtyard's center and sat on its stone rim. A clean mist of water felt light and cool against his face but brought no relief.

"What happened between you and Madelyn? Some of the men told me you went to the Seascape again."

The mere mention of her name made Gareth's breath quicken and chest ache.

"It's ok. You know you can speak to me about anything," Edmund said, sitting beside him.

"I was there, yes," Gareth admitted. "I went to speak to her, tell her of my intentions, and try to end things on a higher note before she left for Bentmont. But before I even made it to the door, I…"

He paused, the words unbearable to speak. Each one made his soul feel like it was dying a bit more. It was too painful to describe what he saw, not without drowning in tears and sorrow.

"I… I saw her, with another man. She…"

"Oh, Gareth." Edmund reached around his shoulders, embracing him. "I'm sorry, lad, truly I am. Your first heartbreak is never easy to endure."

"I feel dead inside. I've never wanted anything in the world except for her affection. Not fame, nor glory, not even the throne. I would renounce my claim if it meant she would be mine."

"Love is a powerful thing." Edmund nodded. "It can make men brave or drive them to madness. But you cannot do this to yourself. You will never gain Madelyn's respect if you react this way."

The sadness in Gareth's heart quickly gave way to anger, both hands tightening and balling into fists.

"She was in bed with another man, Edmund! She doesn't want me. It's folly to pursue her further."

"You can't blame yourself, Gareth. Do you want the hard truth?"

How could it possibly be any harder than the truth my eyes witnessed?

He nodded reluctantly.

"You can feel as down about it as you like, but at the end of the day, she's free to do whatever she desires. You two are not pledged to one another." Edmund stood with a groan, his back aching. "She doesn't belong to you."

An undeniable truth, to be certain, but painful to accept. Tears filled Gareth's eyes, but Edmund refused to coddle him.

"Furthermore," the elder Guardsman continued, "you'll never find a proper woman if you don't start behaving more like a man. I say this not to offend you, but because it's true. Disappearing for days on end because you're in despair is not something a man does. It's the actions of a child."

"You would dare speak to me in such a manner?"

A fire flickered deep behind Gareth's hazel eyes, but his anger was as toothless as the gulls overhead.

"Yes, I would. And yes, I am," Edmund replied sternly. "That fool father of yours never showed you the right way to behave, so someone must. And if you listen, you just might learn a thing or two."

Who does he think he is?

Gareth was stunned. He had expressed nothing but friendship in all the years he knew Sir Edmund. Such a sharp rebuke was as uncomfortable as it was unexpected.

"First off," Edmund said, "you need to let Madelyn go, for *your* sake. She has her own path to walk in life. Now, that doesn't mean you cannot love her, but you need to find yourself a proper princess to wed and have children with. Commoners live different lives from you royal folk. They have different values, dreams, and aspirations."

"The heart wants what the heart wants," Gareth said impatiently, arms crossed. "And what's the second?"

"You need to be more considerate toward others. I'm your friend, and it's my job to look after you. But you've put me in a terrible position by disappearing like that. Your family would have my head if they ever found out."

"My family?" He snorted contemptuously. "Oh yes, because my family loves me *so* much. I doubt they'd notice if I were lying dead on Auburn Row for weeks."

"What about your mother?" Edmund's face was flush with disappointment. "She would certainly notice. You're all she has left in the world, or have you forgotten?"

Thinking about the Queen made his lips quiver. Gareth loved his mother; there was no denying that. Having so much distance between them was regretful since his father's decline.

"I don't want to talk anymore."

"Like it or not, Gareth, you need to—"

"I said I don't want to talk anymore!" His shout carried far throughout the courtyard. "Remember whom you serve, sir!"

It wasn't clear if Edmund's face reflected anger, sadness, or a sense of betrayal, though it was likely a bit of everything. He chewed on the inside of his cheek, carefully weighing his next words.

"As you wish, my prince."

A sudden return to formality made Gareth's heart sink. Before he could apologize, Sir Edmund was heading briskly toward the barracks.

Brilliant, Gareth. You've gone and angered the only friend you have in the world. Now everyone truly hates you.

He called for Edmund to stop and return, but his voice was weak and despairing. It would be useless to try anyway. He stared down at his reflection in the fountain's bubbling waters. He thought it would be simple enough to throw himself in and sink to the bottom if only it were a mile deep instead of a foot or two. A dark, quiet, endless grave was all Gareth felt he deserved.

One of the Citadel's doors was left open to allow fresh air inside. A passing servant glanced outside and noticed the Prince sitting alone. The middle-aged man in yellow and blue silks approached dutifully.

"Pardon me, Your Highness, is there any way I could be of service?"

Gareth remained still, not wanting to be seen crying. "Bring me wine. Bourbon. Ale. Whatever you can find."

The servant hurried away and returned a short time later with a silver flagon.

"Set it down, and leave me," he said.

After executing the command, the servant disappeared, and Gareth found himself alone once again. He expected wine inside but was surprised to find it filled with bourbon. The smell of the fiery amber liquid was enough to turn his thirst into an insatiable craving. His first sips tasted like fine nectar and almost immediately lightened his mood. Gareth gulped down a few mouthfuls, and before long, he felt dizzy and disconnected.

He wanted to walk. Or run. Or be anywhere besides here. It was a tempting thought, but leaving now would surely send Sir Edmund into a full-blown fury. Instead, he decided to roam the palace's expansive and ornate gardens. Rows of rectangular hedges were tall and well-maintained. They formed elaborate winding mazes that led to marble statues, more fountains, and secret alcoves only a lifelong resident would know of.

The gardens seemed to transform under the moonlight and come alive in ways they did not during the day. A soft hum of crickets and an occasional croak of a frog replaced the raucous crowing of birds nested in the trees. Thousands of fireflies glittered in the darkness, accenting the cold light of millions of distant stars with their yellow-green hue.

It was a place of magic and one of the only places where Gareth felt truly at peace. Stumbling and nearly to the point of vomiting, he arrived at perhaps his favorite alcove. It was a small yet cozy nook surrounded on three sides by tall hedges and shrouded by a canopy of viney overgrowth. An old, weathered bench sat alongside red and yellow flowers inside clay pots.

The aged planks creaked and groaned as Gareth lay on the bench and threw his legs over one of the armrests. After a few minutes of discomfort, he removed his dirtied cloak, rolled it into a pillow, and placed it behind his head, content to sleep the rest of the night away. If the fates were merciful, he would pass quietly and be free of the burden of life, or so he hoped.

My father despises me as much as I despise him. My siblings either hate me or could care less whether I live or die. My mother is too consumed by her misery to take an interest in me. The woman of my dreams finds comfort in the arms of another man. And now my best friend is angry with me. Could my life be any more of a disaster?

Gareth sobbed like a child. For someone born into wealth and power and with the world at his fingertips, he could not have felt more worthless and alone. The past several days had exacted a devastating toll on his mind, and not even the familiar warmth of bourbon was of any comfort.

I still have my dirk. Perhaps I should use it.

He lay pitifully on the bench, the collar of his tunic wet with alcohol. His mind began to conjure unnatural thoughts. The gardens would be a good place to slit his wrists and end the misery. It was calm and peaceful here, unlike the raging storm inside his head. Here, there was no pain, only the soft nighttime symphony of nature.

Would anyone notice? Or would my body wither down to the bones before someone found me?

The contents of his flagon were disturbingly low. As Gareth's head grew weary and drifted into slumber, a faint sound of gentle weeping roused him. At first, he thought it was the sound of a gull, but soon enough, he discovered the cries belonged to something else.

Is that what I think it is? Is my mind playing tricks on me?

Gareth rolled off the bench, fell onto the soft grass with a thump, and then struggled to find his footing. The sobbing seemed close enough, but certainly not within the immediate vicinity. Curiously he worked his way back through the maze of hedges and toward another fountain at the garden's center. Once there, the crying was much clearer. It was his mother.

A candle flickered softly from inside Charlotte's quarters above. Recent months had been challenging for her, made worse by her ever-increasing isolation in the wake of the King's more frequent outbursts. None wished to deal with Marcellus Bethard in his current state, least of all her.

I'm sorry, mother. You should never be left to cry alone.

Tired and drunk, Gareth left the gardens and stumbled inside the Westwind Citadel. Its halls were empty of servants, only a few patrolling guards disturbing its tomb-like silence. Shuffling and swaying, he climbed to the upper levels, each step more taxing than the last.

The door to the Queen's chamber was slightly ajar. Warm candlelight poured into the otherwise dreary hall. Peeking inside, he saw Charlotte slumped in a chair near the window. She clutched a small white handkerchief which was moist from tears. He rapped gently on the door so as not to startle her.

"Mother? Is everything alright?" he asked in a near whisper.

When she turned, Gareth saw a tapestry of sorrow draping down her oval face. She tried admirably to smile, though there was little joy to find in much of anything these days.

"Yes, I'll be fine." It was a lie she had grown accustomed to telling.

"I was outside in the gardens when I heard you crying. Please, tell me what troubles you." He sat on a chair opposite the Queen.

"Are you drunk, Gareth? I can smell it." Charlotte saw his soiled and stained clothes, and his face looked nearly as tired and weathered as hers.

"I… yes, I am." He lowered his head and sighed. "I've been having a hard time. But I don't want to trouble you with it."

It was nearly possible to hear the Queen's heart breaking into a thousand pieces. "I'm sorry I haven't been there for you. I've been so overwhelmed with everything as of late," she said mournfully.

"It's not your fault, mother. I know what you're going through with father. And I'm sorry I've been so distant. Life has been a real struggle as of late."

Gareth closed the door and sat at the edge of Charlotte's bed. It was difficult to know what to say, since both appeared lost in their own share of misery. There seemed to be an unspoken understanding between mother and son.

"I appreciate all of your help with your father. I know it's not your burden, and I shouldn't trouble you with such matters. Now, would you like to tell me what's been happening with you? I'm worried."

The question was one he preferred not to answer, though, in some small way, it was refreshing to have someone other than Edmund show concern for his well-being.

"I just feel lost, like my life has no purpose. I've watched my younger siblings surpass me in many ways. They have families and lives of their own, while I'm stuck here without a wife and children, and simply waiting for my father to die before I can make something of myself. I don't live a happy life."

Charlotte's face tightened as she fought back fresh tears. It wasn't easy for a parent to hear their child say such things. She moved to the bed and sat beside him.

"My son…" She touched him on the face. "You're a good man. You're handsome. You have a kind heart and will make a fine king, husband, and father one day. Please, don't despair. Life doesn't work out the same for everyone. But your time will come."

It was nice to hear some encouragement, especially after the tiff with Sir Edmund. But still, Gareth's fears and troubles were not alleviated so quickly.

"But what if my time never comes? Once father dies, and I become king, I'll be even more isolated. Commoners may think kings can do whatever they please, but the truth is, they're less free than even the lowliest peasant. I don't want any of it. I never have."

"I know, Gareth, but don't despair. And please don't do this to yourself any longer. I hate seeing you in this condition. Now, tell me what brought all of this on tonight."

Do I tell her about Madelyn? What would she think of her son and heir being infatuated with a common girl?

There was hesitation initially, but drunkenness had lowered many of his defenses. If there was one thing he knew, it was that honesty would be best. And doing so would help mend the strained ties with his mother, or so he hoped.

"There's this girl…"

Queen Charlotte perked up. It was the first time he saw a genuine smile in what felt like ages. It was good to see her mind shifting away from her suffering.

"Oh? Well, I'm uncertain which maidens are available to court. Forgive me. It's been so long since I was involved in such matters. Is it Lord Eldridge's daughter, Denise? I hear she is quite lovely. Oh, perhaps it's Baron Sheffield's girl, Amelia…"

There was an awkward silence. Gareth shifted uncomfortably, knowing what he was about to say would likely earn him another lecture.

"No, she's… she's…"

"Come now. You know you can tell me anything. Who is she?"

Dashing the Queen's happiness so quickly after it had just returned seemed cruel. But sometimes the truth could create casualties, he supposed.

"She's… she's a Commander of the Blackthorn Knights. Madelyn Everly is her name."

"Oh… I see. A common girl, is she? Or, a nobleman's daughter, perhaps?" Charlotte chewed her lip.

"I wouldn't worry about it, mother. I doubt I will ever see her again. It's probably for the best anyways."

"I know your father hasn't done right by you. He should have found a suitable bride for you years ago, but I promise I will concentrate all of my efforts on it. I want to see you happy."

He touched Charlotte's hand and gave her a half-smile. "No, mother, it's quite alright. I'm more concerned about you. I've seen you cry far too many times."

"Well, there's little I can do, unfortunately. Your father will not let me leave the palace, and he has instructed the Guardsmen to keep me here day and night."

And Edmund never thought to tell me this? Why? What possible reason could he have for not telling me he's been ordered to keep my mother prisoner?

He was angry. Dangerously angry. So much that he was feeling remarkably sober. He resolved his next conversation with Sir Edmund would be a repeat of tonight, only this time, the elder Guardsman would be on the receiving end of a reprimand.

Then again, he is sworn to serve my father, after all. Maybe he was just trying to spare me even more misery.

Either way, such an injustice would not be allowed to stand. Marcellus Bethard may be the king, he thought, but Charlotte Bethard was the queen. And queens were not to be ordered around like subjects nor kept in cages like criminals.

"That's ridiculous, and I will not have it. You are the queen; not a servant, and certainly not his plaything to torment."

An idea came suddenly. If his mother were not permitted to come and go as she pleased, then *he* would be the one to get her out of the

Citadel. Getting away from the King would do them both a world of good.

I would like to see anyone try to stop me.

"Perhaps we could spend some time at the estate in Dellhaven?" he asked. "Leaving Cardale for a while is just what you need. I'll make all the proper arrangements first thing in the morning. We can leave in a few days or tomorrow if you wish."

Before Charlotte could speak, Gareth stood, raised his hand, and interrupted.

"That wasn't a suggestion, mother. You need it, and I'll take you there myself. If father has a problem, he can take it up with me in person."

Tears crept back into Charlotte's eyes, only these were tears of happiness. Many years had passed since she ventured outside the Citadel's walls. Marcellus' paranoia had turned to madness, and he would not let the Queen stray from his sight for fear she would never return. His actions only made such a thing certain, though his mind was too broken to comprehend it. Still, the thought of traveling to Dellhaven excited Charlotte.

"Thank you, Gareth. I know I can always count on you to look after me." She rose and hugged him for what felt like an eternity.

"Get some rest now, mother. Tomorrow, I want you to start gathering your things so you'll be ready. But before I go, I want you to have something."

His fingers fumbled with the clasp of his dirk. Gareth handed her the blade, though she was apprehensive about taking it.

"I... I don't know about this."

Charlotte looked fearfully at the dirk as if possessing such a thing was forbidden. Or perhaps the sight of it had somehow conjured up frightful memories.

"I want you to have it. I won't have father putting his hands on you ever again." Gareth turned and started for the door. "And if he does, you plant it right in his chest and be done."

MADELYN III

"**T**HEN IT'S AS I FEARED." JENSON POWELL SLUMPED IN HIS CHAIR, A clenched fist beating gently against a worn wooden armrest.

"I tried to make them understand. Truly I did. But those pompous fools wouldn't listen," Madelyn said, feeling defeated.

The High Marshal mustered what little of a smile he could, but she could tell it was faux. "I know you tried, Madelyn. It's not your fault. I've come to expect such shortsightedness from Cardale these days."

"But I don't think all is lost," she said. "We do have a sympathetic ear at the Citadel."

"Oh? Well then, this is a most welcome development. Please, continue."

"I spoke with Prince Gareth," she said. "He believed me and expressed a similar concern. He said the Blackthorn may take any steps necessary to safeguard our borders. Gareth will handle it on our behalf should the King or the council object."

Jenson appeared even more unsettled than a few seconds ago.

"Gareth Bethard, you say?" He shook his head. "Forgive me, Madelyn, but the Prince is not exactly… how should I put it…"

"Reliable?" Madelyn shrugged.

"That's one way of putting it. I certainly don't know him as well as you do, but what I do know doesn't impress me much. He doesn't exactly inspire confidence."

"Well, he was very receptive to what I had to say. But unfortunately, Lord Aldred and his lackeys dismissed him just as easily as they did me."

The High Marshal scoffed and grew agitated. "I fear for the future of Betanthia. I truly do. If Prince Gareth allows himself to be run roughshod over, the dynasty may be in its final days. The King is still alive, yet the vultures are already circling, ready to claim the throne for themselves. It will take a strong man to fill the shoes of Marcellus Bethard, and Gareth is simply not that man."

"He did try," Madelyn said half-heartedly.

"Unfortunately, matters like these require more than just trying. If he doesn't learn to be as ruthless in protecting his future throne as Aldred is in usurping it, then perhaps he's not the man to lead Betanthia after all."

Jenson suddenly realized what he was saying, his face turning red, and eyes growing wide.

"My apologies, Madelyn. I should not say such things aloud, much less in the presence of one of my Commanders."

"No need to apologize, High Marshal." She stiffened her back. "But I must ask, where do we go from here?"

There was a brief silence as Jenson's gaze turned to an open window and a blue sky outside.

"Well, I suppose the word of one Bethard is better than none. But as always, it falls to the Order to protect the realm. Let me tell you, this could not have come at a worse time. Our resources are stretched thin as it is. Most of our men are tied up in the Zylmacian borderlands, and our peace with the Droethiens remains uneasy. I have thousands of knights stationed outside Naxonnos. I can't very well pull them out," Jenson said, sighing.

"I understand, High Marshal. But we have to do *something*," Madelyn said impatiently. "With your permission, I want to take a detachment out west. If our suspicions are correct, Lord Valens will need all the help he can get."

Although Jenson nodded in agreement, she suspected something was amiss. It was any guess as to what he was thinking, though every second that passed was another chance the enemy would have to prepare. The Blackthorn needed to arrive, and soon. After what felt like an hour of silence, Jenson finally found a solution.

"The Order will be present on the battlefield. Lord Valens will have every man we can spare. The stakes are far too high."

"Very good. I'll prepare at once." Madelyn turned abruptly and made for the door, but the High Marshal called out before she could manage a half dozen steps.

"You will be staying here, Madelyn, and helping to train the latest recruits," Jenson declared, his words cold and decisive, lacking any emotion. "We'll need to bolster our strength for this conflict should it spiral out of control, and I will require your expertise to get these boys whipped into proper shape, and quickly."

Madelyn turned back to the High Marshal. At first, she was uncertain about what she had heard. Of all the Commanders of the Blackthorn Knights, she was the best and bravest and the only one to never lose an engagement.

"I… I beg your pardon?"

Jenson rose from his seat slowly and somberly. "I will send Commander Marsh to Castle Morden to shore up its defenses. He's a capable leader and would secure the west well."

A sudden, crushing tide of emotion swept over her. She could not believe what the High Marshal was saying. Franklin Marsh was a decent leader but lacked experience and decisive thinking, which set Madelyn apart from others. The situation in the west could prove to be dire, and should their worst fears be realized, Franklin Marsh would not be up to the task.

"But… this is my assignment," she protested. "You tasked me with discovering the meaning of the runes and carrying the message to

Cardale. You trusted me to speak to the King himself! And I did everything you asked. But now? You would lock me inside these walls and let someone else steal my glory? Why?"

"Because it's too dangerous out there. I can not…" he paused, sighing. "I cannot send you on a mission that is certain to be doomed."

Doomed? Was there new information the High Marshal had received that Madelyn was unaware of? Or was he simply overcome by fear? The answer was uncertain.

"But I have never lost a battle!" Madelyn felt tears forming in her steely-blue eyes. "You trained me to fight and lead. I have done so dozens of times, and no harm has ever come to me!"

"Yes, with ten thousand swords at your back! This time I can spare, what, two hundred perhaps? This is a fool's errand, Madelyn. The Order would be in dereliction of its duty if I did not send what I could to protect our borders. But I cannot risk you on this mission, and I need you to abide by my decision."

She shuffled over to a wooden bench beside a window and sat dejected. A rush of sorrow quickly turned to anger, her brooding eyes glaring off toward the horizon.

High Marshal Powell stared at her quietly. She knew it was never easy for him to accept her coming of age, given he had fathered no children, either trueborn or false. The Order was what Madelyn grew up with. It was everything she knew.

She recalled the day Jenson agreed to train her after months of begging and protesting. Madelyn was nearly fifteen and spent years studying the fighting men of the Order as they trained at Castle Thorn, when the High Marshal wasn't looking, of course. She made herself a makeshift sword from an old wooden plank and spent countless hours repeating every motion until it became second nature.

After her first month of formal training, she surpassed men twice her age in swordplay. The High Marshal was proud but always apprehensive.

Madelyn was the closest thing he would ever have to a daughter, which made her first mission a nerve-wracking experience. But Jenson taught her well, and Madelyn was victorious.

"I know you don't like anyone holding you back. You never have," Jenson said calmly, sitting beside her. He placed a comforting arm around Madelyn's shoulders and pulled her close. "I'll never forget the first time I saw you, all those years ago. You were no more than four when I found you outside the gates of this fortress. You looked so sad and terrified, with nowhere to go." He kissed the back of her head. "You looked like you had been living on the streets for weeks, maybe months, and when I saw your sweet face, I knew I had to do something. So I took you in and raised you as my own, even against the tenets of the Order."

With a sniffle and a sigh, Madelyn leaned into Jenson and rested her head on his shoulder.

"Yes, I remember," she whispered.

"I was expecting to raise a daughter, but as you grew, I realized I was raising a warrior. I forget how often I caught you in the armory playing with every weapon you could get your hands on and making your own from whatever you could find. And picking fights with grown men many times your size."

They shared a soft chuckle.

"You were so persistent, too," he continued. "You would ask every day if I could train you to fight like the boys. Sometimes you would ask so much I would lose count. So eventually, you wore me down, and I trained you relentlessly to the point of exhaustion, then pushed you further. And before I knew it, you were besting every recruit in the yard, so it seemed only right to give you a chance to lead."

Madelyn turned and gave Jenson a meek smile, brushing hair away from her face and behind one ear. "I know, and all I've ever wanted was to make you proud... to prove what you saw in me was true."

"You've always made me proud, and you've never had to prove any-thing to anyone, even to me. You have a fierce and unselfish heart, and I know why you want to go out there." Jenson cleared his throat, try-ing valiantly to mask his emotions. "Because in your mind, if you can save even one person from danger, you feel responsible to do whatever it takes."

"You know me better than anyone," she said, sniffling. "And if you truly love me, you'll let me go. It's my duty… it's my destiny to be out there. I was never meant to be kept behind safe walls. You know this. I'm the best Commander in the Order, and if those men out there are to stand any chance against what's coming, they'll need the best."

Somber feelings returned as they looked at each other for what seemed like an eternity. The conversation had now come full circle. Jenson's face tightened as he prepared to confront an uncomfortable truth. Madelyn was no longer a frightened little girl. She was a woman. A woman of the Order.

"Indeed. You realize that should Commandant Valens fail, there won't be anyone to aid you, not for weeks or longer. Are you willing to accept such a risk?"

"I am. I have never lost a battle and don't intend on tarnishing my record."

This is my moment. He cannot take it away from me.

"Very well then."

An icy fire in Madelyn's steely-blue eyes returned. She no longer resembled the little girl Jenson took in, but the warrior woman she had become. With apprehension and perhaps some self-doubt, Jenson rose from the bench and straightened out his tunic.

"Commander Everly," he called out.

Madelyn picked herself up and kneeled before Jenson's feet. "Yes, High Marshal." She placed a forearm on her knee and bowed.

"I task you with taking a company of men and finding Commandant Valens. You are to execute his orders faithfully and defeat this barbarian menace, then return to Bentmont."

"Yes, High Marshal. It will be done."

"Then rise, and assemble your men," he commanded. "You are to leave at once. And speak not a word of this to anyone outside those you have personally selected for your unit."

Madelyn rose to her feet without hesitation. The High Marshal looked stern and proud again but was awash with sadness he could not mask. She gave Jenson a final look before departing the chamber. She thought this could very well be the most challenging mission of her career. It would have been a lie to say there was not a measure of doubt and a healthy dose of fear in the back of her mind.

They've always doubted me. But when I return victorious, they'll never doubt me again.

She rushed to her chamber to gather the equipment necessary for such a lengthy deployment. Her armor was stored on a rack by the far wall. Her steel breastplate had served well on more deployments than she could count, but this time it was likely to see its share of damage. Hopefully, the armor would have integrity enough to withstand whatever the Northmen might throw at it.

Sounds of familiar footsteps echoed in the hall, faint at first but growing louder. There was a pause, then a gentle rapping against the sturdy oaken door. One, then two, then one again.

What is he doing here? And now?!?

It was Corbyn Scott's telltale signal, one he had used many times before. Madelyn could not believe he had come to her bedchamber, not now, not when time was of the essence. It was a wonder she had heard Corbyn's signal in the first place, given the racket of wooden chests slamming and the crash and clang of weapons and tools as they fell to the floor.

"Yes? What do you want?" Madelyn shouted, kneeling beside an open trunk, rustling through its contents.

"It's me," Corbyn said softly. "May I enter?"

"Yes, yes. But be quick about it."

Gingerly the door opened halfway, and Corbyn slunk inside. He wore blue trousers with shin-high black leather boots and a black leather belt fastened around a burgundy tunic. Madelyn did a double take as she turned her head, then cursed silently. She loved how that tunic looked on him, and he was obviously wearing it for a purpose.

"Before you say anything," Madelyn said, flustered. "No, I don't have time for that. The High Marshal was going to send Commander Marsh instead of me, but I changed his mind. Franklin-bloody-Marsh, can you believe it? I'm so unprepared. I need to leave right this instant."

"Where was he going to send Commander Marsh?" Corbyn asked, confused.

Madelyn suddenly realized she had made a terrible mistake. She did not intend to bring Corbyn along; the distraction would be too great, and she would not risk her men finding out about their clandestine love affair, if they did not already know.

"Nevermind, it's… it's just a routine patrol. Nothing you need to concern yourself with."

"Do you want to know how I know you're lying?" Corbyn asked, grinning. "One, because you're terrible at it. You get nervous, and you fidget like a little child in trouble. And two, you wouldn't be tearing through your chamber like this if it wasn't something important. Are you going to tell me what you're really up to?"

The temperature felt like it had increased tenfold, though Madelyn supposed the heat was coming from her reddened cheeks. With a huff, she stood, then sat on her bed. She brushed stray locks of blonde hair behind her ears, chewing anxiously on her lower lip.

"You have to promise me you'll keep this a secret. I wasn't supposed to say anything to anyone."

"Yes, of course. Always." Corbyn sat beside her.

"There's been a terrible attack in the west, and the High Marshal thinks Betanthia's defenses may not be enough to deal with the threat. Since the King's advisors aren't taking this seriously, he's sending me to Castle Morden to assess the situation."

An uncomfortable silence filled the sun-drenched room. She felt Corbyn's disappointment radiating off him. It hurt to leave him behind, but this could be the most dangerous mission she had ever received and needed to remain focused.

"And you were planning on telling me this, right?" Corbyn asked defensively.

"I… no, I wasn't."

Before he could reply, Madelyn raised her hand abruptly.

"You must understand, I can't have you distracting me on deployment. Our ride to Cardale was one thing; there's little danger on the eastern highways. But I'm potentially heading to battle, and a very serious one at that, and I need to keep my wits sharp. I'm sorry. I enjoyed our time in the capital. I truly did. But I need to do my job and bring my men home."

The words were like a sharp slap to Corbyn's face, an unpleasant rebuke he was not used to receiving.

"You're right, this isn't a week-long ride to Cardale. It's a six-week journey to the western border," he protested. "I'm one of the best cavalrymen in the Order, and there's no chance in hell I'm going to let you travel all that way without me."

Why must he be so damned stubborn all the time?

"Corbyn…" Madelyn sighed and rubbed her temples.

She remembered why she turned down Corbyn's advances in the first place. Her entire life was devoted to the Order, every waking minute since the High Marshal found her as a child. All she ever wanted was to excel and achieve what nobody thought possible. And she did just that, but there had always been whispers of scandal and favoritism that tarnished her accomplishments. Succumbing to her feelings for Corbyn had only made matters worse, as the whispers and strange looks became more frequent and less discreet.

"So tell me," Corbyn said, pouting. "Who else is going with you? I imagine it'll take some time to muster a force strong enough to—"

"The High Marshal says we only have around two hundred men to spare," Madelyn interrupted.

"Two hundred?" His caramel-colored eyes grew wide in disbelief. "How are we, I mean, you, supposed to fight anything with only two hundred men? You mean we don't have any sentinels to spare?"

"We have some, but spearmen march too slow, and time is short. I must reach Lord Valens as quickly as possible, so I'll need to ride hard and fast."

The wheels inside Corbyn's head were turning. She could see it. It was no secret the ranks were thin, and resources stretched further than ever. Securing the Droethien border at Naxonnos and the Zylmacian borderlands had been particularly taxing. But Corbyn's realization that so few were left to deploy toward a new crisis shook him.

"Alright, well, you have me. And I have a few dozen lancers under my command here. I don't care what you say; you'll need every man you can get."

He's certainly not wrong. And even then, I fear it might not be enough. I can only pray that Lord Valens is as capable of a leader as they say.

"You're very frustrating, you know?" Madelyn stood and continued to pack her equipment. "You can come along, but you must swear you'll be respectful and professional. I cannot have anyone doubting me or thinking I'm favoring you. Swear it to me, Corbyn. Swear it, or this is where our paths will separate. For good."

"I swear it. I promise I won't even look at you in a suggestive manner. I'm not a fool, Madelyn. I understand the risks, especially with a mission like this. You can count on me."

If you bear any affection for me, then you'll hold to your promise.

"I hope so," she sighed. "I have no problem dismissing you back to Bentmont if I have to. Now, I'm going to have to pick from whoever's here on rotation. Do you know who we have?"

It was hard to say for certain, with the ranks being so depleted. If it weren't for the Blackthorn's reputation throughout Betanthia, and in Bentmont especially, there would be no stopping even a modestly sized mob from seizing Castle Thorn. It would take little to accomplish. And now Madelyn would be stripping the stronghold of over half its remaining men. It was a scenario the Order was ill-prepared for.

"There are only a few cavalry officers around if I recall." Corbyn wrinkled his face. "How about Elite Northcott? I've seen some of his strikers coming and going as of late."

It was a relief to hear a familiar name. Hunter Northcott was an older man and had served the Blackthorn longer than most anyone. Though they never served together in the field, they had developed a healthy bond and respect for one another from their encounters on leave. He was perhaps the most dreadfully unpleasant man to look at, with rows of deep scars accenting a boil-ridden face, which perfectly matched his thick and ugly coastal accent. But he was kind and sometimes felt like an older brother or cousin. Certainly, a mentor, to say the least.

"Excellent, that's the first good news I've heard today. I would prefer more lancers over his light horse, but I'll take him with me any day."

"Let me see, who else is there… Oh, I spoke with Renald Fletch earlier today. He—"

With a scoff and a chuckle, Madelyn interrupted again. "No. Absolutely not. The man is a fool of an officer. I'll never understand why that witless oaf was put in charge of anything other than the privy."

Corbyn could not help but laugh. The man was indeed a halfwit and earned himself reprimands from the High Marshal several times. Yet somehow, Renald maintained his position as an Elite.

"Very well, you won't hear any disagreement from me. There's also Titan, but I would caution against bringing him along. He's quite agitated as of late, based on what I've been told. More than usual."

The mention of his name made Corbyn feel uneasy, which was no small feat. Tylar Bradshaw, or Tylar the Titan, or Titan Bradshaw as he was more commonly known, was a man with a sordid history. No one knew what broke Titan nor when. He was known as a man of honor and integrity, now reduced to a husk of his former self. He was a Commander once but was demoted to an Elite for his rampant insubordination and disregard for the Order's tenets.

"I can't say I've ever had dealings with him." Madelyn shrugged. "What little I do know is by reputation."

"The man is ill-tempered, reckless, and sadistic. He's not the sort of company you want on a long deployment, that's for sure. Couldn't we just commandeer his men instead?"

"I don't know," she sighed. "There aren't exactly any protocols when it comes to that. But he's exactly the sort of company we'll need. I don't need him to follow the rules, I need him to break barbarian skulls. And there's no reason to worry, I'll have you there to protect me."

It was endlessly amusing to watch Corbyn squirm at the prospect of having to defend Madelyn's honor against Titan. She enjoyed a good chuckle at his expense.

Time was running short. Every minute delayed was a minute Lord Valens would be left wanting for reinforcements. And there was no telling how large the barbarian force would be. The uncertainty of not knowing what the Kingdom faced was the most difficult part. Perhaps she and the High Marshal were wrong, and the attack was nothing more than a small rebellion, doomed to fail before the might of Betanthia. There was never a time when she wanted to be more wrong.

Together, Corbyn and Madelyn departed her chamber and made their way outside to the bailey, where they found Hunter Northcott and a handful of men gathered near the stables. Upon seeing their Commander and the First Lance approaching, the enlisted men scattered and returned to their menial duties. Not that it mattered. They, too, would be coming along soon enough.

"Commander," Hunter said, his accent thick and ugly. "What sort of reprimand can I expect on such a fine day? Hm?"

"None. I'm here on business from the High Marshal. Do you have a moment?"

It was more of a demand and less of a question.

"For you, Commander, always." He gave a light-hearted grin, though smiling made him look even more dreadful. But he was a good man, and kind, and that mattered most.

"I've been given a mission out west. I need as many riders as I can get. First Lance Scott and his men are already accounted for, about fifty lancers in all, and I would like to have you and your strikers join me."

After spitting out a mouthful of tobacco juice, Hunter swept a hand across his stubble-ridden chin, flecking away a few lingering drops.

"Aye, Commander, it would be an honor. Most of me lads are away on leave, but I could scrounge up a few, I suppose. When do we move out?"

"Well, before you answer, let me tell you what we're facing. There was an—"

Before Madelyn could say more, Hunter shook his head and raised a hand to silence her. "I beg yer pardon, Commander, but it doesn't make a damn bit of difference where we're headed. If you need me, I'm here. Now, when do we move out?"

Truly, there is no finer knight than you. If only every man in the Order were so selfless.

"This afternoon, if I can find enough riders."

She turned to Corbyn with the same cold professionalism they had grown used to showing when not behind closed doors.

"First Lance, please assist Elite Northcott in rounding up his men. They'll need help gathering provisions if we are to ride before evening."

With a salute, her lover departed and made for the barracks, where he would hopefully scrounge up a number of riders. Hunter went to the stables to see their mounts readied for the journey.

There was only one task left, which filled Madelyn with dread. This would be her first encounter with the man known as Titan. His reputation was not always so tarnished. Quite the opposite, in fact. She didn't know how Tylar Bradshaw earned his nickname, but the stories she heard of his valor were nearly unbelievable.

But Titan also suffered some of the most horrific losses of any Commander in Blackthorn history. When Madelyn was still a girl, she sometimes heard whispers around Castle Thorn, telling of gruesome clashes in the north.

Marcellus Bethard's campaign throughout the upper Plainhold had been costly, and the Blackthorn Knights served as auxiliaries for the King's army. She could scarcely remember the details, it had been so long. But she remembered feeling distraught over the deaths of many men she grew up around.

Madelyn went to the officer's mess hall, where Tylar Bradshaw often lingered. The room was smaller yet more decorated than the hall used by the enlisted men. Without fail, Tylar sat at a small table with a tankard of ale and a pipe filled with a potent herb.

It was shocking to see how many casks of ale he had pillaged, and the evidence of his appetite lay strewn across the bar. Plates of bones from pheasants and ducks and half-eaten potatoes littered its once-clean surface. Madelyn's presence went unnoticed as Tylar puffed rhythmically on his pipe. Plumes of smoke drifted like a morning fog, burning her eyes and lungs.

After clearing her throat and resisting the urge to cough, she sat opposite the intimidating-looking man. Scars and pits covered Titan's face, a literal war map from a nearly endless number of battles. Thick salt and pepper hair covered what remained of scarred and half-missing brows, his vacuous brown eyes distant and glazed over. For a man in his mid to late forties, he looked much older and far more weathered.

"Elite Bradshaw, I trust I'm not disturbing you?"

It was difficult for Madelyn to keep her voice from trembling. She knew rank meant little to such a man; he was as likely to throw her out of the mess hall as to listen.

The burly knight said nothing but continued to sit motionless, staring across the room. An occasional exhalation of smoke was the only sign he was even alive. It was a curious and awkward situation. Madelyn could only wonder what was going on behind his lifeless eyes. She often heard stories of men who had seen too much battle and how the weight of their experience could change them. Sometimes she had nightmares of past campaigns, though thankfully, they were few and far between.

Is he even here, or is he back there on the Plainhold somewhere? Or lost in the northern forests? Can such a man truly escape his past?

She was hesitant to say more, but the High Marshal's orders were too important, and Titan too skilled of a fighter to leave behind. Not like this, sitting alone and rotting away from indifference and too much drink. No, there had to be another way to get through to him. And fast.

"The High Marshal has ordered me to send reinforcements to Commandant Valens in the west. Time is short, and we don't have a lot of men at our disposal, which is why I'm here. I need you to come with me."

Silence was the only reply Madelyn received. Two thin clouds of smoke drifted out from Tylar's nostrils like slithering snakes, but nothing more. A deathly stillness was all the more unusual because her presence still remained unacknowledged.

I'm wasting valuable time. If I can't get through to him, then I'll just have to make do with what I have.

In a move some might consider bold and most downright foolish, Madelyn took it upon herself to pull rank in hopes of rousing Titan from his trance-like state. She swallowed hard and took a deep breath.

"I'm ordering you to gather your gear and ride out with us at once."

Titan still did not flinch, which she mistook as passivity.

"If all you want to do is sit here in a stupor, then fine. Stay here. I'll find another officer who isn't a coward… who is brave enough for the challenge."

It was then that Titan Bradshaw's eyes shifted and locked with hers. She could instantly feel her insides turn to liquid, a sudden rush of fear making her lightheaded.

"Get fucked, little girl. Though I'm sure you're doing plenty of that already," croaked Titan in a deep, rumbling voice.

A large, leathery hand removed the pipe from his mouth and placed it on the table. Without breaking eye contact, he reached down, took up a tankard, and nearly emptied its contents in a few massive gulps. "If you think that little Commander's insignia means a damn thing to me, you're even dumber than you look." He slammed the tankard down, then resumed smoking from his half-expired pipe.

Madelyn's mouth dropped open. She had heard stories and knew Titan was gruff, but their first encounter left much to be desired. How could an Elite of the Blackthorn be so callous? It was as Corbyn said. He was indeed ill-tempered and the embodiment of disrespect.

"If you care so little about the Order, why are you still here? What's stopping you from forsaking your vows and leaving?" Perhaps he would take kinder to a more informal conversation, she supposed.

"They feed me, and they pay me. That's reason enough to stay," Titan replied coldly.

"That is, until you're exiled. Is that what you want for all of your years of service? To be remembered as someone thrown out of the Order he swore to defend?"

Titan leaned in closer and snarled. Scars across his face twisted and contorted, making his appearance ghoulish. "I don't give a shit who remembers me or how they do it. I've paid my dues, and I've had enough of this. All of this."

It was odd, but Madelyn felt pity for the man. She could only imagine what he had seen and what he had done that drove him to such a state. But arguing would be useless, and time was growing desperately short.

"This mission we're going on could be exceedingly dangerous if the High Marshal's suspicions are correct. You would be fine sitting here while your brothers ride off to whatever end?"

"That I would. They're no brothers of mine. All my brothers are dead. If you want to throw your life away for glory or honor or any of that bullshit, then you're welcome to it."

Titan reached for his tankard but discovered it was empty. He cast it down to the floor, the vessel clanging against the dingy gray stone.

"You know, when I was a girl, I used to hear stories about you and how brave you were," she said. "This isn't what I expected, not from a man who spent most of his life in the Order. What happened to you out there, Tylar?"

The question stoked a fire in Titan Bradshaw's cold, brown eyes. He grew agitated and took exception. It was the first indication of any life in him, though Madelyn feared what he might do. Despite her prowess with a sword, Titan could easily wrench her head clean off her shoulders without batting an eyelash.

"You don't have the imagination to picture what I've seen. I've heard all about you, Madelyn Everly. You think you're somehow an expert on warfare because you've won a few battles? Heh!" Titan Bradshaw spat. "I don't linger in the rear issuing orders with a legion of men around me. I fight from the front. Have you ever pulled a man's guts out through his belly? No, of course not. It might soil your pretty little nails."

"I'm no coward. I've fought and bled on the front lines, just the same as you have. But you don't see me slumped in a corner, drinking myself to death."

Madelyn stood and made for the door. Half of her was resentful toward Titan for his disrespect, while the other half feared what he might do if she continued to trade barbs with him.

"You don't know shit," he grumbled. "You know how I can tell?"

Titan rose from his chair and stormed over to Madelyn. It was the first time in ages she felt fear this intense. Her heart and breath were competing to see which could quicken the fastest. He stopped a foot away, then looked down into her ever-widening eyes.

"Because you don't have the stare. Your eyes tell me everything I need to know. You're just a stupid little girl with something to prove. If you want glory, go right ahead and chase it. There's plenty out there."

"Maybe I do have something to prove." Madelyn's spine stiffened defiantly. "But not to you or anyone else. There's a storm coming, Tylar. I won't sit idly by until it's over our heads. I will face it and keep it at bay for as long as possible."

She turned to leave, knowing time was slipping away. The conversation was more than disappointing, but there was little more to be said. Titan Bradshaw was possibly the most stubborn man in Betanthia, and the only one who dared to show such disrespect to her openly. She stopped halfway through the door and contented herself with a final jab for the sake of honor.

"If this little girl is willing to risk her life and you're not, then I guess I know who has the bigger balls."

I can't believe I just said that. Heavens, what's gotten into me?

The audacity of such an insult was perhaps more shocking to Madelyn than to Titan. She quickly decided it was best not to wait for his response. Or, more likely, feel the response of his fists. The harrowing encounter left her with a pounding heart and hands dripping with sweat.

When she returned to the bailey, Corbyn and Hunter looked first at each other, then at her. In her anxiety, she could not tell what they were staring at. Madelyn had turned as pale as a ghost, rivers of sweat soaking through her white blouse. But their eyes looked past her, or rather, through her.

"What is it?" she asked uneasily.

Neither man spoke, then both stepped forward, gripping the hilts of their arming swords. Madelyn looked confused before noticing the ever-growing shadow on the ground beside her. Slowly, she turned and saw Titan Bradshaw standing mere feet away.

He's going to have my head. I know it. Damn you, Madelyn, always trying to prove how brave you are. Now it's going to get you killed!

"That's about far enough there, Bradshaw," Hunter commanded, moving closer to her side.

It was of little comfort to have him and Corbyn nearby. Titan could dispatch all three without drawing a blade if the stories were to be believed. So far, they had all proven true, and Madelyn had no desire to find out if yet another was.

"We're leaving," she squeaked. "You're free to go about your business. I'll raise no complaint with the High Marshal."

As if he would care what Jenson had to say in the first place. How else do you think he got demoted from Commander to Elite? He has no respect for anyone or anything.

"So tell me, little girl, who are you off to fight?" the man known as Titan asked, snarling.

His question seemed more condescending than anything. He might have thought the High Marshal was sending them to quell a rebellion of cattle or sheep for all he thought of her.

"There was an attack near Khorrtal, so the Northmen are likely culprits. We don't know what we're facing," she replied cautiously.

Jenson made her swear not to tell anyone outside of those she chose for the mission, but it was unlikely Titan would go around talking to anyone in the first place. It was easy to see why most chose to avoid his company entirely.

"Northmen, you say?" Titan's mouth twisted and tightened into a frown. "Best of luck to you then. You'll need it if you're subjecting yourself to northern hospitality."

Titan passed by Madelyn and checked his shoulder into Hunter with a thud. As he disappeared into the barracks, the three officers looked at each other with relief.

"What in the world did you say to him?" Corbyn asked, wide-eyed.

"Apparently, it wasn't enough." Madelyn's regret was matched only by her gratitude that Titan reacted calmly to her insults.

He could have killed you at any point, you know. Next time, you might not be so lucky.

After assembling a force of nearly two hundred knights, Madelyn led her men through the gates and began a six-week journey to Castle Morden. If they rode hard and remained on the roads, cutting the time in half was possible. Blackthorn mounts were largely Plainhold Striders, not known for their charging speed but for their endurance. This made them invaluable to the Order and allowed them to move knights throughout Betanthia quickly.

They rode through the congested streets of Bentmont, then out past the city limits. Within the next day, they would arrive at Greenwood Forest, and beyond lay the vast expanse of the Plainhold. Traveling through such a bleak and uninhabited place could prove treacherous if one was not careful. Water was scarce but not impossible to find. Madelyn had learned how to navigate the Plainhold many years ago, though Hunter was far more experienced.

As day turned to night, the band of knights decided to rest their mounts and steal as much sleep for themselves as they could. The sky was a cloudless tapestry of bright stars and a full moon, the largest and brightest Madelyn had ever seen. It would make for good riding weather, which she planned to take full advantage of.

While the knights were fast asleep, Madelyn, Hunter, and Corbyn sat beside a fire and enjoyed a roasted pheasant and a skin of wine. She was not a drinker by any means, but for the sake of solidarity, she partook in a few sips. Together they laughed and shared stories and plans for the future, anything to take their minds off what awaited them in the west.

As the fire dwindled, Madelyn decided it would be best to sleep before returning to the highway. The weeks to come would be trying, and what awaited her in the west would be even more so. No more than a second after she stood to extinguish the remnants of the fire, something stirred in the darkness. It was the sound of approaching horse hooves from the east.

"We're not alone," Madelyn said, drawing her sword, eyes fixed on the black distance.

Hunter and Corbyn took up their swords and stood shoulder-to-shoulder with their Commander. A few knights who were still awake stirred and assembled as well. Some reached for sword and shield should the approaching rider prove hostile.

"Bradshaw?" Hunter asked in amazement.

At first, Madelyn doubted it was Titan. Given their tense confrontation, there was no conceivable way he would agree to join them on the High Marshal's mission. But as the rider drew closer, Madelyn saw the scarred, pitted, and scowl-ridden face of Tylar Bradshaw.

"Titan? What in the world are you doing here?"

Tylar said nothing as he dismounted. He looked at the three of them and scoffed in contempt.

"What does it look like I'm doing? Have you gone stupid, Everly?"

The insult felt like anything but. Madelyn grinned like a fool, though the darkness helped to mask it.

"State your purpose, Bradshaw," Corbyn commanded. "You had your chance to accept the Commander's offer."

"Eat shit, pretty boy," Tylar shot back. He turned casually to Madelyn. "You wanted me to ride with you. I will, but on one condition."

Is he being serious? The most disagreeable man I've ever known wants to make a deal? Now this will make for quite a story.

"State your terms," she said curiously.

"If the High Marshal gives me an honorable discharge when I return, I'll go on this little mission of yours. I've had enough of this life, and I won't be looking over my shoulder day in and day out if I walk away. And I want all my pay and due benefits upon my return. That's my offer, take it or leave it."

A reasonable request, she supposed. Titan's presence on the battlefield would be sorely needed, given their few numbers. And it was no secret that Jenson Powell held Tylar in utter contempt and would likely seize upon the opportunity to be rid of him.

"I accept your terms and will petition the High Marshal on your behalf as soon as we return to Bentmont. If you want out, far be it from me to make you stay. You've earned your retirement."

Tylar seemed surprised initially but was careful not to let it break his rigid demeanor. He gave a curt nod and took up the bridle of his horse, then ventured off into camp. Hunter and Corbyn looked at each other incredulously, but neither held any authority to protest Madelyn's decision.

"Are you sure that was wise?" Corbyn asked as he sheathed his sword.

She smiled, then watched as Titan disappeared into the darkness to rest.

"Is any of this wise? Riding off to a wild frontier while understrength, against an unknown enemy, and relying solely on Lord Valens for support?" Madelyn asked, sensing uncertainty between them. But she couldn't help but smile.

"What's not to like?"

LUCETTA IV

Have I gone mad? Has the unbearable weight of stress and isolation driven all sanity from me? Or am I becoming more like father with each passing day?

Lucetta was frightened, nearly to the point of paralysis. She was too afraid to be alone in her chamber or sit in the courtyard. Merely walking down the halls of her estate was dreadful enough. There was no telling when the woman in black might return.

Accepting the idea that she had seen an apparition was unimaginable. It was not some hallucination, no. The woman in black reached out and touched her, and Lucetta could remember the entity's icy hand upon her face. She felt crazy, as if her grip on reality slowly evaporated by the day. Much more, and she might be shuffled off to the tower for the insane.

This can't be happening. Not to me. Of all the Bethards, why does this curse have to afflict me? Why me and not Gareth? He certainly deserves it more than I do.

But not every day was terrible. There were times when fear and anxiety loosened their grip, and slowly she started to feel normal again. During moments of calm, Lucetta wondered if she was truly crazy, and if the blow to her head had something more to do with it than the physicians said.

One day while walking throughout the estate's grounds, she began to sense an absolute dread creeping back into her mind. Even though Aldred had instructed the guards and servants to keep a close eye on her, she still felt alone and vulnerable. Not even time outdoors was enough to stave off the fear of the woman in black's presence.

That night, her dreams were dark and fragmented. The one thing she remembered was the woman in black strung on the gallows, her lifeless body swaying at the end of a noose. It was a dreadful sight, yet also sad and tragic. Moments before waking, she heard the apparition's voice call out.

"Maybe, just maybe, the fate of your family's kingdom lies not with its princes, but with its princesses."

Lucetta suddenly sat up in bed, the entity's words still echoing in her ears. It was an exhilarating thought that she might be the salvation of Betanthia. But if the woman in black was not malicious, why was she so frightening? It made little sense. She never believed in spirits or the gods, but surely, a benevolent being would be less foreboding.

The thought began to gnaw at her mind like an insect burrowing into a tree. For days afterward, she paced the grounds, utterly consumed by the woman in black's prophecy. Servants had to remind her of breakfast and dinner, or else she might have forgotten to eat.

Today, she settled on much simpler attire instead of the fancy, expensive silk gowns she typically wore. A plain burgundy and white linen dress would suffice. She drew her auburn hair into a simple braid running down the front of her left shoulder. For once, Lucetta could hardly be bothered by appearances.

Indeed, everyone at the estate might have noticed a stark and sudden change in her behavior, but none dared to question it openly. What they thought was irrelevant anyways. The only thing that mattered was what the woman in black said to her. She had not seen the strange entity since that day, but the words it spoke planted so deep in Lucetta's mind she could think of nothing else.

Such a grim sense of purpose filled her with an apprehension she had never felt. Lucetta felt unsafe within the walls of her home, and had wandered the gardens and servant's quarters from sunrise to sunset.

The estate's grounds paled in comparison to the Westwind Citadel, which boasted hedges twice the size of a man and laid out like a labyrinth. Each hidden nook and secluded pathway held its own treasure and had always been her favorite thing about the palace. It was, at times, depressing to be among her own gardens, which were small and plain. But it was better than being trapped indoors, she supposed.

Every movement from a passing servant or caw from a bird overhead nearly sent her into a panic. With nerves becoming more frayed by the hour, Lucetta called for a servant to summon a driver and take her to the palace. There, at least, she would be protected from danger. It was unsafe here, that much she knew. It was a better alternative, even with the possibility of running into Gareth or her mother.

While waiting for her driver, Aldred and a pair of guards approached. At first, she was unsure what to think, and quickly grew suspicious. It was clear someone had informed him. Not even her own servants were to be trusted, it seemed.

"Lucetta, what is going on with you? You've been acting very strange lately, and I would know the truth behind what's troubling you." Aldred's brow furrowed.

Her eyes darted from the guards to the nearby shrubs, rustling from a seaborn breeze. Something was amiss, though she was too overloaded with fear to tell what was benign or malevolent.

"Come now. You need to lie down and get some rest," Aldred commanded, then motioned for the guards to fetch her. "I'm not sure what has gotten into you lately, but it's clear that you're—"

Before the men could take Lucetta by the arms, she jerked away in panic. "No! No, I can't! I can't, and I won't!"

Her attention turned to another man who approached from inside the manor. He was short and thin, with a bald head and a hint of hair on his chin. He wore a flowing brown robe, tattered and stained at the bottom. Slung across his shoulder was a satchel so large he struggled to carry it. He paused at Aldred's side, then discussed something briefly in whispers.

"Lucetta, my love," her husband said softly. "I've brought a physician. He's here to help you. Now, I want you to do everything he says and cooperate, do you understand?"

"No, Aldred, I don't need a physician," she protested, glaring at the guards beside her. "I command you to leave me be. Go. GO!"

"Good day to you, princess," the doctor said. "My name is Dominek. I'm the physician who tends to your parents. You've been under a lot of stress lately. Is that right?"

Lucetta gave no reply but looked around to see if the shadowy entity was watching, its ominous warning still echoing vividly in her ears.

Speak a word of this to anyone, and you will die.

"I can assure you, you're quite alright," he said. "What you need is some rest."

Dominek reached into his satchel, nearly spilling its contents on the ground. "Here, I've brought a tonic that should help relieve some of your—"

"I'm not drinking that!" she shouted with the courage of a child. "Leave here at once. I do not require your potions."

"I can assure you, my princess, you're safe. No one here is going to harm you."

The doctor produced a small flask and a wooden cup. He poured out a few dribbles of tonic and offered it to one of the guards.

"Now, you might feel a little drowsy," Dominek said. "As you can see, princess, it's not poison. He would fall over dead in seconds if it were."

Aldred nodded to the guard, who then drank the tonic, suspiciously eyeing the doctor and his lord. But after a few moments, he showed no signs of poisoning.

"Come now, my love. Enough of this," Aldred complained. "We're only trying to help you. Drink, and get some rest. I won't take no for an answer."

"Aldred…" Lucetta whimpered helplessly with tears in her eyes.

It was the most demoralizing thing she had ever experienced. She scratched the back of her neck until it turned bright red and continued to look for the strange woman, but there were only familiar faces around.

Maybe they're right. Maybe this is all in my head, and I've gone mad from stress. This is all Gareth's fault. If he hadn't angered father, perhaps I wouldn't be in such a condition. Damn him for doing this to me. Damn him!

"Please, my love. I don't like seeing you like this," her husband said reassuringly.

With reluctance, she nodded and agreed to drink the tonic. Dominek poured a larger serving, nearly filling it to the top, then handed it to her. It smelled unpleasant and tasted like spoiled milk. But her eyelids grew heavy within seconds and became impossible to keep open.

When Lucetta awoke, she was tucked safely in bed. It was still dark out, but the sun appeared to be rising. She could only suppose she slept the rest of the day and all throughout the night. Aldred was absent from his side of the bed, likely downstairs in his study or off at the Citadel, tending to early morning council business.

Her slumber was desperately needed and appeared to have done some good. She felt reinvigorated and less threatened by her surroundings. Maybe it was all just a bad episode, she thought, brought on by the stress of her family and fear of barbarian hordes in the west.

Cautiously, Lucetta slipped out of bed, her bare feet gently kissing the smooth wooden floor. Aside from a slight creak of the floorboards, there was nothing. She sighed in relief, then gingerly walked to the wardrobe to change.

"And what do you think you are doing?" the woman in black said. She was sitting cross-legged on Aldred's side of the bed.

Lucetta's heart nearly stopped as she turned and saw the intruder. At first, she wondered how the woman managed to make it inside her bedchamber unnoticed, but was quickly reminded this was no ordinary guest.

"I… I… " Lucetta stammered.

She was so overcome with fear, no words could form in her mouth and instead turned to mush and babble.

"You have spent days wandering around here like a vagrant." The woman rose from the edge of the bed and drifted toward the door. "Grow up. We have work to do."

Work to do? What? I… I don't understand.

"Come, and you will know soon enough," the woman replied.

The coldest chill Lucetta had ever felt ran down her spine. She trembled as if naked in a snowstorm. Not only was the entity an intruder in her home but also in her head.

What? How… how can she hear my thoughts?

The woman was undoubtedly powerful, and Lucetta dared not agitate it further. Instead, she followed helplessly down the hall, then around the corner to her study. The woman's legs appeared to move only slightly. A dark, blurry haze obscured her enough that Lucetta was unsure if the entity was walking or floating. It felt like she was observing the stranger through a dirty lens, the encounter nearly dreamlike.

When she entered her study, the mysterious woman stood beside the desk, looking down at papers scattered about its surface.

"If you are finished acting like a child, sit, and we can begin."

"No. No, not until you answer my questions. You cannot just barge into my home and expect me to follow your every command!"

The woman's orange-red eyes flared so brightly that Lucetta's chill became a burning sensation deep inside her chest. Tiny flecks of sweat formed on her forehead and cheeks, across her chest, and under her arms.

"Very well. Proceed," the entity said.

"Tell me true, who are you? And why have you come here?"

"Who I am is of little importance. And why I have come, well… if you had not interrupted me with your petty questions, you would find out." The woman frowned, the circles around her eyes growing darker.

"Why is it only I can see you? Are you a… spirit?" The mention of such a word made Lucetta tremble.

"I am neither living nor dead. I simply… am. The truth is, I have been with you for some time, watching and studying from afar. However, only now that your mind is permeable can I come to you fully."

Breathing became laborious, as if the air had turned thick as molasses. Lucetta's chest tightened and strained to draw air. The woman cocked her head curiously.

"Does my appearance frighten you, child?"

The entity stepped closer, and as she did, her eyes turned from hellish orange-red to a crystal blue, so bright and piercing they appeared nearly white. Her pitch-black hair softened to a dark blonde hue, a faint hint of rosy warmth filling her otherwise cold and lifeless skin. The black silk dress she wore remained unchanged, however.

"Does this suit you better?" the woman in black asked.

Meekly, Lucetta worked up the courage to give the entity a proper look and nodded. Her presence was still terrifying, but at least now, her appearance was not quite as malevolent.

"Do you have a name?" she asked with reserved curiosity.

"I do not. Names are inconsequential to one such as myself. Call me what you will. It matters not."

"Very well. What is your purpose? Why have you come to torment me?"

"Torment you?" the woman chuckled. "I am not here to torment you. I am here to unchain you."

Lucetta stared blankly, unable to speak or understand what she was hearing. She spent day after day in terror of someone nobody but her could see. And now, the woman in black was trying to say she was here to help? Something was not right.

"I am here because you have no one to turn to and nowhere left to go," the woman continued. "You have no friends or family who care about you. You are isolated and lonely, devoid of purpose. And so, I have come… because you do have a purpose to fulfill. It is written in the stars. The fates have decreed it."

It was one of the most honest and encouraging speeches Lucetta had heard. She always felt there was a greater purpose for her, and somehow, this entity had seen fit to guide her toward it.

"Yes. Yes, I know it. There must be more for me in this life. I refuse to believe I am meant only to be a good housewife while my brother Gareth squanders his inheritance. I want to do great deeds and be remembered as the one who ushered Betanthia into a new era."

"Gareth will not inherit the Kingdom," the entity said coldly.

The revelation was so shocking that Lucetta nearly fainted. Her head grew light and disconnected. She wobbled to the desk and sat, panting for air like a dog. A wall of stifling summer heat was certainly not helping matters any.

"Are you sure?" she asked, rubbing the back of her neck.

"Yes. It is not his destiny." The woman sat on the edge of the desk and stared at her.

"Then tell me, tell me what I must do."

A cautious optimism filled her heart. Perhaps the woman was not a sinister demon after all, but an ancestor or some higher power she could not understand. Lucetta never believed in the gods; their worship was shunned throughout the Kingdom. The practice might very well have been illegal.

The woman in black leaned across the table with a curious and inviting smile. "Your task is simple. You must kill Gareth Bethard."

What? No... no, she cannot be serious.

"What do you mean, kill Gareth?"

There was indeed little love between siblings, but the thought of murdering Betanthia's heir, her own blood, was too much.

"Gareth Bethard will not inherit the throne. It has been written in the stars, so it must come to pass. The fates have willed it. You cannot defy prophecy!"

"No, I cannot do it."

Though she hated her brother more than anyone, the idea of staining her hands with his blood was enough to invite tears. They were not always at odds with each other. Many times in their youth, they were close and loved each other the way siblings should—but those days had passed. Still, she did not wish to see her brother die for the sake of ambition.

"You are in no position to question this mandate, child." The woman's eyes flashed hints of fire.

"No, I cannot, and I will not," she protested. Tears fell from her eyes like soft raindrops. "There must be some other way! Even if Gareth were to die, I still would not inherit the throne. First, father would have to die, then Gareth and Trace. I will not sacrifice my entire family for a crown. I will not!"

The woman in black grew quiet. Lucetta supposed the entity was searching the fates for a different path. She saw faint mists of breath as an icy chill took hold.

"Very well. Not every destination has but a single path. There is another way, but it is more difficult and requires personal sacrifice. Do you have the fortitude to choose the more arduous path?"

"If I must, I must." She stiffened her spine and sat straight. "Yes, I do."

"There is a great storm coming down from the north. Not of ice and wind and snow, but of steel and fire. Will Betanthia survive? That conclusion remains elusive. The fates have many paths, leading to many places. But you must put yourself in a position to capitalize on whatever outcome."

"I don't understand. What is it that I must do?"

"If you do not kill Gareth, then you must carve out an enclave of your own and prepare to strike when the time is right. Should the barbarians be victorious, you must decimate what remains of their armies. Then you shall have a queendom greater than your ancestors could dream of. Your rule will stretch from the Hinterwood to the Forlorn Sea, and across the whole of the Bymist. Should House Bethard win the day, they will be too weak to resist your dominion. They will need your strength and leadership to survive."

The entity's new plan seemed plausible and was worth endorsing.

"And what must I do to forge this enclave? I wouldn't know where to begin."

"Your husband is not the only man in Betanthia with resources. There are others around him you must seek out. If you are willing to do whatever is necessary, the reality I laid before you shall come to pass."

On its face, the proposition seemed straightforward enough. But Lucetta knew there had to be some sort of catch. If killing Gareth was the first option, the second would be more treacherous than the entity made it out to be. Still, if it prevented her from spilling the blood of her family, it was undoubtedly the better option.

"Yes," Lucetta said cautiously. "I'm willing to do whatever it takes."

The woman smiled. "Good. Then I will return to you when the time is right. Until then, rest and recover your strength, Lucetta Bethard. You will soon need it."

It was the first time in years she had heard her maiden name, her true name. It was comforting to hear once again. She watched as the entity stood and gracefully departed without making a single footfall, then disappeared around the corner.

Am I not cursed after all? Maybe the gods are real, and they're the ones that sent this spirit to guide me. I would like to think so.

The encounter left Lucetta drained, both physically and emotionally. But she could not sleep, not at a time like this. Not after hearing what the woman in black had to say. Who were the others she had to seek out, and where would she find them? Where would this enclave be, and how would she create it? Many questions were answered, but now many others also needed answering. It was enough to drive any sane person to madness.

Gareth will not inherit Betanthia. But does that mean he will die anyways? Will he fall on the battlefield or be captured and killed by the invading horde? And what of mother and father? Will they die as well?

She needed a drink, and fast. Thankfully, the servants were always diligent in keeping her supply of wine stocked at every hour. She raced to the table and filled a crystal glass to the top. The dark red wine never tasted so sweet. However, realizing she was becoming so reliant on it was disconcerting. It was alarming enough to see what it had done to Gareth and her father in recent years. And now she was slowly succumbing to her thirst as well.

After swallowing most of the glass, a strange feeling came over her. The woman in black had been looking at something when she first entered, but she could not say what it was. Curiously, Lucetta moved to the desk, each step becoming more cautious the closer she came.

The wine took its toll almost immediately and was a stark reminder of how little she had eaten recently. She set the glass down and peered at the mess of papers.

On top of the stack sat a map of Betanthia, detailing the eastern provinces. Lucetta found it curious because she had not retrieved any of her maps for weeks, possibly months. But this was what the woman in black was looking at.

Her eyes scanned the parchment and noticed a marking that had not been there previously, or so she recalled. To the north of Dellhaven, and somewhere nestled in the protective boundaries of the Siln River, was a dark scratching in the form of an X.

CHARLOTTE II

For the first time in ages, Queen Charlotte felt at peace. It was surreal to be outside the confines of the Westwind Citadel, and she had nearly forgotten what the world beyond looked like. The capital seemed strange and almost foreign to her, it had been so long. Even though Gareth was alongside her, she could not shake a lingering fear that her absence from the palace would incite Marcellus' wrath.

Nearly four dozen Royal Guardsmen escorted her carriage through the streets of Cardale, further bolstered by a heavy presence of city watch. But still, Charlotte grew nervous about the ordeal. Thankfully, Emilee Harper was also making the journey and was there to hold her hand and offer reassurances.

"Everything will be alright, Your Majesty. I promise."

The young maidservant smiled warmly as always, though it was of little comfort at first. Marcellus forbade her to leave the Citadel, and the slightest thought of provoking his anger made Charlotte tremble.

But to her surprise, there had been no incident that morning. Likely, her husband was still passed out from his usual night of drinking and would not notice her absence. But something else caught her attention. The commonfolk turned out in droves to catch a rare glimpse of her. As the carriage snaked through crowded avenues, Charlotte could not help but stare out the window with wonderment.

Could this be happening? Or am I simply dreaming? If it is a dream, I never want to wake up.

She was happy. Truly happy. The people of Cardale had not forgotten about her, even after all this time. Though many cared little for the Bethards, the Queen was always the most revered. It was heartwarming to see smiles and waves along the way, and she made sure to return every one of them. Even Gareth was beaming. He sat mounted on a white destrier and dressed like a true prince ought to be.

"This is your day, mother. Enjoy it!" he said.

It certainly was a dream come true. Although Charlotte was sad her other children were not here to share in the moment, she was grateful to have Gareth.

As the convoy left Cardale, she became sad. The warm reception from the people was invigorating and made her feel loved and important again. She almost wished they could turn around and make another voyage throughout the city before heading to Dellhaven.

They haven't forgotten about me. I would never have imagined it would be so. Thank you, Gareth. Thank you. I'll never forget this day for the rest of my life.

The journey was not unpleasant, despite the heat. Throughout the day, the sun occasionally disappeared behind a patchwork of gray clouds, providing a respite from its oppression. There looked to be rain coming within a day or two, but she would likely be in Dellhaven before then, given the convoy's brisk pace.

"Are you enjoying yourself, mother?" Gareth asked as he rode next to the carriage, smiling. "Isn't it nice to be out in the countryside?"

Charlotte was so overwhelmed with emotion that words escaped her. But she didn't need to speak. Her smile told Gareth everything he needed to know. It was heartwarming to see him happy, especially with how distraught he had been recently. She never wanted to see him so lost and struggling, and she cursed herself for ever being so despondent in the first place.

I'm his mother. He needs me. Marcellus may be vile and cruel, but I cannot let him take the most precious things in the world away from me. I can never let him take my children away.

The sight of Dellhaven was a welcome one. Queen Charlotte could not recall the last time she visited the family estate, but it felt like a lifetime ago. Despite nearly two days of distance between herself and the King, an uneasy feeling still lingered over her. She could only imagine what he might do after discovering her absence.

Come now, you must forget about him for a while, or else everything Gareth has done for you will be for nothing. Besides, Marcellus will likely be too busy with his whores to notice.

Dellhaven was a relatively new town. It was founded by Marcellus' father, King Torbin Bethard, during the first years of his rule. It was built on a scenic stretch of coast and financed by the elite of Cardale as a retreat from the capital's chaos, noise, and squalor. Nearly every wealthy merchant and nobleman had a residence there, and it was the pinnacle of high living, with no other place in Betanthia to rival it.

The Queen glanced excitedly out of her carriage window as the town came into view. There was never a sight sweeter than her home away from home. She wondered how Dellhaven might have changed in her absence. It was sad to think how the world had passed her by in recent years, but no longer. No, not today.

She fidgeted with her dress until Emilee noticed and touched her softly on the hand. Charlotte was a mess of excitement and uncertainty.

"Is everything alright, my queen?" Emilee smiled, knowing how easy it was for her to become flustered.

"I… I…"

Words were simply nowhere to be found. Even though Charlotte was days away from the palace, she could feel Marcellus' eyes upon her, angry, vengeful, and accusing. Something suddenly felt wrong, and not even the four dozen Guardsmen surrounding her could make her feel safe.

But something was reassuring about Emilee's touch. Despite all the breakdowns and fits of crying the maidservant often encountered in her service, she loved Queen Charlotte. Truly. And it showed. Aside from Gareth, she was the one person who was patient, understanding, and kind enough to stick by her.

"I don't know. I just… I'm still worried about what Marcellus will say…" Charlotte chewed her lip.

"I promise you, my queen. Everything will be alright. You're far from home, if you could even call it that in the first place. We're in Dellhaven now, and nothing here can hurt you. We're well-protected. There's absolutely nothing to be worried about. We've arrived for your holiday!"

You have to stop doing this to yourself. You think too much. You worry too much. Let it go, at least for today. You owe it to yourself.

Charlotte poked her head out of the window apprehensively. She saw Dellhaven's walls and dozens of men on horseback beside her carriage. Even the sight of her son riding at the head of the wagon train wasn't of great comfort, though it helped to know he was close.

"Once we get to the estate, I'll draw you a bath. Then, we can walk the vineyards together. How does that sound?"

As proper as Emilee tried to act at all times, she could not help but appear excited. This would be her second visit to Dellhaven since entering the Queen's service, and it was perhaps the best perk of all.

"Yes, I'd like that," Charlotte whispered.

Gareth pulled back on the reins, brought his horse to a halt, and waited until the carriage drew close. Seeing him grown and looking more kingly by the day was surreal. It brought a warm smile to her face.

Though she loved all her children equally, Gareth had a special place in her heart. It was sometimes sad to think of how quickly time had passed. Only yesterday, it seemed, he was running around the palace halls, playing and getting into trouble at every turn.

"Can you smell the salt in the air, mother? We're here! Before you know it, we'll be at the seashore without a care in the world." Gareth smiled and brushed a windblown lock of brown hair from his face.

Charlotte's heart fluttered with excitement. The air did indeed smell of salt, fish, and seaweed. It was cooler here, much to her relief. Summer had been sweltering in the capital, made worse by her daily imprisonment.

"Yes, that sounds lovely," she said.

Dellhaven was less than a mile away now, and the tall sandstone walls excited her again. Gareth brought his horse to a trot and rode ahead to the gates.

"Look at my son, he's so handsome," Charlotte said proudly.

"Yes, he is, my queen," Emilee blurted, though she immediately realized how out of place she was for such a comment. Her face flushed with embarrassment.

"It's quite alright, my dear. You're only stating the obvious."

The Queen leaned out of the window once again as the royal convoy drew to a halt. They were at the gates now, and she saw Gareth conversing with the guards. It was hard to make out what they were saying, but he seemed pointed in whatever statement he was making. The guards bowed deeply, then hastily signaled the wagons to enter.

Dellhaven had become a different town in recent years. The sheer amount of greenery was staggering and more abundant than she remembered. Miles of vineyards and olive orchards stretched as far as the eye could see. They surrounded exquisite chateaus, some standing three storeys tall and made of brown bricks with clay roof tiles. When she last visited, there were only a few estates off the main road, but now Charlotte saw half a hundred or more.

I cannot believe how much this place has grown! It's becoming a proper city in its own right.

The thick scent of salt and a fine mist of seawater were downright therapeutic. Charlotte closed her eyes and basked in euphoria. The cobbled road was smoother here than on the highway, a welcome relief for her aching body.

Residents of Dellhaven emerged from their extravagant homes and came down to the avenue to witness the royal arrival and bestow their courtesies. Though it was home to the rich and powerful, everyone felt small in the presence of the Bethards. She was unsure how to feel after seeing so many people all around. Though witnessing the abundance of wealth and prosperity was thrilling, it was also sad to see how Dellhaven's rustic charm had diminished.

At least it isn't Cardale… and, at least, Marcellus is nowhere to be found.

Twenty minutes passed before the convoy arrived at the royal estate. Charlotte could hardly wait to stretch her legs and be free from the cramped confines of the carriage. As they came to a stop, she climbed out without waiting for the servants to assist her.

Oh goodness, it's even more beautiful than I remember. Lucetta, what have you done!?

Her heart pounded so hard with excitement that she became lightheaded. The sight of the estate, the seashore, the vineyards, and the surrounding gardens was overwhelming. Charlotte felt as if she was going to faint. But before she could, Gareth took her gently by the arm.

"It's been a while since I've seen you this happy, mother."

"It looks so different now, I… I can't believe it!"

While the Citadel was the most lavish residence in Betanthia, she greatly preferred the Dellhaven estate. It was quaint and charming and reminded her of life as a girl in Glimmergulf.

"Yes, there's been some work done to the property. It looks lovely," Gareth said.

The chateau was a three-storey building of white stone with a blue-gray roof. Two additional wings on either side formed a rectangular courtyard. The grounds were immaculately maintained. At the center sat a decorative fountain with a ring of shrubs circling it. Colorful flowers and sculpted trees lined the cobblestone walkway, giving the estate a sophisticated yet relaxed appearance.

Devin Brandybrook, a middle-aged man with olive skin and a head full of curly black hair, greeted the Bethards. Gareth wondered if he was Droethien, though he was likely from Willowsgrove or further south near the coast.

"My queen! What an honor it is to receive you!" Devin exclaimed, bowing flamboyantly. He wore fine blue and gold threaded silk robes and smelled strongly of perfume.

At first, Charlotte barely recognized him. Then came a realization that it *had* been that long since she last visited. How could so much time have slipped away? How much life did she waste while locked away inside the Westwind Citadel? She grew sad for half an instant but also determined not to succumb to her misery and squander a rare opportunity for freedom.

"Devin, it's lovely to see you again. The estate looks beautiful. You've done well with maintaining it."

"My queen, you are as lovely as you are kind. Please, allow me to show you inside for some refreshments." Devin offered his arm, and Charlotte took it eagerly.

A younger man emerged from the chateau and scurried to the wagons as the Queen's maidservant removed several trunks and chests filled with personal effects.

"Allow me to introduce Brendon of Theeds. He will be attending to your every need." Devin snapped his fingers, and the young man quickly turned and bowed.

He was a newcomer to the estate and barely twenty years of age. Brendon wore a red leather jerkin over a white woolen shirt, black linen pants, and leather boots. His eyes were a piercing steely-blue, his sandy brown hair cropped short. With his clean-shaven face, he appeared much younger than he was.

"Oh, that's quite alright, Devin. I have my maidservant with me," Charlotte said politely.

"Very well, Your Majesty. Perhaps Prince Gareth might have need of his services?"

"Perhaps, though, my son has never been one to have anyone fuss after him." She shrugged. "Come now; I'm dying to see how the chateau looks inside."

Brendon of Theeds assisted diligently in offloading the Queen's effects. As he removed a heavy trunk from a wagon, he bumped clumsily into Emilee, who herself was busily disembarking. They glanced at each other and exchanged shy smiles before returning to their duties.

"I can only take so much credit, my queen. Trace and Lucetta have been quite generous with their coin and have spared no expense in renovating the property. They brought in the finest designers and decorations from across Betanthia. I trust everything will be to your liking."

It was curious that neither of her other two children mentioned their work at the estate. Indeed, Charlotte expected Lucetta would do whatever she pleased. Still, it was disheartening to hear that Trace did not consider it important to mention they had drastically altered the chateau. Everyone knew how Charlotte loved it here and made plans to make this her second home. But it seemed getting upset over such a trivial slight would be of little use, she thought.

Devin politely broke from Queen Charlotte and pattered ahead. He opened the ornate glass doors with measured poise and led her inside. She felt a rush of cool air laden with jasmine and a hint of lavender.

Rays of sunshine reflected off a crystal chandelier hanging from the middle of the ceiling, casting pillars of light throughout the room.

Plain sandstone walls were transformed into a tapestry of warm colors. Banners of purple and gold hung from ceiling to the floor, and silvery white curtains rustled gently in a crisp eastern breeze. Several tall oil paintings of past glories and valor hung near finely sculpted marble busts of Bethard kings of old. It was different from how Charlotte remembered. No, it was far more beautiful.

"It's simply marvelous!" She saw the ocean coast through the far windows, its sandy shores a perfect backdrop to a parade of color around her.

She eagerly headed to the master suite in the residential wing. Many of the doors lining the hall were closed. Though Charlotte knew what was behind them all, but it was exciting to imagine how they might have changed.

This place is magical! I could never have pictured it in such a way. My children certainly have exquisite taste.

A pair of wide double doors led into the master suite. Charlotte's heart fluttered with excitement as she opened them slowly, and what was on the other side nearly brought her to tears.

The room was decorated in white and blue from top to bottom. The drapes, bed, pillows and sheets, were all in her favorite colors—even the backs of a pair of tall chairs. A small cherrywood desk sat near an eastern bay window where she could enjoy her reading. An entire section of wall was removed and replaced by a pair of glass doors leading to a stone patio, which hosted a large gazebo.

They did remember me! They may not have told me what they were planning to do, but at least they thought of me.

There had scarcely been a time when the Queen felt so happy and loved. The thought of Marcellus and hardships from recent years slipped further from her mind. For the first time in ages, she felt like the woman everyone once knew.

There was a gentle rapping at the door. Emilee entered, carrying her first haul of bags and chests from the baggage train. She couldn't help but notice the Queen's smile, though glancing around made it obvious why she was so content.

"My goodness, it's beautiful! And your favorite colors too!" Emilee placed a small trunk down beside the bed.

"It's perfect. Like a dream come true!"

"Shall I draw a bath for you, Your Majesty? I'm sure you'll be wanting to join Prince Gareth for some refreshments. Devin informed me the kitchens will be ready to serve at your leisure."

Charlotte agreed. She moved over to the cherrywood desk and ran a hand across it. The surface was as smooth as glass. She opened a drawer and discreetly placed the dirk Gareth had given her inside it.

I won't be needing this here. Marcellus can't hurt me inside these walls. Nobody can.

With Emilee's assistance, she was bathed, dressed, and made ready to join her son for dinner. That evening they feasted on lamb, potatoes, hot bread, roasted carrots, and fresh greens from the estate's gardens. There was little conversation at the table, but as happy as she was, there didn't need to be.

"Something's different, mother," Gareth said between a mouthful of lamb.

There certainly was a lot different at the estate, to be certain. It was a whole new world compared to life back in Cardale. Charlotte thought little of the comment at first but then cocked her head.

"You're happy." He smiled.

Was it so obvious she had been living in misery before leaving the capital? Had her smiles grown so infrequent?

"Yes, yes, I am. And I wouldn't be this happy if it weren't for you."

"I can't take any of the credit, mother. You needed to get away from the Citadel, and badly."

Memories of the night before they left came back to her. Seeing Gareth in such despair was heartbreaking. He was nearly drunk enough to give Marcellus pause. The time away from the palace appeared to be doing him some good already.

"As did you," Charlotte stated. "We both needed to get away from that place. It can exact a heavy toll on a person, especially someone whose heart isn't cold."

"You're right, mother. It certainly doesn't help that the man who resides there seems to enjoy making our lives a living hell."

"Your father wasn't always this way, Gareth. That's what makes it all so difficult. I remember when he was the opposite of what he is now."

"I don't even think of him as my father anymore," her son said coldly.

"Gareth!" Charlotte gasped. "He's still your father, you know. Nothing can ever change that."

"Any semblance of the man he used to be died years ago. I remember when he was kind, brave, and cunning, but those days are gone and never to return. I don't blame him for the wounds he suffered on the battlefield. Truly I don't. But I do blame him for not trying hard enough to look after his family. And to at least leave some sort of legacy behind. People tend not to remember the deeds you've done throughout your life. They remember what you left behind and the state in which you left it."

He's certainly not wrong. I've often wondered what I'll be leaving behind one day.

Gareth had a certain wisdom about him that she could not explain. Charlotte once heard someone say that wisdom beyond one's years was proof of having an old soul. He most certainly had Lord Taybor's blood in him. Sometimes, she could almost see her father's reflection in Gareth's face.

"I can't profess to know what goes on inside his head," Charlotte said. "But I do hope you know that he loves you. I saw his face when he looked upon you for the first time. He cried tears of joy when he held you in his arms."

"Mother," Gareth interrupted. "Those days have long since passed. Whatever man he used to be, he no longer is. I accepted this a while ago. Forgive my rashness, but leaving those memories behind would be easier. Clinging to the past is no way to move forward."

Charlotte picked at her potatoes. "Perhaps, yes."

It wasn't easy to accept that her life turned out the way it did, but some time away from the Citadel's chaos seemed to help. Knowing how Marcellus treated his only daughter and grandchildren, her father was likely spinning in his grave. It was a great injustice, perhaps the greatest of all. But sitting across from her was the one silver lining; Gareth.

Despite the familiar yet new surroundings, rest did not come easy that night. Charlotte learned to sleep with one eye open at the palace, or sometimes not at all if Marcellus was in a drunken rage. Night terrors took hold when she was fortunate enough to doze off. There were times when the stink of his breath and the feel of his fingers around her neck would jolt her awake, panting and covered with sweat. It wasn't until the fourth night at the chateau that she could rest easier.

That morning, Devin treated everyone to a delicious breakfast under the shade of a willow tree. For dessert, he presented a platter of fig tarts, one of her favorite sweets. Charlotte took notice of Gareth and how healthy he looked, even after such a short time. Emilee said he had not consumed a single drink since arriving in Dellhaven, and had confirmed as much with the other servants.

"Gareth," she said as Devin and Brendon cleared the dishes. "Do you remember what you told me a few days ago about how I looked happier?"

"Yes, mother, I remember. And it's true. You look restored."

"Well, I just wanted to tell you I see the same in you. You look..." She paused, searching for the right words, but finding them amidst the sea of her emotions was difficult. "You look like the son I remember.

I'm sorry I haven't been there for you. I'm sorry I've let you slip so far into darkness and despair."

"You mustn't blame yourself for my actions, mother," Gareth said." My life isn't your burden to bear. Come now, let's walk."

"Later, perhaps. I've grown weary."

Though the day was young, Queen Charlotte felt exhausted and in need of rest. She spent the rest of the day in bed, relaxing and drifting in and out of sleep. Her body yearned for it and could have easily slept for a week straight, perhaps even two or three. Certainly, nobody would fault her for it, and nor did they.

With each passing day, her spirits grew brighter. Charlotte spent her time walking through the chateau vineyards and ornate gardens, and made a routine of sitting beside a decorative fountain after lunch. She always enjoyed being out in nature but relished it more as of late. Even at the Westwind Citadel, she was seldom allowed to walk the palace grounds. But here she was free.

One particularly hot day, she decided to walk to the seashore. An eastern breeze was crisp and cool and a welcome relief from the summer heat. She walked barefoot across the beach, hot sand burning the tender skin between her toes. But gentle waves splashed against her feet and soothed them with cool, wet kisses.

Charlotte was reminded of her wedding day, back when times were happier. She remembered it vividly, though now the memories were melancholy. Ever since she was a little girl, she dreamed of marrying a handsome prince on a beautiful beach. So when Lord Taybor told her she was to marry Prince Marcellus Bethard of Cardale, she was lost for words.

The ceremony was magical, a storybook affair that singers would tell of in their songs. On a warm summer day, by the light of a setting sun, she stood on the shore of Silversand Beach, near the outskirts of Cardale. Her father was the first to arrive, along with her mother, Lady Bernice

Taybor. They were dressed in their finest silks and adorned with jewelry that could fetch a king's ransom. Charlotte saw her mother smiling and wiping away tears of joy throughout the ceremony.

King Torbin Bethard and his queen, Patricia Bethard, entered to the most elaborate fanfare she had ever witnessed. When Charlotte saw them, it was as if time slowed to a halt, and reality began to set in that she would be the queen one day. Behind the King came his royal court and, finally, Prince Marcellus.

He was young and muscular, the most handsome man she had ever seen. The wedding was modest in length, but the feasting and celebrating afterward lasted all night. She remembered sitting at the table beside her new husband and King Torbin, though it was a sad memory. Three months later, the King was afflicted with a swift and terrible illness, taking his life in short order. Not even the wisest and most skilled physicians in Betanthia could save him. But on her wedding night, he made her feel like the most important woman alive.

After Torbin Bethard's death, Marcellus became king. Shortly after, his mother Patricia passed away; some said of a broken heart. Marcellus grieved the loss of both parents, though he dared not show a hint of weakness to anyone. Only Charlotte had ever seen him cry, and she comforted her new husband in his time of need and kept his spirits high. During that time, Gareth was conceived, and he was overjoyed to become a father.

When Charlotte informed Marcellus she was with child, he scooped her into his strong arms and twirled her around ecstatically. That was perhaps her most cherished memory, aside from holding Gareth the moment he entered the world. Marcellus held his firstborn son and heir in his hands, then stepped out onto the balcony of the queen's chambers and presented Gareth to a throng of noble lords, knights, and servants, anyone who had gathered in the courtyard below.

"Behold, my son!" Marcellus cried out, holding his newborn baby high.

A deafening roar erupted from the yard, and when the King turned back toward Charlotte, she spied tears of pride in his eyes. Their only regret was that his parents were not there to share in such a wondrous occasion.

The happiest days of my life, she reminisced.

Years passed, and Marcellus gave Charlotte two more children, though he was largely absent after Lucetta and Trace were born. The pain of losing his father drove the King to embark on new conquests in the north and west. But why, she could not be certain. She supposed it was his way of making himself seem worthy in the eyes of King Torbin, as if his father were looking down from the heavens above.

Marcellus spent his days leading his armies against barbarian tribes and expanding the borders of Betanthia. His campaigns were met with resounding victory, far greater than what his father had achieved. For his efforts, the King had been quite successful. But for such glory, he would one day pay a terrible price.

Queen Charlotte stood motionless on the beach as foamy waves lapped against her shins. A sudden wind blew locks of her graying, brown hair into her eyes, but she stood as firm as a statue. She remembered the day news arrived from the northern frontier. A rider brought a dispatch stating her husband had sustained grievous wounds, and the physicians had little hope for his survival.

Weeks passed before the King returned to Cardale on the bed of a covered wagon. When Charlotte saw Marcellus lying there, eyes closed, head bandaged and stained red with blood, it nearly broke her. The man she always dreamed of marrying barely clung to life. But fear and sorrow would not get the best of her, and alongside the finest healers in the Kingdom, she nursed Marcellus back to health. At first, he appeared to have recovered remarkably. But as a few years passed, the damage was plain to see.

No longer was he the kind, handsome, and brave man who pledged his life and love to her. He grew cold and quiet, and then eventually, cruel. Marcellus began to shut himself in the king's quarters, seldom leaving, save for wandering the palace corridors or to fetch more wine or ale. Gradually he lost all care and concern for the Queen and his children. The first time she caught another woman in his bed, she wept, despaired, and mourned. Jumping from the tallest tower in the palace was a constant thought in her mind.

Fond memories of her youth gave way to sad, bleak memories of adulthood. Little made her happy these days, save for her children. A wave crashed against Charlotte's legs, splashing her in the face, a sudden sensation of cool, salty water breaking her from her trance. She was reminded that this was Dellhaven, and was brought here by Gareth. That thought alone brought a smile back to her downtrodden face.

At least I have my son. I would endure all the pain and suffering all over again if I had to… if it meant he would always be by my side.

"Would you care for some refreshment, Your Majesty?" Brendon of Theeds said abruptly, startling her.

She had not seen the servant boy approaching, which made her wonder how many hours she had spent on the beach. He was holding a silver platter with a crystal goblet on it.

"Yes, thank you."

The drink was a strong yet flavorful southern tea, sweetened with lemon, her favorite. It was a reminder of better days when she was young and living under her parent's protection. After what seemed like only a few sips, the goblet was empty.

"Is there anything else I can do for you, Your Majesty?"

"No, Brendon. I think I might rest a while in the shade. My skin is turning red."

"Right this way, my queen. I have an area prepared for you already."

She smiled and followed the servant boy. Being properly catered to made her feel important again, and queen-like. Emilee was an attentive maidservant; none could deny it. But Charlotte had come to expect such decorum from the girl. The respect commanded by someone she had never met was reassuring beyond measure.

"Tell me, Brendon, tell me how you came into the service of my family."

"It's a rather uninteresting tale, my queen. I would hate to bore you on such a lovely day." He led Charlotte to the shade of an astoundingly tall oak that cast its shadow over nearly half the chateau grounds.

"It's quite alright. I would enjoy the conversation."

"As you wish." Brendon brushed a few stray leaves from the cushions of a cozy-looking chair, then tended to a stock of refreshments on a nearby table.

"My parents were farmers," he said. "I grew up helping my father tend to the fields, and my mother with the animals. They would sell their crop here in Dellhaven, but after a few years of bad harvests, my father suspected the fields had turned barren. After my parents delivered their final harvest, they sought work within the city. Suffice it to say, I found work for myself in the kitchens of Lord Andhoff, and eventually, I found myself here."

"And what of your parents?" she asked inquisitively.

"They passed away that winter. Fever took them both."

A tale both tragic and intriguing. Charlotte could not help but feel for the poor boy. He appeared to be a good lad and was thus far attentive in his service. At least here at the chateau, life would not be so hard for anyone under the Bethard's roof.

"I'm so very sorry to hear that. I am glad that you remained healthy. And I trust your time here has been comfortable?"

"Very much so, Your Majesty." Brendon smiled. "You have been very kind, and so have your children."

"Tell me about your birthplace. Theeds, is it? I must admit, I have never heard of such a place. Is it close to Dellhaven?"

Brendon was preparing another goblet of tea. He paused and stood as motionless as a startled deer, then acted as if nothing had happened.

"It is, my queen. I must confess I've been away so long I cannot remember much about my home. Please, forgive me."

"It's quite alright. There's nothing to forgive."

After dinner, Charlotte went on an evening walk with her son. He wore a blue doublet with a black cloak and carried himself with all the poise and grandeur a prince ought to. It was satisfying beyond words to see Gareth doing so well in Dellhaven. Being away from the chaos of Cardale seemed more revitalizing for him than for her. He was smiling again, and there was a light behind those hazel eyes once more.

A chorus of croaking frogs serenaded them, crickets chirping and waves crashing against the sandy shore. The eastern sky had grown so dark that it bled into the blackened waters of the Great Sea. It was easy to forget another life awaited them back in the capital, though Charlotte contemplated leaving it all behind.

"Thank you," she said softly, her voice barely overcoming a loud thrashing of the choppy sea. "Thank you for bringing me here and taking care of me. It means more than anything in the world."

Gareth smiled. "I'm glad you came. Sometimes it's good to forget; I've come to learn."

There was truth behind what he said. Charlotte's desperate desire to cling to memories of happier times proved to be her undoing. But here she was safe, and with the one person who truly cared about her.

"It isn't easy to forget, not when life used to be so… so…"

"Mother," he interrupted. "You mustn't live in the past. Yes, the years used to be much kinder to us all, but if you continue to take refuge among ghosts, you may end up as one yourself."

"You remind me of my father; you know that?" Charlotte could have cried tears of pride right then and there. "He always had a way of putting things in perspective for me. I see a lot of him in you. I wish you could have met him."

A melancholy silence came between them.

"As do I, mother. As do I."

The remainder of their starlit walk was absent of conversation. There was no need for words, just each other's company. Deep down, Charlotte knew nights like this wouldn't last forever. Eventually, they would have to return home, though she tried not to let such thoughts spoil the evening.

You mustn't fret, Charlotte. Savor every moment you can, for as long as you can.

They returned to the chateau, and Gareth decided to turn in early. She suspected his body was still adjusting to an ongoing abstinence from drinking. Though she would have enjoyed his company more, she was sympathetic and understanding. He was turning away from the path Marcellus was lost down, which meant more than anything.

After a glass of red wine, Charlotte felt weary and retired to her bedchamber. It was a welcome surprise when Emilee eased the door open to check on her one final time. It seemed like when Charlotte's loneliness and anxiety were at their worst, Emilee would find her, a connection sadly lacking with her daughter. But thankfully, tonight, she felt strong.

"Is there anything I can get for you, my queen? Or, perhaps you would like me to prepare you for bed?" the maidservant asked politely.

Even in the most casual settings, she always showed the utmost respect, even for a servant.

"I'm alright, Emilee. You're always so good to me. Get some rest. I'll see you in the morning."

If there was one thing Charlotte was sure of aside from Gareth's love, it was Emilee's sincerity. She never felt as if the girl's words were anything but heartfelt.

"If you need me, my queen, I'll be in the next room. Sleep well."

The door shut gently behind Emilee, and after the echoes of her footsteps faded away, Charlotte changed into her bedclothes and lit a few candles on the desk and in wall sconces. The night was so black not even the ocean was visible. The dark always made her uneasy, ever since she was a girl.

Charlotte closed the curtains and sighed in relief as warm candlelight filled her chamber. Something about a moonless night was indescribably terrifying. It was a reminder of times when Marcellus would stumble into their bedchamber at late hours and force himself upon her, drunk and stinking like other women. It was nearly impossible to fight back a sudden rush of fear.

No, Charlotte, not again. You're in Dellhaven. Gareth is here, and you're safe. Nobody can hurt you. Remember it. Remember. Tell it to yourself as many times as you need to.

It was easy to understand why her son turned to an excess of strong drink to calm his nerves. Charlotte would partake occasionally but never to the extreme lengths Gareth and his friend Sir Edmund would. Some more wine might help to stave off her building anxiety, but instead, she resolved to try and find sleep as quickly as possible.

The Queen laid down to rest, a chorus of crickets outside her window providing a gentle, ambient distraction. It was too warm for heavy covers, so a light silk sheet was all she wrapped around her body. She emptied her mind of all thoughts and focused on the soft lullaby of nature.

Moments before drifting off to slumber, a shuffle came from the other side of her chamber door. It was barely audible, but Charlotte distinctly heard it. What would someone be doing outside her room at such an hour? Emilee was likely asleep and would have knocked before entering.

Charlotte grew uneasy. It was a sensation she often felt at the palace and had learned to recognize. She sat up and pulled the sheet close like she did as a girl when the terrors of the night came calling. Unfriendly eyes were staring from somewhere, perhaps through the keyhole in the door. Someone was watching.

"E-Emily? Is… is that you?" Her voice trembled.

There was no response. Even the noises outside her window seemed to quiet, as if an evil force manifested itself and scared away everything in its vicinity. She wanted to hide and pray that whatever lurked outside the door would disappear. But instead, Charlotte rose slowly from the bed, careful not to make a sound.

She moved to the nearby desk with the nimbleness of a cat, ever watchful and listening. She slid the drawer open quietly and removed the dirk Gareth gave her. Charlotte had no idea how to use a blade, but it wouldn't stop her from confronting anyone trying to force their way in.

"Who's out there? Show yourself!" She was trembling and gripping the blade so tight her knuckles hurt. Charlotte crept closer to the door, trying desperately to quiet her breath.

Strange eyes were still there, watching. She was certain of it. Another noise came from the hall, followed by the pattering of hurried footfalls. With the dirk raised high, she wrenched the door open decisively.

But there was no one. Had it all been imagined? Was this simply a manifestation of an overactive mind? No, she thought, it couldn't have been. The sounds she heard were real, they had to have been.

You're safe, Charlotte, she reminded herself. *Nobody can hurt you here. Every man and woman on the grounds has been vetted thoroughly. This is your sanctuary.*

Perhaps it was simply trauma lingering from years of physical and emotional abuse by her husband. There was no way to be certain. The Queen slipped back into bed and slid the dirk carefully underneath one of her pillows. If anyone or anything were to come prowling again in the night, Charlotte would be ready. Or at least, she hoped.

MADELYN IV

THE RIDE THROUGH THE PLAINHOLD WAS GRUELING, AND AT SUCH A furious pace, it would have broken lesser men. Nearly three weeks fell from the calendar before Madelyn and her company of knights arrived in the west. It was a smooth journey for most of its duration, but by its final days, everyone was ready for it to end.

Titan Bradshaw had grown increasingly isolated from the group, though hardly any seemed to notice. Or care, for that matter. While the knights feasted and traded tall tales and jokes, Titan remained content with his own company. Madelyn began to feel guilty about bringing him along. He had every right to stay at Castle Thorn, but instead, he put aside whatever demons that still haunted him and rode out.

"I know it isn't easy for you to be out here, but I want you to know that your presence is appreciated," Madelyn said quietly as they trotted along a worn pathway.

"Spare me, girl." Titan groaned and adjusted himself in the saddle. "I didn't come here for your thanks, or for your company."

"Regardless, I'm glad you're here, for what it's worth."

"The only thing it's worth is my discharge papers," he muttered. "Never would have thought it would be this easy. Ride for a few weeks, and then I'm free."

"Easy, you say? What about this is easy?" Madelyn nearly laughed in disbelief.

"You heard me. Easy. Old man Valens has thirty thousand men. Thirty thousand. If you think this war will last longer than a fortnight, you're stupider than you look."

More than once, the thought had crossed her mind that the situation had been overblown. Maybe the High Marshal *was* being overly cautious. Maybe the things she read in the ancient texts *were* history and nothing more. It was certainly plausible. But Madelyn would rather be cautious, because if the High Marshal were proven correct, the cost would be far greater than anyone could imagine.

"We'll find out soon enough," she replied grimly.

On the evening before they arrived at Castle Morden, Titan supped and sat alone yet again. Laughter and merriment carried throughout their encampment as the knights enjoyed a final evening to themselves. It was sad, in a way, to watch such a mighty man reduced to little more than an outcast.

Titan sat around a small yet roaring fire, roasting a generous portion of days-old venison over the flames. An empty wineskin lay beside his arming sword, which he kept close in case any man dared to disturb his solitude. Most found it wise to keep their distance, but the more time Madelyn spent around him, the less afraid she felt. Titan was a man in pain, but he was no monster. At least, not one that would do her any harm.

"Tomorrow, we arrive. I was hoping you would join us tonight. The men would do well to see you," Madelyn said as she approached his campfire.

Titan Bradshaw scoffed, turning a small spit slowly and methodically. His eyes remained fixed on what was soon to be his meal, and said nothing.

"You're welcome to join us, you know," she said again. "You don't have to sit here and brood all by yourself."

"Fuck you," Titan grunted.

It was challenging for Madelyn to contain her smile. She began to realize his overly caustic attitude was merely a front. But he was still dangerous, she had to remind herself. Even the lowliest dog could snap at its master's hand unexpectedly.

"I can only imagine the things you've seen and the things you've done," Madelyn said. "I know nothing will ever take your suffering away. But regardless of how you feel, I'm glad you're here, and the men sleep a little easier at night too."

Titan chuckled, fire illuminating rows of scars on his face. Perhaps it was better if he didn't smile, she thought. The sight was so unsettling that she still had not grown used to it, even after spending weeks together.

"Make no mistake, girl, once we return to Bentmont, I intend to take my leave. So don't waste your effort trying to be my friend. You'll end up disappointed."

"Trust me, I don't need your friendship." She produced a small wineskin, opened it, and drank before offering it to him. "I need you to follow my commands and kill as many barbarians as possible. That's it. That's the deal we made."

After accepting the wineskin, Titan gave Madelyn a curious look as she returned to the encampment. Few dared to speak with him, and far fewer had the courage to speak so candidly. Even though he was a wretch and a rulebreaker, there was something about the man known as Titan that gave Madelyn confidence.

Within an hour, the knights had turned in for the evening. Madelyn sat alone inside her tent, restless and anxious. Sleeping the night before a mission or battle was often impossible, even for a mundane one. It was difficult to know what to think or what to expect. In one ear, she had Jenson Powell and everything the old Chronican had said, and in the other, she had Titan, who suspected the ordeal would be concluded by the time they arrived.

Who's right, and who's wrong? We'll find out soon enough, I suppose. I pray it's Titan, though.

As the sun began to rise, Madelyn awoke after only a half hour or so of rest. Her head throbbed and ached with fatigue. The strain of completing a six-week journey in half the time was enough to challenge even the heartiest of riders. But it was what the Blackthorn were known for; doing the impossible.

The western reaches of the Plainhold were different from that of the east, where the land was flat and made for smooth riding. As they drove further west, the terrain transformed into rolling hills with little vegetation, and the breakneck pace the knights had started with gradually slowed.

The peak of a final hill between them and Castle Morden came into sight around midday. It was a welcome sign for those who had made the journey in the past. Nora was beginning to neigh and protest. While it was not her first ride across the Plainhold, it was the first time she had gone this far this quickly. Madelyn gently stroked her horse's neck and offered what reassurances she could.

"I know, girl, it's alright. We'll be there soon enough. I'll see that you have a whole bushel of apples all to yourself."

Everyone was in dire need of proper rest, their horses especially. Madelyn supposed there would be little more they could do after arriving at Castle Morden anyways. It would likely be a day of briefings and restocking provisions before joining alongside Lord Valens' army. But the thought of a proper bed was most tempting.

Corbyn gave her a weary smile as he broke ranks and rode to the front of the column, departing from protocols they were careful to observe throughout their travels.

"Are you alright?" His face tightened. "You look like you haven't slept since we left Bentmont."

"I'm exhausted, but I'll be happy once we reach the castle. I could never ride another day, and I wouldn't mind. Not after this." Madelyn shifted uncomfortably in her saddle and grimaced. Her thighs pulsated with dull pain.

"It won't be much longer now. Come on. I'll race you to the top!" Corbyn smiled.

"I can't, and I don't think Nora has much left in her either."

The idea of racing to a gallop made Madelyn cringe. Nora seemed to understand as well and grunted and shook her head.

"Very well, I guess I'll claim victory then. It's not every day someone can best the great Madelyn Everly!"

Were it not for the rising heat and pain radiating throughout her body, Madelyn might have taken Corbyn up on his challenge and shamed him in front of everyone. But she was content to allow him a small victory, just this once.

"I don't know about you, but the first thing I'm having once we reach Morden is a bath," Corbyn complained.

Even sweaty and dirty, he still looked every bit as attractive to her.

"I'll feel much better once I know what's happening out there. I thought we would have received another dispatch at headquarters during our time in Cardale. But, with—"

Madelyn brought Nora to a sudden halt, raising a hand to signal the knights to stop as well.

"Do you hear that?" she asked Corbyn.

It was a low, deep thumping noise, almost too quiet to make out. At first, she thought it might be horse hooves, but it was far too rhythmic. No, this noise was deliberate.

"What am I supposed to be listening for…"

Before the words could escape Corbyn's mouth, his ears picked up a faint, distant disturbance. Hunter Northcott and Titan moved forward and joined Madelyn, unsure why they had stopped.

"Is everything alright, Commander?" Hunter asked. He was silenced by a frantic waving of Corbyn's hand.

"Quiet!" the First Lance whispered.

"Shhh… listen," Madelyn said, her head cocked to the side. "What is that?"

"I…" Hunter stammered breathlessly.

"It means we need to pick up the pace," Titan said ominously, thrusting a bootheel into his steed and racing to the top of the hill.

Madelyn, Corbyn, and Hunter looked at one another, then set off in pursuit. Their knights broke into a gallop and followed closely behind. Titan seldom showed any emotion save for anger, but he was agitated and waved the rest of them forward.

"What is it?" Madelyn shouted as Nora struggled to find a second wind.

"We're late. Too late," Titan said, surveying the land where the fortress sat.

Castle Morden dominated the area for miles, but its splendor was overshadowed by a mass of men descending from the north. An ominous, deep thumping of drums rippled off the surrounding hills, echoing and sounding as if it was coming from every direction. Madelyn could not believe what she was seeing.

"I don't suppose Lord Valens is returning to the castle?" Hunter asked in dismay.

"Not likely. Those are northern drums. War drums," Titan replied.

With a crack of the reigns, he galloped off to the castle, the other knights looking on in disbelief.

"Does this mean Lord Valens was defeated? Is there anyone left inside? What do we do now?" Voices cried out one after another. Fear was spreading throughout the ranks like a sudden, uncontrollable sickness.

Madelyn sat silently on her horse, stunned and unsure of what to do next. Never in her service to the Order had she witnessed such a sight. Against the blue backdrop of a clear summer sky, a dark cloud of barbarians spilled over the rolling hills, revealing its full might. A horn blast rippled like a peal of thunder, and the formation shifted and spread out into a long, nearly endless line.

From her vantage point, she could make out the movement of men along Morden's ramparts. There appeared to be few, far too few to make a proper defense. Madelyn's insides twisted and tightened into a knot until she felt sick. She had faced stiff odds in the past, but what lay before her looked to be insurmountable.

"I… I.." There were no words she could find, to the dismay of her knights. Some were anxiously looking back to the east with every intention of retreating.

"Well, we didn't ride all this way for nothing, now did we?" Hunter quipped with a dry chuckle.

Every instinct within Madelyn's body told her to flee, to ride as quickly as Nora could carry her until Castle Morden was far from sight. It was the first time she had stared down an enemy force and not felt some measure of confidence. Fleeing to Bentmont seemed like it might very well be the wisest decision.

As Titan Bradshaw neared the fortification, Madelyn's senses returned. The man who wanted nothing to do with the Blackthorn, and was here for the most selfish reasons, was doing the most selfless thing by riding to the castle alone. She felt a sharp pang of guilt that cut through her exhaustion and fear.

I can't believe my eyes. He's going down there all alone.

The men inside Morden would most certainly die if she did nothing, a prospect deemed unacceptable. The knights stirred anxiously, some of them whispering among themselves.

I'm the one who's supposed to lead. I'm the one who's supposed to be brave. And the man everyone thinks is a coward is charging headlong while I sit idle. No, this cannot be.

Madelyn rode over to a knight carrying the standard of the Order and wrenched it free from his grasp. She held the black and gold banner aloft for all to see, its horse sigil appearing to gallop as it cracked and snapped wildly in the breeze.

"Knights of the Order! Have no fear! We have Castle Morden! If those barbarians want to take it, they'll have to go through us!"

At first glance, one would certainly think the imposing fortress was impregnable. Despite never setting foot inside Morden, the size and thickness of its stone walls would prove challenging even for the most seasoned Betanthian army. And these were unwashed barbarians, she thought.

But if they could defeat Cedric Valens in the field, could they storm the castle?

She hoped it wasn't true and that perhaps both armies had simply missed one another. While the Northmen appeared to be at least ten thousand strong or more, Lord Valens' army was three times as large. Even under the worst circumstances, it should not be possible for an army of filthy savages to best one of the finest Commandants Betanthia had ever known.

There's no use in dwelling on it now. You're committed. You committed the day you left Bentmont.

"Now, let's show these savages how we fight in the east!"

Knowing time was growing short, Madelyn put her foot into Nora and raced toward Castle Morden, her anxious knights close behind. Before long, they were climbing a long gradual slope of the hill where the stronghold sat. Nora was breathing hard and struggling to keep pace.

"Come on, girl, you can do it. Not much further now."

The ominous mass of barbarians grew larger and more formidable the closer she came. They were less than two miles away and closing rapidly. Upon seeing the standard of the Blackthorn Knights, the men on the ramparts waved the King's colors in reply. The thick, reinforced gate was hastily thrown open, and Titan Bradshaw was the first to enter. Madelyn remained just outside and waited for each man to make their way inside.

Before she entered, she gave an uneasy glance toward the eastern horizon. With every engagement Madelyn had fought, there was always a feeling of fear, but never any serious thought as to whether it would be her final battle. An overwhelming dread she felt as the war drums thumped louder was foreign and uncomfortable. But with all her men inside, there would be no turning back now.

As Nora carried her into the stronghold, the doors were shut and barred, and the portcullis lowered. Madelyn saw men scurrying throughout the courtyard and racing up to the battlements. There were hardly enough to defend such a large castle properly, and many looked to be boys who had never seen a battle.

At least my knights are here. We'll know what to do.

"Is anyone in charge here? Where is Lord Valens?" Madelyn shouted amidst the disorganized chaos.

It was disheartening to see the terror that had swept through the garrison. Once more, she called out in hopes of finding an officer. A man in his early twenties shambled over, his eyes vacuous and distant.

"Yes, I'm… I'm in charge here."

"I'm Commander Everly of the Blackthorn. And your name is?" She dismounted Nora with a groan.

The pain from three weeks of riding cut through her fear and exhaustion.

"Ellis. Lieutenant Ellis Byrne."

"Have you received word from Lord Valens?" Madelyn quickly grew impatient. War drums were booming louder by the second.

"No. We last saw him weeks ago. He was riding to Khorrtal to meet with Commander Holland. They were going to go after the man that killed his son, but… but I was hoping you might have brought word…" Ellis trailed off, muttering to himself.

Then my worst fears have come true. Lord Valens is lost.

"There's no time. Are you capable of leading a defense here?"

At first, Ellis said nothing. He looked around desperately as if the castle suddenly became foreign. Confused and disoriented, he stammered but was unable to speak.

"I'm going to assume command here, alright?" Madelyn touched his shoulder, which seemed to lift him out of his daze, at least slightly. "Take my horse to the stables. I'll handle the wall."

"Where are the rest of the reinforcements?" Lieutenant Byrne asked in sudden agitation.

"We're it—all two hundred of us. But take heart; we're the best at what we do. And this is a sturdy castle. So if your men follow my orders, we'll make it out of this alive."

Titan appeared out of the chaos as the knights raced to stable their mounts and prepare for battle. He stormed over to Madelyn, shoving anyone who impeded him out of the way.

It appeared Ellis' senses returned. He scowled and turned red as a tomato.

"This is Lord Valens' castle, and these men act under my command. How dare you order me about like some common squire! Who do you think you are?"

"I'm the one who's going to keep this castle from falling, you lout. Do you even know what you're doing here? Why are there no archers on the walls? Why don't you have cauldrons of water boiling? Why don't you—"

Before Madelyn could continue, Titan spun Lieutenant Byrne around and hoisted him into the air by the collar. Ellis choked, gasped, and clawed at Titan's hands, but the behemoth's grip was too formidable.

"Here's what you're going to do. You'll get your ass up on that wall and do exactly what you're told, or I'll squeeze your fucking head right off your shoulders. Do you understand me? There's no time for this shit!"

Ellis nodded frantically, shaking and nearly pissing himself with fear, then was released. The drums sounded as if they were on the other side of the gate. Each beat felt like a deep crack of thunder, nearly shaking the walls with intensity. Titan turned to Madelyn, pointing a sharp finger.

"And you. It's up to you to lead us out of this. But if I see you're not doing your job, I *will* take command, ranks be damned. I didn't ride all this way to die because a bunch of peasant boys and little girls weren't up to the task."

Such hostile words were the proper dose of encouragement Madelyn needed. She handed Nora off to a squire and called out to her officers.

"Scott! Northcott! Front and center!" she cried out.

Within seconds, they rushed to her side.

"Here's the situation. We're taking point on defense. First Lance, I want you on the north wall. Elite Northcott, I want you on the south. I didn't see any siege towers, so gather your archers and prepare for ladders and grappling hooks. Titan, you're in charge of the west wall and the gate."

This time it was Madelyn's turn to accost Titan. She jabbed a finger boldly into his shoulder just above his breastplate. "Nothing gets through. Do you hear me? Nothing."

The behemoth snarled and nodded, then turned and shouted to the men above the gatehouse.

"Get some water boiling and some stones ready, if we have them," he roared, then disappeared through a nearby doorway that accessed the battlements above.

"And where will you be?" Corbyn asked, his eyes growing wide.

"I'll be wherever I'm needed." Madelyn pulled Corbyn close and kissed him with a fiery passion, all thoughts of romantic discretion abandoned. "Don't worry about me. Just fight well and stay safe. I can take care of myself," she said, then gave him a push.

Madelyn made her way through the bailey to see if every man had assumed their fighting positions. A faint weeping near the stables caught her attention. She spied a young, frail-looking boy huddled in the corner, shaking and afraid. The pounding drums outside made him flinch and wince with each thump.

"Hey, what are you doing over here?" She knelt beside him.

"I'm scared…" the lad sobbed uncontrollably.

With a gentle, reassuring touch, Madelyn calmed his tears.

"I know, we're all afraid. But I promise you, I'm going to get us through this. What's your name?"

"Spencer. Spencer Morris, m-my Lady."

"Well, Spencer, I rode all the way from Bentmont to help. I'm in charge here and will do everything I can to keep you safe. But I need *your* help."

"I can't fight. I've never fought anyone before." The lad nearly broke into sobs again at the thought of his own weakness.

"Well, not everyone has to fight," she said, offering a smile. "You can make sure the archers are restocked with arrows and the men at the gate have enough wood for fires and water to boil. But if you want to fight, grab yourself a crossbow."

"I'll try, I… I just wish I could be brave," Spencer lamented.

"I bet you're braver than you think you are. You'll find it in you. I know it. And besides, girls like brave men."

Madelyn mussed up his hair and winked, and Spencer gave a pitiful smile, his face flush with embarrassment.

"Commander! Commander, come quick!" Hunter cried out.

The war drums grew faster and faster, and soon the terrible music was echoed by guttural roars and shrill shrieks of nearly twelve thousand warriors as they halted just outside missile range. Running as fast as her sore legs would allow, Madelyn raced up to the battlements and stopped breathless as she gazed at the barbarian army.

The savages stood in several tight formations with mounted officers at the head of each. They possessed no siege engines, but Madelyn saw dozens of ladders and a battering ram at the ready. Suddenly, the drums stopped. Silence fell among the enemy ranks as a hulking man in black armor rode forward.

From where she stood, Madelyn could hear nothing. But then, the entire horde began howling and snarling like wild beasts. She could not recall a time when she felt more afraid, but the ominous threat from Titan still lingered in her mind.

If I see you're not doing your job, I will take command, ranks be damned, he said. This is all on you now, Madelyn.

"Archers, nock your arrows!" Corbyn commanded.

Similar orders were shouted across the battlements by the other officers.

"Steady now, lads, steady," Hunter said. "We have the walls, just remember that."

Madelyn ascended to the very top of the gatehouse. She stood beside Titan and peered out between the crenellations. The enemy horde appeared far more imposing from this height, though she thought it strange they remained so still.

"They're not attacking," Madelyn observed.

"They probably weren't expecting to see a few hundred knights come riding inside," Titan said ominously. He appeared more focused and less angry than usual. "I suspect they're adjusting their strategy,"

"Do you think they'll still attack today?"

Carefully, Titan scanned the breadth of the warband. He shook his head. "Hard to say. If this is the lot that beat Lord Valens, then they know what they're doing. On the other hand, I think they were expecting an empty castle, so I doubt they're going to throw themselves mindlessly at the walls. But I could be wrong. Northerners can be pretty fucking stupid."

The quip made Madelyn smile but did little to ease the tremors in her hands. For what seemed like an eternity, she watched as the barbarian chieftain conversed with several other mounted warriors. She hoped the sight of the Blackthorn banner had filled the Northmen with enough fear to turn back and retire. She hoped Lord Valens might still emerge over the horizon and bring the fight to a swift conclusion.

But such hopes were naive. For better or worse, Madelyn now found herself in the most dangerous situation of her entire life. Outnumbered and surrounded, she looked out at the barbarian horde with bated breath, and at the monster in black armor at its head.

We're as ready as we can be, she thought. *Your move, savage.*

EINARR IV

THE MASSIVE GRAY WALLS OF CASTLE MORDEN LOOMED OMINOUSLY in the distance. Spontaneous cheers erupted as they caught sight of the great stronghold. The warband had spread itself nearly a mile abreast as they maneuvered down a rolling hill into a small valley. From there, they would climb a subtle incline toward the castle before finally reaching flatter ground.

One by one, the war drums thumped rhythmically, their deep bellowing growing louder until it shook the earth. Still high off their two previous victories, the warriors began to quicken their pace in anticipation of another bloodbath. Einarr could only imagine what it must be like to witness their approach from the castle walls. The thought brought him a confident smile.

"We're here, my lord. By the grace of the gods and by your will, we're finally here." Sylvia Stormguard could not have sounded prouder, though Damien's resolve appeared as unshakable as Morden's walls.

"Steal yourself, warchief. This is no Blackwolf Pass. Here, our enemy holds the advantage." Dreadfire's words were grim yet calculated, for he knew what terrible cost fortifications could inflict upon an invading force.

"The castle should be near to empty, I'd imagine," said Zander. "Between Khorrtal and the Pass, we must have slaughtered what, twenty, thirty… forty thousand of them? How many can they have left?"

For once, the wildman said something not even Bonesplitter could dispute, Einarr supposed.

Even to the Supreme Warlord, it stood to reason the garrison would be depleted. Einarr watched as Damien studied the fortification from afar. Though Dreadfire was cautious and difficult to read, he appeared to be just as confident as his warchiefs.

I pray the castle will be ours by sundown, and we can return home.

Any thoughts of a swift victory withered away as hundreds of horsemen appeared in the distance, speeding toward the stronghold. Einarr could not make out the sigil on the banners, but the colors of black and gold were unmistakable to Damien.

"Knights," he grumbled. "Blackthorn Knights."

Gods be good! This siege will not be as easy as I hoped!

Einarr cursed their sudden misfortune. He sometimes heard stories of the infamous military order of Bentmont, and their presence on the field would most certainly upset their plans for a quick, decisive siege.

"Worry not, my lord. We'll take this castle." Sylvia grinned. "A few pretty horsemen won't stand in our way."

The warlord's face showed no such signs of confidence. "No," Damien grunted. "These are not peasant soldiers as we have faced. These are skilled warriors and not to be taken lightly. This fight will be hard, and we must be careful in our execution."

With a wave, Damien brought the warband to a halt just outside of projectile range. Soldiers scurried across the parapet, carrying all manner of weapons and provisions to their posts.

"We make camp here. Set a perimeter and send out foraging parties. Do not let anyone enter or leave the castle unchallenged," Dreadfire ordered.

Zander replied with immediate skepticism. "Come now, my lord. We mustn't let a pile of pebbles stand in our way! Order the attack. We're ready!"

"No, there will be no attack today. We make camp," Damien repeated, this time more pointedly.

"There's no task we can't handle. Have you forgotten Blackwolf Pass? Give me this honor, Lord Damien, and I will easily take that castle." Zander sneered as he watched Morden's garrison readying themselves. Though the walls were lined nearly shoulder to shoulder with archers, the young warchief appeared undeterred.

"Have you ever seen a castle before, you fool?" Marvath snarled. "They're not going just let you walk in and take the damned thing,"

"Listen, Bone-shitter. My men make up, what, nearly half of our force? Where would you be if I walked off this field right here and now? Where would you be? You certainly wouldn't have won at the Pass, that's for damn sure." Zander dismounted and took up his shield and axe. "I've had enough of your disrespect, you hear me? My people fought just as hard as you northerners. We are not lesser men!"

"Perhaps you wish to settle this then, one on one?" Marvath dismounted in kind and took up his two-handed great axe. "I will not suffer your arrogance further. Bymist rats like you have no place here."

With such heated tension rising by the second, Einarr was certain the warband would turn on itself right then and there. He glanced back at Castle Morden, wondering if the garrison might take advantage of such chaos should the situation deteriorate.

"Silence!" Dreadfire bellowed. "You squabble like petty women. If the wildmen are up to such a task, then you have my blessing. Take this castle, and earn your Soul Name, warchief."

Zander showed a mouth full of half-rotten teeth and chuckled, while Bonesplitter spat in disgust and turned away. Damien snapped the

342

reigns of his horse and rode to the rear where he could better observe. Einarr and Sylvia followed closely in pursuit, each dismayed at their warlord's orders.

"Damien, forgive me. But, what are you doing? Truly you must know a direct assault on the castle is suicide!" Einarr was as confused as he was concerned.

"Zander is right," Damien conceded. "We need his warriors, and they are still his to command. If he feels the castle can be taken, he is welcome to it."

Not once had Einarr known Damien to capitulate so quickly to anything, if ever. Something suspicious was afoot, he was sure of it.

"Damien, we both know assaulting the castle is futile now that these knights have arrived," he said. "What purpose will it serve to send the wildmen to their deaths?"

The Zylmacians gathered into formation at the head of the warband, dozens of ladders and a crude battering ram in hand. Most were lightly armored, if at all, and would rely almost solely on their shields for protection. Damien's brow furrowed as he looked on.

"Because I have no need for Zander. I need his men. And if his warriors lose confidence in their warchief, they will obey me without question. Let them witness firsthand what insolence will reap. Ready your kin and stand fast, then sound the attack."

"Damien, old friend. I mean no disrespect, but this is not the way to make a point," Einarr protested. "We need to think long term, and we're going to need every man if we're to—"

"Are you questioning me now? After all, we have been through? After all, you have seen me do?" The ominous black eyes of Dreadfire flashed a hint of fiery red anger.

"No, I have more faith in you than anyone. I simply believe there are better ways to handle this. But as always, I bow to your wisdom."

Einarr and Sylvia looked at each other doubtfully, but little more could be said. The Zylmacians were in formation and ready to attack. With his axe thrust high into the air, Zander shouted one last encouragement to his people.

"Men! This day belongs to the west, and not even the gods will deny us! Sjenohor and glory awaits! For Zylmacia!"

Half a dozen warhorns blasted, and with a deafening roar, thousands of Zander's warriors raced toward Castle Morden. Within an instant, they were greeted by volleys of arrows from the parapet, but their charge proceeded undeterred. With little more than crude wooden shields to protect them, the ravenous wave of wildmen descended upon the castle like a swarm of locusts and hastily threw their ladders against the walls.

"Go! Go! Climb, you fools! Climb! The gods are with us!" Zander shouted as he took shelter against the walls.

His shield was littered with arrows and quarrels. The first to race up the ladders were equally riddled, their lifeless bodies falling to the ground with sickening thuds.

A faint, shrill voice carried itself lightly on the wind. Einarr took notice and scanned the walls to see if he could discover its source. Amidst the chaos of battle, he spied the long golden hair of what appeared to be a female.

"Is that… is that a woman on the walls?" he asked curiously.

"Why yes, it is," Bonesplitter chuckled. "It seems the Bethards have sent only their finest and prettiest to entertain us. Perhaps she might warm all of our beds tonight!"

Stormguard was none too amused. She looked daggers at her Rhivothi brethren and those who dared to laugh. Einarr felt sympathetic and moved to calm her but thought better of it. She was by far the fiercest shieldmaiden he had ever known.

There's one woman who won't be made light of. I feel sorry for whoever finds themselves on the receiving end of her axe.

Damien peered ahead. The defenders appeared to be skilled and highly coordinated, their forces shifting precisely to where they were needed most. When Dreadfire caught sight of the blonde woman, he turned a pale white.

The warlord summoned a page to his side and whispered, then quickly dismissed him. Einarr could only guess what had agitated Damien so much, but with more Zylmacian bodies piling up against Morden's walls, there was little opportunity to think of much else. It wasn't long before the rider returned, except this time, he was standing on a chariot with an elderly woman beside him. The chariot pulled up alongside Damien and stopped.

This must be Lazilyth, the crone he spoke of at the Pass.

Einarr felt his throat tighten in uneasiness. The woman was old. Unnaturally old. Stooped and scowled, she looked as if she had witnessed the passing of centuries. She was clad in a faded roughspun gown of toneless gray, matching the color of her long, thin, wispy hair. Her eyes were a milky white and covered with a hazy film.

Damien leaned down, muttered something to the crone, and then looked back at the stronghold. Even the nearby warriors seemed to share Einarr's reservations about the old woman. She hunched forward and peered through her glazed eyes, scanning the walls in search of something or someone. The light around her seemed to dim and darken as if her presence was somehow scattering it away.

The crone's eyes lit up suddenly. She raised a long, gnarled finger and pointed. Her smile was a toothless abyss of dread, a groaning laugh as deep and ominous as the shifting of the earth's foundations. Whatever she saw also brought an insidious grin to Damien's face.

One person who wasn't grinning was Zander, or his men, for that matter. The Zylmacian warriors on the ram fared no better than those carrying the ladders. Upon reaching the gates, arrows and stones fell from machicolations around the gatehouse. The door sustained no more than a handful of blows before a cascade of boiling water rained down in a torrent. Men screamed in agony as their flesh and eyes burned, though their suffering would be short-lived.

The men on the ram were slaughtered in seconds. Those who followed behind them clustered into a hastily formed shield wall. Again they attempted to take up the ram but were beaten back by an unyielding flurry of arrows. Those venturing up the ladders shared the same misfortune, with only a few able to climb to the top. Once over the crenellations, they encountered an impassable wall of swords that had little difficulty piercing their unarmored flesh.

The assault was beginning to appear as if it were a disaster for Zander, but still, the Zylmacians climbed. Hundreds had taken their ladders around a corner tower and to the next stretch of wall. There, the arrows were not quite as punishing. A handful of wildmen scaled to the top before the garrison shifted themselves accordingly. Zander grew frustrated and ordered a score of men to follow him around the tower.

"Climb, you bloody louts, climb! Faster, faster!"

Half a dozen warriors made their way up the ladder, but none could reach the top. With arrows and bodies falling like hail, Zander roared with frustration, then raced up the ladder as quickly as his legs would allow. Barely a third of the way up, a wildman fell from the crenellations and crashed on top of him. Together they landed in a heap on the ground.

Damien watched coldly from the back of his warhorse as the carnage unfolded. Mountains of bodies were piled alongside the walls and gatehouse. Einarr had seen more than he could stomach and could hold his tongue no longer.

"Enough of this madness!" he cried out. "If they're wiped out, we won't have the strength to fight on! Gods be good, Damien! Use your reason!"

The screams of dying men rippled through the air. In the face of it all, Damien Dreadfire sneered and looked on with seemingly little regard for the unfolding slaughter. But to Einarr's relief, the warlord had seen enough.

"Sound the retreat This battle is over, for now."

A long horn blast carried across the battlefield, followed by another and yet another. Those still alive along the walls raced back to the war-band, their tails tucked in retreat and shame. Einarr heard victorious cheers from the garrison, the taste of defeat bitter in his mouth. Sylvia spat in disgust and retired.

You mustn't let emotion get the better of you, Einarr. We surround the fortress, and they're trapped inside. The day may be lost, but the battle is far from over. No, this is just the beginning.

Later that evening, as darkness swept over Castle Morden, light from thousands of campfires brought a comforting warmth to an otherwise dreary night. Everyone expected Damien to attack come the next day. Each warchief was stationed along a different stretch of wall—Marvath to the east, Zander to the north, and Sylvia and Einarr to the south. The main force under Damien's command held the west.

The mood throughout camp was somber. Though this was the first skirmish of a protracted siege, they expected a more resolute conclusion. The ambush at Khorrtal and the Battle of Blackwolf Pass were swift and decisive engagements. Morden had proven to be a different animal entirely, and victory would be far more elusive this time around.

Einarr took to walking as the Nothanek feasted. No songs were sung, nor music played. The same was untrue for the defenders of Castle Morden. Were it not for hundreds of dead littered around the walls, one might think a festival was underway.

Einarr was unaccustomed to defeat, though he tried to understand Damien's reasoning for ordering the attack. Zander had undoubtedly been humiliated, he thought, and would likely come to heel after suffering such a disgrace. But wildmen were difficult to predict. Einarr half expected them to desert and head west were it not for Zander's insatiable lust for a Soul Name.

With such thoughts lingering in his mind, Einarr continued to walk and offer encouragement to those he encountered.

"This was but one day; a siege seldom ends so quickly. Have faith in the gods, and Lord Dreadfire." The words were foul in his mouth, but the warriors would do well to hear them. For many, it was their first time sieging a castle.

Einarr made his rounds for what felt like hours before arriving at Sylvia Stormguard's encampment. The Rhivothi did not suffer the same loss of morale as their Nothanek brethren, and as they grew drunk on mead and beer, laughter and music returned. It was refreshing not to be among such grim company. Einarr shared a horn of mead with a few shirtless fanatics before spotting Sylvia's shieldmaidens near her tent.

It was curious to see that Rhivothi men did not desire their warrior women like the other tribesmen did. He indeed spied a few Nothanek giving them lustful stares on more than one occasion. Perhaps the Rhivothi were more reserved out of respect for the shieldmaiden's ferocity, he supposed. Or it could be such womenfolk simply did not prefer the company of men and saw little use in wasting their time and efforts.

What a tragedy that would be, he thought, half amused.

"Halt, come no further," Ingryd Bjornsdottir said as she leaned against a wagon. Her gravelly voice rose above steady laughter coming from inside.

Einarr could barely see her in the dim light, as her brown leather jerkin and pants made her blend into the surrounding campsite. He paused and looked around before catching a glimpse of her. Ingryd was a sight to behold, a true northern warrior woman in every way. Her long, blonde hair was drawn up and twisted into a wrist-thick braid. The sides of her head were shaved and covered with blue runic tattoos.

"I would speak with your warchief. Please, step aside," Einarr said.

"If you're here to get that little cock of yours wet, then you've come to the wrong place, I'm afraid." Her hand moved to a dagger on her hip.

"You mistake yourself, Rhivothi. Be mindful who you insult." Chuckling softly, Einarr moved closer to the tent but was halted by the shieldmaiden.

"We don't consort with your kind. Save it for the camp follower wenches."

The laughter suddenly grew quiet. Einarr was unsure what to make of the situation. From over Ingryd's shoulder, he could barely see inside the tent flap, and as he leaned closer, the shieldmaiden shadowed his movements.

"I grow weary of this game. You do know who I am, don't you?" Einarr's brown eyes narrowed and reflected the dancing light of a nearby fire.

"I could give a—"

Before Ingryd could finish, a voice rose from inside.

"Einarr… is that you?" Sylvia asked quizzically.

"Yes, yes it is."

"Come inside and have a drink with us," Stormguard giggled.

With a cynical grin, Einarr stepped past the brooding shieldmaiden. The tent was well-lit by oil lanterns. A fog of freshly smoked herb stirred and swirled about as it met a rush of outside air. The ground was a mess of spilled mead, discarded drinking horns, and bits of leather armor and mail.

Sylvia lay on her side on top of a pile of fur blankets, a small animal bone pipe resting comfortably between her teeth. Her two companions were drunk and lay sprawled out on the ground. Einarr cautiously stepped over the clutter and seated himself between Stormguard and the other Rhivothi women.

"You'll have to excuse Ingryd. She's a fiery soul no doubt, and fiercely protective." Smiling, Sylvia took another drag from her pipe, trails of smoke slinking from her nostrils.

"I took no insult," Einarr said, glancing at the women who were curiously looking at him. "I was making my rounds and thought I would see how you and your kin fare tonight."

"As you can see, we're quite alright," Hilda said sarcastically. She was a known fanatic of Azldyr, and one of the few women Einarr was cautious toward. Her hair was as black as a moonless night and cropped short, one side hanging down to her chin. Half her face was covered in blue runic tattoos, and black liner around her cyan-colored eyes made her look otherworldly, like an apparition.

"Aye, indeed you are." Einarr nodded, then turned his attention back to Sylvia. "I was hoping we might have a word in private."

Stormguard sat up, removed the pipe from between her teeth, and passed it over to Rikke, who had been staring at Einarr the entire time. She had nearly the same hair and eyes as Sylvia but was taller and thicker, a deep scar running diagonally across her face. It did not, however, make her look any less attractive. Quite the opposite, he thought.

"Anything you have to say to me, you can say in front of them," Stormguard said. "Secrets are for the craven."

"Very well," he conceded. "I noticed your displeasure as we retired from the field."

The laughter quickly subsided. Rikke smoked her fill and passed the pipe back to Sylvia. Hilde took a long drink of mead and watched her warchief cautiously, unsure what to expect.

"You could say that, yes," Stormguard grunted, the merriment fading from her voice.

"In many ways, it mirrored my own. I wasn't expecting our first day to end this way. Tell me, do you disapprove of Damien's methods?"

Sylvia made a bitter face and shook her head, the bone pipe clicking softly between her teeth.

"Can't say I liked what I saw out there. Zander is a cunt, but that's no reason to send those men to their deaths. Don't be mistaken now; you'll be hard-pressed to find anyone more loyal to Dreadfire than I am. But if he wanted to make an example of Zander, he should have done it without weakening us all. Now, more Rhivothi will risk death when we attack again because we threw hundreds of Zylmacian lives away. I could care less about those beasts. I care about my people."

"I understand, and I think it was regrettable as well," he said. "But I trust Damien's judgment, even when I cannot see the purpose behind his methods. In all honesty, Zander did this to himself. Being a warchief is an honor and a responsibility. You have to conduct yourself—"

"Do not start that with me," Sylvia said, drawing a dagger and pointing at Einarr's face. "I know what it takes to be a warchief, or have you forgotten I am one?"

"I meant no disrespect, Sylvia. The Zylmacians are unruly, and their allegiance is fleeting. We need Zander to keep them in line. But unfortunately, we have to keep Zander in line. Perhaps some humility will do him well."

Hilde spat in disgust. "You sure are good at kissing Damien's ass. Were you lovers before the war, or do you lack the spine to call out his bullshit when you see it?"

Einarr paused and clenched his jaw. Though he bore no ill will toward any of the Rhivothi, he certainly would not suffer such an insult. "Mind your tongue, woman. I was the first to swear myself to Damien after Borjifa. Or have you forgotten what happened there? Have you forgotten the Night of the Dread Fires?"

Hilde looked uneasy and lost for words. The mere mention of that infamous night was enough to invite fear into the heart of any northerner, man or woman. It was a tale so terrible it was rarely spoken of, if ever. And when it was, it was done in hushed whispers and never openly.

"Enough," Silvia commanded. "We all know why we're here, every one of us. But remember, Einarr, we're here of our own free will. I know both of us will lose warriors. It's inevitable. But I will not see my people slaughtered over foolishness and pride."

"You and I agree, then. I intend to return as many of my people to Skaginlef as I can."

"As you should. I will march home if I feel Rhivothi lives are needlessly sacrificed. Make no mistake about it."

"Then you're just the sort of person to lead your people. I'll speak to Damien about what happened today and see that it never happens again."

"And what about Zander?" Hilde interjected.

It was no secret the northerners bore suspicion toward the Zylmacians. Before the events of Borjifa, the wildmen were counted as enemies by many. Khorrtal felt their wrath on more than one occasion before coming under Betanthian influence. Einarr was unkeen to march alongside men who would just assume to murder them in their sleep instead of fighting as equals on the battlefield. But he supposed that if the Zylmacians could be steered toward Betanthia and away from northern lands, his people would be all the better.

"Zander is a different creature entirely." He shook his head. "And after today, speaking with him would be unwise "

"What about Damien?" Sylvia asked. "Are you concerned Zander might seek vengeance for his humiliation?"

"Damien can take care of himself, but I wouldn't put anything past a Zylmacian. I'll do my best to protect him."

Hilde scoffed. "Could you even protect yourself should the wildmen turn on us?"

The question hung in the air, unanswered. Though Einarr had become irritated at the shieldmaiden's continued provocations, it did not make her any less right. They were at war. Were any of them truly safe? And what if the Zylmacians responded with hostility over their treatment? Few would survive if they decided to turn their swords and axes against the Northmen in the night.

It was becoming likely the warband that took years to forge could come undone after a single afternoon. It was certainly within the realm of possibility. Einarr dismissed himself from the tent, dwelling on the day's events and what might happen tomorrow.

Before turning in for the night, Einarr decided to visit Damien Dreadfire. The Supreme Warlord would prove easy to find. The largest fires burned around his tent, sharpened stakes and spearmen forming a protective perimeter. Not that Damien needed them, he was by far the most capable man in the warband, Einarr reflected. As he approached, a tall, muscled guard stepped forth and offered a challenge, but the Northman stood down.

He threw back the flaps of the tent and stepped inside. It was well-lit with lanterns and smelled of sage. Damien was hunched over a crude wooden desk, poring over a piece of animal hide. Einarr was unaware he could write, but upon further inspection, it appeared Dreadfire was drawing battle plans.

"May I have a word, Damien?"

After scratching a few symbols into the hide, Damien glanced up casually. "You may. What troubles you, my friend?"

"Who said I was troubled?" Einarr objected.

"If you were not troubled, then you would not be here. Come now, speak plainly. This is about today, is it not?" Damien moved his work off to the side. Lantern fire cast foreboding shadows across his face.

"It is," he admitted.

"So then, say what you will."

Einarr cleared his throat. "There's concern among the men about what happened out there. Some say ordering the wildmen to charge to their deaths may prove treacherous. Many died today, and the rest were humiliated."

Damien looked unconcerned. "You must remember, I did not order the assault on the castle. Zander was blinded by ambition and most eager to take it. His hubris is to blame, not my command. If the Zylmacians are slighted, then they have only Zander to blame."

It was a dangerous gamble that Einarr was not fond of making. The wildmen made up half of the warband, and were prone to behaving in ways most would deem dishonorable. Provoking their rage was as wise as slapping a bear.

"I don't doubt your reasoning, Damien. But how can we be certain Zander's men will see it as such? What if they feel slighted enough to cut our throats in our sleep?"

"They know the stories of what I have done to those who have crossed me. The Zylmacians may be little more than dogs, but even a dog knows the price of disobedience."

I pray you're right, old friend. We would be lost without you.

"Come now," Damien said. "Let us speak no more of Zander and his ilk. Let me show you how we will take this castle."

Motioning gently, Damien bid Einarr to come to the table. On the hide was a diagram of Castle Morden and the positions of each warchief.

Arrows and markings stretched across the drawing, accurately portraying how Dreadfire planned to seize the stronghold. Einarr noticed several prominent symbols drawn in front of the gate.

"And these, what are these?" Einarr pointed at the marks.

"These will be our siege engines. The castle is too well-defended for us to storm the walls, even if we attacked all four sides at once. We would still emerge victorious, but our losses would be far too great. No, we will build engines and batter their walls to the ground."

Einarr wondered why Damien did not order the construction of siege engines in the first place, but then reminded himself they had not expected the presence of the Blackthorn. If they hadn't arrived, the castle could easily have been taken with ladders. But the proposal was reassuring enough. Perhaps the presence of siege engines could force a quick surrender.

"We will send hundreds of men, thousands if need be, to the forests near Khorrtal," Dreadfire continued. "I would like for you to oversee this project, Einarr. Your expertise as a craftsman will be invaluable."

"Absolutely, Damien. You can count on me."

Einarr recalled what he had seen of Morden's walls. Their stone blocks were as thick and sturdy as mountains and would present a nearly insurmountable challenge. He was unsure if breaching such impressively constructed walls was even possible.

"I have only one concern," he said, staring at the battle plans. "Morden was built with stones more than twice the size of those used in any fortification I've ever seen. It will take great effort to bring that wall down, assuming we could."

"Fear not my friend. I have a plan." Damien turned the animal hide over, revealing a drawing of a trebuchet unlike anything he had ever seen. According to the calculations, it would stand nearly five hundred feet tall and require two giant treadmills to draw back the throwing arm.

"We're going to need a lot of trees," Einarr sighed, scratching his brow.

"Indeed. This effort will take weeks, perhaps months, but it is the surest way to breach the walls and capture it before winter. I intend for us to return home before the first snow falls. If anyone can make this happen, it is you, Einarr. You have my full faith and blessing to do whatever is required."

It was perhaps the most ambitious plan Einarr had ever seen, even more ambitious than when Damien announced his intention to make war against the Bethards. But here they were, surrounding Betanthia's greatest stronghold after laying waste to an army more than twice their size. Einarr constructed many things throughout his life, but nothing as complicated and imposing as this. But the impossible had already been done, which gave him all the necessary encouragement.

Who am I to question this plan? After all, we defeated thirty thousand men with less than half those numbers, all because of Damien. If this is the way forward, I will help make it a reality.

"You can count on me. I'll begin at first light."

Einarr turned to leave the tent but paused. A question burned in his mind since earlier in the day, which he was hesitant to ask even now. He could not forget the sight of the old woman and wondered what role she would play in future battles.

"Damien, there's something I must know. What did the crone say to you on the battlefield?"

The old woman's groaning cackle still echoed inside his ears. It was a sound Einarr was not likely to forget for the rest of his life. Even thinking about it made his skin crawl and turn cold.

Damien grinned, though it was ambivalent. "She told me the one I seek is here. I will remember her words until my dying day."

"What did she tell you?"

The lanterns flickered and nearly extinguished as if a mountain wind were licking at the flames. Damien Dreadfire's black eyes grew darker and seemed to consume the light around them.

"Fair as winter, yet fierce as fire. The queen of cinders, bid fair to scorch us all."

LUCETTA V

DAYS PASSED SINCE LUCETTA LAST SAW HER UNWELCOME VISITOR. However, the entity's absence did not bring any sense of comfort or safety. It was quite the opposite. The more time that passed without the woman in black revealing herself, the more fear began to pollute Lucetta's fragile mind.

She thought long and hard about what the woman had told her. Someone close to Aldred held the key to all her ambitions, and she would have to discover that person somehow. But Lucetta was entirely removed from her husband's affairs and knew only a few associates of his; the men on the King's high council.

After her first real breakfast in days, she retired to her chamber balcony overlooking the estate's courtyard. An unexpected chill arrived the night before, providing a welcome recess from the torment of summer. Finally, she was able to think.

There were three other members of the high council, aside from Aldred, that she knew of. From her understanding, Sir Tristan Conway was the youngest and somewhat impressionable. They had no interaction, but Lucetta knew well enough that he was a braggart. It would be dangerous to trust such a young and potentially reckless man with plans that could land her in the dungeon.

No, he simply will not do. If he opens his mouth to the wrong people, or to anyone, then all is lost. There must be someone else.

Lord Morgan Lawson was another, but Lucetta dismissed him out of hand. He was a man of honor and fiercely devoted to king and country. Before the words could even leave her mouth, Lord Lawson would already be informing Aldred and, inevitably, the King himself. There would not be enough gold in the world to convince him to go along with such a scheme.

The last man was Sir Bryce Whitewood. The mere thought of him made her skin crawl. He was sixty years old and had laid eyes on her ever since she flowered into womanhood, and possibly before. She recalled stories from her maidservants when she still resided at the palace that Sir Bryce had approached them on more than one occasion and engaged in inappropriate behavior for a man of his station. Her face wrinkled in disgust at the thought of even speaking to such a pig.

Lucetta awoke early the next day with the unsettling feeling that someone was watching her. It was becoming easier to sense the woman in black's presence for reasons beyond her understanding. Aldred was still sleeping, and she gingerly slipped from bed and dressed without waking him.

She wore a low-cut maroon dress made of fine linen with gold trim, accenting her slender yet busty figure. Gold rings laden with emeralds and diamonds adorned her fingers. Her long, curled auburn tresses hung freely and danced across the small of her back like silk curtains. She was a Bethard by blood. Today, she looked every bit of it.

Lucetta paced the grounds of her villa as the first rays of sunlight slipped over the horizon. A passing servant took notice of her wandering and offered refreshment, but was quickly accosted and sent scurrying away. She had heard and seen the guards and servants whispering to each other more frequently as of late.

I see the way they look at me. Each and every one of them. I'm certain they're telling Aldred too. I'm sure they would love nothing more than throwing me in a cell somewhere and forgetting that I existed.

After stealing a moment to gather her thoughts, Lucetta retreated to her chamber where most interactions with the strange woman had occurred. Oddly enough, it was the only place throughout her estate where she felt safe and somewhat normal, though the terror remained.

Lucetta still could not shake the feeling there were eyes upon her, even now, alone in her chamber. Slowly, she walked over to the balcony facing the palace. Only its outline was visible. It stood like a tall, silent shadow against the backdrop of the coming sunrise. From here, she scanned the breadth of her property in search of the woman in black.

Her gaze turned to a row of tall arborvitae near the northern edge of the grounds. They served to keep prying eyes of passing commoners away from her residence, provided they could see over ten feet of stone wall. At first, Lucetta saw nothing, but after allowing her eyes to adjust to the darkness, she saw the outline of a figure appear. A subtle glow of two orange-red spheres sent a spike of cold shivers up and down her spine. The woman in black had arrived.

Lucetta chewed on her tongue while the entity stared back unflinchingly. This was the moment she had anticipated for days. After mustering up her courage to go down to the woman, Lucetta turned and was given the greatest fright of her life. The woman in black was standing only feet away.

The shock was so great, she nearly tumbled backward over the balustrade. Luckily, Lucetta was able to regain solid footing before plummeting to an almost certain death. The entity looked down upon her and smirked.

"Still, you act like a frightened child? Come now, back on your feet. There is work to be done."

The woman in black resumed her less intimidating form, though her soft features did little to stifle fear in Lucetta's heart. After rising onto unsteady legs, she donned a long, flowing crimson cloak and followed the entity through the estate and into a dusky morning. Thankfully, none of the servants were awake, and a pair of guards outside the front gate would never think to question her or inform Aldred of her movements. Or at least she hoped.

"Where are we going?" Lucetta whispered as they walked down Auburn Row.

This was the first time she had ever been outside the estate without an armed escort. It was dangerous enough for a woman, and certainly for a woman of wealth, to walk alone through the city streets. Especially with what transpired the last time she ventured out. Lucetta's mind harkened back to the day she was assaulted, nearly bringing her to tears.

"You already know where we are headed," the entity said softly.

The reply made her shiver, the hairs on her neck standing as stiff as stone pillars. If the woman in black could see and hear inside her head, surely this was a delusion or nightmare she could not wake from. Lucetta was afraid even to contemplate it.

No, she can't mean for me to go there. To see... him...

Together, they passed through empty streets and dark alleyways. Sir Bryce Whitewood's estate was in the government sector and easy to find. The walk was short, though too long for Lucetta's liking. Though it was summer, the air felt crisp and unusually chilly for this time of day.

Finally, she arrived outside the Whitewood estate and instructed the guards to allow her entry. They were hesitant at first, but a senior guard showed her in without further delay.

The residence smelled old, just as old as Sir Bryce and just as unpleasant. Its decor was horribly dated, and much of the furniture looked to be crafted during the reign of King Torbin. The parlor was kept clean enough, but as a servant led Lucetta through the mansion, she was disturbed to find an ever-increasing level of disorganization and squalor.

A distasteful place for a distasteful man.

She walked past piles of discarded parchment stacked on tables and benches lining the main corridor. It was unclear what was more unnerving, the feeling of the woman in black behind her, or the level of untidiness in Sir Bryce's household.

Once outside Bryce's study, the servant gave a sharp bow and returned to his morning duties. Lucetta felt a knot tightening inside her stomach as she rapped gently on the door. There was no immediate reply, so she turned the latch and pushed it open. Sir Bryce was sitting at his desk, scribbling away on a piece of parchment with quill and ink.

"Ah, Princess Lucetta! I did not hear you. Please, come in! I was not expecting company at such an early hour." The old man stood clumsily. He looked even more weathered and decrepit than she remembered. "How may I be of service to you?"

The study was even more filthy than the corridor, she observed. Hundreds of books were stacked in messy piles, along with miles of loose parchment and a few discarded tankards. At first, she heard nothing, her senses overcome with offense. But then she remembered why she had come in the first place.

"I was hoping we may speak in private. And with the utmost discretion, I trust." Lucetta removed her crimson cloak and hung it over the back of a tall chair. She heard Sir Bryce's heavy breathing as his eyes looked her up and down.

"Um... uh... absolutely! Please, sit, sit." He gestured to a chair in front of his desk.

Lucetta would have taken Sir Bryce's seat as a display of authority, except the one he offered looked far cleaner. She sat and smoothed out the length of her maroon dress. The old man waited for her to be seated, then returned to his chair.

"You're looking magnificent today, Your Highness, might I say."

Lucetta smiled and nodded as politely as she could, bile forming in the back of her throat.

"Thank you. Now, I've come here today because I have a certain… venture I'm pursuing, and I need someone who can assist me."

Sir Bryce thought hard, his face crumpling into a ball of wrinkles. "Most peculiar that you've come to me, I must say. Have you not consulted with your husband?"

"My father, the King…" She made sure to add such emphasis. "…has been unwell as of late. Poor Aldred is terribly burdened by having to manage our affairs and those of the entire kingdom. My brother Gareth is absent and has reneged on his responsibilities, so it has also fallen on Aldred to manage nearly everything."

"Hmm, yes, I see. And what of your brother, Trace? He is a man of great resources. Surely he must…"

Lucetta did not wait for him to finish. She rehearsed her responses to whatever objections Bryce may have raised many times in her head.

"My brother is overwhelmed with managing the family finances and his personal ventures. He simply cannot be bothered with much of anything, sadly. Alas, I have no one else to turn to." Lucetta leaned forward and watched the old man's gaze drift slowly down her bodice.

Droplets of sweat formed on Bryce's spotted brow. Lucetta felt dirty, nearly sick to her stomach at what she was doing. With any luck, the wretched old pervert would soon agree, and she could be on her way. But Sir Bryce seemed hesitant, despite the clear and tempting view of her cleavage.

"I'm… em… I will hear you. What sort of venture are you proposing?"

Finally, this filthy villain is beginning to break, she thought, fighting back a disgusted scowl.

"I have drawn plans for a new estate. Dellhaven has grown too crowded and shabby for my liking. Far too many peasant merchants and their ilk around these days. There are lands to the northeast I have set my desires on."

"I see," Sir Bryce said. "Please, continue. Em… Where specifically are these lands you speak of? I cannot think of many territories north of Dellhaven unless I'm mistaken somehow?"

Here's the true test. Will he agree?

"It's a patch between the Siln River and the Great Sea."

Sir Bryce screwed up his face again and thought. "Oh… oh my. Princess, those lands are miles outside our borders. Surely you must be mistaken? All manner of bandits, marauders, and wild folk could reside there for all we know."

Damn it… damn the man… Lucetta cursed. She felt her face turning red.

"It's a small matter, really. I only require a thousand men to secure and protect the territory while establishing the new settlement. Were it not for this nonsense in the west, I'm sure Aldred would have—"

"No, no, I'm sorry, my princess. I'm most sorry," Bryce said, fumbling for words. "What you propose would require a royal decree from the King himself. We cannot send our armies into foreign lands without a proper resolution, em… a declaration from His Majesty. It could spark a war."

Bryce rose from his seat and straightened out the wrinkles of his sandy brown doublet and trousers. When it appeared he would make a retreat for the door, Lucetta stood and slammed both hands down on his desk.

"Sir Bryce." She leaned forward, the top of her breasts plain for the old man to see. "Your concerns are well founded, but I can assure you my request is not improper. Do remember I am the daughter of your king."

"Em… yes, princess, but I am bound by…"

"You are bound to House Bethard, are you not?"

"I am," he stammered. "But my loyalty is owed to your father. Not his children, especially his lesser children. I simply cannot do what you ask of me."

"I'm sure we could come to some sort of arrangement."

Trace will be quite cross with me for pillaging his gold stores again. I know how to spend it better anyways.

The old man paused, his gaze shifting between Lucetta's eyes and her breasts. Clearly, he was fighting an inner conflict between his manly desires and his loyalty to Marcellus Bethard.

"Well, perhaps there is something… em… you could do…" Sir Bryce said, his voice trembling.

No, he… cannot possibly mean…

"Speak plainly, Sir Bryce."

"Nothing, nothing, my princess. Now I must bid you a good day." The old wretch started hastily for the door.

Lucetta grew desperate, knowing her only hope was about to walk out. She would just assume to handle the endeavor herself, but she knew no one in the military. Wandering around Cardale looking for mercenaries to hire was downright insane. She would likely get robbed or killed and left in the streets, like the man rotting on the Camsby bridge.

"I can offer you gold, titles, an estate in my new territory, whatever you desire." She tried not to sound desperate.

Sir Bryce was intrigued and paused before reaching the door. "Yes, yes, a most generous offer, my princess."

"Then it is done," she sighed in relief.

Every man has his price. It appears I have found this old fool's.

"Now that I think about it," he said, scratching his balding head. "Perhaps the best way is not to involve the military. It would raise far too much suspicion if a Commander were to be parted with a company of his men, and I'm sure you wish to remain as discreet as possible, yes?"

She nodded.

"Good, then the use of mercenaries seems most logical. I know a reliable man with five hundred swords under his command. There is but one potential issue, though…"

"And what might that be?" Lucetta inquired.

Deep in thought, Sir Bryce stroked his wrinkled, bare chin. "That many men marching around could raise questions, especially if you mean to move across the border and back. But no one would be the wiser if we were to disguise the mercenaries as the King's soldiers. I could see they are outfitted in the King's colors, with the appropriate weapons and armor, whatever they require."

Smiling with excitement, Lucetta clasped her hands together. "That is most wonderful, Sir! I knew I could rely on you."

"But, I'm afraid it is more easily said than done," Sir Bryce said, a sly grin forming in the corners of his cracked mouth. "It would require me to pillage our armories, which could prove risky and costly. And not to mention inventories are meticulously well-kept."

This old fool means to hold me to ransom! The nerve!

"Tell me what more you require, Sir. Tell me what price, and I will pay it."

Her mood was teetering on the verge of outright hostility. Lucetta leaned her hip against the desk and crossed her arms in annoyance. The old man approached slowly, his eyes glancing down to her bodice, then down to her skirts.

He… he cannot mean what I think he means. Can he?

The old Councilman cleared his throat. "Ahem… you… are quite lovely, my dear. Perhaps… with the right… persuasion, I can make everything happen for you when you need it to happen." He reached out and gave the lightest tug on the strings of her bodice.

Incensed, Lucetta slapped Sir Bryce across the face. He chuckled and shrugged off the blow, then again turned for the door.

"On second thought, I have no need for gold and titles, both of which I have in plenty. After all, I am a wealthy man and a member of the King's high council. So I bid you good day, princess. And I'm afraid I must also inform Lord Aldred of this matter. Attempting to destabilize the safety and security of Betanthia? Now that is something he would be most interested in hearing."

"I beg your pardon?" Lucetta scoffed.

"Yes, I'm afraid so. You intend to send an armed force into foreign lands to root the natives out. Of course, we have no way of knowing the consequences of such actions. But I know this; what you are advocating for, at the very least, is war, and done clandestinely behind the King's back, no less." The old man sneered, knowing he had her backed into a corner.

Dammit, damn him to a thousand fiery deaths!

"You are aware I am the King's daughter, yes? I am a Bethard, and it is my sovereign right to do as I please." Anger and nervousness turned her cheeks a deep shade of red.

"Treason is still treason, I'm afraid. As long as Marcellus Bethard is king, his will alone is the law of the land. Bethard or not, you would be overstepping your bounds."

She was never so embarrassed and enraged in all her life. Sheepishly, Lucetta took leave from Sir Bryce's study and slammed the door behind her. She wept in shame and disgust. That was, until the woman in black passed around from behind her.

"What is this sniveling of yours?" the woman growled. "Why are you running away when you are so close?"

"I can't... I can't do this," she sniffled, trying to save what remained of her dignity. "You're asking me to break faith with my husband and give myself to that deviant. I cannot..."

"You must. You have intelligence, cunning, and beauty. These are valuable traits to possess. And the time has come for you to use them. All of them."

The woman in black circled and stood inches away from Lucetta's face. She felt a piercing heat radiating from the entity, and smelled what appeared to be ashes and sulfur.

"If you do not…" The woman's orange-red eyes grew brighter until they smoldered and swirled into a raging firestorm. "Then this is the fate that awaits you and your people."

The apparition reached out, wrapped its cold and leathery hands around Lucetta's head, and pressed deeply against her temples. The pressure was so great Lucetta thought it might cause her head to explode. But within the space of a second, her eyes rolled back, and she witnessed the most disturbing vision one could imagine.

The Westwind Citadel was ablaze from a raging fire. Lucetta stood in the palace's courtyard, staring at the once proud edifice as it cracked and crumbled from the heat. A red stain bled across the sky as flames lept toward the heavens. Large, thick plumes of noxious smoke smelled of burning wood, and burning men.

Walls of orange flames surrounded her and consumed anything in their path. Everything was blanketed in ash and embers, from the once-green gardens to the people who called Cardale home. Horror-stricken, Lucetta turned to flee but was nearly knocked down by a rider galloping by on a black horse. She stumbled, fell onto the hard cobbles, and crawled backward to avoid being trampled upon.

The rider's untamed hair, beard, and animal skin cloak were unlike anything she had ever seen. He howled like a wild beast, riding into the smoke to seek more plunder. The body of a wealthy nobleman was dragged unceremoniously behind the demonic-looking horse, his features ravaged and ruined beyond recognition. Lucetta scrambled to her feet and fled through the burning gates of the palace, but there was nowhere safe to escape.

Hundreds, nearly thousands of fearsome-looking men overran Auburn Row. They decimated and pillaged anything and everything in sight. She tried to flee to her estate, where refuge might be found, but the streets were running so heavily with blood that her legs could barely move. Inch by inch, foot by foot, Lucetta slogged through the wreckage of what was once the seat of her family's power.

The dense, acrid smoke made it easier to conceal herself amidst the chaos. Shrieks of a frightened woman as she was dragged by her hair from a burning building made for an ample distraction. The poor commoner was promptly set upon by well over a dozen men and stripped of all her gold, jewels, and clothing. Lucetta looked away and continued to retreat to her estate, trying not to think of what unspeakable fate might befall the unfortunate victim.

At last, the gates of her estate came into view. Exhausted and overwhelmed, Lucetta collapsed in a heap onto the ground. Breathing was so laborsome she nearly fainted on the spot. While gasping, straining, and coughing, she noticed a dark figure by the iron gate. At first, it appeared to be floating in midair. After gathering her courage, she crawled forward to see who it might be and noticed a rope wrapped tightly around the person's neck.

Clouds of smoke cleared briefly, and flickering light from the blaze cast a red sliver of light toward the estate. Lucetta gasped in horror as she saw the figure suspended from the front gate was not a servant, relative, or even a random citizen of Cardale. No, it was *her*.

"No… no, this cannot be!"

She cried out as the cold, dead eyes of the corpse stared down at her pitifully. A thick layer of ash and dried blood soiled its lifeless face, but she could still recognize herself. The shock was too great for Lucetta's mind to process. She turned away, clawing and dragging herself across the charred cobbles of Auburn Row. Then, a steady, metallic crunching of armor drowned out all other sounds and grew louder with each step.

Across the backdrop of a burning city, she saw a tall, ominous shadow drawing closer. A passing cloud of smoke obscured the figure's features, but as it came within feet of her, Lucetta saw a suit of blackened steel armor, encasing the largest man she had ever seen. The otherworldly-looking man marched toward her with fierce and bloodthirsty determination.

The eye slits of his horned helm erupted with flames, so bright and hot it made the inferno raging throughout Cardale seem little more than a pit fire. A gauntleted hand reached forward as if to take hold of her neck, but as the man's massive fingers came within inches of her face, the vision was suddenly over, and she was back safely inside Sir Bryce's residence.

The experience was so real and jarring that she wanted to throw up. Lucetta covered her mouth, coughed, and groaned from the burning sensation of smoke in her lungs. When she looked down at her hands, she saw what appeared to be tiny flecks of ash.

"This shall come to pass if you do not do what it takes to earn Bryce Whitewood's favor. Only then can you fulfill your destiny and secure a future for Betanthia. You have no choice now; the fates have spoken. You must obey!"

"I… I don't know if I can…" Lucetta complained as meekly as a child.

"Very well. You will make such a pretty decoration on the gates of your estate until your body rots and is eaten by worms and birds. What a fine meal you will make."

The woman in black turned and walked down the hall. The vision, however, was unforgettable. And worse, the dark specks on her hands were real, not some fabrication of an overactive imagination or clever deception. No, the proof in her hands was real enough. And it unsettled her more than returning to Sir Bryce's chamber.

"Wait," she called out suddenly.

The entity turned and scowled.

"I'll… I'll do it." Fresh tears made Lucetta's makeup smear. She used a finger to dab the mess away.

"Good," the entity said. "And I will be there to make sure you do."

Slowly, the door to Sir Bryce's study opened once again. Cautiously, Lucetta slinked inside and noticed the woman in black was already standing behind him, grinning. Something malicious hid behind her orange-red eyes, yet she smiled and nodded in approval. She called out the old man's name with a voice as loud as a mouse's. Sir Bryce stopped his scratchings and curiously looked up from a parchment stack.

"Do it," the woman in black said mockingly. "Do it. Do it!"

While masking her anger and embarrassment, Lucetta pulled on a string from her bodice until it untied. Sir Bryce raised a curious eyebrow.

"Do it! Do it! DO IT!" the apparition repeated over and over until it made Lucetta's head throb and ears ring.

"Do what you will, Sir. But give me everything I require. And speak no word of this to my father or husband." Her voice was near to trembling, both with rage and fear.

Sir Bryce set upon Lucetta like a lion on a gazelle. Tears welled in her eyes as the woman smiled wickedly and chuckled. The room began spinning and growing unbearably hot, nearly as hot as the inferno from her disturbing vision. The old man tore at Lucetta's bodice until her breasts spilled out. He hoisted her onto his desk and rustled hastily through her flowing skirts. She was in disgust and disbelief, recoiling as his stale, warm breath offended her delicate neckline.

With each thrust, the face of the woman in black grew all the more ghastly as it looked on. Its eyes grew unnaturally large and turned the color of freshly spilled blood, while its skin faded into a dingy lifeless gray, like that of a cadaver. Two rows of yellowed and razor-sharp teeth grew broader and more visible with each mocking laugh. As terrible as the sight was, it was impossible to look away.

Such an ordeal was nearly too traumatizing to endure. The appearance of the apparition had grown so evil and frightening that Lucetta was unaware of Sir Bryce's continued violation of her body. But soon, the woman faded into the shadows, and all Lucetta could think about was her husband and the day of their wedding, and the vows they made to one another. She had promised to be faithful, love him through fortune and tribulation, and provide him with children.

The latter vow was one she could not honor. After months of trying, nearly a year, the physicians told Lucetta she was barren. The news that she would never bear children was devastating, but thankfully Aldred's love and understanding saw her through such a dark time. And now, at the behest of the woman in black, her other vows were shattered forever.

As she felt the warmth of his seed inside her, Lucetta came near to retching. Ashamed and violated, she fixed her dress as the old man stumbled back, wheezing and smiling. The apparition was gone now, though where it disappeared to was a mystery. Lucetta suspected it was still there, somewhere, lurking in the shadows and watching.

"Now, Sir, will you make good on your promises?" Her stomach churned and felt sour.

"Yes, my dear, I will reach out to my man on the morrow and arrange a meeting. Then you can discuss your... um... plans together, and come to an accord." Sir Bryce panted like a dog and stole a moment to fix his britches.

"Good." She hurried to the door, nearly sobbing. "And if you speak of this to anyone, I'll tell my husband and father that you abducted and raped me. They always believe me, so you would be wise to be discreet."

Without waiting for his response, she grabbed her cloak and stormed into the hall, throwing the door shut in a fit of rage. The filth and clutter piled on the floor was a stark reminder that her body was now just as soiled.

"You did well," the woman in black said, stepping out from a parlor.

"Why must you torment me so? What sort of foul and dreadful creature are you?"

"You should be thanking me." The woman sneered. "Your attention was so focused on me, you hardly noticed what that old slob was doing. Consider it a mercy on my behalf."

"A mercy? You force me to prostitute myself and call it mercy?" Lucetta cried through gritted teeth. "Leave me! Leave me, and never return. That is the only mercy I require."

The woman in black laughed, then waved a hand dismissively. "Nonsense. You owe me a debt of gratitude. Were it not for me, you would never have found the courage to take advantage of your god's given attributes. Think of it; you have taken the first step toward fulfilling your destiny. Soon you will have an army at your back and a crown on your head. All because you were unafraid to do what was necessary. Today, you have proven where the real power of House Bethard lies."

This isn't what I had in mind, not at all. All I wanted to do was make Cardale safe and clean, where children don't starve and beg on the streets. And to keep Betanthia safe from attack and secure a future for our house. But now it's all gone wrong, so horribly wrong.

"Your dismay is to be expected, child," the woman said in an unusually conciliatory manner. Lucetta remembered the entity could somehow hear and see what was happening inside her head. "But once this divine plan comes to fruition and you see what magnificent things you will achieve, you will thank me."

The woman's appearance softened as they exited Sir Bryce's residence. Her hair and eyes became light and beautiful as a winter snowfall, and her skin's warm, welcoming glow returned. Finding solace in her transformation was difficult, knowing her beastly form could reemerge at any moment.

"Why can you not look like this all the time?" Lucetta whispered. "Why must you frighten me so? Is there some sort of sick enjoyment you find in tormenting me?"

"The answer is quite simple," the woman replied sweetly, much like Queen Charlotte did to comfort her as a child. "I prey on your fears so you may confront them and become strong despite them. You have always been the true strength of House Bethard, far more than either of your brothers. But one can never realize their true power until they are pushed, tested, and brought to the brink. And now, you have come to see what you are capable of. Your might will continue to grow until not even the gods can challenge you."

It was an encouraging idea, far more encouraging than anything her parents had ever said. Lucetta was beginning to find comfort in the woman's words. However, nothing could make Sir Bryce honor his pledge if he chose not to. And she couldn't march back into his residence and stab him in the heart if he proved treacherous. Royalty or not, such a scandal would be unprecedented if discovered.

Her walk back to the estate felt like an eternity. All the while, Lucetta's thoughts were racing alongside her. A craving for wine was too insatiable to ignore, but what she wanted more than anything was sleep. Sleep, and pretend that when she woke, the woman, the vision, Sir Bryce, the whole ordeal, would have been nothing more than a nightmare.

The monotony of her old life seemed less intolerable now. If only the woman in black were a figment of her imagination or some temporary insanity. Perhaps she might find peace for the first time in weeks since the headaches began and the blurry spot appeared in her vision. Lucetta wondered if the dark, hazy spot was the woman in black all along, watching and waiting for the right moment to reveal itself in full. The notion was too unsettling to comprehend.

After returning to the estate, she took a much-needed bath and washed the old man's filth from her body. Thankfully, the day was still young and no suspicion arose from her absence. The servant girls quickly drew water and heated it to the appropriate temperature. Her maroon dress, which had long been one of her favorites, was too revolting to look at. But as Lucetta thought of having the gown thrown out or burned, she decided instead to keep it as a token reminder that this was real and she was not losing her mind.

The servant girls scrubbed her body gently and washed her long, auburn hair until it smelled as clean and fresh as spring air. The water's warmth was refreshing and helped cleanse Sir Bryce's stink from her skin. The only comfort to come out of such humiliation was the knowledge that, soon, she would have a small army under her command.

"Great deeds require great sacrifice," Marcellus once said when she was young.

I'm sure he never meant this kind of sacrifice.

At first, memories of her father's advice made her ashamed of the unspeakable act committed only hours prior. But gradually, as she relaxed with a fresh goblet of wine, her humiliation slowly drifted away.

When has a Bethard ever sacrificed so much for the greater good, and the sake of our family legacy?

The woman in black's voice responded from deep inside her head. "The answer is, never."

TITAN

THERE WAS SOMETHING ODDLY SATISFYING ABOUT SEEING DEAD savages strewn around the castle grounds. Titan Bradshaw looked down from the gatehouse, surveying the macabre landscape. He was beginning to realize that unless the bodies were cleared soon, they would begin to bloat, stink, and attract swarms of birds. It was a problem in need of swift remedy.

If only we had a trebuchet. I'd sling every one of them back to their master.

The first skirmish was quicker and more decisive than he anticipated, and the result was most welcome. For a fleeting moment, Titan believed they would make it out of the siege alive, though he reminded himself that the men killed today were but a fraction of the barbarian horde. The knights and Morden garrison fought well, but how would they fare if the entire force descended upon the walls?

Northmen… just as stupid as I remember them being.

For now, only light from thousands of campfires gave proof the enemy was still around. Night had fallen, and the dying cried their last hours before. Titan made the most of his downtime and sat quietly atop the gatehouse with a skin of wine and his thoughts to keep him company. He learned he preferred solitude these days. It was easier that way, especially when on deployment.

Throughout his career, Titan suffered more tragedy than triumph. Every friend he made during his training at Castle Thorn died long ago. Most men under his command were dead, though he suspected some still lived. The battle of the upper Plainhold nearly obliterated his entire force only a few years ago. And his most recent deployment to the Zylmacian borderlands claimed the only two friends he had since King Marcellus' final conquest at Borjifa. Neither fame, glory, nor commendations could fill the void in Titan's heart.

The night terrors were the hardest to deal with. After returning from the Plainhold years ago, Titan could not erase the horrific images imprinted on his memory. Each night he returned to the battlefield and watched as his friends died again, and again, and again. It was always the same dream, played out in the same way.

The fighting had been fierce that day, and King Marcellus sent him and his knights to scout for the barbarian army. When they happened upon each other, some of the fiercest and bloodiest fighting in the history of Betanthia broke out. It wasn't until the Order stood on the verge of defeat that the King arrived and decided the battle within the hour.

Even though that fateful day was long in the past, the memories were still haunting. Titan never spoke to anyone at Castle Thorn about the horrors he witnessed. Instead, he withdrew and became the bitter, resentful beast of a man every knight seemed to fear. Nothing about the Order appealed to him anymore. He only desired a discharge and a plot of land in some little corner of the world where he could live the rest of his days in peace.

Perhaps one day, I might find myself in a place like this, minus all the bloody savages. Out in the middle of nowhere where nobody can bother me.

With nearly half of a wineskin in his stomach, Titan grew drowsy. Another attack could surely come tomorrow, and he would need his strength and wits to fend it off. Before leaving the gatehouse tower and turning in for the night, he heard an echo of footsteps coming up the stairs.

"You up here, Bradshaw?" a familiar voice said. It was Hunter Northcott, a man hated a bit less than most but still disliked nevertheless.

"Aye, and I was enjoying the peace and quiet until you showed up," Titan huffed.

"Ah well, you'll just have to make do then."

Hunter grasped his right knee and winced in pain as he climbed the final step of the tower. He flexed it back and forth a few times, the joint snapping and popping. With a sigh of relief, he boldly snatched the wineskin from Titan's hand and took a respectable swig.

"Didn't expect to find you up here. Weren't you planning on feasting with the others?" Hunter tossed the skin back.

"I'll eat when I'm good and hungry. I was enjoying the view." Titan gestured at piles of bodies strewn about the base of the castle.

"Fair enough."

It was endlessly amusing to see the old man squirm. But then again, seeing anyone squirm whenever they crossed paths with him was always entertaining. As humorous as it was, Titan preferred to be alone, and Hunter was intruding on his solitude.

"So… you've fought these northern folk more than anyone I know," Elite Northcott said. "Do you think they'll attack tomorrow?"

Hunter leaned against the crenellations and looked at the array of campfires dotting the landscape like stars.

"Hard to say, but I would give it an even chance that they do, or don't." Titan shrugged, then took another drink from the wineskin. It was nearly empty now, thanks to the old knight's pilfering.

"I'm thinking they were just testing us, and they'll go at us even harder tomorrow," Hunter said.

"Testing? Yes, yes, they were. But you would do well not to underestimate these creatures. They're not going to make the same mistake twice.

Not likely. I had my eyes on that big fucker on the black horse. He's the one calling the shots. If I were him, I would wait until the time is right."

"And what time might that be?" Hunter asked.

"Until we're starved and sickly. This castle may be provisioned for a year or more, but the whole fucking outside is littered with bodies. The last thing we need is disease breaking out, so if they don't send men to claim their dead, we'll need to do it ourselves. And at night, too, so their archers don't pick us off."

Tylar stared off into the darkness, becoming more concentrated and agitated, and eternally on guard for some terror that might come from the night. If there was one thing he could say about the northerners, they were as ruthless and clever as a pack of dogs. If you focused too intensely on one, another would charge from behind and tear you to shreds.

"Aye, you could very well be right. We're in quite the predicament, it would seem," Hunter reflected.

"Of course I'm fucking right!" Titan snarled. "If the girl doesn't keep her wits about her, this castle is finished. It doesn't matter how tall and thick the walls are."

"That reminds me, I meant to ask you something, Tylar. What are your thoughts on Commander Everly? I don't believe you've served with her before."

"She did well enough, I suppose. But the real test will come when that cunt in the black armor sets all of his wolves loose. Today was easy. They were probing for weakness, and it's over the second she shows any."

"Is that a compliment I hear?" Hunter jested, an ugly grin forming across his even uglier face.

"Don't fuck with me, old man. Yes, the girl can lead. And she's not a coward about it either, sitting up in the highest tower and having orders shouted down below. No, she was right there in the thick of it, like a proper Commander should be."

Titan's words showed a certain reluctance, but he spoke true. Madelyn performed well and saw that no savage made it alive inside the walls. She was undoubtedly the day's hero, likely feasting with the rest of the Blackthorn and telling tales of their valor. He remembered once being a celebrated hero in his own right, even before that fateful day on the upper Plainhold, but the memories seemed so distant now.

Nearly twenty years ago, Tylar Bradshaw won his first great victory in combat. He recalled where it all began, at the Battle of Savamange Swamp, which had been especially grisly. Captain Frederick Morrowson led his patrol into a swamp in pursuit of a band of Droethien brigands when they were taken by surprise.

The fighting was fierce, and the Droethiens outnumbered the Order at least twofold. To make matters worse, Captain Morrowson died when his horse fell on top of him after being peppered with arrows. All hope seemed to fade as he drowned in the murky waters of the Savamange. But that was when Tylar, a mere Sergeant freshly promoted, rose to the occasion.

After rallying the remaining knights and fighting out of the muddy, swampy hellhole, Tylar achieved victory. For his efforts, he was promoted to Captain upon returning to Bentmont. He could vividly recall the fanfare he received before, during, and after the ceremony.

"You are a shining example of a knight of the Blackthorn. We should all aspire to carry your courage and decisiveness with us every day, everywhere we go. We are honored to raise you to the rank of Captain, and may your brave actions inspire future officers."

High Marshal Jonas Pierce's words were still fresh in his mind, and it saddened him to see the High Marshal die only a year and a half later. But before that time, Tylar would win more victories and advance himself further within the Order. The Siege of Brimnora was a fight he would assume to forget, though it was perhaps his most memorable.

The barbarians along the northern frontier sacked the border town of Brimnora but retreated inside a nearby fortress when the Order arrived. Titan remembered hunting them for weeks until they finally met each other. The siege was short but terrifyingly brutal.

The Northmen knew little about defending a fortification. But they fought so fiercely that even after breaching the front gate, the Order could still not take the fortress. Wounded three times and with an arrow sunk deep in his shoulder, Tylar pushed into the heart of the melee where the fighting was at its fiercest and hacked the head off the enemy chieftain with a single blow.

Demoralized and with nowhere to go, the barbarians were cut down without mercy until none remained. Then, when the sounds of battle grew quiet and the killing stopped, his men cried out, "Titan! Titan! Titan!" Bleeding and near death, Tylar had emerged victorious once again and earned a name he would forever be known by.

But those were glories of past days, and the younger knights cared little for his legend. After years of fruitless missions and seeing his closest friends killed in battle, Tylar grew angry and disillusioned. As a result, the newcomers only saw a battered, weary, and resentful husk of a man.

"Are you alright, Bradshaw? You've got that distant look in your eye. What troubles you?" Hunter squinted.

Grumbling, he shoved past the old knight and descended the gate-house stairs. He moved across the battlements to the northwestern wall in search of privacy, having grown tired of company.

Why can't they just leave me alone? I'm here to do a job, not make friends.

Moonlight glistened off still-fresh blood staining the crenellations where the ladders were raised. It was a grisly reminder of the day's work and that the battlements might be wet with their own blood come tomorrow. That is, if the barbarians were to attack.

Titan paused and looked at the massive stone heart of the stronghold. Flickering light, songs, laughter, and the scent of roasting meat drifted out from the inner keep. He studied the structure well and long. Should they be driven from the walls and pushed back inside it, his chances of survival would be slim at best.

I didn't ride all this way to die. Not for this fucking Order, and not like this.

There were few options for retreat, especially with Morden surrounded. But the wheels inside his mind were turning, plotting what to do should the walls fail to hold back the barbarian horde. His thoughts were interrupted as the doors of the keep were pushed open.

Merriment made its way into the bailey, and soon roaring fires were lit to accommodate the party. The victorious revelers danced, sang, and boasted about their bravery from hours earlier. Titan scoffed and shook his head as he watched the drunken celebration from above. Part of him felt it was foolish to let their guard down, lest the enemy take advantage and attack under cover of darkness. But the walls were well-manned, and another part of him felt such revelry was necessary to keep morale high. He had certainly done his fair share of drinking since the sun went down.

He caught the unmistakable sight of Madelyn's blonde hair in the light and watched as she laughed and shared stories with the knights and garrison. She reminded Titan of how he used to be with the men under his command, the feeling bittersweet. If there was one lesson Tylar had learned throughout his life, it was that the only permanence was impermanence.

Enjoy your evening, Commander. You've earned it. If you're half the leader I think you are, then perhaps we may make it out of this yet.

The racket was too loud for Titan's liking, and he ascended the steps of the corner tower to find solitude once more. He heard nothing coming from the darkness before him, no sign of attack or sounds of merriment from the barbarian camp. But there they were, and at the coming of dawn, he would be ready to face them again should they feel bold.

After the celebration died down, Titan stole a few hours of rest at the top of the tower. His dreams were dark and full of horrors he often revisited at night. We awoke in a cold sweat, not unusual for him. It was still dark, though the sun was a mere hour away from rising. If there were to be an attack, this would be the perfect time to execute it.

Titan climbed slowly to his feet, stretching and nursing a sore spot on his back from sleeping against the hard stone tower. After rubbing a thin film of crust from his eyes, he peered out to see if he could spy any movement.

"There you are." A voice called out from behind, causing Titan to tense up in surprise. It was Commander Everly.

"Don't sneak up on a man like that, girl. It could mean your head one day."

"I'm sorry. The men were asking about you, wondering why you didn't come for the feast. I brought you some meat and wine. You're probably starving."

It was true. Titan was so hungry he felt like throwing up. Begrudgingly he took the plate and set it at the inlet of a nearby crenellation. He didn't want to show any sign of weakness or hunger to Madelyn.

"I'm sure the men are getting along just fine without me." He took a drink of fresh wine.

"I know you don't like to hear this, but you are a legend throughout the Order. The men *do* feel more confident knowing you're here."

Flattery won't get you anywhere, girl. Not with me. I know I'm as hated as the day is long, and that's fine by me.

"Do you think they're going to attack soon?" Madelyn asked, looking out at the barbarian campfires. Most began to flicker and fade, having burnt themselves out.

"Why does everyone keep asking me like I have all the fucking answers?" Titan shot back in irritation.

"Because I respect your expertise. You've faced Northmen before and won."

"You know what my expertise has earned me?" Tylar's eyes lowered. "It's earned me the privilege of seeing every friend I've ever known die. And die most horribly, screaming and covered in their own blood and shit. So why are you asking me? You're the Commander. You're supposed to have all the answers, right?"

"Well, perhaps if you didn't wallow in self-pity all day, you'd realize you have friends here. You *do* matter to people, whether you believe it or not."

Madelyn stormed out of the tower before Titan could reply, but in truth, he was dumbstruck. Nobody in the Order dared to speak to him as she did. It was uncomfortable to know someone could see through you and call you out so openly.

"Wait," Tylar said, not expecting Madelyn to hear him. But she did and made her way back up the tower.

"Are you just going to berate me some more? Because I won't stand for it. Not after what we did here today." She crossed her arms and gave a sharp glare.

"No, girl. I'll spare you for now." He grinned. "To answer your question, I'm not sure if they will attack tomorrow or the next day. Like I told old man Northcott, it's hard to tell. But one thing you cannot do under any circumstance is think them mindless. They're far more clever and dangerous than most give them credit, as much as it, uh, pains me to say it." Titan instinctively took another few pulls from his wineskin.

"I wish they would realize their folly and retreat, but I know we won't get that lucky." She sighed.

Madelyn returned to the crenellations and looked again at the surrounding fields. She was beginning to develop the stare, as Titan called it. It was disappointing to see someone like her feeling the same way he did. She was young, ambitious, and idealistic, with her whole life in front of her. If there was any injustice in the world, it was seeing her become lost and dead inside.

"I'm afraid, Tylar. I'm afraid of failing these men. I'm afraid of failing the High Marshal and the Order. I'm afraid of what will happen if we can't hold this castle."

At first, he knew not what to make of Madelyn's confession. It was the first time anyone had opened up to him this way in many years. He felt afraid as well, though he couldn't quite say why.

"Whatever you're feeling, whatever fear you have deep down inside you, you must keep it locked away," he said. "You can't let the men know you're scared. Do you understand me? Everyone here is looking to you to lead, especially that worthless shitbag Lieutenant they've got running the place."

Madelyn chuckled. "It does look like Lord Valens left us the riff-raff. If the Northmen don't attack tomorrow, I want to start training these boys to fight. I know they do a decent job teaching in castles, but nothing like we do in the Order. I'd like you to show them how to do it properly."

Titan scoffed and showed his first genuine smile in years. "Oh no, you won't get me roped into duties now. The old man is perfectly capable of training this lot. I've seen him tackle far worse."

"Hunter is good, but I need you to teach them to fight in ways that he can't."

"And what would that be?" Titan raised his chin proudly, amused by the banter.

"With hate. Not wild, unadulterated hate, but focused hate. They will need to become just as savage as our enemy to survive. Are you man enough for the challenge?"

The conversation had taken an unexpected yet amusing turn. Titan was coming dangerously close to respecting her. It seemed she had the same bile coursing through her veins as he did. It was an intriguing offer, and the more he thought about it, the more sense it made.

If these green Morden boys can't hold their cocks correctly when they piss, how can we expect them to wield swords? And they'll certainly be of no use if they're dead. If it means I'll stand a better chance of leaving here alive, then it's worth my time.

"You're a feisty little bitch. I'll give you that." Titan tried to hide his smile by taking another drink. He offered it to Madelyn. "Alright, I'll take you up on it, if it means I won't be the only man who walks out of here alive."

"Good. If the Northmen aren't upon us by morning, can you start training?"

"I suppose I could." Titan belched, then reached for a piece of meat and bit into it. It was cold, but still delicious. "Take that skin with you. I think I best be getting some rest now."

Madelyn hoisted the nearly empty wineskin and saluted him. "Very good then. I'm looking forward to seeing what you can do, Tylar. Have a good night."

"And a good night to you, Commander," he said mockingly, though she seemed to appreciate the sentiment.

Daylight appeared a few hours later, but the enemy did not. Not even when the sun rose and midday passed did the barbarians strike. Instead, they were content to keep the fortress surrounded, with no hope of escape. Titan made good on his promise and ordered all of Morden's garrison into the courtyard, knowing there would be no attack today.

He looked over the meager garrison with utter contempt. Few among the rabble appeared capable. Most were recruits with only the most basic of training under their belt. Some looked as if they had never held a spear or a sword before.

Why in the hell did I ever agree to this?

"Alright, you sorry sons of bitches. Today you're going to learn how to fight like real men. Not like how some pampered lord wants you to fight, oh no. I'm going to teach you how to kill each and every savage that crosses your path with skill and efficiency."

"Excuse me," Lieutenant Ellis Byrne interrupted from across the bailey. "Take care not to insult our lord. He was a man of honor and taught us well enough."

Titan licked his lips and smiled. "So, you fancy yourself a soldier, now do you? Come now, show your men how brave and well-trained you are. Come at me with your best."

"I don't think that's appropriate, I do not require any—"

"So you're a chickenshit then, eh? I didn't realize the lord of Morden preferred to enlist cravens and women in his garrison."

Titan loosened his belt, removed both sword and scabbard, and tossed them onto the ground. He raised a hand and beckoned the young Lieutenant to showcase what Castle Morden's finest could produce. Reluctantly, Ellis drew his arming sword and approached. He screamed wildly and came in close with a lunge, which Tylar sidestepped easily. Ellis swung with a slash, then followed with another and yet another. Each strike met nothing but air as Titan danced effortlessly around them.

Having felt out his opponent, he stepped in during another wild swing and drove a steel vambrace down the sword to block it, then delivered a punishing haymaker to Ellis' face. The Lieutenant collapsed on the ground.

Roughly a dozen knights laughed among themselves. Their brethren in the castle garrison, however, did not share their amusement. Ellis rose unsteadily to his feet and clapped a thick layer of dust from his tunic and trousers.

"Get up. Surely you can do better." Titan was terribly amused with himself.

Overcome by embarrassment, Ellis tightened his jaw and looked as if he might cry. This time he was not so reckless. Both men circled each other, studying the other's footwork intently. Ellis attacked with a lunging thrust but quickly disengaged after Tylar leaped out of the way.

"Get him, Titan, get him!" a voice called out from the crowd.

"Come on Ellis! Come on! You have him!" another shouted back.

Having seen enough, Titan stepped forward and feigned a jab with his left hand, then kicked a cloud of dust into Ellis' eyes and landed another punishing right hook. The young Lieutenant dropped to his knees, and Titan kicked him hard in the chest and sent him crashing to the ground once more. A chorus of victorious cheers erupted from the knights.

"You don't fight with honor," Ellis groaned, spitting out a mouthful of blood.

"Honor? Who gives a fuck about honor? You either live or die, and if you plan on living, then you have to use every weapon and every trick at your disposal."

"There's nothing civilized about hacking and clawing at one another," Ellis protested. "We're men, not beasts."

"By all means, Lieutenant, if you want to die with honor, then you go right ahead. I'm sure when your head is rolling on the ground, it will be most noble indeed. As for the rest of you, do any of you plan on living?"

There was a unanimous show of hands from the castle garrison.

"Good. Then I suggest you listen to everything I have to say."

"Everything *we* have to say," Hunter interrupted. He stepped out from a group of knights and went to Titan's side. "Come on now, Bradshaw, I've trained thousands of recruits in my day. Remember who trained you?"

Hunter's smug satisfaction was irritating enough that Titan considered clubbing him senseless in front of everyone. If there was one thing he hated more than being around others, it was being interrupted. Or made to look a fool.

I wonder if it would be possible to make that ugly face of his even uglier. One punch, that's all it would take.

"Besides," Hunter continued. "A fair amount of work needs to be done, and there's not a lot of time to do it, eh? The Northmen could attack any time now. What do you say we split these lads up and give them a proper workout?"

"You're lucky, old man," Titan said quietly. "Challenge me like that again, and I'll fuck you up so bad you'll need to wear a bag over your head for the rest of your life. Understand?"

With the sun blazing in his eyes, Titan squinted and sneered at the men of Castle Morden. He would undoubtedly have his work cut out with this lot, and there was precious little time. He retrieved his arming sword from the ground and fixed his belt around his hips.

"Anyone else care to say something?"

Silence filled the yard.

"Good. Then grab yourselves some sparring gear. You're about to step into my world."

EINARR V

The backdrop of Khorrtal came into view around midday. It seemed like only yesterday when the warband arrived outside the disputed city and plotted their first strike against Betanthia. Thinking of how far they had come since that day was nearly unimaginable.

They passed by a burnt parcel of land where the battle occurred. Scattered across the blackened soil were charred skeletal remains of those who were put to the sword. Admittedly, there was little pity left in Einarr's heart for what they had done. His lack of feelings over such wanton slaughter was perhaps the most troubling thing of all.

Have I begun to lose myself? No, I must not. I cannot.

There were more pressing concerns than the dead, however. Despite fear in his heart, he rode at the head of the column into Khorrtal. The village had been brought under Betanthian influence only a few years ago, if he could recall the stories correctly.

Even with two thousand men at his back, Einarr was uncertain how they would be received. If the villagers were true to their kin and heritage, songs of their liberation would be sung from this day until the end of time. If not, then surely another bloodbath would ensue.

"Steady men, be on your guard. There's no telling how much sway the Bethards still hold here," Einarr shouted, turning in his saddle.

Fortunately, he was not alone. Damien had tasked Marvath Bonesplitter and a band of warriors to assist in the construction effort and provide additional security. It was comforting to know the Rhivothi fanatics had come along, and Einarr wagered their presence alone would help dissuade any treachery from the locals.

"True enough, Rolffson. It would be a damn pity to have to spill more of our blood. But perhaps they will remember what we've already done here." Bonesplitter dismounted, removed his monstrously large great axe from his horse's saddle, and prepared for a potential skirmish.

To the Northmen's surprise, no alarm was raised and no Khorrtalli warriors had contested their arrival. In a perfect world, Einarr would have assumed it was a sign of welcoming, but nothing was certain in a place like this.

He remembered it was only recently when Damien brought the warband to Khorrtal without incident. The Betanthian garrison stationed there had been deliberately attacked days prior by a host of Sylvia Stormguard's warriors. Some of the enemy were allowed to escape to Castle Morden to bring word of the supposed unrest to Lord Valens.

They did not resist us then, and I pray they will not resist us now.

A small crowd gathered near the outlying homesteads and continued to grow by the second. Many looked afraid and apprehensive. Mothers scrambled to gather their children and seek refuge. Men donned clubs or whatever weapons they could find and stood vigilantly outside their hovels. Einarr took note of their presence but did not sense any hostility.

If their loyalties were with the Bethards, surely they would have resisted our advance the first time around. Kholdyr, shield us from deception and harm.

To his relief, their presence was greeted not with steel but with cautious optimism. The further they rode, the more locals appeared to witness their arrival. When it was clear that Einarr and his men brought peace and not death, a spontaneous celebration erupted. Children broke free from their mother's grasp and ran alongside the horsemen, laughing and playing in the presence of their hesitant-looking parents.

"Brothers and sisters of Khorrtal!" Einarr rode to the village square. Two thousand spears followed closely behind, on guard for any unforeseen treachery. "Do not be afraid. We do not bring you fire and death as your Bethard captors have. Instead, we bring you hope and the promise of a better tomorrow!"

Hundreds of faces stared back in awe as Einarr spoke atop his horse. So many had gathered around, he could scarcely tell them apart from one another. But, unfortunately, not all appeared to be as joyous as the majority were. Some gave ill-favored looks, and he carefully kept a hand ready to draw his bastard sword should the encounter turn hostile.

"In the sight of the gods, we have come to set you free from the yoke of oppression. We demand nothing in return. Your freedom, and that of all Khorrish nations, is yours by right. We ask only that those seeking to avenge your subjugation come forward and join us in our godly quest. Together, we will tear down the walls of Castle Morden and forever free these lands from those who would defile them."

A growing commotion swept over the crowd. It churned and rose like a coming storm, then erupted into a cacophony of cheers and cat-calls.

"And why would our people accept such a fine and generous offer from the likes of you?" a voice called out mockingly.

An old man stepped forth from the crowd, his entourage close behind. He had long, silvery hair and a white beard that retained a stripe of black color, and dressed in a modest tunic and breeches of tan roughspun. Around his neck hung a necklace of what appeared to be Betanthian gold, which drew Einarr's suspicion.

"And who would you be, friend? I am Einarr, son of Rolff, of the Nothanek clan."

"I am Dhuuld Lurrson, chieftain of this community. You have brought turmoil to our peaceful village, Rolffson, and I will not allow our people to suffer any further disturbance."

A few muffled words of agreement echoed throughout the village square, though they seemed cautious and reluctant enough.

"Have the Bethards not brought enough death and suffering to your lands?" Einarr asked. "Have you grown so fat and wealthy in their service that you have forgotten your duty to your people and gods?"

Bonesplitter appeared with nearly two dozen of his fanatics. The Rhivothi nomad sensed the chieftain's unfavorable tone and anticipated the crowd turning at any moment, should Dhuuld command it.

"Tread carefully, Einarr," Marvath said quietly. "Your next words could spark another war we can ill afford."

"If you have come here to insult us, then I say you are unwelcome and must leave at once. What right do you have to march this army into our village?" Dhuuld objected.

"Pray tell me, what right did Marcellus Bethard have when he marched his army into Borjifa? Or have you forgotten?"

The crowd began to stir and whisper. Uncomfortable and uncertain glances were traded among the commoners while Dhuuld's retainers attempted to calm and silence their growing dissent.

"And what would a Nothanek know of such things?" Dhuuld challenged, his defiance undeterred. "What would you know of men like Marcellus Bethard and Cedric Valens?"

"A Nothanek would know nothing, to speak fairly. But we march under the banner of Damien Dreadfire of Borjifa, who has witnessed the full extent of the Bethard's benevolence. I have seen with my own eyes the horrors his people have endured. Have you, son of Lurr? Have you seen death on such a scale?"

Dhuuld scowled and ground his teeth and remained silent. There was little he or anyone else could say, for the name of Damien Dreadfire had spread so far that even Khorrtal knew of his legend.

"Free men of Khorrtal!" Einarr shouted, turning his attention back to the crowd. "Do not fear Marcellus Bethard. Do not fear his wrath, nor those who serve him. We have met the enemy on ground of our choosing twice, and sent Lord Valens and his army to the gods. If you doubt the truth of my words, here is proof for your eyes."

Einarr drew an arming sword from his saddle and removed a cloth covering and bindings. He thrust the ornate blade high into the air, its jeweled and golden hilt glistening in the sunlight. The huddled masses drew closer in wonderment.

"See the truth with your own eyes! Behold, the sword of Cedric Valens!" Einarr threw the blade to the ground, its razor-sharp edge cleaving the compacted earth effortlessly and standing upright.

"You fear the Bethards because you cannot resist them alone. But I am here to tell you, Damien Dreadfire has forged a powerful army that has twice tasted victory. He has united friend and foe, and from many, we have become one."

With an outstretched hand, Einarr's fingers folded back one by one and balled into a fist. He felt an energy building within the people, who were now so vast in number he could hardly tell them apart from his own men.

"You do not have to cower in fear while your Khorrish identity is slowly taken from you. These lands are your birthright, bestowed upon you by your forefathers. Your gods are yours to worship, a right no man may take away. Will you suffer under the boot of oppression and watch as the degeneracy of Betanthia replaces your heritage?"

"No!" a chorus of hundreds, nearly thousands of voices rang out in unison.

The very mention of their conditions over the last several years brought about swift and unexpected anger, though Einarr did not sense their hostility would turn toward him.

"Will you stand and live free as your ancestors once did?" he cried.

"Yes!" the masses roared back.

Their reply was so loud he felt the force of their enthusiasm in his chest.

"Then let the gods drink their fill of Bethard blood!"

Einarr drew his bastard sword, lifted it above his head, and reared his horse, much to the approval of the Khorrtalli. Many embraced and laughed and cheered, understanding they were now free. Einarr could hardly recall feeling more satisfied. This was, undoubtedly, his finest hour, having liberated the vilage without shedding a drop of blood. Surely, Alina would have been proud.

"You speak fiery words, son of Rolff. I didn't know you had it in you," quipped Bonesplitter through the crowd's roar, himself impressed with their reception.

"My tongue doesn't speak the language of steel, Marvath. I'm simply borrowing some of Damien's thunder."

"You speak it well enough. Come now, let me show you soft Teb dwellers how we celebrate in the Hinterwood." Marvath slapped Einarr so hard on the shoulder it nearly unhorsed him.

The crowd's enthusiasm forced Dhuuld and his retainers to withdraw from the square. Einarr could not be certain where they retreated to, but he suspected a close eye would have to be kept on him for the duration of their stay. For now, he was content to bask in the warm energy of thousands of free Khorrtalli men, women, and children.

Celebrations carried on late into the night. Einarr walked among the villagers, feasting, drinking and sharing stories of the warband's victories. Some could hardly believe so few had defeated so many, and he invited any man with doubt to march back with them to Castle Morden.

At first, dozens expressed their interest and intent to fight alongside Damien, but soon the number grew to a hundred, then hundreds. Half a thousand men pledged themselves to the cause before dawn, much to Einarr's satisfaction. That morning, he ventured north of the village to the Hinterwood's outskirts, where they would begin constructing their siege engines.

The first tree to fall was massive. It landed with a roaring, crashing thud, so loud Einarr wondered if the warband could hear it miles away. It was a species of ash, and he decided to use it for the throwing arm of the largest trebuchet, the monster of a machine Damien imagined. He supposed it would be the only wood capable of handling the intense force such a massive siege engine could produce.

A smile came to his face as he smelled the freshly hewn timber. Einarr closed his eyes and took in the scent through his nostrils, savoring it as if he were smelling one of Alina's freshly cooked meals. A few chops of an axe removed a section of bark from the trunk, revealing the wood beneath it. His leathered fingers ran back and forth across it gently. For whatever reason, he could tell if wood was bad or not simply by touching it.

This is good timber. It'll work perfectly.

Bonesplitter chuckled curiously at the sight. "You caress that tree as if it were a tit. Has it been so long since you've lain with a woman?"

Admittedly, the slight made Einarr chuckle as well. He never would have expected humor from a man like Bonesplitter, given his perpetual agitation whenever Zander was nearby.

"Now this, this is what I was born to do. I can hardly recall the last time I was able to build something. If you took as much joy in your labor as I do, you would understand," he replied snidely, feeling emboldened in his element.

"Oh, but I do, Rolffson. Nothing gives me more pleasure than driving my axe through a man's skull." Marvath removed his fur cloak and rolled up the sleeves of his tunic. He tied back his long, sandy blonde hair with a leather band.

"Well, the sooner we finish, the sooner you'll get the opportunity to do just that. Help me remove the branches from the trunk, and I'll start stripping the bark. The throwing arm is the most important part of the trebuchet, and I won't have any hands crafting it but my own."

"Let's be quick about it then. Gods know someone needs to keep their eyes on that treacherous snake Zander and his cohorts."

"The man truly displeases you so much?" Einarr asked incredulously.

Truth be told, he had grown annoyed with the near-endless complaining about the Zylmacians, especially after their humiliation at the castle. As distasteful as he sometimes found Zander and his people, they were brave and hearty enough to charge alone to prove themselves to the warband, Einarr told himself.

"I don't like him, and I don't trust him," Marvath said. "He doesn't belong among our people, nor do any of those rats he marches with. I would rather fight hopelessly outnumbered against the Bethards than march with those scum. It won't be long before we're fighting them anyways, you mark my words. They're scavengers, and the second they sense an opportunity, they'll stab us in the back and take everything for themselves."

The bitterness on Bonesplitter's face was plain to see. The blade of his great axe bit down deeply into the base of a branch, shattering the wood like glass, a plume of splinters flying into the air. Marvath wrenched his weapon free with a single hand, a telling showcase of his power.

"You're being a little harsh, don't you think?" Einarr continued to strip bark from the trunk. "They've fought and bled just as much as you and I."

"Except I've faced the wildmen before, Einarr. They've encroached on the Hinterwood more than once in my life, looking for lands, spoils, and women. Had I not sworn my vow to Damien, I would never have agreed to march alongside them."

"Is that why you're so protective over Sylvia?"

Bonesplitter appeared to take offense to the comment as if an inappropriate accusation had been made. Einarr paused from stripping bark mid-stroke, unsure if he was about to be bludgeoned for his boldness.

"Aye, that's why. I've seen how that lout stares at her, as if she were a fresh cut of meat. Stormguard is kin, more a sister to me than anything else. So yes, I am protective, you might say. Our people were once a single tribe, you know."

"I wasn't aware. I must confess, I don't know too much about the clans outside of those near the Teb. What caused the split?"

He resumed clearing the remaining sections of bark. The wood smelled so fresh it was intoxicating, his excitement and anticipation growing beyond measure. He glanced over his shoulder to spy what the other craftsmen were doing after another tree crashed to the ground. Bonesplitter averted his attention momentarily as well from the sound.

So many had gathered around the site that Einarr could scarcely count them all. The presence of the Khorrtalli would certainly expedite the construction faster than anticipated, he thought. He saw five different sites where men and materials were gathered. The sounds of axes and saws were a symphony to his ears.

"What separated us, you ask?" Marvath's axe resumed its work. "Distance, that's all. Most of the Rhivothi were content to remain a coastal people, while some, like my clansmen, preferred to set out and conquer new lands. Over time we grew apart, but our loyalty to each other never waned."

"If you were once a single tribe, but are no longer, then what do your people call themselves now?"

"Does everything require a name?" Bonesplitter asked with a hint of annoyance. "My people are nomads. We have no village or city that is our namesake. But we are Rhivothi by blood and have always seen it that way. We have answered whenever our kin have called for aid, and the same can be said for them."

"So you and Sylvia have fought together before then?"

"A few times, yes. You ask many questions, Rolffson. Best you stay focused on the task at hand."

Silently they continued removing bark and branches from the massive ash tree. Assisting in the effort were nearly a dozen men, but once completed, Einarr insisted he be the only one to construct the throwing arm. Well over a thousand men would labor in revolving shifts day and night to build the rest of the colossal trebuchet and its four smaller siblings.

One morning while chopping and shaping the trunk into its appropriate form, Einarr reminisced about life in Skaginlef. Though he was only days removed from the fighting at Castle Morden, strangely enough, the war seemed so far away. He was surrounded by many of his kinfolks and lost in the blissful monotony of work he so loved. Einarr felt more at home than he did at any point in the last two years since the Bloodbath at Borjifa.

Solemnly, he reflected on his previous project: the mead hall in Skaginlef, constructed in honor of Alina, his lost love. It was well over twice the size of the previous hall and so elaborate in its design, it became the talk of every neighboring tribe. Travelers would often visit and witness the magnificent hall, bolstering the economy of Skaginlef. For his efforts, the tribal elders offered him a place on their council, an unheard-of feat for someone so young.

Ironically, his last creation was built to memorialize the loss of life, while his newest would be used to destroy it. He rationalized it as a necessary evil. If the war was brought to a swift conclusion by using such a terrifying weapon, then further loss of life could be avoided. But such a hope was, more often than not, naive. Blood would be spilled one way or another, and it was his duty to make sure as many Nothanek could return home as possible.

Days slowly turned into weeks, and each piece of the imposing tre-buchet began to come together one by one. Einarr knew from Damien's drawing that the engine would be colossal, but it wasn't until the frame was erected that he realized how massive it truly was. The trebuchet was far bigger than he had anticipated and easily towered over five hun-dred feet.

Building the frame had taken nearly as long as the throwing arm. Einarr took particular care to make sure it could support the enormous mass of the counterweight, which by his calculations, it would. They would need to construct a series of cranes to lift it into place, which he feared would lead to an unacceptable delay. The four smaller trebuchets were nearly complete, and time was beginning to run short.

Dhuuld Lurrson and over a dozen retainers rode to the construction site one afternoon. This time the chieftain was dressed more appropri-ately for his station, wearing a blend of mail, leather, and steel armor beneath a blue and brown colored cloak. On his hip sat an ornate arm-ing sword, its craftsmanship suggesting it was Betanthian forged.

"Good day to you, Rolffson," Dhuuld said dryly from horseback.

His bearded and weathered face bore the same gruff contempt as when Einarr first saw him, though he was impressed with the colossal trebuchet's construction.

"And to you too, Lurrson. What business brings you to our camp?"

"I would see what my people have been laboring toward these past several weeks, and I can tell their time has not been wasted."

"Quite marvelous, is it not?" Einarr smiled.

"I did not know men could build such things, not on a scale like this. You have talent, Rolffson. The gods made your hands to toil, no doubt."

"Indeed they have. But I suspect you haven't come here to trade pleasantries. Speak your intentions plainly, friend."

"I must confess when you rode into town, I had suspicions. Khorrtal has seen its share of turmoil. Far too much, if you were to ask me. But my riders have indeed seen Damien Dreadfire's host at Castle Morden. And no Betanthian army has arrived to challenge them these past weeks, so it is as you say."

"Your suspicions were well-intentioned, but a Nothanek is no liar. Everything you thought impossible is in fact reality."

"Indeed it is. You have shown me wonders, son of Rolff. It would be a sin for me to deny you my hospitality." Dhuuld straightened up in his saddle.

Courteously, Einarr made to give his thanks but was quickly interrupted.

"And my allegiance."

It was an unexpected yet pleasant surprise. When they first encountered each other, Einarr was certain Dhuuld would resist or impede his efforts. Or even worse, cut his throat in the dead of night. But the Khorrtalli chieftain was not what he appeared to be on the surface.

"I give you my thanks, and Lord Damien will be sure to as well." Einarr gave a respectful bow.

"I look forward to hearing it from him personally."

"Is that so?" Einarr stammered.

"You spoke true when you first arrived at my village. The Bethards must be resisted, and it would be dishonorable for us not to repay them in kind for subjugating our people. Our numbers may be few, but we will stand alongside you in battle, under the sight of the gods."

"Then let us toast to our newfound brotherhood." Einarr whistled to a nearby camp follower. "You, boy! Bring mead, and be quick about it!"

The young man hurried off to a nearby tent to fetch refreshments. He returned moments later with two horns overflowing with mead. Dhuuld and his men dismounted for the occasion.

"Now, let us toast our new accord. The free north welcomes Khorrtal into the fold."

Einarr lifted his horn and saluted Dhuuld and his retainers. Without breaking eye contact, both men downed their drinks. A modest round of applause and cheers rang out by those close enough to bear witness.

"I can offer you three hundred spears. I would give more, but as the gateway between the east and west, we must keep ourselves adequately protected. You have Zylmacians among your ranks, I have heard. You should know our people have suffered dearly against the wildmen for generations."

"Your contribution is greatly appreciated," Einarr said happily. "And you are not the only man with reservations about the westerners."

Marvath nodded, then rested his great axe over one shoulder.

"But together, we have found a common cause, and the Zylmacians have demonstrated their dedication." It seemed as if Einarr was trying to convince not only Dhuuld and Bonesplitter, but also himself.

"If you say they can be trusted, then we will raise no protest," Dhuuld said.

Einarr glanced over a Marvath, who appeared indifferent.

"They can be trusted," the Rhivothi nomad replied begrudgingly.

"Very well then." Dhuuld mounted his horse, followed by his retainers. "I have taken the liberty of dispatching men to gather stones for the siege. There is a quarry not far from here. I find it poetic that stones from that very quarry were used to construct the castle, and now they will be used to destroy it."

The Khorrtalli chieftain's unexpected diligence was yet another surprise. If he maintained this level of awareness and planning, Einarr suspected Damien Dreadfire might grant him the title of warchief soon enough.

"Most fitting indeed," Einarr said, smirking. "The gods are not without a sense of justice, it seems."

"When will you be ready to return to the castle?"

"By tomorrow, we will have the counterweight mounted, and it will be ready to test. Then, we'll disassemble it and bring it to the castle. No engine of this size has ever been built, and I would see that it works beforehand. There would be no greater humiliation than to build something this grand and see it fail on its first use."

"Very well. When you have finished, find me at Khorrtal. We will march alongside you."

With a bow, Dhuuld Lurrson and his retainers returned to the village. At sunrise the next day, dozens of men toiled fervently to attach the counterweight to the throwing arm. They completed their work before midday and loaded the gigantic basket with hundreds of stones.

A nervous flutter took hold in Einarr's chest as the throwing arm was slowly drawn back. Such a task was made possible by two giant treadmills that relied on men to power them. Those inside the wheels grunted and strained, and the clang-clang-clanging of steel ratchets ensured the arm would not come loose and engage.

While looking on with bated breath, Einarr was suddenly slapped hard on the back. Marvath had come to witness the test run and see the fruits of their labor.

"Truly, you have created a wonder, son of Rolff. Now, let us pray the damned thing works." Smiling, Marvath took a bite from a heel of bread. He broke off a piece and offered it, but Einarr declined.

"It will, Bonesplitter. I have yet to build anything that did not work as intended."

I pray I'm right and this won't be the first time I fail.

With the throwing arm locked in place, a boulder was dragged into a sling made of rope and leather. After satisfactory preparation, the crew paused and looked to Einarr for their next orders.

"Something this magnificent deserves a name of its own. Have you thought of one?" Marvath asked with a hint of what appeared to be excitement, though the gruff man was careful enough to maintain his image.

Admittedly, Einarr had given it little thought. His goal, first and foremost, was to make sure an engine this size could even operate in the first place. But Bonesplitter was right enough; such a fearsome weapon deserved a name. Something the men would remember when tales of the siege were told. After a few moments, a name stood out clearly in his mind.

"Ruin."

"Ruin, you say?" Bonesplitter cocked his head, as if he had heard the name once before.

"It was the name of the greatsword wielded by Kuggvord, the last great Khorrish chieftain. With Ruin, he brought Betanthia to heel and ushered in a peace that lasted for hundreds of years. So in remembrance, and in the hope that history will repeat itself, I will name it Ruin."

The explanation satisfied Bonesplitter, who gave an approving nod. With the siege crew looking on, Einarr raised his hand and held it in place. The hour was now upon him. With a hint of doubt in his mind, he gave the signal to unleash the largest siege engine ever built.

The trigger was wrenched free, and with a guttural roar, the throwing arm sprang forward and heaved the stone so far and fast it was difficult to keep sight of. The counterweight groaned and rocked back and forth from the immense weight, but did not fail.

After the trebuchet grew still, Einarr let out a sigh of relief. His most ambitious creation performed flawlessly and would be ready for disassembly and the trip to Castle Morden. Soon, he thought, Ruin would live again and unleash its wrath on Betanthia once more.

LUCETTA VI

DESPITE HER VICTORY, EACH PASSING DAY FELT LIKE A SEPARATE defeat. It was a bold first step, and the most serious gamble Lucetta had ever made. She wondered if it was wise to put so much trust in Sir Bryce, knowing how loathsome of a creature he was. If discovered, the scheme might result in imprisonment, or worse. Far worse, given Marcellus Bethard's penchant for rage.

Weeks came and went since she ventured to Sir Bryce's estate. After the first fortnight, she had nearly given up hope that the old man would make good on his pledge. It was endlessly frustrating and depressing to wonder if she had been taken advantage of, a notion becoming all the more plausible.

Sleep was increasingly elusive these days. Sharing a bed with Aldred had become too agonizing to bear, especially when he sought to enjoy more than her company. He could not understand why she would pull away, shrieking and panicking as if attacked by some grotesque monster. Lucetta could not shake the experience from her mind, and could still smell Sir Bryce's stale breath and feel his warmth inside her. The memories sent a cold shiver down her spine every time.

I was a fool, an ambitious fool who prostituted myself to an old deviant. Curse you, Lucetta, curse you! Perhaps I already am cursed, and this is my punishment.

The woman in black was nowhere to be found, not inside her chamber or anywhere else, for that matter. That was not to say the entity was not watching. On the contrary, the very walls themselves seemed to be spying and studying her every movement throughout the estate, never allowing so much as a single moment of privacy. She wasn't safe anywhere, not even inside her own head.

After yet another restless night, Lucetta shuffled out of bed. Her bouts of insomnia had taken a heavy toll on her body. Dark bags and deep lines grew underneath both eyes, and she had lost an alarming amount of weight. Despite assurance from the woman in black that her intentions were pure and designed to build inner confidence and resolve, the experiences were having quite the opposite effect.

I pray one night I do not wake, so I can be rid of this horror. But then again, if she can follow me inside my head, what's to stop her from following me beyond the grave?

Lucetta shuddered at the thought. Perhaps the time had come to rediscover the gods and take up their worship. It seemed like a silly idea at first, since few in Betanthia practiced the religion of their forefathers. However, if it would mean a reprieve, she would do just about anything to be free. She had already defiled her body in the name of family and legacy; certainly, worshiping the forgotten deities of past ages could be no worse.

The sun was rising, and with it came a new day of torment. Breakfast that morning was the usual fare, but none of it looked appetizing. Lucetta took only a few bites of bacon and fresh bread but left the rest of her meal untouched. Aldred's face tightened as he studied her.

"My love, please, you need to eat. You're nothing but skin and bones. Enough of this silliness."

It might have been that Aldred had come to suspect she was losing her mind, the way he was looking at her. The physicians had no explanation and suggested it was merely the product of stress. But Lucetta knew the woman in black was real. She felt the entity's icy touch and saw ash from a burning city on her hands. It was no hallucination.

"I haven't the stomach for it," she protested. It was impossible to look at Aldred without feeling sick.

"Well, you must eat. Perhaps I can see if there is some tonic or potion to help calm your nerves?"

"No, I don't need anything of the sort. I won't be medicated like some lunatic."

Lucetta rose from the table, flung her cloth napkin onto the remains of her meal and stormed off. The guilt of having been unfaithful to Aldred was agonizing enough, but an argument on top of it was more than she could bear.

After retreating to the second floor, she found comfort inside her chamber with a respectable amount of wine. It was the only way to keep the anger stewing inside her in check. By the afternoon, she was thoroughly inebriated and tried desperately to block out memories of Sir Bryce and his apparent treachery. Sufficient time had elapsed for him to have made good on his promise, but it felt more and more like she had been duped.

It wasn't until she received a letter the following day that some semblance of hope was restored. The mercenaries Sir Bryce contacted were delayed on their way back from the southeastern border with the Droethiens. What pressing matter had kept them occupied for so long was something Lucetta could only speculate. But despite the delay, tomorrow they would finally arrive in Cardale. Receiving the news was relieving and exhilarating, and she had to read the dispatch several times before the gravity of the words set in.

At last, that disgusting wretch made good on his pledge. At least I'll have something to keep my mind occupied now.

That night she stayed awake, wracked with anxiety and impatience. Fortunately, Aldred left early for the Westwind Citadel on pressing matters of his own. The last thing Lucetta wanted was for her husband to poke his nose around and ask questions. Trace was less likely to raise any suspicion, since he too was preoccupied with personal business.

Her greatest fear was the woman in black, and what unspeakable acts the entity might force her to do this time. Lucetta prayed her ghostly tormentor would be merciful. She could not bear the thought of further humiliation.

I am a Bethard, and I still have my dignity. I'll die before I let another man befoul me again.

For the meeting, Lucetta dressed as expected from a woman of House Bethard. She wore a flowing gown of deep purple satin with a long, thin chain of gold links draping down to her breasts. On her fingers were golden rings encrusted with diamonds and rubies, and an exquisite tiara sat majestically on her thick, auburn tresses.

Too sleep deprived to do it herself, one of the maidservants was tasked with applying her makeup. The dark bags under both eyes took some creativity to hide, but the result was impressive enough.

"It's good to see you looking like your old self again, Your Highness," the servant woman smiled.

Have I been such a disaster as of late? I'll wager the other servants have been gossiping about me behind my back.

"Thank you. It looks lovely," Lucetta huffed.

The makeup was satisfactory, though her eyes were a bit too smokey for her liking. It was no matter, though. She paced about the room for an hour before a knock came at her door. Lost in thought, Lucetta heard nothing at first. The anticipation of meeting with the mercenary commander blocked out the outside world. This could prove to be the defining moment in her life. This could very well be the dawn of a new empire, one that could exceed the glory of Betanthia.

A second knock was much louder and drew her attention. Again, her daydreams of glory were interrupted by the reality outside her chamber door.

"Your Highness?" a servant girl asked from outside.

Lucetta's legs turned to water. She had to sit or risk tumbling to the floor. "Yes? Enter, enter."

The door opened with a creak, and the girl stepped inside cautiously. Lucetta spied the long shadow of a figure out in the hall. It was almost impossible to mask her excitement.

"You have a guest, Your Highness. Shall I show him in?"

The words barely left the servant girl's mouth before Lucetta nodded her approval. Then, with a curtsey, the servant dismissed herself and showed the man inside.

He was shorter than his shadow suggested but looked every bit as fearsome. With olive skin and a head of dark, curly hair, the man had an unusual and exotic appearance she had never seen before. He was armored nearly head to toe, not in solid plate, but with hundreds of small, steel scales laced together, giving him the appearance of a dragon. Tucked neatly under one arm was his helmet, which was large and oddly shaped, with mere slits for the eyes and mouth. When worn, it would cover the entire head and neck.

"Good morning to you, Highness." His accent was every bit as exotic as the rest of him. "I am Pavlos, Commander of the White Spear Legion. How may I be of service?"

"And good morning to you, Pavlos. Do you not have a last name?"

He chuckled. "I do not, princess. It is not our custom in the west. Those in the east often find it strange."

"Those in the east?" Lucetta replied curiously.

"Why yes. To my people, everything beyond the Plainhold is east." Pavlos gave a wide smile. His mouth was accented with golden teeth, which made him look even more bizarre and colorful.

Did he just say what I think he said? Did he say the Plainhold?

"You're… you're a… a Droethien?" she uttered, eyes growing wide.

This man and his people had been enemies of Betanthia for countless centuries. Had Sir Bryce sent an assassin instead of a mercenary? She was too frightened even to think.

"Yes, my princess, but do not be troubled. Though our people have been hostile to one another for thousands of years, you will find I am less invested in such matters."

"And where do your loyalties lie, Droethien?" Lucetta backed up closer to the balcony door. Though she could summon the guards with a scream, Pavlos would be able to remove her head and escape before they could arrive.

"I am loyal only to myself, and to my men, and those who keep our purses filled with coin. I left my mother country long ago in search of my own fortunes. But, you see, peace can be as costly as war, and a soldier with no enemy to fight must take his talents elsewhere, yes? I can assure you, my princess, you have nothing to fear." Pavlos bowed deeply, an armored hand pressed against his heart.

"I see. And what was your business along the border these past months?"

"Ah, but who knows the border better than a Droethien, yes? I come from the lands around Naxonnos. It is a broken city, and many have fled to start new lives elsewhere. My men and I were given the opportunity to serve King Marcellus, and we have done so for many years."

"What sort of man would betray his people for gold? Where's the honor in that?" She eyed the mercenary suspiciously.

"I love my people and our rich history, but corrupt and incompetent men rule them. Better to serve a new master than die for a bad one, yes?"

Lucetta was speechless. It certainly made sense that there were some in the world more interested in personal fortunes as opposed to those of kings. But she did not trust this man. Not yet, and not fully. He had a warm and inviting aura, quite the opposite of what she felt when speaking with Sir Bryce.

Perhaps this savage could be put to good use.

"Very well, sir. If you seek gold and glory, you have come to the right place. Should you agree, I will employ you exclusively. You will answer to me and me alone. And in return, I will make you fabulously wealthy and give you a place among my high council."

The Droethien smiled, his golden teeth glistening. "It is agreed!"

Lucetta sighed in cautious relief, then moved to her desk and motioned for the mercenary to sit.

"And where is this council you speak of, princess?" Pavlos glanced around.

"You are the first. And you shall sit at my right hand if you prove to be effective. The rewards will be plentiful if you can realize my vision."

"I assure you, princess, my legion has never tasted defeat! Our swords and spears thirst for the blood of your enemies, yes?"

Pavlos chuckled and reached for a helping of Lucetta's wine. He was confident to the point of arrogance, which appealed to her. She would need capable and proven men to carve out a new swathe of territory without drawing unwanted scrutiny.

"Very good then. I would like to begin right away."

She removed several rolls of parchment from inside the desk and laid the largest one out first. It was a map of Betanthia, with numerous drawings in fresh ink. As impressed as Lucetta was with the Droethien, she had a nagging feeling it might still be a ploy.

As much as I want to trust him, I must be careful. A test of loyalty may be in order.

"There is a parcel of land to the north that I wish to build a new estate upon. It sits neatly between the Siln River forks and should be quite safe. Unfortunately, with the situation in the northwest, our soldiers are too occupied to assist."

"You speak of the invasion, yes?"

Lucetta was dumbstruck. How had a lowly mercenary found out about the attack at Khorrtal? Something felt wrong.

"How did you come by that information?"

Pavlos grinned after a swallow of wine. "A man such as myself knows these things. I have fought all across the borderlands, from Naxonnos to Zylmacia."

"Have you any dealings with the northerners by any chance?"

"Why yes, though there are many different breeds of barbarian. They are all simple-minded and quick to anger. But they have all tasted Pavlos' sword."

"Very good." She poured herself a half-full goblet of wine. "How many men serve under your command?"

The mercenary pursed his lips and thought. "Two hundred and forty-three, princess."

Stunned, Lucetta sat back in her chair, mouth agape. This was not the army Sir Bryce had promised. Two hundred and forty-three men was a force slightly larger than the Royal Guardsmen. How could she conquer much of anything aside from a small village?

"Two… hundred…" Lucetta repeated incredulously.

"And forty-three, yes, princess."

Is this some sort of ruse? Does Sir Bryce mock me?

"That is far fewer than what I was expecting." She huffed, voice tinged with disappointment. "Why do you have so few?"

"Ah, you see, my princess, in my company, every man is free to come and go as he pleases. Sometimes we have near to seven hundred, other times fewer than sixty. Two hundred and forty-three is our number now, but know that each man is worth ten of these barbarians, yes?"

The boast was of little relief, but she would have to make do with what was offered. Lucetta was in no position to turn the man away, certainly not. This would be her only path forward.

"Very well." She returned to the map and pointed at the markings. "Are you familiar with this land?"

Pavlos studied the map briefly but shook his head. "No, princess, I am afraid not. But have no worries. We can scout the area and make sure it is safe first. I have heard much of the north is wild and unsettled. We will find out soon enough, yes?"

"I wish to set out immediately. My family has an estate in Dellhaven where we can operate from. It's well-guarded, and after your men are properly armed and outfitted, you can come and go as you please without raising suspicion. When can I expect your men to be ready?"

"For the right coin, we ride tomorrow."

The mercenary grinned. Lucetta opened a drawer, removed a sack of gold coins, and then tossed it onto the desk. Pavlos picked it up and shook it a few times, the gold inside clinking. Then, satisfied, he placed the sack in a leather belt pouch.

"It is agreed," he said. "I will leave you now and join you again in the morning."

Pavlos stood and bowed, armor and gold clanking. After he departed, Lucetta had to pinch herself to ensure the encounter wasn't a dream or delusion. The wheels of fate were set in motion. With the coming of dawn, so too would come a new chapter in her life.

For once, she wished the woman in black would appear to share in the moment. It was odd to want to be in the entity's company, but there was no one else she could speak to. Not even Pavlos knew the scale of her ambition.

I've done everything you've wanted me to, demon, and succeeded.

She made a toast with another goblet of wine. Perhaps the entity was right and it really was sent to help her overcome her fears. For once, Lucetta felt like she had a friend, strangely enough. The woman still frightened her, although now it was a little less.

"Now, what am I going to call you," she said aloud, hoping the woman would hear.

There was nothing but silence, save for the faint sounds of conversation in the courtyard.

"Since names are of no consequence to you, I shall call you…" Lucetta paused and reflected, feeling saddened all of a sudden.

She always dreamed of children but could never have them. Even thinking about what she might have named her son or daughter nearly brought her to tears. She abandoned the idea nearly as quickly as it came.

Sleep that night was impossible. There was far too much to think about and plan for, so Lucetta found aid in a sleeping tonic. But her anticipation was greater than the potion's effects, and she woke an hour or so before sunrise. A few servants began their morning routines, but breakfast was still hours away. Not that she was hungry, at least not for food. It was destiny she craved.

Lucetta dressed in a flowing crimson and gold gown she wore only for the most important events. Today was just such an occasion. Tight around the waist and low across the chest, it made her feel every bit as proper as a future queen should feel. Her long, auburn hair was drawn back into a simple yet elegant-looking updo. The only thing missing was a crown.

After instructing a servant to prepare her baggage, Lucetta sat down to an early breakfast. The eastern horizon was glowing orange and red with the coming of sunrise, and soon enough, Pavlos would be arriving.

"You're awake early, my dear. And you're looking quite ravishing, might I add." Aldred's voice boomed throughout the empty dining room, giving her a startle. He kissed her on the head and stole a second to smell the sweetness of her hair.

"Good morning, my love. I… I want to apologize for my behavior as of late. I know I've been acting strange and worrying you and Trace half to death. I've just been under so much stress, you see. I've been terribly unhappy."

"I'm very sorry to hear that. But you don't have to apologize. It's quite alright. I'm relieved you're doing better and looking more like your old self by the day." He sat on the opposite side of the table.

"I've decided I need some time away from Cardale," she said. "Life here has become too stressful for me to handle. And I must confess, I still feel unsafe after being attacked in the streets. I'm going to spend some time in Dellhaven, at the estate."

"I think that's a wonderful idea, my love." Aldred's blessing was pleasantly unexpected. "Some time away might be just what you need. When do you plan on leaving?"

This is going well. Too well. But then again, Aldred has always been more attentive to his work and less to his wife. I'm sure he'll be glad to be rid of me for a time.

"This morning. My escort will arrive shortly, and then I'll be off."

"Oh, I see." Her husband seemed taken aback. "I didn't expect that you would be leaving so abruptly. When did you decide this?"

"Yesterday. There's no need to worry, Aldred. I'll be perfectly safe."

They ate in silence, but only briefly. Soon, the clopping of horses and the creaking groan of carriage wheels announced the arrival of the White Spear Legion. Lucetta shot up from the table in excitement but quickly restrained herself. She smoothed out her skirts and gracefully strode to the gates.

Outside, she saw an armored carriage and a parade of mercenaries behind it. The column of riders stretched far past the estate grounds and down Auburn Row. It appeared to be only a portion of Pavlos' men, the others likely awaiting them outside the city walls. They were all dressed in the King's colors and carrying the standards of Betanthia, just as Sir Bryce promised. The sight nearly brought tears to her eyes.

"Good day to you, sir," she said to Pavlos proudly.

The Droethien spoke no reply, careful not to reveal his accent and elicit suspicion. Instead, Pavlos thumped a balled fist against his chest and bowed his head from the back of a white destrier. The men appeared well rehearsed and opened the carriage door without a prompt from their commander. Servants scurried inside to fetch Lucetta's baggage while she loaded herself into the imposingly armored carriage.

"Will you be away long, my love?" Aldred asked hesitantly.

"As long as necessary. Don't worry about me. I'll be perfectly alright."

She motioned for her husband to come closer. Their kiss wasn't fiery nor passionate, but it was enough to let him know she cared. Or, at least, that she wanted him to think she cared. If he were to find out the truth, it would end their marriage and forever stain the Bethard dynasty.

After being secured in the carriage, the mercenary convoy started down Auburn Row. It wasn't until they approached the gates of the Westwind Citadel that she grew nervous. The massive, looming palace cast a long shadow down upon her. It was likely the next time she would see it, it would be at the head of a conquering army. Would the Citadel, which had sheltered countless generations of the Bethard family, be reduced to rubble by her own hands?

It would be fitting to have the house my forefathers built brought down by one of their own.

"Worry not, child. The Westwind Citadel will continue to stand as always," the woman in black said matter-of-factly. The entity sat cross-legged on a cushioned seat opposite of her.

This time, the woman's presence caused neither alarm nor outright panic. In fact, Lucetta was quite excited to see her. It was a strange feeling, given the horrors the apparition had put her through to get to this point. But at least now she had someone to bask in her triumph with, however small it might be in the grand scheme of things.

"I did it," Lucetta boasted, a sly smile stretching across her face. "I did everything you said, and it worked."

"You have done well," the woman said. "But this is just the beginning. The true test lies ahead. You must stay focused."

The ride past the palace was emotional, more so than anticipated. This was the home she was born in, after all. She would be back, she resolved, and would not only restore Betanthia to glory, but take it to heights never imagined.

I will return. And when I do, you will be mine.

"Before we go, there's something I must do," Lucetta said deviously to the woman in black.

Even though the entity could peer inside her mind, it stared at her curiously to see what she was plotting. Lucetta slid open an armored window and called out to the driver.

"You there. Tell Pavlos I wish to speak with him."

Moments later, the Droethien commander appeared alongside the carriage on his horse. His steel breastplate shone brightly and was blinding to look at. Together with a flowing blue cloak, he looked every bit like a Betanthian soldier.

Truly, no one would ever suspect he is a Droethien. As long as he doesn't speak, that is.

"Yes, princess? What is it that troubles you?"

"Nothing troubles me." She smiled. "I was hoping you might handle some business for me before leaving Cardale."

"Oh. But princess, we are so near to the city gates. Might this business wait, perhaps for another time, yes?"

"No, I would have this done tonight. You *are* sworn to serve me, are you not?"

Pavlos grit his teeth, then glanced at the column of riders behind them. "Why, yes, princess. Whatever it is you desire, Pavlos will obey."

It would be a lie to say Lucetta was not excited by the thoughts dancing in her head. For once in her life, she wielded power, real power, and was nearly aroused by the thought of exercising it. At first, she was hesitant to speak, but the exhilaration was too great to ignore.

"And if I were to ask you to kill a man, would you do it?" Her heart rampaged inside her chest, and she shifted and squirmed in a state of near ecstasy.

"For the right amount of coin, I will do anything your heart desires, my princess."

"Good. I need you to make it look natural. No knives. Can you make this happen?"

Pavlos chuckled. "Absolutely. I am a man of many talents. Who is it that I should strike down?"

Lucetta looked at the woman in black, a smile adorning her face. The entity suddenly realized what she was about to command the mercenary to do and chuckled softly in amusement.

"Sir Bryce Whitewood."

The words were as sweet and satisfying as a climax. Lucetta would never have thought she was a killer, or even had a trace of it inside her. It felt indescribably pleasing to know the power of life and death was now firmly in her hands.

"After the deed is done, join me in Dellhaven, or on the highway if you're swift enough. Go now, Pavlos. And do be careful."

With a nod, the Droethien commander rode back to the heart of Cardale at a trot. She watched until he was out of sight, still marveling at how effortless it was to order a man's life to be snuffed out.

So this is what it's like to be a monarch. To command absolute obedience. To wield power. Unquestioned, total power.

The mercenaries made their way through Cardale's protective and imposing walls, its massive gates at the northern highway laid open. They passed without a word from the city guards, the King's standard eliciting no response other than a half-dozen crisp salutes. Soon, the capital, and her old and dreary life, would fade away into the distance.

"Now you are ready," the woman in black declared proudly, as a parent might say after witnessing greatness from their child.

"Ready for what?" Lucetta replied in nervous anticipation.

"To be a queen."

TITAN II

THE BARBARIAN ARMY DID NOT ATTACK THE NEXT DAY AS FEARED, NOR did they attack the day after, much to the relief of the men inside. It was a curious strategy but not an absurd one by any stretch of the imagination. Titan knew the Northmen would likely try to starve them out, but the stronghold was well-provisioned, and he doubted they would want to maintain their siege throughout winter. No, he thought, these savages weren't stupid. There *would* be an attack, eventually.

Titan spent his days training the men of Castle Morden in the art of combat. It proved difficult at first, but thankfully, some of the men he encountered could fight. Alongside Hunter Northcott, he shared the knowledge he acquired over years of service and more battles than he could remember. If these men were stationed at Castle Thorn under the tutelage of the Blackthorn Knights, they would have six months of rigorous training before coming close to a battlefield. Titan suspected he had a week or two at most.

Titan preferred to spend his time alone when he wasn't in the bailey with the garrison. He sometimes wandered up the keep's winding staircase and relaxed inside Cedric Valens' private chamber. No one had been inside the lord's quarters in months, and even now, no one thought to occupy it. After all, an attack could happen at any moment, and everyone needed to stay close to ground level.

When he first entered Cedric's chamber, he was none too impressed. The man was a Commandant and served with distinction under King Marcellus, but his dwelling was surprisingly lacking, considering his status.

The bread stores at Thorn are more luxurious than this sty.

But after finding a stash of wine in a wooden trunk, Tylar's mood lightened. From the windows, he saw small, black specks representing the barbarian army. Their ranks were deep, and they sat coiled around the castle like a serpent, ready to squeeze its prey to death at the slightest provocation.

There was no use in brooding over the matter, not when he had such a comfortable bed to sleep on. It was perhaps the one thing in Cedric's chamber that gave him a lordly distinction. The bed felt as light and soft as a cloud, its silk sheets sleek and cool to the touch.

So this is how those highborn twats sleep at night. I like it. If we make it out of here, I'm taking this bed with me.

Days soon turned into weeks, and there was still no sign of an impending attack. Titan enjoyed his time in Lord Valens' chamber so much, there were moments he forgot they were even at war. Madelyn came up to visit on occasion, but Titan pretended to be asleep the last two times so he wouldn't be annoyed by unwanted conversation.

On one particularly cool afternoon, Madelyn happened to catch Titan unawares. The door to the chamber gave a subtle creak, then a long mournful groan as she opened it and entered.

"You're awake, for once," she said with a grin, both hands hidden behind her back.

Before Tylar could give one of his snotty replies, Madelyn revealed what she was holding. It was a wooden wine cask, similar to one of the dozens he had already consumed.

"I found this down in the cellar. Way, way back in the cellar. I figured you might want to share some with me."

"Depends. Most of the shit they keep here is swill anyways. Makes you wonder where it came from." He motioned for the cask, then removed its cork.

The smell was rich and vivid and immediately noticeable. As he sniffed the intriguing aroma of the wine, Madelyn fetched a pair of crystal glasses from a nearby table. Titan poured each of them a generous serving.

"Allow me to raise a toast…" She hoisted a glass. "…to you. For everything you've done the last few weeks to make sure we'll be able to ride out of here alive."

"In case you haven't learned by now, I'm impervious to flattery." Titan sniffed the wine again, his mouth watering.

"Be honest now. Who in their right mind has ever tried to flatter you?" She smiled.

"Did you come here to insult me then?" His irritation was feigned, and Madelyn saw through it.

"No, I'm being serious. I wouldn't be able to do this without you. I know it's been a while since anyone has shown you any real gratitude, but I'm thankful you decided to ride after us that day, even if your reasons are your own. So, here's to you, Tylar. Cheers."

His chest stung and tightened, almost as if his heart was attacking him. All the years of isolation and scorn from the other knights made the loss of his friends that much more difficult to deal with. But here he was now, sitting with Madelyn Everly, the first person in ages he might consider a friend.

After watching her take a drink, Titan followed suit. The wine was strikingly bold, though slightly rustic for his taste, but nevertheless delicious. It was certainly better than the rubbish he subjected himself to until now.

"Now don't go thinking you're going to tell everyone how you buttered me up like some—"

"Of course not," Madelyn interrupted, then poured another glass. "You're still the terrifying prick everyone has come to loathe."

"You're damn right."

The smallest hint of a smile crept onto Titan's scarred face. The wine was strong, and he could not keep his eternally sour expression for long. Together they sat and talked and, on occasion, laughed, well into the evening. When the last light of day disappeared, Madelyn bid Titan a good night, then began the near-endless descent down the winding stairs. After she was gone, he laid on Cedric's bed and immediately fell asleep.

He woke the next morning to shouts from the bailey below and a rapid crunching of armored footsteps sprinting upstairs. At first, Titan thought he was dreaming, but the noise grew louder until he heard a man's winded gasps outside the chamber door.

"Sir, come quickly!" a knight wheezed, then doubled over in fatigue.

Tylar groaned something indiscernible, then rolled over onto his side. The knight stood dumbfounded while catching his breath.

"Commander Everly sent me to fetch you, sir. The barbarians are stirring!"

Fuck… not now…

Titan shot from bed and nearly stumbled to the floor. Hurriedly, he collected his armor, laying in a heap on Lord Valens' desk.

"Well, don't just fucking stand there. Give me a hand!"

The knight assisted Titan with dressing in his gambeson, mail, steel breastplate, vambraces, and greaves. There would be no time to put on the rest of his plate armor; besides, the heat was unbearable enough.

After taking up his arming sword and shield, Titan slogged downstairs with the grace of a newborn doe, then trudged through the keep and into the bailey. The castle garrison was scrambling up to the walls with jars of arrows and quarrels, buckets of stones, and enough water to boil every horse in the stable alive.

"What's going on?" he shouted over the chaos.

"To the walls, men, to the walls!" Lieutenant Byrne stood at the top of the gatehouse, nearly pissing himself with fear. Titan hastily ascended the stairs and joined him at the battlements.

"What are you screeching about?" he demanded.

From up top, Tylar saw the barbarians scurrying about like bees as a long train of wagons appeared over a nearby hill. Long timbers were offloaded and placed in several specific piles.

I do hate being right…

"They mean to fight then. Good." Titan ran his tongue across his teeth. "It's about time we had a proper battle. I want to see what that big son of a bitch is made of."

"Are you blind?" Ellis squealed. "They're going to breach the walls! They're going to get inside the castle. We're doomed! Doomed! And there's no one coming to save us!"

"Don't shit yourself, man. They're not going to build the fucking things by sundown. Way I see it, we—"

A soft hand on Titan's shoulder caused him to turn suddenly. It was Madelyn, who had come to the battlements as well.

"What's the situation?" she asked, scanning the barbarian encampment.

"Looks like they spent the last month gathering materials, because now they're building siege weapons. Nothing I didn't expect to happen eventually," Titan replied.

"How much time do you think we have?" she asked grimly.

"A couple of days, a week maybe. Who knows. It depends on how many they plan to build. As I was saying, our best course of action is to send men out in the middle of the night and burn as many of those things as possible."

"Do you think the walls will hold?"

"They're certainly thick enough," Titan observed. "Maybe after a day or two of hammering on them, they'll try the gate again. That's the best outcome we can hope for. We can hold them there."

"Perhaps not," Ellis chimed in. "We should send out a rider under a white flag of truce and offer terms."

The proposal seemed so absurd that Titan nearly laughed. The garrison began looking at each other with fear and uncertainty. Even the knights whispered among themselves as they looked at the growing piles of timbers.

"Has everyone in this damned country turned craven, or was I unfortunate enough to find myself stuck in a dumping ground of cowards? I bet there isn't a set of balls among the lot of you," Titan snarled at Ellis and spat in disgust. "I would have thought you'd have grown a spine after all I taught you."

"Gentlemen, please," Madelyn interrupted. "Perhaps we should consider your suggestion, Tylar."

The girl had a way of commanding attention with a mere handful of words. Morden's garrison listened intently, a faint and fleeting hope glimmering in a few of their eyes.

"We allow them several nights to build their engines. They will have used most of their building materials by then," she said. "After that, we send a few men out to set them on fire and retreat to the castle."

"And what if it doesn't work? What do we do then?" Ellis asked doubtfully.

"Then we fight. We show these monsters what good and noble Betanthians can do when put to the test." Madelyn turned to Titan. "You know the Northmen better than anyone here. I need you to organize a raiding party. Pick only the men you think would best blend in. We can't afford to lose a single one."

"I'll do it," he said, looking at the encampment. "I'll get in and out real quick. They won't know what's happening until it's too late."

Madelyn grabbed him by the arm. "No," she said with a hint of fear. "No, I cannot risk you."

"Piss on that. I won't send another man to do something I can do."

Seeing the anguish in Madelyn's eyes was easy, but it was difficult to understand why she cared so much. They had only recently become better acquainted. It wasn't like her not-so-secret lover was being sent out on the mission. Titan watched as she chewed her lip nervously.

Don't tell me you've gone soft, girl. I didn't take you for a sentimental one, but perhaps I was mistaken.

"Very well, Commander," Tylar conceded. "I'll give it a few days. Then I'll send the men out."

Two days came and went, and Titan watched from the battlements as the barbarian trebuchets took form and grew taller and more complete. Four were in total, and a much larger structure was built between them. He supposed it was some sort of siege tower or another device they planned to use to assault the castle. It was too soon to tell. Northmen were as unpredictable as the weather.

On the third day, Titan ordered four men to sneak into the enemy camp in the black of night. They waited until after midnight, hoping the barbarian horde would be fast asleep, their bellies full and content with the day's feasting and drinking. He watched alongside Madelyn, hoping to see the trebuchets erupt into raging infernos, but they only saw the faintest hint of fire.

Come morning, they were shocked to see the flayed and impaled bodies of the four saboteurs staked to the ground in front of the castle. The operation had ended in disaster, and only one trebuchet appeared to have been damaged. Clearly, the fire was doused not long after it was lit, and the men Titan sent forth were captured and murdered for their efforts.

Those inside Castle Morden did not receive the news well. Lieutenant Byrne continued to pace about the battlements nervously, his courage extinguished as quickly as the fires their men lit that night. Talk of surrender was whispered quietly among the ranks, and even the Blackthorn were beginning to have their reservations about holding out against the siege.

The massive structure Titan thought was a siege tower continued to take shape. It became increasingly apparent with each passing day that it was not a tower of any sort, nor a ram or anything else. It was another trebuchet, more than twice the size of any normal trebuchet, at that. It was the largest and most fear-inspiring thing he had ever seen. The sheer scale of the wooden monstrosity filled even his stony heart with apprehension.

"This is madness! We must come to terms while we still have a chance!" cried Lieutenant Byrne on the seventh morning after their men were killed.

Birds and insects ravaged their bodies, making for a ghastly sight. The smell wafting over the castle walls was all the more terrible.

"How can you surrender this castle without a fight?" Madelyn asked incredulously. "These are the thickest, strongest walls ever built, and you would simply open the gates and allow them inside? What makes you think they would offer us anything more than the courtesy of their swords? Do you wish to end up as bird food as well?"

"When last I checked, Lady Everly, this castle is the property of Commandant Lord Cedric Valens. Not you, and not the High Marshal. And before he departed, I was named the acting Commander. Not you! I will do what I see fit with this castle and the men inside. And if you object, then ride to Cardale and explain it to the King."

Frustrated, Madelyn stormed away from Ellis and joined Titan in the gatehouse tower, where he overheard the conversation.

"Coward. What an absolute coward. He won't even give us a chance to defend ourselves!" She leaned against the crenellations, stewing in anger.

"Would you like me to throw him off the wall? Just say the word."

They looked at each other straight-faced momentarily, but Madelyn could not contain her laughter. The sound was so refreshing it even brought half a grin to Titan's face.

"As much as I would enjoy hearing him scream on the way down, no. His men would turn against us, and we'll need all of them. If he's serious about sending someone out there, we'll need to prepare to take full charge of the castle."

"Aye." He nodded in agreement. "I've never seen a man so eager to die, and in such a pitiful manner either. The horde will show no mercy to anyone. Believe that."

"Prepare to open the gate!" Ellis shouted from the back of his horse.

In one hand, he held a spear shaft with a white flag tied to the end. He approached the thick wooden doors and stopped before them, but they did not open. The men inside the gatehouse were reluctant to follow such an order but ultimately relented after Lieutenant Byrne gave the instruction a second time.

The man has gone mad, completely fucking mad.

"Lieutenant, what in the world do you think you're doing?" Madelyn shouted from the gatehouse.

"Someone has to put an end to this folly. This is my lord's castle, and if anyone is going to surrender it, it should be his subordinate."

The metal hinges snapped and popped as they broke free of rust that had formed on them. The doors slowly opened for the first time since the Blackthorn arrived. For the first time in his life, Tylar felt fear, a real and palpable fear that struck at his very core. Every instinct told him to ride as fast as he could through the gates with whoever would follow, and hope to break through the encirclement and head east.

These stable boys will lose their senses when this fool loses his head. When we should be showing strength, he shows only cowardice. Damn him!

Nearly as quickly as the doors opened, they were closed. The nervous men of Castle Morden stood breathless as they watched Ellis Byrne ride toward the barbarian lines, knowing it could very well be the last time they see their commander alive.

"Remember what I told you the day we arrived here," Titan said quietly to Madelyn. "You're going to have to lead these men. There's no other way around it now. This cretin will be dead within the hour. And believe me; the Northmen are going to make a show of it. They know how to make lesser men piss themselves."

"If I can't, if they won't follow my lead…" she said doubtfully.

"Then I'll cut a few of their heads off myself until they listen. I won't take your command away, not unless you fall during the fighting."

Damn you Tylar, have you learned nothing? Don't you remember what happened the last time you got close to anyone?

Memories of his fallen friends came rushing back, but he did his best to suppress them. There was a reason he chose to withdraw from the world. And now, here, in the direst situation anyone could find themselves in, he dared to open himself up to someone else who would likely die before his eyes.

"So don't fuck it up, girl," Titan snarled, then walked away, leaving Madelyn stunned and without words.

After leaving the gatehouse, he walked across the battlements and past rows of anxious men. Each looked more unnerved than the last. He ascended the corner tower in search of solitude but was dismayed to see four archers taking up his space. Titan shoved one of them aside and glanced out between a crenellation as Ellis drew closer and closer to the barbarian line.

Damned fool. He's going to give those savages all the encouragement they need. One look at him, and they'll wonder why they waited this long to attack the castle again.

"I sure hope you men have more brains than your idiot Lieutenant, and more balls than the girl over there," Titan said to the archers. "If not, then you better fling yourselves off this fucking tower right now and spare me the embarrassment of watching you—"

"Wait," one of the men boldly interrupted. "Something is happening."

From the Northmen's front line came two riders. The first was the colossus in black plate armor, the man leading this horde of unwashed beasts. The second was a man of noticeably smaller stature, undoubtedly his second in command. Titan watched as they rode out in tandem toward the impaled bodies.

"Might want to look away, you pussies." He scowled. "You're not going to like what happens next."

EINARR VI

MY GREATEST CREATION, AND MY MOST TERRIBLE.

With apprehensive pride, Einarr looked upon the hulking frame of Ruin. The engine appeared smaller than it was when first assembled, though the shadow of Castle Morden was enough to make anything pale in comparison.

"Well done, my friend, well done. It is even more frightening than I imagined." A menacing yet contented grin crossed Damien's savage face, a rare sight few were fortunate to witness.

"The men deserve the glory. They labored ceaselessly," Einarr said proudly. "I must say, Damien, a part of me fears to see what such a weapon is capable of."

The warlord nodded solemnly, his hand running across the throwing arm's sanded surface. "Indeed. But we have seen firsthand what King Bethard is capable of. So carry those visions with you always, and your resolve will never be blunted."

"Maybe the sight of Ruin will be enough to force a quick surrender? Surely they'll lose their will to fight once the first stone flies."

The thought of another massacre was more than he could stomach, but the onus was on the castle garrison to recognize futility when they saw it. If they chose to fight instead of capitulating, he would have to do what was necessary.

Zifnir, I pray that you bestow wisdom on those men, and our own. This war has seen enough death. Let life win out, just this once.

"There is always a possibility. But those are Blackthorn Knights, and not likely to surrender easily. Perhaps we should see how firm their resolve truly is?" Damien slapped the trebuchet, his massive palms clapping against it like thunder.

"Yes, perhaps," Einarr sighed. "Can you promise me something first?"

"What might that be, my friend?"

"If they surrender, will you allow them safe passage back across the Plainhold?" Einarr's chest tightened. "I've witnessed enough horrors, Damien. We put Cedric Valens and his men to the sword, surely that was enough to appease Azldyr for what happened at Borjifa."

Damien Dreadfire's face twisted as he chewed on his next words.

"Do this for me," Einarr pleaded, though careful to mask his desperation. "What threat could a hundred or so men be to us, even if we must face them again one day?"

He felt an immediate, sinking feeling of regret for making such a request, but it was too late to take it back. Einarr could see hatred in Damien's eyes, the same intense hatred he saw at Borjifa. Though they had slain tens of thousands of Betanthians, Einarr was uncertain if the bloodletting was enough, or if it would ever be enough.

"You have fought beside me faithfully and have asked for nothing in return," Damien said, his tone surprisingly conciliatory, though Einarr could sense his displeasure. "If these men choose to surrender, then I will permit them safe passage. But only if…"

Einarr threw his hands up in agreement, more than content with such generosity. "I understand. Zifnir be praised."

Damien turned to the warband, which congregated in ever-growing numbers. Their anticipation was so electric, Einarr felt it building in the air like moments before a lightning storm.

"Now, let us see what sort of men these Betanthians are," Damien shouted. "Let us loose Ruin!"

His bellowing cry rang out far and wide. Then, for the first time in months, the deep beating of war drums sounded. Each thump and thud brought more of the warband out from camp until their entire force was assembled on the field. Ravenous and thirsting for blood, they snarled and howled like vicious animals while the castle garrison looked down from their walls.

"The time has come, son of Rolff," said Dhuuld as he approached on horseback, his retainers close behind. They carried orange and green banners emblazoned with the runic symbols for Khorrtal and its people. "Are you prepared to witness the fruit of your labors?"

"If it would bring a swift conclusion to the fighting, then yes. Yes, I am prepared," Einarr answered with reluctant determination.

The Khorrtalli chieftain dismounted and approached Ruin with the same wonderment as when he first saw it. Dhuuld reached out and stroked the mighty timbers.

"For every day of oppression and subjugation, for every day of seeing our daughters raped and sons levied into the Betanthian army, and for every life lost, you would honor our people by allowing me to loose the first stone."

The proposition seemed fair enough. Einarr looked to Damien for approval, and it was given with a mere nod. But before Dhuuld could unleash the mighty weapon, the castle gates opened. A lone man on a white horse rode out onto the field and carried a white flag of truce. The sight brought laughter and mocking jeers from the warband.

"Cowards!" a warrior cried out.

"They mean to surrender!" said another.

"What treachery is this?" Dhuuld muttered, looking at the rider in disbelief.

Zifnir, you have heard my pleas! Truly, you have graced us with your presence this day. I am in your debt.

A tear formed in the corner of Einarr's eye. The flag symbolized the end of the siege and, with it, any wanton bloodletting. Damien had given his word, and his word was his bond. But even more, what it symbolized was Skaginlef. With the castle taken, Einarr would be free to return home, victorious.

With their army and stronghold in ruins, the Bethards will be loath to pursue this war any further, especially since the Droethiens will hear of what we've done. Marcellus Bethard can ill afford a war against all of us. Peace will be his only option.

The thought brought a cautious yet encouraging smile to his face. It was easy for Einarr to be optimistic, even after the death and destruction he had witnessed. After all, it was who he was, through and through, even though his optimism was sometimes misguided.

"Will you ride out with me, old friend?" Damien asked as he mounted his massive war horse.

This was his moment to finally make peace. Einarr smiled and motioned for a camp follower to fetch his horse. "It would be my honor, Damien."

After mounting, both men set out toward the Betanthian rider, who was approaching fast. They converged near the impaled bodies of the would-be saboteurs, left to decompose under the sun. Einarr felt his stomach heave and churn from a sweet stench of rot and had to resist the urge to cover his nose in repulsion.

The rider approached cautiously. His mount bucked and recoiled at the macabre display and was hesitant to move closer. Einarr wondered if they could even hear one another over the near-deafening buzz of flies, so thick and bothersome he dared not open his mouth to speak.

"Do you understand our language?" the nervous rider asked slowly, carefully pronouncing each word as if speaking to a child.

With amusement, Damien glanced at Einarr. He paused momentarily, which to the rider must have seemed like an eternity, and then some.

"My people spoke this language when yours were herding sheep and swine," Dreadfire answered, basking in the man's nervousness.

The reply made the rider even more skittish, as if easterners could not comprehend the possibility that Northmen could speak in the first place.

"And what brings you out from such a fine castle?" Damien asked. "I thought you would be content to cower behind your walls, as if they could somehow save you."

"On behalf of Lord Cedric Valens, Commandant of the west and defender of Betanthia, I, Lieutenant Ellis Byrne, seek to discuss terms."

"Terms?" Damien feigned puzzlement. "And why should we discuss terms with you, Ellis Byrne?"

"There does not have to be a battle. No one needs to die here. We may be few, but Castle Morden will claim thousands of lives before it ever falls. If you care for the well-being of your men—"

"Oh, but I do, Lieutenant, I most certainly do," Dreadfire interrupted. "It is the well-being of my men that has brought us here. You see, they have come to seek justice for centuries of conquest and slaughter at the hands of your Bethard masters. What sort of man would I be to deny their rightful vengeance?"

Flustered, Ellis fumbled for words as his horse neighed uneasily. "We both know harvest time draws near. Once winter arrives, we will stay warm inside our keep while your men freeze to death. The winds and snows will—"

"Do you know who you are speaking to, boy?" Einarr barked, determined to terrify Ellis and force a quick surrender.

He recalled what Damien told him after the ambush outside Khorrtal.

Fear is our most potent weapon. Time to wield it, or end up wielding the sword again.

"This is Damien Dreadfire, and I am Einarr Rolffson of the Nothanek. We are true sons of the north, not soft, doughy creatures like you easterners. If you think anything will stand in our way, you have made your second mistake."

"And what was my first?" Ellis asked hesitantly.

"Not fleeing when you had the chance," Einarr continued. "We are not the mindless savages you tell your children about at night. If we were, you wouldn't be staring down the largest siege engine ever built."

Ellis' eyes shifted to the massive trebuchet. With the sun falling fast, Einarr saw the shadow of Ruin growing longer across the field.

"The truth is, Ellis Byrne, you would never have believed that men like us could build such a weapon," Damien boasted. "But now that we have, you are having second thoughts about the integrity of your walls, am I right? Answer me true, boy."

"I came here to discuss terms in good faith, sir. Can we come to an accord?" Ellis asked. Sweat formed into beads and ran down his forehead.

Damien Dreadfire's face tightened and contorted into a brewing cauldron of anger. It was almost identical to how he looked the day Einarr and his riders arrived outside Borjifa, having received word of the atrocity there. It was becoming disturbingly clear that despite all the killing done since that day, it was not enough to fill the void in Dreadfire's heart.

Come to terms, Damien. He's practically willing to hand you the castle unconditionally. Do it, do it now, and end this war.

"State your terms then, craven," the warlord growled.

"I humbly request my men and I be allowed safe passage to the east. In return, we will leave the gates to the castle open."

Gods! He really is going to hand the castle over!

It took every ounce of discipline to not cry out in happiness. Einarr could not have asked for a better outcome.

434

"And why would I allow that to happen?" Damien asked, his agitation growing by the second. "So you and your men can regroup under a larger host and face us under more favorable terms? No. No, I think not. I am no fool. The word of a Betanthian is worth nothing to me. We will lay waste to your walls and butcher every Bethard minion we find."

"Sir, I beseech you." Ellis' face turned milky white in a near instant. "I am asking you with the utmost respect and humility, to show mercy and spare my men. We have no quarrel with you!"

"Mercy?" Damien howled, his eyes turning red as hot coals. "Was mercy shown to the people of Borjifa? Did Cedric the Butcher offer such fine terms before he brought us fire and death?"

Ellis gripped the reins of his horse and looked to flee at any moment. Einarr felt his excitement falling away like dry leaves in the wind as he glanced about cautiously, unsure of what to expect next.

"There is a time for mercy, but it will not be today," the warlord said. "Today, there will be blood."

With one swift motion, Damien Dreadfire unsheathed a massive knife on the small of his back and heaved it at the head of Ellis' horse. The beast groaned and fell dead, pinning Ellis' leg beneath it. Einarr watched as Damien dismounted and removed a length of rope from a saddlebag, cursing himself for ever being so optimistic.

"No, please! I beg you! Please!" Lieutenant Byrne squealed and writhed in pain.

"I find it most curious how every one of you easterners beg and plead for your lives when the end has come." Dreadfire tied the rope tightly around Ellis' hands. "You see, in the north, we do not fear death on the battlefield. We welcome it. We embrace it. And we do so because Sjenohor awaits us if we die without fear in our hearts."

Damien retrieved his knife and lifted the horse carcass off Ellis' leg with seemingly little effort. The Lieutenant screamed in agony, whimpering and babbling incoherently.

"P… please… I… please…"

"For you, at least your death will be swift. Swift, yet magnificent. Embrace it, and perhaps the gods will take pity on you."

Dreadfire mounted his horse and wrapped the rope's slack around his hand several times. Then, after spitting in disdain at the castle garrison, he rode back to the warband, dragging Ellis behind him. Einarr looked upon the soldiers as they scurried along the parapets. He heard frantic shouts and curses for taking their commander in such a manner. A dishonorable move to be certain, but there was nothing more to be done.

The warband cheered as Damien returned to the siege line with Lieutenant Byrne in tow. Einarr followed closely and watched from horseback as he was dragged over to Ruin. The colossal trebuchet was locked and ready to be loosed upon the hapless men inside the castle, and despite Damien's shocking rejection of surrender, part of him wished to see what Ruin could do.

"Truly magnificent, is it not?" Damien studied the engine fondly. "Stories of this day will be told for all time. You should consider yourself fortunate, Ellis Byrne; you will be the first to experience its power."

"I beg of you, sir, please. I came to you under a flag of truce and in good faith!" the officer stammered, struggling to pick himself off the ground.

Damien chortled. "Good faith? Spare me your lies, Betanthian. Faith is not a word in your vocabulary."

"Sir, I beg of you, please! I have offered you the castle. What more could you possibly want?"

"The only thing I seek now, Lieutenant, is vengeance."

A crushing blow nearly sent Ellis' head sailing off his shoulders. The crunching of bone against Damien's steel gauntlets was as loud as a tree branch snapping. He fell to the ground with a thud, spitting out a river of blood and broken teeth. While still conscious, Dreadfire kicked and stomped him with unrelenting aggression.

"P… ple… please…"

Every plea for help only seemed to enrage Damien further. With volcanic hatred, he drew his still-bloodied knife and sunk the razor-sharp metal into Ellis' shoulder. His scream was one of the most chilling things Einarr had ever heard. Dreadfire pushed the knife deeper and deeper, twisting and jerking it from side to side until the Lieutenant nearly blacked out from shock.

The cruelty was too much for Einarr to stomach. Each shriek of pain made him wince and shiver, but he could not look away. He suspected Damien was unleashing his pent-up hatred for Lord Valens onto the hapless prisoner, having been denied the opportunity at Blackwolf Pass.

By the gods, Damien, what do you hope to gain from torturing this man? He showed courage to ride out alone, and showed humility and offered you victory. Just take it and be done.

"Damien…" Einarr tried to stop from speaking, but the words had already left his mouth. Thousands of eyes turned toward him accusingly, as if he were out of place for interrupting. "This is a waste of time. I beg you, kill him and be done, or send him back to the castle. If the day grows too late, we won't be able to see well enough to begin the siege."

Einarr could see the events of Borjifa playing out in Damien's black eyes. There was hatred, a great and intense hatred hot enough to melt stone, but there was also an unmistakable sadness and pain only Einarr could sense. Though he disapproved of such wanton torture, it was difficult not to feel that same pain resonating in his heart.

"Einarr is right," Dreadfire conceded. "We have lingered long enough. The time has come to take the castle, then retire."

Deafening cheers and shouts rang painfully in Einarr's ears. The ravenous warriors moved to their positions, anticipating the long-awaited siege. Many remained around Ruin, anxious to see what the massive engine could do up close.

"As for the Lieutenant here, I think it best to return him to the castle. Surely, his men are missing his company. Load him into the trebuchet."

A pit formed deep in Einarr's stomach, and the world around him seemed to disappear entirely. Raucous cheering of the warband and panicked screams from Ellis suddenly sounded as if they were miles away. He could do little as the Lieutenant was loaded into a giant sling made of thick leather and even thicker rope, the bindings around his hands then tied to his ankles securely.

Einarr looked down at the Lieutenant and sighed. Despite his best intentions for the past two years, he seemed incapable of preventing one atrocity after another. This was not the Nothanek way. This was not what he pledged himself to Damien for. But part of him was becoming strangely indifferent, perhaps the most upsetting thing of all.

"Dhuuld, you may have the honor." Damien raised two fingers into the air, then thrust them toward the castle.

The Khorrtalli chieftain smiled and rubbed his hands together. He approached a thick metal pin holding Ruin's throwing arm in place and gave it a curious look. Dhuuld pulled and strained to loose the pin with all his strength, but it was simply too much for one man to handle. Some of his kinsmen chuckled among themselves.

"Well, don't just stand there," he growled, arms crossed.

Several of Dhuuld's retainers came to assist, and together they wrenched Ruin's pin free and sent the massive counterweight lurching downward with a deep groan. In a flash, Ellis Byrne flew through the air, writhing and screaming. Einarr watched as he soared high across the sky and fell well inside the walls of Castle Morden, disappearing from sight and undoubtedly splattering into a horrific mess. The Khorrtalli celebrated and embraced one another.

Slowly, the two massive treadmills began to turn again, the men inside each wheel grunting and straining with every step. Ruin's arm slowly lowered foot by foot, a loud clanging of steel ratchets ringing like a metronome. A boulder towed on a sled by horses was positioned alongside the siege engine, and another brought forth behind it.

The four smaller trebuchets were loosed while Ruin continued its process of resetting. The first two stones fell short of the wall and kicked up clods of earth where they landed. The third struck true, leaving a dusty, gray wound where it impacted. The fourth flew clear over the wall, missing entirely. Though only one stone found its mark, the crewmen let out a satisfied cheer. They knew exactly how to adjust their counterweights so all four would strike on target.

Men grunted and toiled as they loaded more rocks into the counterweights of two trebuchets, and removing some from the other. After properly resetting and reloading, the four were ready to be loosed again as Ruin locked into position.

"The sun grows low," Damien shouted from a distance. "Bring down those walls."

One by one, the smaller trebuchets roared into action. As all four stones impacted, Einarr saw Damien's expression turn sour. It was unclear whether their attack was having an effect at all. The thick, sturdy walls of Castle Morden stood in defiance with little more than superficial damage.

Einarr's heart raced with anticipation as it came time for Ruin to show its true strength. The engine could throw a man far enough, but whether it could throw a stone capable of penetrating Morden's walls was anyone's guess. Then, with a wave of his hand, Damien ordered the siege crew to set Ruin loose.

The throwing arm howled ferociously as it was unleashed. The colossal stone ripped through the air with blinding speed, slamming against the wall so mightily, Einarr felt the impact in his chest. Several blocks split from their mortar and shifted inward, a spiderweb of cracks clearly visible.

Zifnir be merciful! Einarr thought as he watched the defenders on the parapet stumble and fall.

"Faster you dogs, faster!" Marvath barked as he approached with Valerick the Red. When they were not content with the reloading progress, Marvath extracted the men inside a treadmill and took their place. Together, the Rhivothi drove the wheels faster and faster until the engine was ready for another round.

With each successive hit, the castle wall degraded further until Einarr was confident it would give way. The blocks were beginning to crumble and disintegrate, yet to his dismay had not failed. Doubt began creeping into his mind as he wondered if Ruin could fully penetrate the wall despite significant damage to its facade.

Fires were lit along the siege line as night fell. Einarr ventured away from the engine so he could better see the effect Ruin was having on the wall. He paced and wrung his hands with growing anxiety, made even worse when he spied Damien approaching.

"You look unwell," the warlord observed from the back of his horse.

"I fear I have failed you. The walls must be thicker than I anticipated. Ruin should have easily pierced them by now…" Einarr trailed off, looking apprehensively at the castle.

"I have faith in you my friend, fear not. The gods will not allow us to fail."

Silently, Einarr offered a prayer to Azldyr. He could not recall ever beseeching the war god, but with Castle Morden standing in defiance, few options remained.

Azldyr, god of war, hear my prayer. Grant us the might to smash down the walls of our enemies. Grant us the strength to overwhelm their defenses and exact your divine justice. I call out to you in humility. Bless our righteous mission, and in return, I vow to see your will done.

A faint clanging of ratchets told him Ruin was preparing to loose once more. Time stood still as the largest stone yet was loaded into the sling. After slightly adjusting the counterweight, the siege crew was ready and in position.

"Steady, Einarr. Steady." Damien Dreadfire must have seen the desperation and uncertainty on his face. "Ruin will succeed. I can feel it in my bones."

Though doubtful, Einarr nodded in agreement and turned back to the castle as Ruin roared its might once again. It was so dark he could not see the stone as it flew, but when it struck the wall, a most unexpected noise erupted.

Hairs on the back of Einarr's neck stiffened as a thunderous crash of shattered stone rang out. Bit by bit, the base of the wall split and crumbled, and with its failure, the entire section of bombarded wall came collapsing down. He fell to his knees, looking to the heavens in disbelief. Surely, Azldyr had heard his plea.

Thousands of rabid warriors cheered and celebrated as cries of "Rollfson! Rollfson! Rollfson!" echoed down the siege line. It was the first time he had been honored by the warband, their praise enough to make him forget the terrible murder of Lieutenant Byrne. Damien gave Einarr a rare smile, as if he had foreknowledge of Ruin's success.

"Never forget, my friend, this war is greater than you and I. Truly, the gods are with us. Of that, have no doubt." Damien drew his sword and held it high. This was the moment both men had labored toward for two years. Einarr drew his blade in kind, and after Damien dismounted, he gave the final order.

"Prepare to charge!"

MADELYN V

THE BOOMING ROAR OF THE COLLAPSING WALL WAS EARSPLITTING.
For a moment, Madelyn could scarcely believe what she was seeing,
but the reality was undeniable. As slabs of fractured stone spilled into a
now gaping breach, she searched frantically to see who had survived the
bombardment. Roughly a dozen men lay dead among the rubble, and
she realized Titan Bradshaw was nearby at the gatehouse.

No… no please, not him!

The thought of losing her strongest fighter and newfound friend so
early in the attack was gut-churning. As a thick plume of dust began to
settle, a few disheveled figures emerged from the gatehouse staircase. In
the darkness, she was uncertain who they were.

"Is everyone alright?"she shouted, coughing up dust in her lungs.

None answered. Stunned and disoriented, the men shambled about
aimlessly, coughing, groaning, and retching from the choking haze of
pulverized stone. Debris was beginning to settle, and Madelyn knew
that in moments, their enemy would come spilling into the breach like
a tidal wave.

"Titan! Titan! Where are you?" she yelled, scanning the soiled faces
of those around her.

Somewhere in the darkness, a voice called out. It was familiar, gruff and agitated as usual. Madelyn could not see where it was coming from, but his words were a welcome relief amidst the chaos.

"Yes, yes, I'm here," Titan grunted, brushing off a thick layer of white dust.

The look he gave was grim, and Madelyn felt the same dread washing over her.

"What do we do now? The wall is destroyed, and nothing is standing between them and us." Madelyn trembled, unsure of what to do next. Her first siege defense was ending in disaster.

Her mind harkened to times when the Order besieged outposts and barbarian strongholds. It was satisfying to watch their enemies scramble and scurry while under trebuchet and arrow bombardment. But now she was trapped inside a broken castle, with nothing to shield her from the savage horde. Save for the inner keep, their final line of defense.

"They're coming!" Hunter shouted from the parapet near the breach.

Behind him followed two dozen soldiers who were stationed on the southern wall. It was a relief to see he had survived.

Titan grabbed Madelyn by the shoulders and pulled her in close. "Listen to me. This battle is lost, and by dawn, they'll be through the keep. Take a rope and climb down the eastern wall, and get out of here while you still can."

He... he wants me to run?

His words seemed foreign, as if Titan was speaking Droethien. "I'm not leaving these men here to die," she stammered.

"Fuck all of that. You've got to think straight now. There's no time! Death is out there, and it's coming. Nothing can stop it now. Get your ass back to Bentmont as quickly as you can, and—"

"And what?" Madelyn interrupted. "What would you have me do?"

The question seemed foolish, but she was at a loss for words. A Commander of the Blackthorn Knights should have all the answers, she thought. A Commander was supposed to find victory in even the most impossible scenarios. But there she stood, afraid and uncertain, while the screams and ravenous battle cries of twelve thousand savages grew like an approaching thunderstorm.

"Avenge us." Titan drew his blade and pushed past Madelyn toward the breach. She watched in disbelief as a handful of Morden's garrison followed, some hesitantly and others out of a sheer will to survive.

No, I can't just leave. This is why I came here. This is my duty. There's no running away now.

Madelyn drew her arming sword with wavering courage and headed to the breach. Her fingers were slippery with sweat, and gripping her shield handle was difficult.

"Titan!" she shouted, hoping to get his attention.

Before Bradshaw could turn around, a flash of light shot across the night sky. The giant ball of fire flew clear over the wall and smashed into the courtyard, scattering orange and yellow flames everywhere. Men screamed and writhed as they burned alive, and Madelyn had to shield her face from the raging inferno.

"Take cover, men!" she screamed,

Another, and yet another ball of fire came hurtling into the castle. Madelyn sought shelter at the base of the gatehouse where the stone was thicker and had not given way.

"What are you still doing here?" Titan barked as he withdrew from the breach and took cover.

"I'm not running away! You need me here."

"No, what we need is ten thousand men," he replied sarcastically, but was nevertheless right. "These are from the smaller trebuchets, too. Wait until they use the big one again."

Madelyn looked at him stupidly, as if all sense had left her.

"Yeah, we're fucked," he said grimly. "If you want to die here, then you're welcome to it. But if you're going to stay, then grow a pair and lead these men, or I'll do it myself."

Madelyn gave a panicked nod and gripped the hilt of her arming sword. Balls of flaming pitch flew into the castle one after another without pause. She pressed herself tightly against the wall as they smashed into the bailey and against the face of the inner keep. One of the fiery orbs impacted the stables, the old timbers rapidly igniting. Shrieks of horses as they burned alive joined in the symphony of death playing all around.

Oh no… oh please no!

"Nora!" Madelyn wailed as the dry wood quickly incinerated.

Without any thought for her safety, she sprinted through the courtyard, dodging incoming volleys of pitch and dead and burning men littering the ground.

"No, please, girl, no!" A river of tears poured down her dusty cheeks, turning them from chalky white to a dirty, muddy brown.

But the fire was too intense. Not even the agonizing screams of dying horses were enough to compel Madelyn to go further. Instead, she watched in terror as her beloved Nora slowly roasted to death in her stall. Lost for hope, Madelyn collapsed onto the ground, sobbing. Then it grew quiet, save for the crackling of flames and groans of wounded men.

"Madelyn! Madelyn!" Titan's screams echoed throughout the courtyard. "Get the fuck over here, now!"

"I'm sorry, girl, I'm so sorry," she wept, staring helplessly at the inferno.

With Titan still calling to her, Madelyn stole a second to console and gather herself. Nora was not just a horse; she was a friend and a faithful companion of many years. But now was not the time to mourn, especially not with flaming death raining down around her. Out of sheer instinct, she rose to her feet and wearily trotted back to the gaping wound in the wall. She slumped against the broken stone, panting and distraught.

"What the fuck are you doing?" Titan raged. He grabbed her by the neck and pulled her close. "Hey! You need to get control of yourself, or we're dead."

The best that she could do was nod. This wasn't the end, it was merely the beginning. The Northmen had not charged yet, but Madelyn could feel the crushing weight of defeat pressing down on her. It was impossible to believe the strongest castle ever built could be wounded so grievously.

Madelyn shifted closer to the breach. Once near the rubble, she peeked out to see what the barbarians planned to do next. Trebuchets loomed large in the darkness, illuminated by roaring fires.

Terror filled her heart as she watched the thick arm of the giant trebuchet being towed into position. Slowly the massive timber drew backward until it locked in place. Before she could command her men to remain in cover, the pin clanged and engaged and was released.

The behemoth siege engine hurled a ball of flaming pitch nearly the size of a carriage. Madelyn and those nearby scrambled for cover as it hurtled toward the castle. She ducked inside the gatehouse doorway seconds before impact. The explosion of flames was so bright it appeared as if the sun itself crashed from the sky.

She was nearly sobbing from fear. The distant roar of barbarians and the rumbling of over ten thousand footfalls told her the hour of reckoning had arrived. She had feared this moment when the Blackthorn had first arrived at Castle Morden. Madelyn could have fled right then and there. Indeed, she had given it thought, but there was nowhere to flee.

Instead, she chose to stay, whether out of reluctance or a misguided sense of duty. It was difficult to say which. Men were dying all around, and the rest would most certainly be slaughtered. There seemed to be little stopping it now. It was the most helpless feeling in the world.

Titan roared a whirlwind of taunts and obscenities while standing alone at the breach. Madelyn stepped out from the doorway and saw him there, either like some foolish drunkard or like the Blackthorn heroes of old, growling and snarling like a cornered animal. Titan stood alone while the rest of Morden's garrison looked on with fear and uncertainty. Madelyn knew she had to do something, anything. Her life, and the life of every man there was depending on it,

You've trained and fought and struggled your whole life, Madelyn, she thought, trying to encourage herself. *This is your moment. Tales will be told and songs will be sung about what you do here. What will you think of yourself when this is over?*

"Make ready, men! Make ready!" she cried out, racing to the breach on legs that felt like water. Madelyn clanged her sword against her shield and stood beside Titan as faint silhouettes of barbarians emerged in the darkness. From the corner of her eye, she saw Corbyn rallying the men on his section of the wall and bringing more archers to the chasm.

"About time you grew a set of balls," Titan muttered. "At least I won't die without company."

"I'm sorry," she said. "I'm sorry it has to end like this."

"Fuck it. I'm here, and there's no getting out of this one. Might as well go down swinging," Titan grunted without breaking his gaze on the advancing horde.

Arrows rained down on the barbarian ranks in volleys but did little to deter them. Closer they came until finally, Madelyn could see them in the flames licking at the shattered wall. They were wild-eyed and wild-haired, clad in animal skins and leather, some in steel, and looked more monstrous up close.

"It's been a pleasure, Commander," Titan said cooly.

The words were a meager consolation, but she pinned them to her heart and wore them proudly. Somehow, in the face of certain death,

Madelyn made peace with her fate, and together they charged down the rubble pile and toward the savages who were now scrambling up it.

But they were not alone. As Madelyn and Titan collided with the barbarians, they felt the full weight of the Blackthorn Knights behind them, pushing forward as hard as they could. The sheer force of her body slamming into the enemy hammered the breath from her lungs. Steel and flesh collided violently as hundreds of men clogged the breach, cursing and screaming as they finally had at each other in the most terrible ways.

Maintaining her bearings in the smoke was difficult with so many men clustered at the opening. All she knew was to face the darkness, thrust with her arming sword, and keep thrusting for as long as her arm would allow. But the barbarians kept coming like an unyielding tidal wave, and through their sheer mass, began pushing the defenders further and further back.

"Hold you cowards, hold!" Titan shouted over the clanging of steel and frenzied screams around them.

Rocks and boiling water were loosed from both sections of the broken wall to try and slow the onslaught. It worked briefly, and Madelyn thought they might stop the assault in its tracks. She felt the first glimmer of hope they might actually survive the battle. But it was short-lived. Someone was shouting her name furiously, over and over again. In the deafening noise and confusion, she almost could not hear it.

"Madelyn! Madelyn!" Corbyn called out, waving his hands furiously.

The barbarian advance slowed slightly, thanks to a mass of bodies piling up on the rubble. It provided just enough of an opportunity for Madelyn to withdraw from the front line and run closer to the section of the wall where Corbyn stood.

"Corbyn! What is it?"

"They're bringing ladders to the walls!" he said, voice trembling.

"Which walls?" she asked breathlessly.

"All of them!"

Madelyn's bowels turned to liquid in an instant. With so many men focused on defending the breach, it would be nearly impossible to stop an all-out assault on the walls. Her fears were soon confirmed when she spotted Northmen spilling over the crenellations. Frantically, she raced toward the parapet stairs while Corbyn and Hunter mounted as much defense as they could.

While running across the battlements, she spied young Spencer Morris near the corner tower as he winched a crossbow and locked its string into position. He loaded a bolt, aimed into the sea of barbarians at the breach, and loosed. Without hesitation, he repeated the process over and over again like a man possessed.

I pray you make it out of this. You're not the coward you thought you were.

Madelyn ran toward the infiltrators until she encountered the first ladder in her path. She glanced between the crenellations and saw a Northman mere feet from the top, then thrust her sword down into the man's skull. When she wrenched it free, the barbarian dropped like a sack of rocks into the blackness below and disappeared. With every ounce of strength, she pushed the ladder back from the wall until it fell away.

Several of Morden's garrison were fighting an ever-increasing band of Northmen shortly ahead. Then, the sight of more savages cresting over the opposite wall also drew her attention. There were simply too many of them and not enough men to mount a proper defense. Madelyn felt her heart sink. She lowered her sword in awe of the sheer number of barbarians who commanded the southern wall, and the eastern wall was becoming overwhelmed.

There was only one choice left to make, though it would most certainly result in the loss of more men. She glanced at the keep, then down at the breach. Countless many of her knights would be slaughtered if they broke and ran for the only shelter left, but it was necessary.

"Retreat! Retreat!" Madelyn screamed, her voice becoming shrill. "Fall back to the keep!"

Those who could hear immediately fled toward the towering oaken doors of Morden's formidable keep. Those who did not hear took notice of the retreat and broke as well, and soon there was nothing to stop the enemy horde from storming into the courtyard. Madelyn watched with dismay as those not fast enough to escape were swarmed and cut down where they stood.

"Go, get out of here!" Hunter shouted.

He pushed past Madelyn and ran over to men on the wall struggling to hold their ground. Hunter threw himself into the fight to make sure she had enough of a chance to escape.

"Come on, Hunter, fall back!" she cried while running toward the parapet stairs.

"There's no time, lass! You get out of here!"

There was little use in arguing otherwise. The bailey was swarming with Northmen, and Madelyn had to leap down the last flight of stairs. She nearly slipped trying to regain her footing but was able to sprint to the keep just as the doors were closing. As they were clapped shut, a thick wooden beam was hung to bar and reinforce them. Those trapped outside pounded against the doors and begged to be let in. Their pleas ended in quick order as they were cut down and silenced forever.

So few managed to make it inside. Less than ten of the Blackthorn remained, and perhaps three dozen of Morden's garrison. Not nearly enough, and too few to bother counting. She was relieved to see Titan among the knights who had made it inside. How he had managed to fight his way out of the breach was anyone's guess. Madelyn embraced him and nearly wept.

"You made it. You made it…" she panted, arms clenched tightly around his blood-drenched breastplate.

"Barely. Those fuckers are going to have to try harder than that to kill me," Titan gasped.

The battle had not dampened his mood too greatly. Though the situation was grim and death was waiting on the other side of the door, Madelyn could not help but feel safe around him.

"I don't know what to do."

She looked around the cavernous room and at the exhausted men who struggled to maintain their composure. Familiar faces were around, but Corbyn or Hunter were not among them.

"Corbyn! Corbyn!" she shouted, muscling through the few remaining men.

But he was nowhere to be found. The thought of him being left behind and butchered by the Northmen was too great to fathom. Madelyn's mind raced in frantic despair. Had he been mere feet away from safety before the doors shut, trapping him out there? Or was he cut down during the retreat? Or was he still out there, alone and fighting for his life?

She was in such deep agony that she could not cry. There had only been a handful of nights they stole away to enjoy sleeping in each other's arms. But it wasn't enough. There should have been many more nights, both here and after the battle.

If only I had taken the time to tell him how I felt. If only I would have stayed at Bentmont with him and never came to this accursed place. But it's too late now. Damn you, Madelyn, damn you.

"I've failed them. I've failed all of them. We're not going to make it out of here, and it's all because of me," she lamented, her empty eyes quivering but remaining dry.

Titan would not have it. He grabbed Madelyn by the shoulders and gave her a firm shake.

"Hey, you listen to me. There's nothing more you could have done, do you understand? This battle was lost a long time ago, before we even arrived. You did your best, and no one will fault you for it. But you have to get out now, however you can. All that matters is that you make it out of here, so you can return with an army behind you and avenge every man who died here."

A great commotion outside the keep doors drew their attention. By now, it was unlikely any of her men who were still outside remained alive. It would only be a matter of moments before the barbarians would begin to batter and smash their way in.

What is he trying to tell me? Certainly, he doesn't think I should abandon my post? No, I cannot slink back to Bentmont after leaving everyone here to die. I could never live with myself.

"I don't understand," Madelyn said. "You're not suggesting I—"

"Get the fuck out of here. Yes, yes I am," Titan interrupted. "Cut the chandeliers down and tie the ropes together. You can climb out of a window on the back side of the keep. It's far, but you should be able to jump down the rest of the way."

There had to have been nearly a hundred feet of rope per chandelier, Madelyn supposed, enough to fashion together and make an escape. She nodded, and Titan hurried to where the chandeliers were tied off and struck the rope in two with a single swing of his sword.

"Watch your heads!" he shouted as the massive ornate fixtures plummeted and crashed.

Titan untied the ropes from the heap of metal while a pair of knights cut down the other three chandeliers. They affixed the ropes to a wooden column closest to the window and ensured the coast was clear before tossing the length out the window. Thankfully, they were far enough away that no one could see what was happening, their attention fixed on the keep doors.

"You first," Titan said, ordering Madelyn to make her escape.

Before she could utter a word, a violent slam rang deep and loud throughout the room. The Northmen had begun to batter down the thick oaken doors with a heavy ram. Madelyn looked on helplessly as the doors flexed and jarred with each successive hit. She knew time was growing short, and soon the keep would be crawling with blood-thirsty barbarians.

"No, you go first. If anyone down there spots us, I'll need you to kill them quickly and quietly. The rest of us will follow, and I'll be right behind you. I can't let everyone see their Commander flee. I can't let those we leave behind die knowing we abandoned them."

There was little use in Titan arguing, and the plan had its merits. The Elite sheathed his red-stained sword and drew a dirk, placing it firmly between his teeth. With a nod, he descended the rope, moving as quickly and quietly as possible. Once far enough down, one of the Blackthorn followed, and soon another.

The pounding at the door grew louder and louder. What remained of Morden's garrison grew more panicked and dismayed by the second, and Madelyn knew there wouldn't be time to save all of them. Indeed, they must have been wondering what the Blackthorn were up to. If they knew an escape plan was hatched, there might be a mad dash for the rope, and the whole operation would likely be blown.

Before the last knight descended the ropes, Madelyn pulled him close and gave a final set of orders.

"Get word back to Bentmont as quickly as you can. Tell them what happened here, and tell them to summon all the armies of Betanthia. Go, go quickly now."

The keep doors groaned and rattled as the battering ram crashed into them. Its once sturdy and proud edifice gave way bit by bit as large chunks of wood and small splinters broke free. The faintest hint of dawn was beginning to peek over the horizon and filter in through the keep's high windows. Madelyn knew Titan and her knights would not have the cover of darkness for long.

She glanced out the window and watched as the last knight made it safely down. Every instinct inside her said to run, to climb down the rope and escape to freedom. But looking back at the men forming together near the doors made her feel an overwhelming guilt.

How can I return to Bentmont like this? I've disgraced myself. I've failed my men, and I failed Corbyn. I'll never be given command of anyone again, not after losing the most secure castle in Betanthia. No, I cannot.

Her hands clenched into fists.

Nora is gone. Hunter is gone. Corbyn is gone. All I have left is my honor, and I won't let anyone take it from me. A proper Commander must die with their men.

Nearly in tears, she drew her arming sword and hacked at the rope around the column. She struck a hard blow, then a second, then a third. Finally, on the fourth blow, the rope frayed and separated and fell away through the window. Part of her felt an immediate regret, but the continued smashing of the ram against the door quickly set her straight. Madelyn returned to what remained of the garrison and prepared for what was to come.

"Be brave, men. Everything will be alright."

It was a foolish thing to say, because everything was far from alright, the furthest one could possibly get from it. Some of the troops stood silent and focused. Others chanted and whispered in prayer to whatever gods might be listening, while others openly wept.

Nearly a dozen more strikes landed before the door gave way with an explosive crash. The cries of the barbarians out in the courtyard sounded otherworldly, and the few remaining men inside the keep stood bravely as a horde of sword and axe-wielding savages came storming in to meet them.

"Brace yourselves!" Madelyn screamed as Northmen poured inside in frightening numbers.

She raised her shield and arming sword with trembling hands, though her arms were tired and her muscles burned with fatigue.

The clashing and clanging of sword and axe against armor was ear-piercing. Madelyn's heart pumped so hard it nearly indented on her breastplate, though her adrenaline quickly became exhausted. Her strikes became more feeble with each blow.

Soldiers fell one by one until they were pushed so deep they had nowhere to retreat, except upward. Any semblance of order was abandoned, and the battle was reduced to a wild melee as the sheer number of Northmen became overwhelming.

With nearly all of her men dead, Madelyn found herself surrounded. Some had thrown down their weapons in a futile hope they might be spared. Still, she swung her sword in defiance, though her strength was nearly spent.

A burly warrior charged with a heavy shield bash, sending her toppling to the floor. Though her mind was screaming to get up, her body had given its last.

"That one! That bitch is mine!" screamed an agitated female as she entered the chamber, her shrill cry carrying loud over the wails of dying men.

Madelyn could no longer resist. Her weapon and shield were pried from her hands as she lay motionless, the floor drenched with fresh blood. Ten barbarians put their boots to her, stomping and kicking until she felt nothing. She spat a stream of blood, and her vision blurred and faded. The battle was now over.

Suddenly, a pair of burly warriors lifted her from the ground. The last of Madelyn's men lay groaning and screaming; those who surrendered were dragged unceremoniously from the keep. Madelyn no longer felt fear, she was too exhausted and dazed to care.

"A pretty one indeed!" exclaimed the brown-haired woman. Blue runes decorated the skin under each eye.

It was surprising to see a female among so many unwashed forest dwellers. As they stood toe to toe, the woman examined Madelyn up and down, her face seared with contempt.

"Damien will be quite pleased with you indeed. What's a northern-looking bitch doing in the service of the Bethards anyways? I suppose it doesn't matter. You're coming with me." She snorted and spat on the ground.

The shieldmaiden seemed intrigued, yet burned with a deep hatred despite never crossing paths until now. Madelyn offered no reply or resistance. Her lungs struggled for breath, and her knees had turned to jelly. The barbarian woman reached over, grabbed her by her now unfurled braid, and jerked it back hard.

"You're going to wish you were never born," the shieldmaiden sneered, her words tinged with venom. "Take her to Damien at once."

An ocean of blood pooled in the center of the keep, its surface so slick that Madelyn's feet slipped and struggled to retain their footing. Were it not for a pair of swordsmen carrying her under each arm, she most certainly would have fallen.

The last screams of dying men and the stench of their demise overwhelmed her senses. It felt like the battle had been a dream, a horrid nightmare from which she could not wake. She was carried out through the destroyed doors and into the courtyard, where at least a thousand men gathered. Many thousands more waited outside the castle and along its battlements. The victorious barbarians erupted into celebration as the colors of Betanthia were lowered from the highest tower and discarded like rubbish.

As she was dragged along helplessly, Madelyn saw the corpse of little Spencer Morris lying on the ground, his head and body separated from each other. Her eyes stung as she looked pitifully at him. The smallest man at Castle Morden had found his courage in the end, but the price was high. Much too high for someone so young and innocent.

It wasn't right for you to die like this. You were a gentle soul and deserved a long life. I'm sorry. Please forgive me.

Suddenly, it grew silent, and the masses near the collapsed wall parted. Madelyn struggled to make out what was happening through her pain and exhaustion, but with blurry eyes, she saw the massive frame of the man in black armor riding slowly into sight. The chieftain raised his sword and let loose a bellowing warcry so loud it nearly shook the remaining walls to their foundations.

Cheers and roars erupted, the horde high on victory and drunk on the blood they had spilled. The large man dismounted his horse and stood among them, his face grim yet satisfied. The brown-haired woman smiled. It seemed the scent of fire and dead men was an intoxicating fragrance to her. She grabbed Madelyn again by her long, disheveled braid and yanked her head backward.

"You should have never come here, you Bethard whore."

She shoved Madelyn forward by the back of her head, causing her to tumble forward and crash to the ground. The man in the black armor sneered and looked down at her, his hulking frame casting a deep shadow.

"On your feet." His face tightened into a frown, yet through his searing expression, there was a faint smirk.

A team of barbarians lifted Madelyn to her feet and held her upright for inspection. The chieftain towered more than a foot over her head, perhaps even two. He placed an armored hand beneath Madelyn's chin and forced her to look into his cold, terrible black eyes. After a moment, he turned to a warrior next to him.

"Bring her back to camp. This is the one Lazilyth spoke of."

"Please, if you're going to kill me, then do it quickly," Madelyn pleaded.

"Do you know who you're speaking to, bitch?" The brown-haired woman spat into her eyes. "This is Damien Dreadfire, the ruin of Betanthia! You will not speak to him unless spoken to. Do you understand?"

"Sylvia, be still," the chieftain commanded.

Being tortured or sacrificed to whatever gods the savages worshipped was enough to make her stomach churn, but this man appeared more cunning and sinister. He conquered Castle Morden, the most indomitable structure in the history of Betanthia. Was there a fate worse than death awaiting her? Madelyn could only wonder.

Damien Dreadfire glanced at the warriors around her and gave them an approving nod. They bound both arms behind her back with a length of rope. She squirmed defiantly for a moment but was too exhausted to offer any real struggle.

"What of the other prisoners, Damien?" Sylvia Stormguard asked.

A group of fifteen warriors parted, and Madelyn saw nearly a dozen of her men set down on their knees.

Their faces were too dirty and bloodied to make out who they were, and most had their gazes averted to the ground. Damien approached and stood before them. Some wept or appeared on the verge of weeping, while others looked around frantically, hoping to find an escape. Then their eyes met.

Heavens no… no… not him… anyone but him…

Though battered and caked in dirt and gore, Corbyn Scott's beautiful, sad eyes stared back at her. Madelyn tried to keep herself composed, but seeing her lover on the ground and moments away from death drove daggers into her heart. She gasped and lunged forward instinctively, screaming what little defiance remained in her body and spirit.

The two muscular warriors on either side of Madelyn gripped her firmly by the arms, themselves contented by her suffering. Corbyn's eyes flooded with tears. Wearily he shook his head and tried to tell Madelyn to be still without speaking.

"Kill them, and be quick about it," Dreadfire said coldly.

The warriors drew their weapons and raised them high. Time felt as if it stood still, but even then, Madelyn could do nothing. She watched as swords and axes were brought down one by one, their bloodied and razor-sharp blades slicing through air then flesh effortlessly. But her eyes remained fixed on Corbyn's, and his on hers.

He smiled softly, though it was sad and remorseful. Madelyn basked in the comforting warmth of his caramel-colored eyes one last time before a swordsman's blade cleaved through his neck. Corbyn's head parted from his shoulders and fell to the ground, followed by a torrent of blood. As his lifeless body crumpled, Madelyn screamed, wept, and thrashed violently.

"No! No! Nooooo!"

She wailed and frantically tried to reach Corbyn, but it was too late. He was gone. Madelyn then lunged at Damien Dreadfire, hopelessly trying to break her bindings and strike him in any way imaginable.

"I'll kill you! I'll kill you!"

Some of the warriors laughed, though others appeared to take little joy in the slaughter. Most, however, were too focused on plundering treasures or weapons within the keep. Even the body of her slain lover was not spared. He, too, was pillaged of any effects that remained on his person.

"What are your orders, Damien?" Sylvia asked. She appeared to be quite amused at Madelyn's suffering.

"Men!" Damien's voice echoed throughout the bailey. "Today, you have made your ancestors proud. You have served the gods faithfully and carried out their justice. Your loyalty and dedication to this cause are more than I could have asked for. You have seen fit to avenge the Bloodbath at Borjifa. Together we have put Cedric the Butcher to the sword, and now his stronghold has fallen. This is a day that will be remembered for all eternity!"

A celebratory cheer filled the bailey. Even those who were looting paused and joined in the revelry.

"We must not linger. Gather yourselves and your spoils, and set this accursed fortress alight."

Chants of "Dreadfire! Dreadfire! Dreadfire!" rang out as the barbarians continued ransacking the castle.

Madelyn was dragged from the fortress, kicking and screaming until she nearly lost consciousness. The crackling of small fires throughout the bailey soon turned into a raging inferno. Black smoke began to seep and pour from the keep, what remained of the stables, the corner towers, and any place where timbers were present. The once invincible stronghold of the Bethard dynasty was engulfed in an ocean of fire.

"Please, just kill me," Madelyn whimpered, her voice so frail no one could hear.

Her mind began wandering and thinking about what might come next. The barbarians would parade her around like a trophy, certainly. But the thoughts of what might come afterward were too terrifying to comprehend. Madelyn looked down solemnly at the Commander's insignia on her breastplate.

The proud, prestigious emblem of the Order represented her life's work, and the High Marshal's full faith and endorsement. It symbolized every struggle, every setback, and every triumph that had earned her the right to become the first female Commander. But now, like the fortress she defended, the insignia was dented, destroyed, and left unrecognizable from the scrapes and slashes of barbarian steel.

I've failed them. The High Marshal. Hunter. Corbyn. My knights. The garrison. Everyone. I've failed them all. Maybe everyone was right to doubt me in the first place. I should have never come here.

A long line of warriors snaked out from the open wound in Morden's outer wall, victorious and laden with spoils. After being dragged to the siege line, Madelyn's bound hands were tied to a longer length of rope and fastened to a horse's saddle. Sylvia Stormguard came up behind her and kicked out her knees, sending her falling to the ground in agony.

"Get up, whore," Sylvia sneered. "You've got a lot of walking ahead of you."

The shieldmaiden mounted and gave the horse a slight nudge with her boot. Before Madelyn could stand, the horse was at a light trot, and again she fell on her face. Those watching the spectacle laughed as she was dragged.

"Get up, get up!" Stormguard chuckled after bringing her horse to a halt. "You're lucky Damien wants you unharmed. Come on now, get up!"

Madelyn regained her footing and brushed away blades of grass cling-ing to her dirtied face. A second later, Sylvia nudged her horse forward, and together they made their way toward the barbarian encampment. With every ounce of hope now lost, Madelyn looked over her shoulder briefly and watched as Castle Morden burned.

GARETH V

THE LAST DAYS OF SUMMER WERE FADING AWAY, ALONG WITH IT, HIS troubles. Gareth could scarcely recall when he felt freer of the burdens and insecurities that once consumed him. Being away from the toxicity of the Westwind Citadel transformed him from a troubled boy with no hope for the future into a man who was only beginning to learn who he truly was.

Perhaps the greatest blessing of all was closing the distance between him and his mother. It was refreshing to see Queen Charlotte rediscover herself during their time in Dellhaven. She began to resemble the woman he remembered as a child. And as her wounds slowly healed, she could better help Gareth heal his own.

Maybe something good has come from all of this suffering. Both mine and hers.

Gareth and Charlotte spent much of their time walking along the seashore, through the vineyards, and eating candlelit dinners on the patio. They wore heavy linen and fur cloaks to help stave off the icy breath of autumn. Although it was getting colder by the day, there was a certain apprehension they shared about the changing seasons.

Thankfully, not every day was unpleasant. One warm morning, Gareth decided to go for a ride through the outer reaches of Dellhaven.

It felt like ages since he last saddled a horse. But before he could make it to the stables, his mother called out from a second-storey balcony.

"Gareth! Where are you going?" the Queen asked with a smile.

She looked positively radiant in a gown of royal blue silks adorned with silver jewelry. Her hair was drawn up into a sophisticated updo, likely the work of Emilee's talented hands.

"Good morning, mother! I figured I would go for a ride. I'm dying to get some wind in my face."

"Before you go, can I walk with you for a little while?" Charlotte clasped her hands together in anticipation.

"Absolutely! Come on down. I'll meet you by the door."

He strode back to the chateau briskly, eager to get the walk done and out of the way so he could ride. Before making it halfway back, Charlotte was already downstairs waiting. It was heartwarming to feel so loved and valued, so much that Gareth even began to love himself for once.

"You look beautiful today, mother."

The Queen smiled and looked as if she might cry tears of happiness. Gareth took her by the arm and began their routine walk to the waterfront. The sea was more restless than usual, given the sudden temperature changes. But even when the ocean was at its fiercest, it was still strangely calming.

A merchant galley bobbed in the deep waters far from shore. It was one of many ships frequenting Dellhaven's ports, but the weather was far too uncooperative to attempt a docking. Most of the gulls had migrated to warmer climates, but a few remained. They drifted lazily on a strong wind, cawing and complaining for a fresh meal.

"I do love it here, so very much," Charlotte said softly, her voice barely carrying over the crashing waves.

"What if we never left?" Gareth asked.

At first, the Queen looked at him suspiciously, as if the idea seemed unnatural somehow.

"I don't know," she replied, breathless. "Certainly, we would have to return to the Citadel at some point."

"Do we, though? We're Bethards. Nobody can make us do anything unless we want to. I say we leave father at the Citadel for the time being, and remain here in Dellhaven for the winter."

Charlotte looked leery, almost conflicted in a way. Even though she had been rid of Marcellus for what seemed like a lifetime, there was still uncertainty in her eyes. Gareth suspected that even now, she feared the King's wrath.

"It'll be perfectly fine, mother. If father hasn't sent Edmund or anyone else to fetch you, then I think it's safe to assume he hasn't noticed. You've come so far in our time here. I would hate to see you slip back into despair."

"The same goes for you. I never want to see you so distraught ever again." Charlotte lovingly placed a hand on Gareth's shoulder, the memories still fresh in her mind.

"So let's stay," he said.

"I've never seen Dellhaven in the winter. Does it snow here, I wonder?"

Gareth pondered but was unsure. Aside from an occasional summer trip to the chateau, he spent his entire life in Cardale. The winters there were quite mild, rainier than anything. Once in a great while, there would be a morning frost, but even then, the days were typically comfortable.

"I wouldn't imagine so. We would have to go much further north."

"I've never seen snow, only in paintings. I hope I get to one day." She gave a melancholy smile. So much of Charlotte's life had passed, but thankfully there were still many more years ahead of her, or so he hoped.

"Perhaps one day we can sail a ship up the coast and head north. I would imagine it would be much safer that way instead of—"

Gareth caught sight of Devin Brandybrook coming toward them at a frantic pace. In his hands, he held a piece of parchment decorated with the royal seal. Accompanying him was a Guardsman, as evidenced by his polished steel breastplate and flowing purple cloak.

"A thousand pardons, Highness. This dispatch just arrived from Cardale, and I have been informed it's most urgent.

The Guardsman looked haggard, as if he rode straight from the capital without stopping. His eyes had an unsettling urgency, though he did not speak it. The man straightened his back as Devin passed the sealed parchment to Gareth, who opened it cautiously.

Could this be… no, it couldn't…

As he unrolled the dispatch, the King was the first place his mind went to. Had some unexpected misfortune befallen King Marcellus? Could he have died peacefully in his sleep, or perhaps in some drunken accident? Gareth was almost ashamed to feel excited by such thoughts.

His lips moved silently as he read the message. Charlotte held a hand over her mouth, waiting with bated breath to see if the news was ill. Judging from the look on her face, she was almost praying for news of a calamity.

"Sir… Bryce Whitewood, of the King's high council, was found dead at his estate."

Mother and son exhaled in disappointment. It seemed today the fates would not be so generous.

"Does it say how he died?" Charlotte asked, feigning concern.

"His breath gave out in the night, the physicians say," Gareth said.

The weary Guardsman stepped forward. "The King and the other councilmen have been informed as well, Your Highness."

What any of this had to do with Gareth was a mystery. The high council was not his domain, and he only had dealings with it during Madelyn's visit to the Citadel.

"And why am I being informed of this?" he asked, confused. "The council is Aldred's business, not my own. Tell me, who ordered this dispatch to be sent here?"

"Sir Edmund instructed me to deliver it to you."

Sir Edmund? Why in the world would he...

Bewildered, Gareth dismissed the Guardsman with a lazy wave of his hand. Nothing about the message made sense. His last conversation with Sir Edmund ended in disaster, likely damaging their friendship beyond repair. But now he was sending Gareth a dispatch, carried by one of his men.

"I don't understand, mother," Gareth said, his brow furrowed. "He could have entrusted this task with any courier, but instead, he sent a Guardsman."

"What don't you understand? You two are close friends, and everyone knows it."

"Not anymore, I fear. We had a falling out before we left for Dellhaven, and I feared he would never speak to me again." He scratched the back of his neck.

"Well, clearly, it must not have been so serious." The Queen shrugged. "He still cares about you, or else he wouldn't have bothered to inform you of this development."

"I don't see why sending a rider was worth the trouble. What happens on the high council is none of my business."

Charlotte tightened her face and glanced about. The wheels in her mind were turning, he could see it plain as day.

"Don't you see? This is an opportunity for you!" Charlotte said enthusiastically, but then remembered a man had just died, though he was a loathsome creature. "Sir Edmund must have seen it too; that's why he sent word, not to me but to you."

"Seen what?" he asked.

"There's an opening on the high council now. I remember you telling me you felt as if your life had no purpose. Well, take up the seat for yourself. Use this as an opportunity to learn the ins and outs of politics and how to rule. It will better prepare you for the day you're crowned king."

The idea seemed appealing enough but began to stoke old insecurities. Gareth remembered the painful embarrassment he suffered at the hands of Aldred when he spoke at the council chamber. It was even more humiliating to have Madelyn witness his emasculation, something he would never forget for the rest of his life.

"I'm not sure I have the temperament for it. And besides, the other councilmen have little to no respect for me and dismissed me out of hand when I spoke to them last."

"What business did you have with the council?"

Gareth suddenly remembered the Queen was unaware of the events in the west. The thought of troubling her mind with such information seemed cruel, especially with how far she had come during their time in Dellhaven. Clumsily, he attempted to answer her question without truly answering it.

"It's of no consequence, mother. Not anymore."

"Very well. But I think you have the right temperament to sit on the council. You only need to assert yourself more, Gareth. Your name is not Eldon, Whitewood, Lawson, or any of them. You're a Bethard. That alone should command respect and unquestioned loyalty. If you show strength, they will respond to you. "

He smiled sheepishly. "Yes, I suppose so."

"And besides," the Queen continued, "you have the loyalty of the Guardsmen. If any councilmen shows you contempt, perhaps you might invite Sir Edmund and a few of his men along to a meeting. Men are less likely to slight you if they sense there will be consequences."

Now, this is how I remember you, mother. Sharp, confident, and unwavering. Everything I aspire to be.

"But what about you, mother? If I return to Cardale—"

"Don't worry about me. Everything will be fine," Charlotte interrupted. "This is a golden opportunity to take charge of your destiny. It would be a crime to let it pass you by. And besides, as much as I would like you to remain my little boy forever, you're not. You're a man, and you must start building a life for yourself. As for me, I need to do the same. You've helped me get this far, and now I need to learn to stand on my own again."

Despite deep misgivings, there was little Gareth could say. The Queen had undoubtedly come a long way since she left the toxic confines of the Westwind Citadel. It was time for her to chart a new course in life, just as it was time for him.

"Alright, mother. I'll go," he sighed. "I'll do my best."

The Queen threw her arms around him and squeezed so tight he could hardly breathe. "I know you will. And please, don't worry about me, I will be well looked after. Heavens know there are enough servants around here to care for an entire city. Now please, return to Cardale. Time is short, and Aldred will likely choose another councilman in short order. That man is nothing but business, it seems."

Gareth hugged his mother again, and with a forlorn smile, left her beside the seashore. After gathering his modest belongings, he bid Devin and the other servants farewell and instructed them to take good care of the Queen. After receiving the proper assurances, Gareth rode out from Dellhaven around midday. He dressed in a modest brown doublet with a tan cloak to avoid drawing unwanted attention on the road. The two Guardsmen accompanying him were garbed in similarly discreet attire.

Shortly into the journey, he noticed a train of riders approaching. As they drew close, he took notice of their banners, blue and silver and emblazoned with the eagle standard of Betanthia. Gareth thought it curious for a military caravan to be heading toward Dellhaven.

Near the center of the formation was a heavily armored carriage, which stoked his suspicion. Who was inside the carriage was anyone's guess, but there was no time to learn more. He needed to make it to Cardale before Aldred could fill the vacant council seat with another sycophant.

The ride to the capital was pleasant. Sweltering summer heat gave way to cooler days and even cooler nights. The leaves on the trees slowly transitioned from green to yellow, orange, and red hues. Farmers labored in their fields and prepared for the harvest. Fall was fast approaching.

Within two days, Gareth arrived. It seemed like half a lifetime ago when he was last here. The most telling change was the one taking place inside him. The troubled and insecure boy who left Cardale bore little resemblance to the man who was returning.

One thing that remained unchanged, however, was the capital. Cardale was still the same as it always was, but he could no longer look at it the same way. He had witnessed the squalor and suffering firsthand, forever changing his perspective on the city.

How could I have ever thought living this way was acceptable? Dellhaven has certainly opened my eyes. There's no reason why life here can't be as good as it is there.

The sight of the Westwind Citadel made his throat tighten, and nearly choked off his breath. He swallowed hard, trying desperately to stop the poisonous memories of past months from resurfacing. Gareth resolved things would be different this time around. It was a new chapter in his life, and hopefully soon, for all of Betanthia. He rode through the outer gates of the palace with the grace and courage one would expect from a future king.

"Halt, who goes there?" a familiar voice called from behind.

It was Sir Edmund Thomas, his arms crossed and the faintest hint of a grin on his face. Gareth immediately felt guilt over their last conversation. He wanted to say something clever or humorous in response but didn't have the heart.

"It's good to see you again, Gareth. You look well. I hardly recognize you. Dellhaven seems to suit you."

"Thanks, it's good to see you too." He dismounted with a grunt. "Listen, I just wanted to say—"

Sir Edmund raised his hand. "You don't have to say anything. What's done is done. You were in a bad way and needed time to figure things out for yourself."

"No, I do have to say something. It was wrong of me to take my frustrations out on you. You were only trying to help me. All you've ever done is try to help me, and I haven't been a very good friend in return. So please, accept my sincerest apology."

Smiling, Edmund gave Gareth a quick embrace, then together, they walked to the front doors to the palace.

"I take it you received my message?" the senior Guardsman asked rhetorically.

"I did, and I must admit I was surprised. I didn't think you'd want to speak to me again, let alone try to help me. You and my mother must share one mind; she knew the purpose behind your message almost immediately."

"Sounds to me like the Charlotte Bethard of old has returned. Your mother was always a sharp woman." Pride beamed from Sir Edmund's face. "And, of course, I'm still going to help you. Sometimes I think you forget how much older I am than you. I've had friendships fall apart, then mend. Or sometimes remain broken. But you're a good lad, and I was hoping that, with a little time away, you'd return in a better place than when you left."

"I believe I have, Edmund. I believe I have."

They paused halfway to the entrance of the great hall. Both men looked upon the massive outer doors, pondering what might be

470

happening on the other side. Only a gentle bubbling of the courtyard fountain broke through the silence.

"Before you go in there, there's something you should know." Edmund looked unsettled. "It seems Aldred wasted little time filling the high council's vacant seat. I thought he would have waited until the old pervert was buried first, but he surprised me."

"And when did you find this out?"

"I sent a rider the day Sir Bryce's servants found him, and by the next day, Aldred had already called in Lord Ridley Vakaro to serve as the fourth councilman."

The name was unfamiliar, though Gareth likely heard it in passing at some point. He immediately suspected Lord Vakaro was chosen solely for his unwavering loyalty to Aldred. It was the only company he chose to keep.

Gareth shook his head in disgust. "The man's seat was filled before his corpse was even cold. Leave it up to my brother-in-law to never let any crisis go to waste. Tell me, who is this Lord Vakaro?"

"He's the southern Commandant. I knew him only by reputation during my days in the army. I was on my way out when he was just starting to make a name for himself. Ridley the Rigid, some of the men used to call him. He apparently suffered a great affliction in the womb because the man seems to have been born without a personality."

If it weren't for the gravity of the situation, Gareth might have enjoyed a chuckle. But the development was unexpected and unpleasant.

"I wonder how he came to know Aldred. He wouldn't appoint anyone to the high council that wouldn't fall in line behind him."

Edmund scratched his head. "Of that, I'm not certain. But I'll ask around and see what I can find out. All I know is this; the man is deadly serious. The high council has already ordered thousands of Lord Vakaro's men to reinforce the garrisons at Naxonnos. And get this...

he'll likely be appointed the acting western Commandant should Lord Valens' meet his demise against the Northmen."

"It seems to me there is a consolidation of power taking place. All of this is far too convenient. Think of it, Edmund. Lord Valens is fending off a northern invasion, and another Commandant is bolstering the defense of his sector. Then Sir Bryce dies and is replaced on the council by the same man. It seems to me Aldred is putting many eggs into fewer baskets. Baskets he owns. I'm not certain if there's any historical precedent for something like this, is there?"

"Not that I know of. You're every bit as clever as your mother, that's for certain." Edmund grinned. "But here's another possibility, what if it isn't Aldred that's consolidating power? What if it's Lord Vakaro? If the western army is destroyed, it will need to be rebuilt. And who better to do that than the man whose troops are already supplementing the western border? He'll control half of Betanthia's military."

"Then it seems everything is riding on Lord Valens staying alive. Have we received any dispatches from him since I was away?"

A sense of urgency grew in the back of Gareth's mind. He was beginning to put together the pieces of what appeared to be a sinister conspiracy.

"None that I'm aware of, which in my experience, is a bad sign. Senior officers are quite neurotic about sending status reports, even for the most mundane reasons."

The new revelations were startling, to say the least. Some upstart lord could very well be plotting an overthrow of the Bethard dynasty, taking advantage of the chaos in the west and using his relationship with Aldred to his advantage. Or even worse, what if Lord Vakaro was masterminding the invasion of the Northmen? He could very well be paying them in gold or promising them lands and who knows what else. The possibilities were all too plausible, each more frightening than the last.

Gareth's eyes scanned the vastness of the Westwind Citadel. It looked different now, even from just a few minutes prior. He felt danger seeping into his bones as he stared up at the looming edifice of the palace. The seat of House Bethard's power was now under threat, a direct threat, and there was no denying it.

"I've always suspected I would never sit on the throne. My father's advisors think me too weak to resist them, and apparently, they're making their move at this very moment. And now that the council seat has been filled, I don't have any way of curbing their influence."

"According to whom?" Edmund's eyebrows lowered. "There have always been four councilmen. This is true. But what's to stop you from being a fifth? You're the crown prince, heir to all of Betanthia. I say you take up a seat for yourself. They wouldn't dare deny you or else risk revealing their treason prematurely. Get the jump on them."

The idea was tempting but fraught with danger. Gareth rubbed his chin and thought for a moment.

"I can try, but I can't force them to accept it."

"You just leave that to me, don't you worry." Sir Edmund chuckled, his mind concocting some clever scheme. "Just go in there and assert yourself. That's all you should be focused on for now."

They gave each other a solemn look, then shared a quick embrace. The senior Guardsman marched decisively to the barracks while Gareth entered the Westwind Citadel. He almost felt like a stranger in his home, as if usurpers had already seized the palace. Guards and servants throughout the great hall took notice of his return and offered one respectful bow after another. It was at least a small reminder that it was still his residence.

The walk to the council chamber was brief, far too brief for Gareth to properly collect his thoughts. He was ill-equipped for a confrontation of this magnitude and would go into the viper's den alone. He heard them faintly through the doors, likely plotting and scheming Betanthia's demise.

You're a clever man, Aldred. But here's one Bethard that won't roll over to you so easily. Not anymore.

As Gareth entered, the old metal door hinges groaned, announcing his arrival. The muffled voices inside the chamber turned silent as the councilmen stared back with bewilderment. It was quiet as a tomb, save for a sharp clapping of his boots against the polished floors. He saw Morgan Lawson glancing about the table anxiously.

"Prince Gareth, you've returned! What a surprise indeed." The fat lord's jowls quivered as he stood and simpered. Sir Tristan stood next, following the lead of his older and fatter counterpart. The young and impressionable councilman appeared astonished and uncertain about what to say or do next, except he knew well enough to bow.

At the end of the table sat Aldred. After grinding his teeth contemptuously, he rose and paid his due respects, though more out of obligation than anything. Lord Vakaro was already standing. He loomed behind Aldred's seat, peering down at a stack of parchments.

Ridley Vakaro was a large man, a head and a half taller than any man in the room, and every bit as grim as Edmund said. His skin was deeply tanned from a summer stationed in the deep south. A thinning field of pitch-black hair blanketed his head, combed back, and slicked with oils.

The most noticeable thing was a thick, deep scar from his forehead to his chin. Luckily, the weapon responsible for such horrific damage had not taken his right eye. Not that it made him any less frightening to look at. Lord Vakaro's clean-shaven face was cold and emotionless, much the same as a corpse's.

So this is the man who seeks to supplant my House? He seems to be a far more likely candidate than Aldred, if appearances are considered.

"I trust your stay in Dellhaven was pleasant?" the bulbous Lord Lawson stammered.

"It was, yes. I trust the affairs of the Citadel have been taken care of since I was away?"

Aldred's annoyance was already bubbling to the surface. He was the first to return to his seat, before Gareth even reached the table.

"Yes, of course," Aldred said. "Is there something we can do for you? As you can see, we are quite occupied at the moment."

It was the same condescension Gareth had grown familiar with. For a moment, he felt himself diminishing and withdrawing back into a pit of insecurity and despair he had only recently climbed out of. His heart was clubbing the inside of his chest mercilessly.

"There is. I was informed Sir Bryce has died."

"A most tragic affair," Sir Tristan said halfheartedly. The old man's absence certainly did not seem to be missed, given he was replaced on the council before being interred.

"And how did you come by this information?" Aldred's face tightened.

"I'm the crown prince. I would certainly think the future king should know about the things happening in his kingdom."

"Future king, my prince," Lord Lawson replied after being shot a fiery glare from Aldred.

It was the same dismissal hurled his way as the last time. But the slight did not have its intended effect.

"Thank you for the reminder, my lord. For a moment, I almost forgot I'm the crown prince."

Before the fat councilman could retort, Gareth moved closer to the table and interrupted.

"Furthermore, I want to remind you of your words—future king. Yes, indeed, I am the future king. And judging from my last conversation with my father, I may become the current king much sooner than you would hope."

"Your father is just fine, Gareth," Aldred interjected. "The physicians have told us so."

"There's no way to be certain. I remember even a few short years ago, he could tend to business and function normally. Look at how noticeably he's diminished since then. But thankfully, his eldest son and heir will ensure that House Bethard will continue to survive and flourish."

A few murmurs were traded across the table. Lord Vakaro ground his teeth, but said nothing.

"Very good, my prince," Aldred said dryly. "Now, we have important business to return to. Good day."

Keep your cool, Gareth. He wants this, to provoke you in front of the rest of the council. You have to be smarter than that.

"I agree, Aldred. There is plenty of business to attend to, which is why I'm here. Since Sir Bryce's seat at the table has been taken by Lord Vakaro, I have decided to take up a seat myself. There's no reason why House Bethard should not be represented at its own high council meetings."

A frenzy erupted between the councilmen, save for Ridley. He stood motionless and brooding, and though he didn't speak, his eyes reflected violent anger. Sir Tristan looked like a frightened child as he glanced between Aldred and Lord Lawson, demanding an explanation. The fat councilman was hollering something about protocols while Aldred immediately took to browbeating Gareth, but his words were lost in a sea of shouting.

"My lords, my lords, please." Gareth raised his hands to silence them and had to fight off an amused smile while doing so.

When the commotion finally subsided, a dense fog of fury lingered.

"This is preposterous, Gareth," Aldred scolded. "The high council operates under the King's sanction, to act as an independent body and advise him accordingly. It is up to this council's discretion as to who and how many may sit at the table. Since the days of your father's coronation, there have only been four councilmen. Four, not five."

"Yes, this is terribly unprecedented," Morgan chimed in. "The crown cannot—"

"Yes, my lord, these are unprecedented times indeed," Gareth interrupted. "Hordes of unwashed Northmen are invading our lands, and our king is unwell and deteriorating by the day. We must take bold and unprecedented action to safeguard Betanthia."

Then, Lord Vakaro stirred, no longer content to maintain his silence. "These men might not say it aloud, but this chamber is no place for drunkards who fornicate with commoners. Your presence here is an affront."

Ridley's deep voice rippled throughout the chamber and shook Gareth to his core. This was certainly not a man to be trifled with, but there was little choice otherwise.

These pompous fiends might have been plotting my family's demise right before I walked in here. I can't just turn around and leave now. The whole kingdom is counting on me. Mother is counting on me. I'm counting on me.

It took every bit of strength within him not to tremble. Lord Vakaro's glare burned a hole clean through his spirit, but there was no turning back now. He had come too far, and retreating now would only destroy whatever meager respect the high council had left for him.

"And yet the king you serve now is a drunkard. And a womanizer. And a wife beater. Shall I go on, Lord Vakaro? We all have our failings. Would any man here care to discuss their own while we're on the subject?"

There was silence as the three councilmen looked at Aldred.

"Gareth…" his brother-in-law said, returning to his typical, condescending tone. "We're all very impressed with your display here, but it still doesn't change the fact that you cannot force yourself onto the council. You need an endorsement from another councilman, and, finally my approval. Bethard or not, this is the procedure the current king, your father, has sanctioned. And I will not deviate from it. So again, I bid you a good day. We're all quite busy at the moment."

A faint clinking sound grew louder outside the chamber door. With a half-smile, Gareth moved to the chair at the end of the table, opposite Aldred. As he took a seat, Lord Lawson and Sir Tristan began whispering among themselves in disbelief.

"Aldred, you may have married into my family, but you're no Bethard. So I'll forgive your insults and your lapse in judgment. You and I both know my father is likely not long for the world. Judging by the way you've treated me here today, one might be inclined to think you're plotting to steal the throne for yourself the second he dies."

In a rare display of anger, Aldred rose from his chair and slammed both hands onto the table, a sudden, sharp clap ringing so loud it made everyone flinch.

"How dare you accuse me of such a thing! Don't you ever presume to accuse me of—"

He was interrupted by the sudden opening of the chamber doors. Gareth's half-smile grew into a smirk as he heard the synchronized crunching of heavy steel armor. He didn't have to turn around to know it was Sir Edmund, but he did anyway. The senior Guardsman was flanked by ten of the largest and meanest-looking soldiers Gareth had ever seen, their hands wrapped firmly around the hilts of their swords.

With Sir Edmund at his side and a detachment of Betanthia's finest behind him, Gareth's fear quickly faded. Aldred and his lackeys looked stunned. Even the menacing Lord Vakaro appeared to be taken aback by the unexpected show of force.

"Is everything alright, Your Highness?" Edmund asked, his formality deliberate.

"Quite so, thank you, Sir Edmund." He turned to Aldred. "I know you're a stickler for tradition, but isn't the most important tradition of all the continuity of House Bethard? Don't think of my presence on the council as a detriment. Consider it an investment in our collective future. Betanthia faces dark days; make no mistake, gentlemen. We are at war in the west, and our capital rots from within. I've seen it."

"And how is this an investment?" Sir Tristan asked quizzically.

"Because I will become better acquainted with the finer details of rule, for when my time comes. Your assistance will be most valuable to me. And I do not doubt that we will all become better acquainted with each other in the meantime, which will only benefit Betanthia in the long run. Together, we will see our people through these troubling times."

The Royal Guardsmen looked on intently, ready to defend their prince should the council turn hostile. But the wind was taken out of Aldred's sails, and he diminished where he sat and said nothing. Gareth leaned back in his chair and threw his feet on the table.

"We have a lot of work to do, gentlemen. Shall we continue?"

EINARR VII

*I*T'S OVER. *GODS BE PRAISED; IT'S FINALLY OVER.*

Einarr watched from the siege line as the sun rose over Castle Morden. Damien Dreadfire ordered he stay behind with the reinforcements, having deemed him too important to throw into a pitched battle. Ruin performed flawlessly, and Einarr suspected Damien might have further need of his craftsmanship skills, especially if they were to hold the castle. The walls would need repairs, along with whatever else the trebuchets destroyed inside the fortification. Not that it bothered him. He was weary of killing and much preferred to return to building.

As the commotion of battle gave way to celebration, he knew the keep was taken. Thousands of warriors at the siege line raced to the open wound in the castle wall to join their victorious brethren. Though Einarr was thankful the task was completed, he was more reserved than the men around him. Somewhere in his mind lurked the idea that this victory would not mark the end of the conflict, but was merely the beginning.

Einarr made his way across the field and climbed a large pile of rubble that was Morden's outer wall. He peered into the bailey but had to remain outside the castle. The area smelled of pulverized stone, fire, and dead men. Warriors were packed shoulder to shoulder from front to back, along every section of the wall. It was a relief to see so many survived the battle, which gave him a small measure of pride. Were it not for his efforts, the warband might not have even been able to breach the castle's once-formidable walls.

There was surprisingly little commotion considering the fight was over. Thousands of eyes were focused solely on the shattered doors of the inner keep. Einarr could only guess what it was they were waiting for. He was not kept in suspense for long. Soon enough, Sylvia Stormguard and dozens of warriors emerged with the blonde woman he saw on the walls when the warband first arrived.

The sea of warriors parted near the keep entrance, and Einarr, in turn, climbed a broken section of wall to gain a better vantage point. He saw Damien near a group of prisoners set on their knees, and the blonde woman was pushed and shoved toward them. It was too difficult to make out what Damien was saying, but Einarr had already come to suspect what would happen next.

They're going to die, and there's nothing I can do about it.

Einarr felt strangely indifferent. He knew now that Damien was not the sort of man to take prisoners, and protesting was useless. It certainly did not save Lieutenant Byrne or the men defeated at Blackwolf Pass. He watched as Damien raised his hand and gave the order, but his heart remained steady. One by one, the prisoners were cut to pieces until none remained, except for the blonde woman, the one Lazilyth spoke of.

It was only when he heard the anguished screams of the blonde woman that Einarr averted his gaze to the ground in shame. She must have lost someone important to her, because such cries could only be the cries of love. He remembered the pain and agony of losing Alina, each shriek and sob driving daggers into his heart.

"Einarr…"

He heard Alina's frail voice echoing in his ears. Valiantly, he tried to bury the thoughts of his lost love, but the memories cascaded in, leaving him vulnerable, ashamed, and lonely beyond belief.

"Yes, my love?"

And suddenly, Einarr was brought back to that fateful night. He sat beside Alina and touched her on the arm as she lay in bed, motionless. Thick beads of sweat on her face glistened in the gentle flickering of candlelight. A wet cloth rested on her feverish forehead, its cool caress doing little to stave off the ever-rising heat. Einarr tried with faltering strength to maintain composure as she opened her green eyes and gazed into his.

"Hey… there you are," he said with as much of a smile as he could muster.

He brushed a sweat-drenched lock of Alina's brown hair off her cheek and checked the temperature of the cloth with the backside of his hand. It was becoming warmer by the minute. The growing alarm in Einarr's mind told him that despite every effort, the affliction was only gaining strength. Alina made to speak, but the fever's ferocity robbed her of her words.

"It's okay, my love. Don't speak," he said softly.

Somewhere in her soul, Alina must have known her time was short. Tears began pouring down her reddened cheeks like a melting glacier. With a shaky and weak hand, she reached up to stroke Einarr's bearded face. He gently assisted and pressed his hand against hers. Even her touch was scalding hot.

"I tried, Einarr, I tried…" Alina sobbed wearily.

"I know, my love, you're fighting so hard. I love you so much."

The despair in his heart was overwhelming. He sensed Alina's body could no longer continue the fight. The fever came on too fast and too strong, and not even the shamans nor medicine men possessed the skill to drive it away.

"I'm so sorry…" she cried, then looked around the room as if searching for some desperate relief from her suffering.

"No, no, don't be." Einarr clenched his teeth so tightly they nearly shattered. It did little to stave off the anguish pooling in the corners of his eyes.

"I should… should have told you, but… but the fever…"

A sudden rush of panic made Einarr so dizzy he nearly fainted. There was a great deal of confusion in what she said, and he could not make any sense of it. What secret could Alina possibly be hiding? She was the most honest and loyal person he had ever known.

"Shhh, shhh… It's alright. What was it you were going to tell me?"

Einarr wasn't sure he wanted to hear the answer, but it was better to know whatever truth she was keeping than to have it die with her. Alina stroked his face again, then grabbed his hand gingerly and pulled it down to her body. Hairs on the back of his neck stood on end, and his breathing quickened in uncertainty.

With a sorrowful smile, Alina placed Einarr's hand on her belly. At first, he was unsure what she was trying to tell him. He looked at her, then back at his hand. The truth hit him so hard it was impossible to fight back the tears any longer. Together they cried. Einarr leaned down and cradled Alina in his arms.

"How long have you known?" he asked mournfully, holding Alina and stroking her wet hair.

"Just before… before the…"

"It's ok, my love. You have nothing to be sorry about. I love you so much." Einarr removed the roasting hot cloth from her head and replaced it with a loving kiss.

"I remember the first time I saw you, when I was a boy. I thought you were the most… the most beautiful thing the gods ever created. I wanted to talk to you for years but was so scared."

Einarr gave a bittersweet chuckle as the memories came back.

"Then there was the day I was fishing, right there under the cherry blossom tree. Do you remember? I would never have thought a girl as pretty as you liked to fish, and when you sat down next to me with your pole, I nearly jumped out of my skin and fell into the river!"

Alina smiled weakly, her red face wet with tears.

"We sat there all day, and it was only when the sun started to set that I dared to look at you. The whole time you talked to me about your favorite fishing spots, the best bait to use, and all that. I was completely frozen. I had no idea how to talk to a girl, but you stayed with me until your father called for you to come home."

The memories were comforting, but Einarr wished they were more than just memories. He wished he was back under the cherry blossom tree with Alina, both young and healthy and oblivious to the world.

"Then you touched me on the hand and stared at me with your beautiful eyes. I knew right then and there you were my one… my one and only. You made me the happiest I've ever been, and every day with you has been better than the last. I love you."

Einarr kissed Alina's lips with a passion hotter than her fever. She returned the kiss with as much love and energy as her exhausted body could muster.

She grew weary and drifted off to sleep, her tears claiming what remained of her strength. Einarr held her long into the night until his eyes grew so heavy he could no longer stay awake. He slept lightly and woke on occasion when she stirred.

When sunlight filled the room the following day, Einarr awoke and hoped for a fleeting moment it was all a terrible nightmare. He glanced down at Alina to see if she was awake, but her skin was cold and turned a faint shade of blue. She passed sometime during the night, and he was not awake to say a final goodbye.

Einarr held his love and poured out the agony in his soul. His screams were so loud they could have been heard as far away as Brimnora. He did not find the courage to let her go until near midday. She had passed on now, with their unborn child inside. Einarr knew he would soon have to summon the shamans to ensure she would receive the proper funeral rites in time so that Kholdyr would accept her spirit into paradise.

The sky was mildly cloudy that day, but the sun made sure to shine its warmth on him as he watched the funeral pyre being constructed. The shamans and their acolytes prepared Alina's body well in a gown of white linen, with a circlet of freshly picked baby's breath around her head. The thought of watching the most beautiful and perfect woman burn to ash was too much for his broken soul to endure.

His gaze turned to the peaceful streaming waters of the Teb, and to the flowering cherry blossom tree Alina loved to sit beneath. Einarr joined her on many occasions, sometimes bringing a basket of food and mead for them to enjoy. Now that he thought about it, all his favorite memories of Alina were the times they shared beneath that very tree. It seemed fitting it should be her final resting place.

Before a shaman could put a torch to the pyre, Einarr stepped forward and protested. It was unusual for the Nothanek to bury their dead, but he would have it no other way. The ceremony was brief but lovely. Soft pink petals fell from the tree after her body was buried and covered the disturbed earth. It was as if the gods were offering their condolences, though sadly, they had not seen it in their hearts to drive Alina's illness away.

Despite all the years since that tragic event, Einarr had still not recovered from the loss. The sight and sound of the blonde woman's suffering opened old wounds, and he knew he could no longer subject himself to a campaign less focused on justice and more on vengeance.

I can go no further. I've run my course.

Having seen enough, he climbed down from the broken wall and began walking back to the siege line alone. With each step, the world around him drifted further and further away until it felt like there was no living soul for a thousand miles. The praise and congratulations Einarr received along the way seemed like distant inaudible echoes, with the words drifting away like dry, dead leaves on the wind.

The voice in the back of his mind, the constant and vigilant reminder of what was right and wrong, had fallen silent. His thoughts were as hollow and empty as his heart. Not even returning to Skaginlef was enough to bring any sense of comfort. Still, at least this would be the last time he would have to witness another atrocity under Dreadfire's command.

I have served you faithfully, Damien, but now my oath is fulfilled. I have seen enough bloodshed to last fifty lifetimes.

Somberly, Einarr reached the siege line and called for a camp follower to fetch his horse. Before he could make good on his retirement, a Nothanek warrior came bounding toward him excitedly.

"Einarr!" he called out through labored breaths. "Lord Damien wishes to speak with you. Shall I—"

"You can tell Damien I'm leaving," Einarr snapped back, interrupting the Nothanek, much to his surprise.

The warrior looked utterly perplexed. They stood in the aftermath of another historic victory, yet Einarr appeared to be the only man not sharing in their jubilation.

"Damien is on his way now. Maybe it's best if you speak to him yourself."

Einarr heard the crunching footsteps of the warband as they followed behind Dreadfire. He sighed in frustration and watched as they paraded the blonde woman back to camp, jeering and taunting her all the way. As they left, a column of black smoke rose into the sky from the castle.

"There you are, my friend!" Damien said, giving Einarr a proud embrace. However, he was quick to sense something was amiss. "What troubles you?"

Once, he would have buried his misgivings and remained faithful, but Einarr knew he could no longer remain silent. It mattered not what Dreadfire had to say, and there would be no convincing him to go any further down this path of darkness.

"I've been at your side through good times and bad, Damien. I've never once broken faith. But I can no longer continue like this. What you're doing here isn't justice. It's murder."

Damien scoffed. "They resigned themselves to death the day they decided to serve Marcellus Bethard, or have you forgotten what you saw at Borjifa?"

"No, I remember it well enough. But I've grown tired of you using it as an endless justification for murdering surrendered men. Is it not enough that they've been beaten and humiliated? Could you not ransom them off for profit or take them as slaves, at least? For gods' sake, Damien, must you put every last man to the sword? And what do you plan on doing with that girl? Will you chop her up into tiny pieces and feed her to the crows as well?"

"The girl has great value. She is a Commander of the Blackthorn Knights, and will fetch a ransom so large it will pay for the entire campaign." Dreadfire paused, teeth clenched as he fought to temper his rage. "You may think me a butcher and maybe even a madman, Einarr, but I am no fool." The anger in Einarr's eyes was enough to cool Damien's anger. "What is it you truly mean to say to me?" the warlord asked with discontentment.

"I'm finished. I swore to see justice served for what happened at Borjifa, and I have. Cedric Valens is dead, and his castle is in ruins. I'm going home now."

There was little Damien could do. It was true; Einarr fought and bled faithfully alongside him and was his most vocal champion. It would be dishonorable beyond belief to kill him or diminish him in front of the warband. After a pause and reluctant sigh, Damien placed a gauntleted hand on Einarr's shoulder.

"Take your leave then. I will not stop you. Perhaps some time at Skaginlef is what you need. Some of the Rhivothi plan to return to Rej Rhivoth until spring, so no man will think any less of you for leaving."

"That makes no sense," he scoffed. "Why would they ever want to do that when they're having the time of their lives?"

"Some have families they wish to see again. Others plan to spread word of our victories and rally more to our cause. So yes, son of Rolff, returning home will not diminish you in the eyes of any man."

Not that it mattered. Even if he were the only man in the entire warband to take his leave, it wouldn't change his mind. He was beyond caring for the opinions of others.

"Good," he said without a moment's hesitation.

"I am very sorry to have brought you down this path," Damien sighed. "You knew it would be ugly and difficult the day you swore to avenge Borjifa. Do you remember it?"

"All too well. I'm sorry my beliefs have caused this divide between us, but… at the same time, I'm not sorry. I'm who the gods made me, and I'm a proud Nothanek. We're stubbornly true to who we are. I helped get you to this point, but this path is too dark and bloody for me to continue. I pray you'll understand."

Damien smirked. It was the kind of smirk he had shown several times before, as if he possessed some level of foreknowledge and had been proven right in the end. The smirk made Einarr think Damien had always known this moment would come, and it made his skin crawl and turn to goosebumps.

I've known the man for over two years, but do I even know who he truly is?

"And I do understand." Damien nodded. "If you were not standing here saying these things to me, then it would mean whatever light, whatever… magic the gods put inside you was dead and gone. And that would be just as big of a tragedy as Borjifa, to see this war claim something so rare in this forsaken world."

In a sign of good faith, Damien Dreadfire extended his hand. Einarr stood stunned for a second but returned the gesture.

"Farewell, Einarr, son of Rolff. May the gods watch over you, always. I will make camp at Khorrtal for the winter. If you have a change of heart, you will know where to find me."

"And what of this?" Einarr pointed to Ruin, looming ominously over the battlefield.

"The engine is too large for us to take it with, and we cannot leave it here for the enemy to one day use against us." Damien took one final look at Ruin before turning away and heading back to camp. "Destroy it."

The command was as shocking as it was unexpected. Einarr's hands created many things throughout his life, but he never had to destroy anything he had built. Every creation was meant to last a lifetime or longer. He stared at Ruin long and hard, examining the countless hours of time, effort, and even love, which went into each piece of the trebuchet. However, with each passing minute, he began to feel increasingly indifferent.

Having made his mind up, Einarr fetched a torch used the night before. There was still enough material on the end to cause it to ignite one final time with a few strikes from a discarded flint. The fire erupted suddenly and with an audible rush. Somberly, he studied the white, yellow, and orange flames as they licked at the surrounding air and danced in the free and untamed way only fire can.

There would be no turning back now, he thought. The massive trebuchet represented not only the skill, love, and dedication that defined his life before the war, but also what it had become. Einarr was now an instrument of death. The value and beauty of the life he once cherished so deeply, the Nothanek way, was as hopelessly broken as the walls of Castle Morden.

Or is it? Is it ever too late for a man to find redemption? Can the gods forgive the things we do for love and loyalty?

These were questions in need of answering, but not this day. If he were to find the path of righteousness again, it would have to start where it all began, in Skaginlef. With a sobering self-reflection, Einarr looked at the torch one final time, then threw it down onto the base of Ruin, and watched as the trebuchet erupted into flames.

LUCETTA VII

THE CARRIAGE WAS AS CRAMPED AS THE INSIDE OF A COFFIN. SLOWLY it rumbled up the northern highway, kept secure by over two hundred well-armed Droethien mercenaries. Lucetta had traveled to Dellhaven several times over the years, but this occasion felt like it was taking an eternity. She glanced out the window every few minutes, hoping to see the city walls appearing just ahead.

By the second day, the trip was too unpleasant for her liking. The convoy struck out just after dawn, intent on making it to Dellhaven by nightfall.

If I don't get out of this accursed prison soon, I'll lose my mind.

Brisk morning air pimpled Lucetta's skin. She pulled her cloak tight against her body, its thick fur lining soft and warm. Not that the cold bothered her; she had grown weary of summer long ago. Wearing her favorite heavy linen dresses again brought a smile to her face.

She basked in a comforting breeze fluttering in through the windows, a growing expanse of trees, and a gentle chirping of songbirds. She felt relaxed for the first time since leaving the capital, so much so that her eyes grew heavy. She shifted around on the thinly upholstered seat, then drifted to slumber.

Her dream was a chaotic clutter of jumbled thoughts and disjointed memories that seemed to clump together into an incomprehensible mess. Even at rest, she could not find peace. Moments from her childhood were the only things she could recognize. They were simpler and happier times, when the people around her were loving and caring, and the world made sense. But those days were long in the past, likely never to return.

The carriage driver thumped on the armored body and roused Lucetta from an uncomfortable sleep. As impressive as the mercenaries had proven thus far, their perception of luxurious travel left much to be desired. She stretched her neck to one side, then the other, and groaned from its aching stiffness.

"Yes, what is it?" she barked in annoyance.

"My princess, Pavlos has returned."

The mention of his name caused such a rush of excitement that Lucetta's vision went black for a second. She half expected the Droethien to get caught in the act or perhaps discovered during his escape. But no, he had returned, and far sooner than anticipated.

He must have been successful... he must have, or else he wouldn't be here.

She wanted to ask what happened, but between the fear and thrill of not knowing, the words were lost in her head. Pavlos rode alongside the carriage on his white destrier, a toothy golden smile growing wider.

"A good morning to you, princess. I trust the trip has been pleasant, yes?"

"Yes, it has," Lucetta lied. "Please, tell me. Were you... did you..."

"Kill Bryce Whitewood?" Pavlos looked wildly amused at himself. "Why yes, I snuffed the old man out with his pillow. He was frail and died quickly. Nobody will suspect anything, princess. Pavlos promises this."

She was awestruck. Her mouth hung open, then curled into a smile. Lucetta had done it. Even though Pavlos was the one to have carried out the deed, the order was hers nevertheless.

He's dead! I can't believe it! He's dead, and all it took was a simple command.

"How did you get inside his estate?" she asked, eager to hear every detail.

"Ah, Pavlos has his ways. I slipped in during the guard rotation and climbed to the second floor. From there, it was easy to find him. The old man did not know I was in the room until he was nearly dead."

Lucetta smiled from ear to ear, and she was not the only one. The woman in black sat on the seat opposite her and looked on like a proud parent, content in the coming of age of their children.

A pair of Droethiens raced past her carriage at a gallop, followed by another half dozen. Something was happening on the road ahead, but from where she sat, Lucetta could see nothing. Pavlos drove a stiff heel into the side of his horse and started after his men.

"What is it?" she asked the driver, hands clenched together.

"Riders are approaching, princess. From the north."

"Riders? How… how many?" She toyed with her skirts.

"Only three, princess. Have no worries. Pavlos is taking every precaution so you arrive safely."

She heard the mercenary commander issuing orders, but as the unknown riders drew closer, the commotion ended. Curiously, Lucetta glanced out the window but was careful not to reveal herself to whoever was passing by.

Is it? No, it couldn't be…

To her astonishment, one of the riders was her brother, Gareth. He was dressed in commoner's clothes and accompanied by two men she could only assume were Guardsmen. Lucetta had no idea he was even in Dellhaven or what he was doing there.

Does he know what I plan to do? Is he preparing to have me seized once I arrive and thrown into a cell?

"No, he knows nothing," the woman in black said abruptly.

"Then what in the world is he doing here?" she asked, petrified. "Gareth never leaves Cardale. He has no reason to. All his lowlife accomplices are at the palace, by the docks, or wherever else he frequents."

"It is none of your concern. He did not see you and has no idea you are headed to Dellhaven. You must stay focused now. We will be arriving shortly."

Soon, the town came into view, and the sight was never sweeter. The convoy stopped briefly at the outer gates, a band of guards stationed outside looking on quizzically. Pavlos directed the most senior-looking man to the carriage. At first, Lucetta was afraid, but she quickly reminded herself that, to the outside world, this was little more than a holiday.

Act natural. They'll never suspect a thing.

"Good day to you, Highness," the guard said, bowing. Thankfully he recognized her.

"A good day to you as well."

"Quite a detail you have here," he said, eyeing the length of the convoy.

"Yes, the last time I traveled through Cardale, I was attacked and injured by an unruly mob. Since then, I've taken no chances."

Lucetta was proud of how quickly she could concoct her story, though it was nevertheless true. She supposed the most believable lies were filled with grains of truth.

If only he knew what I'm really doing here, and why I've brought these Droethiens with me.

"I see," the guard said. "You have my apologies for such an unfortunate incident, Your Highness. I assure you, Dellhaven will be far more respectful to you."

The guard waved his hand, and the convoy entered the outer gates. It wasn't long before crowds of curious onlookers congregated along the roadside. It should have been a flattering experience, so many emerging from their estates to pay their respects. But instead, Lucetta looked at them with indifference, and even a growing contempt.

As the carriage arrived at the chateau, she saw a large gathering in the courtyard. She took notice of Devin Brandybrook standing at the head of the estate's servants, many of whom were surprised by her unannounced arrival. Or perhaps the sight of the Droethien mercenaries piqued their curiosity. Even though they wore the King's colors, they appeared to be anything but Betanthian.

"Princess Lucetta! What a pleasant and unexpected surprise!" Devin hurried to the carriage and opened the door.

"Thank you for the welcome. I needed to get away from Cardale. The stresses of life in the capital can be a bit overwhelming at times."

"Say no more, Your Highness! Your quarters have been meticulously maintained, I trust everything will be to your satisfaction."

Pavlos dismounted his horse and joined Lucetta at her side. Brendon of Theeds led the rest of the mercenaries toward the stables, though it was unlikely so many horses could be accommodated. Everything seemed to be going perfectly to plan, until she caught sight of the Queen standing in the doorway.

Charlotte looked confused, as if a squatter had arrived on the property, not her daughter. Lucetta felt her chest tighten and pulse quicken, as if she were a little girl again and about to be scolded.

She's not supposed to be here. What in the world is going on? She hasn't left the Citadel in years! And Gareth was here too. This is wrong, all wrong.

"You must stay calm." The woman in black passed around the side of Pavlos. "Everything will continue as planned, have no fear."

But Lucetta was afraid. Afraid of being discovered and sent back to Cardale in irons. A million thoughts raced through her mind, each becoming more paranoid and far-fetched. But she had come too far and sacrificed too much to give up now.

"Lucetta? I wasn't expecting you. And… you brought so many men with you." Charlotte cocked her head curiously.

"And I wasn't expecting you either, mother. I thought you would still be at the Citadel."

"I needed some time away from everything. I've been here for the last few months. Your brother was here too, but he had to return to the capital on urgent business. Why have you come?"

It was never an easy thing for Lucetta to lie to her mother. Somehow, no matter how carefully crafted the lie might be, Charlotte always seemed to see through it.

So I'll tell the truth. At least, some of the truth.

"For the same reason." She brushed a few stray strands of her auburn hair aside. "I cannot stay locked up in my home every day, and the last time I traveled through Cardale, a raging mob set upon me. This is the only place I can go and escape it all."

"I understand better than anyone," Charlotte said softly. "Come inside."

It was strange to walk through the chateau knowing her mother was there. Even though Lucetta had redesigned much of the interior, everything around her felt strange and foreign. There would be no safety here. If anything, the estate might prove even more unsafe than her home in the capital. There were scores of Royal Guardsmen around, both inside and out. Undoubtedly, one of them was bound to notice the men Lucetta brought with her were Droethiens.

As she walked through the main hall and to her chamber, she heard the rattling of Pavlos' armor as he quickly moved to her side.

"My princess," he said in a muffled voice. "Are you certain it is wise to be here? This was not the arrangement you were expecting, yes?"

"No, it wasn't." She sighed in frustration.

The presence of her mother would be a complication, though hopefully not insurmountable. The Queen had been lost in her despair and would likely not notice anything unusual. But something about her already seemed different.

"Worry not," said the woman in black as she moved to Lucetta's side, opposite the mercenary commander. "Tell your men to remain outside of the town gates for now, until the Queen has departed. You must not fear your mother. She is little more than a temporary inconvenience."

"I know. I'm not worried."

"So sorry, princess," Pavlos asked, his brow furrowed in confusion, "but were you speaking to me?"

It was the most foolish mistake she could have possibly made. This was the first time she had spoken to the entity in front of another person. Lucetta's heart stood as still as her breath as she scrambled to come up with some explanation.

"No, I wasn't. My physician says it's good to reassure myself out loud whenever I feel overwhelmed."

The Droethien pursed his lips and shrugged. The lie seemed to satisfy him well enough.

"Your men won't be able to stay here," Lucetta said, hoping he would forget about her untimely slip-up. "It'll raise too much suspicion,"

"Worry not, princess, it is no matter. We will make camp outside of the city tonight. Tomorrow we will begin scouting. The Queen will not be seeing us for some time, yes?"

Hopefully, she won't be seeing any of us for much longer. Hopefully, soon I'll be in my new lands, building my new queendom.

"Meet me near the southern gate tomorrow. I would like to see you and your men off."

"The southern gate?" Pavlos asked, uncertain if he had misheard. "I beg your pardon, princess, but are we not headed to the north? Why would we stage outside of the southern gate?"

"Because I don't want to arouse any further suspicion," she said. "I can already feel their eyes on us, even now. After I see you off, ride south until you can no longer see the walls, then double back and head north. But be careful to stay far enough away from Dellhaven."

"Yes, yes, a sage move. You are every bit as cunning as you look. If it is your wish, Pavlos will see to it. Rest well, my princess."

With a toothy grin and a bow, the Droethien mercenary dismissed himself. Only when he left the confines of the chateau could she breathe a sigh of relief, and curse herself silently.

How could I have been so careless? If anyone were to find out that I'm conversing with a spirit...

"Let this serve as a warning then," the woman in black said. "You must be more careful and calculating. Rest assured; they will throw you into the tower for the insane and lock you away should they ever discover you."

"No, no, I cannot let that happen," Lucetta whimpered.

Dinner that evening was no less awkward than she expected. Queen Charlotte sat at one end of the table and Lucetta at the opposite. Between them was Emilee, her mother's maidservant. Devin and Brendon were present as well. Lucetta thought it strange that the Queen allowed servants to sit at the same table as her, but she kept her silence to avoid any undue tension.

There was little talk at the table, for reasons she could only speculate. Lucetta suspected her mother was still upset, given what transpired when she was at the Westwind Citadel. Though she would prefer not to dredge up the past, she decided an insincere apology would be best to allay any suspicions about her arrival.

"You look marvelous tonight, mother," Lucetta said after swallowing a mouthful of fresh pheasant.

The Queen smiled but said nothing.

"I wanted to apologize for my behavior at the palace," she continued. "I shouldn't have let my emotions get the better of me. Whatever disagreements I have with Gareth are my own, and I shouldn't have acted so rashly in front of you, especially with everything you've been through with father."

"Oh darling, you don't need to apologize," Charlotte said. "And you didn't need to come all this way just to tell me that. I understand people fight. Especially siblings."

"You deserve as much love and support as you can get from everyone. And you deserve a family that isn't tearing itself to pieces."

"Thank you. I hope this family can start to heal and become one again, especially since your father might not be with us for long. You've seen how much he has deteriorated recently. It may only be a matter of time."

Emilee glanced up from her plate and at Lucetta. The girl looked unsettled and quickly averted her gaze no more than a second after their eyes met. The other two servants, Devin and Brendon, appeared no less thrilled to be in her company.

There was a question burning in the back of her mind, one she was almost hesitant to ask. Lucetta dabbed the corners of her mouth with a fresh napkin, then cleared her throat.

"Is that why Gareth returned to Cardale? Has father taken a turn so quickly?"

"No," Charlotte replied, "your brother received word from Sir Edmund. There was a death on the council, and he's gone to take up the seat for himself."

Lucetta's face tightened. She felt her hands balling into fists but quickly relaxed them. At first, she was angry Gareth would be taking up such a station, but it did not last long. He was a drunkard and a failure, and having him on the council might hasten Betanthia's demise, which ultimately would work in her favor.

"I see," she muttered, pushing her plate aside.

"Sir Bryce Whitewood was found dead by one of his servants. It seems his heart gave out sometime in the night."

A curious, warm tickle ran up and down Lucetta's body. Hearing about the old man's death again was exciting beyond belief. It felt so good to kill him, even if by proxy.

"I'm sure Gareth will do well." She stood up from her seat. "If you'll excuse me, mother, I've grown weary from travel."

Charlotte nodded, then continued eating. Lucetta could not leave the dining room fast enough. Hurriedly, she strode to her chamber, the heels of her shoes clacking throughout the hall. She saw the woman in black step out of a room, though this time, she was not alarmed by the spirit's presence.

"You have become an excellent liar," the woman in black said proudly.

"And why do you say that?" she whispered back through a nearly closed mouth, so quiet it was barely audible.

"Telling your mother how sorry you were, and how much you care. It was quite delicious, if I might say so."

It was somewhat distressing to feel like it was a lie, but the truth was undeniable. Lucetta felt less invested in her family and more in herself, and was almost indifferent to what was happening in their lives.

"The truth is, she is weak," the entity said. "They are all weak, every one of them. That is why you have come so far. That is why you are here! If they had half the strength and resolve you do, there would be no need for any of this. But here you are."

Yes, here I am…

When she retired to her chamber, Lucetta felt uneasiness come over her. Even with the door locked and the drapes drawn shut, she felt prying eyes looking upon her. It wasn't the woman in black she sensed. No, the entity's presence was one she had become familiar with, in a way. This was something different.

It's just your imagination, Lucetta. She wouldn't let anything bad happen to you. She's brought you this far.

After settling down to only a few hours of broken sleep, Lucetta awoke the next morning eager to see the Droethiens off. She dressed in her favorite maroon gown and combed her long auburn hair until it was as straight and smooth as a curtain. She donned a black hooded cloak that would hopefully allow her to traverse the streets of Dellhaven unnoticed.

The estate was quiet, and most of its inhabitants were still asleep except for a few guards at the outer gate. They were Guardsmen, and every bit as sworn to her safety as to her mother's.

"Will you require an escort, Your Highness?" one of the guards asked as she approached the gate.

"No, I'll be quite safe here. I'm just going for a morning walk and catching up with a few friends I haven't seen in ages. But thank you."

"As you wish." The guard shrugged.

The streets of Dellhaven were just as quiet as the estate, with scarcely a soul to be found. There was a cool crispness to the autumn air that she could practically taste. But the walk would be far too long for her liking, and taking a carriage to see her foreign mercenaries off to uncharted territory would expose her to unwanted attention. After nearly an hour of walking, the town's outer walls came into view.

She saw Pavlos and a score of his men gathered underneath a cluster of trees near the gate and was instantly panic-stricken. Her orders were explicit; they were not supposed to remain inside the city. The Droethien commander caught sight of Lucetta and greeted her with a wide smile.

"Good morning to you, princess."

"What in the world are you doing? I told you to meet me outside the walls, not inside them! What if someone were to see us together? The whole of Dellhaven will be in an uproar!"

"Ah, but you worry too much, my princess. One of the guards started to ask questions, but Pavlos convinced him well enough. I said to him, we are from the south, and served under Ridley Vakaro before we were reassigned to the Cardale garrison. As it turns out, he once served under

Lord Vakaro as well. Needless to say, Pavlos has a new friend. Nobody will suspect us, now or ever."

"I certainly hope you're right, because I can already sense my mother's suspicion. Last night I could have sworn someone was watching me in my bedchamber. She knows, Pavlos. I need you to stay here and protect me."

"This is most unusual, princess." Pavlos raised his brow. "The White Spear needs their commander. I cannot hope to—"

"I'll pay you double. Please, I need you to stay close. I won't feel safe unless I know you're by my side. I cannot trust anyone at the estate."

The Droethien made to speak, but instead, let out a sigh. He looked at the other twenty men silently, the wheels in his mind turning. He pointed to two of the mercenaries, muttered something in his native tongue, then dismissed the others.

"As you wish, princess, but Pavlos disapproves of this. I can not lead my men from here."

"I know. You have my thanks and my apologies. My mother shouldn't be here. None of this is what I had planned."

Heavens know I can't afford to anger him, not now, not here. But he's the only one who can look after me. Not even she could keep me from being clapped in irons.

The woman in black may very well have been a guiding spirit, but would most certainly be powerless to stop the Royal Guardsmen from arresting her should the plot be discovered. It was a chance Lucetta could not take.

With her champion and the general of her small army, Lucetta and Pavlos watched as the Droethiens took to their mounts and rode out through the open gates of Dellhaven. In the distance, she saw the rest of the mercenary company, barely visible amidst a faint morning haze.

When the riders reunited with their kin, the White Spear Legion rode south until their silhouettes diminished and faded away. It felt like a knife point was twisting inside her stomach as the gravity of her actions began to set in. What she was about to do was treason, and she knew it.

But only if I get caught. If not, then I will be remembered as Betanthia's savior.

"Indeed you shall," the woman in black said as she passed around behind Pavlos, who stood unawares. "This is a glorious day and will be remembered as the moment it all happened."

"That what happened?" Lucetta asked in a whisper so soft she was practically mouthing the words. She knew the answer but wanted to hear it aloud.

The woman in black smiled mischievously, her eyes pulsating with a deep orange-red glow.

"That a new empire was born."

TITAN III

THE SUN WAS RISING IN THE EAST, AND WOULD SOON BE UPON HIM. Titan made his way down the rope as silently as he could, though the commotion echoing from the keep was enough to provide him adequate cover. After setting foot on the ground, he removed his dirk from his mouth and clenched it tight, eyes scanning the waning darkness for any foe lurking about.

If they were discovered, he would have to move swiftly and silently to avoid raising an alarm. Even though Titan was exhausted, he could still dispatch a handful of barbarians, maybe even a half dozen, but any more would prove challenging. Using the shadows as cover, he moved as stealthily as a cat, ready to pounce on the first Northman who crossed his path.

But the coast appeared to be clear, for now. The barbarians focused so much on bringing down the keep doors that there was scarcely a soul to be seen. Titan looked up and waved his hand, signaling to the other knights that the coast was clear. The first man slid down the rope quickly and took cover behind a stack of wooden barrels.

The second man began his descent, but Titan quickly waved him off. A small band of Northmen were making their way to the keep and were dangerously close. He supposed they must have come over the wall only moments ago, but thankfully, there was still enough darkness to shroud him and his men.

Quickly they passed, having been drawn to the turbulence at the keep doors. The remaining knights made their way down from the window one by one. It was a small mercy they were not discovered, but all Tylar could think about was Madelyn.

Come on, come on… where are you?

Titan looked anxiously up at the window. She should have followed close behind; he explicitly told her such, but for whatever reason, she was still inside. With each knight that climbed down the rope, Titan became more distraught.

"Where is she? She was supposed to be right behind us," Titan whispered to Liam Oliver, the last man he saw make it to the ground.

Liam said nothing but gave Titan a stupid look, telling him everything he needed to know. Tylar's heart raced in sudden panic, and he quickly returned to the rope. With all his remaining strength, he resolved to climb back into the keep and carry her down if necessary. But before he could get a hand on the rope, it suddenly came loose and fell in a heap on the ground. He paused, stunned, a sinking feeling washing over him.

"She's not coming," Liam uttered hesitantly. "She said to get out of here and warn the High Marshal. I tried to talk sense into her. Truly, I did, but she insisted on staying."

Damn foolish girl! Why! Why would you do that?

"And so you just left her? You fucking coward!"

Titan thought of tearing Liam's throat out right then and there, or at the very least, knocking him unconscious and leaving him for the barbarian wolves to devour.

I knew it. I should never have gone first. I should have stayed and made damn certain she made it out. Curse you Tylar, you fool! You left behind the only person in the world that gave a damn about you.

"I was only following her orders." Liam trembled.

Though Titan was beside himself and shaking with fury, nothing more could be done. The girl made her decision, and now she would likely pay for her precious honor with her life. As terrible as it felt to flee, it was her final order.

May whatever gods are out there watch over you, Madelyn. I'm sorry.

Titan gestured for the remaining knights to follow him toward the southeastern tower. Carefully he crept through the shadows and managed to make his way inside, the other knights following closely behind. The climb was treacherous, and he had to delicately walk over the slain bodies of his countrymen and the odd barbarian. Each step was slick with blood, shimmering in the rising sunlight.

After making it to the battlements, he heard a loud crash and an eruption of shouts and screams. It could only mean one thing. The doors to the keep had finally given way, and the unwashed horde of savages was now pouring inside. Somewhere amidst the carnage was Madelyn, outnumbered and with nowhere to retreat. It took every ounce of discipline not to turn around, run back to the keep, and try to save her. As the screams grew louder, Titan's stomach began twisting.

Knowing time was short, he searched desperately for a way out. He could always return and retrieve the rope, but there would be no place inside the tower to anchor it. But thankfully, a ladder sat perched against the battlements, some fifty feet from the tower. Quickly and quietly, Titan and his men made their way to it.

It was quiet now inside the keep. He supposed Madelyn was likely dead by now, and he prayed she was killed quickly instead of being taken alive. Titan knew all too well the hospitality of the northern tribes, the notion sending a rare shiver down his spine.

Damn foolish girl. You cared so much for your fucking honor, and look what it got you. Hopefully, it was an axe to your head and it was over quickly, because if you survived...

The thought was poison, and he tried to block it out. Pausing at the top of the ladder, Titan signaled his men to begin their descent. One by one, they climbed down, careful not to raise any sort of disturbance and betray their escape. When all were safe on the ground, he gave a final look at the keep. He valued his life, to be certain, but not at the expense of a young girl like Madelyn.

You should have died old, and surrounded by loved ones. Not here. Not like this.

But there was no changing what had come to pass. Reluctantly, Titan climbed down the ladder and joined the others below. Though they were safely outside, the danger was no less. If anyone were to spot them, they would most certainly die by enemy archers or be cut down by northern cavalry.

"What do we do now?" whispered Grayson Bennett, another of the remaining knights.

Titan said nothing but scanned the distance to ensure it was safe to venture out. Rays of sunshine spread fast against a bluish-black sky, and if they did not act soon, everyone was as good as dead.

"We head east, I suppose," Liam replied, glancing at the battlements.

"Shut the fuck up, both of you," Titan whispered. "Stay low and move fast. We don't have much time. And keep close."

The survivors ventured out from the castle carefully and in a tight formation. They used what remained of the darkness to mask their movements, clinging to the shadows from distant hills. After making it nearly a quarter of a mile from the wall, Titan spotted a cluster of trees.

Could we be so fortunate? Are those what I think they are?

Upon closer inspection, he discovered they were horses. At first, Titan wondered why nearly a dozen of them were tied off at the small grove. He supposed they belonged to the Northmen who came over the wall after the massive trebuchet did its work and drew the garrison's attention.

"Over there. Quickly now," Tylar ordered while untying a mount suitable for his size.

"Gods be good!" shouted Liam. "We've made it!"

"Keep your fucking mouth shut and have some respect for everyone still in there. We should have left you inside the keep, you moron."

A sudden faint shriek echoed out from Castle Morden. It sounded strangely familiar, much like a woman's shriek. He held his breath and stood as still as the trees, straining to listen as closely as possible. But no other sound followed.

No, it can't be…

Seconds had passed by, nearly a minute. Titan remained motionless, hoping against all hope that his mind was simply playing a trick on him. Was Madelyn still alive? Was she being tortured or perhaps outright executed? None of the other survivors heard the distant cry, though, leading him to believe it was just a figment of his imagination.

"Elite!" Liam said louder than he should have. "Elite Bradshaw!"

Titan snapped out of his nearly despondent state.

"We must go now! The sun has nearly risen!" Liam exclaimed as he untethered a horse.

"You men need to get out of here," Tylar demanded. "I'm going to stay behind. Get back to Bentmont and tell the High Marshal what happened here, and make no delay."

The remaining knights looked at each other in confusion, though none appeared content to stay any longer.

"Have you taken leave of your senses?" Grayson asked incredulously. "You're the only ranking officer left. You have to return to Thorn with us!"

"Madelyn may still be alive. And if she somehow manages to escape, she'll need my help to get out of here. Unless any of you heroes feel like facing the Northmen again?"

The knights said nothing. A few glanced eastward, growing more anxious by the second.

"Exactly," he scoffed. "So mount up and ride. I'll be right behind you."

The men needed no further convincing. They rode hard and fast toward the eastern horizon, leaving Castle Morden behind them. Titan carefully watched the castle and also his brothers until he was alone, save for the company of a few remaining horses. His hope that Madelyn would come racing away from the stronghold and to freedom dwindled with each passing minute.

Damn you girl, damn you. You were brave and your heart was true, far too true for this world. And now you're dead. And for what?

The sun rose, and it was clear he could no longer stay so close to the castle. Titan mounted a white stallion and looked to the east, where his brethren were already well ahead. However, the thought of returning to Castle Thorn without Madelyn was like poison.

How can I return to Bentmont? How can I, knowing she stayed and died a hero, and yet I escaped? No, it should have been me instead. This is your fault, Tylar. You've disgraced yourself.

Titan cursed and fought the urge to weep. He never cared much about what anyone in the Order thought of him, but showing up at the gates of Castle Thorn without Madelyn or any of the other senior officers would most certainly result in him being branded a coward. But he wasn't. He did exactly as the girl ordered.

Though Titan's mind was racing like a stampede of wild horses, he tried to think of where to escape. The nearest town to the south was Mor Seveht, but it was days away, more like a week, in fact. The terrain was rough and unfavorable, with little food or water to scavenge along the way. He considered going southwest and crossing into Droethien territory, which carried dangers of its own.

After spotting figures emerging on the wall, Titan made a split-second decision, broke into a full gallop, and raced to the south. He had been to Mor Seveht once before, perhaps twice, most recently on a rotation back from Naxonnos. It was a lawless place, claimed by no nation and filled with all manner of cutthroats, swindlers, and spies. It was a chance he was willing to take.

So much for a peaceful and quiet existence. The Order will put a bounty on my head once they learn I'm gone. They'll never stop hunting me.

When Titan reached the top of a massive rolling hill, he halted his horse and turned to face the castle one final time. Madelyn's screams continued to ring in his ears. He slapped at the side of his head in a futile hope of driving away the mournful sounds, but it was useless.

"I'm sorry."

Titan set his stallion off into a gallop while plumes of black smoke rose from Castle Morden. There was no telling if he could ever make peace with himself. Each mile he rode seemed surreal. This was the first time in decades he was striking out on his own, though he was not truly free. Deserting his post did not absolve him of the oaths he swore to the Order.

Not that I care. Let them try to come after me.

By the third day of riding, Titan was beginning to starve. Rations in the saddlebags gave his horse enough sustenance to keep moving, as the animal refused to graze on the grasses the further south they went. It was becoming arid and less hospitable, with no sign of shade or water anywhere. He had already discarded his armor and wore only a dingy brown tunic and blood-stained trousers. He knew if the horse gave out and died, his own demise would follow shortly after.

When morning came on the fifth day, he could barely move. It appeared this would be his final sunrise, or so he thought. With no water and the sun's rays searing his already burnt and peeling flesh, there seemed to be little use in going on. Just as he drifted off to slumber, perhaps never to wake again, the thought of Madelyn came creeping back.

She didn't give her life for you to go and get yourself killed like this, you idiot. Get up; you still have some strength in you. Get up! You're still alive, aren't you? And she isn't. Get up!

Out of a sheer will to live, Tylar hoisted himself onto unsteady legs. He used his last ounce of strength to mount his horse, who also seemed to be nearing the end. They rode until the late afternoon. Titan slipped in and out of consciousness several times. When he awoke for the fourth time, he could have sworn a horse-drawn wagon was approaching him.

Could it be? Or have I completely gone mad?

The driver saw something was amiss and quickly brought his wagon to Titan's side.

"Excuse me, sir? Sir? Are you alright?" The middle-aged man gasped when he saw Titan's sunburnt skin and dry, sunken eyes.

"W… water…" he managed to croak.

The driver quickly retrieved a skin of water and held it to Tylar's lips. The liquid was surprisingly cool, or at least felt that way, given how scorched his face was. The sun had been particularly unmerciful, but thankfully his resolve was even stronger.

"What's a fella like you doin' way out here? I'm surprised you even lasted out here all alone. Where you comin' from?"

The questions made Titan's head pound and ache. The driver helped him down from his horse, placed him in the shade of the covered wagon, and offered some salted meat and day-old bread.

"The name's Silas, by the way. Where you headed?"

"Mor Seveht," Titan groaned.

"Mor Seveht, eh? Just come outta there myself. I'm takin' the high pass westward. Where did you say you were comin' from again?"

"I didn't."

"Oh. Oh, well… very well then." Silas tugged at his tunic collar. "Well, um, if you're headin' to Mor Seveht, you should be there by tomorrow just fine. Seems like a fair bit of rest will do you well, eh?"

If there was one thing Titan hated more than Northmen, it was conversation. And Silas seemed to have an endless supply of it.

Perhaps that's why he needs the wagon, for all those stupid fucking words of his.

"I appreciate the food and water, but I must be on my way now."

Titan struggled to stand. Silas reached out and stopped him.

"No no, you need to rest a bit more. You're far too exhausted to be goin' anywh—"

With surprising swiftness, Titan drew his dirk and placed the tip underneath Silas' chin. The move caught the driver entirely by surprise, his eyes as large as the wagon's wheels.

"You talk too fucking much."

"Easy now, easy." Silas put his trembling hands in the air.

"You're lucky I'm not in a killing mood today. And it would be poor manners to gut you after you saved my life, so you get a reprieve."

Both men stood in unison, the dagger blade slowly digging into Silas' chin.

"Take whatever you want. Nothin' I have is worth dyin' for. Just take whatever, and I'll be on my way."

"I'm not too keen on thieving, but since you offered…"

Titan swung with his other hand and landed a devastating blow, instantly knocking Silas to the ground. He was shocked even to have that much strength left in him. It wouldn't have seemed right to leave the man lying unconscious on the ground, especially if his horses were to wander off somewhere. Titan hoisted Silas with a grunt and flung him like a flour sack into the driver's seat.

There appeared to be mostly trade goods in the back, ranging from textiles to some metalwork. Titan briefly rummaged through the cargo and took another skin of water, a hooded cloak to shield himself from the sun, and a small sack of silver coins. Neither of those things would likely be missed much, as Silas appeared well-provisioned for wherever he was going.

After giving his horse a fresh apple and a bit of water, he continued to Mor Seveht. If Silas was right, then he would arrive in short order.

But it was likely he would not be able to stay for long. The Blackthorn would begin looking for him once Liam and Grayson made it back to Castle Thorn, and if word reached the village of a robbery in the countryside, the heat would truly be on him.

Just before noon the next day, Mor Seveht came into view. At first, Titan thought it might be a mirage or some other trick of the mind, but it was exactly as he remembered it. The sight was bittersweet and nearly broke him. On the one hand, it was the first stop on a new path for the rest of his life, provided he could escape the Order's clutches. And on the other, it was a reminder of everything he had lost.

I'm sorry I couldn't save you, Madelyn. But I'll live every day to its fullest so your sacrifice is honored. I'll miss you… my… my friend.

After wiping away the faintest hint of water from his eyes, Titan gave his weary horse a nudge and slowly rode into town. Mor Seveht was just as unimpressive as it was the last time he visited. The streets themselves were little more than well-trodden dirt paths. It was so dry, clouds of dust were kicked up by the wind and drifted throughout town, coating the plain, crude wooden buildings with a thick, tannish-brown blanket.

There were a handful of dwellings, a tavern, and a merchant shanty. Mor Seveht only had one inn; unfortunately, rooms were often scarce. He prayed one would be available, even if it were nothing more than a broom closet. It would be a small mercy to lie down and rest with a roof over his head.

The townsfolk paid him little attention, as visitors came and went regularly. Some took notice of his reddened face and stared curiously, but nothing more. When he arrived at the inn, Titan tied off his mount to a hitching post, and the animal dunked its head into a full trough of water, guzzling it by the gallon. When he stepped inside, his nostrils were greeted by the scent of burned candles and a faint aroma of must and piss.

Not much has changed since the last time I was here, apparently.

The man behind the counter chewed on a mouth full of tobacco, a few brown drops staining his chin. At first, he paid Titan no attention but took notice of his hulking frame as he approached the counter.

"Do you have a room available?" Tylar croaked, his throat still as dry as the Plainhold.

The innkeep looked at him suspiciously. Between scars and sunburns, Tylar looked like a reanimated corpse.

"Gods be good." The man recoiled. "What in the world happened to you?"

Though exhausted, he needed to think of a cover story, and fast.

"I'm a trader from Hok. This was my first time riding through the Plainhold, and I underestimated the terrain. My first horse died, so I had to ditch my wagon, and I barely made it here with my other one."

"Hok, you say? Gods, you must be mad to make that sort of ride, especially for the first time. What were you thinking?"

"I normally make my rounds through Khorrtal, but it's been far too dangerous lately."

The innkeep spat a gobbet of juice into an old pan, then wiped his chin with the back of his thumb.

"Aye, we've been hearing stories as of late. Is it true, are the northern folk coming down into Betanthia? I heard they were crawling all over Khorrtal even a few months ago."

Titan was reluctant to say more, lest his lies become so complex he would give himself away. And the memories were still too fresh and vivid, and far too painful to recall.

"Look, I'm exhausted and near dead. Do you have a room or not? I have enough coin to pay for one."

"Seems it's your lucky day, friend. I just so happen to have one available. It's not the most luxurious of accommodations, but it'll suffice. A few coins, and it's yours."

He retrieved the pilfered sack of silver from his belt pouch and tossed it onto the counter. It landed with a thud and a clink.

"Take what you need. I plan on spending a few days. And bring some food and ale if you have any."

The innkeep pulled the pouch strings, withdrew a half dozen silver coins, and then another two. He examined them briefly, pursed his lips, and nodded.

"Right away. I've got some fresh mutton and some brew in the kitchen, maybe even some chicken. Here's your key. It's the second to last on the right."

Titan stuffed the coin sack into his belt pouch, took the key in his cracked and burnt hand, and slogged down the hall. His room was modest, as one would expect from a glorified outpost like Mor Seveht. He was thankful to have a window and a bed, which didn't look too terribly uncomfortable. Not that it would have mattered, even if it was.

The innkeep entered moments later carrying a tray of meat and bread and a tall pitcher of ale. He set the refreshment down on a small, crude table, bowed his head, and closed the door gently as he left. Titan was so starved he didn't feel much like eating, but he forced down a mouthful of a slightly blackened chicken breast.

The meat was rather flavorless, save for the carbonized gristle he bit into. His stomach immediately erupted into a howling beast, gurgling, twisting, and rumbling. Quickly he devoured the rest of the food, then stared longingly at the pitcher of ale.

Titan wanted nothing more than to sleep, but without sufficient drink, the night terrors would likely be relentless. With a sigh, he reflected on everything he had lost, then placed his cracked lips on the pitcher. He drank to remember. And he drank to forget.

CHARLOTTE III

H ER DAYS AT THE CHATEAU WERE NO LONGER AS COMFORTING, AND the nights even less so. There was something peculiar and unsettling about Lucetta's new companions, something that filled Queen Charlotte with a familiar sense of dread. She had taken to sleeping with Gareth's dirk under her pillow each night, though it would have been better to have guards posted outside her door. It would be wise to do, but she hoped not to raise suspicion.

This doesn't feel right. I wish Gareth was back with me, or I would have gone with him. Who would have thought I would ever want to return to Cardale?

It was surprising to find the following day that the large entourage accompanying her daughter had mysteriously vanished. Charlotte found it curious Lucetta would travel with such a massive host, several times the number she and Gareth brought with them, especially for a mundane vacation. And to make matters even more unsettling, the soldiers appeared to be anything but Betanthian, although they could be sworn to any of the southern lords.

But why would southern troops be this far north? What were they doing in Cardale in the first place?

It was the curse of having an overactive mind, a debilitating state of constant worry that nearly drove Charlotte to take her own life only months ago. But perhaps Lucetta was simply being cautious, albeit overly cautious. It didn't feel right to cast judgment considering her own fears and insecurities and how they nearly destroyed her.

Breakfast was an uncomfortable affair, and more silent than what she was used to. Charlotte grew accustomed to feasting with Gareth outside the chateau amidst the splendor of nature, laughing and sharing stories and plans for the future. But this morning was different. Lucetta sat at the far end of the table opposite her. Between them sat Emilee and Devin, just as the day before. Having servants seated at the royal table was unorthodox, but Charlotte came to cherish their company during her time at the estate. Her daughter's eyes, however, reflected an obvious distaste. Lucetta had the same look of disgust from dinner the night before.

"I just wanted to say how lovely the estate looks," Charlotte said, trying to break the awkward silence. "It's quite remarkable, and I was speechless when I saw what you did to the master chamber. Those are my favorite colors."

Lucetta gave a disinterested smile and picked at her food. "I'm glad you enjoy it, mother. It required my best efforts."

Charlotte wanted to confront her daughter and find out what was happening but thought better of it. This was not the same Lucetta she had always known. Something was weighing heavily on her; it was plain to see. Her eyes had grown sad and vacuous, as if hiding some untold pain. Even Emilee took notice and glanced over at her suspiciously.

"Please, be honest with me." Charlotte chewed her lip. "Is everything alright with you? I don't like seeing my children this way, especially you. You're my only daughter."

A deep conflict looked to be tearing Lucetta apart on the inside. Her eyes continually wandered to the far side of the room and back.

"Not now, mother. I'm feeling unwell. Perhaps later."

Gently, Charlotte motioned for Emilee and Devin to give them the room, and both servants complied with a silent bow.

"I would hear what's troubling you. I'm your mother, and I'm here for all my children equally. Your brother was having his own difficulties, and he shared them with me. I know you two don't care for each other's company, but though it pains me, it's your right to associate with him as you please."

"It isn't Gareth," Lucetta mumbled.

"I'm happy to hear that. I remember how you two fought with each other the day you came to the palace, and I hope never to see that again. So, if your brother isn't troubling you, what is it? Something at home, perhaps? Is everything alright between you and Trace? You two are close. I would have expected you to travel together."

"Trace is fine. He's been extraordinarily busy with his ventures, that's all. But life at home has been overwhelming lately. I'm losing all sense of myself. And Aldred is far too wrapped up in his work to give me any love or support."

It was a story she knew all too well. Charlotte's face tightened and strained to keep herself from crying. "It pains me to hear that. I want you to know I'm here for you. Never feel like you cannot come to me with your troubles. I'll always make time for you."

Lucetta forced a meager smile, then dismissed herself from the table. For some strange reason, she continued glancing off to her side as if taken by an unseen distraction. Charlotte sighed, unable to make sense of what was happening.

I pray my daughter hasn't lost her mind. I can make peace with what happened to Marcellus, but to see Lucetta succumb to the same affliction would be the death of me.

Autumn afternoons in Dellhaven had become one of the Queen's favorite things. Green leaves on the many species of trees began to fade

518

and shift into a tapestry of oranges, reds, and yellows. The musky, sweet harvest scent from the many local fields filled the air like incense. It was magical, something she had never experienced at Cardale.

She walked throughout the estate gardens wearing a dress of heavy blue linen, and a thick black sheepskin cloak. It would only be days before the beds of beautiful flowers would begin to wither in anticipation of winter. It made her sad not to have Gareth here to experience the majesty of the changing seasons, but it did provide an opportunity to spend some quality time with Lucetta.

She should be out here with me. It isn't right that she should be shut up inside the estate, not on a day like this.

With a determined smile, Charlotte returned to the chateau. The years denied her many opportunities to bond with Lucetta, her first and only daughter. It would be foolish to let more time slip away, she thought. And in such a state of obvious despair, it wouldn't be right to leave her alone.

A scent of pumpkin and dried corn filled the manor and gave the Queen a sudden pause. Instinctively her eyes closed, and her nostrils drew in the pleasant aromas that were nearly intoxicating. Excitedly, Charlotte strode to Lucetta's chamber, eager to fetch her for an afternoon stroll.

She rapped gently on the door, but there was no response. Slowly, she turned the polished brass knob and cracked the door open a few inches, peering inside.

"Lucetta? Are you in there?"

Her only answer was silence. Charlotte stepped inside, expecting the room to be empty. She saw her daughter lying peacefully on the bed and wearing night clothes. Even though Lucetta was fast asleep, she looked exhausted and run-down. Charlotte saw dark circles and bags under both eyes, filling her heart with sadness.

Oh, my poor daughter. I hate seeing you like this. I can only wonder what you must be going through.

Every instinct inside Charlotte compelled her to hold Lucetta tight and protect her from harm like a mother bear would protect her cubs. But she was a woman grown, and could not rightfully be sheltered from the harshness of reality. That mistake had already been made once with Gareth, and the road he had to travel to find himself was long and perilous.

It's alright to sleep. Whatever you need, I will do for you.

It wasn't until evening that Lucetta emerged, this time looking a bit less haggard. Her long auburn hair was curled and fixed into a simple updo, and she wore a flowing gown of deep green linen. It brought a smile to Charlotte's face to see her daughter looking somewhat refreshed.

But when she was approached about dinner, Lucetta began to grow agitated. Bright pink lines arced across her left elbow where she scratched the skin raw. And for some strange reason, she had repeatedly stared into nothingness as if being spied upon.

"Not tonight, mother. I must attend to business, something I've been putting off for far too long."

"Very well," Charlotte said, dismayed. "Take whatever time you need for yourself. You can always come to me for anything, whether large or small."

It was the same on the following night and the night after. Lucetta had taken to leaving the estate so often and for such long periods that Charlotte was beginning to suspect her daughter was having a clandestine affair. It would certainly make sense, given her apparent lack of husbandly attention. But there was a certain danger, if the suspicion was to be true, of the commoners finding out. The last thing House Bethard needed was a scandal of this nature.

I need to find out what's going on with her.

Charlotte summoned Emilee and Devin and met with them inside the gazebo under cover of darkness. It was one of the few places where she was certain nobody else would hear them.

"How may I be of service, my queen?" Devin asked, a slight look of confusion about him.

"I don't know how best to say this, so I'm just going to say it. Something is amiss with Lucetta. She's not behaving like herself at all."

"Yes, she has been acting a bit strange; pardon my saying so," Emilee said.

"I need to know what is going on with her, and soon. If she's in some sort of trouble, then I need to help her."

The Queen toyed with her skirts, then smoothed them. Both servants looked at each other, their eyes revealing their uncertainty. Devin cleared his throat.

"We can certainly keep an eye on her, Your Majesty. I'll notify the other servants and—"

"Only the ones you trust," Charlotte interrupted. "I don't want her to find out I'm spying on her."

"I wouldn't call it spying, my queen," Emilee said. "You're only looking out for her like any good mother would do. I'll keep a close eye on her."

When Lucetta was absent for breakfast the following day, Charlotte grew even more concerned. It wasn't natural for anyone to be so exhausted, she thought. Was there some affliction her daughter was suffering from?

I pray not. I don't know what I would do if something happened to her.

After finishing her meal, the Queen went to her daughter's quarters. She didn't get far before catching sight of the strange-looking Guardsman who rode at the head of Lucetta's convoy. As the man passed by, he gave an unsettling smile, his golden teeth glistening in the light.

"Excuse me," Charlotte said after clearing her throat.

The man paused and cocked his head, his smile unchanging yet somehow turning more menacing.

"How did you come into the service of my daughter?"

The man's grin faded slightly, and he shrugged. "It is my duty," he replied, his voice sounding somewhat unnatural.

It was plain as day he was trying to mask an accent, though he did a good enough job that Charlotte could not place it. Before she could think of what else to ask, the man bowed and strode off. There was something peculiar about him, something she couldn't explain. After glancing over her shoulder, Charlotte continued to Lucetta's chamber. The door was closed, and she rapped gently on it several times. There was no response.

"Lucetta? Are you in there?"

She opened the door slowly and looked in, but saw the room was empty. The Queen entered and noticed the glass patio door was slightly ajar. Lucetta must have slipped out after meeting with the Guardsman, if he even was a true Guardsman.

What have you gotten yourself into?

She wanted to cry. The worst was not knowing what was truly going on. It made her feel as helpless as she felt back at the Westwind Citadel, when life was bleak and dark. She closed the door to her daughter's room, then marched steadfastly to the kitchens.

Devin was overseeing the servants as they tidied up after breakfast. The sleeves of his blue tunic were rolled up to his elbows as he helped dispose of refuse and assisted in washing the fine ceramic plates. When the Queen entered, he greeted her with a smile and a bow.

"Your Majesty! How may I be of service?"

"I would like to speak with you when you're finished," Charlotte said quietly.

"My Queen, I am yours whenever you require it. Shall we speak now?" Devin asked, wiping his hands clean on a linen cloth.

"No, it's quite alright. Come meet with me outside whenever you're free of your duties."

Charlotte walked through the gardens, though not even the serenity of the outdoors seemed to offer any comfort. If anything, it made her miss Gareth even more. He would certainly know what to do in a situation such as this, she thought.

Shortly after, Devin made his way to the gardens. He was a dutiful servant and never kept the Queen waiting for much of anything if he could help it. His face had an unmistakable look, one nearly mirroring her own. He was concerned, every bit as much as Charlotte.

"Is everything alright, Your Majesty?" Devin asked. He straightened the wet sleeves of his tunic.

"No, I'm afraid not. I must know what is happening with my daughter now."

"I haven't seen anything out of the ordinary since last night. I suppose I could have her followed if it would please you, Your Majesty."

Charlotte chewed her lip. If Lucetta were in trouble or involved in something dangerous or inappropriate, it would be perilous to allow it to continue. "I have to know what's going on, and I have to know now. This cannot wait any longer. If she leaves the estate tonight, I will follow her."

"Your Majesty, that would be most unwise. Surely we could send Guardsmen to—"

"No," she protested, a slight tremble in her voice. "She's my daughter, and I have to keep her safe. Will you come with me, Devin?"

"My queen, but… I'm no soldier. If there's danger, I'm not certain I could protect you." Devin scratched the back of his neck.

"I'm going. Are you coming with me or not?"

"Of course, Your Majesty. Will you at least allow me to bring some Guardsmen along with us? If there's danger, someone needs to be able to defend you," he said, looking uneasy.

Charlotte nodded in agreement.

"Very well," Devin sighed. "I'll keep an eye out for her this evening, and if she leaves, I'll come get you right away."

Dinner that evening came and went, and Lucetta was nowhere to be found. Emilee informed Charlotte she was asleep in her room, but if the previous nights were any indication, it would be short-lived. Anxiously, the Queen watched from the window of a guest suite on the upper floor, waiting to catch a glimpse of her daughter. Her nails scratched white markings into the polished wood armrests of a high-back chair.

Before long, she saw Lucetta garbed in a dark cloak, making her way across the courtyard. Charlotte immediately rose from her seat and hurried downstairs. Devin was waiting by the front door, his gaze fixed on the estate gates.

"Come, we must go before she gets too far away."

Charlotte and Devin ventured out into the night, each clad in hooded cloaks. They waited for Lucetta to leave the grounds before going any further, but before she did, the strange Guardsman came to her side. Something was unsettling about his golden smile and cold, calculating eyes, something she did not trust. Charlotte watched as they conversed briefly, then left the estate and traveled southward.

Who is this man, and what are his intentions? Lucetta, what have you gotten yourself into?

As Devin and the Queen arrived at the gates, he motioned for two Guardsmen to accompany them. Charlotte was cross at first and wanted to avoid involving too many parties in her daughter's affairs. However, having a pair of skilled fighters alongside them eased some of her anxiety. They left the safety of the estate and started off into the night.

Their walk seemed to last forever. Lucetta and her companion were mere specks in the distance, but Charlotte saw they were headed into a theater under construction about a half mile from the town square. What business she had in such a place and at such an hour was puzzling.

"Hurry, I don't want to lose them," she whispered, even though she didn't need to. There was no one around to hear any of them.

The air that night was particularly brisk. Charlotte pulled her cloak tight to her body and shivered. She saw a faint haze of breath in the full moonlight with each exhale. Not that it mattered. If it meant keeping Lucetta safe, she would go to the very end of the world and back, and more.

The Queen and her entourage hastened their pace, but her daughter was nowhere to be seen. The square was an ever-expanding patchwork of buildings, though the locals were not keen on turning Dellhaven into another Cardale. As such, the town center was entirely vacant, especially at night.

The theater was mere months from completion, but the site was still a mess of scaffolding, stone blocks, and other building materials. At first, Charlotte thought the trail had gone cold, until she saw a faint glow of light coming from the auditorium.

She spied a nearby staircase to a balcony wrapped around the entire theater. It was as pitch black as the night and would provide the perfect concealment. Quietly, Charlotte climbed to the top, careful not to reveal herself.

"Stay here. I'm going to see if I can get a closer look," she told Devin and the Guardsmen.

The three of them appeared hesitant, but they nevertheless obeyed her command.

"Please, be careful, my queen," Devin whispered. We won't be far away."

Charlotte moved across the balcony like a nimble cat, using the shadows and pillars as cover. Flickering lantern light danced gently across the plain stone walls, and along with it came the soft echoes of conversation. She saw Lucetta and the Guardsman standing together with a third man. He wore the King's colors, though Charlotte suspected something was amiss.

What in the world are they discussing at an hour like this? And here, of all places? None of this feels right.

"Our first reports are promising, yes?" the strange Guardsman said, his accent thick. He held a piece of unrolled parchment in his hands.

Their replies were too muffled to make out, and before the Queen could move closer to get a better vantage point, the meeting ended. Both men said something to each other in a foreign-sounding language, then departed. Lucetta walked to the auditorium's far end, where a wide stage was being constructed.

Charlotte followed closely behind, looking down uneasily from above. When Lucetta disappeared behind the stage, she searched for a way down to ground level. A staircase was barely visible at the far end of the balcony. Gingerly she tip-toed down it, careful to avoid making any sound. Her heart was racing and pounding so violently she feared it might be loud enough for anyone to hear.

The area backstage was a mess of construction work. Tall scaffolds sat about everywhere and provided adequate concealment. Charlotte continued onward but paused when she heard Lucetta speaking.

"Are you sure? If anyone were to find out... yes, of course. No, I... I just..."

The Queen chewed her lip and wondered who her daughter was conversing with. She wished Gareth was here to reassure her everything would be alright. Lucetta was involved in something nefarious, and whoever was with her was either an accomplice or the one behind it all.

You can do this, Charlotte. You must, for her sake.

After several deep breaths, Charlotte gathered the courage to peek out and see who the would-be conspirator was. To her horror, she saw Lucetta standing alone in the center of the darkened room, speaking to no one.

MADELYN VI

NIGHT HAD NEARLY FALLEN WHEN THE BARBARIANS RETURNED TO their encampment. A day of being tethered to a horse and forced to walk mile after mile was as exhausting as battle. Madelyn nearly fell several times after her legs became numb, but fear of what the Northmen might do kept her going.

Word of victory must have reached their camp well ahead of their arrival. It looked as if every camp follower and their kin turned out to see the victorious warriors returning with their spoils. There was dancing, cheering, celebrating, and even blessings and prayers from tribal shamans.

Damien Dreadfire and his warchiefs rode at the head of the column and were showered with the most praise. When the barbarians at camp caught sight of Madelyn, they cursed, jeered, and taunted her at every opportunity. Thankfully, they were stayed by a simple wave of Damien's hand. The respect he commanded from even the most uncivilized savages was impressive.

"It's good to be back!" Sylvia Stormguard said. "What do you say we drink ourselves some mead? I don't know about you lot, but I've worked up quite a thirst."

She was met with cheers and hearty laughter. Madelyn looked around the barbarian campsite suspiciously. The crackling and roaring of evening fires and an ever-increasing thumping of drums filled her with a sense of awe. But when Dreadfire dismounted his horse and took control of the rope around her wrists, she half-expected to be put to the sword right then.

"Be still, girl. I will not harm you, not unless you provoke me." Damien studied her, gave the rope a sharp tug, and started into the heart of the camp.

Thousands of tents stretched farther than Madelyn could see, making it feel like a literal forest surrounded her. All around, fires burned bright and hot. Fresh food and drink were shared between camp followers and returning warriors, and many danced to the high-tempo beating of more than a dozen war drums. Some even fought, their thirst for violence seemingly not sated by their sacking of Castle Morden.

Madelyn had never experienced anything like this before, though, at an instinctual level, it felt strangely familiar. Damien paused to share a drink with his four warchiefs. Animal horns filled with mead were passed around, and the victorious barbarian chieftain raised a toast.

"This day belongs to the free lands, and every man, woman, and child who has suffered under Betanthian tyranny. And to you, my friends. Without you, this day would never have been possible."

"To you, Damien," Sylvia toasted. "And for Borjifa."

There was a moment of silence. Damien's eyes seemed distant and sorrowful, though Madelyn could hardly feel remorse for such a ruthless butcher. The five barbarians drank from their horns.

"It's been an honor to fight alongside you," a man with long brown hair and a dark beard said. "The Nothanek have fulfilled their vow, and I have instructed my people that each man may stay or leave as he pleases. As for me, I'll be returning to Skaginlef for the harvest."

"You're leaving?" Sylvia's jaw fell open. "After all we've done together, you're just going to leave? Why?"

"Be still, Stormguard," Damien said. "No one will think less of you, Einarr. We are all here on our own accord, and you have honored me with your loyalty without reservation. If anyone has earned the right to see home again, it is you. Let us drink to Einarr, son of Rolff. He was the first to swear himself to this cause—the first to stand by my side. To you, my friend."

"To Einarr!" the other warchiefs echoed.

Madelyn's eyes met Einarr's for an instant as he turned to leave. Though neither of them spoke, there was an understanding that transcended words. Whatever Einarr saw in her eyes, she too saw in his. It was difficult to believe such soulless murderers could feel anything, but she could not help but sense a deep sadness in his heart.

After sharing their drink, Damien took up the rope around Madelyn's hands and continued on. They were soon descended upon by a troupe of revelers who looked fearsome and animalistic. The men beating the drums were dressed in roughspun, bear and wolf skins, and adorned with the horns of elks and animal bones. They sang and shouted in a strange language. The gentle melody of the women complimented the guttural throat singing and raspy shouts and screams of the men.

Many gathered to partake in the celebration, and for a moment, Madelyn forgot she was even a prisoner. A large, circular procession formed around a massive fire, its majestic orange and red flames dancing nearly in sync with the music. The warriors danced in a state of ecstasy, cheering and singing to the songs of their ancestors. Horns of mead were never in short supply, and a strong scent of venison, roasted boar, and freshly smoked herbs wafted throughout the encampment.

Were it not for the rope digging into her wrists and Damien's iron grasp, Madelyn might have used such an opportunity to escape. It was fascinating, however, to witness how barbarians celebrated. It made the feasting and drinking on the successful first day at Castle Morden seem tame.

After a rowdy number, the musicians began playing at a slower tempo, and the mood grew somber. Dancing and cheering soon ceased, and those gathered stood quietly while the drums and horns played slower. The animalistic singing, if it could be called such, had stopped, leaving only the sorrowful crooning of a tall blonde woman in a hooded cloak.

"This is a dirge for the fallen," Damien uttered softly.

The wolf shaman who led the band of drummers stepped forth and offered a prayer in the old tongue. He held an urn full of a sweet yet pungent-smelling herb and set it alight. He moved in a slow circle around a totem that looked to be carved from a wooden log or perhaps a giant animal bone. It was difficult to tell which. After each line of ritualistic chants, he blew a thick cloud of smoke at the totem, which danced about in the night air before drifting off to the heavens.

"Come. This ceremony is not for your eyes." Damien gave the rope a tug and led her to a command tent near the heart of camp.

After entering, the rope around her wrists was replaced with iron shackles, chained and staked to the ground. Two massive Rhivothi warriors entered and stood vigil by the tent flap, filling her with dread. Madelyn's stomach writhed at the thought of what might come next.

"If you're going to kill me, please just get it over with," she uttered hopelessly.

Damien chuckled as he poured fresh mead into a drinking horn. "I am not going to kill you. You are worth far more to me alive than dead."

After drinking, he offered some to Madelyn, but she declined.

"Very well," he said. "Now, if you would give me your name."

Again she refused the warlord with a shake of her head.

"I never ask twice. For anything. Or for anyone," Damien snarled as he leaned in close. The stench of mead on his breath was off-putting.

"Madelyn. Madelyn Everly."

"Everly? Everly, you say? Interesting, most interesting indeed. Then it is as Lazilyth says." Damien was now smiling from ear to ear, content with the knowledge he possessed. He took another sip of mead without breaking his gaze.

"And what do you find so interesting about my name?"

"There are many things I find fascinating about you, though it seems to me you need a history lesson. Tell me, girl, do you know the origin of your name?

Madelyn shook her head.

"I know it well," Dreadfire said. "Your name, if it is truly Everly, comes from the word Eveldanyr. When the Khorr first came to these lands, they were unoccupied. Not a soul was to be found from north to south, east to west. The first explorers numbered in the hundreds, and many thousands followed soon after. Do you know of these people, the Khorr?"

Damien sat on a weathered wooden chair and leaned an elbow on one knee. Madelyn thought for a second but shook her head no.

"Well, you should. Several cities were named in their honor. Khorrtal is the last to bear the name of its founders. Khorrdell was once the most prominent, but you know it as Cardale. The first wave of Khorrish settlers had many tribes, one being the Bet'erds."

His tone grew scornful and mocking for just an instant.

"They were sheepherders and fur traders." Damien huffed and shook his head, then took another drink.

"They founded the outpost of Bet'mount, or Bentmont as you know it, and over time became prominent traders. They grew so wealthy they built a large enough army to overthrow their chieftains, the Eveldanyr." Dreadfire paused and reflected as if his own eyes had witnessed such events.

"The Eveldanyr were a noble clan, hearty and brave, fair and just. And pure in blood too. Some say they were able to commune with the gods. Others say they possessed knowledge of the arcane arts and could manipulate reality itself."

"And could they?" Madelyn asked doubtfully.

"No one knows for certain. They were wiped out a thousand years ago, or so the stories say. Some have claimed to be descended from the Eveldanyr, but none have been able to prove it. All that is certain is this; without our divine protectors, our people were pushed to the brink of extinction. What you see gathered around us are some of the few remaining Khorrish tribes. The last of the ancient bloodlines. Though we have grown apart over the centuries, we share a common ancestry."

"If what you say is true, what happened after the Eveldanyr were killed?"

Madelyn supposed if she could keep the barbarian talking, it would be easier to gain his trust and help spare her from the sword. Whether the tale was true or not was of little consequence.

"The Bet'herds were clever," he said. "They never wanted anyone to do to them what they did to the Eveldanyr. They knew that to control the future, you must control the past. So they began to change history. The names of temples, rivers, cities, and even their own names were changed. New generations were told that the Bethards ruled these lands since the dawn of time, and speaking of their Khorrish ancestry became punishable by death."

"That's quite a tale," Madelyn said incredulously. "And that's why you're keeping me here as a prisoner?"

"Yes, because enough northern blood has been spilled on account of the Bethards." Damien rose from his seat and moved behind Madelyn. "I have sent many of their minions to the grave, and if the gods are just, I will put down thousands more. You may very well be the last of the Eveldanyr, and I would rather your line not be extinguished by my hands."

Dreadfire ran his fingers through a lock of Madelyn's hair, then smelled it. "Your people, your true people, have suffered endlessly. And

I believe the fates have aligned, and the gods have crossed our paths for a purpose, Madelyn the Eveldanyr. Your ancestors cry out for justice."

He placed his mighty hands on her shoulders. "And I am the instrument of that justice. The gods would be pleased to see you stand at my side and assume your rightful place as chieftess once the Bethards are destroyed. With our bloodlines combined, we could forge a new dynasty that would bring peace and order back to these lands."

He moved and faced Madelyn, his hulking frame making her appear childlike. Damien placed two fingers under her chin and gently raised her head until their eyes met again.

"Join me as my wife, and all twelve thousand warriors outside this tent will swear fealty to you tonight. Join me, and you will sit on the throne of your ancestors, and the sons I give you will sit on it after our time has passed."

Madelyn recoiled as she remembered what happened to Morden's garrison and her knights. The thought of Corbyn made her eyes sting and turn red with tears. "I could never. You're a monster. You slaughtered those men, good men who had surrendered. And you killed them without mercy."

"Monsters are not born; they are made. And the Bloodbath at Borjifa made me. You have never seen what I have seen, nor have you suffered as I have suffered."

"And how do you know anything you've said is true? The Eveldanyr, and me, some long lost queen? I was an orphan. The High Marshal found me outside of Castle Thorn. My parents were probably nothing more than commoners who could no longer care for me. You have no way of knowing anything."

"No." A sinister grin crossed Damien Dreadfire's face. "But she does."

Madelyn felt a cold chill creep up her spine as the tent flaps opened. An old woman tottered in between the two looming Rhivothi warriors. Though each towered nearly twice her height, they both appeared unsettled by her presence. Madelyn's skin turned to gooseflesh as the crone approached.

"Is she the one, Lazilyth?" Dreadfire asked with bated breath. "Is she the one I seek?"

The old woman's eyes were a swirling sea of milky, glassy film. Though she was likely blind or close to it, it felt as if her eyes could see things others could not. Madelyn sensed the crone peering into her very soul as she sniffed and studied her.

Lazilyth's frail, gnarled hand suddenly wrapped around Madelyn's jaw with crushing force. The old woman was unnaturally strong despite appearing a hundred years old, or older. Madelyn's head was wrenched to the side, and the crone slid a bony finger across the birthmark on her neck.

"She has the blood," Lazilyth croaked.

Damien smiled. "Gods be praised. Tell me, what do the fates hold for her and our people?"

"The fates say many things," the old woman replied cryptically. "They are as changing as the seasons, as shifting as the tides."

"Tell me true, woman. I must know the paths before me." Damien's command was stern, but Madelyn saw even he was hesitant to unleash his fury on the crone.

Lazilyth's eyes fluttered and rolled back, turning to a pure white. Her mouth drooped open, and the most haunting and otherworldly groan slowly escaped her throat. A low, rumbling noise shook the ground like an earthquake. The old woman spasmed once, then again, then exhaled as if it was her final breath.

Lanterns began dancing and flickering as if a swift gale swept in. The Rhivothi looked at each other nervously; their hands gripped tightly on the hilts of their weapons. Shifting light cast ominous shadows on the strange woman's face, making her appear more like a corpse than a living person.

In a frighteningly deep and raspy voice, she bellowed. "Many paths… many… many…"

"Tell me." Damien took a step closer, though his face was that of fear. "Is she the one we seek? The one who will restore the line of the Eveldanyr?"

"The blood… is pure," Lazilyth moaned. Her hunched back stiffened and became as straight as a board. "Her fire… burns bright. The seed… must be freely accepted, or it will not take root. The gods will shun the union, and the line will wither and die like fruit on the vine."

What in the world is she talking about? What sort of madness is this? Seed? Do they mean to use me as some broodmare? I have to get out of here before it's too late!

The sight was too terrifying for Madelyn to believe. A stack of parchment took flight, then fluttered to the ground like leaves in a windstorm, though she felt no breeze.

"No," Madelyn said with the courage of a mouse. "I refuse. My body is not yours to do with as you please!"

"Then she is of no use to me," Damien growled. "Since she refuses, better she should die."

The crone suddenly inhaled as if startled by some unseen horror. "Kill her, and doom will be upon you. Death, and fire, and doooom…" Her voice faded and trailed off.

Frustrated, Damien Dreadfire looked down at Madelyn. She saw conflict and uncertainty in his black eyes.

"Very well then. We will keep her captive. Perhaps she will come to know and love her true people in time. Tell me, woman, what do the fates say?"

"Keep her in chains… chains… and she will perish. Bid fare to scorch us all…"

"Perish? How?" Damien and Madelyn said at the same time.

Lazilyth's head began to twitch, jerk, and twist about in unnatural ways. Whatever dark power she was conjuring was too great for her frail body to contain. The two Rhivothi slowly backed out of the tent until they disappeared. The air was becoming thick, difficult to breathe, and smelled of something rotten.

"She will be taken by pestilence… or by the chaos of your broken and routing warriors… keep her in chains and be cursed!"

Dreadfire was aghast. "If she stays, she dies, or it spells our doom. Dear gods, how could this be? I have done everything you have asked of me! I have avenged the slaughter of your faithful! I have brought justice to those who offended you! And now, when I have found the instrument of our deliverance, it is pulled from my grasp?"

In defeat, Damien fell to his knees.

"Tell me, Lazilyth, what must I do? If I cannot kill nor keep her, and if she will not accept the seed, what must be done? Should I release her?"

"Many paths… many…" the old woman groaned and gasped. "The blood must be free. Only then will she return… stronger… fiercer, bolder."

Madelyn's fear was so taxing she grew close to fainting. The crone appeared to be faring even worse. Her body thrashed and contorted violently, her white eyes turning bloodshot.

"I… cannot hold on…" Lazilyth said in her natural voice, the power of her trance waning.

"Then tell me," Dreadfire asked desperately. "Will she return as a friend or as a foe?"

Before collapsing to the ground, she uttered. "F… foe…"

A cold sweat trickled down Madelyn's neck and back. The air throughout the tent suddenly turned light and fresh, and the lanterns became still. Were it not for a subtle fluttering of the old woman's chest, Madelyn might have thought Lazilyth had expired from the tremendous supernatural strain.

"The seer has spoken," Damien exhaled. He ran a hand across sweaty film moistening his bald head. "The fates are a strange and curious thing,

Madelyn the Eveldanyr. They are written in the stars by the hands of the gods, yet… yet they offer many choices; choices that belong to us. The gods allow us to decide which path we will walk down. And so, I would implore you to stay. Stay, and be among your true people, so that you may choose the path of their salvation."

"But she already gave you the answer!" Madelyn protested. "She said I must be freed. I must be!"

"I will keep you for three days. In that time, you will live among us, as one of us. You will not be kept in chains, and you will be given every comfort and courtesy befitting your birthright. But be warned, should you seek to fight or attempt escape, I will break both your legs and leave you in irons. Surely, the gods will forgive me for such an indiscretion."

Damien called to the Rhivothi warriors, who waited outside. Curiously, one of the men poked his head through the flaps and looked to see if the otherworldly act had ended. Satisfied that the coast was clear, both warriors returned.

The thought of being among the barbarian horde any longer than she needed to be was revolting. They were butchers and beastly creatures with not so much as an ounce of civility in them. But if it would mean her safety and her life, three days would be a small price to pay.

"If you can guarantee I will not be harmed, I will accept your offer. For three days, and three days only," Madelyn conceded.

"I will guarantee that and more." Dreadfire turned to the Rhivothi. "Go and summon Marvath and bring him here at once. And you, take Lazilyth to the healers immediately."

One of the warriors bowed and left the tent. The other cautiously moved toward Lazilyth and gently scooped her into his arms. The old woman was exhausted and likely unconscious. Even though the Rhivothi was many times her size, he was visibly shaken by her presence. Apprehensively, he carried the seer out of the tent, and moments later, Marvath Bonesplitter entered.

"You called for me, Damien?"

Madelyn was shocked to see Bonesplitter was nearly the same height and build as Damien. It made her wonder how common it was to find such beastly men in the north. If his size indicated his temperament, then it was unlikely she would receive anything resembling hospitality.

"I did. I have a task for you, Marvath. The girl is someone of great importance, and I charge you with keeping her safe. She is to have free reign of our camp and be given every courtesy."

The massive, bearded man gave Madelyn a curious look. Only an hour ago, she was a prisoner, likely being kept for ransom, but now everything had changed.

"By your will. But I must ask, Damien, who is she that we should extend such treatment to? She is our enemy."

"The fates have been kind to us. She is the last of the Eveldanyr. The crone has seen it." Dreadfire looked at her suspiciously.

"By the gods!" exclaimed a wide-eyed Marvath. He tugged at his sandy blonde beard. "Could we be so fortunate?"

Feeling their eyes scanning and studying her from top to bottom was uncomfortable. But their gaze was not like the lusty gawking she had sometimes experienced throughout her life. No, their eyes were grim and haunting.

"It appears so, yes," Damien replied. "She will have her freedom for three days; then she must decide whether to fulfill or abandon her destiny. We will speak more on the matter later. For now, see that she receives a tent and a warm meal."

Marvath unshackled Madelyn. It felt relieving to be free of the bindings. While the thought crossed her mind to make a hasty escape later in the night, the sheer intimidating size of Bonesplitter was enough to convince her otherwise.

Best not to get on that one's bad side, I suppose.

"Come now, girl," the Rhivothi nomad grunted.

She was taken outside and to a tent close by. It was well within the protective perimeter around Dreadfire's command tent, dissuading any idea of slipping away in the darkness. The area was guarded by scores of the largest and fiercest-looking warriors and lit brightly by dozens of fires.

"This is you," Marvath said, gesturing at the tent.

It was a meager accommodation, but there was a straw bed to sleep on instead of the cold ground. And thankfully, there would be some measure of privacy. Madelyn made her way inside and immediately felt drowsy.

"I would advise against making trouble. You have been shown the only hospitality you're like to receive. Take advantage of it, and it will be the greatest regret of your life. Here, drink."

Marvath tossed a small skin of mead onto the straw bed. She stared at it in confusion, uncertain if it was a kind gesture or some sort of deception.

"Relax. If we were going to kill you, you would die screaming in a pool of your blood. Go on, drink."

"I don't feel like it." It was an obvious lie. Madelyn's throat was so dry she could barely speak, but the thought of accepting kindness from a barbarian made her feel filthy.

"Of course you do." Marvath produced a second, much larger skin, then drank heavily from it. "Tonight, I drink to celebrate the liberation of the north. You? Drink to honor those who died, if you wish. Or drink because you're still alive."

The Rhivothi would not take his leave until he saw Madelyn partake in the mead. It was true; she was alive and had at least that much to be thankful for. Timidly, she opened the skin and took a small sip, enough to satisfy Marvath. The taste was like nothing she had experienced before, though not unpleasant. With a nod, he took his leave.

When she was certain no one was around, she broke down into a fit of tears. The weight of everything Madelyn had lost came crashing down all at once. Castle Morden was a smoking ruin, and everyone inside was dead and gone because of her failure.

Madelyn couldn't bring herself to think of Corbyn, as unfair as it would be to forget him. The sight of his life being snuffed out was too painful to recall. Instead, she thought about Titan and the few men who escaped moments before the doors fell. She hoped that at least they had made it out and could get word to Bentmont before Damien Dreadfire could descend through the Plainhold and into the heart of Betanthia.

Please, Tylar, please be alright. If nothing else, even if I don't survive, I pray you make it home safe.

With tears flooding down her face, she emptied the skin of mead and collapsed. Madelyn was asleep before her head hit the bed. Her dreams were scattered and fragmented, though each seemed darker and more terrifying than the last. She saw the walls of Castle Morden falling and Corbyn dying all over again.

She saw a figure dressed entirely in black, more shadowlike than anything, standing against the backdrop of a raging inferno. It wasn't Damien in his black plate armor. No, this was someone different, yet familiar. Whoever it was appeared to be slender and shapely, face shrouded. The figure had short, cropped black hair covering one eye, while the other glowed like cold, distant starlight. It was a woman, Madelyn could see it plainly.

Before she could identify the mysterious figure, she awoke to a rooster crowing and an axe splitting a log. At first, Madelyn forgot she was at the encampment. She was dizzy from fatigue and as parched for water as a desert.

Am I dying? Perhaps. It would be a mercy if I were.

"Wake up, girl," Bonesplitter grunted. It was unclear how long he was standing outside the tent flap. He held a wooden plate piled with fresh cuts of roasted meats with onions, a generous helping of warm bread, and a horn of water.

"I'm not hungry." Madelyn's voice was weak and thin.

"At some point, you might learn I'm not a fool. You're hungry and you're going to eat, one way or another."

Marvath set the plate down at the foot of the straw bed and held the horn of water with an outstretched hand. Her lips were so cracked and dry even licking them hurt. A grotesque rumbling from her stomach made the large man huff in amusement.

"Come now, girl, you're not being brave or strong or any of that. You're being foolish. Eat, drink, and be quick about it. Once you're finished, we're going for a walk."

It was impossible to hold back her ravenous appetite any further. Madelyn devoured every last bit of food with astonishing speed, so fast it nearly turned her stomach. Bonesplitter smirked and crossed his arms as she finished, panting and gasping as if it was her first meal in a year.

"Good. And now that that's out of the way, follow me. The women-folk are going to get you cleaned up. You smell like a wet goat."

Madelyn was led further into camp, where the wagon train was kept. There, hundreds of camp followers ate and socialized, separated from the warriors. When Marvath approached, some scattered hastily. Whether out of fear or respect was anyone's guess, though Madelyn suspected it was the former.

Four women sat near a wash basin, scrubbing and cleaning clothing, armor, and weaponry the warband had pillaged from the castle. It was heart-wrenching to see shields emblazoned with the Blackthorn sigil in a pile, spattered and stained with blood.

"You there, wench." Bonesplitter pointed at the oldest of the four. "See to it she's cleaned and properly clothed, Damien's orders."

"She can bloody well bathe herself. Can't you see I'm up to my tits with things that need to be cleaned?"

The woman was dainty and somewhat frail, though fierce enough in the eyes to give any man pause. Half her hair was gray, thinning, and drawn back into a loose braid. Her face was a patchwork of crow's feet, pits, and pox scars, evidence of life in the harsh wilderness.

It was surprising to hear anyone speak to a man like Bonesplitter in such a tone. Instead of growing furious, the massive Rhivothi warchief leaned in close to the woman's ear and whispered something, and together they looked at Madelyn in wonderment.

"Very well, I'll get to it right away," the woman said.

It was curious to see that when questioned, Marvath did not react with the fiery anger one might expect from a man so imposing. There was something different about him. Perhaps gentle was too kind of a word, but he was certainly not the sort of man Madelyn expected a murderer like Damien to keep in close company.

"Come, child. You smell something frightful." The camp follower led Madelyn to a separate wash basin, this one thankfully unused.

"I can take care of myself," she said, untying the leather jerkin that served as padding beneath her confiscated breastplate.

"Nonsense. Someone as important as you has no business waiting on herself. My name is Geiva, and I will attend to whatever you need."

She snapped her fingers, and the other camp followers hung several linen sheets between the wagons to provide privacy. Madelyn could disrobe without the ravenous eyes of the warband catching sight of her. She stepped into the basin and sat, and buckets of steaming water were poured inside it. Scrapes and gashes across her body ached and stung, made all the worse when the women began to take brushes to her.

"Is it true, Geiva, about what they say I am?" Madelyn winced as a deep cut on her arm was scrubbed clean. Small flecks of blood dripped into the increasingly dirty water.

"Do I know for certain? I can't say. But that woman Damien keeps alongside him, they say she's a mystic, someone who can see the past and future."

The idea itself seemed ludicrous. Madelyn heard her share of campfire stories while on deployment: tall tales of spellcrafters who could bend light and shadow to their will, swords that could cut mountains to pieces, and fantastical beasts living in the forests and the depths of the seas.

Nobody ever thought the stories were actually real. But what she saw in the tent was enough to give any skeptic pause. It was not some mere parlor trick, no. What Madelyn witnessed was truly paranormal and could only be the work of some unseen force.

"I always heard you northerners were deeply religious, but I didn't know you were so… so deathly serious about it."

Geiva's demeanor darkened. "And what would an easterner know of what dwells in the forests and beyond? You think because we live among the rivers and trees, we're simple people with simple minds? I've seen things you can't imagine."

The women scrubbed Madelyn down thoroughly until her skin was pink and raw. Her hair had grown longer since setting out from Castle Thorn and fell nearly to her tailbone. It was excruciating when they combed the knots and tangles out.

Once cleaned and dried, Madelyn was clothed in a black linen dress with a deep neckline. She wore a leather bodice, a cloak of furs around her shoulders, and a string of small animal bones draped around her neck. Her long blonde hair was vigorously brushed until it was as straight and smooth as silk, then put into a pair of thick braids which began at the crown of her head and draped down the front of her body. Dark outlines were drawn around her eyes, and small, runic symbols painted beneath them with a blue, oily dye.

"Now you look like a proper northern queen. Come, you must see."

Madelyn was led to a nearby wagon containing many treasures, some taken from the bodies of dead Betanthians, and others from

Castle Morden. A tall mirror was propped up against the wagon, likely taken from Lord Valens' chamber. When she stepped in front of it, the reflection staring back seemed as foreign as her captors.

It was easy enough to recognize herself underneath the furs and paint. But unlike the day in Cardale when the Droethien women dressed and adorned her, Madelyn was not pleased by what she saw. The image she saw in the mirror represented everything she came to fear and hate, filling her with disgust.

Three days, Madelyn. You just have to endure this for three days, and then you'll be free. And this is the first. You can do it.

"Do you feel them?" Marvath asked, his towering frame barely visible in the dingy glass.

"Feel who?"

"Your ancestors. They're speaking to you. You need only open your spirit up to them. It's the most powerful connection one can have aside from nature or the gods."

"My parents were Betanthians. They weren't murdering savages. They were civilized people, living in a civilized land."

The Rhivothi warchief scoffed. "Your father may have been born in Betanthia, and maybe his father before him. But your blood is that of old Khorria and has been for a hundred generations or more. I promise you, child, they look down on you as we speak. Listen, and close your eyes. Can you feel them?"

It was curious to behold how superstitious Marvath was, despite being a fearsome beast of a man. She crossed her arms in defiance.

"You don't believe? I suppose you wouldn't. You Betanthians have been denied your true history and your true faith. Come with me. Let me show you something."

When Madelyn refused, Marvath took her around the shoulder. Despite his arm being larger around than her head, he was surprisingly gentle. She was led away from the gawking eyes of the warriors throughout camp. Some sneered and catcalled as she passed by, while others pointed and whispered.

"Pay them no mind. Come, we're nearly there," Bonesplitter said calmly, all the while casting a fiery glare in the direction of anyone who dared to voice their displeasure.

There was something about the Rhivothi warchief that Madelyn could not place her finger on. While it was not unusual for men in her life to want to protect her, it was strange to feel a similar aura of safety around a savage she had only recently become acquainted with. He reminded her of Titan Bradshaw, both in size and temperament. Perhaps they were kindred spirits of some sort, or even long-lost brothers. There was an undeniable viciousness within each of them, to be sure, but only toward those deserving of it. Or so it appeared.

"You're nothing like I would have expected from a Northman. Why are you so different?"

"Different?" Marvath furrowed his brow. "I'm not sure I understand."

Madelyn wasn't sure she understood either. "You're not the blood-thirsty animal I was expecting. Truth be told, you remind me very much of a friend of mine. I'm not sure if he's even still alive. He faced you at Castle Morden."

"Don't mistake yourself, child. I am every bit as ferocious as you might think. But we Rhivothi have an understanding, much the same as our Nothanek friends. We may not be as pious and soft as they are, but we believe all the same."

"What is it you believe?" Her heart seemed to stand still, uncertain if she wanted to hear the answer.

"In the north, we believe everyone and everything is connected. All men and beasts, the skies and seas, every rock and every tree, all living as one. The gods created us to worship them and live as they intended us to."

"And how might that be?"

"Free. The gods did not create us to serve anyone other than them. We do not kneel to other men or lesser beings."

Madelyn shrugged. "But yet you serve Damien Dreadfire?"

"Serve? No, I serve only myself, my kin, and the gods. I follow Damien because he is the last true defender of the old ways. There is much you don't understand, Madelyn the Eveldanyr. You are born of Betanthia, so all you have known is servitude. To Marcellus Bethard, your Order of knights, and who knows what else. Have you ever asked yourself if you're free? Truly and completely free?"

It was the first time she had ever been asked such a question. The more Madelyn thought, the more she struggled to find an answer. She had devoted her life to the Blackthorn Knights and their tenets. It was true; ever since she was found outside Castle Thorn, all she knew was the High Marshal, the Order, and the men. And above all, service to House Bethard.

They arrived at a small grove of trees a short distance from camp. At first, Madelyn thought about running as fast as she could to the east but quickly thought better of it. Bonesplitter would undoubtedly catch her in short order, or at least be able to raise an alarm and summon riders to bring her back.

"Here. Sit." He motioned to a patch of soft fescue beneath the trees.

Begrudgingly, Madelyn obliged. The grass felt cool and smooth to the touch and almost made her forget she was a captive in a strange land, among even stranger people. The Rhivothi took a drink from a small skin then offered it to her.

"What is it?" she asked, smelling the liquid inside. It was potent and unpleasant and made her eyes water.

"Something to relax you. Drink it."

"No, no, I don't want to." Madelyn returned the skin, but a sudden fierceness in his eyes made her think again.

She took a small sip and recoiled at the taste, but took another, much larger drink to satisfy the Rhivothi. She set the skin down and felt a strange warmth embrace her body. Slowly, Madelyn's eyes grew heavy as her breath quickened but then slowed. Most surprisingly, though her eyes were closed, she could still see.

A bright, warm tapestry of colors danced throughout the small grove. She could feel them, like warm rays of sunlight on her skin. All around, there were shapes beyond description. Many were a dull gray, almost shadow-like, despite the intense illumination around her. They appeared human, and though Madelyn found their presence quite extraordinary, she was unafraid.

One of the shadows reached out and placed a hand on her shoulder. There was a comforting energy in the unknown entity's touch, much like a parent or a long-lost friend. She felt a strange connection, as if she had lived a thousand lives before and could only now remember it.

But perhaps the strongest feeling was love. It was pure, wholesome love, the kind she had experienced with Corbyn, the kind that was unselfish and unconditional. With it, Madelyn began to lose all sense of herself. All of her ambitions and ego slowly withered and drifted away until the black embrace of sleep took hold.

She was overcome with fatigue the following day when she awoke. The effects of the noxious drink were utterly debilitating. Her body felt weak and poisoned, and it was challenging enough to eat and not want to throw it back up. But after consuming nearly a skin and a half of water, the queasiness dissipated.

The days had grown noticeably colder now. It made her all the more grateful the Northmen had adorned her with a cloak of animal furs. It was thankfully enough to keep the icy breath of autumn at bay. She sat on a log outside her tent, watching the men tend to their wounded. Tomorrow would be the third day of her captivity, and it appeared the warriors would be breaking camp on the morrow and departing, either for home or their next conquest.

"Well now, aren't you a sight."

A bald man grinned, revealing a hideous collection of half-rotten teeth. He was clad in a thick, dark blue cloak, the same kind worn by some of the Blackthorn. It was likely pillaged from the corpse of one of Madelyn's knights. She looked at him but swiftly averted her eyes.

"It's alright, love. Every woman finds themselves lost for words when they meet the great Zander. I'm the most famous man in all of the Bymist, you know. And one day, all of Betanthia will be mine. Just wait and see!"

Madelyn shifted uncomfortably on the log, turning her body away from the Zylmacian.

"So, are you the queen everyone is talking about? The one who will unite the free tribes?"

His question was met with silence. Were this any other scenario, she might very well lay the man out on his ass for being such a bother. But here, she would have to be especially careful. She was alone among an army of butchers. Zander sat on the log beside her, then inched closer.

"Can't say I've ever been with a queen before. What do you say, love? Wouldn't you like to see what a real king is all about?"

He leaned forward, sniffed at Madelyn's neckline, then tried to steal a kiss. His breath was every bit as repulsive as the rest of him. When Zander reached around to grab a handful of her breast, he was suddenly halted by the sharp edge of a great axe to his throat.

"No, she wouldn't," Marvath snarled. "And you're no real king, and you never will be."

He lifted the edge of the axe, forcing Zander off the log. The Zylmacian smiled and threw his hands up.

"Easy there mate, wouldn't want to do anything stupid now, would you?"

Madelyn saw more men gathering around now, dozens of them, dressed in roughspun and leather, and pieces of Betanthian armor. Many were bald and just as distasteful looking as Zander. She could only assume these were more of the wildmen. Some appeared agitated at the sight of their clansman at the point of an axe.

"Go on, do it," Zander whispered to Marvath. "Take my head off. You know you want to. Kill me, and see how fast my men rip you to shreds."

"If you think a few Bymist rats frighten me, you're sorely mistaken. I could cut my way through every last one of you and not break a sweat."

Marvath lifted the axe blade again, wrenching Zander's chin upward. "If you come near the girl again, it will be the last thing you do. Damien has ordered that no one is to lay a finger on her, do you understand? Or would you care to discuss it with him?"

Zander took a step back, his wildmen waiting with bated breath. Some had discreetly moved their hands to their daggers and axes. If it came to blows, Madelyn might be able to kill one, maybe two of the Zylmacians at most. But without weapons or her armor, the fighting would be exceedingly lopsided.

"What an obedient dog you are, Bonesplitter. No need to bother Damien. The girl is all yours." He looked at her again, sneered, then retreated to his brethren.

The experience was frightening and made her feel even more helpless than she already did. When Zander was good and far enough away, Marvath finally laid down his great axe and grunted his disdain.

"Thank you," Madelyn whispered. It was all she could say to thank the Rhivothi warchief for his intervention.

"I hate that man. Truly, I hate him." He sat on the log, opened a skin of mead and took a swig, then offered it to her. Madelyn declined, her stomach already turning from the smell. "Drink. It'll set you straight."

Reluctantly, Madelyn agreed and took the skin. She placed it to her lips and drank slowly, weary of the flavor. After a few sips, the mead began to soothe her ailing body.

"Is it true what they say, Marvath? Am I really one of these, Eveldanyr? Am I really a queen?" Madelyn wasn't sure she liked the sound of such a possibility.

"It must be true. You bear their mark." He pointed at the birthmark on her neck.

"It's nothing. I've had it all my life. Are all you people so superstitious?"

Bonesplitter chuckled. Seeing such a large and frightening man laugh was strange, especially considering how close he had just come to an altercation with the wildmen.

"Do you believe in the gods, child?" he asked.

Madelyn subtly shook her head, careful not to stir his agitation again. Worship of the ancient deities was largely considered a myth, or at most, a backward and archaic practice.

"Of course you don't. Betanthia abandoned their faith in the gods long ago, and you have been forsaken because of it. But I believe the fates have other plans for you. They've brought you here for a reason."

"What do you mean by the fates? Is that the same as the gods?"

"No, no, they're not," Marvath chuckled. "The fates are… how would one describe it…" He ran a hand through his long, sandy-colored beard. "When we are born, our destiny is written in the stars. There are things we are put here by the gods to accomplish. Sometimes the paths we walk can cross with others in unexpected ways. Damien believes your arrival is a sign."

"A sign of what?" she asked uneasily, uncertain if she wanted to hear more.

"That his quest is true, and has been foretold in the heavens."

"And what is his quest? What does he hope to accomplish by sacking castles and murdering men by the thousands?"

The answer seemed obvious enough, given the events of the last several months, but Madelyn had to know to be certain. She knew she had to gather as much information as possible to share with the High Marshal, if she was to be ransomed.

"To avenge the Bloodbath at Borjifa."

She heard the name the day Castle Morden fell, when she was paraded into the courtyard, but knew nothing of its significance. Madelyn shook her head, unsure of what to say.

"It's no surprise you haven't heard of it. I doubt there is a Betanthian alive that has. Cedric Valens knew, oh yes. He knew all too well."

Nothing good can come from something that's referred to as a bloodbath…

Madelyn felt stupid for such a thought but remembered what the High Marshal once told her.

"The mouths of savages are as sharp as their blades. They will deceive you at every turn if you let them," Jenson Powell said.

Would they truly have done all this over a lie? Could this many men be deceived so thoroughly that they not only faced down a Betanthian army but laid siege to a castle as well?

She hesitated to ask, but had to know the truth. "Tell me, what happened at Borjifa?"

The question seemed to sour Marvath's mood more than the confrontation with Zander. He rose to his feet and brushed away a few stray pieces of bark clinging to his trousers.

"I wasn't there. I know only what I've heard. Einarr Rolffson could tell you, he saw the aftermath with his own eyes, but he has returned home. Believe me when I say it was the most appalling atrocity I have ever heard of. Perhaps when you return home, you might seek the truth of it."

As she watched the Rhivothi walk away, Madelyn pondered the merit of what he said. Could some unspeakable act have taken place, one which had set all of this into motion? Had Marcellus Bethard gone too far in his conquests? There was no way to be certain. Her heart was telling her one thing and her head another.

Soldiers aren't meant to answer these sorts of questions. We take our orders and obey them. That's what we do.

But then a thought came to her. Maybe, if the fates were real, she was precisely the one meant to find such answers. Maybe the roads she traveled throughout her life had brought her to this place for a reason. But if that were true, why would good men like Corbyn be murdered? Why would any divine scheme be dripping with so much blood?

She sat alone for the rest of the day, and the night as well. The stares and jeers became fewer, to the point where she could no longer hear them. Madelyn found solace beside a small fire with a wooden mug of mead. The taste was becoming more enjoyable and paired especially well with a serving of fresh venison.

The barbarians began to break down their camp, bit by bit, in anticipation of moving out and returning home. It would be little use to try and sleep tonight; she was far too anxious to be released from her captors and sent back to Bentmont. The High Marshal would undoubtedly pay whatever ransom the Northmen demanded and would hopefully ride them down after making the exchange.

On the morning of the third day, she walked among the camp followers. Many were families of the warriors or their kinsmen, some very old and some very young. Nearly a dozen children sat around a pit fire listening to a story from one of their elders. The man looked to have once been a warrior from the scars on his face, and an arm cut short at the elbow.

Though he spoke in a strange language, his animated gestures explained the story well enough. It must have been a grand tale of famous battles or the deeds of brave ancestors. The children watched with wide eyes and open mouths as the story unfolded, but when one of them caught sight of Madelyn, everyone gave pause.

She wasn't sure what to think, with everyone staring at her in such a way. It wasn't hatred nor suspicion in their eyes. No, this was something else, something she would not expect to see written across the hardened faces of the northerners. It was fear.

"They're wary of you," Bonesplitter said from behind her, giving her a startle.

"Why would anyone be afraid of me? I'm your prisoner, after all. You took my sword."

"It's not your steel they fear. It's your blood. Word has spread that you are the last of the Eveldanyr. They think you are some kind of sorceress."

The absurdity was enough to make Madelyn smirk. Not that any of it mattered. After this day, she would be a free woman and on her way back to Castle Thorn.

"I don't see why it matters anyways," she said. "Damien is your leader. Even if I were one of these, Eveldanyr, your army would still be his to command by right. Is that not true?"

"If what Damien says is correct and you are indeed an Eveldanyr, then he believes you can unite all the tribes across the free lands. There are dozens, hundreds perhaps, scattered around the north. When once we were a single united people, now we squabble and make war on each other while the Bethards hunt us to extinction. You can put an end to it all."

Marvath placed a gentle hand on her shoulder. "You are the rightful heir to the Khorrish nation. The gods brought you here, now, at this moment, for a reason. This is your destiny. All you see around you is your birthright."

"And that's why he demands I wed him." She paused and sighed. "And what if I still refuse?"

"Then my people, your true people, are doomed. One by one, our tribes will be hunted down by the Bethards and slaughtered, and our ancient culture wiped from existence. You can be a part of something much bigger than yourself. The gods brought you here to lead us back from the brink of extinction."

"Bid fare to scorch you all..." Madelyn whispered, though not softly enough.

Bonesplitter's face showed an uncharacteristic apprehension. It was the only time she had seen the Rhivothi warchief look at her in such a way.

"Do you truly have it in you to see so many die because you could not look past your desires? My people believe there is no greater act than to lay down one's life for another, be it a sacrifice of deeds or blood. Consider this, Madelyn."

She spent the rest of the day alone, though Marvath's words were of little consequence to her. Soon she would return home, and the only regret would be that so many of her knights had to die. As the sun began diminishing in the west, he returned one final time.

"Come. Damien wishes to speak with you."

It was the moment she both anticipated and dreaded. The Northmen seemed true to their word. At least, that was her impression after spending three days among them. Marvath proved himself a man of honor and would most assuredly not let any harm befall her.

When Madelyn entered Damien's tent, the two Rhivothi guards bound her wrists with metal shackles. She offered no protest, given it was likely a precaution on their part.

"Remember what you have seen here, and remember who you truly are. Choose wisely," Marvath said to her softly, then took his leave. He gave a nod to his kinsmen, then disappeared through the tent flap.

It wasn't long before Damien Dreadfire entered. The air seemed to turn colder, as if his arrival brought with it a winter chill. He wore a simple leather jerkin and linen trousers and carried no blade. Even without his suit of blackened steel armor, the warlord looked every bit as fearsome.

"I trust that you were not mistreated?" he muttered, moving to a desk on the other side of the tent.

"No, Marvath was very hospitable," she replied, thumbing at her shackles.

Dreadfire stood behind the desk and placed both palms on the surface. The wood groaned as he pressed his weight onto it. "So, Madelyn the Eveldanyr. I have given you three days, and those three days are at an end. You have eaten, slept, and walked among us. Have you learned anything throughout your time here?"

The question was as treacherous as the Plainhold. Answer it one way, and Damien might assume she would be staying. Yet answer it another way, and it might incite his wrath. Madelyn had to be careful, or she might not leave the tent in one piece.

"I have. Marvath has shown me kindness and respect, which I did not think possible, considering…" Her voice trailed off.

"Considering we are nothing but simple-minded savages. Is that correct?" Damien asked dryly. "I pray you would think better of your true kin. I trust you have considered my offer to take your rightful place as chieftess?"

Although her time among the Northmen had been brief, she felt a certain inexplicable connection to them. Drinking Marvath's tonic amidst the grove gave her a sense of serenity she had never felt before. If anyone in any other place had asked such a question, she might very well have said yes.

But this was Damien Dreadfire, a murderer who had slain Lord Valens and thirty thousand Betanthian soldiers. He killed Hunter, Corbyn, and her knights, the people she cared about most.

How can I betray their memory and side with the one who murdered them? How can I betray the High Marshal when he put his trust in me to lead this mission? No, as right as it may feel in my spirit to be among these people, I cannot betray the Order, nor my honor.

"I have considered it. And with all my heart, I give you my answer." Madelyn swallowed hard. "No."

It was not the answer Damien expected. Pain and anger in his black eyes slowly turned to hate. He grabbed hold of Madelyn's shackles and shook them, the metal digging into the flesh on her wrists.

"How can you betray your true people and side with the Bethards? Has Marvath taught you nothing these past three days?" He sighed and released her. "If you have made your decision, then so be it. The histories will not remember you kindly, Madelyn Everly."

"That is for the scribes to decide. Will you make good on your pledge and free me now?"

The warlord's face twisted and contorted, his teeth grinding in a barely-contained rage.

"You gave me your word," Madelyn stammered. "The old woman said I must be freed."

The thought of Lazilyth was enough to make her skin crawl. What she witnessed was surely enough to force Dreadfire to remain true to his word.

"Indeed, she did," Damien said, the wheels in his mind turning. "And if I release you, it will be a death sentence for my people. And so will keeping you captive. The fates can be strange and cruel. So I will grant you your request, and send you home. After the winter has passed."

Madelyn's feet nearly fell out from under her. She stood dumbfounded, her mouth hanging open as if she had just witnessed some great calamity.

"A… after?"

"Yes, after winter. The snows will be upon us soon enough, and it will take six weeks or more to ride to Bentmont so we can ransom you. The Plainhold will be too treacherous and impassible by then to make the return journey, so you will be staying with us for now."

Panic took hold of her. She gasped and looked around the tent frantically in confusion and fear, desperate for hope or salvation that would never come.

No, I can't stay here any longer! He lied to me. I knew he would lie!

"Calm yourself, girl," Dreadfire commanded. "You will return home but must never be allowed to take up arms against us again."

"I swear I won't. You have my word."

"You are Khorr by blood, yet Betanthian by choice. Your word cannot be trusted."

Suddenly, Damien grabbed her shackles and dragged her outside the tent. She squirmed and struggled, but it was of little use.

"Men! Listen, and hear me!" Dreadfire barked, his voice carrying far throughout the camp. The feasting and merriment halted as a group of warriors gathered around.

"It seems the gods have been generous to us today." He pulled hard again on the shackles, lurching Madelyn forward. Some chuckled and hollered at the sight. "By now, most of you have heard of our newest guest. Here before you stands the last daughter of the Eveldanyr."

Some of the warriors shoved their way closer to get a glimpse of her. Madelyn saw the half-rotten smile of Zander not far away.

"I have made a fine present for her, which she has seen fit to throw back in my face. I have offered her the chance to join us and claim her ancestral right, to rule the free northern people as her forefathers once did. But she has refused. She wishes to return home, and return home she shall. No one is to take her life. When the winter snows melt she will be ransomed, and every one of you will share in the spoils!"

The warband roared heartily, many raising swords and full horns of mead high into the air in approval. For a second, Madelyn felt strangely calm.

All they care about is the gold. They're nothing but petty brigands. Jenson will pay them all they ask for and more for my return.

"But!" Damien raised his other hand and silenced the reveling warriors. "The crone has glimpsed into the fates and has seen disaster at every turn. Should this woman be killed, then the free north will become extinct. Should she remain a prisoner, she will wither and die, and that too shall herald our demise. But should she be freed, she will return at the head of a conquering army."

A hush fell over the warband as they looked at Madelyn suspiciously. She heard them whispering, some likely cursing her for a witch. The sea of warriors parted, and she spied the crumpled frame of Lazilyth as she tottered toward the command tent. It was curious and haunting to see how men twice her size recoiled and diminished in fear.

One of the Rhivothi guards rushed to offer her an arm, but her rebuke was swift. She hissed and spat in disdain and sent the warrior reeling backward. Were it anyone but Lazilyth, there would have been an uproar of laughter.

"Three choices are laid before us, each with the same consequence," Damien bellowed. "I ask you now, what shall we do with this woman?"

The question was met with silence, save for an odd muttering here and there. Madelyn turned and saw the pale, glassy eyes of the crone staring back at her. A menacing smile crept across the old woman's spiderwebbed face, as if she knew what would happen next.

"She will be sent back, but must never be allowed to take up arms against us again," Damien decreed. "Her blood runs ancient and pure. But she has decided to betray her ancestors and forsake her destiny. So to you, my brave warriors, I give you the spoils of war to do with as you please. And if the gods are good, then the bloodline of the Eveldanyr will continue."

What does he mean? I don't understand!

The old woman crowed, her cackling laugh carrying high over the satisfied cheers of the warband. Her mocking smile revealed untold confidence, as if the fates were somehow circumvented.

Before Madelyn knew what was happening, she was yanked back inside the command tent. The shackles were wrenched so hard she stumbled and fell, and was dragged to a thick wooden post at the center of the tent. Damien wrapped a pair of chains around it, then secured her in place.

Without warning, he delivered a clenched fist straight to her stomach, sending her back to the ground. The force was so intense it nearly turned her insides into pulp.

"What are you doing?" Madelyn's voice trembled as she coughed and groaned and curled into a ball. "You said…"

"The time for words is over."

Four warriors entered the tent, each smelling of mead and bad intentions. They chuckled and sneered as Dreadfire reached over and grabbed Madelyn by her hair, jerking her head back.

"If she struggles, put a switch to her. But spare the face, I want the Bethards to know it is her when she returns to Bentmont."

Before she could process what was happening, Madelyn was set upon by the other men in the tent as Damien Dreadfire made his exit to thunderous acclaim. Ravenously they clawed at her clothing, laughing and taunting her as she was stripped naked. Dozens of drunken warriors gathered outside the tent and shoved their way inside, while more lined up in anticipation of their turn.

A spontaneous celebration erupted throughout the encampment. It was the culmination of every victory they had achieved, from the death of Cedric Valens to the sacking of Castle Morden, and now to the tribulation of one of Betanthia's finest soldiers, the one who betrayed her own blood.

A deep bellowing of war drums filled the dusky air, and with it came more feasting, dancing, and drinking. All the while Madelyn Everly's screams rang out as the line outside the tent stretched and snaked for over a mile, further and further back, and off into the coming night.

GARETH VI

IT WAS THE MOST PRECARIOUS TIME IN HIS LIFE. TENSION THROUGHOUT the Westwind Citadel was so thick it nearly became suffocating. As a result, Sir Edmund dramatically ramped up the number of Guardsmen patrolling the palace, both inside and out. He hoped a heightened show of force might remind the high council whom they truly served.

Although Edmund always protected Gareth, he felt anything but safe. There was a growing suspicion and fear of Aldred and Lord Vakaro, and what they might be plotting behind closed doors. So the prince resorted to sleeping with a pair of Guardsmen outside his chamber door and even had a trusted servant act as his food taster. Sound precautions, to be certain. But death was often a determined adversary and could find weaknesses in even the most imposing defenses.

There were no official council meetings since the day Gareth shocked the chamber, only small and informal discussions here and there. He suspected it might be out of spite, or perhaps they were simply holding their own meetings without his knowledge. Either way, he knew at some point, he would have to face those men again.

"I think you should do it," Edmund said reassuringly. "You have every right to call a meeting. Twice as much, given you're a Bethard and all."

Gareth stared out of a window in his chamber, his face long and brooding. While surveying the breadth of Cardale, he wondered what would happen to the city and its people should he fail and Aldred or Lord Vakaro were to seize power.

"And if they refuse?" Gareth asked. "I can't rightly have you haul them in there at the point of a sword. I would lose all legitimacy."

If I even have any in their eyes.

"They wouldn't dare refuse you. They may act tough, but I'd be willing to wager they're terrified. Aldred knows you command our loyalty."

Gareth rubbed his temples. "Yes, but Lord Vakaro commands our whole southern army. How could you stop him from marching on Cardale if he was so inclined?"

"Trust me. He won't. It would be suicide. If he turns on you and a civil war erupts, nothing will stop the Northmen from reaving their way across the entire kingdom. And the Droethiens would likely take advantage of the chaos. No, Lord Vakaro isn't so reckless. There won't be anything left of Betanthia for him to rule. No, men like him prefer to operate from the shadows. The best way to combat them is in the light."

It would be the greatest test of Gareth's life; he could feel it deep within his soul. Everything he had endured so far would be meaningless if men like Ridley Vakaro were allowed to have their way with Betanthia. Would the histories remember this time as King Marcellus' failing or his own?

No, I will not be the one responsible for Betanthia's downfall. A king must defend his kingdom at all costs. What sort of ruler would I be if I willingly allowed this to happen?

"Very well. If you would please, Edmund, tell your men to keep their eyes and ears open. We must be extra vigilant until we know his true intentions."

The senior Guardsman dismissed himself from the room with a proud smile and a bow. Gareth glanced at a shelf containing dusty books he had never read and a half-empty bottle of bourbon. Despite not having a drink for what seemed like ages, his thirst continued to rear its ugly head. He stared at the golden nectar with a watering mouth and wanted nothing more than to drink it all down until the madness of the world faded. But he couldn't. Going back to his old ways was simply not an option anymore.

What would mother think of me? Or Edmund? Or… Madelyn…

It was distressing to realize he had thought of Madelyn so little as of late. Surely by now, she was out west with Lord Valens, far from home and closest to the danger. Even though he feared for her safety, Gareth wondered if it was wise to still love her, given what he saw at the Seascape Inn.

"The heart wants what the heart wants," he once told Edmund. And as tormenting as it was to admit, the sentiment was still true.

She's counting on me to turn Cardale around, and I haven't done anything to accomplish it. Well, starting today, that all changes. I will prove to her, and to the world, that Gareth Bethard is a man of action.

He glared once more at the bourbon, this time in disgust. A fierce determination was welling up inside him, something he had never experienced. He strode into the hall, leaving behind a lifetime of misery and despair that haunted those four walls. Demons still plagued Gareth, though they were a little less oppressive these days.

When he came by a passing servant, Gareth requested he send word to the Guardsmen that he wished to convene the King's council.

"They'll know what to do," he said, grinning.

The servant hurried off with the Prince's message in tow, a faint pattering of footsteps echoing down the hallway. Everyone was treating him differently as of late, and it would have been a lie to say it didn't feel good. Gareth walked to the council chambers, his face beaming with pride. If this was what a future crown held in store, then it was something he was looking forward to.

Who would have thought I would feel this way? I've always shunned the notion of being king, but now... now...

The councilmen were late. Insultingly late. Gareth sat alone at the table for nearly an hour, glancing at the door every few minutes and at a pair of Guardsmen standing next to it. Though loyal, the men's faces reflected the same annoyance. As he prepared to leave, the door lurched open with a low growl. The first to enter was Sir Tristan, though Gareth nearly mistook him for a servant boy. The young councilman fidgeted as he strode across the room, looking like he had seen a ghost.

"I beg your pardon, Highness," Tristan stammered. A thin mist of sweat glistened off his brow despite the refreshing temperature. "I was unaware of your summons, or else I never would have been so tardy."

Gareth wasn't used to someone simpering before him, but he supposed it was better to be feared instead of outright ignored.

"And what of the other councilmen? Will they be joining us?"

"Yes, Your Highness. I saw them speaking in the great hall just a few minutes ago. They should be here any time now."

Speaking to each other in the great hall? What sort of subversions might they be plotting behind my back?

"And what were they discussing?" Gareth asked suspiciously.

"I... I don't know, my prince. I hurried in so as not to keep you waiting. They were whispering to one another... I couldn't make anything out."

It seemed as if his worst fears and Edmund's suspicions were confirmed. A plot was certainly afoot, which made Gareth all the more grateful for the Guardsmen inside the council chamber. But instead of fretting over what he already suspected was true, an idea came to him. It was the first time someone was legitimately afraid to be in his presence.

This fool looks like he's about to soil himself. Maybe I can use this to my advantage and find out what Aldred and Ridley are planning.

"Sir Tristan," Gareth said sternly, albeit feigned. "You sound like a noble and reliable man from what I've heard, with great respect for Betanthia and House Bethard. Is this true?"

"Absolutely, my prince. I'm honored to sit on the high council and serve your family. It's the greatest accomplishment of my life."

"Those who serve my family well will be remembered upon my coronation. Something to keep in mind."

Sir Tristan appeared torn between ambition and loyalty to his brethren, though it seemed the former was winning. The seed was planted, and would hopefully take root in short order. Gareth knew he had to get the jump on any attempt on his life, and with Sir Tristan as an ally, the odds would be much more in his favor. Only time would tell if the young councilman was an asset or another liability.

Minutes later, Lord Lawson lumbered into the chamber, his jowls quivering with each step. His doughy body was wrapped in enough silk to blanket the Citadel. "A thousand apologies, my prince. Some days it's difficult to get about, and my punctuality—"

"Needs improvement," Gareth interrupted. "You've had ample time to prepare, and I would prefer not to drag this out all day."

"Yes, my prince. As you say."

Shortly after, the remaining councilmen entered together. Aldred took up his seat at the head of the table while Lord Vakaro remained standing. Neither appeared to be pleased to have been summoned. Aldred carried a small stack of folded papers in one hand and laid them down in front of him.

"Thank you for coming, gentlemen," Gareth said as pleasantly as he could. "There are several matters I hoped we could discuss together. Firstly, it is the prerogative of House Bethard to declare that bold action be taken to make the streets of Cardale safe and clean once again. No longer will we tolerate filth and crime in our city. Lord Lawson, since your specialty is civil affairs, what news do you have to report?"

The fat lord stammered, then looked at Aldred, hoping to find some support, but found none. His words were little more than indecipherable grunts and mumblings. Gareth looked on, amused, but the sight of Lord Vakaro standing behind Aldred like a shadow gave him pause.

"While Lord Lawson gathers his thoughts, is there anything you would like to report, Sir Tristan?"

The young noble cleared his throat and shuffled through a few papers. Gareth spied an occasional nervous glance his way.

"Thank you, my prince. The merchant quarter has seen a troubling uptick in violent crime over the last several weeks. Robberies have increased severalfold, and murders are continuing an upward trend. Just this morning, three bodies were fished from the Camsby. I have ordered the city watch to double their patrols across all shifts until the violence is quelled."

"Very good. Lord Lawson?" Gareth asked as he leaned back in his chair. The wood gave a soft squeak.

Before the fat lord could speak, Ridley growled and made for the door. There was no hiding the utter contempt seared into his face like a hot iron. As he stormed past Gareth, he shot a menacing glare.

"I don't have time for this farce," Lord Vakaro spat. "I have a war to fight." He looked at Aldred as if to speak. The southern Commandant ground his teeth, then turned and left the council chamber, casting a sharp eye at the two Guardsmen by the door.

War? What war? The one in the west, or is there something else I'm not aware of?

The thoughts were extremely troubling, though the council's apparent lack of transparency was even more disturbing. Something was going on behind his back, just as Edmund suspected. Gareth tried to mask the concern in his eyes and knew he had to discover whatever truth they were hiding.

An awkward silence filled the room. Lord Lawson and Sir Tristan were looking down at the table, their discomfort mounting by the second. Aldred glanced around briefly, then cleared his throat. He thumbed through his papers and then shuffled them into a neat pile.

"I think it would be best if this meeting is adjourned." He rose from his seat.

"But we've only just begun," Gareth protested, his annoyance slowly building into anger. "There are many important matters I would see addressed, matters that have gone neglected for far too long!"

"Gareth." Aldred rubbed his eyes. "Enough of this. Serious things are happening, and none of us have time for your—"

"Excuse me!" Gareth exploded into a fit of rage, most uncharacteristic of him. "It's Prince Gareth! Not baron, not lord, not sir. Prince! Prince Gareth! I ought to have you flogged into pulp for such disrespect! I will not suffer it any further!"

Both Guardsmen stepped forward, their armor crunching, their hands drifting to the hilts of their swords. Lord Lawson looked as if he might keel over from the sudden shock, and Sir Tristan's eyes were so wide they practically fell out of his skull.

"Forgive me, my prince, but—"

"No, no, I will not forgive you," he screamed. "Ever since I reached manhood, you have always sought to keep me down as if I were a lesser son and not heir to the throne! Well, let me remind you, Aldred, you haven't a single drop of Bethard blood in you. My father rules Betanthia, and I will rule when his time is over!"

"My prince," Morgan Lawson interjected. "Aldred meant no disrespect. Now please, Your Highness, may we return to our business? We are most eager to hear your propositions."

One of the Guardsmen pulled two inches of steel from his scabbard, drawing awestruck gazes from the other councilmen. It was a sobering reminder of where the true power of Betanthia lay, a reminder they were not likely to forget.

"I will say this once, and once only," Gareth continued, his temper not yet sated. "If any of you disrespect me in my family's house again, there will be consequences. You may think you hold sway in Betanthia, but ponder this. If I told these men to cut you down where you stood, and you ordered them to do otherwise, who would they obey? I do wonder."

Aldred averted his eyes to the table, his face turning a queasy green. The open threat lingered in the air, leaving the room quiet. Sensing there was nothing productive left to say, Gareth dismissed himself and threw the door shut. As he stormed down the hallway, hurried footsteps came racing behind him. Turning, he saw it was Sir Tristan.

"My prince, a thousand apologies. We never meant any disrespect to you. Please, we would be honored if you rejoined us."

"I have grown weary of talking. If words accomplished anything, there would not be a hungry mouth in Cardale. Northmen wouldn't be invading our lands. I intend to do far more than bandy words with a few useless old men."

Gareth thought for a second and formed an unexpected idea.

Useless old men... old... men. Yes, that's it! Sir Tristan is half Aldred's age, or at least close enough to it. Perhaps if I deal with him more personally, I can begin to reshape the council in my image. Who needs men like Aldred and his sycophant Morgan Lawson anyways?

"You must forgive the other councilmen," Tristan pleaded as he tried to keep pace. "They have no ill will toward you; they've grown proud with age and take their stations seriously. They aren't used to being challenged, but I believe that's precisely the thing this council needs. It's long overdue for us to have a perspective like yours."

Were I naive, I would take your groveling as praise. But I can see you have only your own interest in mind. No matter, I can make use of it, I suppose.

Gareth paused in the hallway, Sir Tristan nearly running face-first into his back. It was risky to put too much faith in a man he hardly knew. The only way to know where Tristan stood was to force him to prove it.

A test of loyalty, as it were.

"And if the other councilmen did indeed have ill will toward me, you would do your honored duty to House Bethard and inform me, would you not? The status quo will start changing for the betterment of us all. I need reliable and loyal men interested in faithfully serving Betanthia."

"Without question, my prince. I'm not some old, dry fool set in his ways. You may count on my unwavering support."

"Good." Gareth raised his chin proudly. "Then tell me, what did Lord Vakaro mean by, I have a war to fight? Does he know something I don't? Did Cedric Valens fall?"

The idea was nearly incomprehensible. Such a turn of events would certainly spell doom for Madelyn. His palms moistened as he thought of what horrible fate might have befallen her should the young councilman confirm his fears.

"I… I haven't the slightest idea, my prince. Truly I don't. Aldred doesn't always tell me everything. Sometimes I feel like he doesn't fully trust me, even though I've been on the council for two years now, I think?"

"You would do me a great service by finding out what he knows. It isn't right that secrets should be kept on the council, and I'm certainly the last one he would ever confide in. If you do this, you'll have my gratitude."

"Absolutely, my prince. I'll do my best." Sir Tristan excused himself with a deep bow and returned to the council chamber.

It took minutes before the gravity of the conversation sank in. Did it really just happen, or was it simply a daydream playing out in his head? The more Gareth thought about it, the more undeniable the truth became. He asserted himself. And not only that, he put fear into the hearts of men who, up until yesterday, held him in utter contempt.

Mother was right. I really can do this! I really do have the temperament to sit on the council.

He spent the afternoon in the King's study, preparing a list of plans he intended to bring to the next meeting. The room had gone unused for so long that, were it not for the diligent cleaning regimen of the Citadel's servants, it might very well be as dusty as a crypt. An oak desk sat at the center of the spacious room, surrounded by bookshelves running from floor to ceiling. Their contents had not been put to use in years.

The list was growing longer and longer, until it required one page and then another. Gareth tried to remember what he saw the night he walked the Scarlet Streets, though his memory was still hazy.

Squalor… crime… hunger. Where do I begin?

As he thought of the best ways to tackle such problems, Sir Edmund walked into the room. Gareth immediately suspected something was amiss, but his friend's warm smile was enough to put his worries to rest.

"Well look at you, all kingly and such." Edmund strode to the desk and slapped him on the arm. "So, what are you up to?"

"I figured I would start working all of this out. Someone has to. I can't imagine my reign as king will be very fruitful if I inherit a broken kingdom with a broken capital."

The elder Guardsman glanced down at the scratchings, then rubbed a hand across his chin.

"Cardale certainly didn't become this way overnight, nor will it change so fast. Be mindful of that. But if you need any assistance, I'll be more than happy to do whatever I can."

Gareth nodded. "Well, there is something I was going to ask you. Have you heard anything about Aldred recently?"

Edmund thought for a second, his face tightening into a ball of wrinkles, then shook his head. "No, nothing out of the ordinary. Say what you will about the man, but he certainly is reliable. Or, perhaps predictable would be a more accurate word."

There was little denying that. Aldred was the same as the day Gareth met him; distant, calculating, and serious. It seemed unlikely he would be the one to hatch some treasonous plot, at least judging by his obsessive devotion to King Marcellus. Sometimes, Gareth wondered if Aldred had convinced himself he was the King's true heir.

"And what about Lord Vakaro?" Merely speaking his name made Gareth's skin crawl. "He said something in the council chamber about having a war to fight?"

Again, Sir Edmund shook his head no. "I'm sorry, but I haven't heard anything about him either. I suppose I could put the feelers out and see if I can remedy that, if you were interested."

"Please do," he said grimly. "I asked Sir Tristan what Lord Vakaro might have meant, but he said the other councilmen have told him nothing. It seems he's being kept in the dark as well."

Edmund scratched at the back of his neck. "Well, I would be careful about getting too close to that one. He has loose lips, from what I've heard—just a word to the wise. As far as our southern friend goes, I'll see what I can dig up. I'll come by later, and we can discuss your list in more detail."

With a nod, Sir Edmund left the study. Gareth was grateful for his friend's diligence, but their conversation brought the fear of conspiracy back into his mind. There would be little use in focusing on the list now, as his thoughts raced from one scenario to another. He returned to his chamber and relaxed with a crystal goblet of tea with a hint of lemon, his mother's favorite drink. He grew accustomed to the taste in Dellhaven and found it a pleasant alternative to spirits.

While lounging alongside the open window, Gareth's thoughts turned to the Queen. It felt like an eternity since he was last in Charlotte's presence. He wondered if she was faring well and if his absence had not been hard on her. Though Gareth missed his mother terribly, Dellhaven was undoubtedly the best place for her. As a crisp autumn wind blew into the room, he gazed out at the breadth of Cardale and sighed.

If only she could see me now, and how far I've come.

But she wasn't the only woman on his mind. As he sipped at his tea, Gareth could not help but think of Madelyn again. Far too much time had passed since he received word of what was happening in the west. He prayed Lord Vakaro was, in fact, making some sort of plot against him instead of having to avenge Lord Valens. If the western Commandant had indeed fallen, it would surely spell Madelyn's doom.

An unexpected knock came at the door, even though it was half closed. Sir Tristan stepped in, hands fidgeting with one another. Gareth saw a shadow in the hall and wondered who it might be.

"Good evening, my prince. I hope I'm not disturbing you." The young councilman's eyes glanced about, then fell to the floor.

"It's quite alright. I was just enjoying some alone time. How can I be of assistance?"

Sir Edmund stepped into the chamber, his face long and sullen. Gareth cocked his head curiously, unsure what to think.

"I have some news I felt you should be aware of." Tristan removed a small roll of parchment from the pocket of his blue cloak. "I wasn't able to learn anything from Aldred. He didn't even want to speak to me, really. But when he stepped out of the room, I searched through his papers, and I found this."

He presented the scroll. Edmund moved closer as Gareth took hold of it, turning it around in his thumb and forefinger. Judging by the looks they were giving him, he supposed the message was anything but good news.

Dare I even open it? Is it going to say what I think it's going to say?

An icy chill crept up his spine, made all the worse by the bite of autumn wind.

"The look on your face says it all, Edmund. Tell me what happened, however painful it may be."

"Very well, lad. It seems your concerns about the barbarian hordes were well-founded. I don't know how long ago Aldred received this message, but based on what you told me about Lord Vakaro, it must be very recent,"

Gareth looked at his friend stupidly. He glanced at Sir Tristan for answers, but the councilman still could not face him. "So, what does this mean? Is... is Lord Valens?" He trailed off.

Edmund grit his teeth, then sighed. "The message says the army of Commandant Valens met the Northmen in battle and were soundly defeated."

The room suddenly felt like it was spinning, along with his bowels. Gareth clawed at the tightness in his chest, though still mindful not to show weakness in front of a councilman. "How many remain? Were they able to retreat to Castle Morden?"

"None," Sir Tristan said. "None survived, none that we are aware of."

They stood together in silence, each hesitant to break it. But there was something else written on Edmund's woeful expression, something Gareth almost did not wish to know.

"Is that all?" he asked. "Did the message say anything else?"

"I'm afraid it gets worse." Edmund glanced over his shoulder at Sir Tristan, then nodded toward the door. The young councilman turned and left, eager to escape the uncomfortable situation.

"Bentmont received word about the battle before we did, naturally. Not wanting to risk the situation we now find ourselves in..." Edmund was visibly pained by what he was about to say. "The High Marshal... dispatched Madelyn and a host of their knights to Castle Morden. With Lord Valens defeated, nothing could stop the Northmen from storming the castle. A few Blackthorn escaped, but

Madelyn stayed behind to ensure they could make it out. I'm so sorry, Gareth."

The world stood utterly still. He couldn't breathe. He couldn't think. It was as if life itself had ended, and his heart had shattered into a thousand tiny pieces.

"Come here, lad. It's alright." Edmund pulled Gareth in close and embraced him.

As badly as he wanted to sob and mourn for Madelyn, his first true love, he could not. There was something deep inside him that would not let such a thing happen. Not yet, at least. He needed answers, and only one man could provide them. Gareth placed the scroll in his pocket, then dabbed at the corners of his eyes with his thumb.

"Aldred knew about this. He knew and did nothing." His eyes turned bloodshot. "I'm going to his estate, and you're coming with me. I want to know what he knows."

Thankfully, Edmund was of the same mind. Gareth took up his sword propped against the wall and fastened the leather belt around his hips. Together they hurried out of his chamber, down the stairs, and across the great hall. As they exited into the courtyard, Edmund motioned to a nearby Guardsman.

"You there! See who's in the barracks, and get them out here, now!"

The subordinate hurried off to the barracks at speed, and before Gareth and Edmund could make it outside the gates, nearly two dozen Guardsmen came flooding outside. As they started down Auburn Row, the soldiers formed a protective ring around both men.

"Make way! Make way, I say!"

The Guardsmen shouted as they parted throngs of pedestrians. Many eyes were upon them, hundreds at first, then soon turned to thousands. The people of Cardale knew something serious was about to unfold. A passing patrol of city watchmen helped to push the crowds aside, though there wasn't any resistance. Everyone knew well enough to stay out of the way of the Royal Guardsmen.

Gareth saw the upper floor of Trace and Lucetta's estate, its sandy facade barely visible in the distance. He felt his hands tightening and balling into fists as they drew closer. A lifetime of frustration with his brother-in-law could no longer be contained. Not after everything he had lost.

When they arrived at the estate, the handful of Guardsmen stationed there looked at one another, perplexed. They knew from the sight of Sir Edmund that it was serious and allowed the detachment through the outer perimeter without incident.

I know you're in there. And now you're going to answer for your treachery.

He found Aldred and his brother Trace sitting at the dinner table with his sister-in-law, Esma Bethard. She was a fair, dainty woman who looked almost childlike next to Trace's girth. She wore a white and baby-blue gown, her pinned-up hair so blonde it was nearly white. When they saw Gareth and the score of Guardsmen, Aldred rose from the table in astonishment.

"What is the meaning of this? You have no right to come into my home!"

Sir Edmund moved to the table and compelled Trace and Esma to their feet.

"Gareth!" Trace protested. "What in the world are you doing? This is madness!"

"Go on now, give them the room," Edmund ordered. A trio of Guardsmen escorted husband and wife from the dining hall while the others stood vigilantly and awaited further instruction.

A whirlwind of emotions ran through Gareth's mind as he reached into his pocket to retrieve the dispatch. He thought about having Aldred killed right then and there. He thought about throwing him into a cell for the rest of his life. There were many possibilities, but first, Gareth needed to know the truth.

"So you knew what happened to Lord Valens, but didn't see fit to share it with me?" He threw the scroll across the table. "Explain."

Aldred looked as if he had never seen the message before. Flabbergasted, he unrolled the parchment and gave it a quick read, though he wasn't fooling anyone, Gareth least of all.

"How did you come by this?" Aldred asked, his voice trembling ever so slightly.

"That's none of your concern. I want to know how long you've known about this and what you plan to do."

"Gareth…"

He stormed over to his brother-in-law, the Guardsmen following close behind. Two passed behind Aldred, placed their hands on his shoulders, and stuffed him back onto his chair. He was shocked and incensed by such tactics.

"How dare you barge into my home and manhandle me like some common criminal! The King is going to hear about this! Mark my words!"

"You don't scare me, Aldred. Go on and tell my father. Tell him you've been withholding critical information on Lord Valens for your own ends. Tell him—"

Aldred stammered and scoffed, his words failing to form in his mouth. "This is preposterous! I would never do such a thing! I have always served your father faithfully!"

A deep, fiery rage inside Gareth boiled to the surface. He unsheathed his sword, the blade singing as it was freed from its scabbard.

"Then tell me why you've kept this information hidden from the rest of the council. Tell me why you brought Lord Vakaro to take up Sir Bryce's seat before the man was even buried. Tell me why you're conducting this war in the west without anyone else's knowledge. Tell me!"

"What are you going to do, kill me in my own home?" Aldred asked incredulously.

It was a genuine possibility. Gareth would have liked nothing more than to open his brother-in-law's skull and spill its contents onto the dinner table. But there were many questions, questions in need of answering, and in short order. Madelyn was dead, and someone would have to pay for it.

"Hold out your hand," he commanded.

When Aldred refused and gave only a quizzical look, a third Guardsman strode over, wrenched his arm outwards, and held it down on the table. The elder councilman squirmed and shouted but was no match for the brute strength of Cardale's finest.

"Now answer my questions. Tell me the truth." Gareth placed the blade's edge directly in front of Aldred's outstretched hand, a mere inch away.

"There's nothing to tell! I was never scheming to supplant your father's rule. All I have ever done was—"

In an instant, Gareth lifted the sword and brought it down with blinding speed, the blade biting deep into the polished table. Splinters flew as he wrenched it free, then placed the edge on Aldred's wrist.

"The next lie you tell will cost you."

"Alright, alright!" Aldred begged. "After the first message we received about the attack at Khorrtal, I instructed Castle Morden to send regular situation reports. When I learned from the acting Commander that they lost contact with Lord Valens, I immediately sent for Lord Vakaro. He's the only Commandant with men close enough to assist, but we received word the castle had fallen before we could muster a sizable enough force. That's the truth, I swear it!"

Plausible or not, the explanation did little to soothe the burning hatred inside Gareth's heart. He suspected Aldred was not telling him the whole truth and doubted he could learn anything more through intimidation. With a sigh, he returned his sword to its scabbard.

"I intend to get to the bottom of this, one way or another. Under no circumstance should we have lost an entire field army and the most secure castle in all of Betanthia. Someone is to blame, and whoever it is will be held accountable."

Gareth withdrew from the dining room with a wave of his hand, the Royal Guardsmen falling in line behind him. Esma stood around the corner, looking as terrified as a startled deer. Trace held his wife close, looking on in shock as if a band of marauders raided his homestead.

It was curious to note Lucetta was nowhere to be found. Gareth would have assumed in all of the commotion, she would have at least shown her face and demanded an explanation. She was not the kind of person to ignore any slight. So the only logical explanation was that she was absent.

Could it have been her on the highway to Dellhaven? It must have been. Who else would command so many men for such a journey? But if that's true, what is she doing there all alone? And mother is still there...

Suddenly the war in the west seemed trivial, but he could not become distracted. Lucetta was another issue for another time, even though Gareth knew his sister never did anything without intention. As he left the estate, he looked around to see if she had emerged, but still, there was no sight of her.

"He knows more than he's telling you. I would bet my life on it," Sir Edmund said, breaking Gareth out of his head. "Men like him don't crack easily. You must catch him in the act in order to out him."

"Indeed," he growled. "I want your men to follow him, day and night. Wherever he goes, I want him to see a purple cloak not far away. Make it no secret he's being followed. Perhaps that might dissuade any ideas of further treachery."

"And what about Lord Vakaro?" Edmund asked. "Do you trust his intentions are as noble as Aldred says?"

"Absolutely not."

They passed through the outer gates of the estate and back onto Auburn Row. A sizable crowd had gathered, though they were careful to maintain their distance. Another patrol of city watch arrived and helped to bolster security. The Guardsmen again formed a protective circle around their prince as they headed back to the Citadel.

"I agree," Edmund said, eyes scanning the crowd as they walked. "With that one, we might take a more subtle approach. I know a few reliable men from my days in the military, men who could infiltrate his inner circle and report back what they find. I might also suggest doing this with Aldred as well. When people are scared, they make mistakes, especially when they think no one is looking."

"Make the arrangements," Gareth said coldly.

The walk back to the Citadel took longer than anticipated, but the crowds dwindled the further they ventured away from the estate. When they arrived at the palace, Gareth parted from Edmund's company and returned to his chamber. As the adrenaline rush subsided, he grew exhausted and eager for rest.

Shutting the door softly, Gareth stood still and reflected on everything that had transpired. All of the uncertainty and the full weight of Madelyn's loss came crashing down, sending him collapsing to his knees in a fit of anguish. He could no longer hold back what he did not wish to show the outside world.

His thirst came roaring back, stronger than ever. The half-empty bottle of bourbon was calling out like a long-lost friend, beckoning Gareth to drown his sorrows the way he had always done. He stood on watery legs and stumbled to the bottle, nearly tumbling over in despair. Uncontrollably, he poured the drink down his throat, each swallow burning and stinging like fire.

"Madelyn… why…" Gareth wailed, beating his fists against the stone wall until his skin broke and bled.

The alcohol took hold shockingly fast. The room was spinning, and along with it, his stomach. Months of sobriety had ended, and Gareth felt all of the progress he made in Dellhaven beginning to crumble.

I'm sorry, Madelyn. I'm sorry I didn't do more when I had the chance. I'll miss you.

A gentle autumn breeze drifting in through an open window. He stumbled over to it, the bottle clenched in his unbattered hand. It would be easy enough to step onto the sill and set sail on the air, until the embrace of the ground below would steal his pain forever.

Gareth glanced out through the window, then down at the bottle. He thought of Madelyn and his mother, the two women who meant more than anything in the world, and what they would think if they could see him in such a state. Madelyn would certainly be disappointed, and Charlotte would be heartbroken.

No, he thought, a sudden and unfamiliar sensation building in his heart. *I cannot succumb. They're counting on me to be strong and to lead. Even though Madelyn is gone, she's still counting on me to avenge her. How can I do that if I'm dead or despondent?*

He held the bottle with an outstretched arm, studied its contents, and imagined all his failings and fears inside the vessel instead of bourbon. Gareth threw it out the window with a vengeful cry, as hard and far as his arm would allow. The glass spun and spiraled through the air, then exploded into nothingness when it impacted the grass below.

The distant sky was a menacing tapestry of black, gray, and dark blue. Storm clouds were forming against the backdrop of a setting sun, a distant peal of thunder signaling their arrival. It was a fitting sign of the wars to come and the arduous trials that lay ahead.

There would be time enough to mourn for his love, but it would not be now, Gareth decided. Now would come a time of blood, and death, and hate.

EPILOGUE

THE DAYS BECAME NOTICEABLY SHORTER, AND THE NIGHTS GREW colder and colder. It was a telltale sign summer had become a distant memory, and now the harvest was calling. Ryland Meeks didn't seem to mind much. The barkeep was one of the few in town who happened to enjoy the changing seasons. Cold days always brought in more patrons than usual, each seeking a seat near a roaring fireplace and a cup or tankard of his finest vintages to warm their bellies.

Life in the border town of Mor Seveht was difficult, and so was supporting a family of six. It wasn't a wealthy town, far from it. Ryland sometimes wondered why anyone would settle here and sometimes questioned his own decision. Mor Seveht seemed to be in all of the wrong places, all at the same time. It sat just outside the western edge of Betanthia, mere miles from Droethia, and a day's ride from the Zylmacian borderlands.

To say Mor Seveht was a dangerous place was an understatement, but surprisingly, it was relatively peaceful. The comings and goings of Betanthian soldiers and Blackthorn Knights failed to dissuade travelers from coming to sell their wares and find a warm bed to sleep in. It was an interesting patchwork of different people from different ways of life, and all were grateful such a place existed.

The tavern was lively this evening, though thankfully not too busy. Several of the usual customers were present. Turr Saahl sat at his favorite spot at the far end of the bar, slowly nursing a mug of mead. He was an older gentleman and kept well enough to himself most of the time. The same couldn't be said for Largan Whyl and Clive Cross, who laughed and boasted at a table near the fireplace, each of them thoroughly embalmed on some of Ryland's most potent whiskey. A few other nameless faces sat scattered about the room.

After thanking a trio of departing Droethien travelers for their patronage, Ryland cleared their tablet. With a damp cloth, he scrubbed and cleaned away crumbs of food and dribbles of wine speckling the tabletop. He heard the footsteps of his children upstairs as they chased each other around playfully. Living above the tavern and knowing his children and wife were so close was often nerve-wracking. Ryland kept a loaded crossbow and a short sword behind the bar in case of trouble from an overly intoxicated patron. Thankfully, he had yet to use either of them.

"Another round, Ryland, and keep them coming!" Clive belched as he lifted his tankard clumsily into the air.

A sudden ripple of laughter filled the tavern. Four young men sat in the corner and played a dice game. Three of them gave their winning companion a mocking jest as he cleared the table of his spoils. The victorious man shoved one of his friends stiffly, then gleefully departed with a fist full of gold coins.

"Glad those Droethiens are gone," Clive said as Ryland moved back behind the bar. "They sure do stink up the place with their perfume and whatever else that smell is."

"I remember a time when you wouldn't ever see one, and now they're everywhere," Largan stated. "I swear, the Droethiens don't even need to send their armies to conquer Caldakas. All they need to do is send their merchants. They do a good enough job of siphoning off our gold."

Ryland reached under the bar for a fresh bottle of dark brown whiskey and poured two generous servings.

"I certainly won't complain about the business," he said. "It's not easy supporting a family here. If it weren't for their merchants, my children wouldn't be eating as well as they are now."

Largan spat. "Heh! Bugger them all, I say. I can't even walk down the street without at least one of them trying to sell me something. There really ought to be a law against trinket peddling around here."

Despite being a trading post of sorts, Mor Seveht had no real marketplace. Goods were bought, sold, and traded on an as-needed basis, often right in the streets. It was still a developing town and lacked much of the infrastructure one would expect when traveling anywhere in Betanthia. There wasn't even a town watch or lord to keep the peace. Only the presence of the King's army along the frontier kept order, though their numbers seemed fewer as of late.

"Be careful what you wish for," Ryland cautioned. "We don't need the Bethards sending in some fat, privileged lord to oversee things around here. I quite enjoy not having to pay the King's tax, don't you?"

"Suppose you're right," Largan grunted, then begrudgingly sipped at his whiskey.

"Well, if what I hear is correct, we might soon have bigger problems on our hands than merchants or taxes," Bate Yordson called out from across the room. He picked up his cup of wine and moved closer to the conversation. He was a stout man with stringy blonde hair and a patchy beard, and a tunic that was becoming more purple with each cup he consumed. "I hear, something's come down from the north."

"Another one of your tall tales, eh Bate?" Clive said, unamused.

"No, this one is for real!" Bate grabbed a chair from another table and slid it closer.

Ryland smirked as he washed the cups and flagon the Droethiens left behind. The remaining men in the corner cursed and derided each other as they left their table and made for the door, but thankfully it was all in good fun. He certainly didn't want to break up a fight as he had to the week prior.

As they left, a tall man in a dark brown hooded cloak entered. He approached the bar and leaned against it. The old planks flexed slightly and groaned from his weight. Ryland had seen the man skulking about Mor Seveht recently but thought nothing of it. There were often many shadowy travelers who came and went, and most without incident. Turr Saahl turned and looked briefly but resumed staring into a nearly depleted mug.

"An ale," the hooded man said in a gravelly voice. "And be quick about it."

"Right away, sir."

Ryland sensed something unsettling about the man, but business was business. As he poured out a tankard of auburn red ale, the man dropped a few silver coins onto the bar.

"You're full of shit," Largan said, his drunken agitation growing.

"No, it's true!" Bate protested. "I heard it from my cousin Dawson's friend, who sends grain shipments to Castle Morden. He told me that one day he was taking one of his regular deliveries over there, you see. And, and you're never going to believe this, he said he saw smoke coming up from the castle! Black smoke, as black as the night he said!"

Ryland set the frothing ale down on the bar and retrieved the silver coins. The man in the hooded cloak picked the vessel up and emptied it with a few mighty gulps, then slammed it down.

"Another," he croaked, then tossed down more coins. One of them rolled across the bar and nearly fell onto the floor.

Cautiously, Ryland poured another drink. The large man snatched it away and walked off to the far corner of the room where the young men sat. Everyone in the tavern paused and fell silent as he passed by.

"You must think we're pretty stupid to believe something like that," Largan said accusingly. "Last week, you were going on about how you saw a ghost rider on the Plainhold, and now you're telling us Morden got sacked? Give it a rest."

Bate scoffed and looked around. "I wasn't lying about any of that, but… but that's beside the point. I'm being serious. My cousin would never lie to me!"

"But what about his friend? How do you know he's telling the truth?" Ryland chimed in, smiling.

A torrent of wine spilled down Bate's chin and onto his wet tunic as he took several large, flustered gulps. Muffled chuckles filled the tavern.

"I did hear about some thieving outside of town not too long ago," Turr said, his voice thick with intoxication. "Friend of mine knows a guy named Silas. Says a rider put a knife to his throat and robbed him, big ole brute of a man, he says. But whoever it was, he didn't take much."

Ryland looked over at the man in the hooded cloak suspiciously. He was not one to put stock in drunken boasts, but something about the man's face made him feel uneasy.

"When's the last time you didn't hear about some kind of thieving out here? Did you forget this is Mor Seveht?" Clive retorted.

Ryland had heard hundreds, perhaps thousands of stories about bandits, fantastical sightings, and whatnot. Each time the tales seemed to grow more and more extravagant, with each man trying to best the other and add a sense of importance to an otherwise unimport- ant existence.

"And what about you, friend?" Bate asked the man in the hooded cloak. "Seen anything interesting on the way into town?"

"Go fuck yourself," hooded cloak replied, growling.

Ryland heard everyone in the tavern exhale at once. A few patrons glanced at each other, some not taking kindly to the sudden agitation. Bate stammered for words, but before he could reply, Largan grabbed him by the shoulders and shuffled him off to the other side of the room.

"Excuse me?" Bate belched.

"Come now, gentlemen, it's just some friendly conversation. No need to get heated." Ryland said cautiously.

The pattering of footsteps above had grown silent. He felt a sour pain in his gut, knowing his children were listening. He hoped Bate could keep his fool mouth shut and not instigate anything, especially with a behemoth of a man.

Don't think I won't throw you out of here. I won't have any fighting in my tavern. No sir.

Ryland's hand drifted slowly to the crossbow underneath the counter, but his fears were soon allayed. Bate was set down at the bar, his face flecked with purple droplets. Largan approached and ordered a fresh mug of ale, then brought it over to the colossus as a sort of peace offering.

"Our apologies for Bate's behavior. The more wine he gets in him, the more irritating he becomes. We don't want any trouble."

Hooded cloak said nothing but swallowed the mug in a few monstrous gulps. He slammed it onto the table with a thud, then stood and moved slowly across the tavern. Ryland's hand moved back to the crossbow, though he was uncertain if it would affect a man of such size.

Everyone inside the tavern looked on silently, though Bate was clearly the most troubled. It seemed that this time, his big mouth would end up costing him, or so Ryland suspected.

Perhaps I'll need that sword, though it might only make him more angry.

But the large man said nothing and strode to the door, the floorboards creaking with each step. "If any of you twats knew what was good for you, you'd leave and get as far away as possible."

The warning was unsettling. Maybe Bate's tale wasn't so fantastical after all. Maybe this stranger had seen it with his own eyes, but there was no way to know for certain. All Ryland knew was, he had a family to look after, and if danger was on its way, then he would have to be on his.

"Tell me," he asked the tall man. "Tell me what's going on out there. I have a wife and children."

Hooded cloak ground his teeth. The light of a roaring fire revealed scars and deep pits across his face, and a sullen and sorrowful expression.

"If I were you, I'd find yourself a nice plot of land somewhere far from here, and soon. Death is out there, and it's coming." The man placed two silver coins on the bar as a tip. "This is the end."

A sudden tightness formed in Ryland Meeks' throat. He swallowed hard, uncertain if he wanted to know more. But he had to, for the sake of his wife and children. They were counting on him to keep them safe and alive.

"The end of what?" he asked timidly.

The tall man pulled down his hood, his face even more terrifying in the full light. His eyes were glassy and vacant and grew wet with a faint hint of tears. He sighed, then turned for the door.

"The end of everything."

A WORD FROM THE AUTHOR

Thank you so much for taking the time to read *The Hellborn King*, book one of *The Hellborn King Saga*! I hope you had as much fun reading it as I did writing it. If you enjoyed this book, please leave a great review (or rating, at least) on Amazon or Barnes & Noble, as well as Goodreads. It only takes a few minutes, and it's the best way for you to support my work and get the word out. Doing so will help ensure that I will be able to continue publishing long into the future. From the bottom of my heart, thank you for your fantastic support!

— Chris